Final Mission:

ZION

THE PALE HORSE SAGA

autobahn
BOOKS

Final Mission: ZION

THE PALE HORSE SAGA

CHUCK DRISKELL

In honor of Martin Nils "Marty" Richert, my uncle and a retired Air Force colonel. A kind and humble man, he was awarded the Distinguished Flying Cross for his brave actions during the rescue of a Marine pilot during the Vietnam War. Marty later served with distinction in Berlin, Germany before the Berlin Wall came down. He regularly traveled into the former East Germany and has told me many fascinating tales that captivate me to this day. I credit Marty for planting the initial seeds of my love and fascination for Germany. He's a great man.

Never was anything great achieved without danger.
     —   *Niccolo Machiavelli*

Part One:
THE CALL

Chapter One

1915, the Ottoman Empire

THE feeling in the field tent was one of bitter defeat. It was seconded only by the anger that comes with it, especially to a group of men accustomed to winning. Neil Reuter, easily the youngest person in the tent and only four months removed from basic training, situated himself in the darkest shadows at the rear of the shelter, listening as the normally refined Brits argued vehemently with one another. It was readily apparent that things here in Gallipoli were not going as planned. The intense heat of the humid Turkish night did nothing to help the situation, covering each man in a film of irritating sweat.

Breathless runners came and went, carrying messages from the bloody battle line. Neil watched as the lead British general, a man whose name he didn't know, read the most recent message, cursing and hurling the balled note at his nearest subordinate. Outside, small arms fire crackled in the distance. The distant sounds of the battle were overpowered by the nearby screams of the wounded, making Neil's seventeen-year-old skin crawl. From the triage area he could hear a man begging someone, anyone, to shoot him, to please put him out of his misery. Neil pressed himself against the musty canvas of the tent, closing his eyes, trying to envision himself back in the cool sanctuary of the Shoshone reservation in the Sierras, surrounded by family and friends, free from this stench of death that hung in the air like an evil fog.

A fresh argument shook him from his reverie. Neil opened his eyes and looked to the stately figure that was General Horace Yeager, puffing his pipe as he coolly watched the impassioned exchange between his British counterparts. Yeager was known as a brilliant field tactician, invited here by the British commander whom he had come to know at an international war college of some sort or another. For the moment, so it appeared, General Yeager was keeping quiet, allowing the Brits to wrangle with one another unhindered.

Just four short months earlier—although, at this moment, it seemed a lifetime ago—Neil had been chosen as the general's driver and assistant following his basic and advanced training at Camp Redwood. As another runner pushed through the folds of the tent, carrying a note that must have been worse than the former, Neil again closed his eyes, recalling the early May day he'd been selected for what now felt like a Godforsaken duty.

They'd just graduated training and were given weekend liberty—their first time off in three months. Every man in Neil's platoon headed into town with pockets full of money, prepared to unleash holy hell on the saloons and women of unsuspecting Eureka, California. Every man but Neil, that is—he stayed back. He'd been summoned to the unit dayroom, reporting as ordered at rigid attention. His senior drill sergeant appeared from around the corner, moving toe-to-toe and staring at Neil through gun-slit eyes. From nowhere, the drill instructor unleashed a solid right to Neil's stomach, dropping him to a knee, leaving him gasping for precious air.

"That's to bring your highfalutin ass down a notch," the drill sergeant inexplicably admonished, his rigid finger pointing down at Neil.

Neil had opened his mouth wide, unable to breathe for a full half-minute as his stricken diaphragm spasmed. He finally managed a few wispy breaths, gasping a dutiful query about what he'd done wrong.

"Ain't done nothing wrong other than got yourself a cherry-ass job right outta the chute, private."

Neil, breathing raggedly by this time, turned his purple face questioningly up to the drill sergeant. The NCO grasped the shoulders of Neil's uniform blouse, lifting him back to the position of attention. He moved close enough to clue Neil into the fact he'd eaten something heavily laced with onions for lunch.

"I just don't want you thinkin' you're somethin' special," the instructor growled, eyes slightly twinkling.

"Drill sergeant," Neil managed to croak, huffing glorious quantities of air by this time. "Might the private inquire as to what this job is?"

"General's driver and assistant," the normally coarse drill sergeant replied crisply. "You're gonna be carryin' a Tinker Bell briefcase around while the rest of your platoon's out soldierin' like men."

Neil's head had begun to shake back and forth as he mouthed the word "no," processing this unheard of change of plans. He'd joined the Army with his best friend Jakey—Jakey was off in town having a blast by this time—and the Army just couldn't separate them this soon.

I won't allow it.

"No, drill sergeant," Neil finally managed. "You can't let them do this. All due respect, but I don't want to be a damned general's driver. That's *not* why I joined. Private Herman and me joined up to serve together."

The senior drill sergeant jabbed his finger at a poster depicting the familiar flag-festooned, stony-faced human symbol of American pride. "You know what G.I. stands for, Private Reuter? Do ya know? Stands for 'government mother-fuggin' issue,' and what it means is good old Uncle

Sam there can do whatever the hell he wants with you, whenever the hell he wants, however the hell he wants. Got that?"

Neil managed to quietly assent.

"And guess whose name, rank, and serial number is on your recommendation?"

"I'm guessing it would be yours, drill sergeant."

"Bet your narrow injun ass, it is. I recommended you only because you learn damned fast and stand taller than most of them duds in your platoon. Fact of the matter is, it was gonna be you *or* Jew-boy Private Herman, but you edged him out. So either way, you two was gonna be split up." He again stepped in, striking Neil's nose with his campaign hat. "None of this talk matters, 'cause you ain't got no say-so. You got that, boy?"

Neil blinked several times, mind racing. "I understand, drill sergeant."

The drill sergeant almost smiled. He walked Neil to his bunk, had him gather his things, and took him straight to the train station without giving him a chance to say his goodbyes. Neil reported for duty the following day.

While at first he had felt ambushed, he'd grown to appreciate his new assignment, traveling, hearing important conversations, being exposed to life outside of California. He wasn't quite ready to call it an honor, especially not now, not here in Gallipoli. But before his arrival here, things had been bearable, building toward something, though what it was he didn't quite know.

Through it all, Neil had corresponded with Jakey Herman by post. Jakey, who had a special way with words, never once failed to make Neil laugh out loud with his letters. Neil's mind came back to present, back to this battle, morosely wondering if Jakey could make him smile at this moment.

Along with Neil in the general's entourage were two other soldiers who served between Neil and the commander. Neil's direct chief, and the general's retinue—his bodyguard—was a grizzled old master sergeant, Jimmy "Buck" Wingo, a Tennessean and veteran of the Spanish-American War. Wingo often bragged in his hoarse voice about how he once beat President Teddy Roosevelt, then a soldier, arm wrestling "not once, not twice, but three damn times!" Each time Wingo would exuberantly relay his favorite tale, ever-present brown tobacco juice would dribble from his grinning mouth as he finished by saying, "Sumbitch couldn't stand losin'. Jus' kept comin' back fer more."

Senior to Wingo was Major Frederick Hamilton, the general's attaché and a man who Neil quietly studied due to his ubiquitous polish and razor-sharp wit. Even with prestigious degrees from Washington

University and Northwestern, the well-educated major knew his place, always standing several paces behind the general, ready when needed. In his four months of traveling in this oddly matched quartet, Neil typically turned to Major Hamilton for advice, respectfully addressing the refined officer and appreciating his willingness to share occasional unsolicited counsel with him.

The American visitors had now been in Gallipoli for four days, since the start of the current battle. Earlier in the day, when the sun was still up, the tide had begun to turn for the worse. It was then that Major Hamilton and Sergeant Wingo sought permission to join the fray, hesitantly agreed upon by General Yeager. But when Neil had attempted to join them, he was promptly stopped by all three men.

"You got a few more years'a growin' a'fore you go wadin' in to somethin' like this," Wingo had said to Neil with a wink. "Don't worry, boy. We'll bust that cherry soon enough."

Major Hamilton had nodded his agreement. "It's the big leagues out in those sooty trenches, sport. Be patient—we'll find you some fun soon enough." And with that, the two men had waded into the lead-filled fight. Other than wearing the same uniform, the two men couldn't have been more different: a hard-boiled war veteran with a grade school education, side-by-side with a classically educated, distinguished officer. The two soldiers drew from two completely different, yet equally effective, sets of expertise.

They'd been out there now for eight hours, through the heat of the August afternoon and into the blackness of the sticky night. Neil had worried about them until another messenger arrived. This one burst into the tent, his right hand holding a blood-stained muslin bandage to his helmetless head—a folded note in his other hand. He handed it to a British colonel who, grim-faced, passed it to the commanding general. The general's face and body sagged upon reading it. He pressed his lips together, whitening them before finally speaking to General Yeager.

"Horace...your two men..." The British general looked up, collecting himself. "They've been killed."

"Dear God," General Yeager breathed, stumbling backward before falling onto a cot. He sat there and took large, steadying breaths as the messenger muddled his way through an explanation.

"It's the Turkish bastards up in that pill box, sir," the messenger said. "They've got two field guns and a sniper with a blooming perfect eye."

General Yeager ground his teeth together, staring up at his friend. "Why don't you hit them with your damned artillery?"

"We've got no artillery!" the British general replied, opening his arms in exasperation. "This was supposed to be a doddle, not a bloodbath!"

"The Turks in the lower trenches are softened up, sir," the messenger persisted. "It's the demons in that pillbox that are shredding us. We knock them out and we'll take the whole of the high ground, billy-o."

It was almost as if Neil were hovering above, watching the scene from an opera box, like the ones at the Gunter Theater back in San Francisco. He saw himself hiding in the corner, turning his head at the mention of the unchallenged pillbox. Then, taking slow steps forward— not unlike the mysterious character appearing at the end of the critical first act—Neil saw himself step into the middle of the tent. He didn't come back to his own body until he heard the soft words escaping his mouth, occurring spontaneously as he said, "I can take that pillbox, sir."

"Who the hell are you?" the British colonel boomed.

"Private Neil Reuter, sir. I'm the fourth soldier with General Yeager."

Yeager lowered his head into his hand, seemingly still stunned over the tragic news he'd just received. "Reuter's my assistant," he muttered. "He's just young."

"I may be young, sir," Neil replied in a respectfully challenging tone. "But I *can* take that pillbox."

The second in command, the British colonel, took a step in Neil's direction, cocking his head in a warning manner. "You're out of line, private. I'd suggest you belt up and move outside with the rest of the attachés before you *do* get sent out on that line."

Neil's adrenaline surged as he took his own step toward the threatening colonel, staring at him while addressing General Yeager. "General Yeager, sir! I said I *can* take that pillbox, and I beg you to allow me to try." He snapped to attention and turned his heterochromatic eyes to his superior. "Your verdict, please, sir!"

General Yeager stood, linking his thumbs in his Sam Brown belt. His chest expanded as he inhaled, looking Neil up and down before turning to the British commander. "George? You mind if my boy here makes what will probably be his death run to that pillbox?"

The British general snorted. He moved his objecting colonel back with his right arm while his mouth turned upward at one corner. "Cheeky lad. Guess we were all like that once. Makes me a mite envious." He removed his Webley revolver, flipping it around and proffering it to Neil by the barrel. "Here, boy, take this for close range, assuming you make it that far."

Neil stared at the revolver a moment, carefully reaching around the general and, in a deft movement, spiriting the general's bolo knife from his pistol belt. He took several steps backward, eyes downward as he began to disrobe, ignoring the surprised protests as he hurriedly stripped to his undershorts.

"Private," the colonel yelled, "what in God's name are you doing?"

Neil ignored him, stepping from the tent, one side of his sweaty body illuminated by the flashes of fire in the distance. Next to the tent were the bullet-riddled bodies of Wingo and Hamilton, arranged on two medical litters. Neil glanced at them before searching the dim area, finding a muddy puddle underneath a portable water reservoir used to fill canteens. He dove into the shallow puddle, rolling and squirming, covering every inch of his body in the tiger paste of Gallipolian mud.

As the assembled cadre stood around him, mouths collectively agape, Neil walked to the messenger. "Where's the pillbox?"

Wide-eyed, the messenger gestured to a small rise on the horizon and spoke a few words. Neil nodded before lifting the bolo knife, pressing it to the back of his own left forearm and slicing across. He lifted the bloody gash to his mouth, sucking his own blood as the whites of his eyes glowed in the black of the night. Afterward, he stepped to the corpses of his fallen comrades, covering both hands in their warm blood, combining it with the mud on his face and head.

"He's a bloody fockin' savage!" the colonel yelled. Even General Yeager gaped at Neil as if he were otherworldly.

Neil gripped the knife in his right hand, blade back in icepick style, moving before the British general. Neil's eyes were wide and alert, his voice as sharp as the bolo knife. "Keep watching, sir. When you see my signal, you send *everything* you've got."

"What signal?" the Brit asked. But it was too late. Neil Reuter was already gone, his mud and blood-covered figure gliding silently away on bare feet, melding into the war-torn night like a vapor.

* * *

General Yeager, bewildered at the display he'd just witnessed from the normally unassertive Private Reuter, hurried back into the tent, retrieving his field glasses. Back outside, shoulder-to-shoulder with the assembled group, he pressed the field glasses to his face, scanning the battlefield, able to see glimpses of figures during the brief flashes from grenades and Bangalore torpedoes. He peered through the field glasses for a period of minutes, his eyes aching from the intense concentration.

There was no sign of Reuter.

The machine guns in the pillbox continued to fire, spraying the battleground with lead. Occasionally a tongue of flame could be seen darting from the pillbox, followed by a single report from what was probably the sniper's Turkish Mauser. True to the messenger's testimony of the sniper's accuracy, the rifle would fire and the cracking report would be heard after a moment, usually followed by agonized screams or, worse, deadly silence.

Even a crawling man would have reached the pillbox by now. As the assembled officers began to murmur that the crazed American private had most likely met his end, Yeager felt his chest tighten with ache. What had begun as an exciting jaunt to the Ottoman Empire to see his old friend had resulted in the loss of his entire personal staff. These were men with families and, in the case of young Private Reuter, futures.

The general lowered the field glasses, allowing his chin to dip to his chest. He stayed that way, eyes closed, trying to make sense of this dreadful day.

Why were humans so destructive? Why kill each other when what this world needed was extreme cooperation? Yeager attuned his ears, saddened by the dreadful cacophony.

Curses.

Shooting.

Anguished cries of pain.

Then…

The largest explosion of the night rocked the Gallipoli Peninsula. A fireball fifty feet high went up as rounds and explosives could be heard igniting secondarily.

When the chest-pounding shockwave had passed, Yeager jammed the field glasses to his face, scanning frantically. Then he saw something. Yeager watched, rapt, as a darkened figure leapt from the front of the fiery pillbox, starkly silhouetted against the vivid orange flames licking up behind him. The lean shadow dove into what must have been a frontal trench, his knife-laden hand striking up and down, stabbing viciously. The stabbing figure moved laterally in the furrow, fiercely meting out his death blows. The figure finally emerged, again backlit by the flaming pillbox, his skin shiny from perspiration and blood. He held the British general's bolo knife high in the air, shouting a piercing cry into the night sky.

After struggling to moisten his mouth, General Yeager said, "George…something tells me that was your signal."

General George Cresswell, like Yeager, had been watching through his own field glasses, his jaw slack. He lowered the glasses, appearing to struggle with what he'd just witnessed. Then he turned to the group and in a thunderous yell said, "Get off your arses, gents! Take those brave boys forward and seize that blasted hill!"

The British general turned to his old American friend, General Horace Yeager, skipping the handshake, bear-hugging him before both officers charged forward, pistols drawn as they willingly joined their men on the advance.

* * *

Six Weeks Later

A chilly September wind pressed in from the Pacific, ushering in the smell of the sea to San Francisco's Presidio. The lush green grass of the Army installation's expansive lawns seemed to glow under the sun and extensive blue sky. Separating the lawns from the walkways were the ever-present whitewashed knee-fences found on all Army posts, designed to keep soldiers from taking unwarranted shortcuts in one of the military's many little methods to maintain good order. Neil Reuter, dressed in his khaki cotton uniform—now adorned with the rank of corporal—crossed Lincoln Boulevard, following the walkway to the headquarters building, snapping off smart salutes as he passed officers. Inside, after removing his headgear, he turned right, his polished boots clicking on the gleaming floors. The general's comely civilian secretary beamed upon seeing him.

"Good morning, Corporal Reuter. I must say, that was fast."

Neil nodded. "The general calls."

"Go right in. He's expecting you."

General Yeager, wearing his dress uniform, sat behind the wide desk. He was leaning back, hands laced behind his head. "Reuter, my boy, how the hell are you?" he asked.

The general's affability set Neil on guard.

"Fine, sir. As are you, I hope?"

"Fine, fine." General Yeager stood, motioning Neil to the sitting area on the far side of the room. Never before had Neil seen anyone under the rank of full colonel welcomed into the general's semi-circle of comfortable chairs. The chairs faced a large window, behind it the sloping lawn that led to the crashing waters of the South Bay.

"Something to drink?" the general asked, motioning to a gleaming coffee urn.

"No, thank you, sir," Neil answered, sitting rigid, palms on knees and feeling quite uncomfortable.

"I'll get right down to it, then. Corporal Reuter...much as it pains me, I'm letting you go."

Neil blinked several times. "Sir?"

"It's not easy for me, son. I lost Wingo and Hamilton...now you." He straightened. "But I can't keep you hidden here for myself. As much as I'd like to, yours is a different kind of star, and it's on the rise."

Neil was silent, unsure of what the general meant—also unsure of how to respond.

The general hitched his thumb. "There's a school being put together at Fort Johnston, back east, in North Carolina. I'm sending you there."

"Sir, might I ask what sort of school it is?"

"They call it unconventional warfare, son. I certainly don't have to explain to you what *that* means."

Neil broke eye contact, glancing downward in mild embarrassment.

"There's a growing segment among the Army leadership…and you can count me as one of them…who believe wars aren't always going to be fought shoulder-to-shoulder, directly between two opposing lines." The general leaned forward. "There's a better way to do things in the killing fields."

Looking up, Neil said, "It's best not to get in a fight in the first place, sir."

"Fights happen, Reuter."

"Yes, sir."

"You're going to that school, and you're not only going to learn, you're going to teach, too. I've already seen to that." Yeager chuckled. "Aren't those fellas going to be surprised?"

Neil didn't respond.

"I'm recommending, after the school, we send you to officer candidate school. Get you schooled up on more than just fighting. We need officers like you leading our young men. There's a war brewing, you know."

"Yes, sir," Neil said, looking beyond the general.

"Reuter?"

Neil joined eyes with him.

"This is the beginning of a new life for you, an important life. And life's what you make it."

Neil tried to understand what the general meant. "I'll honor your wishes by doing my best, sir."

"Can't ask for more than that." The general stood, offering his hand. When Neil took it, Yeager pumped hard and pulled him close. "Son, I gotta ask you one more time. How the hell did you do what you did at Gallipoli?"

Neil allowed a hint of irritation to enter his voice, giving a clue to the man he would someday become. "I can't really say, sir. Some things a man is taught, some things he just knows."

"And you just *knew* how to do that?" the general asked, wearing a skeptical face. "The blood, the way you got to that pillbox undetected, the hawk-like shriek?"

"Sir," Neil said, pulling his hand away. "Do you remember learning to breathe?"

"Of course not," the general snorted.

"It's like that."

The general knotted his lips together, clearly unsatisfied but eyeing Neil the way a proud father views his son who has grown beyond his sphere of control. "Good luck to you, Corporal Reuter."

"And you as well, sir."

"Enjoy your new life. I'm convinced it'll be stimulating. I'm even more convinced you'll do amazing things."

The general's words couldn't have been more prophetic. Neil Reuter did begin a new and important life that was marked by many astonishing moments. It was a life that would take him around the world, doing things most men would never dare dream. It brought him power. It brought him wealth.

It brought him misery.

Chapter Two

July, 1938 – Twenty-Three Years Later

IN A MANSION PERCHED HIGH ABOVE SAN FRANCISCO BAY, Neil Reuter couldn't understand what in the hell could be making such a racket. He withdrew his head from under the pillow. The wispy light from the gaps between the heavy drawn drapes pierced his brain, making him lurch in agony while he fought down a wave of nausea. After finally marshaling enough saliva to moisten his mouth, he shouted for Agnes, the sound of his yells making his brain recoil inside of his skull.

There was the noise again—a loud, thudding sound. And no reply from Agnes, damn it.

Neil swung his feet over the side of the bed and moaned as both of his hands automatically shot to his temples. From the hook next to the nightstand, he donned his silken robe, realizing he had slept with nothing on. After a moment of slit-eyed searching, he located his pajama bottoms, pulling them on and tying the waist cord. Using his hands to find his way—because his eyes were again shut—Neil shuffled to the bedroom door, opening it as he braved the luminosity of the main hallway.

Boom. Boom. Boom.

It was the knocker, the damned bronze gargoyle knocker, given to Emilee by the San Francisco Flower Club when he had first purchased the estate known as Hillside. Some pest was at the front door, going to town with it, and it didn't sound like they planned on leaving until someone yanked it from their hand.

Sonofabitch, where the hell is Agnes?

Neil shuffled over the thick oriental runner, choosing, as he always did, to take the right curving staircase down into the three-story grand foyer. The architect had designed the striking space for Emilee to host *vernissages*, whatever that meant. There was movement behind the stained glass on the front stoop and, as Neil reached the foyer, a glance at the ten-foot-tall weighted clock showed him it was 12:45 p.m. Lunchtime for normal people. Agnes would be across the main yard, in her quarters, having a long lunch. No doubt she was leaning forward, rapt, as she listened to the crucial mid-week episode of *Big Sister* on the RCA radio Emilee had given her three Christmases ago.

Neil, finally able to see clearly, glanced down at himself. He made sure the robe was pulled tightly around his torso. As he always did when receiving an unknown guest, he opened the top drawer of the door-side

Victorian cabinet, removing the chunky Obregon pistol, gripping it behind his back as he moved to the door. With a twist of the bolt and another wince at the metallic snapping sounds, he opened the door, using his left hand to shield his throbbing head from the potent midday brilliance of the Northern California July sky. As his eyes adjusted to the intensity of light, he saw the outline of a woman wearing a large hat. As she came into focus, he noticed that she wore a fashionable red suit and clutched a small purse over her midsection.

"Yeah?" was all he managed to mutter, still shielding his eyes.

"Neil?" A soft voice. A kind voice. A concerned voice.

"Unfortunately, that's me," he answered flatly, without a trace of self-deprecating humor. Now that he could see, Neil lowered his hand and studied his visitor. She had dark hair and the smooth, eggshell skin of a porcelain doll. Her lipstick was perfectly matched with her trim suit and she couldn't have weighed more than a hundred pounds soaking wet. She was as pretty as any woman Neil had ever seen but, at that moment— consumed by leaden grief; ridiculed by shame over a recent incident; and suffering a blistering hangover—Neil didn't notice. To him, this woman was simply an irritating roadblock to his glorious, alcohol-induced coma.

His visitor bounced on her toes, urgency in her voice as she spoke. "Neil, don't you remember me?"

"No, I don't."

"I grew up right behind your home on O'Farrell." She tilted her head, seeming frustrated at his lack of recognition. "I'm Meg Herman, Jakey's younger sister."

Neil raised his eyebrows just a fraction. He hadn't seen Meghan Herman in…his brain struggled to recollect…well, at least since he went north and joined the Army. That would have been more than twenty years before, and at that time she'd been only seven or eight.

"I can barely remember you. What do you want?" he asked.

She seemed exasperated with his brusqueness. "Can I at least come inside?"

Equally annoyed, he motioned her in, dropping the Obregon back into its drawer when her back was turned. He asked her to sit, appropriately, in the sitting room. It was much too bright for Neil's liking and still decorated exactly the way Emilee had decorated it. Neil only chose the room because the wet bar was close by.

The wooden floor creaked under his weight as he shambled the shiny, well-worn pathway to the center of the marble bar. Without asking Meghan if she wanted one, he poured Russian vodka into a tall glass, filling it halfway. After spiriting the tomato juice from the icebox, placed there three hours before by the well-trained Agnes, Neil topped off the glass, sprinkling several dashes of pepper on top of the concoction.

Without leaving that spot, he turned the glass up, drinking two-thirds of the drink, allowing it to flood down his throat and open his sinuses at the same time. He stood there with his eyes closed for a long moment, eventually letting out a breath as he began the slow crawl back toward his place among the living human race.

Breakfast.

Neil staggered back into the sitting room, frowning at Meghan as she sat primly. Meghan returned his frown with an expression that was a combination of concern and unease. He sat diagonally from her, choosing the most uncomfortable, thinly padded chair in the room. He did this to remind himself to make this...*whatever* this was...brief.

"They still call you Meg?" he asked as he closed his eyes and again massaged his temples. There was already a heavenly hint of the alcohol hitting his bloodstream. Just a hint.

"Yes, I go by Meg." She smoothed her skirt and crossed her ankles as she leaned forward. "How have you been, Neil?"

Dammit.

It had been the same question, the very same damned question—identical tone, wording, and inflection—for two damned years. Always the same. At least a hundred women had asked him those exact words, and all of them had cocked their head the way Meg Herman had just done, like he was some sort of failed science project that still managed to rouse their deepest curiosities.

He leaned back, his face tilting to the ceiling as the alcohol continued its infiltration of his circulatory system. *Keep coming...*

"Neil, I'm so sorry about your wife." Meg's brown eyes widened, rimmed by the sparkling of the tears that pooled on the verge of cascading.

Neil looked at her. "And my son," he said monotone, a disinterested actor reading from a script he knew forward and backward.

"Your son?"

"Emilee was pregnant when she was murdered."

Meg's painted lips parted before she put a gloved hand to her mouth. "Oh, God, Neil. I hadn't heard that. I...I'm just so very sorry."

Neil eyed her, his expression displaying neither hostility nor gratitude. He was simply there, marinating in his lone joy of alcohol. His only desire was to drink himself to oblivion, to forgetfulness, to nothingness, to that vacuous nirvana he'd come to know, and love, and depend on. Everything in between was simply a function of physiology. Eating, sleeping, relieving himself: just like his damned heart still beating on its own. It all just happened, seemingly on full automatic. While he'd never entertained suicide, a piece of his subconscious he stayed well away from knew that he was taking the slow road to killing himself. In reality, although most people who knew him believed he was a drunk, Neil wasn't addicted to booze. It's just that alcohol was his only true choice—and he needed to maintain some semblance of direction over his life that had spun decidedly out of control. He turned the drink up, draining every drop of the simplistic bloody Mary, trying his best to suck down the last fleck of pepper.

"I have some things to do," he said, standing and walking away.

"Neil, wait."

Neil faced Meghan Herman. He swept his hand in her direction as the skin on his distinct face tightened from the strain. "Look, Meg, I guess I appreciate the sorrow that everyone feels so compelled to express. Maybe someday I'll truly be able to welcome it. I'm not trying to be callous, honest. But I've got to—"

"Neil—"

"Wait," he snapped. "As I was saying, to be honest, I can't help but notice that most of my women callers aren't married, and I can tell you right now that I will never—do you hear me?—*never* get married again." After the words fired out like machine gun bullets, Neil's mind shot back to the regrettable incident down in Santa Monica, making him wince.

No. Not that. Not now.

He took a calming breath, softening his tone. "Look, Meg, I don't mean to be rude. But if I have to endure one more visit from a woman who thinks she's going to ensnare me into her—"

"Jakey's dead."

The two words stopped his coming diatribe like a reinforced brick wall.

Neil's mouth moved to speak but nothing came out. He instantly pictured his best friend, Meg's older brother. Many years before, their friendship had begun with a fistfight and, from that day on, the two had been inseparable. Following Neil's appointment to the Unconventional Warfare School, he'd immediately recommended they recruit Jakey. It wasn't long before the two of them were in Europe together, serving side-by-side while the Great War claimed so many thousands of lives around them. Afterward, Neil and Jakey came home together, building similar professional lives. They'd even occasionally worked with one another, off and on, until three years before, when Jakey headed back across the Atlantic on a private mission. When Neil last spoke with him, Jakey had been busy frustrating the British gentry in tumultuous Palestine.

Feeling numb from the waist down, Neil dropped back into the uncomfortable seat, focusing on Meg Herman. "How?"

Meg's cheeks glistened with tears. The twitches in her face told him she was on the verge of sobbing. Finally, she unbuckled her clutch and removed a tattered envelope. Handmade from stained paper, it was folded twice and had a broken wax seal on the back. She unfolded the heavy stock paper and placed it on the table, sliding it across but allowing her gloved fingers to linger on it for a few extra seconds. Neil took it. Upon seeing the word "Barkie" scrawled across the front in Jakey's horrid penmanship, he knew it was genuine. Jakey Herman was the only person on earth who knew Neil as "Barkie." It was an old, silly joke from their teen years but, with Jakey, the moniker had stuck. The envelope was postmarked Innsbruck, Austria. The date wasn't legible. Neil flipped it over. On the back of the envelope, under the broken closure, was a simple phrase:

Give to Neil Reuter in the event of my death.

"When did he give you this?" Neil demanded, carefully flattening the dog-eared envelope.

"I received it from a friend."

"Who opened it?" he asked, fingering the wax seal.

"It was that way when I received it."

"How did they know who I was?"

"Jakey's lady friend had heard all about you from him. She and some of her friends made sure I received the note."

Neil let out a breath and removed the single sheet of paper. It was covered on both sides in Jakey's scratch, and its contents made Neil's eyebrows go up.

July 2, '38
Barkie-Boy:

Do you still get mad when I call you that? Probably the last time you'll hear it, especially if you're reading this letter. But, as you and I know so well, the sun also rises again.

I need a giant favor. And after what you've been through, you're just the man. I need you to go to the city I've been working in and move a few hundred children to safety. They're well hidden but they will run out of food and supplies 75 days from the date I write this.

If this important envelope made it to you in S-F, it means my job isn't done. It means I bought the farm. The whys and wherefores of the mission will be explained to you. Will you do it? I need you Pale Horse. We need you. These are innocent people: women and children. And after all you've been through, I thought you might like the distraction.

You must liberate them to the transport ship by September 15th. Not before and not after. It's too dangerous to have them out in the open. All you need to do is find secure transport from→

The note obviously continued, but the subsequent page wasn't there. "Where's the next page?" Neil asked, flipping it over.

Meghan Herman dabbed her eyes with her handkerchief. "That's exactly the way I received it."

"But that's the most important part. He was just getting to whatever it is he wrote me about," Neil said, shaking the paper. "He was telling me where the children are."

"Maybe someone removed the page," Meghan said, shrugging. "Probably to ensure that you'd follow his wishes and travel to Innsbruck."

"So, they're in Innsbruck?"

"Maybe. They're probably somewhere close by."

Neil closed his eyes and massaged them with his fingers. "Look, I'm willing to bet that all of this has been handled by whoever took the pages from this note."

"No."

"No?"

"It hasn't been handled."

"Will you *please* stop speaking in circles?" he said at length.

"I'll tell you what I know." She took a deep breath. "Jakey's been smuggling Jewish children out of Germany and Austria. He was in the process of getting a large group of children out when he was killed. Those children have no one to take them to their ship." Meg motioned to the note. "He mentions the date the ship will sail, September fifteenth. You have to go and move those children."

Neil looked away, considering this. "So, let me get this straight," he asked, speaking deliberately. "You want me to go to Austria and move the children?"

"Yes."

"Where are they being moved to?"

"Ultimately, Palestine."

"Why Palestine?"

"So they can be adopted and cared for by people who will love them, I suppose. And also..." She hesitated.

"Go on."

Meghan Herman took several steadying breaths. "Because many of us believe the rumors that the Nazis will try to eradicate our people."

Neil had no response for that.

"Will you go?" she asked.

Despite Neil's drinking, he couldn't help but read the countless articles about the German annexation of Austria through the *Anschluss*. In addition, for several years now, Neil had read the news about the frantic Jewish flight from the Thousand Year Reich. They feared the worst after the passing of the Nürnberg Laws, and with good reason. It was because of the ever-increasing pressure on the Jewish people that Jakey had dedicated the final portion of his life to getting them—and obviously their children—to freedom. Unfortunately, it seems his final "shipment" was stuck in transit. Neil shut his eyes, trying to dissolve the images of starving children from his brain.

"Neil, will you go?"

"I can't do that, Meg," Neil said dismissively. "Maybe he was delirious when he wrote this. Besides, there are hundreds of people better qualified than me to get those kids out. Hire a good German to do it."

"We can't."

"Why not?"

"This was Jakey's passion—his life's work. He left this note for you, Neil. If it couldn't be him, it had to be you." She leaned forward. "Do this for Jakey."

Neil lowered his eyes back to the note. "This is insane."

"It may be insane, but it's what your best friend wanted."

"But why me?"

"Indeed," Meghan said with a note of disdain as she looked him up and down. "But I suppose my brother knew what he was doing. Neil Reuter, will you go?" she persisted. "For Jakey? For the children? For their parents and loved ones, who don't deserve to grieve like you've had to?"

Neil felt the impact of her last words. "I don't know, Meg."

"Well, read his note again and think long and hard about it. I'm in town, staying at the Whitcomb down on Market." She stood and smoothed her skirt, looking down at him as she placed a delicate hand on his shoulder. "Those children need you, Neil."

"I'm not good enough for this," he answered, lowering his eyes to the floor.

"Jakey thought you were. And he's left you with time."

"Where's the ship supposed to sail from?"

"Jakey had contacts in Innsbruck. They'll give you all the details."

"Who?"

"His lady friend, and a doctor. They'll help you."

"Meg, for the last time, why can't someone else do this?"

"Who, Neil? Our ships are being turned away by even the United States and Canada," she replied, her voice strained. "These are Jewish children we're talking about. They're in Austria, of all places. There's no one there to help them, and even if there were, they're too scared to do it. Jakey wanted you."

Neil looked up at her. "And what happens if the children aren't escorted away by September fifteenth?"

"From what I've heard, their caretakers will bring them out of hiding if the deadline passes. And once they're found, and they will be, they'll all be sent to a camp." Her cheek twitched. "They might as well be shot on sight."

Neil closed his eyes.

"I'm sorry I was rude to you. But you need to snap out of it." Meghan Herman leaned down, kissing him on the cheek as her gloved hand ran back through his dark hair. "Just do what Jakey has asked of you. It'll be good for you." With that, she turned and made her way out, exiting just as Agnes reappeared.

Agnes Gentry, Neil's maid of ten years—she of the drawn, saturnine face—stood at the entry to the reading room and covered her mouth with the back of her hand, watching the front door as it was pulled shut. Short and slightly overweight, in her trademark blue uniform, she pointed to the door.

"Did that woman wake you?"

Neil didn't hear the question. He held the edges of Jakey's incomplete note, staring at it, his mind racing.

"Mister Reuter, *who* was that lady?" Agnes demanded after a period of silence. Her tone turned motherly. "And is that *lipstick* on your face? And you, wearing only your robe and pajama pants, in here alone with her. My goodness."

Since Emilee's death, Agnes had grown to be a surrogate mother to Neil. However, she was far too embroiled in the radio soaps she favored, and to her, any drama between a man and a woman probably denoted something lurid and scandalous.

"What on earth just happened here?" Agnes demanded.

"If you want to be useful, mix me a damned drink."

She walked to the front of the foyer and peered out the window.

"Did you hear me?" Neil asked.

As Agnes huffed loudly on her way to the bar, Neil moved to his leather office chair and reread the note.

For the next three hours he sat there, drinking. Drinking and reading the note.

And remembering.

Chapter Three

FOUR solid days of drunkenness ensued. During each day of his bender, the position of the sun or the moon meant nothing to him. Neil would drink until he passed out. When he came to, he would usually vomit before resuming the binge.

Drink; puke; rally; nibble a biscuit; wander the gardens; the periwinkle makes a helluva bed; ant bites aren't as bad as people say; bee stings are, though; ankle's the size of an old telegraph pole; stagger up the stairs lit by the architect's oculus, whatever the hell oculus means; hate Latin; there's a damn good reason it died as a language; people oughta quit trying to act so smart and let it rest in peace; more fever dreams; Lex Curran again; no, please; not that evil bastard; wake up and he's gone; again; gotta get that sonofabitch out of my mind; sort of hungry; even thirstier; well then, Aggie, hand me my pajama pants if seeing one bothers you so much; and put my damned drink by my bed; why? because I'm thirsty, that's why; awake again; stagger down the street; sorry mister, dogs do it wherever they like, why can't I?; need a drink…time to head on back; and when did this hill get so steep?; so tired; haven't slept well in months; now here's a good spot; blackness; blackness; blackness; someone shaking me; damn it Agnes, every time I find sleep you have to wake me; I don't care if the gardener uses manure or not, it's damned comfortable; up to the bath; tub's slippery; ouch; no big deal; is that my tomato juice in the water?; but why is Agnes screaming?; oops…blood…not tomato juice; bah, just a superficial scalp wound; it's nothing; well, I slipped because the damned tub is slippery, that's why; am not that drunk; hand it to me; oops; okay, see Aggie? now that's tomato juice; refill me and, yes, I'll hold the damned towel on my head; a long sip; ahhhh…good old Agnes; back to bed, bandage wrapped around the head like back in the mustard-gas trenches; sleepy time; damned fever dreams; Lex Curran, staring at me; pointing; mocking; bastard;

"Bastard!"

Neil Reuter sat straight up in the bed and shouted for two minutes straight. He bellowed until he eventually coughed blood from his abraded vocal cords. Agnes rushed in after hearing him from her quarters across the yard. She quieted him, insisting that he allow her to call Dr. Walsh. Neil shook his head, slinging the wet sheets aside as he shivered feverishly.

"But you're not well," Agnes persisted. "Worse than normal, even."

Neil's voice was a ragged whisper. He asked her to prepare some coffee and take the entire day off.

"It's nine in the evening."

"Then just make strong coffee and, please, leave me."

She placed her hands on her hips, unmoving.

Neil couldn't shake the image of Lex Curran, wearing his trademark zoot suit and sneering at Neil. In the dream, Lex wore boots with the suit, cowboy boots, made of snakeskin. Neil rubbed his eyes, trying to rub the haunting image away. "Please just put on the coffee and go to bed. Give me until the morning and check with me before you call the doc. I'll be fine."

"Should I...should I prepare another drink?"

Neil balled the damp white sheet and coughed into it, leaving a Rorschach spattering of blood. "No," he rasped. "Pour it all out. Every damned bit. Just pour it out and make the coffee." He was still drunk, if that was even the right word, but even through that haze of the deepest inebriation, there was a clarity Neil had only felt a few other times in his entire life. It wasn't unlike standing atop a tall mountain on the clearest of days, staring down at every little detail of the earth below and plotting your route home.

Neil could see his path. Turn, by turn, by turn.

Agnes stood there. "I really think you should allow me to ring—"

"Just pour it all out, Agnes," Neil said, cutting her off. He paused, patting the hand that gripped his shoulder, forcing a drawn smile. "And sleep well."

Agnes's eyes were wide as she stared at him in disbelief. She reluctantly left his room.

It took Neil a full hour to make his way down to the dining room. He sat at the end of the long table, sipping black coffee and smoking cigarettes. The so-called superficial wound on his head was a clean gash to the skull, and it throbbed like a bass drum. After rewrapping it, Neil found a photo of him and Jakey in Paris, recalling a few of the assignments they'd completed together during the War. He thought about the European trips they had taken afterward, before Emilee, when, between jobs, they would steam back to France, spending a month carousing and telling stories. The intention had always been to collect as many girls as they could but, in the end, they wound up simply enjoying each other's company, the way best friends often do when they don't get enough time together.

Sitting there, the thick sepia image pinched between his fingers, Neil tried to imagine what had happened to his old friend at the end. And, as he pondered and reminisced through the silent nocturnal hours, he brewed two more pots of coffee and nibbled on a full loaf of soft white bread. By the time the tangerine sun brushed long strokes across the eastern edge of Hillside, Neil had eaten half of the bread, consumed twelve cups of coffee and smoked thirty-one cigarettes. His insides were wrecked. Dr. Walsh arrived at ten in the morning, at Neil's behest, and used nine stitches to close the cavernous gash in Neil's scalp. Neil sat there, placidly smoking, never once flinching from the needle. He ate a proper lunch and spent the next three days on a routine schedule, rising early, swimming in the heated pool, actually going to the office, then retiring early to bed at night.

Without alcohol, despite the tremors and the shakes.

Neil was determined to prove to himself that he wasn't a drunkard. The alcohol had served its purpose, blunting him from his daily pain. He'd first begun to use it to obscure the visions from his past, and then the business with Emilee turned him into a hard-core drinker. But through it all Neil knew, deep down, his dependence was not an addiction. Regardless, his body had come to depend on the alcohol, leaving him occasionally sick as he dried out.

Neil didn't care—he soldiered through.

As a few visitors came and went, word of Neil's newfound sobriety got out. And that's when the boys from the War Department began to call. First, it was the local contact, then that sonofabitch Preston Lord rang. Neil ignored both calls. He also decreed that he would see no more visitors. As far as Neil was concerned, this unfortunate chapter of his life was finished.

By the fourth day, Neil's shakes had finally abated. He arose with the sun glaring through his picture window, the starched sheets of his bed crinkling as he pulled himself to a sitting position. Neil inventoried his body and mind, sitting there for a full fifteen minutes, trying to reach a decision. Finally, feeling lucid for the first time since before his wife's murder, Neil felt much of his old self had returned. The grief was there, of course, but pressed backward by a newfound calling.

He went into his bedside table, finding the tiny key concealed under the ledge. Neil walked to the dresser and, using the key, opened *the* drawer, staring at the contents. He lifted the piano wire and walked outside on the balcony, slinging the coil like a discus, watching it land in the ivy bed on the eastern edge of the house. Neil took the small vial of cyanide into the bathroom, dumping it into the sink and running water behind it to ensure its dilution. He went back to the drawer where he removed the hollow-point bullet from the revolver, dropping the bullet into the tub drain, sliding the now-empty revolver under his mattress. Neil walked back to the drawer and, in place of the items he'd discarded, placed a photo of Emilee. He touched the picture, allowing his fingers to linger there for a moment. With a nod, he closed the drawer.

In the bathroom, Neil filled the sink with warm water. After sharpening his straight razor and soaking his overnight beard, he lathered the porcelain cup with face soap and shaved slowly and deliberately, staring into the mirror, into his fraternal eyes, one blue and one sea green.

That done, he brushed his teeth before taking a steaming shower. His mind raced the entire time—raced with excitement.

Breakfast consisted of a grapefruit and plain toast with strong black coffee. Neil retired to his study, opening the drapes to take in the beauty of the flower garden as he again studied Jakey's incomplete letter. After rereading the note for the umpteenth time, he considered the mementos in his study. Items from his German father: a camera, a pocketknife, a hand-carved pipe. His mother's Shoshone keepsakes rested safely behind vitrine glass: her adult necklace, a baby's rattle, an earth pigment painting of her parents. In the past, whenever he'd been close to opening *the* drawer, Neil would come to the study and stare at his physical memories, remembering his parents, hearing their words.

Their words had settled him each time.

He crossed the room, reaching behind a stand of books, retrieving a long knife. He unsheathed it, running his finger over the nicked blade, his mind crossing continents. He smelled the sulfur, heard the screams, felt the slick warm blood. The recollection of that night caused him to perspire. This was the bolo knife, from Gallipoli. Years later, Jakey Herman had used it to gut a German soldier, a German soldier who would have killed Neil otherwise. Neil twisted the blade, catching light from the window. His cheek twitched as he catalogued the memory of Jakey for the moment, placing the knife back into its hiding place.

Neil had decided, concretely, to acquiesce to Jakey's request. Neil knew he could stay here and die. Or he could go to Austria and die. Or, perhaps, he would go there and live. Either way, if he stayed here he might as well go retrieve his bedroom pistol, find another hollow point, and end it now. Life in San Francisco was over. The game he'd played, which was once stimulating, was now a distant and haunting memory.

It disgusted him. Neil needed to cleanse his soul.

He lifted the letter, twisting it without reading it. There was something peculiar about it, other than the fact that it was missing a page. Neil had known Jakey long enough to be certain he had, indeed, written it. But there was just something about the contents of the first page, an inconsistency of some sort, niggling at a corner of Neil's mind.

He stayed in his study until mid-afternoon, sitting in his favorite chair and thinking, nodding to himself occasionally as he crafted the plan in his mind. After the sun crossed over the house and began its unhurried summertime descent to the Pacific, Neil stood and walked to his desk, picking up the mirrored brass telephone. He summoned his accountant and top financial man, J. Harrison Musselwhite IV, telling him to be at Hillside at seven-thirty the following morning.

All of the solitude and rational, sober thoughts had paid off. Neil now had a plan.

Chapter Four

NEIL HELD A STEAMING MUG OF COFFEE as he watched J. Harrison Musselwhite IV pace the pea gravel in the flower-enclosed sitting area. They were in the garden on the northeastern corner of Hillside, at the highest point, with the smell of lilac thick in the still, dewy morning air. The shimmering water of San Francisco bay was far below them, golden under the rising sun. An unusual southern wind had warmed the fledgling day to a comfortable temperature near seventy degrees, yet Harrison was sweating as if he were trudging through Death Valley.

Harrison stopped suddenly, sending small pebbles flying from his highly shined cordovan wingtips. His right hand gripped his hat, twirling it nervously. As he gaped at Neil, his mouth opened and closed two times. Without speaking, he shook his head and resumed his pacing. Neil watched as Harrison stopped again, mopping his brow with his handkerchief as he shot another bewildered glance at Neil. Neil wasn't surprised at Harrison's shock over what he had just been told. The financial man obviously thought Neil was insane.

Perhaps he was correct.

At sixty, Harrison was nineteen years Neil's senior. Long and lanky, Harrison had more loose skin on his face than an aged hound dog. His drawn mien and periorbital puffiness gave many people the impression that he was slow and incapable. But a close inspection would reveal green, vigilant eyes that rarely missed even the smallest of details. With a degree in accounting from the University of Arkansas, sent there by a father who worked day and night in a lumber mill to make sure his son could have the things he never did, Harrison had come west as a bookkeeper for the railroad before opening his own firm in Sacramento. It wasn't long after that when a young man named Neil Reuter recruited him for his growing Bay Area shipping company.

Neil trusted Harrison unreservedly. He was one of the brightest men he'd ever met. Harrison's wise counsel helped Neil to grow the company beyond anything either of them would have ever dared dream.

From the tin on the Adirondack style table next to him, Neil removed a cigarette and lit it. He turned his mug up, swilling the remainder of the cooling coffee, then took a long drag of the Lucky Strike. He gestured to the adjacent chair.

"Will you please stop pacing and sit down?"

Harrison nodded curtly and sat. Unable to halt his frenetic activity, his sweaty hands twirled and wrung the blue felt hat, adding a curl to the brim.

"Promise me…" Harrison started before choking on his words. He stopped and seemed to struggle to swallow.

"Water?" Neil asked.

Harrison waved him off, collecting himself. "Neil, your parents are dead and gone. And, well, I know the situation with Emilee was traumatic, to say the least."

"And my son."

Harrison cleared his throat again and spoke lowly. "Yes, and your son." He turned his body in the white garden chair and jabbed a crooked finger at Neil. "But you can't do this, Neil. You just can't. Not at least without taking sufficient time to think about it. You want to travel around the world, fine. Want to take a sabbatical and live in the desert like some reefer-steeped shaman, that's fine, too. Or maybe you just ought to go out on that boat of yours and get stinking drunk." Harrison tilted his furrowed face skyward, summoning calm. His voice settled when he resumed his speech. "You can leave everything at the business to me, or—because you know I don't have any ego about it—we can bring in someone else to run the company." Harrison smoothed the brim of the hat in his hands, afterward shaping its peaks. "Neil, you may see things differently in a year. Plus…and this is the most important part…the company isn't going to fetch near the multiple it would have before the crash. You'd be committing corporate suicide to sell it right now."

Neil nodded at Harrison, acknowledging his advisor's point. Drawing in on the cigarette, Neil listened to the tobacco crackle under the heat created by the suction of oxygen. After picking a piece of tobacco off of his tongue, he asked Harrison a question.

"Approximately what am I worth?"

"Pardon?"

"What am I worth?"

Harrison leaned back into the angled chair and closed his eyes for a moment. "Why are you doing this?"

"Damn it, Harrison," Neil said evenly. "Answer the question."

Harrison snorted—the sound of a sane man forced to communicate to a crazy one. "Business and personal?"

Neil pitched the cigarette into a fully blooming rose bush and stood, creating a shadow over Harrison. "If I liquidate everything. Your best guess."

Harrison dropped the hat crookedly onto his head. "The company, the estate, the cars, the boat, stocks, bonds, your minority interest in the bank, the property in Santa Cruz, the property in Salinas, your miscellaneous assets…I'd hazard somewhere close to two million. Maybe even two-and-a-quarter."

Neil digested the figure and began to walk. Waving his hand, he motioned Harrison to sit still—he wanted a moment alone to think. He walked from the sitting area, through the curved path of the flower garden and onto the damp green grass of the northern plateau of the Spanish-style estate. Neil could see the towers of the newly completed Golden Gate Bridge, a thick fog bank enveloping the lower half. The top of the fog bank was visibly sheared off by the southern wind, but the land on the southern side of the mouth of the bay, near the Presidio, was protecting the lower half of the fog over the water.

"Two million dollars, maybe two-and-a-quarter," Neil said aloud. In his fifteen years of professional business, he'd never once stopped to estimate how much wealth he had amassed. It would have been like stopping midway through a good round to pronounce his score in golf—an absolute no-no. A veritable curse.

He clearly remembered his pay when he was a young soldier at the Presidio—four dollars every two weeks.

Four measly bucks.

Then, he'd had only fifty-something dollars when he arrived back in Northern California after the Army. He recalled the men he was told to contact, then the companies they told him to work with. He remembered his first shipping order. And his second. It wasn't long before money began to tumble in. His days were long, sometimes loading and unloading crates and cartons from sunup until sundown.

Did he know, back then, that his success was no coincidence?

Turns out, it was guaranteed. The guarantor? Uncle Sam, himself.

After dark, Neil would do as he'd been told, traveling about and reporting on the things he learned. The company—despite being a cover—had grown under his leadership. As his position in society developed, he became more influential, able to learn critical societal secrets that others could not. Despite his Indian blood—which few knew about—Neil had blossomed into one of the bay area's most well respected businessmen.

Yet, he realized now, the vast sum of his net worth didn't add one bit to his personal view of who he was. If anything, it cheapened his self-opinion. For years Neil had convinced himself that his success was due to his own hard work. Sure, he'd been helped along—and for the longest time he made himself believe that the success of his company, the rapid growth and the legal crushing of his nearest competitors, was borne of his own hard work. From its start, with one piddly slip down at Pier 23, to its current position as the largest shipping company in California, Neil had been consumed by the company's growth. But the trappings of his life, like the estate at Hillside and their small yacht, had been Emilee's desires, not his. Unfortunately, had Neil had his way, he'd have slept at the office every night.

But now, since her death, Neil realized Emilee's motivations—the home, the yacht, the cabin down in Santa Cruz, and all of the other niceties she'd been involved in purchasing—hadn't been about her desires to be showy at all. Rather, those purchases had been her futile, desperate efforts to draw him closer to her. And, despite all that, he'd still put her behind his career.

"Sonofabitch," he said aloud, tilting his head back, feeling his self-loathing welling up inside him. His money, his burgeoning company and his position in society had nothing at all to do with his own intelligence. He could have done a horrible job and the company would have still grown like a weed. The men behind his ascent even made him hide his Shoshone heritage. His entire existence in San Francisco was all a fancy ruse, nothing more than a cover—no different than a fake moustache and five and dime wig.

And what had all this cost the government? Couple of million? What's a few million bucks to Uncle Sam, especially when the old man is protecting his interests?

And Emilee had been so damned proud. *If she'd only known the truth*, he thought, shaking his head.

Well, it's all over now.

And, to Neil, blowing it all up felt good.

He strode purposefully back to Harrison, now sitting erect with his Fedora cocked in the fashion of the day.

"How quickly can you arrange for everything to be sold?" Neil asked.

"When you say everything, do you—"

"*Everything*, Harrison. Other than what I can pack in a suitcase." Neil's face was stone, his dual-colored eyes blazing as he watched his already shell-shocked right hand man register the blow of such a request.

Harrison's tone turned formal. "You've lost your mind, sir."

"Maybe so. How long?"

"Months. Perhaps more."

"I want it done this week."

"Pardon?"

"*This—week.*"

Harrison snatched the hat from his head, standing quickly. "If you do that, it's viewed as a fire sale, and everyone will know you've gone utterly mad!"

"That happened a long time ago." Neil's face and expression softened as he gripped the older man's bony shoulder. "Just do it, Harrison. And do it very quietly."

"Is there a…is there a new woman that's made you do this?"

Neil's grip became hydraulic. "No, Harrison. There isn't, and will *never* be, another Em."

Harrison lowered his eyes and didn't respond other than a slight nod.

"Do you want to buy the company?" Neil asked.

"No, sir."

"I'll give it to you at a tremendous discount."

"No, thank you."

Neil stared out over the bay. "Well, Eugene Remington and his partners will buy it. I have no doubt. Take your time today to determine what the entirety is worth, ships, inventory and all, then offer them a twenty-five percent discount contingent upon closing by Friday. Tell them they have to buy everything in the business, down to the lead pencils and rubbish containers, along with all my personal property."

Harrison shook his head, clearly nonplussed but trying to follow along. "They'll never manage to arrange financing that fast."

Neil lit another cigarette, speaking with smoke escaping his mouth. "You don't actually believe that."

"Perhaps it's hope."

Neil smiled. "I think even I could arrange financing, especially if I knew I could make twenty-five percent at the stroke of a fountain pen."

"Very well, sir. It's your company, your things."

"There's another contingency."

"Sir?"

"Discretion. They must keep this from their employees, and we from ours." Neil held up his index finger for emphasis. "I don't want a whiff of this getting out until the papers are signed. And you make sure the lawyers know that, too. There can be *no* escape hatches in any of the contracts."

J. Harrison Musselwhite, IV pinched his craggy lips together and nodded. He looked taken aback and panicky.

"Call in a lawyer you trust to take care of my personal holdings and what not."

"Fine," Harrison said distantly.

"You'll be well taken care of," Neil said. "You've done so much for me…for our company."

Harrison shook Neil's hand and walked back to the chauffeured company Lincoln. Neil called after him. Harrison stopped. Neil strode over, bear-hugging his trusted advisor, clapping him on the back. Harrison pulled back after a moment, eyes wide. Neil, in all of his time with Harrison, had never done more than shake his hand.

"Neil, please tell me you won't do something…" Harrison's voice cracked. He couldn't finish his sentence.

Neil smiled reassuringly. "Harrison, I'm fine. Better than I've been in two years."

The elder man studied Neil for a moment before he entered the Lincoln. Neil could see his employee's ashen face as the car headed to their offices down on Sansome.

Adding a touch of levity to the situation, Neil thought about the call Harrison would soon make to Southern California, to Eugene Remington, the able competitor based at the Port of Los Angeles. And wouldn't Eugene be floored when he received that unexpected phone call? Neil would bet another twenty-five percent of the take that once Remington's wife laid her eyes on Hillside, they'd be making plans for a hasty move to San Francisco.

That made Neil again think of Emilee.

He threw his cigarette on the ground, crushing it out under his black split-toe shoe. He then dropped back in the Adirondack chair and stared in silence out over the bay for a full hour.

Overriding his sorrow was the thought of hundreds of children. He didn't know where they were hiding, but he knew it must be miserable for them. And scary.

There were 52 days remaining before they would miss their ship and come out of hiding.

* * *

Neil's preparations were complete on August 2nd. He had just under a month-and-a-half to get to Innsbruck and lead the hidden children to their freedom. The hired car idled behind Neil. He handed his second bag to the driver, asking the man to give him a moment. Neil turned, stuffing his hands in his pockets, looking at Agnes Holloway. She stood there in the pea gravel drive, a hand over her mouth as was her habit during times of great stress. He stepped in front of her, lifting her chin with his finger. His smile was gentle—unusual for him.

"Are you going to be okay, Aggie?"

She choked on her words. "The real question is, will you be okay?"

"Of course I will." Neil's hand slid up her face, his thumb wiping the burgeoning tears away. "Thank you, Aggie. Thank you for all you've done for me, and for Em. She loved you like a mother, you know that."

"I know she did," Agnes answered, voice cracking.

"And, Aggie," he waited until she joined eyes with him. "I want to apologize for the way I've acted since Emilee's death."

"Why?"

"It consumed me, made me someone I don't want to be. I just want you to know I'm sorry. You never had a proper chance to grieve over Em for having to tend to me and my drunken escapades."

Agnes dipped her head, shaking it.

"Was the money okay?"

"Oh...the money's fine," she answered, stomping one foot and sending pea gravel skittering over Neil's shoes.

"Then what is it?"

There was a long pause as she joined eyes with him, her eyes darting between each of his eyes. "You're never coming back. I have no idea where you're going or what you're planning, but I know...*I know* in my heart that you're never coming back."

Neil made no effort to convince her otherwise. Instead, he pecked her on the cheek. "Aggie, the pension I provided you is taxable."

"I don't know what that even means."

"But the large box of cash that I placed under your bed...it's *not* taxable. Just don't ever deposit it or spend too much in one place, okay? Buy a nice safe and keep it there, then use it for your spending money. It should last you many, many years."

Agnes Holloway's jaw ceased operations.

Neil lifted his finger for emphasis. "You'll eventually be questioned about my departure, and that's fine. Hold nothing back. But please, *until then*, not a word. And don't mention the cash," he said with a wink. "Don't *ever* mention the cash."

With a final wave, he entered the back of the car, instructing the driver to take him to San Francisco Municipal Airport, located south of downtown. Neil stared at Agnes Holloway, his longtime maidservant, as the car crunched out of the gravel drive and away from Hillside.

Forever.

Chapter Five

IT WAS A FEW MINUTES BEFORE SIX IN the evening in Washington D.C. A summer thunderstorm had just blown through, racing northeast with the speed of an automobile and still trailing light rain as lightning cracked in the distance. Behind it, the bureaucratic city was left catching its breath in cooler temperatures and unseasonable wind. With its driver taking advantage of the wet roads, a speeding inky black Lincoln slid to a stop in front of the State, War, and Navy Building.

The building, like most government structures in Washington, was enormous. Decidedly old French in its design, making it somewhat unique, it had drawn the ire of many a discriminating eye over time. Mark Twain once termed it "the ugliest building in America."

Preston Lord, the Lincoln's primary occupant, had shown prescience years before when he lobbied to be stationed in the new government buildings down at Foggy Bottom. He knew, all too well, that the State, War, and Navy Building was inefficient in design as well as bursting at its seams. The original tenants, the War Department and the Department of the Navy, would soon be vacating because of the heavy overcrowding. It was so bad that, on the first and third floors, secretaries and low-level bureaucrats were forced to move their desks, en masse, into long rows in the hallways. Even the basement—it was nothing more than a leaky, damp, rat-infested hole—was now being used by the lowest rung of senior officials.

Lord lurched from the backseat of the official Lincoln, flicking a cigarette in an arc as he crossed the wet sidewalk. Above him, the soaked American flag with its 48 stars, lit in the stormy dark afternoon by dueling triangles of spotlights, furled and popped with each strong gust.

The Department of War's very first Observation Director, Lord entered through the main entrance on Pennsylvania, stomping his feet before hustling across the lobby. The armed guard mumbled a greeting and allowed Lord access to the curved stairwell, which he took two steps at a time. On the second floor, he made his way through two levels of security before padding down the long, portrait-laden executive hall, the footsteps from his handmade shoes dampened by the thick burgundy carpet. Though he had walked this corridor hundreds of times, Lord had never once stopped to view the oil paintings of the stuffy-looking men, nation builders, none of whom ever lived to see their portrait hung. Because Preston Lord, like most of his compatriots in Washington, had little concept, or appreciation, of history. Most in Washington were concerned with two things: where they were now, and where the next election would take them.

The Observation Director was different from most, however. A sharp-nosed, hatchet faced, ruthless man with degrees from two prestigious northeastern universities, he worried *only* about the present, and his unscrupulous climb to the top. He didn't concern himself over the next election. He knew his instincts were cat-like—he'd always be able to land on his feet.

Working as a rogue only added to Lord's mystique. Precious few knew of his battery of shadowy agents—hard men with high intelligence quotients and little regard for human life. In fact, Lord purposefully kept most of the facts of his team to himself. In his mind, this protected him, and would guarantee his position from administration to administration.

Though he was trust fund wealthy, Lord felt no allegiance to his family—he hadn't spoken to his mother or two brothers in years. They'd called his office; they'd sent letters and telegrams—he stopped answering when he realized there was nothing to be gained by it. He wished they would leave him alone or, better yet, just die. To Lord, family was a colossal waste of time. Most traditional things were.

The only true diversion Lord enjoyed was sex, of the masochistic variety. He was unquenchable, preferring married women due to their necessity for discretion—and for the glorious fact that they *always* had to leave. Their leaving was the second-best part of the liaison; he had no desire to share his home, or his non-sexual time, with another soul.

And because of a planned sexual rendezvous this evening, Lord wished the phone call he'd just received would have come tomorrow morning, *after* he planted his seed in that panting round-assed, wedded secretary from Justice. But now he'd have to stand her up because, in Washington, there was no such thing as a regular life schedule. And Lord had long since grown used to a timeless, calendarless way of life, going all the way back to his first day working as a page for an insipid junior congressman from South Dakota.

Lord reached the end of the executive hallway, glancing around to see no one. After quickly thumbing through the papers on the two secretaries' desks, finding nothing of great interest, he placed his hand on the knob of his boss's door and listened. Following ten seconds of scant sounds, he took a great breath and burst through the door. Seated at his large desk with his feet propped up, reading from his daily periodical brief, was Henderson Wolfe Mayfield, known by the public as H.W., known to his friends simply as "Wolfie." Mayfield, the former congressman from Tennessee, was now the United States Secretary of War, appointed to the office by President Roosevelt three years earlier after Mayfield's predecessor died of a stroke while eating Lady Baltimore cake at a state dinner.

Upon rudely infiltrating his boss's office, Lord noticed Mayfield's rubescent face. Lord kept coming, purposefully stepping around the expansive desk to see the crystal tumbler, warm in the Secretary's hand, half-filled with potent Kentucky liquid.

"Don't you knock?" Secretary Mayfield growled. A devout Methodist, he kept his drinking highly secret, even from his wife. Over the past three years, Lord had always chuckled at the copious numbers of peppermint wrappers and Listerine bottles that filled Mayfield's trash bin. With a reputation as one of the hardest workers in Washington, the Tennessean was known to work well past midnight five and six nights a week. Lord, however, believed it was all a ruse designed to allow Mayfield to do the two things he lived for: drink heavily and read.

Secretary Mayfield placed the tumbler in a drawer, carefully pushing it shut. He stood, brushing past Lord and closing himself in his restroom. The running water didn't completely cover the sound of his gargling. Several minutes later, the Secretary of War emerged, his face and leading wisps of hair damp. He walked to his window, staring at the rain-slick lawn and, in the near distance, the White House. The clouds were quickly dissipating, with a few hints of pink twilight showing in the west.

"I should hope you've a suitable motivation to burst into my chamber unannounced," Mayfield said in his deep drawl. He turned and glared. "Impudence at its essence."

"I received a call from one of my men in California. A disturbing call."

Mayfield gestured to the sofa as he took a seat in a high-back chair. "A call about what?"

"About Neil Reuter."

Mayfield's eyes flicked to his right before coming back to Lord's. The Secretary had to keep up with thousands of people, projects, operations, bills, conflicts. Added to all of those things, he still had to perform each of the duties that went along with being a married father of four—and a closet alcoholic. Despite his innumerable obligations, Lord noticed Mayfield's recognition at the mention of Reuter's name.

Because Neil Reuter knew where all the bodies were buried.

Literally.

Mayfield nodded. "Yes, Reuter. The, ah…shipping fellow. I remember something about him. Go on."

"Well…" Lord fingered his fedora, stalling.

"Well, what?"

Lord smiled a torturous smile.

"What?"

"He's gone."

"Gone?"

"Yes, sir. Gone."

"I remember Reuter," Mayfield said, shooing with his hand. "He's been a drunk since that tragedy with his wife. Probably shacked up in some whorehouse, or passed out in an alleyway somewhere. He'll turn up."

Lord continued to grin as he slowly shook his head.

Mayfield frowned, his voice growing edgy. "What's this all about?"

"He's not laid up drunk. He's not out whoring."

"Then where is he?" Mayfield demanded, poking a rigid finger into the arm of the chair. An impatient man, he despised being brought along slowly. And Lord thoroughly enjoyed torturing him by doing just that.

"*Where*, damn it?"

"Reuter has fled."

"Fled?"

"Yes."

"Why do you say that?"

"I'll come back to it." Lord sat on the edge of the chair. "Do you remember the name Lex Curran?"

"No, I do not. Get to the damned point. What makes you say Reuter has fled?"

Two "damns" in mere seconds.

Lord knew he was on dangerous ground. The drinking was Mayfield's little secret, but the man almost never cursed. As a matter of fact, the only time Preston Lord had ever heard him swear was two years before – and the object of that vicious ass chewing, a former high-level bureaucrat, was now the assistant manager of a struggling grocery store in Fairfax. Abandoning his irksome game, Lord explained.

"If you will recall, Lex Curran is the man accused of murdering Neil Reuter's wife. So, back to Reuter—I received a phone call a short while ago...disturbing to say the least." Lord lifted his left hand and checked off items by pulling down his fingers. "Reuter sold his business, his estate, his boat, his cars...everything down to the last rake in his gardening shed...and yesterday, he *disappeared*."

"Sold everything?"

"Every *single* thing he owned," Lord replied sharply. "Do you have any idea what that portends, what he could do to us?"

The florid color Mayfield's face had held earlier was now replaced by ghostly white. He pulled his mouth shut, clearing his throat before speaking. "How did you find out?"

Lord shrugged. "Routine check turned it up."

Mayfield stood. He walked to the drawer and removed the tumbler of whiskey, downing all of it, his discretion apparently lost in the moment. "And this Curran fellow, why did you mention him?"

"Do you really want to know?" Lord asked, unable to keep his thin lips from twisting in a smirk.

"Yes."

Lord reset his countenance. "I'm not trying to be cute. You truly might not want to know this, for your own protection."

"Just say it, damn you."

One curse word in three years, and now three today. Guess I touched a nerve. "After the murder, when the police were forced to release Lex Curran due to lack of evidence, I snatched him."

"You what?" Mayfield bellowed.

"I snatched him. I did what I felt was right." Lord shrugged. "And, turns out, I was right."

The Tennessean stormed across the room, grasping Lord's hand-tailored suit jacket and lifting him by the lapels and growling his words. "Your reckless, cavalier ways will land me in a federal prison."

Lord was eye-to-eye with the hazel-eyed Secretary. "Unhand me…right now."

"Why did you do such a thing?"

"Because, if you will just calm down and think back to that time, you'll recall I wanted Reuter neutralized after the murder of his wife. He was too much of a risk. But *you* wouldn't allow me to take Reuter out, so I grabbed Curran as my insurance policy."

Mayfield loosened his grip. "You've kept a United States citizen captive—for two years?"

"Absolutely. And, after a little bit of pain, Curran confessed to what he did. Cried like a little baby, and he's been crying ever since. C'mon, it's not like I've been holding some cherubic choirboy against his will. This guy is a gutter-dwelling rapist and killer. Hell, I did the citizenry a favor. To hell with that bastard."

Mayfield released Lord and shoved him backward, spitting his next words. "These methods of yours, they're not only unconstitutional, they're criminal."

"There is *no* justice among men."

"Don't start laying famous quotes on me. Where's Curran now?"

"Just before I came over here to see you, I ordered him shot and killed." Lord stopped the coming rebuke with an upheld hand. "And, no, I cannot recall my order. The wheels are in motion on an order that can't be undone." He took a step closer. "Because, Secretary Mayfield, I want your ass to be on the line…with my own. That way, you'll be more motivated to jump behind this little plan I've developed."

Mayfield took a step back, aghast. "You ordered Curran *killed?*"

"You heard me, Wolfie."

The Secretary of War staggered back to his desk, plopping down as he stared off into nothingness. "Why?"

Lord mumbled to himself something about how the seniormost officials are often also the most naïve. He then spoke slowly, enunciating loudly like he might to someone who recently learned English. "Because, sir, I want the general public, and the local authorities, to think Neil Reuter did it."

"But why?"

"Because no one knows where Reuter is," Lord laughed, throwing his hands up. "He's fled, don't ya see? And now if he turns up and starts talking about all the things he's done, we'll simply say he's crazy over his wife's death, and a murderer to boot."

"Reuter knows too much. He could ruin us all."

"Funny how you could barely remember him a few minutes ago, and now you're an expert on the man." Lord gestured around. "I have men in every major city of this country, and many more scattered around the world. Once Reuter's located, I can neutralize him in mere hours."

"You're mad."

"Hey, I wanted him gone after his wife's murder. You're the bleeding heart who ordered him spared. So, in essence, this is *your* fault."

Secretary Mayfield glared at his shadowy subordinate. "Where do you think he went?"

"The man's crazy—always has been. He's got Indian blood, you know. For all I know, he could've just gone out into the wilderness to dig his own grave and die in it."

"And if not?"

"He's hours from being wanted for murder. We'll find him."

The secretary reached into the back of his drawer. He poured another glass of liquor, taking a long sip with closed eyes. "God help us if you don't."

Chapter Six

THE STATE-OF-THE-ART DOUGLAS DC-3 LIFTED OFF, the twin radial engines droning loudly as the fully loaded airplane clawed its way into the damp evening sky at Chicago's Air Park Airport. Traveling under the name Frank O'Ryan, Neil pondered all that lay ahead. Facing rearward, he unbuttoned his Glen plaid suit jacket, adjusting himself in the seat. After almost a full day in Chicago, he was ready to get this long leg of the flight over with.

Once he eventually landed in New York, Neil was scheduled for a morning meeting in Manhattan. After that meeting, he would hopefully have an impeccable new identity that no one could possibly trace. Neil would then travel by ship to England. Once in England, he'd have to find transportation to Austria—no small task.

When the airplane leveled off over the southern rim of Lake Michigan, the engine noise abated somewhat. Neil pulled the flexible seat lamp over his lap and opened his loose-leaf notebook, resuming the transcription. He quietly spoke the German to himself as he translated Mark Twain's *Huckleberry Finn* into proper German text. Neil's father had been a first-generation German from the small farming town of Lich, located in Central Germany. While his mother's people had raised Neil in the ways of the Shoshone, his father had insisted they speak German in the home. During the war, Neil had used his experience from both upbringings. Since then, however, he'd hardly spoken German. Now he had the desire, and a life-dependent reason, to speak the language once again. And he'd need to speak it like a native. He worked hard to make sure his *CH* sounds were crisp and guttural, and to burr his *R's* in the Austrian way.

Feeling a bit fatigued, Neil reached between the seats and removed his brown leather bag, pushing his service .45 to the side as he retrieved a fresh pack of cigarettes. He slit open the pack with his thumbnail and lit one.

"May I have one, please?" the lady across from him asked, leaning forward and touching his knee. In front of her, on the small teak table that separated them, was a tumbler half-full of clear liquor, which she swirled expectantly. She had boarded in Chicago. Neil made her as thirty years old, or perhaps a year or two shy of the milestone age. She spoke with a foreign accent and her eyes appeared faintly Asian. Neil handed her a Lucky Strike and couldn't help but notice her firm, generous bosom as she leaned forward, the cigarette perched in her mouth as she awaited a light.

"What's your accent?" Neil asked offhandedly as he flicked his lighter.

She puffed the cigarette coolly, leaving a tight red ring of lipstick. "I am Russian," she said, resuming her perusal of the newest Look Magazine. She didn't thank him for the cigarette; she didn't smile.

And she didn't look at him again.

Neil examined her clothes, eyeing the trim blue suit that contrasted nicely with her auburn hair. Judging by her suit, her shoes, her handbag and her demeanor, she came from money—rare for the few Russians Neil had ever met in the States. He blinked several times, wondering why he was even intrigued. He resumed his translation.

Much later, Neil jolted as he felt movement around his hands. It was her, the Russian. He had been dozing with his legs stretched out when the Russian lady had spirited the notebook from his lap. He tried to grab it but she'd already pulled it across the table.

"Excuse me?" he said, holding his hand open for the notebook.

"What is all this?" she asked, holding the book under the light, moving her index finger over the scrawled German, loaded with a number of the very German scharfes-S characters and umlauts.

"It's German," he said, snatching the notebook back. "And it's *private*."

"Cigarette," she commanded, snapping her fingers.

"Direct, aren't you?" he asked, producing two cigarettes. The man across the aisle from them stirred. The Russian woman's makeup and hair were as perfect as they had been when they had boarded the aircraft five hours earlier.

She stared at him, her face so neutral and unreadable that it was almost unnerving. After several drags on the cigarette, she leaned forward, tapping the black linen covering of the novel. "Who translates Huckleberry Finn into German?"

Neil stuffed the notebook and the novel into his bag, careful not to allow the nosy Russian to see his Colt. As he worked with his bag, he spoke. "I own a small publishing company. We're translating the book into German. I do much of the work myself."

"Liar."

"What did you just call me?" Neil asked, raising his eyebrows.

Rather than answer, the Russian woman pressed the switch of her lamp, reclining in her seat. She pulled on the cigarette once more before crushing it out. As she closed her eyes to sleep, a sly smirk remained on her face.

For the next seventy minutes of the flight, Neil tried his absolute best not to stare at her. It wasn't that she was not attractive—she was—but Neil was proficient at reading people, their motives and their emotions. And while this Russian was a cool customer who could probably make serious money as a card sharp, his instinct told him her interest in him was more than casual. So, even though he knew it was rude, he kept on staring. And, as the plane began its descent, the Russian opened her eyes, seeing his gaze. She returned the stare, neutrally.

Neil turned away first.

* * *

One hour later, a damp, salty wind blew in from Flushing Bay, rushing over the tarmac of Long Island's North Beach Airport in Queens. Neil leaned into the heavy breeze, holding his trilby hat in place, his body buffeted by each gust as he awaited his two pieces of luggage. In the distance, another DC-3 roared down the runway, crabbing sideways into the crosswind as it finally levitated into the wet, morning sky. Neil turned to look in the direction of Manhattan, unable to see anything beyond the dingy Queens skyline. From this distance, Manhattan was obscured by the gray and fog of the passing weather. This would be Neil's quickest ever visit to the world's center of commerce, a place he and Emilee had visited several times.

Just as his heartache was about to strike full force, the airline employee appeared with his luggage, a rolling trunk and a standard grip. Neil tipped him as the Russian woman reappeared and stood very close to his side on the blustery tarmac. As a brief tempest of stronger wind made her grab his arm for support, she leaned to him and spoke into his ear. "I wish I had gotten a chance to know you better."

Neil pulled his head back so he could get a better look at her. "Thanks for saying that," he answered, not really knowing exactly what she meant, or how else to respond.

She curled her finger, beckoning him in as the roar from another airplane filled the area with a thunderous drone. "Tread carefully now," she said, squeezing his upper arm. "What you're doing doesn't begin in Austria. It starts right here, today, in New York. Word is already out about your estate sale and identity change."

Neil frowned, narrowing his eyes as he pondered how in the hell this Russian, who had boarded in *Chicago*, could know what he was doing. The woman, still gripping his arm, leaned in again.

"You can make no mistakes, understand? There will be but one chance. Many powerful people want you dead."

"Who? What are you talking about?"

"The people who killed your friend, Jacob. They're after you now."

Neil knew he'd been burnt so he decided to drop his ruse. "Nazis?"

"Yes, Nazis. Americans, too. Trust no one." She patted his cheek. "No one, at all."

"Including you?"

The Russian twisted her lips into a small smile before turning serious again. "Please, save our children."

With that, she turned, barking instructions to the driver of her hired car as she motioned with her elbow-length gloved hands. The short man hustled her suitcases into the back as she held her overcoat tightly around her waist. Before she entered the Cadillac, she looked back one final time at Neil. There was no facial expression other than a distinct voltage in her wide coffee eyes.

Neil watched the black car drive away, spinning its tires as it disappeared, headed west into the morning traffic on Astoria Boulevard. Alarms were going off in Neil's mind and, after a moment, he realized he had been holding his breath.

Who was she? How did she know what he was doing? This was foreign ground for Neil. He wasn't used to being made and, in fact, had never dealt with such a situation before. He analyzed what she had said: *tread carefully; it starts here; no mistakes; only one chance.*

"And many powerful people want me dead," he whispered.

She hadn't made a lucky guess, because she mentioned Austria. His paperwork, in the event she'd somehow gone through it while he had slept, only went as far as New York. Everything else was booked in another person's name and he didn't have the itinerary yet.

Neil thought back through his planning for a moment. He'd left no loose ends. After a moment of reasoning, he tabled the strange encounter. He'd have to worry about it later.

His focus now turned to what needed to occur on this dreary Thursday morning. It wasn't until his own hired car was fifty feet over the East River that he realized there was something peculiar going on inside him. Something different…

For two full years he had been dealing with Emilee's death, mostly by drinking himself into a stupor. Initially there had been the typical emotions involved with a tragic death: shock, anger and sorrow. On the second day after her murder, the slimy, underworld hood named Lex Curran was identified as the chief suspect. The police arrested him before Neil could even get back to San Francisco. Upon arriving, he rushed straight to the police station, forced to sit in the police captain's office for hours on end. Neil was a simmering volcano. After nightfall, there was a commotion outside of the office. The captain appeared, stepping into the office and pulling the door shut.

"We have to release the man we apprehended."

Neil had bolted from his chair. "Do you think he did it?"

"I do, but I think his cronies are coverin' for him. We've also got a witness, but he didn't identify a picture of your wife." The captain shook his head. "May take a day or two but we'll get Curran...just need to do our due diligence and upend these alibis he's managed to come up with."

"You *definitely* think he did it?"

"Absolutely and without a hair of reservation."

Neil didn't respond. His mind was already made up about what he would do. But it was at that exact moment when Lex Curran and his attorney had slithered from the back of the station, the lawyer barking orders and acting as if it were his citing of numerous statutes that had done the trick. Until then, Neil had no idea who Lex Curran was, didn't even know his name. But upon seeing him, he knew in a flash the man was guilty. Curran's sneer was wicked, his eyes knowing as he smugly sauntered around the station.

Neil was going to take great pleasure in killing him.

While Neil had stood there, transfixed, gazing at the killer of his wife and unborn son, Curran turned his head and obviously realized who Neil was. Curran shrugged off his lawyer's oily grip and walked to the office.

"Looks like I'm a free man, Reuter," Curran drawled. "Guess I'll go back to the neighborhood...see what other kinda trouble I can get into."

To say Neil leapt at him was an understatement. No sooner had Curran spoken the words than the police sergeant and captain lurched in anticipation of what might happen. They were a second too slow.

Neil threw his coffee at Lex's face as he dug his hands into the soft flesh around the criminal's neck, the two men going down in a scrabbling heap in the hallway. Neil's powerful hands were like steel traps, trying to exterminate the man he knew had raped and killed his wife. Once the policemen were able to get Neil off of him, the coffee-drenched Lex Curran exacerbated the situation by blowing kisses at Neil while Curran's lawyer dragged him away.

As they walked to the lawyer's car, Curran's lawyer even tried to have Neil arrested for assault. The captain wouldn't hear of it, earning the threat of a lawsuit from the lawyer. Outside by the car, Curran begged every reporter present to take pictures of the claw marks on his neck where Neil had managed to draw ten points of blood.

"And he burned me with hot coffee," Curran added.

The murder of Emilee Stonington Reuter was an immediate boon to every newspaper in the Bay Area, but that didn't mean the reporters cared for the man who had presumably killed her. One reporter "boo-hooed" after Lex mentioned the hot coffee. Seconds later, the reporter was hunched over, holding a bloody nose.

Neil went after Curran that night, after midnight. He never found him. He repeated his actions the next day. Again, Curran was nowhere to be found. The police proved Curran's alibis were false. Additionally, they produced several pieces of incriminating evidence and put out a warrant for Curran's arrest.

They couldn't find him either.

Jakey came home for a month, primarily to look after Neil. Using every trick they knew, the two men rousted the entire underbelly of San Francisco, twisting arms and offering bribes for any scrap of information on the fugitive. Their efforts were fruitless.

Lex Curran had vanished.

Neil recalled one heart-rending evening many weeks after the murder, when he sat in his study, alone with his vodka and sorrow. He'd heard the crunch of gravel and the squeak of brakes, peering out of his window to see the headlights go out on the plain brown Plymouth parked in front of the mansion. Neil stood in the turnout at Hillside, trembling with anger and rage as he listened to the precinct's captain, Yarborough, explaining Curran's disappearance. The chief detective on the case, a Greek fellow named Kalakis, sat in the car. The window was partly open, the detective no doubt listening to every word.

Captain Yarborough was a short barrel of a man with a quarter inch of steely hair and a florid face dotted with ruptured capillaries. He lit both of their cigarettes and leaned back on the fender of the unmarked car, narrowing his hazel eyes at Neil. When he spoke, his boyhood Scottish accent lilted through only at the tail end of his sentences, like a curlicue at the end of a beautifully penned word.

"I know a bit of what ya done in the military, and I think I know what ya prob'ly did to Lex Curran."

Neil shook his head. "No, I didn't. If I had, I'd be sleeping right now."

The policeman studied him, the only light from the gas lamps on the house throwing top-down shadows on their faces. "I believe ya, Mister Reuter."

"I really don't care if you do or don't. That bastard's disappeared and I fault *you* for letting it happen."

"We're bound by th'law. I don't like it anymore'n ya do. Believe me." The captain held the cigarette in the corner of his mouth and folded his arms over his indigo uniform. "But I know what you're gonna do if'n ya ever do find Lex Curran. God knows if I was in your place I'd probably do it tonight, if'n I could find the slippery bastard."

Neil stared at the ground as he pulled on the cigarette.

"But, listen to me, Mr. Reuter...look at me, please."

"What?"

"You're too important a man to all those who depend on ya to throw your life away over south wharf, career criminal trash like Lex Curran."

The captain's face broke into a knowing grin as he glanced around. "Ya follow?"

Neil simply stared.

"I think ya do," the captain said, sweeping his arm at the mansion. "So, why don't ya use some'a this money of yours to put a quiet bounty on this fella's head to find him. And when ya do, just make sure when ya kill that focker, you're sufficiently insulated. Use someone ya trust and have a tight, undeniable alibi. Maybe ya could be outta town or attendin' a party with hundreds of people. I can promise ya that, if'n we have anything close to a shade of gray on ya, there won't be an investigation."

Neil flipped the cigarette onto the pea gravel and straightened, towering over the short policeman. "Thanks for the advice." And, as Neil turned to go back inside, he paused and turned. "But if I ever do find Curran, I'm going to kill him, and it's going to be long and slow. There's no way I'd ever give someone else that pleasure."

Captain Yarborough removed the flask from his wool uniform coat and took two hard swallows. He nodded his understanding and lifted his flask in a toast to Neil; then he and Detective Kalakis drove away.

Since Emilee's death, Neil had spent a fortune searching for Lex Curran. During the first year he went to Curran's bar once a week, bracing the new owner who had innocently purchased it at auction from the city. As if he could still pick up on Lex Curran's scent, Neil would charge into the bar's storeroom and office, the new proprietor protesting feebly. After finding it clean, Neil would usually mumble an apology before plopping down at the long, sticky bar, drinking vodka on ice, ignoring the stares of the old geezers who sat there, day in and day out, soaking their livers the way a janitor drenches a dirty mop. As the months droned on, Neil's searching decreased while his drinking increased. After a year, when the San Francisco Police had all but given up, Neil's drinking outweighed his searching by 10-to-1.

By the time Neil departed for Austria, he'd all but given up his search.

Lex Curran was long gone—taken from Neil, in a way that was perversely similar to the way Emilee and his unborn child had been taken from him. All he wanted was a chance to avenge his family. Emilee had been so good to him, so patient with him, never deserving to die the way she had. His character demanded he avenge her, and the only way he had been able to tamp down his raging regret had been with alcohol.

Neil's eyes were rimmed with redness. He gnawed on his lip as both his hands dug into the rear bench seat of the hired car.

And though he couldn't describe it, Jakey's letter had triggered something inside of Neil. He had been nearing his personal rock bottom when the note had arrived. Something had been about to give—though

Neil didn't know what. He wanted to think he wasn't the type to take his own life in an overt manner, but drinking himself to death would have been perfectly acceptable, and he had been well on his way. One of those drunken days, Neil would have eventually blacked out from the vodka and never woken up. But Jakey's message had awakened him in a different way, and he now had a purpose. A mission.

A mission he had to fulfill before he died.

The hired car ground to a stop in a line of cars just like it. Chelsea Piers buzzed to the right of the cars, while Manhattan's West Side loomed to the left. Neil wiped his forehead with his handkerchief, fortifying himself with deep breaths.

There was work to be done.

Chapter Seven

SALVATORE KALAKIS, KNOWN TO HIS FRIENDS AS SAL, exited the bus at Columbus and Stockton Streets, hustling through the bay area mist into his police precinct. In the detectives' room, the familiar smell of male body odor and gun oil mingled with the diluted aroma of Harry Cato's weak coffee. Cato's special brew irritated Sal to no end.

How early does that fella get in every day?

Sal vowed to be in prior to six tomorrow. For today, he would have to wait until the tepid Cato-coffee was gone before racing to the percolator to make a proper pot, strong and bitter and with a dash of sea salt, in the Greek style like his mother had taught him many moons ago.

Eyeing the pot as he stepped to the communications table at the back of the room, Sal grumbled when he noticed no one had consumed even a single cup. "Damned Cato," he growled. Sal grabbed a Chronicle, still warm off the press, taking it back to his cluttered desk. He scanned the headlines and second page for anything that might interest him.

Germans, Neville Chamberlain, more Germans—the lead story was yet another piece about an anti-Jewish law passed in Germany. That damned psychotic Hitler was thirsting for someone to go to war with. Sal had served in France during the Great War. He still walked with a slight limp as the result of a knee mortar that had lived up to its very name. Now the Germans were back on the charge—led by the Nazis this time—building a war machine and enlisting every man, woman, and child. At least there was the relative solace of the sports page, which he spirited out from the thick paper. After skimming the headlines, he glanced around for Harry Cato. Not seeing him, Sal tiptoed to the back of the room and poured half the pot of coffee out the open window, laughing at the surprised protests from the sidewalk on Columbus Street two floors below. Sal pinched off his grin and hurried back to his desk.

He was just settling into the comfort of the sports page when a young patrolman burst into the room, carrying with him the distinct smell of the ocean. "You Detective Kalakis?" the kid gasped, his splotchy cheeks expanding and contracting with his heavy huffing.

"Yeah, why?"

The policeman bent over and rested his hands on his knees, gasping oxygen as perspiration gathered in a great droplet under his rounded chin. He looked as if he had just run a marathon.

"Got...a...message...for...you...from...Cap'n...Yarborough."

"Get your breath, kid."

The young officer took a few more great breaths, finally able to speak normally. "Cap'n took the call from us in the middle of the night."

"Took what call, and why didn't he radio me instead of forcing you into an early heart attack?" Sal asked, his forced gruffness replaced by brusque concern.

"Said he only wanted you to hear it, for now," the policeman answered, taking a final massive breath before resuming a normal posture. "He said to tell you…" his eyes went skyward as he paused. As if trying to divine the message from thin air, the young cop opened his hands. His mouth opened, but no words escaped.

Sal redlined at the kid's hemming and hawing. He jerked the paper so hard the sports page ripped in half. "You gotta be kidding me! What? What? What did he tell you to tell me?"

"Just making sure I get the name right." The patrolman seemed to recollect it as he nodded confidently. "Okay, I got it. Cap'n said to tell you, and *only* you…he was very specific about that."

Sal spoke through clenched teeth. "Spit it the hell out, kid."

The patrolman nodded, finally seeming to grasp that Sal was about to decapitate him. "A man named Lex Curran…he's been missing."

"No shit, he's been missing," Sal snapped. "What about him?"

"Well…we found him a few hours ago, hung up on the rocks, out near the Pacific."

"Found him?"

"Yes, sir. And he has a bullet hole smack dab in the middle of his forehead. There are distinct powder burns around the bullet hole."

"What?" Sal blared, standing so quickly that his chair shot straight backward. The chair rolled with such force that it struck the communications table and sent Harry Cato's remaining coffee splashing all over the grimy green linoleum.

"The powder burns, detective, typically mean that the murder weapon was fired at close range."

"Where exactly is the body?" Sal asked, ignoring the greenhorn patrolman's patronizing forensics tip.

"South of the new Golden Gate Bridge, out on the Baker Beach side. I can show you."

"Let's make tracks," Sal said, grabbing a set of keys from the board on the wall as he motioned with his hand.

A minute later, Sal put his foot in the floor of the Ford Coupe and didn't let up until he saw the frenzied seagulls circling, indignant that they were being denied such a fine feast. Sal instructed the patrolman to stay up on the dirt road and to keep any curious onlookers at bay.

Captain Ciril Yarborough stood on the jagged rocks as the water splashed ten feet below him. A cigarette dangled from the Captain's lips and his hat twirled nervously in his hand while his bald head absorbed the sun. Sal could tell that his superior was itching to show him the body bobbing in the water just below him.

"Took ya so long?" Yarborough asked.

Sal struggled over the enormous, mossy rocks until he found a spot where he felt halfway safe to stand. In a small eddy below them floated the familiar figure of Lex Curran, face up. He was bloated—a hole in his forehead. Just behind his head floated enough loose attachments of skin and skull that Sal immediately knew the bullet had been high-powered. Several brown fish brazenly nibbled and tugged at the loose skin.

"Can't say I'm too sorry this guy's no longer among the living," Yarborough pronounced, the cigarette clamped between his yellow teeth. "Ya bring any coffee?"

Small waves lapped at the rocks, and mist flew in the air from the larger waves that crashed just around the point. Sal shook his head as he stared at Lex Curran, his mind struggling to imagine why Curran would finally surface—here—dead.

"You kept this quiet?" he mumbled to the captain.

"I did. How much time did ya burn on this bastard?"

"Two years, almost to the day," Sal answered automatically. "Who found him?"

"Fishermen called it in. Trolled around the point and saw the gulls in the moonlight. They didn't see the body. Just called and said something was dead over here. With the new bridge there's been a fair number of jumpers and the currents take their bodies all over the bay." Yarborough dragged deeply on the cigarette before flicking it in the water. "I was monitoring an all-nighter, about to go home, when patrol called me. I put a lid on it and waited for ya."

"Thanks, Cappy," Sal said without smiling. "Anything to indicate where he's been?"

Yarborough knelt down, using his pen to push aside the top of Curran's shirt. "See the upper chest? Scars...old scars...lots of 'em. Were those there before?"

"We didn't strip him, but we did turn up pictures of him from a beach trip and I don't recall any notable scars on his torso."

"And the bugger's lost quite a piece a weight since he ran away, even bloated like he is. My guess is someone held Curran a while, and his recalcitrant nature finally got to his captor."

Sal knelt down on the other side of the eddy, lifting Curran's sleeve. The skin on his hand was loose, like an oily rubber glove too large for the hand it covered. There were striations around the wrist. "Handcuffs?"

"Looks like that t'me."

Sal dropped the arm back in the water. "Reuter?"

"Ya read my mind."

"Have you sent someone to grab him?"

"A'course. Sent the partner of the patrol who came and got ya. Sent him with strict orders to keep it quiet."

Sal nodded. "Did he get him?"

Silence.

Sal looked up at his captain, standing on the adjacent, higher rock. His face was bright with the aura of the eastern sun on one side, a dark shadow on the other.

"Cappy?"

"Salvatore…Neil Reuter is gone."

"Do you mean gone, as in dead, or gone as in out of town?"

"I mean, *gone*, gone. Poof! Vanished like a magic man." Yarborough answered with his full accent and a mock magician's gesticulation of his hands.

Sal glanced back down at Lex Curran's puffy body before climbing up to Yarborough's rock. "Was anyone at his estate?"

"The kid that went to Hillside got back to me ten minutes before ya did. Said a woman named Agnes Holloway—I guess ya remember her, Reuter's housekeeper—she said the estate had been sold last week. Sold lightning quick. Said Reuter gave her two years' salary and a fancy new Oldsmobile. Said she has to vacate her cottage in a couple of weeks. Said she's going to Saratoga to be near her daughter."

Sal struggled to process everything, twisting his face as the realities began to strike him. "Wait a minute. Reuter *sold* his estate? He sold *Hillside*?"

"Accordin' to the housekeeper, he did," Yarborough answered, his face a mix of frustration and amusement.

Sal pressed fingers on his eyes and wished he had some coffee in his hand to help him wake up. This was all way too much to take before caffeine.

Damn you, Harry Cato.

"Did she say where Reuter went?" Sal asked.

"Wait, there's more," Yarborough replied, clearly enjoying himself.

"C'mon Cappy…you're killing me."

"When the patrolman pressured the housekeeper a tad, she told him that General Logistics, Reuter's company, was sold, too—lock, stock and barrel. Sold to some outfit from the southern end of the state. She said the company was sold, along with *everything* else Reuter owned. All facilitated by his finance man, Musselwhite." The captain eyed Sal Kalakis. "Sal, th' housekeeper said Neil Reuter left town last night."

"Where?"

"Said she didn't know. Said she thought he left on an aeroplane."

Sal felt his equilibrium falter so he repositioned his feet for balance. Neil Reuter, grieving widower, a man who many felt would seek to avenge his wife's death, had cleaned house and liquidated everything…and now he was gone, scot-free.

And just a foot below Sal was the reprehensible Lex Curran—missing for the past two years—now reduced to fish food.

Yarborough jerked his head to the trail. "Let's log this in official-like and leave our uniformed boy wonders here so they can bag and tag this piece o' shit. Ya can buy me some breakfast before ya hit up the housekeeper and Musselwhite."

"You gonna let me work this?" Sal asked.

"Do ya honestly think I woulda gotten splashed by freezing water for two hours if I wasn't? This is your baby, Sal. Ya stay on it. I'll give ya all the underlings ya need."

As Yarborough climbed the rocks and walked to his car, Sal stood there staring at the glazed eyes of Lex Curran. He wasn't at all sorry for the man. In Sal's estimation, it had most certainly been Lex who had raped and murdered Emilee Reuter. They'd found even more evidence after his disappearance, and if they'd had a trial, Sal was a hundred percent confident they'd have gotten a conviction.

But it appeared someone else had tried and convicted Curran, and the sentence was what looked like a .45 round through the skull. Fair enough.

"Come on, boyo!" Yarborough yelled, slapping his palm on the sheet metal of the car.

Caffeine addiction took precedent over personal rumination.

* * *

The massive hulk of the gleaming, state-of-the-art RMS Queen Mary towered over Neil as he stood beside his hired car. Neil paid the driver, instructing him to find a porter and have the bags placed into the quarters reserved for Freeman Jennings.

A low fog from the Hudson River had rolled in, just off the surface, adding a sense of atmosphere to the frenetic scene. Neil stared at the massive ship from a hundred feet away, watching the beehive of activity at Chelsea Piers as leathery dock workers scurried like ants, struggling to load cart after cart onto the ship, preparing it for its speedy voyage over the North Atlantic. Neil's eyes moved up the ship, from the waterline, over the polished black hull, to the sparkling white of the superstructure and finally ending at the shiny crimson steel of the three rearward-raked smokestacks. She was a beautiful ship.

The great vessel made Neil briefly think about his forty-five footer and how, on rare Saturdays when he was in town and had time, he and Em would sail north, anchoring in the calm waters of Richardson Bay just behind Sausalito. There, they'd listen to her favorite slow jazz and make love all afternoon. She would taunt him playfully afterward, telling him if they wanted to have a child, he would need to slow down and live life like a normal man.

"Anxiety can affect your ability, *our* ability, to make a baby," she once told him, cocking her eyebrow at him the way she did when she was being half playful, half serious.

"And who says that?"

"I heard it from Beatrice Fairfax," she answered.

"Ugh…not her."

Em had laughed and knocked Neil's captain's hat from his head. She'd always known how to handle him.

Oh, what Neil would have given to go back to that moment. To pull her to him, to hold her that way forever. He had been a decent husband to her, nothing more. He'd provided everything she'd needed, bought her whatever she'd asked for, given her attention when she requested it—but he never went out of his way to truly demonstrate his love for her. He never left her a simple love note on her pillow. Didn't brush her cheek at unexpected moments. He never even popped her on her bottom. Emilee would have probably fainted had he come home in the middle of the day, or during a business trip, to surprise her with his presence. And when he *was* with her, he was typically distant, his mind occupied with his work and all that went with it.

On the day she died, Emilee had been combing the city, searching for an antique chest of some sort. She was probably planning to use it in the nursery. Antiques were a hobby of hers, especially of the mid-19th century prairie variety. Finding items from that period gave her joy.

According to the police, she drove to the South Shore area on that late June morning, visiting two stores in search of the simple, rough-hewn piece of furniture. A witness testified to seeing Lex Curran approach her on the sidewalk from the side door of his unopened bar. They spoke for a moment before the witness said Curran grasped Emilee's arm. She slapped his face two times as Curran pulled her into the building. The witness, an unemployed carpenter on his way to the "work-wall" that morning, said he thought it was a domestic dispute, so he minded his own business. The witness was a neighborhood resident—he knew all about Lex Curran— and he knew a violent altercation would have been in the cards had he confronted Curran.

Emilee's body was discovered in her car, twenty miles away. She had been strangled to death. Neil found out a day later that she'd been eight weeks pregnant. Only her closest friend had known. Neil had been so busy he hadn't even noticed her morning sickness. She was waiting to tell him, wanting to make certain the pregnancy took. Neil didn't know for certain the sex of the child; but over time, in his grief, his belief that the unborn child was a male became engraved in his mind.

The unemployed witness, the only one who saw Lex Curran and Emilee together, came forward after reading about the murder in the afternoon newspaper. Before he was even asked, he described her maroon Ford four-door to a tee. The police, in an effort to bolster the case against Curran, didn't release Emilee Reuter's name or photograph. Unfortunately for the police, the carpenter, a known drunk, was unable to identify her picture in three different photo lineups of ten.

No other witnesses came forward.

The inability of the carpenter to identify Emilee Reuter, which came to be known as "the lineup debacle," was the reason Lex Curran had initially walked—along with several false alibis. The witness later saw a picture of Emilee Reuter, swearing to anyone who would listen that she was indeed the one, and his ability to separate facial characteristics from the photographic lineups was hampered by a vision defect—a side effect of his liver condition. A doctor confirmed this, but the damage to the investigation was already done. The police later found two other witnesses who placed Curran near the scene where her body was discovered but, by this time, Curran had disappeared.

There was other evidence, too. Few people doubted Lex Curran's guilt.

Now that he was sober, Neil couldn't get Emilee's death out of his mind. He wanted to savor the horrid thoughts, but to keep them tucked away in a dark recess of his brain, available for when he truly needed them. Because, despite Agnes Holloway's predictions, Neil would come back—come back with a vengeance. He planned to use every fiber of his being to find Lex Curran, and kill him. The people in Washington had already proven that they were unwilling to assist. They were obstinate even, their replies distant and cold, the murder nothing more than an annoyance to their busy lives.

The one thing Neil had never tried—and it had never occurred to him, not in his grief and drunkenness—was a threat to his bosses over their lack of cooperation. He knew the Department of War probably wouldn't react well to such a thing. But if Neil truly didn't fear death, then why wouldn't he play his ultimate trump card? With everything he knew, with all of the sordid details, the raw realities, the killings—he could bring Washington D.C. to its very knees. He stopped on the street, cupping his hand over his Lucky Strike as he lit his memento Thorens lighter in the wind, glancing at the etching on its face, thinking of his friend Jakey.

"Give it to 'em with both barrels, Barkie," Jakey would say, grinning crookedly at him. "Why hold back? Why *ever* hold back?"

Neil puffed the cigarette and returned his friend's smile.

"Okay, Jakey. I won't...I won't hold back."

Neil flipped his lighter shut and turned away from the Chelsea Piers, walking south to 20th Street, taking the street to the east until he reached 10th Avenue. He would have liked to have walked farther; the exercise felt magnificent to his cramped body which was knotted and sore from sitting in one place for nearly a day's time.

It was now after nine in the morning. As the last of the workers from the docks and meatpacking districts scurried to their places of business, Neil stretched his body on the street corner. His suit was wrinkled and matted. A heavy five o'clock shadow accented his somewhat menacing appearance. He untied his silk tie and stuffed it in his pocket. In this seedy district, the rougher he looked, the safer he'd be. Neil walked on, idly wondering if Manhattan would ever be safe for pedestrians.

After paying a newspaper boy three shiny pennies for The Times, Neil stepped into the café he'd been told to go to, glanced around, and took a seat at the rear booth. He ordered black coffee, plain oatmeal and dry toast. Neil scanned the paper's headlines, mostly concerning tensions over Czechoslovakia and their region of Sudetenland, along with Hitler's lust to take it. Following the hours of tedious translation on the airplane, he didn't feel like reading, dropping the paper to the sticky table and focusing on the coffee instead. His contact arrived five minutes later.

The man was nothing, absolutely nothing, like Neil would have expected. He had been told the man he would meet was New York's finest forger of European documents. Neil had expected a shadowy gentleman, perhaps with a sneaky Machiavellian air and a smart suit. Instead, the man who slid into the booth was a Hasidic Jew at least fifteen years Neil's senior. He had bulging, expressive eyes, each mapped by red lines all leading from the corners to the brown centers. His face was dominated by a wide, toothy grin that exposed great gaps between each of his khaki teeth. His skin was shiny with bodily oil or sweat, Neil couldn't tell which. And he smelled heavily of this morning's coffee and last night's onions and garlic.

"You are Mister Jennings?" the forger asked with a thick accent, offering a sweaty hand over the table.

Neil took the hand and nodded. "Do you have everything?"

"Ah...right down to business, I see. Of course I have everything, of course, of course," the man answered, tapping the breast pocket of his coat. "But first, we shall converse."

"I have until noon," Neil answered with a wave of his cigarette, still a bit dismayed about the slovenly appearance of the man he was sitting with.

"So, you are the man who will rescue the children, yes?"

Neil dragged on the cigarette. "That's the plan."

"I want to hear all about it. Now it is time that I must eat. My *mogn* calls, you know."

Narrowing his eyes at the forger, Neil felt he was not only an interesting character to look at, but he also had a peculiar way of speaking. It probably had something to do with his native language, whatever it was.

The forger signaled the weary waitress and ordered a large plate of food, including fried potatoes, four runny eggs, a sliced green apple, oatmeal, buttered toast, and two orders of orange juice. "My good friend here will reimburse you for the food," he said, pointing at Neil. Neil nodded and asked for a refill of his coffee. The waitress scurried away.

"Aren't you supposed to follow strict eating laws?" Neil asked.

The forger either didn't hear him, or pretended not to hear him. Instead, he leaned forward, patting his chest again and whispering even louder than he spoke at his normal tone. "These documents are absolutely flawless. The best available anywhere in the world, or beyond if you so please. Hitler and his closest minions wouldn't be able to spot the forgery. In fact, I would wager my firstborn that these official papers are of higher quality than those actually turned out by the legions of ignorant followers in that vacuous excuse for an Austrian government." The forger made a shushing motion by placing his finger over his lips. "If there is any question about you, friend, it will be because of your own numerous misgivings, not these documents."

"What do you mean? And why are you whispering?" Neil asked, glancing around.

The waitress clunked the two glasses of orange juice in front of the forger and splashed coffee into Neil's cup before shuffling away. The forger continued, speaking conspiratorially. "Germany and Austria have become police states, and in police states the authorities can do as they wish. If they have any suspicion," he poked the tabletop with a thick finger, "they will detain you and will get the truth from you. Believe me, they will."

"I'll be fine," Neil answered as he crushed out his cigarette.

"Ah…American resolve. It is a good thing. A very good thing. It will take you far in life, especially where you are going…into the belly of the beast." The forger again leaned forward. "Or, it might lead you to an agonizing death. But only God knows your fate."

"May I see the papers?"

"But it's not even close to the noon hour."

"I might have till noon, but I'm not sitting here till noon. No offense."

Dejected, the forger removed a calfskin pouch from his inner pocket, pushing it over the sticky table. Neil opened it and, as the plates of food arrived, he scrutinized the Freeman Jennings U.S. passport, thumbing through each of the pages, satisfied with the various stamps from places such as Cuba and Portugal. He placed it on the table before studying the Austrian passport and accompanying papers. The three attached pages, detailing Neil's new Austrian identity's background, were on a linen paper with a watermark bearing the name of *Eisenbeiss Papier*. Neil held it to the light.

The forger motioned his dripping fork to the paper. "You see, it's the little things like that watermark that could out you. But I know these things. That's the paper that has been used by the Austrians since thirty-four, the year of my near-fatal surgery by that unskilled Cossack doctor from Guria. I was a hair from death."

"Yeah...about the brand of *paper*."

"Yes...yes. You show up with standard paper or, God forbid, American paper...well...you can imagine what sort of fate might await you."

Neil flattened the papers on a clean area of the table and studied his name and address. His cover name was Dieter Dremel. His address was 2 Berchtoldshofweg, Innsbruck. His occupation was listed as a Logistics Expert.

"Dieter Dremel?" Neil asked, looking up with a sour expression. "Sounds like a character in the comics."

"Yes, it's rather nice, isn't it? Especially coming from such an execrable language. And that address represents your home." The forger added a copious amount of pepper to his runny eggs. He jammed a full egg into his mouth and continued to speak as a rivulet of yolk danced on his bottom lip. "Dieter Dremel once lived there but departed the chaos of Austria twenty years ago and moved here to the United States."

Neil focused on the papers again. "And how do you know that?"

The forger slathered additional butter onto the toast, loading it so heavily that he had to crease the bread and eat quickly to keep it from running off. "Because my second cousin is in Salzburg," he answered with his mouth full. "We've been working on this for some time."

Neil frowned. "Some time?"

"Yes."

"How long?"

The forger caught a bit of escaping butter with his thumb, sucking it before answering. "Days, weeks, what is the difference?"

Jakey's letter was in Neil's pocket. Since it had been previously opened, Neil could understand how...whoever these people were...a

Jewish movement…could have been planning this for weeks, but certainly not before Jakey's death. Meghan told him Jakey had died in July, leaving the children with about two-and-a-half months of food.

And where do you hide that many kids with three months of food? An aircraft hangar? An old factory? It'd have to be enormous. And how could they avoid detection for so long?

"Your mind is awash in thinking, yes?" the forger asked with a mouthful of food.

Neil reached across the table, grabbing both of the forger's wrists, making him stop his eating. "Listen to me. Exactly how long have you been working on this? It *is* important."

"A little over two weeks."

Neil released him. "Who do you work for?"

The forger glanced around before leaning forward, making a pulling expression with his greasy fork. "Tell me what you know."

"I know enough to know what I'm traveling to Austria to do. But I need to know more about your organization."

As he worked on another piece of toast, the forger grinned as he spoke. "It's not an organization. We're a people, a tribe. And like any good tribe that is threatened, we pool our resources for the greater good." He peered over his spectacles, whispering again. "There are such well-known people involved with this that, if I were to tell you, it would make your Brylcreemed hair stand on end."

"Who?"

"Famous people. Notable people. And skilled people, like me."

Another thought passed through Neil's mind. "About this address in Austria: won't the locals be suspicious if I just show up?"

"Dremel was a loner. He moved from Innsbruck but retained ownership of his house and land. As far as the government knows, he has been maintaining a part-time residence in Salzburg, paying his taxes, keeping up his good standing. He is not a Jew and our friends in Innsbruck have tended the property." The forger produced a ring of keys and slid them to Neil. "Those will get you inside the residence. It's cozy and rustic, with a spectacular view," he said with a conspiratorial wink.

"Won't the neighbors think it's strange to suddenly see me after the house has been empty for so long?"

"Worry not—the home is quite secluded." Again, the forger jabbed the fork at the counterfeits. "Those papers will get you to Austria. Once you're there," he said with a cocked caterpillar of an eyebrow, "the rest is up to you. And please hurry. You have until—"

"September fifteenth, I know."

"Getting them safely out of Austria will be a major feat. That's why you must arrive early. The southern border with Yugoslavia is heavily patrolled."

"I'll get it done." Neil shifted in his seat. "Any chance they could run out of food and water early?"

"No."

"How can you be so sure?"

"They will ration it to the day. This has been done at least a dozen times before. The Jewish flight from the Reich didn't just begin, you know."

"And couldn't the children be discovered in the meantime?" Neil asked.

"Not according to your friend, Jacob."

"Where are they hidden?"

"Only your contacts in Innsbruck know."

Neil's mind jumped back to his cover. "What about the real Dieter Dremel? What if I run into someone who knew him?"

The forger swallowed a mouthful of food. He sat straight, jerking the napkin from his bulging neck and wiping his hands. From inside his jacket pocket, he produced a heavy picture, backed by a thin piece of cardboard. In the photo was an unsmiling man, standing erect in front of a large building. Neil could immediately see the resemblance between himself and Dieter Dremel.

"Do you see?" the forger asked, fingering a piece of food from between his teeth. "This is not some slipshod operation. Your cover, your home and your papers have been painstakingly thought through. Again, any failures in Innsbruck will be your own."

Neil stared at the forger, underwhelmed by his appearance, irritated by his peculiar method of speaking, but sufficiently impressed by the man's diligence. He removed the envelope of money from his jacket and slid it across the table. The forger stared at it a moment, and then with a sausage finger, he slid it back.

"Herr Dremel, I don't want your money."

"But I was told to pay you."

"No, thank you. But you can pay for my food." The forger's mouth twitched upward as he leaned sideways in his booth, unbuttoning his vest to allow his massive midsection a few more inches of breathing room and sighing afterward.

Neil studied his new papers and the photo, not hearing another word the forger said until the forger touched Neil's hand.

"Let's hear your German."

"Why?"

"Just talk."

Frowning, Neil relented because he knew he needed the practice. "*Hallo, mein name ist Dieter Dremel. Ich bin Österreicher.*"

The forger's bloodshot eyes widened before his great belly shook with building, wheezing laughter.

"What?" Neil demanded. "What?"

The forger scratched his cherry nose as his laughter wound down. "That accent of yours, oh my, oh my. Well, I'd suggest you'd be wise to come up with a compelling back-story," he said, breaking into laughter again.

"How bad is it?"

"I lived in Vienna—a place from here forward you shall call *Wien*. And that accent will stick out as badly as I would wearing my Rekel and Shtreimel at a Berlin Nazi rally," he said, wheezing with more laughter.

"Thank you for the papers," Neil said, readying to leave. The forger grabbed his arm.

"As I said, I have a cousin in Salzburg. He's only a *trepl* below me in talent. If you require additional forgeries, or even counterfeit legal documents, go to him." The forger produced a business card and pressed it in Neil's hand. "He's in hiding. You must first call the man on the card. He will put you in contact."

Neil stuffed the card into the pouch, placing everything into his inner jacket pocket. After nodding his thanks, he dropped a five-dollar bill on the table, leaving without another word.

For the next three hours, he walked the streets of Manhattan, stretching his legs, strolling all the way to the north end of Central Park, speaking German to himself and wondering how on earth he was going to accomplish this mission without getting found out.

Chapter Eight

THE RMS QUEEN MARY STEAMED THROUGH THE mouth of New York harbor, signaling with her great steam horns to the well-wishers waving their handkerchiefs from the railing on Ellis Island. It was mid-afternoon. Neil was in his modest cabin room, wearing only his wrinkled suit pants and his undershirt. He finished unpacking his bags and laid his suit coat on the bed, pulling the lone chair next to the single mattress. He sat and removed the pouch of identities from the jacket pocket of his suit coat. Neil worked his finger through a tri-fold crease on the other side of the jacket, revealing a hidden pocket from which he extracted a thin smoking tin. After spreading one of his clean undershirts on the bed, he opened the tin and removed a felt bag, carefully pouring out its contents over the undershirt.

Before him, sparkling like tiny flecks of molten sun, was the sum total of what remained of his personal fortune. Seventy-nine diamonds of assorted size, all of the highest cut and clarity. It would have been far too great an undertaking to try to move nearly two million dollars in cash, even if he were to use hundred-dollar bills. Such a large amount would have been bulky and hard to secure, and would have no doubt raised someone's suspicion.

The diamonds, however, fit neatly in his pocket and their worth was essentially universal. General Logistics had sold quickly—Neil knew it would. And after Musselwhite convinced Remington to take the entire estate, Neil arranged for the diamond exchange through Meghan Herman, at the same time she informed him of the New York forger.

The old man who'd exchanged the diamonds for Neil had been located in a dim little shop just outside of San Francisco's Chinatown. Neil had immediately wondered how the shop ever attracted a single customer. The front window was so dirty it had become opaque, and had he not been given explicit instructions on where to go, Neil would have never found the place. Two women, both in their fifties, had ushered Neil in, keeping their heads bowed but stealing occasional glances at him. After having Neil sit, they both began to deafeningly yell the word "papa" in the direction of the rear of the store. Neil heard what sounded like a mattress creaking, followed by what must have been assorted curses in a language he didn't understand. And then the old jeweler appeared, wearing an undershirt and silk pajama pants while both of his bony hands scratched his stomach and exposed ribs. He was small and wiry, with parched lips that he licked incessantly.

"My daughters," the old man said as he poured a cup of tarry coffee from a silver pot.

"We've met," Neil answered, watching as the two peculiar women giggled like teenagers.

After the man's painstakingly slow cup of coffee, and very little small talk, he and his two daughters counted the bills from the many stacks of cash. The man whispered a figure to both girls; they both nodded their agreement. Then, from a locked safe, the old man removed three pouches of glittering diamonds, keeping them segregated into piles, probably based on size and value.

The jeweler had poured another cup of coffee, nibbling a hard biscuit as he worked arithmetic on a brown paper sack. He drew two hard lines underneath the total and, with a slight cackle, he shaved fifteen percent off of the diamond exchange for his trouble, marking it in large numbers. Neil looked at the list of diamonds, marked by their weight, their cut, and their clarity. He nodded his approval of their value, taking the old man's word for it. And how would he have known if he was being taken advantage of? He wouldn't, and had simply decided to trust Meghan's advice.

Next, he asked the jeweler about exchanging the diamonds for cash in Europe and was told the best rate of exchange would be enjoyed in Belgium. The jeweler told Neil to expect another haircut, probably at least fifteen percent and perhaps twenty. But Belgium wouldn't work for Neil; he needed reichsmarks. He asked about Germany or Austria.

"If you must go there, exchange the diamonds in Austria," the old man answered, waving his hand as if he didn't approve. "The Austrians: such rough, boorish people. Neither they, nor their banal cousins to the north, know the true worth of these precious stones. Expect to be offered half of what you might get in Brussels."

"Any Austrian cities you might recommend for the best value?" Neil asked.

"Salzburg. At the very least, they somewhat understand the fruits of the earth there. You'd be best advised to find a Jew, if there are any left who dare show their face."

Another blast from the ship's horns broke Neil's reverie. He stared at the cluster of diamonds scattered about on his undershirt. With his index finger, he traced a line through them, watching as they absorbed and refracted light, thinking of all of the things that needed to occur if he had any hope of pulling this off.

"Find a Jew in Salzburg," Neil said aloud, chuckling at the situation's absurdity before he carefully replaced the diamonds and stuffed the tin back into the hidden coat pocket. He rubbed his face, dreading the hundreds of lonely hours he was going to endure on this ocean liner.

His mind moved across the Atlantic to London, where his mission would really begin. From London, there were no contacts and no plan. It would be Neil Reuter, and Neil Reuter alone. He closed his eyes, remembering the days during the war, when one of the men laying cover-fire for him first dubbed him the Pale Horse. The man, like Neil, had American Indian blood—a Cherokee. He claimed when Neil ran back through the flying lead of the front line, his feet never once touched the ground. That next morning, as they'd boiled wild onions with the scant meat of a pigeon, the Cherokee had bestowed him with the sobriquet, telling Neil about Cherokees who'd performed similarly under duress.

"Pale Horse," Neil said aloud, glancing at his tired reflection in a mirror. "Let's hope you can conjure him again." He touched the stitches on his forehead, that drunken day seeming months ago. He removed them in only a few seconds using a pair of cuticle scissors.

Neil lit a cigarette and spun the round porthole window open on the vertical hinge, flooding the cabin with moist, salty air. Leaning against the cabin's outer wall, he stared at the flat nothingness of the Atlantic, feeling the slight vibrations as the great ship effortlessly sliced through the waves off the coast of Long Island. A solitary cloud obscured the afternoon sun, diffusing it to a lemon corona. The sound of seagulls, unknowingly committed to following the ship across the Atlantic, occasionally squawked from aft, probably circling a child who was rewarding them with thrown pieces of bread. The child made Neil think of his unborn son, and of Emilee.

She would have liked to have been with me, he thought. By this time their son would have been one-and-a-half years old. Maybe he'd be playing, or perhaps taking an afternoon nap. Emilee would walk up behind Neil and rest her head on his shoulder, like she always did when feeling pensive. Sometimes they would go to bed during the day, especially on holidays or weekends. But it wasn't typically sexual; Emilee preferred that during the nighttime, unless they were out on the yacht. The daytime bed sessions at Hillside were about conversation, and opening up. Emilee would sometimes share Neil's cigarette, nodding as she dragged on it, listening to his limited tales from the Great War, rubbing his dark hair as she soothed him while he opened up a Pandora's box of tragic, horrid memories.

Neil remembered the time she told him that she had feelings, premonitions, that they were doomed to a short life with each other. But Em always felt it was he, and not she, who would die early. She would scold him about working too hard, recounting for him her father's death by that old printing press, his hand clutching his chest as he collapsed and died in front of his two employees. Neil would comfort her, talking about his own good health and pronouncing himself strong as a bull. And then

Em would feel better, and the subject would be tabled until the next session, when it would come up again.

It would have been worse, far worse, had she known about his true occupation.

Neil always felt Emilee suspected he did something more than just run General Logistics. She'd never said anything, but when he would return from a business trip with no gifts and scant details about what had transpired, he would see the knowing look of anxiety in her eyes. And in the end, Emilee's premonition was correct – only it was she, not Neil, who would be ripped from the earth far too early.

Determined not to begin another period of melancholia, Neil pitched the cigarette out the porthole and glanced around the cabin. All this sitting around was going to be hell. He needed a drink. Desperately.

No…yes…no, dammit.

Just as he was considering a room service call to the steward, a loud, merciful knock came through the shiny teak door. Neil didn't expect any sort of trouble on this voyage, but he also didn't anticipate any visitors. He glanced at his bag containing his Colt, thought better of it, and opened the door.

"Message for Mister Jennings," the short steward said. The man handed him a buff envelope, bowed politely, and hustled off into the labyrinth of corridors. A strong, masculine script addressed the note to Freeman Jennings. Neil frowned, knowing the passage had been purchased in this name, and also knowing that he had told no one, other than Meghan and the forger, of the alias. He found a letter opener in the room's desk and sliced the envelope open…

Dear Mr. Jennings,
I hope you will please do me the favor of accompanying my wife and me for dinner this evening. We will meet you for cocktails on the fantail deck at eight p.m. I will be wearing a red rose on my lapel.
Cordially,
Gregor Faust

Neil reread the note and blinked rapidly. He didn't know anyone named Gregor Faust.

"Could there be two Freeman Jennings on this vessel?" Neil asked aloud. "No," he replied after a moment's thought. It wasn't a common name, and the coincidence would be too fantastic.

Sufficiently flummoxed, Neil ran a hot bath as he retrieved a dark suit and shoes. He rang for his steward, handing him a generous tip of a half-dollar, instructing him to steam the suit and apply a glossy shine to the shoes. He wanted to look his best for Mister Faust, whoever he was.

* * *

The passenger known as Freeman Jennings nodded to the doorman as he stepped from the art gallery near the stern of the great ship. The fantail deck was awhirl with the chilly winds and salty smells of the Atlantic Ocean. No sooner had Neil reached the gleaming brass railing when an attendant arrived and nodded to him.

"Mr. Jennings?"

Neil had just jabbed an unlit cigarette between his lips. It took him a fraction of a second to remember his cover; he turned and raised his eyebrows. "Yes?"

"Mister Faust has requested that you visit together in his stateroom. He sent apologies and said there is too much chill in the air for his wife."

Neil nodded. "And where might that be?"

"Please follow me," the attendant said after cupping his hands and struggling in the heavy winds to set Neil's cigarette aflame. A tall, boyish-looking man with bad teeth, the attendant had to duck as they passed through several sections of the ship with low beams. Eventually, after what Neil felt like was a negotiation of the full length of the ship, they arrived at a forward stateroom. The door was adorned with a gold number two. The attendant knocked, spoke a few words and disappeared.

As the door opened wide, Neil faced a man several inches shorter than he, and at least fifteen years older. He wore a beautifully tailored blue suit, adorned, as Faust said it would be, with a fresh red rose. Faust had a broad, well-bred smile framed by full cheeks. His head was mostly bald, surrounded by a narrow Caesar crown of black flecked with silver. The man oozed wealth.

"Good evening, you must be Freeman Jennings?" he asked with an accent Neil couldn't immediately place.

"Yes. And you're Gregor Faust," Neil said as he pressed the cigarette into a hallway ashtray.

"Indeed. Please do come in."

Faust ushered Neil into the large suite, rimmed on the front by an expansive row of sectioned windows. Outside, several lights from the bow of the ship could be seen, ahead of them the northeastern blackness of the Atlantic. Neil could only imagine the impressive seascape view during the daytime. If there were a finer stateroom on the ship, Neil would like to have seen it. He spun around slowly, drinking in the exclusive suite, adorned in white with accents of gold and jade. Standing across the room was a tall, statuesque woman with dark, swept-back hair and shiny olive skin. Neil couldn't help but notice her green eyes and high cheekbones as he correctly guessed she wasn't from the United States.

"My wife, Petra," Faust said. Neil stepped to her, took her hand, and bowed politely. Petra nodded without affectation before crossing the room and sitting on the sofa.

There was an awkward silence before Neil spoke in Faust's direction. "You'll have to excuse me, but do we know each other from somewhere?"

Faust's smile was indulgent. He motioned Neil to the chair opposite the sofa where Petra sat. As Neil settled in, Faust retrieved a wooden box and placed it on the table before them. "Cigar?" he asked. Neil shook his head and instead tapped out a cigarette. "Cocktail?" Faust then asked. Again, after a moment's hesitation, Neil shook his head.

Neil watched Faust as he walked to the bar and poured two vodkas over ice, adding a twisted slice of lime to each.

The tinkling of the ice. The bubbling sounds from the vodka being poured.

Neil's stomach began to do flip-flops at the sight and sounds of his former salve. Faust placed his and his wife's drinks on the table and sat next to her, leaving sufficient space between the two of them. He removed a long cigar from the humidor and clipped it, taking his time as he spun the cigar while using a gilded lighter to set it aflame.

"Cuban," Faust said, puffing and spinning. "My weakness."

Once the cigar was lit, Faust sat back and placidly smoked. Petra stared straight ahead.

Neil realized with a slight amount of discomfort that these two people had no problem, none whatsoever, with great periods of silence. Neil used Faust's gilded lighter to light his cigarette. The two men smoked as Petra cupped her drink in both hands, taking small sips with a wisp of a smile as she stared off into the distance.

The situation felt quite awkward.

Two times Neil readied himself to speak, and both times stopped himself—these people had invited *him* here. No matter how long it took, he planned to let them be the ones to break the silence. Faust puffed away, finally placing the thick cigar on the rim of the ashtray with a few audible smacks of his lips. He took a long sip of his drink, sighed loudly, and settled back into the white fabric of the sofa, unbuttoning the jacket of his suit.

"Your name is Neil Reuter," Faust pronounced.

Neil simply raised his eyebrows. He was homing in on the accent. Swedish? Perhaps Danish.

"We are friends, dear friends, of Meghan Herman," Faust added.

Neil said nothing.

"My wife and I live in Finland, but often spend extended periods of time in the United States. We have great interest in Meghan and, until recently, Jacob."

"Is that so?" Neil asked. He turned to look at Petra. She stared at him with a neutral expression, expressing neither interest nor boredom. It befitted her simple elegance. Neil appraised her more thoroughly, quite taken by her smooth complexion and her trim, neck-length black hair which was pushed straight back. Even though Petra was most likely pushing fifty, there was something quite captivating about her. She could have easily been visually cast in a play as Cleopatra. Neil caught her eye and smiled politely. She turned away.

Faust leaned forward, taking the cigar into his hand and resting his elbows on his knees. "Do you think you can get the children safely out of Austria and to the ship?"

"I'm not sure what you're referring to."

"Oh come on, Neil," Faust chided. "I realize you need to maintain your cover, but we're part of the movement. You met with a forger this morning in Chelsea, and you were approached by a Russian woman who flew with you from Chicago. Your cover isn't blown—it's perfectly safe." Faust inclined his head. "And this is the last leg of your journey when anyone will accompany you. That is, until you reach Innsbruck. But from England to there, you're on your own."

"Interesting."

"So, can you move the children safely?"

"I have no way of knowing that yet."

"Neil, this is of the highest importance imaginable," Faust said. "I'd at least like to hear your opinion."

"If it's so important, Mister Faust, why does it fall on me? I know nothing of this operation other than what I've been told by Meghan Herman, the Russian woman, and the forger in Manhattan. And none of them told me anything that might clue me in on the difficulty of the job." He leaned forward. "And, if you'll pardon my bluntness, I'm concerned that your people on the ground in Innsbruck don't have the ability to do this themselves, or to find someone who can."

Faust grinned triumphantly. "Ah, finally, an opinion."

"While I might have an opinion or two," Neil said, his mouth growing dry, "I'm not up to speed on what's needed in Austria and, again, I'm almost certainly not suited for what my friend wanted of me."

"You *are* suited for it. Please understand that a great deal of this mission involves the transportation of the children and their keepers *away* from the Reich. Each time this has been done, arranging for the ship was the easy part. But moving the children inside the Reich is where the difficulty lies. And you *do* have the skill and wherewithal to handle it."

There was a period of silence. Finally, Neil said, "I'll give this my best, of course—and I want to help the children—but something about the entire affair seems a bit off kilter."

Faust stood and crossed the stateroom, his heels clicking as minuscule pieces of ash fell from his cigar, leaving a trail on the gleaming floor. He disappeared into what must have been the stateroom's sleeping berth before returning with a handsome aged briefcase. Faust flipped the top portion open and retrieved a slim, bound booklet, sliding it over the center table. It was the same type of booklet one might see in a boardroom containing a corporate report, held together on the binding edge by a fabric-coated rubber band.

"I apologize, Neil," Faust said. "You won't like this report."

Neil kept his eyes on Faust's as he allowed his hands to clasp the booklet. He briefly met Petra's emerald eyes before turning his own to the booklet. On the front of the heavy, black card stock of the booklet was a single strip of white paper. In the center of the strip, typed, was his Christian name: Neil Michael Reuter. Neil placed his cigarette between his lips and narrowed his eyes as the smoke ascended and enveloped his head. He flipped the booklet open.

On the first page, glued, was a black and white photo taken three years before by the San Francisco Chronicle. He remembered the day clearly, the photo taken for a feature article Neil had been ordered to cooperate with—it was considered good for his cover. In the photo, Neil wore a dark suit and stood in front of his company's headquarters. Below his name was a listing of both his personal and physical information. Neil glanced up, seeing the Fausts staring at him with great interest. He turned the page.

There was a paragraph about his parents; a paragraph about their German and Shoshone backgrounds; a shockingly accurate summary of his net worth; and finally, two full paragraphs about Emilee's murder. The second paragraph addressed Lex Curran, delving into his documented sexual deviancies and his disappearance. Neil grew hot with anger, turning to Gregor Faust.

"Where the hell did you get all this?"

Faust's tone was apologetic. "It was easily obtained. I do understand that the inquiry is overly personal, but it was essential we obtain as much information as we could."

Neil took in a great breath and let it out slowly. He crushed out his cigarette and turned the page. There he found several run-of-the-mill paragraphs on his military service, but the third paragraph struck him in the chest like the Queen Mary's anchor:

Neil Reuter, after enlistment, was hastily commissioned and served in France during the Great War. He ascended to the rank of captain, as an intelligence officer. In 1917, it is believed that Reuter deliberately misled two British brigades through a critical intelligence report, thereby paving the way for an American brigade to secure a key victory in the conflict at Dormans during the Second Battle of the Marne. The faulty report was later amended, its author hidden, and swept over by American intelligence in the fog of the War's final weeks. Reuter's actions allowed Lieutenant Colonel Archibald S. Stone of the United States Army, the commander of the victorious brigade, to be rapidly advanced through the ranks. He was ultimately promoted to four-star general: a rank he still holds at the publishing of this report. It has been stated by several general officers who were a part of the campaign that, had the two British brigades been utilized in the action, further loss of life may have been avoided.*

(The action at Dormans resulted in 97 American casualties and 812 [est.] German casualties.)

Neil poked the page. "This is fabricated horseshit and whoever wrote it doesn't know his head from his ass."

"Really," Faust replied. It wasn't a question. "The report was researched and written by one of the finest investigative firms in Washington D.C. We've not had them miss on anyone yet."

"They missed." Neil summoned patience. "Their facts are skewed. I did write the intel report based on the information I had at the time. But by the time we were afforded a clearer picture, the British were more than busy defending our flank. Thirty-Second Brigade had to move forward, and it was *not* my call. What the hell does this have to do with anything?"

Faust puffed the cigar as he motioned him to turn the page. After several rote paragraphs about Neil's business, there was a section titled "Vital":

It was recently learned, through a painstaking series of circumspect inquiries, that General Archibald S. Stone's younger sister, an arresting woman named Lana, married widower A. Walter Yance, of Philadelphia. He is 32 years her senior. Yance owns a sizeable majority of Advanced Chemical, the second-largest chemical conglomerate in the United States. His title is president and chairman. Commonly thought of as a modern industrialist, Yance is one of the most respected businessmen in the U.S., and is the fifth wealthiest man alive on the planet.

Most importantly, Advanced Chemical, as well as three other businesses Yance owns majority interest in, comprise well over half of the total revenue of General Logistics, Reuter's shipping business.

It is the opinion of this team of investigators that General Archibald S. Stone deliberately rewarded (pre-arranged?) Neil Reuter for the faulty intelligence reports, through his wealthy brother-in-law, with the considerable western shipping contracts of Advanced Chemical. It should also be noted that Yance's company, Advanced Chemical, counts on the United States Army for seventy percent of its business—both directly and indirectly. Advanced Chemical produces nearly all of the high explosives used in hand grenades, artillery shells, tank rounds, and landmines. General Archibald S. Stone would easily be in a sufficient position to sway the Department of the Army's purchasing practices.

Neil flipped the booklet shut and smacked it onto the hard, white table. He glanced at Petra, who had turned away at the first sign of his anger. Neil searched for words, finally cutting his eyes back to Gregor Faust. Faust held his chin high, seemingly ready to take a berating, and appeared unashamed of his investigators' theories.

"Who the hell do you think you are, trying to strong-arm me based on a series of suppositions that are nothing more than a nifty grouping of coincidences? And don't you know, *Faust*, that if you dig long and hard in any business dealings between large companies, you're bound to find incidences of past collaboration?" Neil again removed his cigarettes from his breast pocket and lit one after snatching the lighter from the table. "Perhaps it's different on top of the world, up in snowy Finland?"

The three people sat there for a moment, the quiet enveloping the room like a chilly fog. Neil leaned back in his chair, trying to determine why Faust had even shown him the report. What was the point? What was to be gained? Now Neil's blood was up, making it difficult to control his thoughts.

Finally he stood, crossing the room and smacking a crystal tumbler to the marble top of the bar. As it had earlier, the ice tinkled as he dropped it in by hand; the vodka made a satisfying chugging sound as he poured it, filling the tumbler to the brim. Neil took a long sip, drinking a third of the drink before holding the cool crystal to his cheek, his eyes closed as he accepted the liquid's searing fire in his throat. He felt much, much better.

And worse.

"So why," Neil started, his voice velvety after the familiar liquid, "are you showing me this concocted report, even *after* I have agreed to help?"

"Because you cannot go back," Petra Faust said in her thick accent. They were the first words she had spoken to him.

Neil turned to her, his eyebrow cocked, unable to muster any anger toward her. "I hadn't planned to."

Faust relit the cigar, puffing quietly. "But even if you change your mind, you cannot."

"What are you getting at?"

"It sounds a bit callous, but the lives of those children are worth far more than your discomfort."

"I don't disagree. But that doesn't mean you have to come up with bullshit that slanders me in the process."

"I'm not so sure it's bullshit." Faust dipped the mouth end of his cigar into his drink before putting it into one side of his mouth. It modulated his voice as he spoke. "And you didn't read the final page of the report." Faust reached over his wife and grasped the booklet, handing it to Neil.

Neil took the report along with his cigarette from the ashtray. The Fausts glanced at one another before turning their eyes to the windows of the front of the stateroom. For whatever reason, they didn't seem to want to watch. Neil felt his fingers tingling as he opened the booklet and flipped to the last page:

Final Analysis: Neil Michael Reuter is highly intelligent and influential. He is recognized throughout San Francisco as a shrewd businessman and a philanthropist, and was known as a loving, albeit distracted husband. Like many people, though, Neil Reuter is not above corruption, as is detailed in the manner in which his company grew to its current size. Additionally, it appears Neil Reuter may have had additional dealings with the government, though these seem to be well concealed. According to numerous war veterans, his nickname during the Great War was the Pale Horse, presumably because he could slip in and out of enemy territory like the blowing wind. Finally, and perhaps most potentially damning to his business, or worse, is the evidence of an eight-year affair between Neil Reuter and Lana Stone Yance, aforementioned youngest sister of General Archibald S. Stone and much younger second wife of A. Walter Yance.

Neil Michael Reuter is capable, intelligent and dependable. Risk factors include his possible alcoholism, his ongoing affair, and instability over his wife's murder. An additional risk factor is the likelihood of additional government dealings, all of which seems to have been scrupulously cloaked. All things considered, especially taking in his Germanic and Indian heritage, his superior military experience, and lifelong friendship with Jacob Herman, he would make an ideal operative for the mission's needs.

Neil didn't look up from the final page. He read it and reread it, his mouth parting several times, but no words ever escaping. Affixed inside the back card-stock cover of the report was a small manila envelope with the word "Reuter-Stone photo" typed on the bottom. Neil lifted the flap and used the fingernail of his thumb to slide out a black and white photo, captured in exceptional clarity. He knew, the instant he saw it, when it had been taken. It had to have been captured only three months earlier in Los Angeles, at Santa Monica's Edgar Hotel.

The picture showed Neil, on his back, in one of the hotel's signature massive poster beds. Silken sheets were swirled around him, two pillows jammed under his head. Astride him, and quite nude, was the alluring Lana Yance, her head and body arched backward in laughter, her perky, upturned breasts pointing skyward. In the photograph, Neil certainly did not appear the part of the grieving husband.

Neil pushed the picture back into the envelope and turned his eyes to the Fausts. They both now stared at him the way they might watch the climax of a good Saturday matinee—their faces bright with anticipation. Neil searched for words but found none. He turned the drink up, draining every drop before carefully placing it in the brass sink. Finally, report firmly in hand, Neil walked to the door and let himself out.

Petra turned to her husband, her expression betraying nothing. Without a word, she retired to the sleeping berth, unclasping her pearls as she went.

Chapter Nine

THE MASSIVE CLOCKS OF THE SHIP STRUCK MIDNIGHT as August 5th was ushered in. The clocks' deep tones even rattled the assorted stemware in the Observation Bar Lounge. The RMS Queen Mary was scheduled to adjust time by one hour on each of the first five days to offset the five-hour time change that would be experienced on the voyage to London. Those who remembered were busy adjusting their timepieces while an attendant dragged a chair to the giant clock. He stood on the chair as he manipulated the hands one hour ahead to one in the morning.

Neil Reuter didn't remember to adjust his watch.

He was at the curved walnut bar, facing his sliver of reflection in the mirror between a bottle of Beefeaters and a single malt scotch he'd never heard of. With heavy eyelids, Neil listened to the soft music played by the heavy, raven-haired woman on the stark-white grand piano.

Perched precariously between Neil's fingers was a tall glass, ordered special, containing vodka, ice, and two lime wedges. The ice had caused condensation on the outside of the glass, something Neil was grateful for as he rubbed it on his warm forehead and cheeks. He turned the glass up, drinking all but a third and becoming concerned because he hadn't seen the bartender in quite some time. After a minute of frantic scanning, he saw him pass at a distance, carrying a carton of supplies. Neil snapped his fingers, then yelled, motioning for another as he finished off the one in his hand. He crunched the ice and ate one of the lime wedges, peel and all.

"What a night," he muttered, loving and hating how he felt.

Neil didn't know what bothered him more: the falsehoods in the report—or the report's deadly accuracies. He opened it again, flipping the pages as he skimmed their contents. This had been prepared by a team of highly educated assholes, probably Ivy Leaguers. They had undoubtedly spent weeks, maybe even months, turning out something that, in the end, was nothing more than a sleazy blackmail piece. They had to know their little coup de grace, their finishing touch of the purported long-term affair with Lana Stone, was nothing more than reckless speculation. There could have been no other evidence. None.

Because Neil had *never* engaged in an affair with Lana Stone.

He finished turning the pages and came to the rear cover, touching the envelope that contained the photo. After the bartender placed another heavenly drink on the bar, Neil slid the photo out and held it carefully between his thumb and forefinger. At the angle the picture had been taken, someone with a camera had to have been in the room beforehand and either hid behind a drape, or concealed the camera and operated it by wire. Neil had seen cameras of that sort before and, in either instance, the premeditation of the act concerned him.

The detail of the sordid photo was not only disturbing, it shamed him to no end. The muscles of Neil's stomach could be seen as he tensed in a half sit-up position. Lana's dark lipstick contrasted with her pearl-white teeth as she was caught laughing, making the moment seem all the more decadent, like something captured from the guiltless debaucheries of a Roman orgy. Her hands were on Neil's chest, the tone of her arms displayed as she held on like the rider of an unbroken steed. The satin sheets were swirled around them, and from the angle of Lana's thighs, it seemed she had opened her legs as wide as humanly possible.

But the look on Neil's own face bothered him more than anything. In contrast to Lana, he wasn't smiling. His expression, as a tangle of dark hair hung over his glistening forehead, was one of immense concentration and effort. His lips were pressed tightly together, his brow lowered almost menacingly. To the unknowing observer, it would appear Lana Stone was in sheer ecstasy while her gentleman lover concentrated with all his might to please her.

But the sad part, at least to Neil, was that he had been too drunk that night to remember all the particulars.

Oh, he remembered the incident, and what led to it, not unlike the foggy familiarity of a mediocre book he'd read years before. The basic plot was still there, but the intricate detail—especially the climax—that the author languished so hard to create was long gone, awash in the many threads of life that had since come and gone—or, in Neil's case, had been cleansed away by copious gallons of Russian vodka. He closed his eyes, searching for a better recollection, trying to grasp the minutiae from the recesses of his mind.

It had been unpleasantly cool and damp in Los Angeles that week. It was either at the end of April or early May; Neil couldn't recall. The sun had barely showed itself during his visit.

Neil recalled chemical magnate Yancey Stone's bullish attitude as they had lunched on Monday. After Emilee's murder, Stone had never mentioned a word of condolence, and he certainly didn't break the trend on the Los Angeles trip. During lunch, Neil recalled his disgust over Stone's sheer greed as they discussed his latest ventures. He could remember watching the man as he sat there, cracking crab legs and sucking melted butter off their meat, taking great delight in the detailing of how his pricing practices after the market crash had crushed three of his competitors and how, once the competition had eventually failed, he inflated his prices to never-before-seen levels. He told his customers it was due to the unfortunate phenomenon known as depression inflation. And what could his customers do about it? He was the only one left.

Neil wouldn't forget how, deep into the morning hours after the first night of the retreat, Yancey Stone had ordered his efficient Japanese assistant to rush out and retrieve three women, one African and two Asian, like he might order species of lobster for tomorrow evening's feast. Neil wouldn't forget the devilish look on Yancey's face as he disappeared to the penthouse with the women, pinching one on the bottom as he licked the nape of another's neck, leaving a sparkling trail of drool. Neil wouldn't forget seeing Lana Stone arrive from back east the following day, and watching as Yancey pecked her on her cheek without a trace of contrition for what he had done the night before. Neil wouldn't forget Yancey Stone's leaving the retreat early, probably rushing back to Philadelphia to take care of whoever his mistress of the month might have been. And Neil Michael Reuter would never forget how, on that cool and vaporous Tuesday night, his suite had echoed as someone had pounded on the door, snapping him from his near-religious communion with the tall bottle of 90 proof.

It had been her. Yancey Stone's wife, Lana. And she was drunker than Neil.

He'd never paused to try and recall the details of that embarrassing night, but now as he did, the particulars were clearer than he might have thought. Lana Stone pushed her way into his suite, wearing a sequined cocktail dress and a matching head wrap. The dress hung on her, and although he tried to look away, Neil could see the outline of her breasts and nipples just below the plunging neckline of the look-at-me getup.

A tall, lithe woman, she'd immediately kicked off her heels. While she had no doubt looked better earlier in the evening, Neil was still taken by the affluent woman's unhurried, unworried presence. He had asked her if she was okay, wondering if she'd been crying due to mascara trails on her cheeks. Lana Stone, as she always did, appeared to be without self-consciousness, simply laughing at his question.

When he offered her a damp towel for her mascara, she wiped her face and then tossed the towel out the open window. Without speaking a single word, she grabbed Neil's bottle and turned it up, chugging three ounces like she might guzzle cool water on a hot day, leaving a sticky ring of lipstick around the neck. She lowered the bottle and wiped her lips with her forearm, turning her animal eyes to Neil. Her first words were a shock:

"I'm very sorry about your wife, Neil."

Neil had nodded his thanks and glanced at the door. "Lana, if someone saw you come in here…"

Lana Stone, the personification of an upper-class upbringing at the finest schools—the wealth, the exposure to culture, and a hint of typical rich-girl flouting—began to giggle. Her giggles grew to belly laughter, making her snort as she held a finger under her nose and clutched her trim midsection with her other hand. Finally, containing her hilarity, she stepped to Neil and kissed him, pressing her warm tongue into his mouth as she squeezed his cheeks tightly in her hands.

Oddly enough, that had not been their first-ever kiss.

Neil pulled back, shaking his head back and forth as confusing, drunken-dampened emotions raged war in his body and mind. "Lana, stop…"

"Stop?"

"Yes. Please."

Neil paused his recollection, finally understanding one of the main reasons for his giving in. Like a good battlefield commander, Lana had flanked him. Every single woman that had come at him after Em's death—and there had been mobs of them—had approached him as if he were an injured bird. They'd tried to soothe him, baby-talking him, treating him as if he might shatter to pieces at any moment. But Lana had come on to him full-bore, using all the subtlety of Mae West as Diamond Lil.

"What? I shouldn't run around on my husband?" she had asked, stepping away and opening the bar under the radio, from which she spirited a bottle of scotch. "Ahhhh," she said. "How about some joy juice?" She broke the seal and poured three fingers in one of the crystal tumblers, taking a mighty pull and afterward licking the rim with her long tongue.

Neil had resumed his spot in his chair and held his own drink. He had been quite unnerved, watching her as she prowled his suite, padding silently in her bare feet like a tigress. She stopped on the far side of the bed and unpinned the wrap from her head. She poked her lips out in a pout and ruffled her streaky blonde hair, staring at her reflection in the mirror. Lana pulled one of the pillowcases off its pillow, dipping it in the icy water of the vodka's bucket. She turned her head slightly as she used the damp linen to wipe the remainder of mascara from her face. After winking at herself, Lana Stone crossed the room and perched herself in Neil's lap, running her long fingers through Neil's dark hair, mussing it.

"My husband sleeps with nearly every woman he meets. He has for years. If I were to challenge him, I would be both divorced and shunned, even by my own blood relatives." She drank half of the scotch and allowed her hands to move to Neil's chest, unbuttoning his shirt before rubbing the thin cotton of his undershirt. "In our nine years of marriage, I've been a good wife to him, always appearing where he wanted me, offering him children in case he wanted them...and always...always," she said, turning Neil's chin to her, "...looking the other way."

Neil shuddered as she ground her bottom into his lap. She cooed and told him she knew he liked it. He did like it—and he was ashamed of himself. Neil had felt the blood coursing through his body, warming his neck and face as glass-shattering images of Emilee flashed through his mind.

He swallowed thickly before he spoke. "Lana, I'm not judging you. Not at all. But we can't do this. My business, all of my workers, depend on your husband's trust in us. In me."

She leaned to him and moved her lips to his ear, whispering. "But he'll never know. Ever. And you need something to take your mind off of your wallowing grief. It's been too long, Neil. The time is right. The time is tonight."

Neil had stared into her eyes, his breaths coming quickly. He could smell her perfume and the faintest hint of her tart perspiration. She moved her hand down his stomach, reaching underneath herself, gripping him softly.

Then she abruptly changed tactics, grasping him roughly as she nibbled on his lip.

He held off for another ten seconds before carrying her to the bed and making torrid love to her. She was an expert lover, bawdy and unafraid, doing things with him, to him, that he had never even heard about, even from the most coarse of soldiers during his days in the Army. She had taken him into her mouth, clawing at his chest and stomach while turning her body to accept his pleasuring. Lana licked him all over, giving instruction of where she wanted his hands at all times. In the end, she liked him behind her, adjusting the tilting mirror so they could watch themselves. They went on that way for nearly an hour and, after more drink, repeated the act. Lana was insatiable.

And Neil, drunken Neil, a grieving man, was still a man after all.

Since that night in Santa Monica, he withdrew into himself even further, ignoring three phone calls and a less-than refined telegram from Lana.

But there had been *no* long affair. That part of the report was entirely inaccurate. There had been only the one interlude before the night in Santa Monica.

Neil stared at the photo before sliding it back in the envelope. The bartender asked him if he wanted another; Neil waved him off.

Now his mind was busy recalling his first kiss with Lana—the first piece of the puzzle. It had been years before Emilee's death, in Philadelphia, back when he was happily married, before his business had grown, before other activities he participated in had matured. He and

Emilee were at the Stones' Christmas party. It was a celebrated affair, known through all of northeast society as one of the most exclusive, and just to have received one of the gilded invitations was a distinct honor. He and Emilee made a week of it. They'd stayed in New York, seeing the shows, eating well. The party was their last event before going home. At the soiree, late in the evening, Lana was on the verge of passing out from too much champagne. Neil caught her, literally, on his way back from the side courtyard where he and some of the other men had been sharing cigars and speaking of world events. Lana had been staggering down a columned hallway and he steadied her just as she was about to careen into an ornate table.

Just after he gently led her to a sofa in one of the sitting rooms, Lana grasped the lapels of his tuxedo and kissed him, pulling herself up to him as she locked her mouth on his. She couldn't have been but, what, maybe twenty-three at the time? Neil remembered the way she expertly clamped her legs on both sides of him like a vise. He pulled back, carefully, and was wiping her lipstick from his mouth as Yancey Stone's top operations man walked by, pausing with his mouth open as he viewed the shocking scene.

"Wait!" Neil called after the man, but he was gone, scurrying down the long hallway like a child running to tattle on an older sibling. "Shit!" Neil growled as Lana giggled, holding her finger under her nose the way she later did in Santa Monica. As far as Neil knew, the ops man never mentioned it to anyone, at least, so Neil thought. He'd never heard one peep about that incident. Not one.

Until Faust showed him the report.

That must have been it. The investigators had somehow talked to the man and, after getting the pictures of Neil and Lana in Santa Monica, they made the deduction that the affair had been long-term. Two rich assholes ignoring their marital vows and carrying on like teenagers in heat.

But it wasn't true.

Neil had never once been unfaithful to his wife, and his actions with Lana Stone in Santa Monica shamed him. Two-timed or not, she was still married. He tried to blame her, in his mind, but he couldn't pull it off. Though he was drunk, he'd known exactly what he was doing that night. He had been complicit.

And that's why he was stinking drunk on this night.

In the depths of brain, in an uncontrollable recess of his true self, Neil hoped this mission would be his undoing. In a perfect world, he would accomplish the objective just before someone put a merciful bullet through the back of his head. Or, better yet, Neil would safely move the children and then come back for Lex Curran. When he found Curran, Neil would bring along two bullets: one for Lex, one for himself.

Neil placed the glass behind the bar and staggered back to his cabin, cursing himself for weakness.

Chapter Ten

THE DETECTIVE'S FLAT BLACK COUPE SAT on Vallejo Street, parked in front of Neil Reuter's former mansion, Hillside. The orange setting sun was slung low, nearly below the horizon in the direction of Half Moon Bay. The unusually warm weather had begun to dissipate on this day and, as the sun dove for the Pacific, the chilly bay air settled over the hilly city like a familiar blanket.

Sal Kalakis sat on the hood of the coupe, numbly staring at a yard full of children playing kickball as if it were their last day of freedom. His mind was racing. He was confused. He sat there for a full half-hour until the sun was down, slipping his coat on and jerking a weed from the sidewalk.

After climbing into the coupe, Sal chewed the weed as he drove to Chappy's, a well-known dive and popular police hangout. Chappy's served three items, and three items only: draft beer, whiskey, and peanuts. Not a week went by that a policeman wouldn't tell Chappy about something he should add to the menu. And not a week went by that Chappy wouldn't direct the suggesting policeman to the hand-painted sign behind the bar. The sign read: "We only serve beer, whiskey, and peanuts. You want something else, go somewhere else."

Several detectives whooped when Sal entered the crowded bar. Nearly every patron smoked, their jackets and ties off, their sleeves rolled up. To the right of the table where Sal was headed, two standing vice detectives screamed at one another, their fists on the table, neck veins bulging like purple cables. A third vice detective, a fellow Sal knew, held the combatants apart with both arms—although his effectiveness was somewhat impeded by his own laughter. After reaching his table, Sal turned to watch the scene. Thankfully a fourth officer, a lieutenant, broke up the argument and the normal din resumed.

"What's with them?" Sal asked Captain Yarborough.

The captain lowered his beer and wiped his upper lip. "Arguin' over whether the Babe's record'll ever get broken. Ya believe that?" He chuckled. "Th'only way that'll ever happen's if science fiction comes true and they create some sorta injectable miracle serum."

Chappy arrived with two draft beers, sloshing them as he slid them onto the table in his haste. Sal took a long sip before leaning back in the chair and loosening his tie. "What a day. What a flipping day."

He had just completed a five-hour interview of Eugene Remington, the proud new owner of Hillside, General Logistics, and just about everything else Neil Reuter once owned. Remington had been busy settling into his home office, working while Sal peppered him with questions.

"So, did ya solve it?" Yarborough asked in that tone he used to pester his detectives.

Sal cut his eyes over before staring back into his beer. "Musselwhite, Reuter's financial guy—on Reuter's behalf—sold everything, and I mean every-damned-thing to this fella Remington."

"So?"

"So, I checked him out. Musselwhite's straight up and down...a clean, hard-working businessman."

"So?"

Sal took another gulp. "And I made Remington the same way: honest, straight-forward, successful. A rich sonofabitch, yes...but a square guy. I'd wager he's telling the truth about snapping up the Reuter empire so quickly. He got it at an incredible discount. I'd have done it, too."

"If'n ya had money...and brains."

Sal fake-smiled. "Cute."

"Yer point about all this is?"

"My point is that it appears Neil Reuter liquidated his assets, all of them, so he could murder Lex Curran and disappear with a pile of dough. Sound reasonable?"

"A'course it does," the captain answered. He tapped two Chesterfields out and handed Sal one, lighting them both with a sulfury wooden match that he lit on his thumbnail.

"And that's it, Cap. That's all I've got so far."

Yarborough puffed the cigarette and tapped the ash into one of the empty mugs. "Why now, Sal? If Reuter knew where Curran was, why would he wait two years and do it now?"

"Maybe Curran just surfaced?"

"So instead'a killin' him right away, Reuter puts everything on hold so he can liquidate his estate?"

Sal shook his head. "That's the same thing I keep coming back to also. Doesn't make sense." He hitched his thumb toward town. "But, don't forget, the coroner said it appeared Curran had been held against his will, with all the striations and torture marks."

"And you believe Reuter woulda done that?"

"Hell, no. He couldn't have waited."

"I agree," Yarborough answered. "That night we went up to his home, I believed him immediately when he said he wasn't the cause'a Curran's disappearance."

"I remember," Sal said, nodding.

"The man burned rage for Curran. I didn't make him as a fella who woulda waited around when that lizard surfaced, or had the tolerance to hold him captive."

Sal sipped his beer. "Maybe he got a read on where Curran was being held without anyone knowing it. He might have decided to do it the careful way. People change their minds, especially when the risk of jail is looming."

"The timing about all this just doesn't make sense," Yarborough muttered.

Sal tapped the notebook in his pocket. "I did learn something interesting. Reuter had a visitor. It wasn't till after that that he liquidated. And the killing, assuming he did it, happened immediately following the liquidation."

"Who was th' visitor?"

Sal removed the miniature notebook. He kept one solely for each case he worked, and right now this was his one and only. He flipped back to the first series of pages, from his previous day's interview with Agnes Gentry, Reuter's longtime maidservant. Sal licked his thumb, flipping the pages until he found the one he wanted.

"Here it is. The maid told me about a dame who visited Reuter, and then he went on a serious bender."

"Who was she?"

"The maid didn't know her name. Said she was a younger woman, early thirties, maybe. Said she came to see Reuter and right afterward he went on a wicked binge—worse than normal. Then, he wakes up one night, dries out, and starts settling his estate."

Yarborough leaned back and laced his fingers over his round stomach. "God, I wish I was rich. Get drunk for a week. Sober up. Sell all my shit. Get drunk again. Whadda life."

"The dame, boss, the dame."

"What's yer point about her?"

"Maybe she's who he's with."

"Maybe she was his wife's old friend, simply stopping by to see how th' poor widower was doing?" Yarborough countered. "And her presence set him off."

Sal studied his notepad a moment. "Gentry, the maid, said the good-looking dame brought him a letter...a letter, chief...and Reuter later told Gentry the woman was a childhood acquaintance, and to mind her own damned business." He thumped the pad. "Gentry told me that Reuter held on to that letter through the whole bender, reading it constantly to himself, sometimes working himself into a fit of either misery or some sort of peculiar rage."

"I don't see the significance," Yarborough said with a shrug. "No way to know what was in that letter. My guess is it was some sort of sympathy note and the letter brought back memories of his dead wife."

"She's the key, Cap."

"Th' wife?"

Sal crushed the cigarette onto the tabletop and glared at his captain. "I've not slept in over thirty hours, boss. Would you mind not pricking me around more than usual?"

"Okay, okay," Yarborough said, holding his palms up. "So th' young lass delivered some sorta message. This sent Mister Reuter on a week-long drunk, then th' lad woke up, sold everything, blew a tunnel in Lex Curran's head, and disappeared."

"I think she told him where Curran was hiding."

Yarborough frowned at that but didn't disagree. "Well, have ya found out who she was?"

"If she was a childhood friend, she shouldn't be too hard to find, right?" Sal stood. "Tomorrow, I'll do a little more background on the honorable Mister Reuter."

"Have another beer, boyo."

"I haven't seen the wife and kids in days, and tonight's my wife's stew."

"Stew?" Yarborough curled his lip. "B'lieve I'd stay and drink."

"You haven't had her stew," Sal answered with a wink. He slid his tie in the pocket of his jacket before heading out of the bar. The single beer made him sleepy. Because of his need for food and rest, Sal made a conscious decision to put the Reuter investigation to bed for the evening.

There would be plenty of time for it tomorrow.

His detective's coupe rolled quietly down Lombard before Sal popped the clutch and stabbed the gas, tires squealing as he bullied his way into the evening traffic.

* * *

Four Days Later

Everything pointed back to the mysterious girl. Other than a peculiar series of dead ends that Sal seemed to encounter whenever doing any sort of governmental background on Neil Reuter, the early crux of the case most definitely seemed to be Reuter's nameless female visitor. Reuter's housekeeper, Agnes Gentry, recalled his mysterious visitor telling him that she was staying at the Whitcomb Hotel. Apparently, Gentry came in at the end of their meeting, and to her it first appeared to be nothing more than an attractive young woman telling a gentleman which hotel he should find her in. The housekeeper, no less than three times, informed Sal of her shock at the young woman's brazenness. Each time Gentry mentioned the flagrancy, she also complained about the lack of morals in this "libidinous, lascivious generation of youth."

Then, she made certain—*absolutely* certain—that if Sal were to find any evidence of a relationship between Reuter and the beautiful girl, Gentry wanted to be the very first to know.

"Why?" Sal had asked, purposefully torturing the nosy old soul.

"I know what's good for my Neil. And that…that *tart* is not it."

Sal had been unable to contain his laughter.

Per routine, Sal checked the Whitcomb and, sure enough, a young lady who matched the description of Reuter's lady caller had stayed there. Her name was listed in the register as Meghan Herman. She had stayed there for nearly two weeks and the savvy concierge was able to validate Reuter, upon seeing his picture, as one of her guests. They'd chatted in the hotel lobby—nothing else.

While at the Whitcomb, Sal interviewed a number of employees, none of whom had anything useful to tell him other than the fact that Meghan's phone bill was excessive. Unfortunately for Sal, there were no records of the numbers she called—just a bill for nearly $40.

The balance of his past week was spent tidying up all other angles of the case, none of which proved helpful. That pointed the needle back at Meghan—she was now in the spotlight. The star of the show. Meghan with an H.

But Meghan Herman had proven difficult to find, even with the telltale H.

The neighbors from where she had grown up, which happened to be directly behind where Reuter had first lived, had long since moved. Sal checked her school records, finding out about her admission to Cal Berkeley. He phoned the registrar, learning that Ms. Herman had graduated with a degree in business. According to the registrar, Meghan and a group of other women had campaigned fiercely to be allowed to matriculate with a business degree—something which, until that time, had been reserved solely for men. However, the school had lost touch with her since. They didn't have her current address.

With nowhere else to turn, Sal eventually used the oldest trick in the detective's handbook. When all else fails, when no one knows where a particular person might be—forget universities, forget family, forget friends. Instead, follow the money and call Uncle Sam and the one department who jealously tracks the whereabouts of every penny-earning American citizen with great fervor: the Bureau of Internal Revenue. It was always Sal's last resort due to all the red tape. After establishing that he was indeed a detective and, yes, he did pay his taxes, it only took a few minutes for the snippy clerk to pull Meghan Herman's most recent address. She lived in Boston, Massachusetts. No husband was listed.

The Boston Police Department assisted Sal in reaching her. They arranged a Tuesday call for him from their precinct, which Sal currently awaited while enjoying a cup of coffee in his own precinct. He was drinking *his* coffee—*not* Harry Cato's. Sal had made the brew so strong he already had a minor case of the shakes.

"Call for you, Kalakis!" came the voice from the other room.

"Put it through to my desk."

Sal snatched up the earpiece on the first ring. "This is Detective Kalakis."

"Hello, detective. This is Meghan Herman. The Boston Police politely insisted I speak with you."

"Yes, ma'am. Thanks for calling. In the interest of time, I'll be direct."

"I'd appreciate that."

"You recently visited the home of Neil Reuter?"

"Excuse me, detective, but before we begin, might you tell me what this is in reference to?"

Sal cleared his throat. "It involves the murder of a man named Lex Curran."

"He's dead?"

"So, you know who he was?"

"Of course. My brother Jacob and Neil were best friends."

Sal had heard the same from others. He put a check mark beside Jacob Herman's name on his pad. "I understand you hadn't seen Neil in many years?"

"Correct. But I still followed all that happened with the murder. So tragic."

"Indeed, ma'am. So, after Curran was found dead, Neil Reuter was nowhere to be found. In fact, he's still missing. And you, Ms. Herman, were one of his last visitors. Might you tell me what you discussed?"

"I came to San Francisco, personally, to tell him my brother had been killed."

Sal straightened. How had he missed this? He cleared his throat. "Would you mind detailing that for me?"

"I'm afraid I can't provide much in the way of detail. I received word from the Austrian embassy that my brother had been killed in an explosion."

"Austria?"

"Yes, detective."

"Why was he in Austria?"

"I have no idea. Jacob and I weren't all that close."

"Was he working there?"

"I don't know. Jacob exited the military a number of years ago and since then, I don't really know what he'd been doing."

Sal scribbled furiously. "And I understand you brought Neil a letter."

"Yes. It was just the telegram informing me of Jacob's death."

"Was there anything more to the telegram?"

"It was infuriatingly cold and bland, detective. The only detail it gave was the explosion."

"Did it say where in Austria he had been?"

"No."

"Have you tried calling the Austrian embassy?"

"I'm Jewish, detective. I have a feeling I won't get much help."

Trying not to sound dejected, Sal said, "Do you have any idea where Neil Reuter may have gone?"

"No, sir."

"A guess?"

"I truly wouldn't know."

Sal talked to her for ten more minutes, learning nothing meaningful. Afterward, following a solid hour of transcontinental phone calls, Sal reached the appropriate person at the Austrian Embassy in Washington. The man's name was Leinster, the embassy's legal liaison. He spoke with hardly any accent at all. After twenty minutes of questioning, Sal decided the man knew more about Jacob Herman's death but wasn't going to budge. He told Sal exactly what Meghan Herman had said—Jacob Herman was killed in an explosion. Sal learned the accident happened in the state of Tyrol. When Sal asked which city, Leinster promised to investigate and get back to Sal.

"How long will that take?"

"It depends on my communications back to Austria, detective. My guess is a week or two."

Sal hung up the phone, feeling he'd been stonewalled.

He scribbled the word "AUSTRIA" in bold letters, all around his yellow pad.

Frustrated, Sal went for a walk, despite the rain.

* * *

In Boston, Meghan Herman departed the police station and made certain she wasn't followed. She then made a phone call before hurrying to the American Express office on Bunker Hill Street where she sent an urgent telegram.

It cost Meghan four extra dollars to send the telegram to a ship at sea.

Chapter Eleven

THE GREAT SHIP SHUDDERED UNDER HER POWERFUL, one-foot diameter steam horns blasting their baritone call, signifying that land was now in sight. It was the seventh and final day of the voyage, August 10th, just after sunup. Neil was sober and well aware that he had 36 days remaining before the children's ship set sail.

After the meeting with the Fausts on the first evening, Neil drank for two days before drying himself out again, eating properly and occupying his time with calisthenics and completing his tedious German translation of Huckleberry Finn. Other than when he exercised, he kept to himself, taking his meals in his room and occasionally practicing his speaking with a German-born steward he had met on the afterdeck. But when England was sighted, Neil finally made his way back to the main deck, coffee cup in hand, leaning over the railing as the cool, salt air pushed his hair sideways over his head. And, as he viewed the seaside resort of Plymouth slide by in the distance, Gregor Faust appeared as if from the fog of the ocean's surface, touching Neil lightly on his arm as it rested on the port rail of the ship. Neil turned, not sure whether to walk away or simply punch the squat man in his mouth.

"There's one other thing," Faust said, as if their conversation had never ended. He appeared pale and nervous.

Ignoring him, Neil turned his eyes back to the coast.

"Not out here," Faust persisted. "Come inside."

"Piss off."

"You'll want to hear this," Faust said, walking away. Neil reluctantly followed.

The passengers who weren't already above decks were rushing through the passageways to get to the main deck. After many days of sailing, the sight of land is a blessed relief, especially to those who might have suffered from claustrophobia or seasickness. Neil followed Faust as he moved through the Observation Bar Lounge, past the ship's library, to a sitting area in the nearly empty Verandah Grill. They chose the first grouping of slung back leather chairs with a square table in the middle. The Grill was ornate, covered in high drapes and paintings, and topped with an arched, glass ceiling. At night it was transformed into the Starlight Club, the most popular destination on the ship. A waiter appeared immediately.

"We're only two hours from port," the waiter said. "Can I get you gentlemen a celebratory drink? Bloody Mary perhaps?"

Faust brusquely asked for privacy. He turned to Neil, clearing his throat and tugging on his collar. "When exactly did you leave San Francisco?"

"Why?"

"It's important."

Neil's eyes swiveled around the bar. His past two weeks were a blur, especially when throwing the confines of the ship into the mix—a place where days don't matter. "It was the Tuesday afternoon before we sailed. I flew out that day and it took me two days to get to New York. Why?"

Faust shook his head as if disappointed in something. He spoke what must have been a Finnish curse word.

"What?" Neil asked.

"Dammit!" Faust said, slapping his own leg. "I told them you were too unstable. It was right there in the report."

Neil didn't care for Faust, and right now the man was irritating him to the point that he wanted to flatten him. "Faust, what the hell are you talking about?"

Faust's eyes were rimmed in red. "You vengeful, prideful bastard."

Neil maintained his calm. "What *exactly* are you referring to?"

"You could have slid into Austria unnoticed," Faust admonished, his breath heavy. "Slipped in and saved our children." Tears rimmed Faust's eyes as he spat his words. "But you had to go and make it a damned suicide mission. People are depending on you. This is bigger than one man."

Neil opened his hands, feeling his anger growing. "Spit it out, Faust. What are you talking about?"

Faust tried to say something but was stricken by a sudden coughing fit. He tried to clear his throat, covering his mouth with his handkerchief. Seemingly unable to speak, he removed an envelope from his pocket, a ship-board telegram, the envelope marked by a gold embossment of the Queen Mary. Hesitantly, Faust placed it on the glass-covered table as he hacked into his handkerchief.

Neil took the envelope and, after the report from the other night, wondered what other tricks Faust had up his sleeve. Irritated by the coughing, Neil snapped his finger to the waiter, motioning for him to bring Faust some water as his cough became more violent. Finally, gasping for air, Faust leaned back and sipped the water, eventually taking large breaths as his eyes bulged. Faust was beet red as he turned his bug-eyes to Neil and used his thick hand to shoo the waiter away again. He seemed anxious that Neil read the telegram.

The envelope had already been slit open. On the back, Neil noticed the message had been received the night before and signed for this morning. He pulled the card-stock paper two-thirds of the way out. Neil read downward, reading it three times without taking a breath.

Lex Curran murdered. Found Aug 4. Dead at least a day or two from gunshot. SFPD and DOW manhunt for Neil Michael Reuter underway. Source tells me DOW suspects Reuter on run to Europe under false identity.

The Verandah Bar spun like a carousel. Neil gripped the telegram, twisting it as if the angle might change the meaning of the words. Eventually he managed to breathe, wetting his dry mouth as he turned his blue and green eyes to Faust.

"Who sent this?"

"Meghan Herman," Faust rasped.

"How did she know?"

"She visited you. The police are probably talking to everyone close to you." Faust's tone changed to accusatory. "Your selfish actions have jeopardized everything."

"Is this authentic?" Neil asked, shaking the card paper. "Not another motivational trick you're pulling?"

"I wouldn't create a hoax over something this important."

Neil's shaking wasn't immediately noticeable. It took several seconds to come on. His hands began to twist the telegram, pulling it apart at its middle. All of the sleepless nights, the vomiting sessions, the nightmares, the utter hatred, the voices in his head—the indescribable contempt he held for Lex Curran—were now vanquished and, in Neil's eyes, unjustifiably.

Lex Curran, his reason to live, had been taken from him.

Ripped away.

"Noooooo." The sound came from below Neil's throat. It was involuntary, a moan from the depths of his soul. He turned his attention to the glass ceiling, morosely viewing the broken sky as he took a minute's worth of deep breaths. Finally, he folded the ripped telegram, tucking it into the breast pocket of his charcoal pinstripe. He collapsed backward in the chair.

Neil Reuter wished he were dead.

"Did you do it?" Faust asked.

It was just what Neil needed to hear. He straightened, aiming a finger at Faust's face. "All of the digging you did obviously revealed nothing about me. I've spent two agonizing years mourning my wife and son, thirsting for revenge against that bastard Curran. He ruined my family, and damn near made me kill myself in the process." Neil's head dipped; his eyes closed; his bass voice uncharacteristically feeble. "Everything's now ruined. Everything…"

The two men remained still and quiet for a moment. Faust reached inside his breast pocket, offering a clean handkerchief to Neil. Neil pushed it away.

"You're telling the truth," Faust breathed. "You didn't kill him."

Neil lifted his head.

"I know this is difficult," Faust said. "But if you didn't do it…then who, Neil, *who* would have done such a thing?"

Faust was correct to ask such a question. Neil thought back to his personal liquidation, considering all of the things he knew, the things he'd been ordered to do—and the damning evidence locked away in his brain. Everything was coming at Neil with the force and speed of a locomotive. He was stuck somewhere in a muddle of despair, anger, and bewilderment.

"Regardless of who did it, Neil," Faust said, opening his wallet, "there's something I want to show you." From inside the wallet, he pulled a black and white photograph of a girl of perhaps five. She had a thin, lively face with enormous, expressive eyes. "You might hate me, and with good reason. Regardless, this is…this is my granddaughter," Faust said, his voice cracking. "She was six in this picture. She's almost ten, now."

Neil viewed the picture before looking at Faust again.

"They lived in Düsseldorf. Her father, my son-in-law—and a damned capable man—was on one of the initial Nazi lists of probable Jewish threats. According to the Nazis, he was a militant Jew who might pose some sort of threat to their Reich."

Neil's mind was still awash in Lex Curran's killing. He twirled his finger to hurry Faust along.

"When the Germans and Austrians came for him, he supposedly resisted. They murdered him *and* my daughter, after…" Faust began to tremble. "After they raped her. I have many eyewitness accounts of the savagery they endured." He gathered himself, holding a fist over his mouth as his eyes again filled with tears. "But our dear little Fern made it out with a family friend. She's hiding with the group of children you're going to Austria to rescue."

Despite being overcome with his news of Lex Curran, Neil dipped his head, defeated. There was so much tragedy. Faust gripped Neil's arm, squeezing it tightly. He pressed the picture into Neil's hand. "Keep this, Neil. Her name is Fern. She's as innocent as your son who never got a chance at life. You remember her as you move forward, dammit. And when you find her, you hug her tightly for me. And you bring her out."

Neil was silent.

Faust sniffed a few times and managed a smile. "You see, not everything's ruined. I'm truly sorry about all that happened to you. And I regret hiring that report out on you. That was a mistake. Despite all that, you're doing something far bigger than just yourself. Put your own grief aside to help Fern, and the hundreds of others. Perhaps your suffering can prevent theirs."

Neil stood, walking to the window, watching the ocean slide by. He pressed his hands back through his hair, summoning strength. Faust was correct. This was bigger than Neil. Somehow, he'd have to press through.

Faust crossed the Verandah Bar to Neil's side. "Are you okay?"

"No. But I will be."

"You think about that child. Think of your own pain and imagine hers."

Neil wiped his face, nodding to Faust.

"Now, I don't know this for certain, but I would imagine there will be people waiting on you when we dock. The Department of War is after you, too. I can't begin to imagine the resources they have at their disposal."

Neil lifted the picture of Fern. He considered it for a moment, imagining his own son at her age. A tremor passed through his body.

Then, he heard Jakey…

Press on, Neil. You've come this far. Don't stop now.

Neil stood stone still, eyes closed. His mind reached back, before pain and sorrow, before Emilee, before the war and before his emergence at Gallipoli. The air was sweet smelling and cool in the summertime mountains of eastern California, the forest floor a carpet of pine needles. He remembered the heavy hand of his Shoshone elder, resting on Neil's adolescent head, instructing him in his deep and caring voice.

"How can anyone find you if you aren't there?" The elder studied Neil, not expecting a response. With his finger, the elder made a line across the sky. "The hawk glides without a sound." Gestured to the edge of the wilderness. "The fox pads through the forest, instinct telling him where each paw should strike the ground, inaudible to his prey." He aimed his hand at a rocky cleft between two mountains. "The lynx roams his precarious territory, knowing what he must do to survive, eating prey, avoiding predators, keeping rivals at bay. Adapting. Thriving."

The elder grasped young Neil's shoulders, turning him to face the forest, the mountains, then tilting his head back to the sky. "So, young hunter, which shall you be?"

Neil opened his eyes, nostrils flaring as he considered Faust and his warning. Pocketing Fern's picture, Neil nodded to Faust. "I'll get Fern out." He walked from the bar, headed below decks, his speed increasing with each step.

The Pale Horse ran again.

* * *

As Neil hurried to his quarters, he noticed a porter three doors down, gathering luggage for passengers who'd already left their cabins. Neil stepped into his own cabin, spinning the porthole window on its horizontal hinge and measuring its size. No, that wouldn't work. The only way he might fit would be to remove the window altogether and, judging by its construction, Neil didn't have the time or the tools.

He sat at the desk and scrawled a note to Gregor Faust. Then, after securing his pistol, his identifications, and the diamonds, Neil quickly stuffed his clothes and shaving tackle into his two pieces of luggage. Confident there were no identifying items in his luggage, he removed the two metal tags with Freeman Jennings' name and address. Neil then summoned the porter.

"I want you to find Gregor Faust and give him these two bags, and do it before the ship gets into port," Neil said.

"Before, sir?"

"Yes. I'll be busy until we port. I'm headed up to cabin class and saying my goodbyes to a young woman I met during the cruise."

"Gregor Faust?"

"Yes. Go now, please." Neil tipped the porter handsomely, disappearing in the opposite direction.

Hurrying through the maze of passageways, Neil made his way up several levels to the main galley. After a modest tip, a sous chef provided Neil with a rubber mat and oilskin. Neil locked himself in the nearest bathroom and created a pocket-sized waterproof bundle for his critical items. He used string to bind the oilskin, repeating the process on the outside with the thin sheet of rubber, wrapping it all around in an effort to make it waterproof. Neil fastened his Colt behind his back, running his belt through the trigger guard to ensure its security. Knowing he'd done all he could do, he began to search for his exit point.

One level above the galley were five staterooms, not as nice as Faust's, but significantly larger than Neil's cramped quarters. The five sprawling cabins each had an outer door that opened to a small indentation on the side of the ship, creating a viewing deck. Neil knew this because one of the rooms had already been vacated and was open as a maid cleaned inside.

He smiled at the woman, told her he forgot something, and stepped through the room, acting as if he were the guest who had stayed there. Instead, Neil eyed the coast of England as it slid by, assuming the beaches in the distance to be at least a mile away. He stepped outside on the port side of the ship, looking down—it was at least twenty-five feet to the water. He swiveled his head, peering upward. Several levels up, numerous arms could be seen resting on the railing, heads craning over, fingers pointing. This was not the side of the ship to jump from, starboard was. No one would be looking in that direction—there was nothing to see. Neil tipped his hat at the maid, hurrying across the ship, finding an identical set of rooms on the opposite side. Most of them were unlocked and vacated, their occupants probably above decks, awaiting their port call.

Neil noticed a steward, busying himself with a cart of dirty towels. Neil passed the young man, moving aft until he found what he was looking for. After stuffing the waterproof packet deep in his pocket, he set a trash bin aflame, making certain it was at the base of a granite and tile stairwell. The fire, other than the smoke, would be innocuous. Neil waited for the smoke to build. When it did, he pounded on several doors and yelled "Fire!" The steward shot around the corner, his eyes wide with fear. Neil yelled that the aft companionway was blocked by flames, and to hurry forward to inform the fire-fighting team.

A couple appeared from one of the cabins. They seemed to have dressed quite hastily. Neil feigned panic as he informed them of the fire and told them to get above decks. Once they moved forward, Neil entered the unlocked middle cabin and peered upward from the railed indentation. Just as he thought, he was unable to see another soul on this side. Everyone was standing on port, watching England's south shore.

Stepping over the railing, Neil checked his items one last time. Despite the rushing wind and the sound of the waves below, he heard his own pulse thudding in his ears. Though twenty-five feet doesn't sound like much, it's high enough to be quite scary. The water next to the ship's hull was roiled and foamy and Neil's primary fear was getting sucked under. He checked to see how far forward he was from the stern of the ship and the churning screws. Marking his distance, Neil leaned outward. His skin prickly with fear, he jumped straight out before dropping to the water below.

The water took Neil's breath.

He'd originally intended to submerge in the event a stray passenger thought they saw someone jump but, as it turned out, the Queen Mary did everything for him. Just as he feared, he was sucked under.

The hydraulic force of the ship's motion was otherworldly and sent a spike of childlike panic through Neil. The suction from the twenty-foot screws pulled at him like the current in a raging, flood-fueled river. Fighting his fear, Neil focused on the fact that his body was being twisted and tossed about by an irresistible force. He understood the physics of what was happening, knowing he would be unable to successfully fight the impelling vacuum created by the massive steel screws.

Neil was a strong swimmer and, after years of swimming in the cold and often violent Pacific, he understood riptides and how to get away from them. Using his best underwater stroke—taught as a combat sidestroke—he thrust *with* the pull but at an angle, the pulse of the screws growing in his ear. With each stroke, he felt himself being pulled into the screw's immediate vortex and, just as he felt his arms were going to be the first part of his body to be chewed up by the massive propeller, Neil's sidestroke pushed him into the ship's wake, away from the starboard screw that had tried to dice him to bits.

Though he was desperate for air, Neil knew there would be an overflow crowd at the stern of the ship. Remaining on the starboard side as the rudder passed, Neil thrashed to stay submerged beneath the foamy churn for twenty more seconds. Finally, lungs on the verge of bursting, he allowed his head to surface as he gasped air, also sucking in tiny amounts of spray, making him cough spasmodically as he tried to get his wits about him. He swiveled his head to the RMS Queen Mary, watching the great ship as she churned eastward. She was a hundred feet from him. Then two hundred. Then five hundred. Neil could see a wisp of smoke coming from the balcony where he had jumped—the scant evidence of his harmless crime.

The ship kept steaming. She never slowed.

He had escaped in such a way that, unless they took the time to fingerprint the massive ship, no one would be able to absolutely confirm that Neil Reuter was ever aboard. Sure, some of the stewards or passengers might positively identify him if shown a picture, but given the general pandemonium of a docking ship filled with thousands of passengers eager to disembark, Neil liked his chance of anonymity—at least for a few hours.

And those few hours should give him the time he needed to escape England.

After a brief spate of relief, Neil again became acutely aware of the frigid cold of the North Atlantic. It penetrated him to the bone. Even in August, the water seemed as cold as that of San Francisco Bay. He pressed his hand to his chest, checking the security of his oilskin package. After jerking his wingtips from his feet, Neil began a freestyle stroke to the shore, picking a landmark in an effort to judge the current. Once he saw he was being swept slightly eastward, Neil turned thirty degrees in that direction, accepting the ocean's energy. He soon felt himself moving at a faster rate.

As he crept closer to the Isle of Britain, Neil estimated it would take him about a half-hour to reach the shore. He could no longer feel his hands or toes, but if he kept moving, he felt certain he could survive the cold swim.

While he swam, he surprised himself by thinking of Fern, the frail Jewish granddaughter of the Fausts. "Fern," he muttered as he stroked. "Fern. And Jakey. And Emilee. And my son."

But, for whatever reason, he kept coming back to Fern.

"Fern." *Those expressive eyes.*

"Fern." *Needs my help.*

I'm coming, Fern. Your grandfather is an asshole, but that has nothing to do with you. Don't you worry your little head…I'm coming, and I will get you out.

Neil swam on.

Chapter Twelve

PRESTON LORD HAD BEEN IMMERSED FOR TWELVE HOURS.

He was in the basement of Washington D.C.'s Greeley Building, a covert storage center for sensitive Department of War records. Before him lay hundreds of files and documents he'd already pored over. He swilled the remnants of what was once good coffee before shouting to the attendant, a young Marine sergeant. The attendant appeared from the rows of shelving, sweat on his forehead.

"Sir?"

"Bring me the file on Three-Team-Romeo...the *sealed* file. It would have been sealed in thirty-five or maybe thirty-six."

"Sealed file, sir?"

"Yeah...it's a file with a wax seal on it. Do you want me to draw you a damned picture?"

The Marine glared at Lord, then turned on his heel and hurried away.

Lord stood and stretched, his hands touching the low ceiling of the dark basement. He walked to the back wall, shaking the nearly empty coffee percolator, tossing it down on its side. A yellow rectangle filtered through the solitary window at the top of the back wall, lit by the sidewalk lamps around the building. While it was only warm in the basement, muggy August heat smothered the District of Columbia like an unwanted blanket. Everyone was sick of summer, the season they'd all pined for mere months before.

The cramped quarters didn't bother Lord—he'd be leaving soon. Whether or not he found anything meaningful on Reuter, he was taking a government airplane somewhere. Action often rattled the bushes and flushed out the prey, and he could feel the inaction of this case harming his desires.

"Sir?"

Lord ambled back to his table, taking the file from the sergeant without a word of thanks. He sat, looking irritably up at the muscular young Marine. "Leatherneck, you want to make yourself useful?"

"Am I not useful, sir?"

"Don't be fresh. Go upstairs and get me a fresh pot of coffee. As a matter of fact, go to the all-night deli over on G Street and get me some breakfast."

The Marine shook his head. "Sorry, but I'm not able to do that, sir. My after-hour orders, unless I'm properly relieved, are to stay in this records room no matter what."

"I'm properly relieving you."

"Afraid not," the Marine answered with a grin. "I take my orders from Marines."

Preston Lord slid his chair back and stood. "You either do it, or here's what I'll do: I'll walk over to that phone and call Colonel Harry Ballantine, your *Marine* superior about six levels up, and I'll rudely awaken his ass. I'll tell him you stunk of liquor and derogated me repeatedly this evening. I'll tell him that when I threatened to call your commander, you struck me in the face and said you'd kill me."

The Marine's lips parted but he didn't speak. Lord moved closer.

"If you even think I'm lying, you're in for it. I'll take my coffee mug and I'll smack myself in the forehead to get a nice little bruise, just for effect, and then I'll chuckle as the M.P. truck hauls you away down to Fort Belvoir where you'll rot in a hole for the next twenty years for assaulting a senior member of the United States Government."

The Marine stammered for a moment, finally licking his lips and producing his words. "Sir, these threats are uncalled for and unprofessional and..."

"And what?"

The Marine grew quiet.

"You're not gonna say it, Marine, because you know I'll follow through. And, believe you me, I will," Lord said, his voice low. "I always do what I say. Now, move your ass."

The Marine lingered for a moment before bolting from the basement. He was back in five minutes with a fresh pot of coffee, two Danishes, a banana, and an English toast sandwich.

"You spit in this?" Lord asked.

"I thought about it."

Lord chuckled and sat back down. He didn't offer a word of thanks, nor did he offer to reimburse the sergeant. He unwrapped one of the Danishes and glared at the Marine. "Piss off."

Fifteen minutes later, when Lord was halfway through the once-sealed file, one of his men, LaSalle, sprinted through the basement, sliding to a stop. LaSalle was breathless.

"Yeah?" Lord asked.

"Got word from San Fran. Two Joe-citizens identified Neil Michael Reuter getting on an airplane the night in question."

Preston Lord stood bolt upright, throwing his coffee cup into the mortar wall of the basement. "And why the hell, *ten* days later, am I just now hearing this?"

"The people who pegged him just returned from holiday. The airline didn't have record of where they connected to, but they were on the list of people our canvass team was waiting to speak to." LaSalle glanced at his notepad. "Their description was spot-on, sir. Reuter was headed east, with one stop in Chicago."

"Under his own name?"

"Negative. He was traveling as Frank O'Brien."

Lord pulled on his jacket, securing the sealed file under his arm. "And where was the flight ultimately headed?"

"New York City."

ENGLAND

Chapter Thirteen

THE YOUNG LADY SAW HIM FIRST. She was twenty-two, her husband twenty-four. They'd met almost a year ago to the day at a summer garden party in Kent. The engagement was originally planned to be a long one, while the fiancé slogged through the requisite associate years at Lloyd's in his quest for his junior partnership and a life of fine living. But a bit of coital carelessness in the spring had necessitated a hasty wedding, as well as a vicious ass chewing from the father of the bride.

Once daddy learned about the pregnancy, he'd done a bit of checking on the groom-to-be. Aside from knocking his daughter up, her father was more concerned that the boy better quickly transform into a loving husband—because he sure as hell hadn't been a faithful fiancé. There were a string of comely secretaries at Lloyd's, each having fallen prey to the fiancé's charms, eager to spill their guts for a mere sovereign. During his chat with the groom-to-be, the bride's father, aided by a Webley Mk VI in his hand, did a fine job of making his point.

That unpleasantness behind them, the blissful couple was now on the beach, the first to arrive that morning. They were in front of the Yardley Resort in the East Sussex beachside town of Seaford. A thin film of haze, coupled with the cool morning breeze, had warranted cover-ups over their bathing suits. Their cabana was directly behind them, the one in which they had just made hasty love after a nearly sleepless night. The groom was still in the small cabana, readying himself to take a brisk dip when the bride, not even showing yet, sat straight up and called to him. He emerged from the cabana in his swimming trunks, munching an apple.

"Look," she said, pointing slightly to the left.

A man in what looked like a suit had tumbled in with the three-foot waves, now resting his face in the grayish sand as the murky water lapped at his sock feet. Behind him, further down the beach, white cliffs towered over the restless ocean, leading clear around the southeastern edge of Britain to Dover. The groom walked to the man, running the last piece. The man's skin was pallid, almost bluish from the frigid ocean. The groom patted him on the back as the man coughed weakly between the chattering of his teeth.

"Cor blimey! What happened, fellow? You fall overboard somewhere?"

The man lifted his head, his face coated with sand as he mumbled, "Didn't think I would make it."

"From where?"

Peering at the new bride standing in the distance, the man coughed for a moment before rasping, "Can you keep a secret?"

"American, eh?" the groom asked. "Sure, I can."

"Last night I was on a pleasure cruise with friends, on their yacht. Well, the owner learned about me and his lady friend...about our *friendship*. Heartless man he is, he threw me overboard at gunpoint." The man glanced wearily back out at the sea, shaking his head. "I must have swum miles!"

Empathy coursed through the groom as he patted his new friend on the shoulder.

Kindred spirits.

The American rolled to his back, massaging his hands together. Half of his body was coated in sand and sea foam. "I'd rather that fella not know I made it back here, understand? I think it wise for me to quietly slip back to the States."

The groom helped the castaway up. "I'll just tell my wife you were alone on a small boat that flipped over."

"Thank you," the American mumbled. "Thank you so much." He staggered up the beach with the young groom, patting the lump in his suit pocket, appearing exhausted but relieved.

Once the husband told his brief tale about the overturned boat, he led his new friend into the cabana, giving him a dry towel and some fresh water. As the American dried himself, he cocked an eye at the groom, looking him up and down.

"Say, you're about my size. You wouldn't happen to have an extra suit I could buy, would you?"

* * *

Preston Lord had rushed away from the records basement and now stalked back and forth in one of the executive staff chambers at the War Department. The windows were wide open, not as if that helped. Even in the middle of the night, it was still eighty degrees in Washington, and a cool breeze was about as likely as an endearing, pro-Semitic speech from Adolf Hitler. There was a knock at the door. Lord beckoned. It was Special Agent LaSalle.

"What do you have for me?" Lord snapped.

LaSalle loosened his thin tie, shaking his head. "The three liveries that serve the Chicago airport are still being questioned, just in case. All zeroes there. I'm positive he didn't get off in Chicago."

"That's all you've got?"

"No, sir. A livery driver in Queens pegged a photo of Reuter right quick, but said he was traveling under a different name."

"What's the name?" Lord demanded.

"Said our guy was boarding the Queen Mary. Said the passenger tipped him to stow his bags."

"The name!" Lord roared.

"Freeman Jennings," LaSalle said with a grin.

"Got him," Lord breathed, closing his eyes. "Where does she port, and when?"

"She sailed from New York to just outside of London."

"When does she *port?*"

"Today."

Lord's eyes flew open as if operated by tightly coiled springs. "What time?"

LaSalle checked his watch. "Soon." He stopped Lord. "Slow down, I've already got six men headed out to the docks. We'll get him."

Lord collapsed into one of the leather wrapped chairs. A grin came over his face, but after a few seconds, it disappeared, replaced by a look of unease. "Do *not* underestimate him. Lock down the ship upon arrival; break the arms of those Brits if you have to. Tell them to direct their fallout at me. Don't let a soul off that ship, even the crew, until you have the manifest and know the head count." He aimed a finger at LaSalle. "Do—*not*—underestimate—him. Watch all sides of the ship in case he tries to jump."

"Got it."

Lord's eyes danced around the room. He opened his folio and searched through the pages, finally lifting his hand for silence. "And as soon as our men get him off the ship, tell them to take him to 22 Larch Road, in Dartford. It's near the port."

"Interrogation?"

"No." Lord paused. "Elimination."

LaSalle nodded his understanding.

"And, LaSalle?"

"Yes, sir?"

Lord smiled. "Tell them to make it painful. I want to know he was broken first. I want tears of anguish. I want fingernails ripped off, eyelids cut away. In fact, tell them to scalp his Indian ass."

After what appeared to be a mighty swallow, LaSalle nodded.

"Move!"

LaSalle dashed from the room.

Lord kicked off his handmade shoes. Using the slickness of his socks, he skated to the stocked bar, rewarding himself with a whiskey and water. As he toasted the empty room, he lifted his glass to the northeast and spoke one phrase.

"Goodbye, Neil Reuter. Burn in hell."

Chapter Fourteen

AFTER UNSUCCESSFULLY TRYING TO PERSUADE the young groom to take something for his suit and clothes, Neil purchased a ticket for a private berth on the morning express train into London. Once aboard, he found the attendant to get his voucher punched. Afterward, Neil locked himself inside the rectangular compartment and slid the ticket between the small aisle window and the curtain. He hoped for some privacy, and he also knew the fewer people who saw his face, the better.

Neil tugged off the tight split-toe shoes given to him by the generous young man. While the two men were roughly the same build, the groom's feet were at least two sizes smaller than Neil's. His first priority in London would be the purchase of new shoes.

As the train began to chug away from the station, the requisite whistles and yells were replaced by the metronomic clicking from the tracks. Neil had purchased a pack of British cigarettes at the station and lit one with matches from the berth. The cigarette tasted awful, especially after all of the saltwater spray he'd inhaled during the swim. He crushed it out and vented the berth with the outer window. After removing his new coat, he reclined in the bench seat, forcing himself to relax. His muscles ached from the grueling swim—he stretched and massaged his shoulders with each hand. The news he'd been given earlier in the morning weighed heavily on his mind. As fresh air swirled through the room, he deliberately focused on his pressing tasks before allowing himself to think about Lex Curran.

Neil laid the rubberized packet on the table jutting from the outer wall of the train, holding his breath as he untied the string that held everything together. Seawater leaked out. He wiped away the water, gingerly opening the oilskin. Neil deflated as he saw even more water pour from the creases. He'd been concerned that it wouldn't be waterproof but, given his circumstances, he'd had no choice.

The note from Jakey was wet around the edges but salvageable. He opened the Freeman Jennings passport, still legible on the top half, but stained by the seawater on the bottom and all the way around. Neil placed it on the opposite bench so it could dry in the morning rays of the summer sun. He opened the envelope containing the Dieter Dremel identification and papers; again, water spilled out. The name and address were legible, but barely. Neil knew enough about the Nazi police state to know that waterlogged documents and a bad accent weren't going to endear him to the Gestapo.

Essentially, his fake identities were now useless.

Also in the packet was the photo Gregor Faust had given him. It had actually fared better in the Atlantic than the documents. Feeling a peculiar connection to the girl, Neil dutifully dried the picture, laying it in the eastern sun with his other papers. He then broke down his Colt, drying it, making a mental note to find gun oil at some point.

The diamonds were fine. He blotted them dry before turning his attention to the lighter. He pulled it apart and, using a napkin, carefully blotted the water from each of the pieces. Once it was situated next to the drying documents, Neil made sure he still had the keys the forger had given him. He did, and was satisfied that he'd made it through the swim with all of his items, even if some did happen to be damaged.

It was time. Neil stared at the wet shipboard telegram.

"Lex Curran is dead," he said aloud, after rereading the telegram. He said it over and over, his tone hardening. Each time he said it, his right fist beat the thin cushion. Neil felt as wronged as he had since Emilee had been ripped from him two years before. He'd never had the words to describe to anyone the inconceivable level of injustice one feels after a senseless murder. There is no way to prepare for it, no way to explain it. And while time does help a person cope, Neil never felt as if the wound healed. He simply learned to live with it. But now Curran, too, was gone. And not only did Neil never get the satisfaction of killing him, he'd been set up for the murder.

If Curran was indeed dead, he reminded himself. A big if.

He had to keep the notion alive that the entire production on the ship, including the telegram, could have been an elaborate setup to keep him moving. But for whatever reason, Neil had a feeling that this telegram was the real McCoy. After a half-hour of stomach-churning rumination, Neil's hunger pushed him into action. He pulled on the tight shoes and exited the berth, locking it and finding the nearest attendant.

"Where's the dining car?"

"Two cars back, sir."

Once he made his way rearward, he purchased two deviled ham sandwiches, crisps, two glasses of water and a cup of coffee. The cashier also gave Neil a small bottle of olive oil. While it wasn't gun oil, it would prevent the saltwater from damaging his Colt.

Neil stared long and hard at the rows of bottles behind the bartender, focusing on the vodka.

As the train rushed on toward London, with sixty more minutes to go, Neil made his way back to his berth, balancing his food and drinks on a tray.

There would be no alcohol this day.

* * *

Upon the express train's arrival at Embankment Station in London, Neil stayed in his berth, scanning the platforms for any type of surveillance or waiting police. He noticed two beat cops, chatting idly as the passengers exited and made their way to the station. They didn't seem to be examining the crowd for anyone at all—except comely young ladies—and were obviously engrossed in a funny tale, judging by their hysterical laughter. Neil gathered his things, moving rearward before leaving the train with the throngs from 2nd class. He felt naked without a hat, dipping his head as he passed the bobbies, never earning a glance.

After finding a London cab, Neil instructed the cabbie to take him to a department store that sold shoes. As the cabbie wended his way through the back streets, a thought came to Neil.

"How long would it take to get to the port where the ocean liners dock?"

The driver cocked his head, eyeing Neil in the mirror. "Port o' Tilbury?"

"Where the large cruise lines dock."

"Yeah, that's it. Prob'ly half-hour this time'a day."

Neil displayed a handful of still-damp pound notes he'd exchanged on the ship. "Take me there, please, but don't go all the way in. Park outside."

"S'your quid, mate."

The taxi driver picked his way through the streets north of the Thames. Neil's first impression of London was positive. The famous images he'd seen so many times in newsreels and magazines were there, right out in the open. It seemed to be a populous city, with streets and sidewalks teeming with people, cars, and even horses. The cabbie knew what he was doing, and inside of ten minutes they were racing eastward, outside of the city rush. Ahead, Neil could see the cranes and massive ships signifying the port.

As they approached, Neil reminded the cabbie to stop short of the port. After a final turn, they noticed the long line of cars.

"Are these people here to pick up passengers?"

"Yeah. Place gets rammed when a ship's in."

Neil gripped the door handle as the cabbie eased his way through the mass of cars. "Stop here. I won't be long." He began walking before coming back to the cab and leaning in the open passenger window. "May I borrow your hat?"

"You want me hat?" the cabbie asked, cocking his head.

"I'm trying to surprise someone." Neil reached in his pocket and flipped a pound coin to the cabbie. "An advance on your tip." The cabbie produced an oil-stained tweed newsboy cap. It was too small and clashed with his clothes, but Neil managed to cinch it down over most of his hair. "How do I look?"

"A mite ropey with that getup, but it'll do," the cabbie said, displaying a row of scattered brown upper teeth.

Once he was out of sight of the cab, Neil tried to light a cigarette with his dried-out lighter, realizing he needed to refill it with Naptha. He cadged a light from a passerby. Then, holding his hand with the cigarette over his mouth for further concealment, Neil tucked into the crowd at the gate. He eased his way forward, getting a good view of the ship he'd just called home for over a week. Passengers were disembarking, but only in ones and twos, wearing disgusted looks on their faces. No less than ten reporters stood at the exit, their cameras flashing as they engaged the angered passengers, trying to find out who the authorities were looking for.

"I've missed a half-day of my holiday," protested one well-fed older lady in her New England accent. She spoke slowly for the assembled reporters. "They wouldn't make special exceptions for anyone, herding us all into the ballroom while *only* two extremely rude men cleared people to leave. I'll be speaking to my congressman about this," she told them haughtily, as if her testimony would make the front page of tomorrow's *Mirror*. "*We* won the war with England, you know. *We* shouldn't be treated this way." She began to walk away.

"Hey lady! We were told that all the men on the ship questioning the passengers are *American*," one of the British reporters remarked.

The large woman stopped, her jewels clicking. "Well...yes, I suppose they were. Still...it shouldn't happen here. Because...well..." She appeared at a loss for words, finally deciding to shuffle to her waiting car and no doubt a large lunch somewhere in the city.

Neil knew exactly what was going on and who they were looking for. He focused on the RMS Queen Mary, watching the empty decks, scanning slowly from the top deck. He moved his eyes fore to aft, slowly making his way down.

There!

From the Verandah Grill, where Gregor Faust had told him about the incident that had spawned this manhunt, a man emerged. He removed his fedora, running his hands back through his hair as if he were exhausted. After lighting a cigarette, he yelled over the railing at a grouping of men at the gangway. The men yelled back, giving the thumbs-up signal. Neil focused on them, some of them in uniform—the London police.

So the Americans had called in favors, and were now tearing apart the Queen Mary—pissing off every passenger in the process—performing a systematic search for Neil Michael Reuter, aka Freeman Jennings. Neil thought about the nearly ruined Freeman Jennings passport in his pocket, deciding that it was now definitely useless. Staying in London for any amount of time would be tantamount to a suicide mission. He excused himself, pushing through the crowd until he reached a reporter's side.

"Hey pal, I'm waiting on my brother," Neil asked, scratching his upper lip to conceal the lower half of his face. "Any idea how many of the passengers have made it off yet?"

The reporter was busy snapping pictures, never even turning his eyes to Neil. "Less than half. They'll be here all day if'n they keep this pace up."

Neil thanked him before heading back to the cab.

"Where to?" the cabbie asked.

"I may need you for a while this afternoon." Neil handed the cap over and instructed the cabbie to take him to a fine jeweler. After that he would go to a department store to acquire new luggage and proper clothing, including new shoes of the correct size. Damn if Neil's feet didn't ache. He leaned back into the seat and pressed on his closed eyes. Now that he was a federal fugitive, mass transport was absolutely out of the question. The authorities probably thought he was still on the ship, so it could be some time before the net was fully spread over the city.

"Does London have a newsstand that would have American newspapers?"

"Just ahead."

Neil asked him to stop. The only paper from San Francisco was the previous Sunday paper, August 7th. Back in the cab, Neil told his driver to head to the jeweler as he delved into the paper, his heart sinking as he saw the small piece on the bottom of the fourth page:

POLICE REMAIN STUMPED OVER LEX CURRAN MURDER

The sub-headline ruled out the possibility of suicide. So, it was true. Neil crumpled the paper, placing it below his feet. He had no desire to read on. Feeling nauseous, he decided to focus on the tasks at hand—first of which involved not getting caught. If Neil's description wasn't already out to the London authorities, it would be in short order.

The money in his pocket wasn't enough. He needed to exchange a diamond to secure enough sterling to buy a change of clothes and find someone to transport him to mainland Europe. He considered hiring a fast boat, but the shore was an easy area to patrol and would probably be closely watched by the military due to Germany's increasing belligerence.

Neil thought about the growing number of Jews, and even German citizens, especially those with something to fear, who were now fleeing Nazi Germany in their search for a better life. Someone here in London had to be profiting from that burgeoning need. Had to. But who? Other Jews? Possibly.

But who could move in and out of Germany with relative ease? Who would have access? An idea coming to him, Neil leaned forward.

"Is there a German neighborhood around London?"

"Yeah, a couple."

"Which one's the biggest?"

"Shoreditch."

Neil leaned back, scratching his stubble. "Yeah, Shoreditch. That'll be our last stop."

Though he didn't feel like sleeping, he knew he needed rest. Surprisingly, he fell asleep seconds after closing his eyes, getting a nice catnap as the driver made his way westward on Victoria Embankment, following the Thames back into the city.

Chapter Fifteen

PRESTON LORD RAPPED ON THE ARLINGTON apartment door. He waited. It was still quite early in the morning, the shadows in the stairwell heavy due to the low sun that hadn't yet ascended above the adjacent buildings. He knocked again. After a moment, he heard the soft thudding of approaching feet. Lord guessed she'd only been asleep a few hours—who knew what the little minx had done last night? He took a step backward, opening his arms as he heard the chains and locks clicking. The door opened.

"Well, did I make your day?" he asked.

The woman was expressionless. She wore a long silver gown, revealing bare feet with painted red toenails. Her short blonde hair was matted on one side, matching the red sleep lines on her face. Though she wore no makeup, this woman in her mid-twenties, with her full lips, small nose and large green eyes, was strikingly attractive.

"Well, did I?"

"You should've called," she mumbled.

"I know he's out of town, Shirley. In fact, he's out of town being a bad little lawyer. I'd wager he had two or three Cuban *putas* last night."

"He doesn't run around," she replied with her eyes closed.

"Yeah, okay…neither do you, right? Besides, do you know how wicked a city Miami is?"

Shirley's head made a bumping sound as it thudded against the door.

"Are you gonna let me in, or what?"

Fifteen minutes later, the twosome stood under a cool shower, their tongues entwined. Minutes before, all Lord had done to wake her up was give her the pharmacist's bottle of the peculiar white powder known as cocaine. In fact, it was cocaine that first brought Lord in contact with this beautiful young creature. Apparently, she'd developed an affinity for it when she and her husband had lived in Memphis. Lord had met her one night in a Georgetown tavern. After an hour of cajoling the married beauty, he'd discovered her weakness was the organic powder he could so easily obtain from one of his sources. Lord had known from the second he spotted her across the bar that she was naughty—a naughty young lady with secrets. Now, all he had to do was tease her with a taste of the miracle powder and she'd do anything he wanted.

The wife of a young associate at a good D.C. law firm, she often complained that her husband gave her no money to spend, hence Lord's mental hold over her. Lord had the cash; Lord had the cocaine; she had the goods. And, oh, how sweet her goods were.

After she'd snorted a bit of cocaine into both nostrils, he'd made her brush her teeth and that's when they'd gotten in the shower. She'd just greedily knelt before him when he cocked his head at a sound.

"You hear that?" he asked.

She pulled her head back. "What?" she asked, rubbing her hand under her nose and sniffling the way she always did for a number of minutes after inhaling the cocaine.

Lord yanked open the shower curtain. "The phone! Answer it!"

"What if it's George?"

"To hell with George!" he yelled. "He doesn't know I'm here. It might be my guys."

"You *told* someone you were coming here?" she asked, water striking her in her wide green eyes.

"Just go answer the damn phone."

Lord let the water cascade over himself as he waited.

"It's for you," he heard her say.

Without using a towel, he walked into the entryway of the apartment, dripping water on the carpet runner. "Yeah?"

"This is Greenwood, sir."

"Who?"

"Greenwood, from London…they patched me through."

"I'm busy, Greenwood. Get on with it."

"He wasn't on the boat. We tore it apart and checked every soul as they debarked."

"How is that even possible?" Lord roared.

"We think he may have gotten wind and jumped."

"Jumped?"

"Yes, sir."

"Have you considered the fact that he could be hiding? That ship's huge."

"We have people camped out in and around the boat. He can't hide forever. But we're pretty sure he bailed overboard. There was a small fire about an hour before they put in," Greenwood said. "A ship hand gave us a description of the man who reported the fire—according to the manifest his name is Freeman Jennings—and he wasn't among the passengers who debarked."

"Was he the only person on the manifest who was missing?"

"Yes, sir. Other than an old lady who died during the voyage. But she's in the ship's icebox…I saw her myself."

"Cute," Lord said. "What are you doing now?"

"As you told us to do, we're using our influence and putting out the word in London and every town the ship passed on its way in. We've spread his picture, his real name, the works."

"Whatever actions you've taken, double them. I want every damned Brit to know what he looks like, do you understand me? And tell those limey bastards to shoot to kill."

"Yes, sir."

"As I said, I'm incredibly busy. Don't call me back unless you've got that Indian's scalp in your hands." Lord jammed the earpiece into the handset so hard that it broke the cradle.

"Hey, you busted it," Shirley protested.

"Buy another one." Lord eyed Shirley the way he might eye a rare cut of meat. She was feet away, a towel covering all but a portion of her right breast. Lord congratulated himself for having the prescience to come here this morning. Now, his frustration with Reuter's aggravating disappearance could only be worked off.

Properly.

Lord removed her towel and lowered her to the sofa.

* * *

London pulsated with nervous energy. The talk of impending war was everywhere. On street corners, skinny young boys hawked afternoon newspapers in shrill, glass-cutting voices; and next to them, working completely independently, civil volunteers tried to yell over the paperboys, enlisting the citizenry to prepare for the Hun they felt was bound to storm ashore at any minute. It must have been going on that way for months because the Londoners kept their eyes straight ahead, ignoring the criers like they might any common nuisance of living in a big city. It was as if they weren't even there.

Neil had expected a New York feel in London, with glitz and glam, posh restaurants and exclusive shows—but that wasn't what he observed. Not at all. Perhaps it was the growing fear of the Nazis. Or maybe it was just their Victorian-influenced culture. London was indeed large and lively, but a bit more spread out, and certainly quite old. And while many of its citizens wore the pinched faces of those expecting impending doom, the city seemed to possess a charm and hospitality all its own.

The Londoners dressed similar to Americans, with some noticeable differences. The men seemed to prefer a more formal look, going with three-button suits or vests in heavier, woven wools. Fedoras were common, but many men chose to go with the larger homburg, possibly in deference to their prime minister, Neville Chamberlain—Neil had never seen him without one. Women's dresses were a bit more concealing than what Neil was used to in San Francisco. All in all, Neil found the people to be rather polite for such a large city.

Deciding to stop and observe for a moment, he leaned against a stone wall at the corner of Park Lane and Stanhope Gate, just on the eastern edge of Hyde Park. He lit a cigarette. From his pocket he removed the seawater-stained picture of Gregor Faust's granddaughter, Fern, certainly taken in happier times. Neil shut his eyes for a moment, imagining how she might look right now, living as a persecuted captive. In the picture, she was thin, but appeared healthy and bright-eyed. Neil tried to picture her after weeks of running following her parents' death—her eyes would bulge slightly from their dark sockets, and her shoulder blades would be visible, like coat hangers under a filmy dress. But the grief of losing her loved ones would have been the worst part for Fern—Neil knew all about it.

He was tricking himself into getting angry, but sometimes he needed to do this for extra incentive. Jakey was his primary motivation, but the end result would hopefully assist people like Fern. People who were persecuted unjustly—namely, the Jews. Neil remembered when, as a boy, he was invited to the Hermans' home for one of the traditional Passover meals of delicious Matzo balls and accompanying latkes. He recalled how the modest Herman family had devoutly prayed throughout the day and night during that time of year. Neil went home, finding his father resting in his worn tweed chair, wearing only his stained undershirt and tattered trousers, the requisite bottle of beer in his hand. He told Neil, with a measure of restrained disdain, that the Hermans were Jews, and they didn't believe in the same God the Reuters believed in. That their people had shunned Jesus—killed him. But, as far as Neil could ever recall, he never remembered his father worshiping any God. It wasn't until Neil met Emilee, a Methodist, that he had any true exposure to Christianity. His father had seemed more irritated over the difference of the Hermans' religion, and not his faith in his own beliefs.

But it didn't matter what faith Jakey Herman was; Neil would have gone anywhere for him, no strings attached. Jakey had saved Neil's life and, other than Emilee, was his only true friend. They'd always joked about their heritage: Neil's Shoshone blood and Jakey's Jewish ancestry. "We're brothers from two tribes," Jakey used to say.

Neil touched his breast pocket, the one with the torn telegram announcing Lex Curran's murder. Also in the pocket was the note from Jakey. He'd asked Neil to do all this, and Neil intended to follow through.

Suddenly, it hit Neil. "I'm in London," he whispered. "I sold everything, evaded capture and I don't have too far to travel." He'd been so busy and preoccupied that he'd failed to congratulate himself for making it this far. In terms of distance from San Francisco to Austria,

London was ninety percent to his goal—the longest section was well behind him. But Neil had no illusions about this last ten percent. There would be no freedoms once he reached Hitler's Reich.

The sudden appearance of a police car, a Humber Snipe, brought Neil out of his reflection. The police car screeched to a stop across Park Lane. A bobby, who moments before had been patrolling the block on foot, walked to the passenger door of the Humber and leaned in. Neil had already passed by him twice as he visited the jeweler and the department store, both times earning a quick glance and a grunt. He'd not been concerned about his image being circulated since the Americans were probably still searching the Queen Mary.

But now Neil's concern began to grow.

The two policemen in the car talked to the bobby before handing him a sheet of paper. The bobby straightened, staring at the paper before stabbing it with his finger. Neil could only see the back of the paper, but the sunlight shone through, displaying a great deal of ink. It was either a sketch reproduced by mimeograph or an actual photograph.

Neil lifted his new suitcase, his eyes turning southward. His taxi was parked several blocks away in Mayfair, right next to Christ Church. Another police car squeaked to a halt between him and the taxi. Neil began to walk, turning toward the Tube station at Hyde Park, away from the police. He glanced over his shoulder, watching as the bobby scanned the area. He shouldn't have turned because, when he did, the bobby locked in on him. He pointed and, over the din, Neil heard him yell, "There he is!"

Neil had two simple choices: stop and face the music—or run. Normally, when incorrectly accused of anything, Neil would vigorously fight the charge. But Lex Curran's murder had left him on edge, and on guard. It was just too convenient for Curran to disappear for two years, only to surface—literally—when Neil was departing town under a shroud of secrecy.

Something about it smelled like a fabrication. And a setup.

The second choice, to run, was Neil's best option, and he took it. He sprinted down the two flights of stairs into the Hyde Park Tube tunnel. At the bottom, a bored attendant sat behind iron bars, reading a newspaper. Neil smacked a pound down, asking for a ticket. ·

"Where to?"

"Day pass. Whatever."

The attendant shrugged and slid a ticket over the cool granite counter. Neil ran into the station, leaping the turnstile as he rushed to the platform. Only a few teenagers milled about.

"How long 'til the next train?" he asked, breathless.

The closest teen turned to him with Bassett hound eyes. "You a yank?"

"Yes. How long?"

"I dunno. Five minutes, maybe ten."

Neil ran.

Police whistles could be heard, coming from the stairwell. They would be descending, probably five of them, if not more. One had certainly gotten on the radio, and he would have broadcast a positive identification of the fugitive American in this area. The American agents would hear this and, if Neil were correct, *their* orders would be to shoot to kill. Most of them were probably still out at the docks, a good thirty minutes away. As Neil leapt from the platform and onto the tracks, heading east, he gave himself twenty minutes before all of London would be teeming with Scotland Yard, intent on capturing him. Worse was the bevy of American agents from the Department of War, bound and determined to end his life. Either way, if Neil didn't shake these locals immediately, he didn't like his chances.

Now well into the tunnel, he stopped, looking back to the light of the Hyde Park station. No one was following him yet, but he could hear the commotion as the police questioned the teens. He swiveled around. Ahead of him, at roughly twice the distance, was the light of the next station, Green Park.

Neil caught his breath, watching, measuring his options.

The police from the Hyde Park station still weren't following him. That could mean only one thing: there were cops awaiting him at the next station.

Or a train was barreling in his direction.

Either way, he was trapped.

Slow your mind. Think clearly. Focus.

Standing in the darkest shadows of the north side of the tunnel, he allowed his eyes to adjust as his mind hearkened back to the summers at the Shoshone Indian reservation in the southern Sierras. At night, he and the older boys used to play a modified game of hide and seek. Neil could remember being surrounded, just like this, the circle closing in on him. And while it was just a game, Neil remembered the agonizing fear as the boys grew closer. At the last instant Neil would make a desperate move and would get caught every time. Until one summer when the elder, who had watched Neil get nabbed by his friends, took him aside and showed him the technique to escape the situation.

"You have to disappear," the old man told him in his heavily accented English, a mild look of mirth on his face.

"I'm not magic," Neil had replied, exasperated.

"Magic has nothing to do with it."

"Then how do I do it?"

The elder took Neil into the woods every evening for two weeks, spending hours helping Neil perfect the art of concealment and escape. Each night he adorned Neil with an extra decoration on his breechcloth tunic, not unlike a military award for superiority in a particular discipline.

"While you might be there in body," the older man told him, "you have to be elsewhere in spirit. If your spirit is hidden well enough, they will *never* find your body. And you will live to see another day." He showed Neil how to use the trees, the water, the earth and even the wildlife to escape. After every lesson, the elder would always finish with one statement. "It ends with your spirit. Do not concern yourself with your body. Your spirit must be gone."

There was, indeed, nothing magic about the elder's lessons. Essentially, one has to believe in his concealment or escape in order for it to work. Neil later learned the power of visualization in his business life, too. Athletes used it. Actors used it. And the elder Shoshone had taught it to Neil. That had been in July. The other teenagers never found him again that summer. Nor the next.

Neil closed his eyes, summoning his inner spirit. Keeping his eyes shut and a hand dragging the wall, he patiently began to shuffle in the direction of the Green Park station.

Chapter Sixteen

SAL CONTINUED TO COME UP ZEROES ON THE Reuter case. Captain Yarborough was under pressure from the chief to move the case forward or turn it over to another team, and it was only thanks to Sal's Greek doggedness that the chief had extended the deadline by another week. But since finding Meghan Herman, Sal had come up with nothing. The lack of any other evidence screamed to him that there was something incredibly meaningful hiding out there somewhere—he just hadn't found it yet. When there was virtually nowhere else for him to turn—at the exact moment Neil Reuter was busy extracting his spirit from a London subway tunnel—Sal showed up bright and early at a spick and span barbershop on Folsom, directed there by the wife of J. Harrison Musselwhite, IV.

The bell on the door in the two-chair establishment jingled when Sal entered. Musselwhite was the only man in a barber chair, probably the first customer of the early day. The striped apron was spread around him and his face was well lathered with white shaving cream, freshly whipped in a mixing bowl that sat perched on the counter behind him. Next to the mixing bowl and behind Musselwhite, a barber, a good distance into the fourth quarter of life, sharpened a straight razor on a leather strap, tapping his foot out of time with tinny music coming in over the radio. The barbershop was quite masculine and smelled of fresh mint and Listerine.

"Dan'll be right in, friend," the old man said with a genuine smile and what sounded like an Irish lilt. "Go ahead and have a seat. Newspaper's on the table, there. Coffee in the back, if'n you please."

Sal removed his fedora, showing what little hair he had. "Dan wouldn't have much work to do on me. I just need to chat with your customer, if you don't mind."

Upon hearing that, Musselwhite opened his eyes, turning them to Sal. After seeing him, he closed them again, nestling into the chair and exhaling. He seemed mildly perturbed that what was probably a relaxing weekly ritual was being derailed. "Mornin', detective," he said, his voice flat. "Surprised it's taken this long for you to come back to see me."

"Yeah, well, I've been real busy chasing dead ends."

The other barber emerged from the rear, wiping his hands on a towel. Sal would have given two-to-one odds that he was the old barber's son, and that even he was pushing sixty. The barber brightened upon seeing Sal and yanked an apron from a hanger. Sal shook his head. "No haircut for me, pal." He dug into his pocket and handed the barber two quarters.

"Lemme rent the chair for fifteen minutes." The barber took the money, shrugged, and disappeared again into the back room.

Sal leaned back in the chair, staring into the mirror ahead of him, studying Musselwhite. The accountant seemed perfectly relaxed, his eyes closed again as the barber went to work, slowly scraping the skin of his cheeks below the short sideburns. The sound of the razor on Musselwhite's face was akin to paper being slowly ripped.

"Mr. Musselwhite, exactly why did your former employer sell everything and leave town?" Sal asked.

"I told you already, detective...I don't rightly know. Anything I give you will be a guess, and no better than your own guess." He paused. "And I'm hiding nothing. Got no reason to."

Sal believed him. "Tell me about Reuter. Things I may have missed."

Musselwhite opened his eyes briefly. "How would I know what you've learned? I could speak about Neil Reuter for months."

"Humor me. Stream of consciousness."

Musselwhite closed his eyes again. "Well, he's a reader, a voracious one. Perhaps his books or magazines would give you a clue to his whereabouts. He likes chess, and he'll readily learn and play most any strategy game such as backgammon or poker. Only if he has time, mind you. And if you beat him, he won't speak to you for a few hours. He's not big on losing. He's not big on food either. Eats to live...doesn't live to eat, unlike me. He had a small yacht, but that was for his wife. Neil likes success but hates the notoriety." Opened his eyes. "*Hates* it."

Sal jotted that down.

"Drinks too much, too...especially since the murder, but I think he did it to help himself cope. He drank before the murder, too, but it would come and go in spurts. Probably something from the war. Neil enjoys helping charities...deserving ones...and is well-known for enlisting others and matching their donations only if—"

"Wait a minute," Sal interrupted, stabbing his notebook with his pencil. "About the military..." Sal gathered his thoughts as the scraping of the razor continued. "Did he often talk about the war?"

"Never. Not once."

"Not *once?*"

"That's what I said, detective. I don't forget that type of thing."

Sal frowned as he flipped to the half page of notes he had taken while on the phone with the Army's personnel division. He scanned them, remembering that the man in Washington had informed him that Reuter had been an officer, serving in logistics, in France.

"Do you know anything else about his service?" Sal asked.

"No, but he had a few Army friends that would sometimes come around. Maybe you should pester them."

Sal let out a long, slow breath, his cheeks expanding into a facial globe like an old trumpeter's. "Mr. Musselwhite, Reuter's wife is dead. He's gone. His stuff has been sold. His personal effects have vanished. Plus, the man had no real friends that I can find. So, how in the hell am I going to find the name of any old Army buddies he might have had?"

The barber had finished scraping the gray hairs from Musselwhite's face. Using a pair of tongs, he produced a scalding towel from a steaming pot, unapologetically wrapping the financial man's face. The sudden intense heat made Musselwhite's entire body tense. Sal winced. Once the apparent shock from the searing high temperature had settled in, Musselwhite spoke one muffled word.

"Agnes."

"Excuse me?"

"Agnes Gentry."

"The housekeeper?"

"Yep."

"She'd have names of visitors?"

The towel, essentially a face-turban, nodded up and down. "I'd wager she has a detailed list. She never wanted to be caught off guard by Neil. He didn't like to be blind-sided by unwanted guests, so I'll bet you she has a list of all approved guests."

"Sonofabitch," Sal mumbled. "If that turns out to be the case, then I oughta be fired. I never once thought to ask her."

Musselwhite removed the towel from his face. "Since I'm now unemployed, maybe I should come down and apply for a job as a detective."

Sal donned his russet trilby, adjusting it. "Thanks, Musselwhite. I'll let you know when I find him."

J. Harrison Musselwhite, IV watched him go, waiting until the bell stopped jingling. "So much for the peace and tranquility of retirement. Let's do it all again, Elmer, this time in peace."

* * *

Eight time zones and more than 5,000 miles away, Neil opened his eyes and estimated the Green Park station to be several thousand feet away. Someone was leaning out over the tracks, aiming a light in his direction, but he was too far away for them to have any hope of seeing him. If a local train were to come to either station, Neil imagined that the police would keep it from proceeding. But an express train was a different story, and Neil didn't want to wait around to find out which type of train was first up.

He continued to scurry down the north side of the single track, running his hands along the damp wall. He ducked below a solitary green light, carefully avoiding its luminance. Several enormous rats skittered over his new shoes. After a moment, his hand slid into a recess of several inches. Widening his eyes, he tried to make out the indentation in the darkness of the tunnel. He put the suitcase at the base of the notch so he could use both arms. As his hand worked over the rectangular outline, Neil could feel the alternating temperatures of the resident stone and the warmer recessed surface, making him hopeful it was a door.

He controlled his breathing, focusing on his spirit. This had to be the way out, the portal to his exodus.

You must believe...

A commotion grabbed his attention from the Hyde Park station. At first he heard yelling and more police whistles. He turned to look, immediately recognizing the horrifying round white light of an approaching train. It vibrated with speed, clearly not about to slow down. Neil focused his eyes on the frantically waving figures on the platform, feeling his chest tighten as the train blew through the station at a high rate of speed. It was coming directly at him, and Neil estimated he had ten seconds before it would turn him into one helluva mess.

The hawk, the fox, the lynx. Which will you be?

Neil's mind raced. He could flatten himself against the shallow indentation, but he wasn't confident the train would clear him. If not, it would grind him against the wall, leaving a trail of American hamburger and a mangled suitcase. There were sparks showering from the train's carriage, at its electricity source. The light on the front was powerful, illuminating the space like the brightest of days. Neil whipped his head back to the indentation, mere seconds from being crushed, confirming that it was indeed a door. There was no door handle, but a plate where the handle would be, marked by a bolt-lock in its center.

Neil pushed on the door. Nothing. He threw his body into the door.

It didn't budge.

It's a football field away...

The pushing wind from the barreling train assaulted Neil, making his ears pop as the air pressure changed in the confined space. Instinctively, he jerked the Colt from his waistband, raking the slide and pulling the trigger as fast as he could, hoping the saltwater hadn't fouled his bullets. He pulled the trigger again and again as the tongues of flame flicked from the end of the Colt. The heavy .45 caliber bullets punched holes through the plate like it was school paper.

With the impossibly loud train feet away, Neil lowered his shoulder and ran into the door, falling over the lip as he lunged into the blackness. Instinctively, he reached back through the opening, yanking his suitcase in just as the train passed.

The passing train was so deafening Neil was unable to even think. He lay there in a muddy puddle until the train passed, leaving an eerie silence in its wake. Neil's heart thudded in his chest while his ears rang from the train's roar. He patted his face, his chest, his legs.

Ten fingers...ten toes...

Neil staggered to his feet and pushed the door shut. He was in another tunnel, this one quite ancient, with four-way arches and solitary bulbs hanging low, half of them lit. Piping and plumbing of all sizes ran in every direction. Hot steam shot out at various spots, making the underground space feel like a haunted Russian bath.

Neil knew he only had a minute or two. If he were to simply turn and run, they would probably realize he hadn't been run down and then they would catch up to him in short order. He needed something to slow his pursuers down. He began to scour the space, picking up occasional parts before discarding them. After a full minute of searching he found a ten-foot section of pig metal pipe. He rushed back to the door, propping the pipe against it, wedging it against a notch in the brickwork behind him. With the pipe in place it would take a tank's force to open the old door from the subway tunnel.

But they'd still see the bullet holes. They would know he was still alive. He had to get far away—and fast.

Neil turned and jogged in the opposite direction. He knew he was headed north. After what must have been a block, the tunnel intersected a cross tunnel, this one leading to the east and west. Neil continued forward. He repeated this until he had gone twenty blocks to the north, at which time he turned east, going twenty blocks again. Exhausted, especially from running with his new suitcase, he bent double, stopping to rest. Once he'd caught his breath, and realizing he was soaked from sweat and steam, Neil began to look for an exit. He suddenly felt a rumble that shook the earth beneath him. He froze, realizing it must have been another subway line on the opposite side of the wall, the sound heavily dampened by the thick stone. Neil crossed the wide passageway of his own tunnel, singeing his hand on a scalding pipe as his slid underneath.

A steel rung ladder protruded from the far wall, which Neil climbed, struggling to use only one arm while the other held his grip. He unlatched a hatch at the top, cautiously emerging into a well-lit hallway. He spent a moment dusting off his clothes before walking to both ends of the hall, finding a squat door at the second end. Neil took several deep breaths, emerging from the door onto a bustling street. The late afternoon streets teemed with men and women heading home or to their second-shift job. It was the perfect time for Neil to blend in and disappear.

Keeping a lookout for police, Neil stopped an affable-looking older man, asking him how to get to Shoreditch.

"Ah, an American," the man said with a smile and a wink. He personally guided Neil a block south, stopping at a wide avenue and pointing east. "This is Oxford Street, m'friend. Stay on it with the sun to your back. It's only a few miles to Shoreditch." The man clapped Neil on his back.

"Will the street be this crowded the entire way?"

"In this fine weather? Billy-o, arseholes and elbows," the man replied, tugging on the brim of his hat.

After thanking the Englishman, Neil pulled his new fedora down tightly, keeping his head down as he carried his grip smartly to the east.

Chapter Seventeen

WILHELM KRUGER WAS NEIL'S AGE, older by only six days. In the Great War he had been a pilot, flying a Fokker D VII in missions over France and Belgium. On one particular summer day back in 1917, one with the correct weather and wind, one that he had awaited for many weeks, Wilhelm, or "Willi" as he was known to most people, took off after his mission brief, his Fokker loaded with a hundred-kilo bomb underneath and two *senf*-slathered bratwurst rolls in his lap. He had munched one of the bratwurst sandwiches, chewing happily as the cool wind at altitude added to his sense of well being over what he was about to do.

Willi waited until he passed the forward line of battle before jinking to the right and diving to the treetops. After running at full throttle and skimming the leaves on the tops of the elm trees, he jettisoned his bomb directly into a non-threatening rear echelon area of the Allied forces, banking so he could watch the volcanic explosion that sent tents, rifles, legs and heads spinning high into the air. Willi leaned his head back, cackling before he throttled down to save his precious fuel. He flew on the deck, pressing ahead to the east of Dunkirk, feeling the air cool and thicken as he popped out over the grayness of the famed strip of water the Brits called the *English* Channel. Arrogant bastards.

After what seemed an hour, with the aid of the tailwind he had been waiting weeks for, he sighted land just as his Fokker began to wheeze and sputter. Before his tank was completely dry, Willi climbed high enough to spot a lumpy field. His engine quit shortly thereafter, sending him gliding in for a bone-shaking landing. He got the wheels down for a hundred meters, but the overgrown grass had prevented him from seeing the marshy underbelly and, once the landing gear was seized by the water, it sent the Fokker keeling forward, hammering Willi's large nose directly into the hard leather-padded rim of the cockpit. Figuring he would be overrun with soldiers, he clambered clumsily out of the airplane. After attempting to stem the blood from his thoroughly broken proboscis, he began waving the once white hankie, unaware that it now looked like the flag of the Japanese Empire—white with a blood red orb centered in the middle.

Willi's assumptions, as usual, were incorrect, because the only onlookers he garnered that afternoon were two boys who had been out playing, coincidentally, a game of war. They approached him fearlessly, running their hands over the taut skin of the Fokker and openly making fun of Willi's broken English—and nose.

Once again using the handkerchief to stem the free flow of blood from his nose, Willi asked to be taken to their parents. As it turned out, one of the boys, the owlish one with oversized eyes, was the son of the town constable. The constable locked Willi away after beating him with a rake handle. Two days later, the constable and a group of other locals hogtied Willi before driving him into London, like farmers with their prized fattened pig. After another beating from his new captors, they deposited him in a hole that smelled fouler than Willi's pigpen of a barracks back in Hannover.

Willi stayed "in the hole" for the better part of six months, eagerly telling the military brass everything they wanted to know about his airplane, his training, the collective mission, and the general state of turmoil in his motherland. When repeatedly asked about the rogue bombing of a medical detachment well behind the front line of battle on the day of Willi's defection, Willi had shaken his bullet-shaped head, claiming it was done by Klaus von Wieseck, a radical ace from his squadron who flew the exact same type of aircraft Willi did. While Willi knew good and well that he, himself, had done the dirty deed, he hated Klaus with a passion, even providing the investigators Klaus's home address in the hopes they might send a spy to kill him.

Before Willi's defection, Klaus had taken every pfennig of Willi's poker money. Willi suspected Klaus had done so by marking the cards. He spewed Klaus' address so many times it got to where the investigators would open every interrogation with the phrase, "We know all about Klaus von Wieseck..."

Before and after every beating, before and after every interrogation, Willi expressed an interest in becoming a full-fledged English citizen. He told them he was married with no children, but that his wife had sampled every man in Hannover. This wasn't exactly true. Willi suspected Katarina might have once sent a postcard to her teenage beau, but that was about it. He, on the other hand, was well known to every nurse and attendant at the airfield in Koblenz. And he could easily be identified due to a small birthmark he'd been bequeathed in a particularly private place.

Such rampant philandering was Willi's primary motivation to defect. He'd been tipped off that his wife's father, a full colonel in the tank command, had gotten word of Willi's indiscretions and was going to have him drawn and quartered as soon as the war was over.

Drawn and quartered—or British food for the rest of his days?

Willi did not have a difficult time coming to his final decision.

Now, more than twenty years later, the limited English citizen was well known in the Shoreditch area because of his inner-city farm. Between two rows of buildings, Willi Kruger had developed a market garden that was capable of producing impressive quantities of needed produce, especially when considering the conditions he was forced to operate in. His three farm hands, including his freckly Irish wife—she happened to be fifteen years his junior—worked their collective fingers to the bone. They bottled milk, collected eggs, imported hay and feed, and spread manure at a pace that would make even a good, hard-working German farmer proud.

On this particular day, a grimy-faced Willi Kruger had just finished selling a half-dozen eggs to a sixteen-year-old English girl from two blocks over. As he gave her a few coins of change, he winked at her and told her to come back "any damn time she wanted...for any damn thing she wanted." No sooner had the teen hurried away than a tired-looking man wearing a serious expression and a soiled pinstripe suit appeared.

"Can I getcha?" Willi asked, wiping his hands on his canvas apron while speaking in an adopted English accent that was still quite German.

The man whipped out a five-pound note, pinching it between his two fingers. "Fifteen minutes of your time, in private." The man spoke German.

"Nellie!" Willi screamed, stripping off the smeared apron as his other hand dug in his pockets for his cigarettes. "Take over," he said, hitching his thumb to the cash box.

"Where ya goin now?" she asked in a tone somewhere between weary and pissed off.

"Never you mind, woman. Do what I tell you, when I tell you," he answered, leveling a rigid finger at her. Willi turned to the man and winked at him. "Gotta treat 'em like livestock to get 'em to produce."

His visitor seemed unimpressed.

They walked through the back alley, with the visitor tiptoeing over the slop and the manure. Willi entered the rear of the bordering house through a screen door, motioning his guest inside. The room was dim, with a small table and an aluminum counter on the far end. This was the back of Willi's small home, the working end. He reached into the icebox and retrieved a beer for himself, biting the top off.

"Getcha a beer?"

"Have any coffee?" the man asked, eyeing the pot on the stove. Willi didn't ask if he took cream or sugar, instead just splashing the burnt coffee in an ancient mug. The visitor sipped it and winced.

"The money," Willi stated, making a pulling motion with his fingers. He took the bill, eyeing it before cramming it into his shirt pocket. "What do you want?" he asked, no longer trying to speak with a British accent.

"I understand you have an airplane," the man said. His German was odd.

Willi narrowed his eyes at the funny accent. His wife knew a kindergartener's German, and this man's accent wasn't too dissimilar from hers. "Who told you that?"

"The very first person I asked when I walked into this neighborhood."

Willi frowned. "And who are you?"

"That's not important," the man answered, tossing the coffee into the sink and leaving the mug. "What is important is the amount of money I'm willing to pay you to fly me to Innsbruck, Austria."

Willi had been in mid-swig, and he quickly lowered the beer to keep from spilling any more than he did. He coughed several times before wiping his mouth and foamy moustache with the back of his sleeve. "If I did have an airplane, stranger, getting you to Austria would be next to impossible, and would cost more than you've ever dreamed." He narrowed his eyes. "I don't have an airplane, and it doesn't matter anyway because—"

The man pulled several bands of twenty pound notes from his pocket, stacking them one by one on the table. By the time he was finished stacking, Willi was staring at more money than he had made in the past three months.

After Hitler had seized power in Germany, and the German economy had roared back to life, Willi had seen a sufficient need to create a smuggling business. He'd first utilized an old boat and a series of train hops through France. Several years ago, he'd invested in a rattletrap airplane, an old Curtiss. He used it to fly into Germany and bring back human cargo, Jews mainly. He brought them, their babies, gold bars, paintings—they always carried something he didn't expect.

But in the past year, just after he and his partner shelled out all of their savings for the new airplane, the smuggling business had begun to sour. There were now numerous competitors, mostly military, from Germany. They had the equipment, the know-how, and they were on the inside—able to get clearance for their flights. Subsequently, Willi's funds had all but dried up. But, today his ship might have come in. If this fellow, who was by no means a German, had enough loose cash to throw on Willi's breakfast table like it was nothing, how much more might he have?

Trying to focus on the man and not the money, Willi allowed his hand-rolled cigarette to dangle as he softened his face. "Your German sounds strange, friend. Where are you from?"

"I'm not from Germany," the man answered. "I'm from Austria."

Willi chortled. "Well, either you lived on the top of a mountain and never spoke a word to a soul, or you've spent the last thirty-five years of your life in New fockin' York, 'cause I know an American accent when I hear one."

The guest nodded with closed eyes. "Yes, I've been away for a while." His eyes opened. "Now, can you get me safely to Innsbruck?"

Willi studied him through slit eyes. "You a bluebottle?"

"What?"

"Police? Polizei? Government man? Law enforcement?"

Neil shook his head. "I have no interest in you, at all."

"Are you?"

"No," the visitor with the odd accent answered. He tapped the money. "Five hundred pounds for flying me to Innsbruck, Austria."

Willi ran his hand through his thick mop of tangled hair, collecting a coarse film of grease and oil. He used the collection of human lubricants on the ends of his moustache, twirling them until they curled, glistening. "Double," he said loudly.

"Excuse me?"

"You heard me, *Kumpel*. I want double."

"If I agree to that...we leave today."

Willi's face opened into a wide, harrowing grin, exposing rounded, rotting teeth. He grabbed for the money before the visitor swiped it away.

"You get paid when we get there."

"Come on, I need a down payment," Willi protested.

"Not a coin before we fly."

"But I need to buy petrol for the flight."

"I'll pay for it at the airport."

"We won't be flying from an airport."

"Where do we fly from?"

"A private strip."

Relenting, the man asked, "How much?"

"Fifty quid'll do me for now. Then half before we fly. We'll have to refuel along the way."

"Where?"

"Wherever we happen to be when the engine starts sputtering," Willi answered dryly.

"How's that?"

"Relax," Willi said. "I've got secluded refueling spots scattered all over Germany." Cocked his eyebrow. "And, if you're interested, I've got *Muschi* spread all over Germany, too. For a small price, I can set you up with a nice lady friend to come to Innsbruck and look after you. She might even help you get by with that horrid accent, all while servicing you during the evening hours."

The man frowned at Willi's ribald suggestion. "Forget the women. When can we fly?"

Willi removed a tattered silver watch from his shirt pocket, glancing at it. "Can't go in the daylight. Need to wait till dark. Maybe midnight?"

"I can't wait that long."

Willi eyed the man. "Seem kinda skittish, you do. Got the heat on ya?"

"I'm paying *you* so how about *I* ask the damned questions?" The man rubbed his dark stubble and glanced around.

"Speaking of paying me…"

The man smacked fifty pounds into Willi's grubby hand.

Willi performed the same moustache-rubbing ritual as before. "If we fly during the day, we'll get shot down. Trust me. Both sides are on high alert. My bird's a night flyer."

The man nodded. "You know somewhere I can get a bite to eat without drawing any attention?"

"Pub right around the corner…Compton's," Willi replied. "Sit in the back. Tara there'll fix you up."

The man edged closer. "We're not waiting till midnight. We go at first dark, and no funny stuff."

"We're far north here, friend. Be at least eleven before it's dark." Willi's horrid smile reappeared. "Just settle yourself a bit, okay? As long as you're payin' me, I really don't care who you are…even if you're Jack the focking Ripper."

He hitched his thumb. "Pub around the corner?"

"Compton's. Get the corned beef hash—best in London, owner is some sorta meat expert. I'll be by just before sundown. We've a nice little drive ahead of us."

The man stared at Willi for a moment before picking his way back through the muddy garden.

After the man rounded the corner, Willi danced a silent jig in the small kitchen and removed another of his beers, biting the cap off and drinking with fervor. The man was American—Willi would wager the entire 500 pounds on it. Willi also again wondered how much money the man had on him if he was willing to pay five times the going rate for such a flight. Yes, Austria was farther than Willi had ever ferried anything or anyone; but he had flown in and out of Munich before. And Austria, depending on their destination, wouldn't be much farther.

This isn't a setup of some sort, is it?

Willi rubbed his chest, feeling the tightness that occurred when he considered what might happen if the Germans ever caught him. He thought about the man who had just visited him. He wasn't police. No, that ignorant *Arshloch* was some sort of profiteer, into something illegal. That's why he was slipping deep into the heart of the Reich like a cat burglar. And it was quite obvious that he wanted to keep his presence in England undetected.

Willi pulled open a kitchen drawer, sliding out a false back to display a poorly hidden rear compartment. He moved away several stacks of bills, each in different currencies, before removing his moldy-green Parabellum P-08 nine-millimeter pistol and a falling-apart box of green bullets. Letting him keep his service pistol had been one of the only concessions made by his captors upon his release. And since that time, Willi had only fired the pistol once, killing a massive cat that had been enjoying nightly feasts of his hens. But that had been years before and the Luger-designed product, given to him at the end of flight training, desperately needed to be taken apart and cleaned piece by piece. Willi chugged his beer, finishing it before retrieving a small, oily wooden box that held his cleaning utensils.

He sat at the kitchen table, cleaning the weapon, drinking a fresh beer, and pondering exactly how, and when, he was going to kill this fancy American and take all his money.

* * *

It was just past lunchtime in San Francisco. The manic weather of the past week continued as a blinding rainstorm had just given way to a mild and sunny afternoon. The extreme warmth was unusual for the bay area, the strong rays of the sun pulling visible vapor from the damp streets. Sal stepped from his unmarked car and inhaled the smell he associated with his childhood—rain on heated macadam. Smiling, he walked to the locked gate at Hillside and peered through the decorative iron bars.

Surely Agnes Gentry still lived here. Sal was almost to the intercom when he heard footsteps.

"Who the hell are you?" a rough voice asked.

Sal turned, watching as two men in suits approached from the street. The shorter of the two men had obviously endured at least one broken nose in his time. He had reddish hair and a boyish face that belied his age of probably mid-30s. The taller one, at least 10 years older than his friend, fancied himself as a ladies' man, based on the cut of his clothes and his swagger. Sal guessed they might be with some branch of law enforcement.

"You hear me, bub?" the shorter one asked, his accent distinctively Bostonian. The two men stopped several feet away from Sal.

"Sorry, guys," Sal said with a grin, automatically producing his badge, "but I don't usually make it a habit to explain myself to *dickheads* who I don't know. I'm here on police business and I'd advise you both state *your* business—or piss off, before you end up spending a night in *my* jail."

In a lightning move, the shorter of the two belted him in his stomach. Now Sal knew where the man had gotten the broken nose. He'd once been a boxer, and the body blow Sal had just taken had robbed him of his wind and almost certainly bruised his liver. Sal kept his feet, his hand moving to his holster.

The taller of the two men grasped Sal's arm, wrenching it behind his back and making him grunt in pain. As he did, the shorter one reached into Sal's jacket and came out with his pistol.

This was a bad situation. Very bad.

The tall man put his mouth to Sal's ear, speaking in a southern accent. "Dickheads, huh? How 'bout I pop your shoulder outta joint?"

Grinding his teeth, Sal tried to formulate a response. After a moment he simply wheezed, "Who are you?"

Crooked nose was in front of Sal, with Sal's pistol in his left hand. He used the pistol to kick his own hat backward, eyeing Sal with an open face. "Never mind who we are, Zorba. You got any idea where Reuter is?"

Sal finally had his breath. "Neil Reuter? I was hoping you might know. I'm with the Saturday Evening Post. Reuter's a month behind on his bill and I'm here to coll—"

Sal's words were cut off by another hydraulic blow to his gut.

Definitely a boxer...

He slumped forward, unable to get a breath. The tall one torqued Sal's arm again. "Where's Reuter, asshole?"

Sal shook his head, his mouth opening and closing for air. He heard the one with the broken nose tell the taller one to ease up. The man kept his grip on Sal's wrist and collar, but released the tension of the hold. After what seemed like a minute of trying, Sal was finally able to gasp glorious breaths of air. The shorter one waited a moment before asking the same question for a third time.

"And I'd suggest you answer without being fresh if you want to avoid more pain."

Sal offered a defeated nod but was unable to speak.

"Talk," the short one commanded.

When Sal recovered his wind for a second time, he gasped his words. "I don't know where Reuter is."

"Got any leads?"

"Hardly anything."

"Hardly means you've got something," the taller one said, giving Sal's wrist a squeeze.

"I do, but I'm still trying to run it down."

"Tell us," the short one demanded.

"But I haven't proved it out, yet."

"Boy, I'm warnin' you," the tall one growled, jerking Sal's arm up again.

"Ow! Okay, okay." Sal lifted his eyes to the short one. "We got word that two guys have been milling around Reuter's estate. They've been acting suspiciously, hiding back behind the bushes and..."

"And what?" the tall one asked.

"They've been seen sliding their hands down inside each other's trousers. Sick stuff."

"What?" the short one yelled, screwing up his face.

Sal brightened. "Yeah, and you know what? Come to think of it, they match your descriptions. Tall and ugly, and the other one's a crooked-nose midget."

"Hold him tight," the short one said. He pushed up his right sleeve and ripped the air with a vicious right hook, catching Sal in his cheek and making his knees go limp.

When Sal's head cleared, he was down on all fours. He lifted his head to see a dark Ford roaring away. Something black flew from the Ford's window, tumbling into the wet grass beside the driveway. After staggering to his feet, Sal retrieved the item, his pistol. His head slowly clearing, he walked—still quite unsteadily—to the unmarked car and sat inside. He lifted the radio, keyed it, opened his mouth—but said nothing.

As the shorter one had been punching Sal, he had seen the man's shoulder holster and .45 automatic. And down on the man's waist was what looked an awful lot like a leather pouch containing credentials and a badge.

If they were cops, they weren't FBI—that was for sure. The by-the-book feds didn't come hard and heavy like that. And they weren't staties, either. Sal would've known. He searched his mind for more agencies but couldn't come up with anything realistic. He decided to file away what had just happened in the "shame folder." Unfortunately for Sal, his shame folder was bursting at the seams.

They called me Zorba. How'd they know I'm Greek? I could pass for Italian, Armenian, lotsa backgrounds. They knew who I was beforehand. So, who the hell were they?

Sal eyed his swollen cheek in the rearview mirror. It was red and hot and was going to be a real beauty in a day or two. Using his thumb and index finger, Sal grasped his rear upper molar and wiggled it. There was movement, but not too much.

"Let's hope that tightens back up," Sal muttered, stepping from the car as he rubbed his cheek. He lifted his hat from the mouth of the driveway, brushing it off and donning it. Then he walked back to the gate and rang the bell on the two-way intercom. Thankfully, Agnes Gentry answered.

A moment later, the electric gate hummed open.

Chapter Eighteen

NEIL FOUGHT TO STAY AWAKE. He lit a cigarette and rolled down his window. It was just past 10 P.M. as Willi announced their arrival in the dark crossroads of Eynsford. They turned off the main road, making their way down a dirt trail between rows and rows of some sort of knee-high crop. The moon was partially obscured, occasionally illuminating Neil's arm resting on the door of the truck as he smoked in silence. A solitary triangle of light floated toward them on the right side of the vehicle. Willi's truck squeaked to a stop. Without a word, the German got out. Neil pushed open the door and stepped out, stretching and taking in his surroundings. The light was above the door of a large barn. There was little else to see.

Neil was sick of traveling and dreaded the long flight that lay before him. As Willi walked into the barn, Neil continued to stretch as he pondered all he'd endured on this day. The news about Lex Curran's murder was by far the most sapping, more so even than the cold morning swim. Combined together, the horrible news, the brutal swim in the frigid Atlantic, and then the police chase underground, all without the benefit of proper rest, had left him feeling like he'd been awake four days, and not just one.

He hefted his grip from the cluttered rear of the eighteen year-old Model TT truck, the exact same type that had been sold in droves back in the States. Resting the grip on the tailgate, Neil opened it and removed the olive-oiled Colt 1911 that had worked so well in the tube tunnel. He reloaded the weapon and chambered a round. Neil checked the dual safeties of the Colt before stuffing the heavy pistol into his waistband.

He could hear Willi calling him. Neil walked to the triangle light, watching as the pilot pushed open two colossal barn doors. Neil helped him secure the doors and then watched as Willi proudly swept his arms over the purplish silhouette of his private airplane, stored in the large working barn along with murmuring goats and pigs. It was a De Havilland Hornet Moth, Willi told Neil, using the tone an arrogant salesman might use if he were truly in love with his exclusive product.

"She's a state of the art bi-wing aircraft with side-by-side seating and enough room for your luggage, and then some," Willi pronounced majestically. As the German began to light lanterns, Neil could see the airplane had been brush-painted flat black, and was devoid of any markings which might denote it as British.

"Whose barn is this?" Neil asked.

"See the farmhouse over there?"

Neil turned, squinting through the darkness. "I guess."

"The barn and house belong to my partner," Willi answered. "Now, where's my money? I have to pay him for fuel and storage."

Neil stepped away and counted out half of the full price, minus the fifty he'd already paid, just as they'd agreed upon. Willi took the money and walked away with a kick in his step, headed to the farmhouse. While he waited, Neil studied the airplane and its external working parts.

Though he wasn't a pilot, it fascinated him how airplanes were such straightforward pieces of machinery. Each component had a particular purpose, and its failure would almost certainly result in catastrophe. The entire contraption was an artful concinnity of singular pieces, working together to effortlessly defeat a force so many had died trying to tame since the beginning of time.

In an automobile, if a tire blew, a person simply steered to the side of the road and changed it. Neil used his hand to move the elevator up and down. But if this part flew off, Neil and Willi would be done for. Though he was no pilot, Neil knew airplanes couldn't be flown without an elevator.

He opened the swing-out doors on the right side of the aircraft, loading his grip in the rear compartment. Since tonight was cool, Neil assumed it would be chilly at altitude. He unbuckled his new suitcase and removed his just-purchased waistcoat, folding it and wedging it under the seat. While he had a few moments alone, Neil pulled the Colt from his waistband, placing it under the seat, in the folds of the jacket. He looked to the farmhouse, narrowing his eyes.

Willi the German, with his simpering smile and smart-ass ways.

Do I trust him?

It took Neil less than five seconds to formulate a simple answer—no. However, allowing Willi some measure of credit, Neil rarely trusted anyone until a great amount of time had passed—especially a person who makes his living by breaking the law. But there was a palpable element of scheming about his new friend. Since his time in the Army, Neil had made a living by judging people and their motivations. There was something about Willi, an air of duplicity that Neil had picked up on from the first moment they'd met.

Or perhaps Neil, exhausted and on the run, was simply being paranoid.

Still, thinking through what was about to occur, Neil knew he was entering Willi's world. He'd been taught—preached to, in fact—that when stepping onto another's turf, you've allowed yourself to be more vulnerable. And not only was the airplane Willi's lair, now Neil was headed into the teeth of the tiger that was the growing threat of Nazi

Germany. And as soon as they crossed the channel to continental Europe, he would need to be permanently on guard.

Neil's eyes danced as he ran through a list of potential scenarios and outcomes. After several seconds, he jerked the Colt from the waistcoat, cocking the hammer before replacing it. The grip safety would keep the pistol from going off unwantedly, but at least now the weapon was ready for immediate use. Ten more minutes passed before Willi returned, grinning like the proverbial Cheshire cat.

"The hell took you so long?" Neil snapped.

Willi inspected Neil's baggage, cinching the strap over Neil's case. He turned to Neil, sensually rubbing the skin of the airplane. "Just like my baby here needs servicing every month or so, Frau Janzen needs an occasional servicing, too."

"Who?"

"Frau Janzen, the wife," Willi said, hitching his thumb to the farmhouse. "My partner who owns this barn is a Dane. I fly. He stores my baby, gets me the fuel, and shares in the profits of our little tax-free import-export business. Herr Janzen was an airplane mechanic during the war, so it's a good partnership." Willi's decimated teeth were tough to see in the scant light as his mouth widened again. "A very good partnership," he said, making a vulgar gesture with both hands, "especially when he's away while I'm here."

Neil snorted. "You and the wife?"

"Oh, yes, me and the wife. Viktor is off drinking tonight, probably won't even be home at all. He quit touching her years ago. I suspect I'm not the only one she takes, but when I am…" Willi shook his head and stacked both hands over his heart.

Neil curled his lip—*there's another reason not to trust this asshole.* "Can we just get on with it?"

"Impatient, are you?"

"Yeah, I am. And I'm about to get really pissed off."

"Say no more."

After Willi went through what Neil felt was a cursory amount of pre-flight checks, they pushed the surprisingly light aircraft from the barn. With Willi's guidance, he and Neil walked it across a grassy yard, over a gravel path, and onto a rough meadow of threshed grass. Once there, Neil could hear the cooing and clucking of sleeping hens in a nearby coop. Willi spun the tail of the aircraft ninety degrees to the left and then walked to each wingtip, peering down the outer edge of the wing. High above, the quarter moon was now fully visible. Willi adjusted the tail once more and then set out in a jog, straight ahead, blending into the inky night. It was another minute before Neil saw a flame and then could make out Willi's shape as he ran back to the aircraft.

Willi arrived breathless, quickly adjusting several controls from outside the airplane. He instructed Neil to sit in the left seat. "Hold your hand right here," he said, moving Neil's hand to a lever. "When the engine catches, push it slowly in. Not before." Willi flipped two switches upward and moved to the front of the airplane. He turned the prop slowly, several times, the sucking sounds of the pistons clearly audible. "You ready?" he asked.

"I guess."

Willi spun the prop. The engine coughed twice before going silent. He repeated this three times. The engine never caught. Cursing in German, most of which Neil understood, Willi leaned back inside and adjusted several controls. He told Neil to be ready. Again, he moved to the propeller, spun it, and this time the engine caught, belching acrid smoke that briefly filled the cockpit. Neil eased the throttle forward until the engine roared. Willi sprinted around the prop and wing strut, knocking Neil's hand away as he jerked the throttle back out.

"I didn't want you to take it all the way!" Willi yelled. "You're lucky she didn't jump chocks or flip forward." The engine idled roughly as Neil climbed out, allowing Willi to take the left seat. Neil sat in the right seat and pulled the door shut.

"Gotta hurry before the flame goes out," Willi said, pointing down the runway at the light he had created. Because the aircraft was a tail-dragger, Neil had to touch his head to the ceiling of the airplane to see the flame.

Willi throttled the aircraft to the hilt, holding the brake. Neil could feel the wind from the propeller try to lift the tail of the aircraft, but he could see Willi pulling the stick to him, preventing dangerous upward pressure from occurring at the elevator. Finally, satisfied with whatever he was watching on the gauges, Willi released the brake. The small aircraft lurched forward as Willi occasionally turned to gain reference to the light at the end of the bumpy grass strip.

Once the tail was up, Neil could see the flame growing closer, a simple but ingenious tool for night takeoffs that guided Willi, not only in the direction to keep the aircraft pointed, but also indicating to him the dead-end of the runway. Running off either side or passing the light at the end of the runway would almost certainly not produce a desired result.

The small airplane levitated after the rough run over the grass, the bumpiness giving way to the smooth cushion of air at ground-effect level. Neil watched as Willi worked several knobs and spun a wheel by his seat. Seemingly satisfied with the dimly lighted gauges and controls, Willi snapped his fingers and yelled for a cigarette. Neil removed two, handing him one and lighting both. As Neil smoked, he looked out the side window, seeing the occasional light flash by between long washes of darkness.

Willi had a map on his lap and a device in his hands. He said the device was brand new, an E-6B "whiz wheel," and it would compute everything he needed to navigate to Innsbruck. Once he'd made a few calculations, he twisted a dial on the floating compass on the top of the control panel. He leaned to Neil, yelling to be heard.

"Ten minutes to the channel, then about four or five hours until we refuel. I could possibly make it all the way to Innsbruck, but winds this time of year are unpredictable, and I don't think you want to be smashed into the German side of the Zugspitze!" Willi flashed his trademark busted smile.

"You're the pilot," Neil yelled in response.

The English Channel appeared right on time, an unending stretch of blackness, forcing Neil and Willi to trust in the Hornet Moth's instruments. Neil grew more comfortable in Willi's abilities, watching as he dutifully monitored his controls. After a second cigarette, Willi poured coffee from a small thermos. Neil declined, his eyes sleepy as he continued to watch his hired German.

He seemed like a capable pilot.

With the blackness enshrouding the aircraft, and the smooth vibration from the engine, Neil Reuter slipped into a deep sleep, never even extinguishing his freshly lit cigarette.

Willi did it for him.

CONTINENTAL EUROPE

Chapter Nineteen

NEIL REUTER JERKED FROM HIS SLUMBER as the Hornet Moth cruised at three thousand feet, the moonlight glinting off the numerous canals, making the earth look like the illuminated grid of a checkerboard. He glanced at Willi, still looking rock-solid with coffee in hand. "Where are we?" Neil yelled while rubbing the side of his face.

"Crossing over the arable fields of postcard Holland!" Willi yelled, toasting Neil with his coffee.

Neil nodded and closed his eyes, sleep coursing back through him immediately. The next time he awoke, he stirred before leaning his head against the cool window, staring out at the blackness.

"That's the Ardennes forest," Willi said. "You've heard of it?"

"No."

"It's huge. We're over the Belgium portion right now."

Neil fell back asleep. An hour later, he started from a dream.

"Now over Koblenz," Willi pronounced.

Neil had visited Koblenz once before. He peered out the right side window, seeing the spotlighted great fort at the confluence of the Rhine and the Moselle rivers.

"Beeindruckend, nicht wahr?" Willi asked.

"Yeah." Then, as if he were drugged, Neil fell asleep again. He dreamed of the Fausts, his contacts from the Queen Mary, picturing them eating a great feast while he was bound and whipped before them. He stared back in a type of self-induced masochistic fascination as Petra Faust eyed him with that neutral gaze of hers while he was savagely lashed. Through it all, Neil was somehow aware that it was just a dream. Later in the dream, as his whipping intensified, Neil watched as Petra sliced a hunk of extra rare roast beef. After a sip of her red wine, when Neil teetered on the verge of bleeding to death, her mouth turned upward and she licked her scarlet lips, beckoning him with the curl of a finger. Her painted fingernail left a trail of scarlet through the air like lipstick on a mirror.

"I need you," Petra said in a lusty voice. "We all do."

Then, Petra somehow transformed into Lana Stone, sitting nude before Neil. Her pose was far from ladylike. And, somehow, it all seemed reasonable. Lana blew a kiss to him, telling him to love her the same way he had in Santa Monica. Before he could act, Neil heard maniacal laughter and turned. Standing behind him, dressed like a Great War doughboy, was Lex Curran. He had a long trench knife raised high and ready to strike.

"Now it's your turn, Pale Horse," Curran said, cackling.

Neil awoke with a shudder, only to find Willi holding the stick with a single finger, smoking a cigarette in the faint yellow light of the cockpit. There was smugness all over his face. Willi pronounced their location as somewhere over the growing metropolis of Frankfurt.

"How long?"

"Maybe an hour before we refuel," Willi said with a wink. "Maybe less."

After shaking off his dream, Neil chatted about the airplane a bit before willing himself back to sleep. With so much ahead of him, he knew these intervals of sleep would come in handy later. By the time he was again snoozing, they were pressing southeast over the fruitful grapevines in the Franconia winemaking region near Würzburg. After a few more moments, Willi peered out of his side window, eventually turning in the direction of a moonlit landmark.

Neil felt the banking of the aircraft, opening his left eye only to see Willi focused upon his task. There was something about the rush of the wind and the vibration from the aircraft that lulled Neil, again and again, into a comfortable sleep.

Following another brief doze, Neil sat up, stretching as best he could. He lit a cigarette, pulling open the vent window to wake him up. He accepted a cup of coffee from Willi's thermos. It was lukewarm, but good and strong.

Judging by Willi's increased activity, Neil could tell they were preparing to land.

* * *

After spotting the distant lights of Nürnberg at his one o'clock, Willi veered twenty degrees to the left, throttling back just a hair. He kept it straight and steady, flipping a switch to eliminate every light source inside the cockpit as he descended to five hundred feet AGL, flying strictly by stick and rudder as his eyes scanned for the radio tower in Velden. After ten minutes of flying low, Willi sighted the tower—red light blinking on top—off to his left, chiding himself for being five kilometers too far to the south. A light wind was probably the reason and, at this speed in the blackness, he had no way of calculating its force as it crabbed the aircraft in a diagonal line.

Once he had the bead on the tower, Willi furtively removed the Parabellum pistol from his jacket pocket and tucked it under his left leg. He glanced over at the American. The man was staring out of the right side of the aircraft, seemingly still half asleep.

He won't be half asleep for long, Willi thought as a devilish grin ignited his face.

The former Luftwaffe pilot made a beeline for the radio tower, peeling right when he was about a kilometer away. He knew this runway very well, and the sequence of landmarks that needed to be lined up to find the proper heading was absolutely critical. Willi found the first mark out of his side window, which was the assemblage of straight tracks signifying the rail depot. He aligned the aircraft along the westward tracks, looking to his eleven o'clock for the grain tower. Once he found it, he used the rudder only to adjust heading, pushing down on the stick but maintaining his speed.

The runway was quite long, something that would work in Willi's favor. Since he had no idea exactly what the wind was doing, the landmarks necessitated that he land to the northeast—typically incorrect with the winds at this time of the year—but he had no choice. There were no landmarks to come in from the opposite direction at night, and no lights marking the runway. So, in the event he was landing downwind, he had to counter this with a fast landing, which would prevent an unwelcome stall.

Now Willi once again illuminated the control panel. Having accounted for the height above sea level of the refuel point, Willi descended through two hundred feet AGL, making out the lighter shade up ahead that represented the gravel and tar runway. Keeping the nose straight was requiring a slight amount of left rudder pressure. The good news was that Willi could now tell he was landing into a light headwind, a rarity in summertime at this heading.

He pulled the knob of the throttle, easing back as he grasped the lever for the flaps, lowering them to their first position while the Hornet Moth approached the end of the runway. Realizing he was a bit high, Willi slipped for a few seconds—a method for burning off altitude without adding a great deal of unwanted speed. Following the next setting of flaps and allowing the aircraft to decelerate, Willi forced the aircraft down a bit, making it touch down as he bounced upward half a meter before settling into a fast roll down the strip. It wasn't a pretty landing, but a good pilot knows how to fudge certain situations, and not being absolutely certain of the wind conditions, Willi was more than willing to be unconventional. In the end, he would have rated his landing as *sehr gut*, especially considering the circumstances.

But now there were more important things to consider, like how much money this American was carrying. Willi watched from the corner of his eyes as the man again tried to stretch in the cramped space. As the aircraft slowed to a crawl, he saw the man's hand go to the door lever.

"Stay close," Willi yelled over the rush of the wind and the engine.

"Where are we?"

"Not far from Nürnberg."

"Is anyone here at the airfield?"

"Only hares at this early hour. No one else."

Willi kept his eyes on the American as he exited the aircraft, stretching in the cool, predawn morning before urinating into the high grass at the edge of the runway. A piece of Willi wanted to simply throttle up and take off. He could be in Nürnberg in fifteen minutes, and could ransack the American's cases without fear of retribution.

But what of the American's valuables that might be on his person? Earlier, his money had come from his jacket, and while the American's heavy coat was underneath the seat, he might have moved the money to his wallet. Willi recalled seeing it earlier—a big, thick wallet.

And Willi *wanted* that wallet.

He allowed the engine to remain on idle. He had plenty of fuel to make the short hop to Nürnberg. And if he were to leave this American—or kill him—he didn't want to try to hand-prop the Hornet Moth by himself. After slipping out the open door, Willi, like his passenger, stretched before relieving himself. As he did, he mentally prepared himself for what he was about to do. They were standing well away from the noise of the Hornet Moth and the American was just tapping out a cigarette.

"Another for me?" Willi asked, wiping his hands on his trousers and offering up his tainted smile in the indigo moonlight.

The man tapped another out, cupping his hands around a match. Willi waited until the American was lighting his own to whip the Parabellum from behind his back. There were ten feet between the men, and Willi's directives were stern and simple as he spoke over the distant drone from the prop.

"Do not move," Willi demanded, flicking his cigarette to the tarmac.

The American lowered his own cigarette, his brow furrowing. "What in the hell are you doing?"

"Put your wallet on the ground. Then empty your pockets of all money, that fancy gold lighter I saw earlier, and anything else of value you might have. I want your watch, too. And I *will* be searching you, so don't try to be cute."

"Why are you doing this?" the man yelled.

"I believe in insurance," Willi retorted. "Once we're in Austria, I'll give it all back."

"My ass."

"I promise. But I don't trust you and this will guarantee me that you'll cooperate."

The American shook his head in disgust, finally motioning to the De Havilland. "Everything's in my jacket, in the airplane." He tossed his cigarette and began walking toward the aircraft, shaking his head.

Just as the American was mere feet from the Hornet Moth, an electric current of fear shot through Willi. He should be the one retrieving the American's possessions. And why would everything, watch included, be in the man's jacket? Something wasn't right.

"Stop!" Willi yelled. When the American heard the command, he lunged the last few feet to the passenger door of the airplane.

It was a confirmation to Willi—the American was making a move. Willi lifted the old pistol and popped off a round. Even over the idling engine, the singular cracking of the nine-millimeter round sounded like a thunderclap, booming in Willi's ears as an arrow of flame erupted from the barrel. The impact of the round threw the American up against the airplane. He leaned against it for a moment before turning, sliding down the strut of the landing gear to a sitting position.

"I told you to stop," Willi yelled in German, shaking his head as if he were admonishing a child. He stalked to the man.

The American's head was slumped forward as his left hand held his side.

"You better not move a damned—"

As Willi spoke, the American's right arm elevated, holding a handgun much larger than Willi's ancient Parabellum.

And, unfortunately for Willi, he had lowered his Parabellum after shooting the American.

Willi didn't have time to react.

The gun at the end of the American's right arm exploded into white and orange light, and the immediate sensation for Willi was that of being struck in the chest by a cannonball. The bullet impacted him squarely in his sternum, lifting him from his feet and propelling him straight backward before skidding to a stop at the edge of the runway.

Willi spent his last brief moment on earth speculating about this American. Who was this man, who could withstand a bullet to his back and still be able to grab and fire a pistol with pinpoint accuracy?

Willi's curiosity, as well as his life, ended seconds later.

Chapter Twenty

PRESTON LORD STARED INTO THE TUMBLER containing at least two ounces of single malt scotch. He swirled the drink, watching as its syrupy surface rippled, the product of years of coaxing to achieve just the right flavor. Using his middle finger and thumb, Lord lifted the tumbler to his lips, turning it upward. The warm liquid with the carefully cultivated taste bypassed his mouth altogether, rushing down his throat and into his stomach, joining the ten ounces he'd already ingested. He'd be drunk for many hours to come.

Lord's Georgetown apartment was well appointed for that of a bachelor. Pieces of furniture from various periods and countries mingled effectively to create an academic-meets-adventurer effect. While tastefully decorated, he'd not purchased or placed a single item on his own. The apartment's furnishings, right down to the books on the bookshelves, had been chosen by the oldest daughter of a Connecticut senator. A well-known Georgetown decorator—she'd gotten all her best clients *after* her father was elected—she'd also been married, of course. Lord's relationship with her began innocently enough, and she'd commanded a hefty fee for her interior design skills. Their affair began within days of his first payment to her, although the relationship had been sadly brief. For all her decorating skill, the woman had been simply lousy in the bedroom. This had been a surprise to Preston Lord, given the woman's history—he'd expected a tigress. She'd not reacted well when he'd broken it off. Without a word of explanation, he showed her evidence from three of her previous affairs, along with the address of her husband's firm.

"Shall I mail these photos to him, or tell him in person?"

The decorator slinked away quietly, never to be heard from again. That had been several years before. Dozens of women had since followed.

Tonight, he'd added another notch to his bedpost, even though his mind wasn't on sex—at the moment. He placed his hand on top of the brown expandable folder, using his fingernail to peel at the label that denoted a code and not a name. He'd been through the sealed file three times, reading and rereading the report about Neil Reuter's assassination request.

There was little news from San Francisco. Two of his men had encountered the detective from the Lex Curran case, but he was just sniffing around with nothing of substance. In Lord's mind, the focus was now on Europe.

Earlier, after hearing that Reuter had escaped the ship and dodged those fatuous fools in London, Lord internally pronounced his rogue employee as free and clear. They wouldn't find him again, at least not in England. And for the moment, until he caught his next break, Lord had more pressing needs.

Physiological needs.

His tryst in the morning had left him wanting more. Shirley the cocaine addict was quite a dish, but she was old news. He could have her anytime he wanted. He needed new meat.

So, today, just before six in the evening, he'd had the official car take him directly to Boudreaux's Bar, instructing the driver to park up on the curb, right in front. The evening was cool and comfortable after another passing storm, meaning old Boudreaux had pushed the pane windows open, leaving the youngish patrons to gawk at the important-looking Lord as he strutted inside while his driver waited.

Lord had been dropping hints to Cornelia, a junior secretary at Foggy Bottom, for weeks. And when he saw her face light up upon seeing him, he knew he had her. Lord paid for her drinks, whispered a nasty suggestion into her ear, and promptly escorted her outside.

Since that time, hours earlier, there had been little time to hunt for Neil Reuter.

Lord turned up one more slug of the scotch as the toilet flushed. He twisted his head to watch the voluptuous Cornelia exit the bathroom, the honey light illuminating the reddish delta below her navel.

"I really need to get going," she said. "My mom's probably worried sick."

Preston Lord stood. He, too, was nude. He glanced back at the Reuter file, pondering what he'd read. There was no point in Lord's running off to London right now. Reuter was too smart to use his own identification. If he *were* still in London, especially after being spotted, he'd have gone dark. But getting into Germany, even for someone as talented as Neil Reuter, wouldn't be easy. He'd trip up somewhere.

And that's where Lord would nab him.

What worried Lord most was someone else discovering Neil Reuter's real identity. Clues might exist, especially since Reuter had vacated his post in such haste. And preventing a startling discovery by some nosy investigator would be Lord's first order of business.

But before he sunk days, maybe even weeks, into such a manhunt, Lord aimed to empty himself of all lust and desire, lest it become a distraction on down the line.

He turned his head back to Cornelia, the secretary whose mother had moved to D.C. from lower Georgia just a few years before. Cornelia was young enough that she wore her few extra pounds well, tautly hidden on her Rubenesque frame. His eyes alternated between her large breasts and her face. He watched as her own eyes moved downward, her mouth gently opening as she watched his manhood levitate.

"Are you sure you want to leave just yet?" he asked.

She couldn't hide her flush as she responded in her southern accent. "You certainly have a lot of stamina. But my mama's probably waiting up."

"To hell with her. Stay the night," he commanded.

Cornelia didn't respond. He moved his hand to her body, manipulating with his fingers.

"Will you stay?"

Biting her bottom lip, she nodded.

An hour earlier, Lord had learned that Cornelia liked it rough. Until then, she hadn't known it, either. Now he grasped her wrists, twisting them behind her. She grunted.

"What do you want?" he asked.

"You," she gasped.

"No. Tell me what you really want."

"Treat me like a whore."

He threw her on the couch. She rolled over, eager for him.

As Lord tongued the dark corners of Cornelia's body, his active hands alternating between soft pets and rough pinches, his mind went—for the last time on this evening—to Neil Reuter. He was probably asleep in some outer-London boarding house, waiting until the heat died down before he made his next move. It was likely that he would have to arrange for a forger to create his identification, and that could take upwards of a week. Lord would decide, tomorrow, whether to start right here in D.C, or go to California. Europe would probably be Lord's eventual destination, just not yet.

But more pressing to Lord was getting his nickel's worth out of this naughty siren that lay beneath him, writhing under his ministrations like a purring Siamese cat. He moved upward, straddling her. From the coffee table, Lord took the chunky candle he had lit a half-hour before, holding it above her breasts.

The candle was full of hot wax.

Though Cornelia's screams were piercing, they were tinged with pleasure.

* * *

Willi's body skidded to a stop at the edge of the runway, knocked there by the enormous power of the .45 ACP bullet. With Willi no longer a threat, Neil's mind lurched to witnesses. Had anyone heard anything? One gunshot could be written off as a car backfire. Two shots, especially in such close succession, would most likely get the attention of a nearby person blessed with any measure of street smarts and awareness. Willi had said no one was here at this time of night. Hopefully he'd been correct.

Neil struggled to stand, using the wing's strut to pull himself up as the sharp pains cut through his ribs like rusty blades. He reached across his body, probing as far as he could reach with his left hand, feeling the oily slickness of his own blood until he found the small entry hole. He moved his hand back toward the front of his body, feeling around under his arm until he found the exit wound. It was much larger than the entry wound, punctuated by shards of rib protruding outward. Despite his pain, Neil rummaged around in the airplane before unstrapping his suitcase and retrieving a brand new undershirt. Leaving the suitcase in the airplane, Neil balled the undershirt tightly, using his right arm to press downward on the wound.

Feeling somewhat lightheaded, Neil scanned the nearby area and saw nothing other than a simple hangar several hundred feet away. There were no cars, no houses, no lights. Even if no one had heard the gunshots, Neil didn't like his chances of walking away. Sooner or later, someone would discover the body of Willi the German. Once they did, finding Neil—especially since he was weakened by his injury—would be a cinch.

Neil stared at the De Havilland Hornet Moth for a few seconds. Then, in a move motivated more from desperation than brass balls, he lifted himself to the lower wing before situating himself in the left seat.

* * *

Moments earlier, a man stirred nearby.

South of the airstrip was a rolling field, marked by scattered hay rolls and bounded by a gently murmuring brook. Beyond the stream sat a cottage, built solidly from brook stone and ancient wood. In the sunlight, it appeared neat and orderly, like something from a Bavarian postcard. At five in the morning, it looked especially cozy and inviting. A stranger standing outside in the moonlight would see wisps of smoke emanating from the chimney. They might even catch a whiff of the strong coffee being brewed and the sugared ham searing in the iron skillet. The home's owner, Thomas Lundren, was fervent when it came to tidiness as well as timeliness.

After lowering the heat of the wood stove under the thick slice of ham, Thomas sprinkled the ham's topside with a dash of salt. He glanced at his watch before tucking it back into his wool shirt, then walked outside, across the well-kept yard to the small barn. There he retrieved the morning's quantity of hay and oats before pumping the trough full of clean, cold well water. Finished, he glanced at his watch again, greeted his horse and two goats with vigorous petting, and hurried back through the yard to turn the ham. Arriving inside just in time, he used a fork to turn the heavy slice, closing off the stove's heat passage and marking the time once again.

There was a bark of screeching tires from across the field. Thomas looked up.

From experience, he knew an airplane had just landed. Thomas poured a cup of coffee—strong and black—sipping it as the ham sizzled and occasionally popped in the still hot iron skillet. After another minute, he removed the ham, poured off the excess grease, and placed two pieces of split bread into the skillet, warming them and allowing them to soak up the remaining flavor. Satisfied, Thomas sat at the small table with his breakfast, murmured his Lutheran prayer, and began to eat with gusto. That's when he heard the second distinctive sound, a pop.

Thomas frowned. He raised his head and peered out the window in the direction of the *Flughafen*. Used primarily by recreational pilots, the local Luftwaffe reserve unit occasionally utilized the airport for exercises. At nearly seventy years old, Thomas' senses were still keen. Prepared to write the sound off as a backfire, he began to chew his ham again.

And that's when he heard the second sound, another pop, but this one throatier.

Thomas Lundren knew a gunshot when he heard one.

Or two.

Hunters? It's possible, but doubtful. Thomas knew every hunter nearby and none of them would dare hunt grouse near the airfield. When there were so many good fields down by the flats of the Auerbach Stream, what would be the point of hunting up by the airfield?

Someone could have shot at a deer, but a person rarely gets two shots, Thomas reasoned.

And Thomas heard two distinct sounds. Meaning, two firearms, neither of which sounded like a rifle.

He swallowed his piece of ham and unconsciously sipped his coffee. With a small nod, he stood and retrieved his Gewehr 88, an old, accurate rifle created through an amalgam of concepts and parts from the Mauser and Mannlicher corporations for the German Army back in 1888. After donning his field jacket, Thomas checked the right pocket to make sure his bullets were there; they were—7.92 millimeter, cold and hard, clinking together as he touched them. He pulled on his cap and stepped outside, listening, his eyes staring in the direction of the *Flughafen* as he buttoned the toasty field jacket.

The air was thick with the distant droning of an engine. Other than the occasional chirp of crickets, the only other sound he could hear was the occasional dinging of the bell that hung outside the barn.

Thomas was a thirty-year veteran of the Middle Franconia Polizei. After his military service ended in 1894, he joined the police force, eventually rising to the highest position in the district. Now retired and a widower, he lived a simple and modest life on his small pension, taking great pleasure in caring for his animals and flowers, tending to them like the children he and his wife never had. Once a week, as was his habit, Thomas went into the city to run errands and to see his old friends, most of them retired police. Every Thursday they met for coffee. Thomas was the quietest of the group, listening far more than he spoke. He would typically leave the gathering and walk to the theater for the matinee, sitting alone to watch whatever feature might be showing. Then, after the movie, he would visit the market, purchasing his needed items before returning to his small house, repeating the process week in and week out.

This was his routine. Thomas prayed he could maintain it until his death. And he knew his death wasn't all that far away.

A moderate man, Thomas detested Adolf Hitler and his fanatical regime. But to say so aloud could make an old man disappear, and Thomas was wise enough to stick to his routine, and to keep such opinions to himself. He knew that the entire Nazi reign would end badly. A man needn't live seventy years, Thomas thought, to know a fanatic when he saw one.

Regardless, Thomas was certain the goodness of man would somehow prevail—though he probably wouldn't live to see Germany return to democracy.

After his forced retirement, Thomas and his wife Greta had moved here, settling in for what they thought would be a quiet final chapter of their lives. Unfortunately, Greta passed away after a short illness when they'd only been here for a year. Since then, Thomas had been alone.

Very alone.

Thomas was not a party member, thereby putting him at odds with the current leadership. Despite pressure, Thomas had never acquiesced to the party. Had he done so, he'd have been able to work again, despite his advanced age. But, no matter how lonely or miserable he was, Thomas couldn't set aside his morals. Rather, he kept his mouth shut and never spoke a cross word to anyone about the Nazis.

A wise strategy.

But deep in his heart, more than politico or retiree or moralist, Thomas was still a policeman. He would always be a policeman. And when he heard the two pops and the idling engine this early in the new dawn, his sixth sense knew that something unpleasant had occurred across his brook and over the *Landkreise*-owned meadow.

After chambering one of the bullets into the bolt-action rifle, Thomas set out in a determined walk across the stones of the brook, and then across the rolling field. His pace was deliberate and he showed no fear. The lawman sense inside of the man calmed him.

It excited him, too.

Chapter Twenty-One

THE PAIN IN NEIL'S SIDE was unlike anything he had ever before experienced. It felt as if he were squeezing a fiery orange lump of coal into his tender flesh—every small movement was disrupted by lightning bolts of electric agony. Taking enormous breaths, he remembered Willi's actions back in England. The stick had to be pulled back when revving the aircraft, so the tail wouldn't rise due to the propeller's slipstream. After noting that, Neil moved both feet back and forth on the rudder pedals, clearly understanding what they were for. His actions during the Great War had occasionally taken him up in airplanes, and even though the pilot sat behind him then, with no means of communication, Neil had always studied in fascination the movement of the stick and rudder as the pilot danced his tango with the swirling atmosphere.

Knowing he would bleed to death if he didn't act quickly, Neil chose not to waste time. A quick glance at the fuel gauge told him the tank was below its last quarter. That was okay. He didn't need to go too far, just far enough to gain adequate separation from the dead thief lying mere feet from this aircraft.

Upon landing, Willi had spun the aircraft back in the proper direction, so all Neil needed to do, or so he thought, was to accelerate and take off. He grasped the throttle, pushing it in before widening his eyes due to the great roar from the engine. Riding as a passenger and piloting an airplane are two very different sensations, even though one sees and hears all the same things. The rush from the prop seems louder, every vibration more obvious.

A bullet hole in one's side adds even more manic anxiety to an already tense situation.

As the aircraft gained speed, Neil pushed the stick to the right as the airplane tried to veer left. This, while natural to someone who drives an automobile, was incorrect, though he didn't yet know it. His actions caused the wing to dip and, as the torque and other forces created by the Gipsy-1 engine overwhelmed the small aircraft, the wing scraped the rough pavement.

The De Havilland spun a full circle, executing an ugly ground loop.

And the inertia of the spin, along with the jarring of the aircraft, made Neil yell out in pain.

When the energy of the amateurish maneuver was gone, the De Havilland was facing twenty degrees from where Neil had started. The right wheel was off the runway and, after sputtering several times, the engine resumed its idle.

Mercifully.

* * *

After he had passed over the brook and five hundred meters of field, Thomas heard the engine revving. The clear sound allowed him to focus his keen eyes on the horizon and, when he did, aided by the cold light of the partial moon, he could see the outline of an airplane beginning to move. Thomas stood there, coughing like he had recently begun to do when winded, and watched as the aircraft began to accelerate. After fifty meters, he could see something was wrong as the aircraft turned sharply, one of its wings dipping and the unlit lights on the wingtip sending a hail of sparks into the night's blackness. The airplane spun like a top, shuddering to a stop with the engine still running.

Thomas stopped coughing and shook his head in bewilderment before quickening his pace.

* * *

After the wave of pain-induced nausea passed over him, Neil thought about the physics of what had just occurred. The airplane had felt like an unbroken colt under his unqualified control. When he had applied power, the airplane naturally wanted to pull to the left. Neil thought perhaps it had something to do with the rotation of the propeller. But as he peered out the window in the scant light, he could see what he already knew; the stick controlled the rectangular devices on the trailing edge of the wings. But those devices needed wind and lift to work. The only significant wind on this night was provided by the propeller, and the propeller's wind was rushing down the fuselage. Working it out in his mind, Neil looked into the blackness where his feet were, moving the pedals to and fro. He allowed himself a pained smile.

Let's do it again.

* * *

Thomas arrived at the runway and scrutinized the aircraft, still idling a hundred meters away. It was sitting askew, headed diagonally in relation to the runway, and the right side of the aircraft was slightly lower since the right wheel was in the grass. The retired policeman's eyes turned to the shed at the end of the runway: no lights, no movement. And just as he was turning back to the airplane, which was getting louder as the engine once again revved higher, Thomas noticed the dim outline of something on the edge of the runway. It appeared to be...

A body!

Mein Gott!

He hurried in that direction, confirming the shape was indeed a person—a man, lying in an odd position with one hand twisted unnaturally under his back. Thomas squinted to see a pool of shiny liquid coming from underneath the body. When he stepped closer, he sensed that there was nothing that could be done for this man. Thomas held his hand over the man's chest, just beside the wound, feeling nothing. He repeated this at the area of the carotid pulse. There was no heartbeat.

Murder!

Thomas stood and spun around, lifting the old rifle to the ready. He hurried up the left side of the runway, the hard walnut stock cinched into his shoulder. Keeping his keen eyes on the cabin of the small airplane, he watched as the aircraft rocked back and forth as the pilot tried to coax the right tire over the lip of the runway.

Just as Thomas reached an angle where he could make out the faint image of the pilot, the airplane lurched onto the runway as the two men joined eyes. Thomas could see the pilot's face, ashen with panic. He noticed the man's dark hair, parted on one side, and could tell by the hunched way he was sitting that the man was tall.

But more than fear, the old lawman saw something else in those two seconds—he saw pain. Real pain.

There were two gunshots.

Perhaps the pilot, too, had been shot.

As the aircraft skittered across the runway, fishtailing right and left, Thomas knelt on one knee and aimed the old Gewehr 88 squarely at the back of the tail, at the center mass of the airplane. He took a deep breath, coughing once before holding his breath as he steadied his aim...

* * *

Seconds earlier, Neil pushed the throttle all the way to the stop. He knew that once the aircraft moved he would need to use the pedals, and not the stick, to turn right and straighten his direction on the runway. Then, unlike last time, he would have to fight the pulling of the aircraft, and would have to be gentle as he did so.

"Instinct!" his mind screamed. "Don't over-think!"

Neil remembered what Willi had told him back in England. "Airplanes want to fly. All they need is enough speed."

Just as the airplane lurched over the edge of the runway, movement to his left caught Neil's eye. As he straightened the aircraft, an older man appeared, his features only somewhat visible in the moonlight. He had a hawk's eyes and, despite his obvious age, stood tall and erect like a noble and capable man.

Neil was certain the man had heard the shots and seen Willi's body. But more concerning to Neil was the long rifle the man held at the ready.

As the aircraft approached the other side of the runway, Neil pulled the throttle and applied right rudder to straighten. After swerving several times, he got the feel for the pull of the aircraft and kept it as straight as he could while it wanted to turn left. Again he depressed the throttle all the way, accelerating. Surprising him, when the tail popped up, the airplane suddenly tried to turn right, making the craft teeter several times until Neil tediously applied the proper inputs with his feet. Once again, he was headed somewhat straight and, since the tail was up, he could finally see the remaining length of the runway.

His right tire drifted to the edge again, but now he could see where he needed to be, and with the growing speed, less input was needed to point the aircraft in the proper direction.

With the moon in the top of the windshield, Neil felt the slight lift as the airplane began to ride the cushion of air rushing over and under the wings, and that's when he heard a crack and saw glass fly in the cockpit. A gauge, squarely in the center of the control panel, and just to Neil's right, had shattered. The shattering glass made a small cut on the top of Neil's right hand. He ignored it, focusing instead on keeping the moon in the exact same place as he saw the threshold of the trees flash by underneath him.

When the aircraft was several hundred feet in the air, Neil looked backward to his suitcase and the back of the aircraft, seeing nothing out of the ordinary. He gently moved the pedals back and forth, doing the same with the stick. Everything seemed to be working properly and he was beginning to get a feel for the aircraft. There was a lever beside his seat that controlled the flaps. Willi had explained their purpose in England. Neil lifted the lever, releasing the trigger underneath as he lowered the lever to the floor. The airplane lost lift, making Neil feel like it would careen to the ground. But he watched the airspeed indicator, seeing it increase. The flaps had been holding him back. He eased back on the throttle slightly as the De Havilland began to ascend rapidly, light on fuel and human cargo.

Neil rotated his eyes to the shattered gauge, unable to discern what it had been used for. The old man's bullet had missed Neil by a foot. That thought faded quickly as Neil's adrenaline plummeted, probably due to the throbbing pain in his side. The place Willi's bullet had entered, on the right middle of his back, hurt, but nothing like the exit wound at his ribs.

Neil felt like vomiting. He slid the small window aperture open to ventilate the cockpit with the cool morning air.

He knew by the floating compass that he was heading west, somewhere north of Austria. Gently, Neil turned the stick left until the waning moon was on the right side of his aircraft. He located the altitude gauge, not knowing if it was set for ground level—which had to be higher here—or what would have been almost sea level back in London. No matter. He spun the tick mark to set his current altitude, and throttled back until it began to dip. Then he throttled up, repeating the process until he found a sufficient power setting that would hold this altitude. This was an incorrect way to trim the aircraft. Neil didn't know that, but it actually worked, albeit in a crude fashion.

After lighting perhaps the best cigarette he had ever tasted, he grunted as he settled into his seat, glancing left at the faint strip of orange on the horizon. It would be daybreak soon. By that time, Neil needed to have a great deal of distance between himself and Willi's body. The old man who saw what had happened could be a problem, and would know the killer escaped in a black airplane—one with a bullet hole running straight through it.

But the authorities would have no clue of which direction Neil went. Perhaps they would put out a description of the airplane, but that would be about it. If they learned who Willi was, it was unlikely they would travel to England to try to determine who he was associated with.

The growing light displayed the ground moving steadily underneath him. Mile after mile passed, each one a small victory for Neil. He was far enough up to see the outlines of the farms, and could see the occasional road pass by underneath. As he finished his cigarette and allowed the nub to be whisked from his hand in the small vent window, Neil finally confronted his main problem, larger than the holes in his side or the man who had just seen and shot at him.

Neil's greatest concern was where—and more importantly, *how*—he was going to land this airplane.

Chapter Twenty-Two

THOMAS FIRED ONLY THE SINGLE SHOT AT THE AIRPLANE. He stayed in the same shooting position long enough to see the airplane gently bank and turn to the south, the rounded rudder gliding like the dorsal fin of a shark through the starry sky. After watching the airplane until it was no longer visible, Thomas stood, ejecting the warm shell and dropping it into his left pocket.

He walked to the dead man, peering over him before kneeling down. His body was still quite warm, emanating wisps of vapor in the chill morning air. Ambient light from the approaching sunrise aided Thomas' vision as he examined the fresh corpse. Grasping the man's pants, Thomas rolled him far enough to expose the hand trapped underneath him, and that's when he saw the Parabellum. It appeared to be old and military—a gun Thomas was most familiar with and perhaps the most common handgun in all of Germany. Feeling as if he had gone back in time twenty years, Thomas searched the man by starting with his pockets. He found no identification, but he did find a wad of odd-looking currency. Later, when he was back at his house, Thomas would learn the currency was British.

And that's when Thomas would become keenly interested. He liked to be keenly interested.

But before then, Thomas checked the man's other pockets, finding cigarettes, a lighter, some keys and several coins. He didn't, however, find any identification. Thomas kept one note of the currency and one of the coins, tucking them into his jacket pocket with his bullet casing. Finished, he patted the dead man on his shoulder, murmuring a few words about justice, and stood.

Thomas searched the area, finding the dew-soaked remainder of a freshly smoked cigarette in the grass just off the tarmac. He soon found another, probably blown to the grass by the wind of the prop. The sun still wasn't visible on the horizon, but the eastern sky was now morning purple, allowing him to walk back to his house without fear of stepping into an abandoned well. When he arrived, he dumped out his mug of coffee and poured another cup, closing the opening on the stove so the burning wood's heat would only escape from the front. Thomas sat at the table, pushing his cold breakfast away. After a scorching sip of the strong black liquid, he examined the paper money and the coin, immediately realizing it was British. Thomas spoke passable English, certainly enough to recognize the twenty-pound note.

"English money and a German military pistol," he said aloud, rubbing his freshly shaven face. He stared at the money for a number of minutes, his fingers drumming a tattoo on the table. Thomas Lundren was deep in thought.

His mind made up, he stood and crossed the kitchen into the small den, retrieving a large book from a shelf. From the book he took an old map, tan from age but folded perfectly. He smoothed it on the tabletop. After another sip of his coffee, Thomas retrieved a pencil and a long piece of string from a drawer in the kitchen. He leaned over the map, using his thumb to hold the string over Velden—his location. Pulling the string due south, all the way to the southern border of Germany, Thomas drew a heavy lead line, terminating at the resort town of Bad Tölz. He then drew a lighter line to the left of Bad Tölz, near Weilheim, and one to the right, at Rosenheim. This created a triangle to his south: the alleged murderer's possible flight path. The largest cities on the alleged murderer's route were Regensburg and Munich.

Those cities were where he would begin, if his plan panned out.

Thomas took a red apple from the bowl on the table, slicing pieces with the clean blade of his pocketknife as he worked out his plan. Upon finishing the apple, he brushed his teeth, washed his face and combed his hair. After placing the British money in his pants pocket, he locked the house and drove to his former home city of Nürnberg.

There was someone there he needed to see.

* * *

Thirty minutes later, Thomas Lundren parked the old Opel Blitz in front of the Middle Franconia Main Polizei Bureau. Nervous, he tugged his hat onto his head before wiping his face with his handkerchief. He stepped from the truck and glanced around, briefly recalling the decades he spent in this very bureau. The horse carriages were now replaced by loud, intrusive automobiles. On the outside of the building, the gas lamps had been traded for electric lights, probably operated from the convenience of a single switch. Power and phone lines ran to the building, snaking in from all directions to create an unsightly tangle. From an open window upstairs, he could hear music, courtesy of one of those radios everyone now seemed to own and worship. The world's modernization had all happened so fast.

But to Thomas, no matter what sort of advancements came along, the operating principles were still all the same. Hard work could never be replaced by technology. Ever. No machine would ever replace intuitiveness and elbow grease. There would never be a device that could listen to a defendant, analyzing the person's testimony for the slightest signs of guilt. No scientist would ever come up with an invention that would comfort a victim on a cold and rainy night. There would never be a device to track a suspect wherever he or she went. Police work was hard work. Human work. Thomas' work.

Or at least it had been, until he was made to leave.

He crossed the parking lot, noting that the chief was there. His car was adorned with insignia and Nazi flags. Thomas took the stone stairs at an even pace, keeping his head low until he approached the high desk in the lobby. Behind the desk was a large portrait of Adolf Hitler, right where the state crest once was. Doing his best to suppress his grimace, Thomas eyed the desk officer, a man he didn't know.

"Heil Hitler, how may I help you?" the officer asked.

"Yes, heil," Thomas said with zero enthusiasm. "I'd like to see Chief Gerhard Michener. I realize it's quite early but I did see his car outside."

The sergeant placed his pen on the desk, offering an unapologetic smile. "Yes, he is. Comes in no later than six. But you'll need an appointment to see him, and his rank is now *Generalmajor*."

Thomas didn't blink. "Please tell the Generalmajor that Thomas Lundren is here."

The desk sergeant frowned, but before he could respond a senior sergeant stopped behind him, his arms loaded with papers. "Well I'll be damned if it isn't the old chief!"

The younger sergeant watched as the senior man put down the papers and hurried from behind the desk, taking Thomas' hand and pumping it up and down. "Thomas Lundren, when you retire, you damned well retire! We thought you might be dead."

Despite his anxiety, Thomas forced a polite smile. "Henry, good to see you. You look well. How is your family?"

"They're just fine. Years ago I'd heard you came to the city on occasion, but it's been so long since I asked anyone and...well...I hate to say...I'd kind of given up."

"I would, too," Thomas said softly.

"What are you doing here?"

The younger sergeant motioned to Thomas. "He's here trying to see Generalmajor Michener."

"Then send him up! The chief will be thrilled."

"No, Henry, thank you, but this is not a social visit," Thomas said. "I want him to be notified that I am here. If he agrees to see me, we will meet formally. I have a serious request."

The older sergeant's face creased. "Is everything okay?"

"No, it's not. Will you please call him?"

The older sergeant turned to the junior man. "Ring him up." Frowning, the older sergeant retrieved his stack of papers, nodding at Thomas. "Good to see you, chief. Highlight of my day. I mean that."

"Thank you, Henry, and you take care," Thomas said as the friendly officer disappeared through a door. The younger sergeant made the call, waited a moment, and then murmured into the phone, nodding his head as he listened. He placed the earpiece into the holder and motioned to the door. "He wants you to come on up. I presume you know the way?"

Thomas nodded his thanks and went through the door he'd been through thousands of times. As he ascended the two levels of worn stairs, their centers curved downward from decades of friction, Thomas smelled the familiar odors of ink and old registry books; of bad cologne and sweat; of shoe leather and reams of paper; of cigarette smoke and saddle soap; taking him back so many years to when this had been his kingdom. When he'd had a purpose.

Back when he had mattered.

From the day Thomas retired, when they presented him his very first Modell 1883 pistol with his name engraved down the barrel, he had walked out the door and never looked back. He'd had to. When a man is forced out, it's best to go along with the wishes of his superiors and respect their decision, even when politics are the catalyst. He had approached his retirement the way he approached everything in his life, with a kind of steadfast certainty only few men could muster.

It would have been far easier with Greta by his side.

But when he had heard those pops this morning, when he had seen the body, when he had joined eyes with that man in the airplane, fate had intervened. This mystery was brought to Thomas and laid on his doorstep. All of his retirement serenity disappeared like a fabric stage backdrop attached to a heavy weight, replaced by one final act of ambition in Thomas Lundren's dwindling life. This was a case only Thomas *could* work. Only Thomas *would* work. Even if it killed him.

He reached the outer office and immediately noticed that Michener had yet another beautiful young secretary. From the day Thomas had hired him, Michener had always loved the *Fräuleins*. With bottle blonde hair and her business skirt a few centimeters too short for social grace, she stood and offered the Nazi salute and greeting before she personally welcomed Thomas warmly.

"Won't you please have a seat?" she cooed.

Thomas watched her as she busied herself. She filed her nails and simultaneously paged through a clothing catalog while sipping a cola through her straw. Thomas noted the rings of strawberry lipstick around the waxy paper.

The secretary looked up to see him watching her. "This is my morning break," she said with an anxious laugh. She adjusted the miniature National Socialist—Nazi—flags on her desk before again flipping the page to what looked like brassieres.

Thomas turned his attention to the floor as he collected his thoughts.

Several minutes later, he heard his old office door click and open. He looked up. And there *he* stood. Generalmajor Gerhard Michener was a big man with a barrel chest and a florid face. His salt and pepper hair was severely parted down the middle and pressed down tightly. He wore a dark, elegantly cut pinstripe suit and a brilliant red tie, confirming for Thomas the rumors that Michener was planning to run for public office soon, National Socialist Party of course. True to his forced, over-the-top nature, Michener's face beamed as he flashed a hundred-watt grin and fired his right arm up.

"Heil Hitler!"

Thomas stood. "Sieg Heil," he muttered.

Michener then ushered Thomas into his office with a magnanimous, overdone greeting.

"No calls, please," Michener said to the secretary, winking once Thomas was past. The secretary blew him a kiss before going back to her catalog.

Thomas stood before the great desk, his worn trilby hat in his hand as he waited to be asked to sit.

"Please, Thomas, over here," Michener said, motioning Thomas to the sitting area by the window. The entire office had been thoroughly redecorated. Michener had gotten rid of the bookshelves that contained Thomas' case files, replaced by oil paintings and certificates of merit. The sitting area had once contained a coffee-stained worktable. It hadn't been unusual for Thomas to order a weapon be disassembled right there, so the signature of the barrel rifling could be studied in the good light of the south-facing window. Now there were oriental rugs, leather chairs, wood paneling: it felt more like the office of a head of a large corporation. Before he even sat, Thomas counted seven Nazi flags, displayed at every conceivable spot. Behind Michener's desk, between the two windows, was an even larger painting of *der Führer* than the one downstairs.

My, my, my…

Thomas sat, placing his hat in his lap and both hands on his knees.

"Gerhard, I want you to know this is a formal visit."

The brilliant smile dimmed slightly, along with Michener's tone. "Yes, that's what I was told. But before all that, how have you been, old friend?"

Thomas eyed Michener. "As you can see, I'm impotent against the hands of time, leaving me aged but otherwise just fine. Thank you for asking."

"How many years since Greta passed?"

"Too many."

"My sympathies."

Thomas nodded.

"Have you joined the party?" Michener asked, arching his eyebrows.

"No, and if you'll excuse me, I'd rather not discuss politics. Now, about this visit..." He watched as Michener shifted uncomfortably. Rather than draw it out, Thomas said it quickly.

"I am the *only* pseudo-witness to a murder, one which may or may not have been discovered by now. And I want you to use your authority and to instate me as sole and lead investigator for the case. I want it all to myself, and I want complete—and *absolute*—authority to do as I please." Thomas maintained eye contact, his green eyes locked with Michener's twin browns.

Tiny rivulets of sweat emerged on Michener's tanned forehead, trickling slowly downward. His mouth opened and closed several times before he finally stood. With his matching red pocket square, he mopped the sweat away before stepping to Thomas and gently touching his shoulder. "Thomas, are you feeling well?"

"Aside from ailments common to people of my advanced age, I feel perfectly fine," Thomas stated flatly, staring straight ahead.

Michener moved in front of Thomas. "Well, since I know Greta's death was a terrific blow, and hearing such a request from you in this...this unorthodox manner..."

Thomas coughed several times into his handkerchief. He stuffed it into his shirt pocket, clearing his throat. "Gerhard, I'm asking for a significant favor. I know this. And I'm not intentionally trying to put you in a bad position." Thomas paused, crafting his next phrase. "But without me being forced to say more about *why* you should grant it, know this: your best option is to give me approval to do this. It won't affect you, your lofty position, or your political desires."

Michener's head twitched as his eyes narrowed. Thomas knew that Michener was enough of a political animal to recognize the emergence of a power play, and a veiled threat. He also knew that Michener probably thought Thomas had no cards to play. But, in reality, Michener had no idea at the royal flush that rested against Thomas' sternum.

Rested like a coiled viper.

If Thomas hadn't been an expert poker player, many years ago, he might have tipped his hand with a knowing smile. He chose not to—he knew it would play out with the most impact as a total surprise. But Michener should have known that Thomas wasn't stupid enough to walk into the *Generalmajor's* office—the same man who pushed him out—and levy a threat without sufficient backup.

Michener pinched his bottom lip between his two fingers as he again sat. He shook his head. "Before we get to this supposed murder, I'd like to address my appointing you. That would be...well, in a word, impossible."

Thomas shut his eyes and shook his head only once. "No, sir. If you were to study the powers granted you by the Polizei Act of 1872—an act that still stands, despite the National Socialist Party—you would find that all pensioned retirees, in good standing—and I do fit the bill, despite being forced out—are designated, for *life*, as inactive reserve. Meaning, I can be fully reinstated through the simple use of an article-twelve and—as you and I both know for this district—the signing authority for an article-twelve is the high captain...or, *Generalmajor*, as you're now titled." Thomas lifted a bony finger, stabbing it at Michener. "And that, Gerhard, is you."

Michener offered a wan smile as he tapped a cigarette from an engraved silver case. He slipped one between his lips, lighting it and inhaling deeply. As he exhaled, he spoke. "I know the provisions, Thomas. But thank you for the lesson. May I be perfectly frank?" Thomas didn't move. After several seconds, Michener continued. "The simple fact is that you were pushed out by the *Ministerpräsident*, and *not* me, because you stayed too long. It had nothing to do with your resistance to the party. You were too set in your ways and butted heads, far too often I might add, with men more powerful than yourself." Michener took another long drag before massaging his forehead, breaking eye contact as he spoke. "It's because of this, I simply cannot do it."

Thomas was not the slightest bit disappointed. This was the answer he knew Michener would give and, being a political climber, had to give. Like the fine poker player he once was, Thomas had calculated all of this beforehand.

He allowed a silence to settle over the room before speaking. "Gerhard?"

"Yes?"

Thomas awaited eye contact, ready to unleash his royal flush.

"Go ahead," Michener said, seemingly unworried.

"If you do not do this, I will inform the current *Ministerpräsident*, who doesn't trust you I might add, of the bribe you took in nineteen-twenty-three, from the Holtzheim family." Thomas let that sink in for a few seconds. "You took it to spoil the investigation of their out-of-control eldest son who raped and killed that poor Swiss girl. *You* made it look like she drowned. A thorough investigation will reveal the money you received during those horridly lean years, and how you used it to purchase your garish country estate at Höhenfels. If I remember correctly, you told people, quite offhandedly, that your wife had 'family money.'" Thomas' mouth smiled, although the rest of his face did not. "But you and I know your wife's family never had two pfennigs to rub together, don't we?"

Michener's bleary eyes widened. After a moment of silence, he swallowed and began to speak, stabbing a finger toward his predecessor. "How dare you come here and make such an—"

"And," Thomas said, cutting him off, "I will inform your wife and *Schutzstaffel Obergruppenführer* Siegfred Kraling of the sexual relationship you had with his wife while he was deployed in Prussia. It was proven to me by a now dead officer, and I kept the telltale proof. You impregnated her and paid a nurse to perform an illegal abortion. The nurse, fearing you might ultimately harm her, photographed you both without your knowledge, and I have the evidence in my possession. The SS commander is a powerful and jealous man, Gerhard." Thomas leaned forward. "He will have you killed...if your wife doesn't first."

The royal flush was now fanned out on the table.

Michener's breathing became loud and ragged as he stubbed the cigarette out. *"Mein Gott!"* he exclaimed as he crossed the room and stared out the side window, eventually leaning against the mullion for support. "You come here and unashamedly threaten me, the high chief?" Michener turned, still holding himself up with his left hand. "You're bribing me, dammit!"

The buzzer clicked and the secretary asked if everything was all right.

"Go powder your nose!" Michener boomed, regaining a measure of his swagger. The intercom clicked off before the sound of high-heels tapped out of the anteroom.

Thomas sat motionless until Michener had calmed a bit. "I overlooked the bribe and your reckless affair when I was here. I did it against my own good judgment, and it shames me to this day, especially the case with the murdered girl. By the time I knew about it, the paint had long since dried. And despite these heinous acts, you were always a loyal protégé, except in the very end..." Thomas fought to remain neutral in expression, "...when you left your knife hanging from my back."

Michener looked as if he might break down in tears, shaking his head as he again stared out the window, no doubt calculating his options. He eventually turned, his eyes completely red and moist. "You believe those things about me?"

"They're absolute fact, of which I have indelible proof."

Michener's lip trembled as he eyed his predecessor for a half-minute. Finally he dipped his head, his voice almost a whisper. "What else do you want from me?"

"Nothing at all, Gerhard. My life is now nothing more than tedium. It's like the scratchy hollowness at the end of a phonograph record of beautiful music, playing over and over, never ending in its vacuity. For me, all I want is the thrill of working one more case. I want to hear that beautiful music one more time...just once more is all I ask. It's a selfish request after a long life of what I hope was selfless service."

He coughed.

Michener, a man who was accustomed to far more potent power plays, cocked his eyebrows. After a moment he actually smiled, probably due to Thomas' raw human appeal. Michener walked to his desk and sat, digging through his file drawers until he found a certain piece of paper. He dipped an ink pen before filling the form out in a beautiful script.

Looking up, he held the paper across the desk. "Very well, Thomas. You shall have what you want. And, of course, you shall give me every shred of the evidence you bribed me with."

"Later."

"I trust you. Now, please, Thomas, tell me about this murder."

Chapter Twenty-Three

IT WAS FULLY LIGHT NOW. There were puffy rain clouds to the west, glowing orange as the eastern sun bounced off their condensation. But for Neil, his southerly path was all clear. He had allowed the aircraft to climb slowly, registering just over eight thousand feet on the altimeter. His side still hurt, but the lightning pain had been slowly replaced by fiery throbbing. It felt as if someone were holding a low-burning hand torch to the tender skin and not letting up. Neil kept his arm clamped over the wounds as best he could, having bunched his shirt to stanch the bleeding. He lit his final cigarette, angered with himself for not purchasing more in the Shoreditch pub. Then his mind drifted to Jakey. He would be the very first one to find humor in his lifelong friend piloting an airplane over Bavaria while suffering from a leaky gunshot wound.

Neil grunted, unable to laugh at the lunacy of the situation.

His thoughts of Jakey were interrupted by a cough from the engine. It caused the aircraft to shudder before again running normally. A minute later, the sputter happened again. Neil's eyes searched the control panel, focusing on one instrument in particular.

The fuel gauge now showed empty.

"Damn!" He'd been so consumed with his pain that he'd forgotten to keep an eye on it.

Neil pulled hard on the cigarette and peered out all three sides of the cockpit. The remains of an enormous city were beginning to disappear in the distance off the right side of the aircraft. Directly ahead, at quite a distance, loomed the large white peaks of the Alps.

As Neil scanned the earth below him, the engine stopped sputtering, wheezed several times and died completely. The propeller seized to a halt almost perfectly straight up and down. The loud sound of the engine and prop were now replaced by the cool rushing of air.

Danger filled the cockpit.

To some people, danger is a foreign sensation, causing immediate panic. But for years, Neil had operated in a climate of danger. Sometimes at low levels, other times when loss of life was imminent. This was one of those times. Had there been a danger gauge in the cockpit, the needle would have been pinned in the red.

I'm probably going to die, he thought, *so I might as well go out kicking.*

He felt the stick getting mushy. His inputs on the rudder pedals effected no significant change, and in seconds the airplane shuddered violently as it stalled and nearly rolled on its back. The airplane yawed left and began a rush to the ground, elevating Neil's stomach into his throat.

Clamping the cigarette between his lips, he willed himself not to provide input. Yet. He knew that airplanes needed speed to remain in the sky. And since the aircraft was now plummeting, it was gaining speed. After hearing the rushing wind grow to a roar, he pulled aggressively on the stick, feeling nauseous as the Hornet Moth completed an ugly and unintentional split-S maneuver. What had been zero gravity a moment before now tugged on his face and insides, making him feel like he might burst through the bottom of the airplane as he successfully pulled the airplane from the dive.

Neil used the dark strip of horizon as his level, the loud rush of wind staying constant as he kept a small amount of downward pressure on the stick. He was now headed north—the way he had come. In the distance and to his left, he could see the large city sprawl again, underscored by the impressive spires of its churches and cathedrals.

But he didn't want to go that way.

A glance at the altimeter showed Neil that he had burned off two thousand feet with his inadvertent death-defying stunt. He lost even more altitude when he banked hard to the left, pulling on the stick to execute a tight turn back to the south. Now, once again headed to the south in the direction of the looming mountains, Neil watched the altimeter closely, knowing he had to sacrifice altitude for distance. He had flown for a little more than an hour since the incident at the airstrip and, judging by his average airspeed, Neil estimated that he had traveled a hundred miles and change—more than enough distance to avoid the manhunt that would occur.

But only if he could land and walk away.

As he passed through four thousand feet, Neil scanned in earnest for potential places to land. Ahead in the distance were two bodies of water. One appeared to be a medium-sized lake. It was slightly to his right. To the left was a smaller lake, and between them what appeared to be a connecting river bounded by acres and acres of lush-looking farmland. Judging by his speed and altitude, Neil felt he would overshoot it if he continued on his same course. He also knew that pilots liked to land into the wind. So how the hell would he know which way the wind was blowing? Neil looked to his left, scanning the ground for people, livestock, anything. He was anxious, knowing that in a matter of minutes he would be on the earth—in some state—whether or not he was ready.

Smoke...

He noticed smoke from a stove chimney drifting in the direction he was flying. It wasn't being sheared off upon exiting the chimney, but the wind appeared to be steady enough to make a forty-five-degree stream of smoke to the south, meaning the wind this morning was from the north. Hopefully it was blowing enough to matter to the aircraft he was piloting. It was time to pick a spot and land this airplane.

Then the realization of what he was about to attempt to do hit him.

From his time during the Great War, Neil knew that landing an aircraft was supposed to be what separated the men from the boys. It was the one basic, yet critical, action that took years to master. The razor's edge difference between a pilot's life or death. And here he was, a man who had simply flown a great deal as a *passenger*, with two ragged holes in his body, over a country that was fast becoming his country's enemy—again—banking an airplane whose owner was now dead, working out the physics of the problem as if it were an experiment in a laboratory.

But this was no experiment.

The ground coming up at him made that perfectly clear in Neil's mind.

He tapped his pocket with his left hand, cursing when he remembered he was out of cigarettes. A cigarette would help mightily right now.

As the smaller lake passed to his left, Neil was now low enough to see the canoes and fishing boats tethered at small docks around the water's edge. He began to bank east, alarmed at the way the airplane plummeted. From the east he continued his turn around to the north, into the wind. The sun swapped sides and, as Neil leveled the wings, the greenhouse effect warmed his face from the right side. He was quite low now, and the surrounding trees and scenery filled his peripheral vision, making him feel as if he were dropping like a stone. Neil pushed forward on the stick to gain speed, afraid he would stall again the way he had done earlier.

At this altitude, a stall would be his undoing.

With the nose in a downward attitude, Neil could see the brown, loamy earth approaching him quickly. He had flown in enough airplanes to know that he always felt pilots were landing too fast, only to have them pull up at the last moment, seemingly preventing a catastrophe. But there had to be a reason they did that, and Neil followed suit. He kept the stick forward, now amazed at the way the bales of hay whizzed underneath. He even saw a scarecrow. The eastern sun was still fairly low and, once Neil was near the ground, the cockpit darkened slightly as the foothills and forest to his east blocked the sunrise he had enjoyed for the last hour.

He suddenly remembered the flaps Willi had used when landing at the airstrip. They were operated by a lever and helped the aircraft fly slower. Neil decided it was too late. He didn't dare divert his concentration from what he was doing. He'd just have to land without them.

Now mere feet above the ground, aware of the rushing sound from the speed he had gained, Neil leveled at what he estimated to be twenty feet above the ground, knowing he'd probably made an amateur mistake. But he held it there, bleeding off excess speed, keeping his eyes on the horizon. The fields went on and on—there was plenty of room. As the speed decreased, Neil was startled when it felt like the bottom suddenly fell out on the airplane. He pulled the stick into his belly but it was too late.

The Hornet Moth dropped the final twenty feet, the right wing dipping slightly.

Neil yelled out in pain at the jolt when the wheels bounced from the earth, sending twin rooster tails of earth as the airplane bounced ten feet back into the air. He pressed the stick forward. As the craft moved nose-down again, Neil's eyes went wide when he saw where he would hit next. He instinctively pulled back on the stick—it was of no use. His speed was too slow to generate lift and the steeply cut drainage ditch rushed at him, making Neil feel as helpless as he ever had. He let out one final shouted protest at his helpless situation.

The impact jerked the propeller from the aircraft, leaving it stuck in the ground like an Olympian's javelin. The far side of the drainage ditch tore the landing carriage from the airplane, also ripping off most of the lower wing as the fuselage skittered forward, dirt and grass spewing from the unintentional plow. The violent impact hurtled Neil's luggage forward as he was thrown against the control panel and the left window. The remaining aircraft came to its rest, right side up, facing ninety degrees left of the direction he had been heading.

Even though he could not hear it, all of the sounds he had been exposed to through the night were now replaced by sheer, eerie silence. No more engine; no more propeller; no more gunshots; no more rushing of air; no more yelling. Just the thick heaviness of clear, uncut quiet.

Neil's freshly healed head wound had ripped apart. His eyes were closed. He was not moving.

After a full minute, the silence was replaced by the sounds of running feet and urgent voices.

The voices belonged to his welcome party.

Welcome to Nazi Germany.

Part Two:
INTO THE REICH

Chapter Twenty-Four

THIS WAS A FEVER DREAM. It had to be. Even through his closed eyes, the darkness was rimmed by red when the white jags of lightning flashed. *Did I just fly an airplane? Did I crash?* Neil Reuter pressed his parched, cracked lips together, his mouth coated in an acrid dryness and the taste of rusty metal. He heard the haunting voices, one of them shrill and urgent. He also smelled smoke. The aroma wasn't typical wood smoke; it was more like the smell of a fire when petroleum objects were added. Neil opened his eyes, seeing the blur of hands and arms before feeling the collateral splashes of several buckets of icy water. There was a great deal of jostling, a click, and then everything came clear when he was tugged from the blackened wreckage.

The metallic taste in his mouth was quickly replaced by manure-tinged dirt. He spat, unable to breathe deeply enough to repel much of the filth. Through the fog of his condition, Neil's mind curiously hearkened back to his boyhood, when he'd tasted hurled earth during heated dirt-clod wars with the kids from down the street. Spitting again, he decided right then he'd sell his soul for a sip of good clean water.

With a groan he turned his head, staring at a heavy woman of probably 50 years of age. With deep lines in her weathered face, she peered at Neil as if he might be a space alien. She wore a tight kerchief over her head and held a curved pipe clamped in her mouth. Neil rotated his eyes to see a boy in his teens, mouth agape, standing between the woman and a girl of perhaps twenty.

Farmers. Their clothes were a dead giveaway; sewn together with heavy fabric and absolutely no concern over fashion. These people had come to work their fields this late summer morning, only to find a crashed airplane and an idiot inside who was somehow still breathing. Neil knew that any minute now, the father would come along and that would be that. Neil felt he *might* live to see the bowels of a German prison, but judging by the level of dehydration he was experiencing, he might not.

It's not simple dehydration…it's shock and blood loss…you know that…

"Help me up," Neil said, offering his left hand to the boy. He watched as their eyes went wide upon hearing his American English. Getting his bearings, Neil switched to German. *"Helfen Sie mir, bitte."*

The boy grasped both of Neil's arms and pulled. As Neil made it to his feet, an unbearable wave of pain flashed through his body. He was lightheaded from loss of blood, and the pressure the tug put on his injury made his vision darken. Neil's head felt like an over-inflated balloon and, just before he fainted, he managed to speak the German words, *"Bitte nicht weitersagen, dass ich hier bin."* It meant, "Please, don't tell anyone I am here."

He thudded to the ground.

After an indeterminate amount of time, Neil came to again, his eyes staring straight up into the cobalt sky. He listened as best he could to a brief discussion among the family—the discussion seemed to border on an argument. He twisted his head to each of them, watching their gesticulations as they debated. From what he could understand, the children appeared to be taking his part more than the mother.

Finally, the older woman dismissed the boy and he leapt over the ditch, sprinting off through a tilled field. Neil nestled his head into the cool earth as he waited. *Where's the Pale Horse now? God, Jakey would fall down laughing if he could see this scene. Oh, sure, he'd be concerned about my injury, but my flying an airplane would be too sweet for him to let go...*

Neil lifted his head to look at the two women. They were both peering off into the distance. Through his pain, Neil cranked his head around, seeing the boy returning with a horse and a small wagon. The old horse moved about as fast as a hunched-over, elderly man's shuffle and, after a good ten minutes, the teen led the nag back to where Neil lay, breathing raggedly.

Though Neil didn't know it, the gash on his head was splayed open, displaying his skull for a full inch of its run. Fortunately, he was no longer losing blood from that wound, aided by the poultice of horseshit-laced-dirt filling the gash. But his side was a different story—it continued to ooze dark red blood. The family loaded him into the cart, causing Neil to again pass out from the pain of jostling. As they gradually made their way back to the small farmhouse, Neil woke up, grasping the older woman's arm and repeatedly begging her not to tell anyone about his being there.

"Don't tell your husband, please. I'll pay you," he murmured in German. "I have enough money to give you five years' earnings of what you would make with this farm." Neil then switched to English, babbling incoherently about children who were counting on him.

When they were halfway there, he fell unconscious and didn't wake again for the duration of the slow march.

As if they were doing a normal day's work, the family loped back to the barn with the old nag, carrying with them an American man who spoke strangely accented German. For the entire distance, amounting to a twenty-minute walk, the family never uttered another word.

* * *

Thomas Lundren led two junior officers and an ambulance down the rutted road to the airfield at Velden. The lone airfield worker had found the body shortly after Thomas' meeting with Michener. The airfield worker had notified the local constable, who had already been called by Gerhard Michener. Michener had instructed the constable to shut down the airfield—an impossibility for landing aircraft since the airfield had no radio—but it was no matter. There had been no flight activity on this day.

By the time Thomas arrived, a steel gray sky had moved in, casting a gloomy pall over the day. Making the day far worse for Thomas, however, was the unmistakable silhouette of the local constable. He swigged from a small pewter flask, quickly tucking it inside his vest as he scowled at Thomas and his trailing entourage.

Thomas despised the man.

"Heil Hitler!" the constable roared, popping his heels and extending his arm.

Thomas knew the constable's exuberance was deliberate. Though he didn't want to, he dutifully returned the salute.

"Thought you retired," Constable Bernard Sauer said with a sneer.

Thomas turned to the two junior officers, handing them a bundle of small white flags attached to pointed sticks. "Search every square meter on and around this entire runway. If you find something you think could possibly be evidence, flag it but *don't* touch." Thomas instructed the medics to wait before doing anything.

Turning back to the constable, Thomas managed to be polite. "Bernard…I appreciate your coming and providing security. You can go now."

The constable was *Ordnungspolizei*—known as "Orpo"—ordinary police but reporting under the Interior Ministry of the Reich. He was most definitely a party member and was the de facto law for the sparsely populated areas of Velden and nearby Vilseck, mainly because no one else wanted the job. With the large military *Kaserne* and the long stretches of farmland, about the only service he provided was locking up drunken servicemen who happened to stagger too far from their post. Known to be as crooked as a German Shepherd's back leg, Constable Sauer was quite overweight, with a neck that oozed out over his tight collar, rippling upward to his moon-like alcoholic's face. Deep-set in the center of the flat face were two beady eyes, both of them icy blue with oversized black pupils.

Thomas and the constable had a history.

Back when Thomas and his wife had first settled in Velden after his retirement, Constable Sauer had shown up within a week, attempting to shake Thomas down for protection money. Thomas had played along that day, never telling Sauer his name or what he had done for a living.

"And what will this money buy me protection from?" Thomas had asked.

"All sorts'a things," Sauer had replied, slurping tobacco juice that tried to escape the corner of his mouth. "These soldiers around here—no good shit-eaters, all of 'em—will bust in your barn and steal you blind. The monthly payment'll ensure that I look out after you and the missus."

"Then what are my taxes for?"

"Taxes don't buy you shit from me. This here's a *local* insurance policy."

"Really," Thomas had said. "Do I pay you now?"

"Right now and every month, by the first. Not a day later."

Thomas offered up a tight grin. "Wait here, please."

It had been a warm spring day. Thomas was in his early sixties at that time, and his suspenders hung around his waist as he crossed his yard with no shirt on, all skin and bones. He stepped inside the house and told Greta to go to the bedroom. When she'd locked the door, he retrieved his gift police pistol, which he held behind his back. Thomas wasted no time in exiting the house. He crossed the yard quickly then revealed the weapon, leveling it squarely at Constable Sauer's head. Sauer wore a pistol of his own, in a hip holster hanging low from his fat body as if he were some American cowboy. Thomas got the jump on him that day. Sauer stood there in shock, tobacco juice now oozing from his open mouth, dripping from his chin onto the dusty grass.

"Constable Sauer, I was the high policeman in the entire state of Middle Franconia for fourteen years. My only regret is never hearing about you before because, if I had, you would be in prison right now." Thomas stepped closer, his heart visibly beating against his thin skin. "Now get in that damned car and don't you *ever* set foot on my property again. You have been duly warned. If you ever do come back, for *any* reason, I'll consider it a threat and I *will* shoot you dead." He motioned with his pistol for Sauer to get moving and, not without an ominous stare, Sauer did.

They had seen each other a few times since then and, when they had, Sauer had allowed Thomas a wide berth. They'd never spoken a word since that day. Thomas knew what kind of man Sauer was, but it was no longer his place to intervene.

Until today.

Constable Sauer looked Thomas up and down, his upper lip curling when he saw the badge on Thomas' belt. "Didn't know the polizei hired dead men."

Thomas didn't engage in an argument. A problem with the local constable was the last thing he desired. He took the paper from his chest pocket and unfolded it, turning it for the constable to see.

"I have been deputized with absolute power to investigate this shooting. Thank you for securing the airfield, constable. Your work is done here."

"I ain't gotta leave, though."

"Actually, you do. I'm securing this airfield for my investigation and I don't want you here. I've asked you kindly, several times, to go." Thomas paused for a moment. "If you don't leave right now, I'll arrest you and turn you over to the *Kripo*. I doubt they will care for a fat Orpo from the hills."

Sauer straightened, his eyes aflame. Defiantly, he spat on the ground before jostling to his dusty black DKW Reichsklasse sedan. He left with a screech of tires, spinning a half circle on the runway and roaring back to the east.

Thomas breathed a sigh of relief as he mopped the perspiration from his face. As he often did when frustrated, he pictured his Greta, imagining her tousling his hair the way she liked to do when he was troubled.

I'll get through it, dear.

Thomas turned to watch the policemen as they scoured the grounds. He didn't expect to find much else of significance, but one could never be sure. "Did you find the shells?"

Both men said no.

"No shells at all?" Thomas asked incredulously.

"No, sir," the nearest one said.

"Keep looking." Thomas summoned the medics to take pictures. He then carefully inventoried the dead man's effects before turning to the medics.

"Please go ahead and load the body. And tell those jackals at the county morgue that I've inventoried every item in his pockets." Thomas thanked the medics and sent them on their way.

A small civilian plane could be heard. Rather than land, the pilot circled in a steep bank, no doubt curious about the commotion. After two passes, the engine changed pitch and the airplane flew off to the west. Watching him go, Thomas decided to finish the search and reopen the airfield.

It took Thomas about fifteen minutes to find the shell casings. They'd been blown backward, rolling all the way to the end of the runway. He first found the smaller 9-millimeter shell casing from the Luger. It wasn't shiny at all and was marred by an oxidized green scabrous pattern. The man had been lucky the bullet even worked. Not too lucky, though. Because the man with the Luger was now headed to the morgue.

Adjacent to it, nestled into a tuft of grass, was a larger shell casing. This one was shiny and well kept. As he'd done with the oxidized casing, Thomas lifted this one with a pencil. Stamped on the bottom was "45 AUTO – WINCHESTER."

An American pistol with American ammunition. Thomas didn't get excited, though. American .45s, along with the other weapons that used this round, weren't uncommon in Germany—especially in the underworld.

Thomas had worked a killing in Munich once and each of the six men in the shootout had carried M1911 pistols.

"Find something, sir?" one of the two policemen asked.

Thomas closed the small bag with the bullets, made a notation on the outside, and sent the two policemen back to the station to log the evidence and to begin the paperwork for the murder. He instructed them not to turn the paperwork in until he had a chance to review it. As the policemen drove away, Thomas removed his hat and rubbed his sweaty head.

"This one's going to be quite a challenge," he murmured to himself. Although he had been out of police work for many years, Thomas knew a complicated case when he saw one. A good detective knows almost immediately, as did Thomas on this humid, late summer's day.

He replaced his hat and went to the maintenance shack, greeting the airfield employee who'd been standing in the door of the hangar, watching with great interest. As it turns out, he was the airfield's lone worker, named Antonio. Thomas had seen the young man from a distance on many occasions. Antonio had an open face and bright, expressive eyes, though he seemed to be mildly slowed by some sort of disability. Thomas didn't feel it took away from Antonio's intelligence at all—it just seemed to add to his response time when queried, and was the type of thing that might cause people to write him off too quickly.

Thomas liked him.

"Do you have a chart showing all airfields south of here?" Thomas asked, watching as Antonio walked to a large map on the wall. That map was broken into labeled grids, each label referencing a map of greater detail.

As Antonio busily gathered the maps, Thomas looked around. The small hangar was nothing more than a maintenance shack and was crammed with bins of parts and small machinery. It smelled of petroleum, probably because every square centimeter of floor, wall and ceiling appeared to be smeared in oil. Wearing his American-style ball cap pushed back on his head, the affable young man returned with three rolled maps, then cleared a spot on the flat work table.

"Only three?"

"Yes, sir," Antonio answered after a short pause. "One is due south, covering Munich and the surrounding area. The other two are south, but much farther to the east and west."

"Let's start with the Munich map."

Antonio rolled it out on the table, placing wrenches on each corner to keep it flat. Finally he placed a small screwdriver on the map, its tip pointing to the airfield where they currently stood.

Thomas reached into his suitcase, retrieving the map he had drawn on earlier. After unfolding it, he took a heavy wax pencil and, using a level that had been hanging on the wall, he recreated the same triangle on the aviation chart. After that, he and the young man located every airfield inside the triangle, circling each of them with the wax pencil. When finished, there were thirteen airfields, airports, and landing strips in the zone Thomas had initially created. Working out the distances in his mind, Thomas felt it would take him over a week to visit all of them. He turned to Antonio.

"Are you a pilot?"

"No, sir."

"Do you have a telephone?"

"Yes, sir, an old one back there by the water closet."

Thomas nodded, stepping to the phone and jiggling the receiver. "Hello, ma'am. Please ring me to the Middle Franconia Main Polizei Bureau, Generalmajor Gerhard Michener."

Thomas waited several minutes as the call was patched through various lines. Antonio asked if Thomas was thirsty and retrieved two cold cups of cloudy well water. Finally, Michener's voice could be heard and Thomas spoke confidently into the old phone.

"Generalmajor, this is Special Investigator Lundren...I need a fast airplane with a good pilot here in Velden. Probably will need it for today and tomorrow, maybe even the day after. And I need it this afternoon." He listened to the expected objection for a moment before he hardened his tone.

"Considering our little talk we had this morning, Generalmajor, I'm confident, especially given your impeccable connections, that you *will* find a way. You have two hours." Thomas placed the earpiece back in the cradle and breathed in deeply through his nose. Michener was probably pounding his spotless desk, cursing him for all he was worth at this very moment. But Thomas knew Michener would come through, at least until he had the blackmail material in hand.

Thomas walked back through the jumble of parts and equipment to where Antonio stood.

"Were you angry at that man?" Antonio asked.

"That was just a business call."

"You live across the field, don't you?"

"I certainly do. I've often seen you up here working, trimming the grass, clearing sheep from the runway."

"The sheep love the grass here. But when a plane comes, they can cause problems."

"I imagine so," Thomas remarked. "You hungry?"

"Yes, sir."

"How would you like to walk over to my house for a bite? I could fry up some *Schnitzel mit Buttergemüse*."

"I'm not supposed to leave."

"Well, I'm in charge of the airfield today," Thomas said with a wink. "I hereby give you permission."

Antonio's radiant smile offered sufficient answer.

The two men crossed the meadow to the Lundren farm. As they walked, Thomas learned that Antonio was originally from Italy, having moved here as a child. When they arrived at the farmhouse, Thomas' coughing was so severe he had to excuse himself to the bedroom. For the first time since his cough began, he noticed flecks of blood on his handkerchief.

Chapter Twenty-Five

Two Days Later
NEIL OPENED HIS EYES. He felt the softness of a quilt before being overcome by hot, searing pain through his side and abdomen. The room was dim, lit only by the low honey light of a kerosene lamp across the room. Sitting on each side of the narrow bed were two young people. As the miasma of pain and bewilderment cleared, he recalled the basics of what had happened.

And these were the people who'd rescued him.

Upon seeing Neil awaken, the boy stood, his eyes wide. "Where are you from?" he asked. The young woman, who Neil assumed to be his older sister, shushed him and called for her mother.

The older woman entered the room, her craggy face twisted downward into a frown. "Why don't you want anyone to know you're here?" she asked in heavily accented German. She loomed over him, hands on her hips, her bosom heaving.

After a painfully deep breath, Neil spoke. "I was flying an airplane." He managed to shrug. "I ran out of gas and crashed."

The woman leaned over the bed, pushing downward on the pillow next to his head, making the spring mattress jar and sending spikes of pain through Neil's body. "That airplane is down in my field clogging up my irrigation ditch. And while we carted you back here, you babbled on about us not telling anyone. My daughter tells me you were speaking of children. So, what is all this? We've missed almost two crucial days of harvest."

Neil's mind was working better than he thought it might, especially since he could understand the woman's fast, guttural German.

"Two days?" he croaked.

"That's right. We wrapped up those holes in your side, occasionally stuffed your mouth with horse pills, and you've been sleeping and moaning ever since."

Neil asked for water.

The young woman stood and disappeared, coming back with a pitcher and a glass. She held the glass for Neil as he managed to prop up on his left elbow. The water was heaven-sent. He sipped it slowly, taking the time to use it to lubricate his entire mouth before swallowing. Temporarily sated, he collapsed back into the down pillow.

"I guess these are your children?" he asked the woman.

"Who are you and *why* are you here?" the woman demanded.

Realizing she wasn't going to be easily distracted, Neil gestured to the young woman and the boy. "Have them leave the room."

Their mother pointed to the window. "Gabi, you go on and start at the lower field. I want three full rows of *Rosenkohl* out of the ground by sunset."

The woman snapped her fingers at the boy. "Peter, clean up and get your butt off to your maneuvers." She retrieved a pressed uniform from a handmade armoire, along with socks and shined boots, handing them to him. Neil focused on the outfit, realizing it was a Hitler Youth uniform.

The boy took the items and disappeared but the young woman, Gabi, remained, alternating her eyes between her mother and Neil. "I want to stay."

"You go now."

The young woman viewed Neil for several seconds before turning back to her mother, shooting her a piercing glare in the way only a daughter can do. "But I'm an adult and I want to hear what—"

"Go!"

Gabi stalked out, slamming doors, breathing choice words. The mother waited until a screen door slammed shut before turning back to Neil, rattling the bedpost so hard it hurt. "You better start talking, mister. And I want the truth."

"It's complicated," he said.

"I'm not stupid. Explain it to me."

"Well...who I am and why I'm here shouldn't matter, but if you'll help me, I'll pay you. I'll pay you a great deal."

"That doesn't answer my question. Why don't you want anyone to know you're here?"

Neil ignored the question, grunting as he shifted to a cool area of the feather mattress. "Here's what you're going to do. I will give you money, plenty of money...but you have to help me get better."

She took her pipe from her work apron and clinched it between her stained teeth. Neil could see where the upper and lower teeth had grown outward from holding that pipe in the same position for so many years. "Help you get better, how?" she finally asked.

"I need my jacket from the airplane."

"The one with the *gun* in it?" she asked, crossing the room and hefting Neil's Colt in her calloused hand. "It was on the dirt after your crash landing." She tapped the letters stamped into the hardened steel. "This gun is American and it smells of fresh gunpowder." She replaced it. "Don't try to mislead me, either. We hunt birds and boar in the winter. I know all about guns and rifles."

Neil did his best to focus through the growing pain. "I'm not going to try to mislead you," he said, surprised his German was coming so clearly. "I *am* American, and it cannot be known that I am here. As I said, I will pay you, but I need your help."

"Pay me with what?"

"Give me my jacket."

The woman lifted his dirt-mottled jacket from the firewood bin. She tossed it to him. Neil let out a loud breath when he found the tin buried deep in the inside pocket. He opened it, removing the velvet bag. From the bag he pulled a large diamond, pinching it between his thumb and forefinger, holding it between their riveted gazes.

"This will do for starters."

"A rock?"

"A diamond," he corrected.

"Still a rock," she declared, dragging a wooden match over the stone of the fireplace and puffing her pipe.

"We can discuss its value later." He glanced around. "Where am I?"

"My son's bed."

"Where are we, geographically?"

"In the middle of nowhere, really. This land's been in my husband's family for more generations than anyone can remember."

"Husband?"

"He's long since dead."

"Where's the closest town?"

"Hausham."

"Is that in Germany?"

"Is now, although most everyone here still considers ourselves Austrians."

Neil remembered seeing the mountains, the Alps, dead ahead before he turned and crashed. "Closest big city?"

She clicked her tongue. "Depends how big you want. Rosenheim's the next biggest. And if you want really big, then there's Munich."

"How far is Munich?"

"'Bout sixty kilometers."

"Would Hausham or Rosen...Rosen-whatever have a good jeweler?"

"Rosenheim." A variation of a smirk appeared on the woman's leathery, sun-cracked lips. "Do I look like I'd know the answer to that? I haven't been out of this valley for fifteen years. We sell most of our take to the co-op. What we need, either we buy through the catalog or Gabi gets over in Hausham." With a shake of the head, she turned and began to walk away. "So I don't know anything about any damned jeweler."

"I'm not going to live," he pronounced, moving his hand to his wound. "This hole in my side is too big."

"You've lived this long."

"I won't make it long-term. This isn't going to heal on its own."

"Everybody dies, mister." She grasped a picture off the same dresser that held Neil's Colt. The photo was old and stained, displaying the faint ghosting of an unsmiling man. She tapped the frame with a thick finger. "My Albert died forty years before he should have, drank himself to death. Maybe you men are just too stupid to live long lives."

"I won't argue that."

She turned to leave.

"I need your help, ma'am, *please*."

She stopped, leaning over the fireplace and tapping out the burnt tobacco from her pipe. Her eyes stared out the window at the growing light of a Saturday morning. Neil felt she was about to acquiesce.

"Why should I help you when you won't tell me the truth?" she asked.

Neil nodded. "Okay. I'm not supposed to be in Germany. I'm here illegally."

"Why?"

"It's a long story that I promise I'll tell you later. For now, I need you to keep my presence a secret. Enough?"

"Maybe. What exactly do you want from me?" she asked, not turning her gaze to him.

Neil propped himself up, grunting through the pain. "Have your daughter go sell a few of these diamonds, then talk to a doctor you trust. Pay the doctor to come here, and fast."

"There's no doctor around here I would trust. Only one nearby is that crooked Dornier Guriard, and all he's worried about is his position with those damned Nazis. Thinks he's gonna be the local *Kreisleiter*."

"Well, is there anyone else who can patch me up?"

The woman eyed Neil for a moment as she chewed her cheek inside her mouth. "Yeah, I think I know one person who might have the ability."

"Good, because it—"

"How much is that rock worth?" she asked, cutting him off.

Neil clenched the diamond in his palm. "Get your daughter up here and let's find out. If infection sets in, I won't have days, I'll have hours."

* * *

After making a deal with the dubious Frau Heinz, it was Gabi who had the task of selling several of the diamonds. Neil had sat in the bed, drenched in sweat from his pain, watching through the warped glass as Frau Heinz and Gabi pumped water from the yard pump, carrying it bucket by bucket to the adjacent barn. It was there, presumably because they had a warming flame, where Gabi had taken a bath. Neil watched with guilty interest as the mother led her daughter back across the yard, shuffling in wooden clogs and wrapped in a thick blanket.

Another half-hour passed before they came back into the bedroom, politely knocking as they had begun to do. Frau Heinz had entered first, beckoning her daughter. Gabi seemed hesitant, finally coming in with her head bowed. She wore a flowered dress, displaying a trim midsection and a larger bust than Neil might have imagined. Her blonde hair was pulled into a woven mound at the rear of her head, and around her shoulders was what appeared to be a handmade shawl. It didn't match, and it was obvious the dress was thirty years old and severely out of fashion, but the young woman's natural beauty and radiating vitality more than made up for it. Her breaths were shallow as she looked at Neil for approval, eyes alight and hopeful for a flattering remark.

"*Sehr schön*," Neil whispered, a remark about her beauty. Gabi had beamed, clasping both hands in front of her. Frau Heinz had frowned at that point, no doubt feeling there was a bit too much of a spark coming from what she probably still viewed as her little girl.

"Yes, well," she had said after clearing her throat, "let's discuss this before Peter comes back. He doesn't need to know about selling diamonds and what not."

In Neil's pain, he'd forgotten his instructions to the boy for concealing the airplane wreckage. "Is he having any luck?"

Frau Heinz shrugged. "He's cutting evergreens from the south boundary. It's hard work and takes time. When we were in the barn, I could see he'd covered about half of the wreckage. I'd imagine he'll get it mostly covered by sunset."

"What time is it?"

"Mid-afternoon," Frau Heinz answered.

"And the jeweler?"

"We need to hurry before he closes," Frau Heinz replied. "Besides, the veterinarian will be here after sundown."

Peter had come in from the fields an hour after the women had left. With a note of pride, Peter informed Neil that the shattered airplane was now completely camouflaged. Despite Neil's agony, the boy brought in a checkerboard, placing it on Neil's covered legs. As Neil disinterestedly allowed Peter to beat him, he did his best to occupy his mind by learning more about the Heinz family.

He learned that Frau Heinz's husband had died shortly after Peter was born, of cancer—or at least that was the story Peter had been led to believe. Neil guessed what Frau Heinz had said, about her husband drinking himself to death, was probably the unvarnished truth. But Peter had no recollection of him, knowing only that his mother vowed never to marry again.

According to Peter, their farm was quite large, occupying the upper plain to the east of the two natural lakes: Tegernsee and Schliersee.

"Any idea how far Innsbruck is?"

Peter shrugged. "Over the range. Few hours by car, maybe?"

I'm close.

Echoing his mother, Peter informed Neil that Hausham was the closest town with basic items for subsistence. Peter typically went there with his sister at the end of every month, and conspiratorially related how the two of them would share forbidden cigarettes on the bumpy ride home. Peter still attended school, a co-op of the farms in the area. The school claimed a total of sixteen children that comprised almost every grade in the spectrum. They wouldn't start back until mid-September, after much of the harvest was complete.

"When did your sister stop going to school?" Neil asked.

Peter smacked the black disc on the back of the checkerboard, demanding his *König*, which Neil dutifully gave. He didn't want to play again after this thrashing.

"My sister completed her last grade three or four years ago."

"Did she not want to go to university?" Neil asked.

Peter looked up. "Why?"

"That's just what some people do."

"No one around here goes to school longer than they have to," Peter answered. "Unfortunately, our mother insists I finish *Realschule*." After a bit of discussion, Neil learned this was roughly equivalent to finishing high school.

They chatted a bit about the local area. Peter informed Neil that all of the young men had gone off to Munich to be in the Wehrmacht.

"I noticed your uniform," Neil said. "Hitler Youth?"

Peter twisted his lips, barely nodding.

"Do you like it?"

He shook his head.

"Why not?"

Shook his head again. Forcefully. Something about this subject bothered Peter. Neil decided to table it for the time being. He changed the subject and enjoyed his time with the young man.

An hour later, they had heard the sound of the puttering engine followed by squealing brakes. Peter was sitting next to his new houseguest, listening, for the fourth time, to the altered tale of how Neil had crash-landed the airplane. Peter thought Neil's wound was from the crash. Neil, per Frau Heinz's instruction, relayed the entire story as if he were simply a normal pilot who suffered a critical failure.

The front door slammed. Frau Heinz's large body ushered in a blast of barnyard air as she immediately shooed Peter out, instructing him to do his chores while supper was prepared. Once Peter was out of the house,

Gabi came into the bedroom, having already quickly changed into her long nightdress and an equally long robe. She took the chair Peter had sat in. Frau Heinz walked behind her daughter, glowering at Neil before she dropped a pile of reichsmarks on his wool blanket.

"That's the sum total, right there."

Gabi touched Neil's arm, giving it a light squeeze. "How did we do?"

"I'm sure you did fine," he grunted, still in considerable pain. He struggled to smile at Gabi before turning his mind back to the next task at hand.

"How much should I pay your friend for the surgery?"

"He *isn't* my friend, he's the local veterinarian. And how would we know how much to pay for surgery on a human being?" Frau Heinz asked.

"Tell me how much some common items cost. I don't know anything about the value of a reichsmark, so maybe I can use it to get a frame of reference by knowing what you pay for other things."

Gabi and Frau Heinz told him the value of their old Adler truck. They spoke of the price they received for the cow's milk to the co-op, and the subsequent price for each liter to the other consumers. Additionally, Gabi knew exactly what beer and cigarettes cost, making Frau Heinz momentarily cock her bushy eyebrow at her daughter. They gave him the prices for a loaf of bread, a pair of work overalls and, finally, helping Neil more than anything, Frau Heinz was able to estimate the price of a bottle of Russian vodka at six reichsmarks. Back in the States, Neil paid between two and three dollars. After listening to the many other items, some of which were helpful, he hastily decided that a dollar was worth somewhere between two and three reichsmarks, splitting the difference and deciding on 2.50 reichsmarks per dollar. Neil assumed that a farming veterinarian, at least back in the States, made a decent living. Perhaps as much as a hundred dollars per week. Per Neil's formula, the vet likely made 250 reichsmarks per week. Thus, in order to perform an illegal surgery—and keep his mouth shut—Neil planned to pay a month's wage, one thousand reichsmarks for the surgery.

Assuming Neil was still alive to pay him.

"The vet's a flag-waving Nazi," Frau Heinz warned.

"Will he keep all this quiet?" Neil asked.

"He's a greedy *Schwein*." She thought about it for a moment. "Yeah, I think he will...if you pay him enough."

Gabi chatted with Neil for the next hour as they awaited the veterinarian.

"Where the hell is that man?" Neil had grunted after the sun had fully set. "I don't know how much longer I'm going to last."

It wasn't long before Neil passed out from the pain.

* * *

Special Investigator Thomas Lundren waited patiently as the pilot, a diminutive man who walked with the swagger of a man twice his size, poured a steaming mug of coffee. Almost mechanically, the pilot lit a cigarette and stretched in the late afternoon light. After a few moments, he shared a look with Thomas as they both shook their heads. It was beginning to look as if this initial search would be fruitless.

Disregarding a personal abhorrence for anything other than early-morning caffeine or alcohol of any type, Thomas poured a full cup of black coffee for himself. He was exhausted and needed the energy. He sipped the coffee slowly as he and the pilot stood there in the open hangar, both of them watching as the tangerine sun inched downward to the distant horizon.

They were at Zorneding Airfield, the final airport on their list. An intermediate landing strip well to the east of Munich, it was significantly larger than the one in Velden. Zorneding was used by a few businesses and mainly wealthy Müncheners with enough income to own their own sport aircraft.

The air chief, a burly man with a mop of oily black hair, had greeted them upon their arrival, whistling at the Junkers JU-88, outfitted in civilian markings and swastikas. Gerhard Michener had come through in fine fashion, scaring up the lightning-fast aircraft in only an hour after Thomas' phone threat. The airplane actually belonged to the party and was used to shuttle political bigwigs around Germany at high speed.

Upon meeting Thomas for the first time, the short pilot, a Luftwaffe reservist, had bragged that he had flown everyone from Marlene Dietrich to Heinrich Himmler. "In our dear Reich, if someone needs to get somewhere fast, I'm the man they call," he'd said, jabbing his chest with both thumbs.

Thomas knew he'd found the correct man.

Once the air chief had fastened the cowling on another airplane, he wiped his hands with a rag and ambled over. Formal introductions were made and, after a brief over-his-head conversation about the JU-88, Thomas politely asserted himself.

"Sorry to interrupt, but we're tight on time." Thomas motioned to the runway. "Have you seen all aircraft that landed here recently?"

The chief nodded. "I haven't missed a day in months."

Thomas lifted a single finger. "What about Thursday, probably in the early morning? I'm interested in all activity, but that's the timeframe in question."

"I was here all day. When the weather's good, Thursdays and Fridays are among our busiest."

Thomas stepped closer. "It was a black biplane, enclosed cockpit, seats side by side. No markings that I know of. Did it land here?"

The pilot lowered his mug of coffee, squinting his eyes as he cocked his head. "Funny you ask that."

"Why?"

Thomas' pilot, who had been a disinterested observer so far, even appeared mildly intrigued as he lowered his cup of coffee.

The air chief lifted his own mug to the sky, making a line from north to south. "Thursday morning, just after first light, I'd just gotten the coffee made and was waiting on our first customer to show up. I heard an airplane and thought I might be getting some early business. I remember this, because I was surprised—it's very rare to get a customer that early."

"Did he land here?" Thomas asked.

The air chief shook his head. "Nope. This runway points due north and south, and the airplane came right over me, true as the ass end of a compass needle. He was heading south, puttering along in an efficient cruise."

"A black biplane?"

"Damn right," the air chief said, nodding. "I've never seen one of that manufacture either." He turned to Thomas' pilot. "Had kind of a pointy nose and a moth-like stabilizer. I used my 'nocs to get a good look at it. She was pretty and ugly all at the same time. Probably underpowered with that skinny nose." Shaking his head, the air chief seemed to be talking to himself as much as Thomas and the pilot. "I know every small aircraft in this area, but I've never seen that one, not in person anyway. Pretty sure it was from an English manufacturer."

Thomas reminded himself to breathe, thinking about the British monetary notes in the pocket of the dead man. His hand moved to his own pocket, touching the note he had brought with him. "English, you say?"

"Yes, sir. Can't tell you who makes that aircraft, but they've been making the same rudder and stabilizer design since the war. Shot down a DH-Four myself," he added with a trace of pride, glancing at Thomas' pilot and winking. "Same exact rudder."

"You're certain about this?" Thomas asked.

"Yes, sir. Thing about it was," the air chief said, "I couldn't figure where the fella was gonna land."

"Why do you say that?"

"Well, if he'd been planning to go over the mountains, even through the lowest pass over at Kufstein, he would have to have been higher than he was cruising."

Thomas' pilot removed the cigarette from his mouth, puffing smoke as he spoke. "He's right. Any pilot worth his salt would have slowly climbed to the correct altitude after takeoff. You don't go lolling along low and slow and then climb at the face of the mountains. That's nuts. Too many potent wind currents to deal with, and besides, it's just not efficient."

Thomas eyed both men. "So he landed?"

The air chief arched his eyebrows. "Well, that's what you would think. But that's what puzzled me. There're no landing strips south of here before the mountains."

"You're certain?"

"Yeah," the chief said, walking to the carafe and cursing when he realized there was only a splash left. He poured it anyway, walking back, apparently deep in thought. After considerable silence, he said, "Either your guy was scouting something—you know, looking around this area for a reason—or maybe he didn't know what the hell he was doing, or where he was."

"Please explain," Thomas said.

"Well, you wouldn't want to land that bird on anything other than hard-pack or pavement. And like I said, there's nothing between here and *die Alpen*."

"What are the possibilities?"

The air chief raised his fingers one at a time. "He was looking for something; or he put that bird down somewhere unadvisable; or maybe he turned east or west to go land elsewhere; or he climbed up and landed over in Austria. Whatever he was doing, it was peculiar. That's partly why I remember—the other reason being the strange airplane."

Thomas rubbed his forehead, feeling the stack of hay growing larger by the moment. "So, if you two had to guess?"

The two men conferred in quiet tones, as if their pilot talk was some sort of sub-rosa privilege, not suitable for mere mortal ears. Finally, Thomas' pilot spoke up. "We think he put it down somewhere south of here."

"Before the Alps?"

The air chief nodded.

"Why?"

"It makes the most sense," Thomas' pilot replied. "Maybe there's a suitable strip of hard-pack or a small, private airfield that's not on the map."

Thomas twisted his head to the air chief, who shrugged. "The maps don't cover private strips. No telling who has one."

"So you think he's nearby?" Thomas asked.

The two pilots glanced at one another. "We do," the air chief replied solemnly.

"The killer is nearby," Thomas breathed.

Chapter Twenty-Six

THE OPERATION OCCURRED WELL PAST THE HEINZ FAMILY'S BEDTIME, around 11 P.M. on Saturday night. The doctor, a veterinarian named Hörst Baldinger, had arrived earlier to find the man unconscious. The vet opened the man's shirt and probed the wounds with his fingers, viewing them discriminately like he might when buying pork or liver at the *Metzgerei*. The wounded man awoke from the pain and asked Hörst if he could perform the surgery.

"*Ja*, I can patch this up. But I can't promise your end result," Hörst replied.

Once the man told Hörst how much he was willing to pay, he sprang into action. He was cautious about how much anesthetic to administer to the man. He had tables for farm animals, by weight, but he had never induced unconsciousness in a human being. When a farm animal died due to an overdose of diethyl ether, the veterinarian would simply shrug and tell the owner that it was allergic to the anesthetic. Nothing he could do about that. And while Hörst didn't know this man, he did want his money, so he chose to be somewhat judicious with the amount of the diethyl he gave. Apparently Hörst was too careful; the man woke up just as the vet was shoving the last splinter of rib back in place.

Frau Heinz and her daughter Gabi stood in the doorway to Peter's room, watching in horror as their guest's back arched clearly off the bed. His yell was thunderous, shattering the reverie of the quiet farmhouse. The boy, Peter, had been asleep in the other room but rushed in to view the terrifying scene.

Hörst placed the cup over his patient's nose and mouth, pumping three times as the misty anesthetic mixture sent the man blissfully dozing back into blissful unconsciousness. The vet turned to the family, ogling the daughter for a moment. She'd really filled out over the last few years and Hörst planned to make a move on her the next time he saw her in town. He'd bedded several young women over the years who were simply too dumbfounded by his aggressiveness to say no. But for now, her and her mama were being a nuisance to his work. Hörst stabbed a crooked finger in their direction. "I asked you once to leave. Go in that kitchen and make some coffee, damn it, and leave me be. I need to sew him up and then he needs rest."

The family hustled away as Hörst retrieved his cigarette with a bloody hand, tapping the ash before drawing deeply. He'd never worked on a bullet wound before; never worked on a human, for that matter. Nevertheless, he knew this man was lucky. The bullet struck him in the back, below his right lung. It had traveled diagonally, only a few centimeters under the skin. The problem, however, was the wreckage it caused to the victim's ribs and adjoining cartilage. While it was impossible to know the exact extent of the injury, the vet felt that at least two ribs had been affected. Those ribs would take, at minimum, a month to begin to heal properly, if they *ever* did. The question was the distance between the shattered rib pieces, and whether they were close enough together for the body and blood to go to work and knit their way back into some semblance of structure.

Using a strong, tightly woven filament made for horses, Hörst sewed the large exit wound first, followed by the smaller entry wound, making both pucker outward. The patient would be left with tremendous scars, but aesthetics paled in comparison to the twisting and pulling pressures the wound would be exposed to, especially during coughing or sneezing. After using a sponge loaded with warm water to wipe the area, the vet drew on his bloody cigarette again, nodding to himself. His work here was done. He used a clean white sheet to dry the man's wounds before cinching a tight bandage around his entire midsection. The vet then quickly irrigated the man's scalp wound, sewing it up with a lighter gauge filament.

The family was huddled around the kitchen table when Hörst finally emerged. He nodded to them, mumbling a vague explanation before helping himself to a cup of coffee. He rummaged around in the cabinets without asking, finally finding an ancient bottle of brandy and adding a great slug to the coffee.

"I need to get going," Hörst said after several gulps. "Where's my money?"

"Not yet," Frau Heinz answered after removing the pipe from her mouth. "Our guest was very clear that you must remain until he awakens. He will need to speak to you and be the one who pays you."

Hörst chuckled and swilled the remainder of the laced coffee. After smacking the cup down on the wooden counter, he hitched his thumb to the room where the man lay unconscious. "Hildie, why are you protecting that man in there? I heard his accent when I arrived. I know he's English, or American, maybe. That was a bullet hole in his side, and not a puncture from a piece of machinery, or whatever that bullshit excuse he gave me was."

"A bullet?" Peter asked.

"Quiet," Frau Heinz said.

Hörst began to pace. "He won't wake up for hours. I want my money."

Frau Heinz stood. "You'll wait."

"Then maybe I'll just *take* it, damn it."

Peter stood. "Don't talk to my mother that way."

Hörst's tone turned wicked. "I admire your bravery, boy. Now step aside before you wind up unconscious like your mother's boyfriend in there."

"Hörst Baldinger, you cowardly sonofabitch," Frau Heinz growled. "Don't you dare threaten my son."

"Right, Hildie...right you are. I shouldn't do such a thing, especially since there's no man here to protect him." He cocked his head, a smirk forming. "Unless you're the man of the house. Is that it, Hildie? Should I treat you like a man? Because, if you're going to act like a man, then maybe I should whip your ass before I take the money...that's how we men—"

"Stop!" Gabi yelled. Hörst turned to see the girl brandishing a large pistol, aiming it at his head.

"Why, you dirty little bitch," the vet whispered, leering at her and licking his lips.

"Sit down and shut up until that man wakes up," Gabi said, adjusting her fingers on the pistol. Her index finger moved over the trigger.

"You couldn't use that pistol if you had a book of damn instructions in front of you," the vet snorted.

Gabi pulled the hammer back with her thumb.

The vet's eyes went wide in shock. Plaintively, he turned to Frau Heinz. "This is uncalled for."

"Uncalled for?" she yelled. "You're on a rural farm, Hörst, and you know damn well we're within our rights to shoot you for threatening us." She snapped her fingers, taking the pistol from Gabi and holding it on him. She didn't uncock the hammer.

"I've never been treated this way," Hörst protested, glaring at Gabi before coming back to his chair and helping himself to more brandy.

Frau Heinz wagged the pistol. "You hold every farmer in this valley hostage, every day of the year. Do you think I haven't figured out that you've paid bribes to the licensing bureau to prevent any competing veterinarians from moving here? Do you think I don't know that in other areas, people pay thirty percent less for livestock husbandry than we pay you?" She used her stout leg to kick his chair, just below his crotch. "And do you think I won't tell everyone in the valley these things if you don't sit here, drink that liquor, and shut the hell up?"

Hörst was ashen. "Those accusations are false. And I'm a party man, so you better be careful how you talk to me."

"I'm not scared of you."

He pointed to the pistol. "Is that loaded?"

"Care to find out?"

"I didn't mean no harm," he said, pouting like a child. "I get ugly when I'm tired...when I've had a nip. Never hurt a soul." He finished the coffee before pouring another cup, again integrating it generously with the liquor.

Frau Heinz spoke to Peter, telling him to go back to bed.

"Was it really a bullet hole?" Peter asked.

"We'll talk tomorrow. Off to bed."

Peter grudgingly complied.

"I'm staying up," Gabi said. Her mother didn't protest.

Hörst turned to Gabi, eyeing her up and down. "I kinda like the way you handled that gun, girlie. You're all grown up now, ain't ya?" he asked, drinking in her breasts for a few seconds. He looked up and winked at her.

Gabi mouthed the insult, *"Alter Wichser."* Translated, it meant "old wanker."

Chastened by her ribald slur, Hörst turned away, sipping his brandy and coffee in silence.

* * *

Thomas sat perfectly still as the converted Junkers fighter-bomber knifed through the Stygian night. There had been a moon earlier, but somewhere north of Munich they'd flown under a high layer of clouds that remained above. The pilot smelled faintly of alcohol, but Thomas was not a man to worry over such things. He was staring aged death in the face every day of his life, so what harm would flying with an egotistical, drunken pilot do?

Their plans had changed. Earlier, after three hours of fitful sleep in the hangar, Thomas called the bureau, speaking to the night officer. The sleepy-sounding man had perked up upon hearing Thomas' name.

"I have an important message for you, Special Investigator Lundren."

"What is it?"

"It's from the coroner. Let me find it...okay, here it is." The night officer began to read at a slow and broken pace. "Herr Lundren, as you thought, the victim died of a gunshot."

"Go on."

"Also, upon a closer search of his clothing, I discovered a pocket watch." The policeman paused. "It was tucked into an inner pocket and had an engraving of a name...Wilhelm Spadern Kruger."

"Wilhelm Kruger," Thomas repeated, not recognizing the name.

"Very good, young man. I assume they are doing a check on him right now?"

"There's a good bit more in the note," the policeman said. "A records search revealed that a man of the same name was discovered to be a deserter in *der Weltkrieg*. If this is indeed him, and the age of the corpse does seem to match, the Bundeswehr claims he stole his assigned aircraft and defected to England."

England! Thomas covered his forehead with his hand, his mind racing.

"The coroner's note continues, sir. A birthmark in the corpse's groin area matches the medical records of Kruger as relayed to me by the records bureau in Bonn. Given the age and birthmark, I'm absolutely certain of his identification." The policeman cleared his throat. "That's all, sir. That's the end of the message."

After Thomas made sure he had the spelling of Kruger's name, he committed the officer to silence, thanked him and hung up the telephone. As Thomas stood there in the hangar, the blunt reality of what he had heard began to sink in.

"*Mein Gott*," he declared to no one, taking a massive breath followed by a cough. "A German deserter, back on our soil, dead from a gunshot. And a night-black airplane racing away." This was bigger than a simple murder. It had to be. With the Reich now acting as an imperial power, coupled with the worldly snubs; with all that had gone on at the Olympics; with the youth rallies; with the daily calisthenics programs; with the medals for fertile mothers; with the appalling treatment of the Jewish people—and, of course, with the impending war that everyone in the world knew was coming—with all of these things occurring, to know that a defector had come home in a stealthy aircraft and had been shot dead while his killer raced away. Thomas had been in law enforcement long enough to know that a mystery such as this probably ran wide and very deep.

As he considered the possibilities, allowing his victim's identity to penetrate his brain, Thomas had paced the darkened hangar, rubbing his day-old beard. This wasn't as simple as two men having a disagreement, no. But what could it be?

He attempted to start out by thinking small. He tried. He failed. This was not small—his every intuition, honed by many years of service, screamed that it was a component of something momentous. They could have been British agents, here to soften the Reich before a strategic infiltration. Or, perhaps, cooperating spies and, as often happens in the popcorn matinees, one turned on the other.

But there was a problem. A big one.

If the murder was indeed a piece to a much greater puzzle, the Reich would demand to know what Thomas knew, and then they would quickly relieve him. They would want this handled by the Gestapo, or perhaps some special branch of the SS. There was no way they would let a retired state police officer, and non-party member, head up such a case. And especially a retiree in poor health.

If Thomas were to play this by the book, he knew he should have hung up and called the Nürnberg Office of Special Affairs, which was nothing more than an outpost of Nazi quasi-police thuggery.

He also knew their special investigators would take over the case.

They would pat Thomas on the back, offhandedly ask for his opinion and then not listen to a word of it. They would give him a civilian medal and send him home, promising to call with an update Thomas knew would never come.

Yes, Thomas should halt his investigation this very moment. He should go straight back to Gerhard Michener, slap the special papers down on his desk and resign his temporary commission. He should tell Michener everything he knew. Afterward, Thomas should go back to his farm, take a nap, and then resume his daily chores. He should remain there quietly, never bothering a soul until he died from this agonizing cough. Thomas knew he should do all of these things if he wanted to avoid the sticky tentacles of the Reich.

He knew he should.

But he didn't.

Instead, Thomas picked the phone up and rang the night officer again. He repeated his instructions that the policeman should keep this quiet. Thomas also instructed the policeman to destroy the message from the coroner.

"How?"

"Burn it."

Next, Thomas called the coroner, an old working acquaintance, at his home. He learned that the only people who knew about the inquiry into Wilhelm Spadern Kruger were himself, the officer Thomas had just spoken with, a clerk at the records bureau, and another doctor in Bonn who'd told him about the birthmark.

Thomas was uncharacteristically forceful with his sleepy colleague. "Did you tell the clerk why you were inquiring, Konrad?"

He could hear the man lighting a cigarette. "No, Thomas, I didn't. I remember how you liked to decide how to disseminate such information."

"What about the Bonn doctor?"

"No. And he wouldn't talk, anyway. I know him well."

"Thank you, old friend. Thank you. I destroyed your communication so please keep good records."

"It's all safely in my office."

Thomas made plans to see Dr. Konrad Güppertal, the coroner, very early the next day—which was now only hours away. As the pilot began his descent into Nürnberg, Thomas tried to recall the last time he had felt so alive. The sound of the powerful V-12 engines coupled with the rushing wind covered his voice as he answered his question in a normal tone.

"The last time I felt this alive was twenty-five years ago, in a shoot-out, when I was actually closest to death."

Thomas enjoyed a private grin before he stifled his cough. Leaning his forehead against the glass, the old policeman watched the growing number of lights rushing by beneath him.

Chapter Twenty-Seven

FOLLOWING THE SECOND ROUND OF ANESTHETIC from the veterinarian, six more hours passed before Neil finally awoke. His pains were still intense, but at least they were of the throbbing variety and unlike the bouts of searing pain he had endured before the surgery. Before making a sound, he checked his faculties, remembering where he was and why he was here.

"I flew an airplane," Neil whispered, remembering but still unable to believe what he had done. The anesthetic left a sulfury medicinal aftertaste in his mouth and sinuses, not to mention a skull-splitting headache emanating from the gash on his head. He rubbed his eyes, doing his best to clear his vision. When he moved, he no longer felt the clicking of the bone fragments. Instead, there was soreness with each motion.

After wasting four matches with his impaired movements, he finally managed to light the paraffin lamp beside his bed. Neil slowly eased his legs over the side of the bed, waiting until the dizziness passed. Taking great breaths, he carefully stood, waiting until he felt steady enough to move. Eventually, short step by short step, Neil shuffled through the bedroom and opened the door.

Despite the slow speed, it was good to be on his feet.

The two women of the Heinz family, and the veterinarian, were asleep with their heads down on the kitchen table. The door made a slight clicking sound. Only the daughter, Gabi, stirred. She raised her head, her face red and lined from where it had lain on her arm. She stared at Neil for a moment before her mouth creased upward into a smile.

His head aching from the anesthetic, his side searing from a bullet wound and the subsequent surgery, Neil still managed to feel admiration for this strong farmer from southern Bavaria. Despite his pain, he had noticed the deft way she'd handled the diamond situation yesterday afternoon. And he didn't even know that she'd held his Colt on the veterinarian while he was asleep.

Neil stood wavering in the kitchen, with Gabi staring at him and wearing an expression that both scared him and made his heart soar all at the same time. After licking his parched lips, he barely lifted his left arm, acknowledging her. The wooden clock on the shelf showed the time as nearly four and, judging by the enveloping darkness, Neil was lucid enough to deduce it was four in the morning.

Gabi shook her mother's arm. Just as Frau Heinz was raising her head, her hair matted straight up one side of her head, Neil felt the room begin to spin. Gabi reached him just as he began to fall. She managed to get one of the chairs underneath him, cushioning most of his fall as he sat there, wheezing and trying to breathe.

"Damned fool!" Frau Heinz whispered. "What are you doing up?"

Neil's head bobbled back and forth as his body shuddered with paroxysms of coughing. When he recovered, he gasped his words. "I felt the urge to stretch my legs." He frowned. "What's my pistol doing out here?"

Frau Heinz held it. "Never you mind."

Neil beckoned Gabi close, telling her about the balance of money he'd placed in the checkers box. He told her to pay the veterinarian, who'd just awoken. After the man had been paid, Neil motioned him over, gripping his arm.

"Thank you for patching me up," Neil grunted. "I do appreciate it."

The veterinarian was counting the stack of bills for the second time. "My pleasure," he said without a thread of genuineness.

Neil summoned surprising strength, pulling the vet closer. "Don't tell a soul I'm here. Wash me from your mind."

The veterinarian tried to pull his arm away but Neil held it firm, the tension causing the joined hands to begin to quiver. After a long moment, Neil released the arm and watched as the vet rubbed it with his hand. Neil saw the fear in the man's eyes, but also saw something else he didn't like. It was a type of shrewdness. Neil raised his index finger, staring at the man.

"Not a soul."

After the veterinarian had taken his leave, Gabi and Frau Heinz led Neil back to bed.

As sleep began to wash over Neil, he reminded himself that he had 32 days remaining. If he didn't find them, those women and children were going to come out of hiding.

And die.

It was sufficient reason to focus on his own healing.

* * *

Three Days Later

After helping his precinct close another case involving a murder-suicide, Detective Sal Kalakis finally was able to turn his full attention back to the Neil Reuter investigation. Following the beating he took at the hands of the two goons at Hillside, Sal had closed every single angle he'd found on Reuter.

He was now back to the tip from the Musselwhite fellow—tracking down Reuter's military pals.

As Musselwhite had thought, the housekeeper had indeed kept records. Right away, three names stuck out to him – these had to be the guys Musselwhite was talking about. Good old Agnes had penned "Army" right by their names on her approved callers list, each word made pretty in her flowing Palmer script.

The first two names were too plain and common to do much with. "Harold Baker" and "Michael Smith" probably numbered in the hundreds—even locally—so Sal didn't bother scouring the directories. Canvassing had never been Sal's long suit. Besides, he didn't have to waste time with the two plain names because the third one was far more unique: Cleveland Mixton.

Sal was alone in the Ford coupe, so he sang the words, "Here I come, Cleveland Mixton."

Only minutes before, Sal had crossed into Arizona after the long, two-day drive. The windows were down, whipping his cigarette smoke into the hot desert air as he held one hand lazily on the steering wheel while the other dangled out in the wind and sun.

Flora, the detective bureau's research assistant, had checked census records and found two Cleveland Mixtons living in the entire United States. One lived in—not too surprisingly—Cleveland, Ohio. He was ninety-five years old and a surviving Union Army private from the Civil War. Sal would've loved to have chatted with the man, but somehow he didn't think he was his guy. The only other Cleveland Mixton lived in Bouse, Arizona. This one was forty-one years of age, part Quechan Indian. He was a United States Army veteran of the Great War and was currently employed as a mine owner/operator.

Bingo.

So, Sal had informed Captain Yarborough that he wanted a travel chit, accepting it between a hail of Glaswegian curses so beautifully woven together that Sal had wished he had one of those *Popular Mechanics* voice recorders to save them for later. He would've liked to share the obscene soliloquies with some of his fellow detectives, or perhaps a few of the drill sergeants down in Monterey.

"You guys think you're good at curse words?" Sal would ask, his finger hovering over the switch. "Have a listen to this."

He chuckled, his mood brighter because he was getting close.

The tattered Reuter-case notebook was wedged under Sal's gabardine wool pants leg. He eased off the gas as he pulled into the greater Bouse metro area, half expecting to see an old west gunfight break out at any moment. A few sun-bleached, abandoned buildings loomed. Sal slowed to five miles per hour, creeping through the small town. At least there were no tumbleweeds or saloons with swinging doors.

Despite its deserted feel, the town did have a gas station, just ahead on the right. Sal wheeled in, his tires ringing a bell inside as he stopped next to the pump. An old man shuffled dutifully out, pumping gas before even asking Sal how much he wanted. Sal stepped from the car and shrugged.

"Well, fill 'er up I guess."

After the car was topped off, the old man soaked a sponge in a bucket, preparing to clean Sal's dusty windows.

"Hey, old timer, you happen to know where I can find Silver Shot Road?"

The man straightened for a moment, his eyes flicking to the east. "Yep." He went back to his work and wet the windshield.

Sal studied the man a moment. His hair was light gray and his skin the deep brown of saddle leather. "You mind telling me where?"

"Nope."

Sal stretched his stocky body, chuckling at the man's mildly disobliging manner. After crossing the empty fueling lane, Sal retrieved a joyously cold bottle of Coca-Cola, popping the top with the twine-held opener, guzzling nearly half of the bottle in one pull. After three hours with no liquid, and breathing the dry desert air, Sal walked a frenzied circle as the carbonation went to work on his mouth and sinuses. When he recovered, he waited until the man had finished cleaning the windshield before he asked for clarification.

The old man wiped his hands on the rag. "Why do you want to go down to Silver Shot?"

"I need to see someone. Police business."

"Police?"

"Yes. I'm from San Francisco."

There was no movement in the deep tan lines of the old man's face. He might have been part American Indian; his dark hair had lost its pigment, but there was no mistaking the sophisticated shape of the old man's face and nose. He studied Sal a moment before looking to the cooler and then back to the pump. "Be a nickel for the cola and a dollar-five for the gas."

Sal handed the man a dollar and a quarter. "Keep it." He finished his drink and handed the man the bottle. "Why do I get the feeling you're avoiding my question about Silver Shot Road?"

"Ain't avoiding it," the man said. "It's just...well, there's no one there. Not no more." There was immediate dampness—and pain—in the man's light brown eyes. Sal saw it as clearly as the azure sky that spread out above them.

"You alright?"

The man breathed deeply in through his nose, motioning Sal to follow. He walked to the slightly elevated sidewalk, placing the Coke bottle into a wooden crate and then sitting on a faded glider. There was just enough shade to protect them from the sweltering sun. Sal took a spot on the other glider, feeling oddly relieved to sit down although he had been sitting for the better part of two days straight. The man removed a pack of Lucky Strikes from his pocket, tapping one out before offering the pack to Sal. Sal took a cigarette, flicking his lighter open and lighting them both. The old man smoked for a moment before finally breaking the silence.

"Silver Shot Road ain't nothin' but a rock path that leads here off'a Seventy-Two. Ain't even on the map, but my son got it registered with Yuma County so he could have his mine's address on it instead'a the highway." He rocked back and forth, waiting.

"Your son?" Sal asked.

"That's who you're lookin' for, ain't it?"

"Your son is named—"

"Cleveland O'Reilly Mixton," the old man said, interrupting Sal.

"And you knew I was looking for him because he's the only one who lives on Silver Shot Road?"

The man pulled on his cigarette, exhaling even lines from his nose. He turned his eyes straight ahead, his chin trembling slightly. "Yes, sir. I guess when you mentioned Silver Shot, that's what tipped me. But the real reason I knew, especially since you're police, is…" He took another drag, finally getting the words out, "…is because my son, as good as he was to me and as much as I loved him, was nothin' more than a cold-blooded killer."

The cigarette tumbled from Sal's mouth, putting a small hole in the crotch of his gabardine suit pants.

Chapter Twenty-Eight

THE WAIT WAS EXCRUCIATING but Sal couldn't just up and leave the old-timer. After a tedious, long-winded tale about his son's death from an aggressive form of cancer, the old man clammed up when a truckload of what looked like wildcatters came through. Sal had seen a number of new wells on his way in. The rowdy men filled their truck with gas and nearly bought old Mr. Mixton out of Coca-Colas and cigarettes. After they had gone, Sal tried to get the old man to continue but he wouldn't. Each time Sal would ask, the man would shuffle by, busying himself with some mundane task. Finally, at high noon, the old man locked the door of the small station and flipped the hanging sign around to indicate he was closed for lunch. He opened the passenger door to the police Ford and got in.

"Need a ride?" Sal asked, puzzled.

"If you want answers, we might as well go down to Cleveland's house. I need to be back here by one."

Sal hadn't expected further cooperation, but happily pitched his cigarette into the road and cranked his car. They drove eastward, down the gentle grade of Route 72, past the thirteen buildings that constituted Bouse. Mixton seemed to have regained his composure, grousing about the lying, no-good bureaucrats of the U.S. Army.

According to the old man's tale, his son, Cleveland, had lived here since '31. Then, about three years ago the Army announced plans to open a training facility just outside of Bouse. Big news for such a desolate area. Freshly widowed and ready for a change of pace, the elder Mixton sank his life savings in the purchase of the shuttered gas station. The old man thought he could live out his golden years near his son while making an easy living off the needs of the U.S. Army.

"So, after I done all that, the Army changed their plans…didn't even notify anyone here…decided to develop their outpost down in Cochise County instead. Somethin' about not messin' up the oil boom. By the time I heard, I'd been in business six months." The old man's leathery hand gripped the frame of the passenger door. "Soon after that, Cleveland got sick. Died fast." The old man shook his head as his tone deepened. "And there ain't no oil around here, 'cept for a few drops. Just me and the snakes…all of us dying our slow death."

"Snakes?" Sal shot back.

The old man shrugged.

"Sounds tough," Sal replied, not knowing what else to say.

"Yeah, well...none of us is promised a good ending."

Sal agreed, though he kept it to himself.

Silver Shot Road was just as the old man had described it. As the Ford bumped and scraped down the steep rutted path, Sal wondered if he would ever make it back out. If a highly unlikely rain shower were to emerge, the SFPD car would definitely be stuck until further notice. Wouldn't the captain love taking that call?

"Hey, Cap...I might be here in Arizona a day or two longer than expected. Why? Well, your detective's coupe is stuck in the desert mud, down by a silver mine."

To hear Cappy's resulting symphony of curses would make the ass chewing almost worth it.

Silver Shot Road was about a half-mile long, cut into the side of a steep canyon, running a ridge downward, presumably to the mine. The only sign of life were a few utility poles joined by a single cable that roughly followed the road. After they passed around a sharp left turn, Sal could see the small house, if that's what a person wanted to call it. It had four walls and a slanted roof, set there in a dull orange valley, surrounded by rocks and cacti and nothingness. The house's frame was wooden, while the walls and roof consisted of corrugated sheet metal. There were two window openings but no glass.

"That looks like a nice respite from the heat, especially with the metal roof," Sal quipped.

"Cleve wasn't much into possessions."

The road leveled as they neared the house. Numerous hand-painted signs warned against trespassing. Staring at the structure, Sal spoke to the old man. "You could just wait in the car if you like."

The old man stepped out, tilting his face skyward as if drawing energy from the sun. "Nah, I kinda like comin' down here. I'm seventy-eight years old. If I ain't learned to face death yet, I never will."

Sal exited the car and followed the old man to the porch, which was nothing more than springy plywood sheets tethered over cinderblock. Then, startlingly fast, a long brown snake emerged from the front window, slithering downward before speeding sideways, off in the direction of the mine.

"Sonofabitch!" Sal yelled, jumping off the porch.

"Just a coachwhip. He's a good one, too, clearin' out the rodents for us."

Sal had no use for snakes. None. "I don't mind rodents one frigging bit. But I *do* mind snakes."

He held his hand over his heart, trying to calm himself. After a few more seconds, and seeing no other snakes, he eased his way over the porch and inside.

The house was roughly twenty feet square. There was a cheap table with three chairs—only one of which looked used, primarily because the seat was brown with dirt and oil. There were two cabinets over a sturdy piece of flat wood and, in the corner of the room, a steel bed with a thin mattress. Otherwise, the only other items in the house were books, hundreds of them.

The books were stacked floor to rusty metal ceiling, perilously leaning to the left or the right. Sal picked one up, a red hardcover titled *Burma*. The pages were well worn, with twenty or so turned down at the corner, each page containing numerous underlined passages. He knocked over another stack by removing one from the middle. The book was *Working With High-Explosives* and, like the other, it was marked throughout.

"Guess Cleveland liked to read," Sal said, placing his hat on the table as he mopped his head.

"This ain't what you came to see," the old man said. It wasn't a question. "Slide that bed out."

Sal was still uneasy about more snakes, but grasped the bed and cautiously pulled it out.

"All the way."

After sliding the bed nearly across the room, Sal looked at the old man.

The elder Mixton moved into the space where the bed had been. He knelt down, pulling out several loose wall screws by hand. That released a warped piece of the wall's sheet metal, which Sal quickly realized was a false front. Behind the sheet metal was a floor hasp held by an enormous, ancient padlock. The man produced his keys and unlocked it.

"The door's heavy. Do you mind?"

Sal unlatched the hasp and lifted the square door about an inch. He hadn't seen the outline on the floor—it had been artfully concealed. He lifted it all the way, estimating its size as thirty inches square. Sal then peered into the darkness of the cellar, pushing the terrors of snakes from his mind as his curiosity centered on what the hell was down there.

"Well, go on," the old man said. "It's still got 'lectricity 'cause I still pay the bill. Pull cord's on the right as you go down the ladder."

Sal eased his way into the dark square, realizing when he was fully on the ladder that the cellar was deeper than he expected. At the bottom, he waved his arm to his right, finally grasping the string. He whispered a prayer that there would be no more snakes.

"Boy, what the hell're you waitin' on? We gotta leave in less'n thirty minutes."

Sal shut his eyes and yanked the string. When he opened his eyes, he quickly forgot all about snakes. Hidden beneath the ramshackle hut was a fastidiously organized military bunker.

The walls of the cellar were carved into the rocky earth and bolstered with angle iron struts and strong timbers. The neatly swept floor was cut straight from the desert rock. To Sal's right was a workbench and, sitting before it, a quality swivel chair like the ones in the lab back at the precinct. On the bench were a number of tools and implements, as well as an ancient-looking box. Sal first walked to the box, opening it and narrowing his eyes. Inside were small tubes of glue, pigments in various skin tones, assorted watches and eyeglasses. It seemed to be the type of thing an actor or a makeup artist would own. He lifted the top tray to find a high-quality wig of sandy-colored hair underneath.

"What color was Cleve's hair?" Sal asked, directing his voice upward.

"Black. You're looking at the wig."

Sal didn't answer. Instead, he closed the box and walked to the back wall. It was partially hidden in the shadows cast by the single hanging bulb. On the wall was a sloped rack with a number of oily-clean weapons: shotguns, rifles, pistols. Sal lifted one of the pistols, an old Colt Army Special revolver that Sal was familiar with. Sal examined it and realized that it had been outfitted with a new barrel. The pistol was unloaded. Sal clicked the cylinder out, holding the barrel to the light. He had carried this same type pistol for years, remembering the twists of rifling from the hundreds of times he had cleaned his own. This barrel, however, was far different. The rifling was far more extreme than a normal model—called a gain twist—probably making the pistol hyper-accurate, but only from close range.

Sal spoke upward. "Sir, you said your son was a killer?"

"I did," the old man replied.

"Did you know that before he died?"

"No, sir. I assumed it after findin' that keep you're in."

"So you don't know for certain?"

"I knew my son. But, no, we never talked about it."

Sal believed the old man.

Continuing his search, Sal looked over the other weapons; none were uncommon, but all had a reputation for reliability and accuracy. It was a professional's collection and, judging by the Colt he had just viewed, probably modified to suit the shooter's tastes. Somehow Sal didn't think these were used to protect a useless mine that had probably been cleaned out of all its precious ore ninety years earlier.

Sal walked back to the trap door, calling out to the old man. When he appeared above the trap door, Sal asked the senior Mixton if he knew how to drive.

"Boy, I was driving the first horseless carriages when you were droolin' on your mama's teet."

Sal tossed his keys up. "Your gas station isn't far. When I finish here, I'll walk back." The old man stared at him for a long moment before Sal assuaged him. "I won't steal a thing and I'll leave it as I found it. I promise."

"Gonna be hot as hades," the man said as he disappeared. "Hope you're up to it."

Sal waited until he heard the familiar sound of the flathead Ford V-8 crank, and then the crunch of grit and rocks as the Ford bounced its way back up the rutted path toward the ghost town of Bouse.

For the next half-hour, Sal scoured every square inch of the space, finding nothing other than tools for a skilled gunsmith, along with several additional costumes and a package containing a fake beard. He looked over each of the weapons and was particularly taken with a beautiful Belgian FN-Herstal 1889 bolt-action rifle. The rifle was highly modified and probably accurate over an incredible distance.

One thing struck Sal—where was the ammunition? Unless there was another hiding spot, the ammo certainly wasn't here.

Once he was finished searching the bunker, Sal realized how incredibly thirsty he was. The dry desert air had parched him, making him wonder if there was an old well or some water source close by. He pulled the light cord and ascended the ladder, but something stopped him at the threshold from the tidy bunker to the hovel upstairs—it was the gap in the reinforced floor. It was several inches thick, hence the heavy trap door. Sal reached down and pulled the light cord back on, climbing back up and peering into the gap in the floor. The gap could be seen on all four sides of the doorframe, nothing more than the space between the reinforced bunker and the chintzy construction of the shack above it.

Sal turned, examining each crevice on the four sides. He stopped on the one behind him, the one a person would not naturally look at due to the ladder's orientation. There was something in there, behind the grime and shadows. Using his pinky, he gained a purchase on the object's edge, sliding it to him.

It was a book, a thin book.

Sal pulled it out, blowing away the slight accumulation of desert dust. There were no markings on the outside. He opened it to a page in the middle, noticing that the pages were clean and white. This was not an old book as the coating of dust might suggest. Sal glanced at both pages, digesting the handwritten words laid down in an easy-to-read, decidedly male script. He looked at the first entry on the left page. Its words took his breath.

107.34: San Diego, California, number 14, CM, MS. Simulated holdup by the bay as CSJ walked to his house from his mistress' home. Clean. Headshot from close range after full confession. Stayed in town for six days before we pulled out. The police and newspaper found the mistress and proceeded in that direction. The manner of death, and the killer, were an afterthought. UPDATE: 199.34: complete success. Locals closed case as a mugging gone awry.

Sal reread the passage three times. He wanted to go on but knew he needed water. Struggling to wet his mouth, Sal locked the trapdoor, replaced the bed and staggered out into the blaring sun. Hand shading his eyes, he glanced around for a well or a reservoir—anything to give him just a few ounces of water. Seeing nothing, and wondering how the hell Cleveland Mixton had stayed alive out in this wasteland, Sal glanced at the journal. Was this what it appeared to be? He pondered the weapons, the tools, the costumes...

And he remembered the old man's revelation about his son—*a cold-blooded killer.*

Already overheated by the sun, Sal found a sliver of shade next to the shack, scanning the area for snakes before he sat down. Resting his elbows on his knees, he used his already damp handkerchief to mop his head and face.

"This is an assassin's journal," Sal said aloud. Unable to resist, he flipped the book open, reading a few other passages. They seemed to be in chronological order, each coded at the beginning before brazenly describing a killing. Sal had been ignoring the big question since he'd been shown the cellar, but now decided to ask it: *Had Cleveland Mixton been working all alone, or did this somehow tie back in to Neil Reuter?*

Despite his burgeoning curiosity, Sal's physiological needs overtook his desire to know the truth. He needed water. Badly.

Sal stood, removing his soaked shirt and undershirt, wrapping the undershirt around his head before trudging up the hill. On his way out, he noticed an ominous sight. Above the eastern cliff, towering over the old mine, circled three turkey vultures, their red heads visible from hundreds of feet. They seemed to be staying aloft from the currents propelled upward by the ridge, patiently waiting for Sal to collapse, presenting his offering of a fattened, fleshy lunch.

Nearly delirious, Sal extended his middle finger, cackling as he yelled, "Not today, you pricks! I'm not dying today!"

Sal was correct. He would not die...*today.*

* * *

After staggering the seemingly eternal distance back to the gas station, and stashing the journal along the way, Sal drank nearly a gallon of water from a rubber hose before uttering a single word. Finally sated, and feeling like a taut water balloon, he spent a few minutes discussing the bunker with the elder Mixton. Sal was certain the old man had no idea about the journal. Finally, he thanked the old man for his cooperation, told him nothing of the journal, and asked him not to disturb Cleveland's home.

"I'll be back next week," Sal said, shaking the man's hand.

He left the elder Mixton with his phone number and work address before driving to retrieve the journal. Sal then drove an hour north to Bullhead City, allowing the whipping wind to air-dry his sweat-soaked clothing. In Bullhead, he located a ranch-style motel, reserving a room for the night. Sal purchased some sandwiches and sat in the room, reading in front of a whirling fan.

It was now mid-afternoon and, with the drapes pulled shut, Sal read each journal entry slowly, processing the locations and apparent codes as he munched a minced chicken sandwich. If Sal had the code right, the twenty-seven entries all took place between 1928 and 1936. None had occurred since 1936, which seemed odd because, before then, the longest gap between a presumed killing was only five months. Sal had to guess that the onset of Cleveland's cancer was the reason the killings stopped.

Cleveland Mixton's journal contained twenty-seven descriptions of what Sal felt had to be calculated, contracted assassinations. In each of the simple entries, Mixton detailed what the killing was set up to look like, and then usually provided an update regarding the investigative authority's eventual view of the death. In each entry, there was a number beforehand, like the 107.34 before the San Diego killing Sal initially read about. Sal theorized the number was most likely the date from the Julian calendar, the 107 signifying the 107th day of the year, and 34 signifying 1934. Therefore, 107.34 would indicate the killing took place on April 17th, 1934, assuming Sal had counted the days correctly, and that 1934 wasn't a leap year.

Twenty of the entries indicated killings in the United States. One took place in Canada. Three in Mexico occurred all at once, although in that particular entry the names of the victims all seemed American, so perhaps it didn't involve locals. One occurred in London. One took place in Venezuela and one in Berlin, Germany. No wonder Cleveland Mixton's mine had been a failure. The man was never home.

Also included in each cryptic description was a set of initials. In every entry "CM" appeared, presumably the initials for Cleveland Mixton. Sometimes his initials were accompanied by one or more of the following: MS, HB, or PH. Sal thumbed quickly through his notebook, going back to the names of Neil's frequent visitors; they were Harold Baker (HB) and Michael Smith (MS). After reminding himself to breathe, Sal shook his head as he thumbed through his notes, searching for anyone with the initials PH. Neil Reuter would have been NR, and nowhere in any of his notes did Sal have anyone with the initials PH.

Nowhere in the journal were the initials NR.

After reading each of the entries, Sal lay on the bed and thumbed through the pages, reading the occasional notes between the entries. It seemed that Cleveland Mixton had been taking orders from someone else, although he never editorialized his comments. His occasional reflections seemed quite machinelike, as if he were built to do nothing but follow orders. There was an entry in 1934 regarding the possibility of the team being "busted up," but then, two months later, an entry for a "high profile" killing in Alabama indicated business as usual.

In one of his last entries, before the final killing in Venezuela of a man with an apparent Hispanic name, Cleveland detailed over two pages the team's desire to eliminate "Harry" and their efforts to prove they had the mettle to pull it off. Sal scoured his mind, having no idea who "Harry" might be. Sal did know that "Harry" was the name to symbolize the letter "H" in some phonetic alphabets, although in the U.S. military's phonetic alphabet, the word "How" was used instead. In his notebook, he made notations of "PH" as an unknown assassin and "Harry" as a possible victim. After each he added an enormous question mark.

Sal studied the journal until well after sundown. He had already made the decision not to call this in. If he were to do so, a professional assassin's journal, especially one from across state lines, would certainly be commandeered by the feds. Along with the entire investigation. Sal didn't want that. This case was *his* baby. He'd give it up, but not just yet.

And at some point soon, Sal was going to find the thread of Neil Reuter's involvement and piece all of this together.

"Maybe he was the money man?" he pondered, standing and stretching. "Maybe it was him giving all the orders. What could he have gained from having these people killed?" Sal thought about Reuter's estate, his wealth…

It appeared Reuter had done nothing *but* gain.

The detective ran the faucet, throwing gloriously cool water on his face, then mopping it off with a towel. Attached to the motel was a small restaurant. In their window they had a sign advertising the "coldest beer north of the ekwator," spelled exactly that way. Sal decided to check it out for himself, and he did so with the journal again tucked safely in his waistband.

The beer was good. And very cold.

* * *

Sal made it back to San Francisco in just under fourteen butt-numbing, sweat-soaked hours. For the first time since the summer solstice, he noticed the days getting a tad shorter as he raced up the spine of the San Francisco Peninsula, the bay shimmering like molten gold off to his right.

He arrived in the city at just after eight in the evening, heading straight to J. Harrison Musselwhite's home. Fortunately, when Sal pulled into the driveway of the tidy Pacific Heights cottage, Musselwhite was in the front yard, a black garden hose in his hand as he watered what looked like a bed of freshly planted fall flowers. In Musselwhite's other hand dangled a bottle of Pabst. He swigged it before motioning with the bottle to Sal's dust-covered police Ford.

"Sounds like she was on the verge of overheating. Were you pushin' her?"

The flathead V-8 of the Ford ticked loudly as the cool evening air rushed over the searing metal block of the engine, making it contract as if someone had doused it with cold water. Sal tipped his hat backward, nodding. "Had my foot on the floor since first light. Drove from Bullhead City in Arizona."

Musselwhite twisted his entire body to Sal, raising his eyebrows. Luckily for Sal, the garden hose's range was a few feet short of his dusty shoes. "Th'hell were you doin' in Arizona? You think ol' Neil's down there hiding out in one of those cliff dwellings?"

Sal tapped out a cigarette, ignoring the question. "Where could I find Neil Reuter's calendar? I'd like the one for thirty-six, and the years before if you could please produce them."

After another pull on the beer, the financial man with the hound-dog face walked behind a row of neatly trimmed boxwoods, shutting off the water. He set the beer bottle on the edge of the porch and ambled back to Sal, stuffing his hands in his pockets and shaking his head. "Neil's secretary kept his calendar. He took them when he left. Took every one. I saw him do it."

"Shit," Sal breathed.

"Why?"

Frustrated, Sal shook his head. He wanted a headache powder and the comfort of his own bed. Maybe, if he pushed the right buttons, he might even convince Mona to rub his shoulders.

"Why, detective? Why his calendar? What are you hunting?"

"I need to know when Neil was in the office, and when he wasn't."

"You want to know when he was in the office, or in town?"

"In town would be helpful."

"Why?"

"A hunch."

"I can't help you if you don't give me some direction."

"Look, Mister Musselwhite, I can't really tell you what I'm on to, but I can assure you it's something." Sal lit the cigarette and shook out the match.

"Not saying your former boss was dirty, but he appears to have at least been...*adjacent* to something untoward that was going on. Something big."

"Adjacent, huh? Pretty slick way of puttin' it. I, myself, have been adjacent to quite a few things in my day. My bet is you have, too."

"Any ideas, Musselwhite? Any at all? How can I determine when Neil Reuter was in town, and when he was out? I'm open to all your brilliant ideas—and I mean that."

"Now see...that's a better way of getting what you want."

"Pretty please," Sal added, hopeful he was about to get a break.

He was.

"*My* calendars, detective, just like every other book and ledger I kept, are spot-on. I have every single appointment calendar from every year I've worked, post-college," Musselwhite pronounced. "An accountant never knows when that might come in handy."

"Your calendars?"

"Yep. And every time Neil was out of the office, I would have noted it, along with where he was going, because I would have been in charge of the staff on those days."

"You're kidding?"

"Why would I joke about it?" Musselwhite asked, lifting the Pabst from the porch and finishing it off.

Sal resisted the urge to hug him as he ignited with energy. "Where are these calendars?"

"Upstairs, in a box. Along with the rest of the junk my wife gives me hell for keepin'."

"Would you be willing to let me borrow them?"

Musselwhite studied Sal. "You truly believe Neil had nothing to do with Lex Curran's death?"

Sal made a show of crossing his heart.

"I'll go get 'em, detective. But if I get a speeding ticket, or a parking ticket, or anything...you know who I'm comin' to see for some help."

"You got it, Mister Musselwhite. I'm your man."

Fifteen minutes later, Sal headed home with seven years' worth of handsome, leather-bound calendars from Musselwhite's days at General Logistics. Musselwhite must have paid a pretty penny for such fancy books. On the cover of each one was the year in raised gold numbers. The calendars were thick, containing two full pages for each week. And Musselwhite wasn't exaggerating when he said they were spot-on. Sal opened one, just to sample it, reading full paragraphs of information for each day's entry. But he resisted the urge to begin matching dates. After being out of town, he needed to set aside at least a few days to relieve his wife of being the heavy hand with their two teenagers and one adventurous ten-year-old, all of whom were probably on the verge of making her feel homicidal.

And Sal also had a motive. He really needed that shoulder rub.

Chapter Twenty-Nine

ON THE SIXTH DAY AFTER HIS SURGERY, Neil slept longer than he had since some point before Emilee's death. The first three days after the surgery had been horrible, and the most he managed to sleep was only a few hours at a time. The fall he had taken after the surgery had opened two of the stitches. After the vet had re-sewn them, Neil had wanted only water until just yesterday, when he drank a cup of broth with small bits of vegetables. Perhaps it was the calories from the broth, or maybe he was finally healing; but for whatever reason, on this Friday, he had begun to feel markedly better.

After perusing a horribly one-sided, pro-Nazi German newspaper in the morning, and comprehending nearly every word, he managed to sleep for the balance of the afternoon and evening. Neil had just awoken, refreshing himself by guzzling a full glass of cloudy, slightly sweet well water. The air pressure in the room suddenly changed. Through the darkness Neil could see a white gown, realizing it was Gabi, the daughter, slipping into the bedroom like a ghost.

Over the previous days, Neil could have sworn he had awoken to feverish images of Gabi, sitting on the edge of his bed, pushing his sweaty hair off of his forehead, or mopping his face with a cool rag, murmuring comforting words to him.

She tiptoed through the room and took a place on the chair next to the bed. He turned his head to her and offered a small wave. "What time is it?"

"Almost midnight," she whispered. "You slept for a long time. We checked on you every now and then…we even heard you snoring."

Neil chuckled. His pain had subsided a great deal and the sleep had done him good. The discomfort was still there, but now only occurred when he moved. "Where is everyone?"

"Asleep. I wasn't able to."

"You need to get some rest," Neil said, looking away. Talking to her like this, in the dark of the night—in secret—made him feel awkward.

"Where will you go when you leave here?"

"Why do you ask that?" he asked, sitting up. "Have you or your brother told anyone I was here?"

"No," she answered calmly. "I was only wondering."

Neil nodded, mildly embarrassed for being accusatory. "No one can know I'm here, Gabi. For your sake, and for your family's."

She leaned forward and grasped his right hand with both of hers. And even though she did a man's work on the farm, her hands were delicate and cool and smooth. Her thumbs massaged the tops of Neil's hand in a nervous action and Neil could hear her breathing coming in short murmurs. "The evergreen branches started to brown, so we spent half the day taking your airplane apart and hauling it up behind the barn. The only piece left down there is the front portion with the engine."

"You did all that?"

"Yes, with Peter and Mama."

"Is the engine hidden?"

"It's mostly under the mud so, yes, no one will find it. We covered what had been showing with dirt and rocks."

"Why didn't someone check with me before doing all that?"

"You were sleeping. Besides, we're quite capable," she said with a proud smile.

Neil gave her hands a squeeze. "I do appreciate it. But there's another day's work I've cheated your family out of. I promise I'll make all this up to your mother when I leave."

Gabi pulled his hand onto her knee. He stared at her. She was on the precipice of saying something, but it seemed stuck in her throat.

"What is it, Gabi?" he asked, attempting to tug his hand back. She held it firm. "Come on now, I can tell you have something to say."

Her hazel eyes were alight with energy, her words hitting him like a strong right hook. "Take me with you."

His reply was in English, albeit with a stutter. "Pardon?"

"You heard me."

Neil untangled his hand, switching back to German. "Gabi, that's...well...that's impossible."

"No, it's not. It's quite simple. When you leave here, you take me with you."

He leaned over and poured another glass of well water from the pitcher. He took all of it in three gulps and dropped his head back on the pillow, wishing the water had been vodka.

"Has the weather started to turn?" he asked. "It feels a bit cooler."

"Don't ignore me," she said. "Where will we go? Who are the children you keep mumbling about? Are they your children? Are you married?"

"Please."

"Are—you—married?"

"No. Not anymore."

"Then it's settled. I shall come with you."

"Gabi," Neil breathed. "You just see me as a mysterious foreigner whose life is some sort of bizarre adventure, but that's *not* it at all. I'm about to do something—"

"Dangerous? I know that. Do you think I'm stupid?" she asked, her voice rising.

"Shhhhhh." Neil turned the paraffin lamp up a tad. "Of course you're not stupid."

"This is Germany, the Reich, gripped under the violent hand of those criminal National Socialists. And here you are, an *American*, and you crash into our field in a blood-soaked English airplane, with a bullet wound, and you think I don't know that you're doing something dangerous?"

"Bullet wound?"

"Peter is the only one who didn't know," she said flatly. "And even he heard it from your veterinarian doctor."

"Gabi, listen to me. You have everything you need right here. My life...it's over, Gabi. It's all over. I've got one thing left to do and then I'll have nothing left to give." He rubbed his forehead, his eyes averted. "You don't want to spend time with someone who has an outlook as utterly bleak as mine."

Her voice cut the still quiet of the night like a blade. "Do *not* tell me what I want."

He parted his lips to speak but she cut him off with a raised finger.

"You talked, now it's my turn. I'm twenty-two years old, and I would rather die *this* year just to know, if only for a few months, that I lived a real life. I don't want to get married to some yokel farm-boy and have five babies that will probably die in a coming war or, perhaps worse, to live a life tilling our fields and praying for rain or sunshine." She wiped tears that had begun to stream down her face. "I want to see new things and taste new foods. Before I die, I want to feel the ocean on my feet and I want to meet people who are different from me, who speak strange languages. I want others to know me and respect me, and I'd like to do something unusual or dangerous that doesn't involve livestock or a damned rickety old tractor. I want to do risky things that bring me close to death and leave me exhilarated afterward." Gabi jerked a handkerchief from her gown pocket and mopped her eyes. When she spoke again, her voice was low and velvety and, in the honey light from the lamp, Gabi Heinz looked as pretty as any creature Neil had ever laid eyes on.

"Before I die," she said, "I'm going to leave a mark on this world so, someday, people will remember me." She stood. "Because otherwise, I'll simply be a walking dead person whose body will end up as part of the soil in the Heinz plot in that sad little cemetery over at the base of Kratzer Mountain."

Neil stared up at her, watching her chest rising and falling. He opened his mouth to speak but she held up her finger again.

"I won't die here. Do you hear me? I won't." She moved to the door, eyeing him for what seemed like an eternity. As she did, her face softened and the tears again began to stream. "Don't talk. Just think...think about me...about us...about what I said."

Gabi left his room and pulled the door shut.

Neil didn't sleep again that night.

* * *

Feeling loose and relaxed, Sal removed his hat as he strode into the San Francisco Public Library at Market and Van Ness. Under his arm was a stack of Musselwhite-authored, anally-retentive calendars along with Sal's case notebook. In his free hand were two sharp pencils. Mona had come through with the backrub, and more, much more. So, even though Sal was short on sleep, he was long on afterglow. And Sal could go all day, and well into the night, on quality afterglow.

The main floor of the library hummed with the Monday crowd. The tables were packed with men in their best clothes, probably unemployed, scouring the rolls of daily job opportunities. Seeing them, Sal felt a pang of guilt, though he didn't know why. He wasn't lazy and had certainly earned his position, but many of those men probably had as well. The economy wasn't their fault. He shook the thoughts from his head and hurried down the center staircase into the basement, headed straight for the periodical records room. The still basement air smelled of newsprint, mildew and perfume.

"Mornin' detective," Eunice said, drinking him in over the lenses of her wire rim glasses. Sal was well known here, and used the library for research more often than he utilized the SFPD archives. The library had better information, it was quieter, and Eunice was more helpful than anyone on the police payroll. She was probably around forty, quite stout and painfully plain. She always wore too much perfume. Sal enjoyed flirting with her just enough to give her a thrill without making her think he was serious about following through.

He donned his hat again just to remove it with a flourish. "Eunice, m'lady, how does this day find you?"

"In a foul mood, detective. My eastern shipment hasn't arrived yet. And if it isn't here by eleven, you just might witness the most open-and-shut murder of your career." Eunice lowered her glasses to hang by their chain and leaned forward over the counter. Her colossal bosom, covered fully and tightly by her modest dress, strained as she pressed her only assets together with her arms.

"Careful, Eunice, careful," Sal said, cocking his eye at her. "Planning a murder is against the law."

"It is?"

"Well, if your attorney is worthless."

Her maroon lips tilted upward at their corners. "Then cuff me, detective. Cuff me and do with me as you please. I dare you."

"I may just give you a reprieve for good behavior," he said, winking. Sal opened his notebook and removed a piece of paper. He slid it to Eunice.

"Business so soon?" she asked with a pout.

"Your day is coming, dear. Be patient."

"Promises, promises."

Sal tapped the piece of paper. "I know you may not have all of these newspapers, but the incidents I'm looking for occurred in those areas. Pretty big news in some of the cases. Could you bring me the newspapers of those cities and dates, as well as the next few days' worth, if you have them?"

Eunice slid her horn-rim glasses back on and perused the extensive list. "Goodness, detective. It'll take me an hour to gather all these together, assuming we have them." Her eyes came back up. "What will you give me in trade?"

Sal pondered this for a moment. Finally, he lifted his left hand, using his thumb to wiggle his wedding band. "Mona got to me before you did. But would you settle for knowing that, had she not, well…you and I would be sharing some adventurous nights together?"

Eunice squeezed her lips together as her face and neck flushed. She glanced at the list again before beckoning him close and whispering conspiratorially. "Just so you know, I don't think you could handle what I have to give."

Sal pondered her statement for a moment before wiping imaginary sweat from his brow. "I have no doubt, Eunice. But it wouldn't be for a lack of trying."

Eunice, a satisfied grin plastered on her face, sauntered into the back to begin retrieving all of the copies on Sal's list.

Good old Eunice.

Fifty-five minutes later, Sal sat at an eight-seat table, all alone, with a stack of newsprint a foot and a half high. He removed the top newspaper, the *Denver Dispatch*. Sal opened Cleveland Mixton's journal to read the entry:

12.35: Golden, Colorado, number 24, CM, HB. Automobile accident and fire at the lower foothills of the eastern range. LPS confessed to the shooting, a bona fide piece of shit. He cooperated until he realized what we would do. HB strangled him and the wreck went smoothly thanks to HB's exp. Good thing we planned in advance. No witnesses and clean as a whistle. We were southbound by car just as snow hit and then took train from Lubbock. UPDATE: 16:35: officials wrote off as a tragic accident.

At the beginning of the entry, 12 indicated the twelfth day of the year, January 12th. Sal lifted the three copies of the Denver newspaper. After looking through the edition from the 13ᵗʰ and finding nothing, he had a faint sinking feeling that the entire journal might be some sort of sick delusion, but that was quelled by the Post's morning edition from the 14ᵗʰ. Apparently, due to the snowstorm, no one saw the accident until well into the day on the 13ᵗʰ.

Denver Icon Perishes in Fiery Crash

Golden— Prominent businessman and philanthropist Lawrence "Larry" Swayfelt died tragically in an automobile crash just outside of the town of Golden. According to Swayfelt's wife, Evelyn, the Denver railroad magnate planned a full day on the mountain range "to shoot a few hundred rounds, the way he did when he was frustrated." Officials believe his car may have struck a patch of ice or snow in the early moments of the fast-moving snowstorm that dumped seven inches on the Denver area.

Swayfelt's automobile, a 1934 Lincoln, was found twenty feet below the road, hung on a rock formation. The auto was completely burned. Since the wreck occurred on the western side of the mountain, the flames and smoke weren't visible to any nearby homes. A passing motorist saw remains of the wreck after the storm cleared. After consulting dental records, authorities were able to positively identify the body as Lawrence Swayfelt.

After several rote paragraphs about his business, Sal cocked his eye at the closing section of the story...

In August of last year, Swayfelt was fleetingly investigated following the death of former U.S. Congressman Ulysses Powell in southern Texas. The two had been together on a group hunting trip. According to numerous witnesses, Swayfelt was the last person seen with Powell. Swayfelt vigorously denied any involvement with Congressman Powell's death, insisting that the congressman accidentally shot himself when crossing a split-timber fence. The authorities soon exonerated Swayfelt, writing Powell's death off as an accidental self-shooting.

Before the accidental shooting, Congressman Powell was rumored to be pondering a presidential run in 1940. A colonel in the Great War, he was outspoken about his distaste for an industrialized Germany.

Questions later arose about Swayfelt's trips abroad: to Venezuela, Germany and Morocco. Despite these questions, no connections to the death of Powell were ever made. However, sources at the U.S. State Department said Swayfelt had been a person of extreme interest before his death, due mainly to his friendship and fascination with the newly installed National Socialist government in Germany.

The newspaper article supported the diary entry. If the article was accurate, Swayfelt had been an extremely wealthy Nazi sympathizer. And if Sal's assumptions were accurate, Swayfelt was killed by an assassination team that made the murder appear accidental. Also, the diary stated that LPS confessed to the shooting—he'd killed the congressman.

Sal took a series of deep breaths.

He read the follow-up from the next day, noticing how the *Denver Dispatch* backpedaled just a bit without coming right out and admitting it—the way edgy journalists are skilled at doing. He made a note to have Eunice find the edition from the 16th, so he could read about the police's pronouncement of the wreck being accidental.

Sal inventoried what he had learned from the one story. First, his Julian calendar theory was correct. That much was certain. And unless Cleveland Mixton's journal was some sort of sick re-imagining of accidental deaths, the journal seemed, indeed, to be a recounting of twenty-seven murders. But why were the victims murdered, and at whose command?

And, again, did this somehow involve Neil Reuter, or was Sal chasing a rabbit trail unrelated to Reuter?

The detective lit a Chesterfield and smoked for a moment. The Seth Thomas clock could be heard ticking on the wall. It was nearly lunchtime and the basement had cleared out. He twisted his head to look at the counter; Eunice was nowhere to be seen.

After a bit of reflection, Sal decided he had made himself wait long enough. It was time to work on the individual represented in the journal as "PH." Could the initials somehow be related to Neil Reuter? In Cleveland Mixton's journal, PH appeared in three separate entries. Once for the killing in Venezuela. Once for a killing in New York. And once for a killing in Glendale, California. Since Venezuela's newspapers weren't available at the library, Sal decided to start with the New York killing and thumbed through the pile of newspapers until he found the *New York Times*. He placed the three copies before him, then flipped through Mixton's journal until he found the entry.

360.34: Sagaponack, New York, number 20, CM, PH. PH himself came along as this one was deemed personal. No confession was sought as command indicated absolute guilt of espionage and traitorous actions. JKQ had hosted a party. After all guests were gone, PH entered alone, shooting him three times. I heard the first shot at least an hour before the final two. UPDATE: 101:35: officials have not closed case. State it appeared to be a robbery but also suspicious. PH tells me their suspicions are of no concern—that he left zero evidence.

The *New York Times* had nothing on the following day. Sal opened the edition from two days after the murder and found the article on page 3. It wasn't as helpful as the *Denver Dispatch* story had been. Possibly because Sagaponack was out near the eastern end of Long Island, and also because the police seemed to be more tight-lipped about the case. What Sal did learn was the deceased, "JKQ", was a man named James Kenneth Quinby, a forty-four year-old inventor with hundreds of successful patents. The *Times* writer was a stick-to-the-facts type, and other than listing the man as a popular and wealthy member of Hamptons Society, it gave Sal no indication of why anyone would want to kill a socialite from a wealthy enclave of Long Island.

Especially for espionage.

Sal crushed out the Chesterfield and stared at Musselwhite's calendars. He could have easily cross-referenced the dates immediately after taking them from Reuter's former financial man. But true to his pattern of investigative activity, Sal first liked to prove global theories—in this case, actual murders occurring—before he went on the hunt for firm evidence involving those global theories.

The first global theory, in Sal's mind, had now been proven. The journal certainly appeared to be the diary of a member of a team of assassins. Thus far, it seemed that Cleveland Mixton had indeed been a cold-blooded killer, as well as the author of the journal. Despite their common names, now Neil Reuter's other "old Army buddy" visitors, Harold Baker and Michael Smith, would be worth checking out.

But, for now, Sal wanted to focus on "PH".

He glanced again at the date of the Quinby murder and then removed Musselwhite's 1934 calendar from the pile, riffling to the second to last page, briefly admiring Musselwhite's handwriting and organized system for note-taking. Then Sal ran his index finger across the dates as they neared Christmas.

And there it was.

In clean script, as plain as the half-smoked pack of cigarettes that lay before Sal, Musselwhite had made a notation on December 21st:

Neil out until 1/2 (NYC)

Sal reread it three times, reminding himself to breathe. Then he checked the dates of the other murders that contained the initials "PH".

The Venezuela killing had occurred in July of 1933. He hurried through the pages of Musselwhite's 1933 calendar, unable to quell the frantic tension that was coming over him. Distantly, as if she were down in a deep well, Sal could hear Eunice calling to him. He ignored her—*not now, Eunice! Haven't you ever seen a man learning about a quartet of professional assassins before?*—as he located the date in question and saw Musselwhite's familiar black continuance line leading from the previous page. He licked his thumb and flipped back a page. There it was:

Neil out of office for holiday (Mexico)

"Detective Kalakis!" Eunice yelled again, apparently unworried about her personal volume since there was no one else downstairs.

Holding up his finger to buy another minute, Sal hurried to find the final entry. Two positives proved a strong coincidence; three would convince Sal that "PH" was somehow Neil Reuter. He'd still have to find what PH stood for, but if he were gone during the Glendale killing, Sal would be convinced that Reuter was his man.

The killing took place in April of 1935. Sal thumbed the diary to the time period, knowing full well that Glendale, a suburb of Los Angeles, was only a long day's drive from San Francisco. But the killing had been on a Wednesday, so Reuter would have been out of the office all day. He located the week, traced a line across the paper, and stood straight up when he saw the entry:

Neil in Los Angeles

"It's him," Sal whispered to himself. "Cleveland Mixton, Harold Baker, and Michael Smith were a killing team...with Neil Reuter." Sal's shaky fingers tapped out another cigarette as he stared at the mess of books and newspapers spread out before him.

"Detective!"

He shook his head as the piercing voice shattered his reverie. "Damn, Eunice, where's the fire?"

"I've been trying to get your attention," she said from behind the counter.

"Okay, mission accomplished, now what?"

She mock glared at him. "You had an urgent phone call come in while I was at lunch." She pulled on her glasses, lifting a yellow note. "A Mister Weeks wants you to meet him outside the Reuter Mansion, wherever that is." Eunice opened her hands in a "don't shoot the messenger" pose.

"Did he say when?"

"It says he's there waiting." Eunice held the slip of paper out for Sal to take.

"Who took the message?"

She looked at the note again. "I don't recognize the writing. Looks messy like a man's, but there's too many people here for me to make a guess as to who took it."

He nodded and jabbed the cigarette between his lips. "Would you set all this aside for me?" he asked, motioning to the newspapers.

"You really owe me now, buster."

Sal pocketed the note, lit his cigarette, and donned his fedora. As he turned to go, he winked at Eunice and said, "I shall return, Madame."

Chapter Thirty

A VARIETY OF DETAILS DASHED THROUGH SAL'S MIND as he made the ten-minute drive to Hillside. While headed up Pacific, he pondered the similarities he had found thus far between all the victims in the Mixton journal: All were male. All were high profile. All were associated with a government or political angle. And each of their deaths was orchestrated in such a way that the authorities wouldn't suspect an advanced motive.

The assassins were supreme professionals.

How did they get that way?

Were they a team for hire, or a part of a much larger organization?

A misty rain began to fall, fogging the windows of the car. Sal was almost there, turning right on Taylor before seeing a black, four-door Lincoln with two of its whitewall tires on the curb across the street from Hillside. He pulled in front of the car, which was parked illegally, facing him. Sal used a rag to rub off the condensation while the driver of the other car eyed him through his own rain-streaked windshield. The detective exited in the rain, pulling on his hat and grabbing his raincoat from the trunk. The rain was light nuisance rain—typical for San Francisco. Sal walked to the window of the Lincoln, tapping lightly. The man inside pulled the handle to open the door.

Sal stepped back and let him out. "I'm Detective Sal Kalakis. I was told you were looking for me?"

"Yes, detective. Good to meet you. The name's Lord, Preston Lord." The two men clamped damp hands.

"The note said your name is 'Weeks'."

Lord smiled affably. "In my line of work, it doesn't pay to announce my Christian name to the nosy old spinsters at a public library."

Sal wasn't amused. "Aside from your being parked illegally, what's this about, Mister Lord?"

Lord motioned to a towering balsam tree hanging over the stucco wall surrounding Hillside. "Let's step over there and see if that's a bit drier."

Little rain reached the ground under the massive conifer. Sal studied the man who stood before him. He was trim and wore exquisitely tailored clothes, although they were cut from swaths of a normal, bland cloth. It was almost as if he wanted to fit in with the common man, but couldn't quite bring himself to wear something off the rack. Lord had intelligent, grayish-blue eyes and a sharp nose. His hair was fashionably short, and the shear marks in the hair above each temple displayed to Sal that Lord's barber used a high-quality pair of scissors.

Government or not, this kid Lord came from money. Sal would bet his pension on it.

"Who did you say you were with?" Sal asked.

"Department of War," Lord said, clasping his hands in front of him. "I understand you're investigating Neil Reuter?"

Sal nodded. "Yeah, doing it on my own, too. For a while it was just a dark mystery, but now that I've found a few pieces it's turning into a puzzle. A real conundrum, but solvable." He reached inside his inner jacket pocket and removed his Chesterfields, handing one to Lord as he took one himself. "What's your interest in this?"

Lord used his lighter to light both cigarettes and glanced up Taylor Street, past the main entrance of Hillside. He turned back. "Reuter appears to have been a little more than a wealthy businessman."

Sal didn't respond. He smoked and narrowed his eyes, waiting.

"Have you learned that, detective?"

"Are you here to try to take my case from me?"

Lord shook his head. "No, no, not at all. Sorry. I should have told you that first thing. I don't want to intervene, or to try to take any credit. In fact, I'm here off the record. I'd like to quietly pass on some information that might help you."

"Lemme see some ID first." Sal studied the waxy Department of War identification before nodding. "Okay. Let's hear it, Mister Lord."

Lord exhaled a stream of smoke. "We think Neil Reuter might have been involved in the murders of several people, and may have had a hand in others. Many others."

Sal fought to remain expressionless. "Go on."

"We're trying to piece it together, but it seems that perhaps Reuter was involved with some acquaintances from his time in the Army, and that their actions may have been grave, and completely rogue." Lord stopped and stared at Sal. "Have you found any such corroborating evidence?"

"My investigation is the business of the San Francisco Police, unless you have an order from a judge that I share information with you."

Lord didn't respond for a moment. He tossed his cigarette over the stucco wall and stepped an inch closer to Sal, his eyebrows lowering as his voice took on an edge. "Based on those newspapers you pulled this morning, I'd say you're following a similar line of thinking."

Sal didn't care for any man, no matter who he worked for, stepping into his personal space and taking on an aggressive tone. He poked Lord's chest and said, "Back up, bub. I may be a cop, and you may be a fed, but I won't hesitate to drop an ass-whipping on you."

"The way you did my two men?"

"Those pricks were *your* guys?" Sal asked, remembering the two lugs who'd worked him over in this very spot.

"They didn't know who you were."

"Like hell," Sal said. "Goons like that oughta be behind bars. Now, I said back up."

"I apologize if they were rough with you. One of them boxed in the Navy and has always been quick to use his hands."

A boxer...I knew it. "Thanks for the apology—now back the hell up."

Lord stepped back, showing his palms. "Look, detective, if you want to be a Bolshevik, then that's your choice. I actually expected that from a local cop. But you should also realize that I have my own agenda...and it's back in D.C. I couldn't care less about San Francisco." He smiled with his mouth only. "So, if you don't want to give me what you have, then I *will* make it my mission to give this case to the FBI. In fact, it won't take more than one phone call."

"You said you came here to give me something."

"I will. And, in return, I want to know what you know. We think a few of these items might have critical associations to national security. But as far as the local murder case and your locating Neil Reuter, and even connecting the dots to the other killings, you can have all that. I'll allow you to publicly break the case, even the federal connection—*when* the time is right. Hell, they'll probably make you chief of police." Lord took a step back. "But you have to tell me everything, and I mean everything."

"Give me something first," Sal said noncommittally. "Just so I know you're on the up and up. And when you do, I'll decide if I want to move forward."

Preston Lord gnawed on the inside of his cheek before nodding. "In the war, Neil Reuter was, perhaps, our most highly-decorated intelligence officer."

"That's not what I heard," Sal said. He dropped his cigarette onto the damp sidewalk and ground it under his foot. "I actually spoke to *your* people and they said he was just an above-average officer. There was nothing about him being superior."

Lord smiled knowingly. "You think records can't be altered?"

"Give me something else."

"Reuter was a shadow...a natural at the intelligence game. In the war, he'd go far behind the enemy lines and assimilate. He'd impersonate German soldiers and sabotage their equipment or even assassinate their officers."

Eyes narrowed, Sal listened intently. "What was his actual job?"

"At first he was simply an intelligence officer, but he was so good at getting to the nerve-center of the enemy, he eventually became a type of sapper, able to cripple the enemy without ever firing a shot. No one knew how he did it...that's why they called him the Pale Horse. He was a bit of a ghost. It was as if he was able to take on the very soul of an enemy sol—"

An alarm clanged in Sal's head. He halted Lord with a raised hand. "*What* did you just say he was known as?"

"Pale Horse. Why?"

"P…H," Sal whispered, adding a pause between the two initials as he stared through the mist toward the bay.

"I don't get the significance," Lord said, irritation in his voice.

"P-H," Sal breathed over and over. Finally, as Lord stared at him quizzically, Sal turned and walked across the street. When he reached his car, he turned back to Lord. "Let's get out of this rain and grab a bite. Whadya say?"

Lord shrugged.

"C'mon," Sal said. "Follow me…it's a short ride." He cranked the car, pulling up the street until Lord could get his Lincoln turned around. Though he was indeed hungry, Sal also wanted a few minutes to think about what he'd just learned.

Pale Horse!

The two cars drove away from Hillside, the intense mist swirling in the cars' wakes.

* * *

Thomas Lundren stood all alone, staring at the yellowish lights of his house in the distance. The rolling meadow dropped several meters between the airfield and his piece of land, putting him nearly on the same plane as his stone chimney. He thought about Greta, his wife who had passed away, and how she would scold him over what he was putting himself through.

"Why are you doing this?" she would ask, pleading with her tone rather than using a mass of strong words. All he would have had to do was look at her. One look was able to make a woman like Greta, a loving wife, his soul mate, understand. She would have given his hand a squeeze before nodding, resigning herself as she walked away, dealing with it through silence.

But Greta was gone, and all Thomas was left with was an aging body that seemed to be quickly failing. Time wasn't on his side. This was his final chance to follow his true calling—one last time. However, on a solvability scale of one to ten, this case was about a two, and the needle was edging downward, not up. If he didn't find something, and soon, he'd have to give it up.

It would be time to go home—go home and die.

Thomas had driven back to the farm from Nürnberg earlier, deciding to check on things and stay the night in his own bed. But that was only a convenience. The farm was fine, being tended by the closest neighbor. Thomas found his animals in fine shape. His primary reason for coming home was to visit the young man employed at the airfield, Antonio. He had been questioned already, but something about his answers didn't sit right with Thomas. There had been decided apprehension in his replies, especially when talking about the man who'd been found dead.

The officer who'd questioned Antonio, once Willi Kruger's identity had been learned, had the feeling Antonio somehow knew the deceased.

Earlier, before driving back here, Thomas had phoned Antonio, requesting an evening meeting. Antonio agreed, telling Thomas he first needed to go home to attend to his mother, an invalid. Despite the brief phone chat, Thomas could tell Antonio was nervous.

It was fully dark at the quiet airfield when Antonio finally arrived, pedaling a squeaky bicycle up the dirt road from the opposite direction of Thomas' home. The one exterior light on the shed showed Antonio's black hair damp with perspiration, his shirt sticking to his back. Antonio greeted Thomas, unlocking the shack and switching on the lone inside light. The boy was tense.

"Are you okay, son?"

Antonio jerked his head around, his bleary eyes wide with fear. Struggling to swallow, he nodded.

Thomas instructed him to sit. The career policeman pulled up a tall stool, sitting well above Antonio. "Son, after you were questioned last week, some other critical facts have come to light."

"They have?"

"Yes, they have," Thomas said in a steely tone, one that he'd not yet used with the affable young man. "And unless you come clean about everything you know, right now, I'm going to have to take you back to Nürnberg, to the main police station."

The young man's swarthy face contorted, twisting into a mask of agony as he covered it with both hands. "I'm sorry, sir. I never lied to you. I promise."

Thomas wanted to pat the kid on his shoulder, assuaging him. An excellent judge of character, Thomas had known Antonio was a good sort from the moment he'd met him. But this was a major case, and Thomas had to let Antonio taste the fear. Had to…

Let 'em sweat—the age-old rule.

After a gulf of time had passed, Thomas' voice was firm but soothing, like that of a favored uncle or a good judge. "Do yourself a favor, son, and tell me everything. If you do, there's an excellent chance you won't get into any trouble."

Give him a glimmer of hope.

Antonio took a chest-expanding breath. "I'll tell you everything."

"Let's hear it," Thomas replied with a frown. *Keep the pressure on.*

"Sir, I promise I never knew who bought the nighttime fuel from us. Never."

"The nighttime fuel, yes. Keep going."

Antonio pressed his hands backward through his thick wet hair, struggling to speak through his anxiety. "The former airfield custodian, Mister Brand, he died of a heart attack before I got the job. When I started, the commissioner explained the nighttime fuel to me and just told me to keep it going."

"Tell me the details of the nighttime fuel, son."

"Five or six times a year, I would come in and find an envelope of money under the door. The person who refueled during the night had a key to the lock on the fuel pump."

"Did you know the person or know anything about them?"

"The one who took the fuel at night?"

Thomas nodded.

"I was never here when they came."

"You didn't answer my question," Thomas snapped.

"No, sir. I *never* knew anyone who took the nighttime fuel."

"Do you think the dead man was the one who would buy the nighttime fuel from you?"

"I don't know," he replied, tears streaming down his cheeks. "But there was no money the morning of the killing, and no fuel had been taken."

"Okay, good." Thomas allowed Antonio a moment to gather himself. "Is there anything else you can think of?"

Antonio rotated his large eyes upward. "The commissioner told me something once."

"Tell me."

"He said the man who purchased the fuel was German, and not a nice person. He said if I ever happened to be here, to stay away from him and just let him have the fuel."

"He said he was German?"

"Yes."

"Are you sure?"

"Yes."

We're in Germany, so of course the buyer would be German. So, why would the commissioner make such a distinction unless the man taking the nighttime fuel didn't live here in Germany?

Thomas tugged on his whiskers. "Did the commissioner say anything else about him?"

"Never."

Thomas believed him. "Antonio, did you get a share of money from the night fuel sales?"

"Yes, sir. Whenever it happened, I would call the commissioner and he paid me a few extra reichsmarks."

"Was it always reichsmarks?"

He nodded. "Yes, sir. And I would log the gas as a regular fuel sale."

"How much over the normal price was the fuel?"

"It was three times the normal cost."

Thomas arched his eyebrows. *Three times the normal cost—only someone doing something illegal would pay such a price.* "Very good, son." Thomas asked Antonio a dozen more questions, satisfied that he knew nothing more. He removed his notepad, exultant that this could very well be the break he needed, especially once he talked to the man who had set this deal up—the commissioner.

"Antonio, I need to chat with the airfield commissioner. I think he might know the fuel buyer's identity."

Antonio was nervously chewing on a fingernail, his eyes averted.

"Who's the commissioner, Antonio?"

"He'll hurt me."

"Son, I can find out through district records."

Fresh tears welled in Antonio's eyes.

Thomas touched his shoulder. "I can approach him in such a way that he won't know you told me any of this. In fact, if you think you need protection, I can provide that, too."

"He already warned me against talking, sir," Antonio said in a fearful whisper.

"When?"

"Every day since the murder."

"Indeed?"

Antonio began to cry.

"Who is the commissioner?"

Antonio looked up at Thomas and shook his head.

"Tell me, son."

"It's Constable Sauer, sir."

Constable Sauer, the local law who Thomas had first run off with a pistol, then run off after the murder. A leaden blanket of defeat fell over Thomas, crushing him. He had only one enemy in the entire district of Nürnberger Land, and it was Constable Sauer. Thomas massaged his closed eyes with his thumb and forefinger, wondering how Sauer had managed to be named administrator of the tiny airfield.

"Please don't tell him I told you, sir."

"You can relax, Antonio," Thomas said, forcing a smile. "I have no interest in speaking with the constable."

Setting aside his disappointment, Thomas thought about the British money he'd found in Willi Kruger's pocket, combining it with what Sauer had told Antonio about the buyer. Thomas stood from the stool, rubbing his chin as he glanced at the map hanging in a dimly lit area on the wall. "Would an aircraft need to refuel if it had flown here from England?"

"England?"

"Yes."

Antonio stood. "Other than large airplanes, I think most would."

Thomas thought back, remembering the timeline on that early morning. A realization struck him. When he was making breakfast, he'd heard the chirp of the tires as the airplane landed. It wasn't another minute before he heard the gunshots. Assuming the aircraft had flown directly from England, and there was nothing to indicate to Thomas that it *hadn't*, it might have been low on fuel.

That's why the pilot landed. *Of course.*

Thomas couldn't believe he hadn't thought of this. He did a full circle, trying to contain his thoughts from spinning out of control. He focused on Antonio. "How long would it take to refuel a small airplane?"

Antonio opened his hands, his jaw slack. "That's hard to guess. Ours is a hand pump, so it depends on the operator and how much fuel they needed."

Thomas closed his eyes, struggling to remain calm. "Then just take a wild stab."

"Fifteen…twenty minutes."

Thomas' hand again rubbed his mouth and face, his whiskers scraping audibly under his fingernails. "Was any fuel used that morning? Was any fuel missing?"

Antonio shook his head. "Like I said, sir, there was no money left for me, and no fuel was missing. You can check the log if you like," he said, pointing to a clipboard hanging by the door.

Thomas felt it was better than a fifty-fifty chance that the men in that airplane had come here to refuel and something had gone wrong. And that meant, when he joined eyes with the man who was obviously struggling to pilot the airplane, the airplane was low on fuel.

His mind hearkened back to the air boss at the airfield in Zorneding. He told Thomas that anyone flying as low as that black airplane was—with the Alps looming ahead—was either looking for something or didn't know what they were doing.

Thomas would bet on the latter, especially after seeing the airplane do a ground loop.

He thanked Antonio, pumping the boy's hand before exiting the shack and starting back to his house.

"Wait! Herr Lundren, wait!"

Thomas stopped and turned. "Yes?"

"I'm not in trouble?" Antonio asked, his face a mask of confusion under the triangle of light.

"No, son, you're not," Thomas said with a smile. "In fact, I thank you for your help."

Thomas marched in the direction of his house, stepping confidently in the dark night, unworried about stepping into the old hidden well. His mind was already back in Nürnberg. A week earlier, Thomas' pilot and the Zorneding airfield employee, with the help of a book on modern aircraft, both confidently identified the airplane in question as a De Havilland Hornet Moth. But the one thing Thomas had paid little attention to was the range of the Hornet Moth.

The book was in his temporary locker at the police station, along with a handful of other items that had not helped him to this point. As excited as he was, Thomas knew he needed to rest. His coughing fit after his brisk walk confirmed it. He turned in after drinking some water and reciting his prayers. Tomorrow morning, he would drive back to the city in the hopes that the book would help him determine the range the Hornet Moth could have achieved on a single tank of fuel.

Chapter Thirty-One

IF A PERSON DIDN'T ALREADY KNOW about Grinelli's Trattoria in North Beach, they probably wouldn't have gone near the place. With one grimy window fronting Stockton Street, the restaurant looked more like a failing laundry than an eating establishment. But Sal, like many locals, knew all about it, and when his brain worked overtime, his hunger did as well. Grinelli's family-style lunch was easily the best deal in the Bay Area.

It was just past one in the afternoon. The two men sat at the round table in the back corner. Disgusted with himself and his gorging, Sal jerked the napkin from his collar and leaned back in the booth, pushing the last few bites of lasagna away. He loosened his belt and stared at Preston Lord.

"Okay, bud, I've told you everything I'm gonna tell you until you give me the goods."

Lord lifted Sal's cigarettes and Sal nodded. The Department of War man tapped one out and toyed with it in his narrow, delicate fingers. "I'm incredibly impressed that you learned as much as you did. You're a helluva detective."

Sal stared at him, silent. He was immune to false flattery, unless it was coming from the mouth of a beautiful woman—all bets were off, in that case.

Lord pointed the cigarette at Sal. "So why haven't you told anyone about all this?"

"Because I knew the feds would send in someone just like you to take over."

Lord's thin lips twisted into a smile. "As I said, you can have the glory, detective. You've actually uncovered a great deal of information we didn't even know."

"Like what?"

"Well," Lord said, placing his hand on Cleveland Mixton's journal, "these killings were never authorized. Neil's team began to take it upon themselves to defeat so-called enemies of the state. They began to think of themselves as crusaders."

"But you employed them."

"Yes, but not as assassins. Reuter and his men were supposed to be DOW undercover."

"What do you know about the victims in this journal?"

Lord lit the cigarette and shrugged. "All types. Killers, a few spies, several businessmen who authorized killings of their own in their quest for power…that type of stuff. Truly unsavory people." He motioned to the journal. "I've no doubt every single one in that diary fits the same bill." Lord dragged on the cigarette, cocking his head. "Give Reuter's team some credit. Like weeding a yard, they were doing American citizens a favor."

Sal defied his full stomach and leaned forward. "You're telling me you didn't authorize *any* of those killings?"

"That's precisely what I'm telling you," Lord replied crisply.

"If you had authorized those killings, would you admit it?"

Lord twisted his mouth into a grin again. "What do you think, detective?"

"I thought so." Sal settled back into the booth, quiet for a moment. "So the United States government is complicit with setting up and employing a team of assassins? That's insane…I don't care how revolting the targets are. It goes against the bedrock of freedom and justice our country was founded upon."

"Are you really so shocked, detective? Defending this country involves more than a powerful military. There are millions, and I mean many millions, of people who want to impose their will on us. Our freedoms and successes drive them mad, and they'll stop at nothing to bring it all to a halt." Lord dragged on the cigarette as he stared at Sal. "Is killing in the name of freedom too high a concept for you to grasp?"

Sal took the barb in stride, ignoring the question. He opened the journal to one of the killings that had involved Neil, the so-called "Pale Horse," on Sagaponack, out on Long Island. "James Kenneth Quinby, a guy that Neil Reuter allegedly killed. I found all sorts of information about this guy being a society member who made his money off of hundreds of patents. What's his story, and why was it personal to Reuter?"

"You're asking me to admit certain things," Lord said flatly.

"Then speak hypothetically. No admission."

Lord smiled as he placed the cigarette in the groove of a gleaming white ashtray. "Okay, detective, this is all hypothetical. Jimmy Quinby…yes. I'm hypothetically quite familiar with that one." He relaxed into the softness of the booth, looking away as he began to recall. "That dirty sonofabitch was the quintessential trust-fund scumbag. I grew up with a silverish spoon, detective, but Quinby took the proverbial cake. His inheritance was so big and so deep that he set up a research company, employing all manner of scientists doing nothing but searching for new technology two shifts a day, seven days a week. He was like Edison times ten."

"Something wrong with that?"

"No, detective, except that he took personal credit for each invention he patented."

"So you killed him for being a prosperous, glory-seeking asshole?"

Lord ground the nub of the cigarette in the ashtray. "*They* killed him for brazenly speaking to the Russians, to the Germans, and for attempting to contact the Japanese."

"Why was he doing that?"

Lord leaned close. "Quinby's company had made incredible advancements in a technology which uses radio waves to detect objects such as airplanes and even ships, much farther out than the eye can see. Others were on to it, too, but Quinby had the best technology. So, instead of selling it to his own country and making himself wealthier, he had to act like some half-ass spy from a Saturday matinee."

Sal ran his finger over the passage. "But this says it was personal for Neil Reuter. Why?"

"We're going to be in a war soon, detective. You, me, and everyone else in this great nation. That invention could save us or break us in the air, or at sea." Lord fingered the pack of cigarettes. "But Quinby got greedy and contacted our soon-to-be enemies. While I have great interest in finding Neil Reuter, there is no denying the man is a patriot. Anyone who betrays our country, like Quinby did, automatically becomes Reuter's enemy." Lord slid another cigarette from the pack. "And that's why I think Reuter has gone to Germany."

"Germany?"

"You realize I'm now giving you the meat of the story?"

Sal shrugged.

Pulling the journal to his side of the table, the Department of War man flipped to the latter portion Sal had shown him earlier, where Mixton outlined the group's desire to kill "H." Lord's index finger traced the passage. "See right here? 'H' stands for Hitler—Adolf Hitler."

Sal didn't follow world news very much, but he certainly knew who Adolf Hitler was, as well as his beliefs of Aryan dominance. And Sal, possessing the olive skin and dark hair of a true Greek, didn't much care for the fanatical Nazi leader.

"You think Reuter's gone to Germany to kill Hitler?"

Lord stood and pulled on his overcoat. "Most assuredly. I think he finished his business here, killed Lex Curran, and has gone to Germany with every intention of assassinating Hitler, possibly even as a martyr."

Sal grabbed the dangling belt of Lord's overcoat to prevent him from walking away. "And after killing all of these American citizens, why the hell would you *care* if he did that?"

"Why would I care if he killed Hitler?"

"Yeah."

"I like Hitler," Lord replied.

Sal screwed up his face. "You like Hitler?"

"Indeed."

"He's bat-shit crazy. He's violent and he's quickly becoming our enemy."

"He's the lesser of two evils, detective. Hitler in Germany, Stalin in Russia. Have you read about the purges in Russia, detective? Read the accounts. They'll make your skin crawl." He nodded as if he'd made some sort of decision. "As of now, we're pulling for Hitler. At least until Germany and Russia tear each other apart, at which time we'll go in and pick up all the pieces."

Sal frowned at the glee on Lord's face as he spoke about what would probably amount to millions of deaths. "But what about Hitler's beliefs? Doesn't he think people like me should be deported from Germany, or worse, because of my skin tone?"

Lord detached Sal's fingers from his belt. "We'll deal with little Adolf in due time. For now, we want him on the throne, doing our dirty work for us."

"Where are you going?"

"There's something in the car that you *need* to see. It'll demonstrate to you exactly what I'm talking about. After that, you're on your own."

Sal had not told Lord everything. In fact, all he admitted was his discovery of Reuter's past. He held back the part about Meghan Herman. Because Sal still didn't quite trust this Preston Lord fellow.

He watched the Department of War man walk away before digesting some of what he had heard. First, if Neil Reuter had indeed been running a killing team, there was no way in hell Lord and the DOW were going to allow Sal to maintain his investigation. Perhaps they would allow Sal the latitude to prove Neil killed Lex Curran, maybe even give him an award for what he had uncovered, but it seemed fanciful to think they would permit him to take the case and all the glory that would go with it.

Sal stopped thinking, squinting his eyes as he pondered Lord's solitary revelation.

Neil Reuter was planning to assassinate a world leader?

The reality hit Sal like a sledgehammer. If Lord really thought Neil Reuter had left the country to kill Adolf Hitler, and if the United States wanted Hitler to live, then that would mean Neil Reuter and his entire team were enemies of the state.

They would have to be killed.

Sal blinked as his mind lurched into high gear. This was extremely weighty knowledge—the type of intel that could get a small-time detective in big trouble. Concurrent to those thoughts, Sal heard the rumble of an engine and saw a streak of black through the grimy window. It was Preston Lord's Lincoln speeding away.

Sal's eyes searched the table. *The notebook...*

Just as Sal slid to the edge of the booth seat to hurry outside, Mama Grinelli, the proprietor and de facto hostess, arthritically shuffled over.

She was carrying a shiny black briefcase.

"Detective, your nice friend told me you left this in his car."

Sal's lips parted a split second before the solid-state timer triggered two pounds of Baratol high-explosive. Grinelli's Trattoria, the four employees (three of whom were named Grinelli,) Detective Sal Kalakis and two people in the pawnshop next door were all killed instantly. Even in the murky weather conditions, the flash from the blast was reportedly seen all the way across the bay in Sal's hometown of Oakland.

In an unrelated incident, and drawing little attention from the police due to the shocking death of one of their own, a spinster librarian named Eunice Gregory was found in her apartment several days later, multiple stab wounds in her chest. She had been beaten about the face, and there was also evidence of sexual assault in a deviant fashion. An only child with deceased parents, her funeral was so poorly attended the funeral parlor owner directed some of his employees to act as friends during the brief ceremony.

The Grinelli's explosion and the murder of Eunice Gregory were never solved.

Chapter Thirty-Two

THOMAS LUNDREN SAT IN A CORNER OFFICE OF the police station. The office had been vacated by a detective who had succumbed to a heart attack three months earlier. Resting before Thomas on the desk was the aircraft book. With it were a new map, a piece of yarn, and a sharpened pencil. The legend on the map displayed a distance ruler. Thomas pulled the string taut above the ruler, marking it in increments of one hundred kilometers. He made twenty tick marks, though he didn't think he would need all of them. He retrieved a green apple from his bag, slicing it as he stared at the aircraft book, the page open to display a color rendering of the De Havilland Hornet Moth.

Described as a civilian aircraft, suitable for recreational pilots and businessmen, the Hornet Moth was one of the affordable frontrunners in the new age of private aviation. Thomas read downward to the aircraft specifications, searching for the range. It was listed as 1,050 kilometers—maximum. That would represent ten-and-a-half tick marks on his string. He used his thumb to hold the string on London, knowing that might not be where the flight originated, but playing the odds since it was far and away England's most populous city. Thomas pulled the string taut, finding the tiny dot of Velden on the map. The distance was almost exactly 800 kilometers. While he wasn't a pilot, Thomas would imagine that the pilot of an aircraft with a maximum range of 1,050 meters would certainly want to refuel no later than 800 kilometers into his tank.

In his next supposition, Thomas assumed an airplane used a bit more fuel during takeoff than it would while cruising. Because it had endured two takeoffs, he subtracted fifty kilometers from the maximum range, giving the pilot two hundred kilometers to work with upon leaving Velden. Since the air chief in Zorneding had seen the airplane fly over, Thomas held the string on Velden and pulled it directly over Zorneding. His eyes followed it southward, stopping at what would represent the Hornet Moth's 1,000 kilometer range. The termination point was almost directly between the towns of Hausham and Miesbach—closer to Miesbach—just north of the political border with Austria.

And very close to the base of the Alps.

Using the pencil, Thomas circled Miesbach before standing and taking large bites of the sliced apple. As he chewed the delightfully tart fruit, he stood beside the window and stared out into the bright day, his gaze facing south. Somewhere, perhaps near Miesbach, the mysterious pilot had come back to earth.

Now all Thomas had to do was find him.

* * *

Montauk Army Air Corps Base's pilot lounge was small but comfortable. Girlie magazines were strewn about, mixed in with assorted newspapers and magazines such as *Popular Mechanics.* Preston Lord focused only on the girlie magazines—not because he was horny, but because he didn't want his mind occupied with anything more complicated than a picture. He'd taken the mother of all ass-chewings from Director Mayfield after informing him that he'd "cleaned up" the situation in San Francisco by "discharging the root of the problem." Mayfield had spewed like Krakatoa. Lord was unfazed—ass-chewings were nothing new to him.

He enjoyed cinnamon chewing gum, smacking it loudly as he sat on the sofa, lifting his eyes to the window. Since he'd been here, the sky had turned from sable to indigo; indigo to pink; pink to auburn; and finally, several hours before, auburn to baby blue. It was now nearly mid-morning, and just as he was about to find a phone to call Director Mayfield to ask where the hell his transportation was, he watched as a shiny silver Martin B-10 bomber glided in from the south, its wheels touching the ground with puffs of white smoke and a bark he couldn't hear through the thick glass. The airplane slowed, taxiing over several adjacent taxiways before stopping on the large tarmac just outside of the pilot's lounge.

Lord stood at the window watching as clumps of airmen and soldiers, unused to seeing this particular type of aircraft at Montauk, gathered at the fence line on the far side of the tarmac. Per Lord's rigid instructions, posted guards kept them at bay. After the aircraft's engines were silent, Lord opened the door, motioning the exiting crew of three to the pilot's lounge. When they reached him, he was staring at a major, a first lieutenant and a buck sergeant. Lord pointed at the major, an intelligent-looking fellow who stood about five-feet-seven in height.

"Major, I only want to talk to you. Tell your men to go find a cup of coffee somewhere else."

The major stopped, placing his hands on his hips and frowning. He wore a bomber jacket and, underneath it, the summer tans of an Army Air Corps officer. "I don't know who you are, pal. And I take my orders from officers, light colonel and above." His voice grew in tone and edginess as he spoke, and his eyes moved up and down Lord, no doubt drinking in the civilian clothes and Lord's youthful appearance. "So unless you've got some silver oak leaves in your pocket, I'll send my men wherever I want to send them, whenever I want to send them."

There's a bit of a Napoleon complex at play here, Lord thought with an inward smile. If he had the time to find Montauk's degenerates, Lord would lay five-to-one odds that the major drove a very large automobile. Unfortunately, though, there was no time. He pointed a rigid finger at the lieutenant and sergeant. "You two stay there." He motioned the pilot inside, removing the order from inside his coat. After unfolding it, he smacked it into the major's hand.

"Read."

The major pushed his garrison cap backward as he read, his eyes darting back and forth until he reached the line which Lord knew would draw a reaction. With alarm, the major looked up at Lord. "Are you crazy?"

Lord snatched the letter back from him. "Yes, I am. Now tell them to piss off. This is a job of the highest national security. I have complete authority. I'm briefing only you." Lord pushed the door open, hitching his head to the major.

Ten minutes later, the pilot sat opposite Lord, three maps spread out on the table before them. The major—his name was Clayton Paige, from Montana—leaned his head into his right hand, a cigarette perched in the same hand above his mussed brown hair. He appeared perplexed.

"What if the wind isn't right? The water legs will be stretching her range to the max."

"Then I guess we'll swim or die," Lord said without inflection. "But it's almost September. The eastbound winds should be picking up."

"Barely," the major grumbled. "This is a hare-brained scheme if I ever heard one. And there's a regular route that's already all laid out for Trans-Atlantic flight."

"I don't want the regular route—it's too long," Lord replied. "We fly my route."

The major snatched the far map. "Where will we land in England?"

Lord touched the map, west of London. "Oatlands Hill, right in the middle of bloody nowhere. They'll be expecting us. It's a bit more than four thousand miles, and we should average two hundred miles per hour groundspeed. With four quick stops we—"

"Quick stops?" Paige bawled. "That dog won't hunt."

"Damn right, *quick*. Land. Refuel. Go."

"We'll need maintenance. We'll need time to rest. Get food. And we may not have the parts we need in the event—"

"Negative. As long as that scrap-heap still flies, we keep moving."

Major Paige grew quiet and stared at Lord.

"So, twenty hours of flight time, and half-hour stops in Nova Scotia, Greenland, Iceland and then, if we can make it all the way, terminating at

Oatlands." Lord placed both palms flat on the map of the United Kingdom and looked up. "Well?"

Major Paige sucked on the last of his cigarette. He shook his head. "Insane. Absurd. Illogical. Ridiculous. If I were stupid enough to try this, I'd need to remove every single non-essential item to make us light." He stared out the window at his airplane, looking like he was working the numbers in his mind. Finally he nodded, turning back to Lord. "With some luck...serious luck...we might make it as long as nothing breaks."

Lord smiled thinly. "They're topping her off to the brim. I've had food and coffee placed aboard. I want to leave in fifteen minutes."

Paige shook his head. "That's way too soon. Need to brief my guys on the mission, get their thoughts, and take our time as we strip the excess gear."

Lord held his hand on the pilot's shoulder to prevent him from standing. "Your crew...that's three hundred and fifty, maybe four hundred pounds we'll be saving."

"What is?"

"Your crew."

Paige's brow dropped. "Come again?"

"They're staying here, getting a four-day furlough. They've already been whisked away, and will never, and I mean *never*, hear a word of this."

Paige wasn't breathing. His only bodily action for a period of twenty seconds was to blink twice. "You mean to tell me, you're wanting me to fly this without my crew?" His voice climbed to a yell as he spoke. "That's impossible!"

Lord's fake smile returned. "I can take the helm every now and then. Come on now, don't act like it's brain surgery or something. I'll simply hold the steering wheel, or stick...or whatever the hell it is... steady while you grab a bite or piss out the window." He stood and threw a ten-dollar bill at Paige. "Use the head if you need to. And there're cigarettes and other junk down at the canteen. We leave in fifteen, and if you breathe a word of this to anyone, I will have you shot—today—right here and now—for treason."

Major Clayton Paige picked up his garrison cap, molding it with his hands. "Let me see those orders again." He read them. Finally, with a resigned nod he walked into the hallway from the lounge's other door, disappearing in the direction of the canteen.

Twenty-three minutes later, leaving a thrift sale of heavy aircraft parts and equipment scattered on the tarmac, the fuel-laden, stripped-down Martin B-10 lumbered into the sky, its engines sipping fuel as Captain Paige applied only the power necessary to gradually climb away from Montauk.

* * *

As it turned out, twenty hours was an optimistic projection. Just before reaching the northwest coast of Iceland, the oil pressure on the starboard engine had dropped, indicated by the gauge and evidenced by the streaks of black on the cowling and wing. Fortunately for Preston Lord and Major Paige, they were enjoying favorable winds and didn't have far to go. With sweaty palms and a stub of a soaked Swisher Sweet clenched in his mouth, the major was able to baby the Martin onto the rumble-strip temporary airfield at Keflavik Naval Base.

Lord, wearing a captain's uniform, instructed Paige to keep his mouth shut if anyone were to ask him anything and, as it turned out, the only talking either of them had to do was with the maintenance supervisor. The oil line hadn't ruptured, but a small return line had simply disappeared altogether. The supervisor, a Navy master chief, insisted that they ground the aircraft. But after some of Lord's special monetary palm grease, and a story about two loose dames waiting on them in an English burg known as Barnard's Castle, the chief studied the other engine's return line. He disappeared on a battered BSA motorcycle, arriving back an hour later with an adequate handmade replacement.

They had already been several hours behind schedule when they landed in Iceland, following longer than expected stops on Nova Scotia and Greenland. Thus, by the time they were flying again, they were a grand total of five hours behind schedule. The last leg of the flight had been without drama until Major Paige began tapping the two fuel gauges, somewhere over the pastoral fields of central Britain. "Gettin' too low to press on. My map's showing another hundred miles and change. That's gonna be way too close to nut-cuttin' time. We have to put down for gas."

Lord was sitting in the co-pilot's seat, chewing his cinnamon gum and reading a Civil War book that compared the tactics of both sides. He didn't look up when he spoke. "Negative. This *is* nut-cutting time. We keep going. We press on to Oatlands Hill."

Paige bumped the yoke, making the aircraft shudder. "Look, pal, I don't give a shit what that sheet of toilet paper in your pocket says. Friggin' Roosevelt could have his wide ass in that same seat and I'd tell him the same damned thing. This is *my* bird. I'm signed for her, down to the last dink bolt, and I'm tellin' you we'll be lucky if we make it eighty more miles." He jerked the map off the center console and scanned it. "In other words, when we're up here in the atmosphere, what I say goes. And I say we're comin' down at the first airfield near this current heading."

Lord folded the page and closed the book. He lifted the flask from its perch behind the landing gear lever and swigged it, offering it to the major who refused. Then Lord said, "Major, this job that you're pulling for me goes so deep into the bowels of our national security that the president would finally…and thankfully…keel over if he were to know anything about it."

Obviously ignoring Lord, Paige stabbed the waxy map. "Bromyard will work. Only about twenty more miles, which, at our groundspeed…" he squinted, calculating, "oughta be about seven or eight minutes." He lifted up out of the seat, scanning the horizon under the high gray cloud cover before aiming a finger at their eleven o'clock. "And there it is." He turned to Lord. "Sorry pal, but I gotta put her down there and get some juice. We'll be back up in fifteen minutes."

Lord removed a sleek black Beretta 1923 pistol from the bag at his feet. He slid the chamber open halfway, making sure that nine-millimeter short round was indeed seated. It was. He lifted the pistol, aiming it at the major's forehead.

Major Paige grinned straight into the barrel's menacing eye. He pulled the sticky, unlit cigar from his mouth. "You ain't gonna shoot me no more than I'm gonna crawl out on the wing and start pissin' the gasoline we need."

"I'd like you to maintain heading and altitude, and listen to me."

"You got two minutes 'fore I put the gear down and descend. And while they're fueling us, you and me's gonna have us another type'a conversation…a real man's conversation."

Lord lowered the pistol to his knee, keeping it aimed at the Army flyer. "We cannot put down *anywhere* other than Oatlands because of the extreme secret nature of our mission. Once we land, *at Oatlands*, there will be an escort awaiting us. They will take you away and debrief you, post haste."

"You mean, assumin' we make it there."

"Yes. That is an assumption," Lord answered, he continued to aim the pistol while he swigged from the flask. "But no one can know that we're here. Do you hear me? No one. While England might be our ally, I cannot have her airmen seeing us land anyplace where we're not expected."

"There's U.S. bombers all over the place right now. Why would we be any different?"

Lord closed his eyes and massaged the bridge of his pointy nose with the fingers of his free hand. "Trust me, they would know."

"What if someone on the ground sees us flying right at this very moment?"

"I'm not concerned about that. I *am* concerned over where we land."

"So why all this secrecy? What's the hurry?"

"Mine is a suicide mission, some might say."

"It's gonna be a suicide mission if we don't start pickin' up a twenty knot tailwind, mister."

Lord didn't respond.

Paige glanced again at the airport before turning his head slowly back to Lord. The silence seemed to get to him. "What kinda suicide mission?"

"Tomorrow, major, I'm to oversee the assassination of Prime Minister Neville Chamberlain."

Major Paige seesawed the yoke three times, making the aircraft porpoise violently. He twisted his face into an incredulous mask. "You're gonna do what?"

Lord removed his finger from the trigger, resting it on the trigger guard. "You heard me, and it has to happen tomorrow morning. He's prepared to make a deal with Germany, with Hitler, that will effectively give the Nazis carte blanche into the remainder of continental Europe, and that's something we cannot have."

The gray airstrip at Bromyard disappeared underneath the left wing. Major Clayton Paige seemed to be having trouble swallowing. He motioned for the flask of Irish whiskey, turning it up for so long that Lord could hear the air bubbles rushing inside.

Paige wiped his mouth with his sleeve and told Lord to take the yoke. "Hold her nice and steady. Any movement will bleed speed."

"Like that stunt you just pulled," Lord muttered, still holding the Beretta in his right hand and taking the yoke in his left.

Paige flattened the map on his knees and jerked a flat instrument from his pocket. After measuring the distance and peering out of the side window several times, he pronounced the airfield at Oatlands Hill to be seventy miles away. "And we're running at about forty-five hundred feet AGL. If we conk out, I'll have to put her down on a road—or a field, if we're lucky." His voice fell low as he talked to himself. "If we can hold this altitude…and with us being so light our glidepath'll be about eight to one…theoretically, in no wind, we could glide the last six, seven, maybe even eight miles if I feather her along just right."

"Let's hope that won't be necessary," Lord said, having heard every word over the open intercom.

Major Paige edged the throttle backward, wincing as he adjusted the trim. When the altimeter began to creep downward, he made a clucking sound and continued to seek the proper settings. Seconds turned into many minutes. The two men didn't speak. Just as a light rain began to assault the windshield, Lord pointed to a tower at their two o'clock. "There's a marker for you. Where does that put us?"

As Paige went to the map, the aircraft shuddered as the starboard engine wheezed and sputtered. "Oh shit," muttered the major. "There she goes." He scanned the map, sliding his finger to the left. "We're about seven miles out."

"That's fine," Lord replied, unconcerned. "You said we could glide the last seven."

"Perfect world, Mister Lord. When you find a perfect world, make sure you let me know. That distance doesn't take into account vectoring for the runway. Plus our little tailwind, once our speed drops, will work against us.

And… this is the biggie…we need to pass the airport and come back, landing into the wi…*shit!*" He groaned as the other engine began to hitch and wheeze. Major Paige used his right hand to ease the throttles back as he began his descent. He rubbed the sweat from his chin, moving his head back and forth as he peered through the silver streaks of rain.

"The gas pickups are at the front of the tanks, by design. With any luck, a downward attitude might find us an extra half gallon in each tank."

Lord stood, leaning all the way forward as he scanned the horizon for the airport.

Paige jerked Lord's headphone from the jack. He held it up in front of him and yelled, "Go down to the forward gunner's area at the bay window and talk me in!"

Preston Lord was now officially nervous. The engines had coughed to life again, but by the time he reached the gunner's area, seated himself and found the jack, both engines had cut out once more. "Paige, can you hear me?"

Aside from the whisper of wind over the gunner's nose canopy, silence reigned.

"Paige!"

Obviously distracted, the major's voice cut like a surgeon's scalpel. "I'm busy up here. You talk. Where's the airport?"

From the snug and uncomfortable nose seat, Lord scanned the wet landscape in the distance. He guessed they had descended several thousand feet since the engines had quit, and they were low enough that he could clearly see the spots on the cattle in the fields below him. The rain had caused a light fog to emerge, making his viewing more difficult. After a minute of looking and yelling back and forth, he saw the long gray strip of asphalt slightly to his left. "Airport, at ten o'clock!"

Major Paige slowly banked the aircraft. "Tell me when I'm on heading."

"Right there, dead ahead!" Lord yelled back. "You see it?" He held his breath as the aircraft leveled. All he could hear was the constant air rushing over the bubble window he stared through. The same air that held them aloft was also fighting against them, trying to keep them from making it.

"Do you see it?" he screamed at Major Paige.

"Yeah," came the grunted reply. "No way I can land into the wind. We're going straight in, and I think we're still gonna come up short."

"Should I stay here?" Lord asked.

Paige chuckled into the headset. "Not unless you wanna die first."

Lord hustled back to the cockpit, standing behind the co-pilot's seat, peering through the low-profile windshield at the runway. They were at least a mile out and very low. It didn't seem they had a chance. If they came up too short, they would be in the trees.

"What can I do?" Lord yelled.

"Sit down and buckle in," Paige said, his voice eerily calm. "The die is cast, now. Just hang on for the ride. We're teetering just above stall speed."

Lord obeyed, plugging his headset into the console and watching the coming runway. Their aircraft was only a hundred feet above the treetops and the runway still seemed an eternal distance away.

"See those big round levers?" Paige asked, manipulating the yoke as he fought against the mushy low speed.

"These?"

"Can't look. They're big with round wheel-like rubber things on 'em."

"Got them," Lord answered, struggling to control his breathing.

"When I say 'down,' jerk 'em both down. *Not* too early, 'cause landin' gear is like a boat anchor. Wait for my call because I may decide to keep her clean and belly in. Got it?"

"I've got it."

"At least we won't have to worry about a fuel fire," Major Paige remarked.

"What's that?"

Paige ignored him, wincing as he pulled the yoke all the way into his stomach. Lord looked ahead, seeing the trees disappear underneath them, screeching as the underbelly of the Martin scratched the top limbs of the last ones. Lord alternated his view between Major Paige and the runway they weren't going to reach. He guessed they were seventy feet above the ground.

"Not yet. Not yet. Not yet," the major uttered, tugging the yoke and fighting the stall. When they were nearly in the grass he yelled, "Gear down!"

Lord jammed both levers down, hearing the landing gear as it moaned in an effort to lower itself before their flight ended. He looked out the window, seeing the green earth rushing up at them.

Major Paige again pulled the yoke all the way into his midsection and yelled, "Hang on!" The three red lights by the landing gear turned green the second the Martin Bomber struck the high grass two hundred feet shy of the runway. Fortunately for them, the engineers who built the airport had added a layer of packed gravel to each runoff at the end of the runway, and it provided enough of a supported surface to cause the Martin to bounce twice before it roughly skittered to a stop at the very end of the runway.

Everything was quiet other than a grating buzzer and the huffing breaths of the two government employees.

They made it.

Major Clayton Paige still held the yoke to his abdomen, as if there was more flying to be done. After a moment, he released it and flipped a switch, silencing the buzzer.

"All those thousands of miles and we came up a pitching niblick short of our goal," Paige laughed.

Lord lowered his head to the yoke, amazed he was still alive.

The major rubbed his hand down the control panel, patting it eventually, like he would a trusted pet. "I sure tore the shit outta your gear, darling. But you'll fly again." He turned to Lord. "Hope you can get me a letter explaining that." He then whispered "holy shit" at least thirty times as what they'd just done settled in.

Lord unbuckled his seat belt and stood, stretching before clapping the major on his shoulder. "You should get a medal for this, major. Thank you. Truly fine work. You're a helluva pilot."

"Luck always helps."

Lord ducked down, peering through the windshield at the black automobile racing down the center of the runway, straight at the Martin. He stepped backward.

"That your contact?" Paige asked, unbuckling his seatbelt.

No answer.

"Is that your guy?" Paige persisted. He turned to Lord when he didn't get an answer. The major's eyes widened upon seeing the Beretta again.

This time, the handgun was inches from his face.

Preston Lord shot Major Clayton Paige at point blank range, the bullet going in through the tip of his nose and terminating in his cerebellum. The major slumped between the seats. Lord put a cushion under his face to catch the blood before it fouled the controls.

"Thanks for the lift," Lord said quietly, patting the pilot on his upper arm. He stepped to the center of the aircraft and worked the lever to open the door. When he did, there was a youngish man in a gray overcoat, pointing a revolver at him. The man slumped and put the revolver away upon recognizing Lord.

"Is the airport secure?" Lord asked.

"It's completely deserted, sir. Has been for two years."

"Good. Call Harrison to get the body of the pilot out. Make this airplane spotless and repair it if need be. Have it flown to a busy military airfield after dark, one near London." Lord managed to light a cigarette in the mist and wind. "When I say spotless, I mean it. Then wait a full day and dump the pilot's body in an alley behind some rough pub row in the East End of London. Do it in such a way that the authorities won't be able to tell he'd been moved. Maybe drop him in a few feet of water." He offered a wry grin as he pondered the investigation. "Typical pilot. Cocky little bastard must have said the wrong thing to the wrong bloke."

"Yes, sir," the man replied. He stepped to the car, spending several minutes dictating instructions into a radio while Lord smoked and urinated in the grass.

"Done, sir," the man called out.

"Good," Lord answered, walking to the car and climbing into the back seat. He broke the seal on the waiting bottle of scotch and took a slug from the bottle. Then he melted into the plush seat and spoke with closed eyes. "Take me to the finest hotel in Mayfair. I need a day's worth of sleep before I get started."

You just pushed a man and aircraft to their limits in your hurry to get here, and now you're going to laze around in a hotel room for a full day?

As Lord chuckled indulgently, the Jaguar raced away from the sealed-off airport, turning east on the motorway.

Chapter Thirty-Three

IT WAS THE FIRST TIME NEIL DRANK COFFEE SINCE his accident. Gabi and her mother were working in the barn. Peter was in school. While Neil's pain had begun to subside, Frau Heinz had made it abundantly clear that he was to keep his "ass in the house" no matter what. So, after sleeping longer than he would have liked, Neil arose to find an empty house, and that's when he decided to brew a pot of coffee. The first cup was bitter and smelled akin to horse piss. But the second cup, especially after the caffeine went to work on him, brought back the potent liquid he'd started his days with for the past twenty years.

He sat at the small kitchen table, staring out over the sun-drenched lower fields as a sheepherder from the nearby community tended to his flock. Frau Heinz allowed the herder to use certain fields, depending on where each field was in the growing rotation.

There were only 18 days remaining before the deadline, before hundreds of children had a rendezvous with a ship in the Adriatic Sea. While his healing seemed to be progressing nicely, he was beginning to concern himself with the task ahead, and right now his mind fretted over how he might arrange for transport of the children out of Austria. Neil's line of thinking kept coming back to a train—a method of transport perfect for hundreds of people. The biggest challenge would be making sure the train could cross the Yugoslavian border unmolested. Certainly his contacts in Innsbruck would have some helpful ideas. After all, Jakey had done this many times before. Neil was hopeful he'd be ready to leave for Innsbruck next week. This would allow him a number of days to get the children to their destination.

Trying to distract his worried mind, he read some of the previous week's paper, *Der Stürmer*. Every single article lauded the National Socialist Party and their efforts. The newspaper was also hyper-critical of Jews and communists, while being heavily slanted against most other countries. Based on the unified tone, it was almost as if some propaganda minister had instructed the reporters on exactly what to write, and then scrutinized every word before going to print. In Neil's opinion, the slanted drivel made for utterly mind-numbing reading. He tossed the paper aside and straightened as Frau Heinz entered the house.

"You're sleeping better," she said, washing her hands.

"I want you to start waking me at dawn."

"Why? You should sleep so you can heal enough to get the hell out of my house."

He chuckled. "Wake me anyway."

Neil watched her as she stared out the window while toweling her hands. Afterward, without moving, she closed her eyes, taking several regulated breaths—a private moment. Neil had been a guest in the Heinz household for long enough to know when something was bothering her. He pushed the adjacent chair out with his leg. "Have a seat."

"No time. Need to fix a bite for everyone and get back to it."

"C'mon and have a seat," he said, using a tone he'd hardly used since the accident.

She turned to him, giving a resigned nod. Neil poured her a cup of coffee, twisting his chair to face her. "What's wrong, Hildie?"

She stared into the coffee and shook her head. "Nothing's wrong, just life."

"What about it?"

"Owning a farm, doing the job of two parents, having a grown daughter with a sharp tongue…things you wouldn't know about."

Neil sipped his coffee. "Educate me."

Her brown eyes were damp. "Some days I can take the weight. Things like my note at the bank, and the coming sale of wheat at the auction, and helping Peter with his schoolwork and those damned Hitler Youth obligations. Some days I can handle Gabi's incessant bitching, challenging me, and questioning of how I do things. I can do things like unclogging the water drain, and I can handle knowing I haven't had a partner in years and I'm all alone with my thoughts and feelings—some days I can take all of it." Her mouth twisted as the tears began to flow. "But other days, like today, it all just seems so black, and I wonder what the damned point is." Frau Heinz lost it, her body shuddering as she began to cry in earnest.

Unsure of what to do, Neil leaned over, wrapping an arm around her. Frau Heinz's cries went on and on. She sobbed into Neil's flannel shirt, years of frustration pouring out with each wail.

She pulled back after a few minutes, wiping her face and eyes with a kitchen towel. "Look at me. This isn't who I am, blubbering on like a schoolgirl." She smiled weakly, uncharacteristic embarrassment on her face.

"So what is it?"

"What's what?"

"Something set you off."

Another tremor passed through her. "No matter how tough a woman can be, and no matter the amount of tasks she can fulfill, there are certain tasks that only a husband…a *father*…can accomplish."

"I could imagine," Neil said, thinking of his own shortcomings since Emilee's murder. Despite how adept he was at certain things, there were many things only a woman could do well. He studied Frau Heinz. She was still troubled, as if by something in particular.

"What *exactly* are you referring to?"

"Peter didn't tell you?"

"Tell me what?"

Frau Heinz shook her head. "I figured he'd talked to you about it because he's dreading it so. And I don't trust that crooked little brigade commander, or whatever title they bestowed on him."

"Hildie, what exactly are you talking about?"

She stood, dumping the remainder of her coffee into the porcelain sink. "The Hitler Youth programs Peter has to attend…"

"Yeah?"

She walked to the table by the door. On it were two baskets with her personal correspondence, invoices, letters. Neil had never gone through any of it. She came back with a letter, removed it from the slit-top envelope and tossed it on the table. Emblazoned on the header were a bold swastika and assorted stamps and seals. Neil pinched the letter in both hands:

To Master Peter Heinz:

Congratulations, future leader! You are one of select Hitler Youth who have been chosen to attend the Grand Rally, 5.9.38, at the Imperial Party Congress Grounds in Nürnberg. The fact that you've been chosen to attend should be considered the highest of honors. Unless you possess a valid, verifiable excuse or infirmity, your attendance is required.

Your Brigade Commander will have additional details. We look forward to rallying with you in Nürnberg.

Blood and honor!

Most Sincerely,
Baldur von Schirach
Reichsjugendführer

Neil had read about the weeklong rally in the newspaper. Actually, other than the slanted stories about Czechoslovakia and its Sudetenland, the rally was the story that had dominated the headlines. He handed the letter back. "I take it you don't want him to go?"

She stared at the letter as if it were doused with poison. "Of course not. Don't you realize what goes on there?"

"Propaganda? Brainwashing of impressionable adolescents? Drinking? Smoking? Cursing?"

"Well, at least you're wise to the ways of the world." Frau Heinz massaged her temples and rested her head in her hands. "That maniac, our so-called blessed Führer, is promoting, and even *rewarding*, all young Aryan women who produce pure-blooded babies. He thinks we'll someday run out of bodies, which can only indicate he means to go to war."

"I agree." Neil thought back to his own research on the man. His mind changed gears. "Are you worried about Gabi becoming…you know?"

She lifted her head, frowning. "No. Not Gabi. Not at all. Gabi can take care of herself. It's Peter I'm worried about. That brigade commander of his is a twenty-year old snot from Hausham. His daddy is probably the richest man in the entire district." Frau Heinz grabbed Neil's sleeve. "There's talk that the party is bringing in tens of thousands of young women. That these boys are going to be used to try and impregnate every single one of them like…like…" She couldn't find the words to finish.

Neil arched his eyebrows. A Roman orgy was most likely the phrase she was searching for, and perhaps even the Romans would have blanched at something as sordid as this—if it were indeed true. A giant, state-funded orgy to impregnate the adolescent masses and create more *Lebensborn*.

And Neil thought he'd seen it all. He turned up the last drops of his cool coffee, an idea striking him.

"Alright, enough of this. Gotta get lunch made," Frau Heinz said as she began to stand. He stopped her.

"Hildie…what if I go with him?"

She clucked her tongue, dismissing the thought as she moved to stand again.

"Wait," he said, motioning her down again. "I'm completely serious."

"I can tell." She motioned to his side. "But you're in no shape to go, and besides, your accent would be a dead giveaway. You'd get arrested and then me and my family will be up shit creek with the gestapo."

"You're telling me you don't have anyone in this country who doesn't speak without an accent?" He paused, his eyes cutting to the side as he thought of who he might be. "I'm his uncle. I've been abroad in…in Canada…yes, Canada. And now I've returned to support the Reich."

She narrowed her eyes at him. And while she wasn't ready to allow it, he could see the relief begin to creep over her face. "I don't think it's a good idea. If you get caught…"

"Yes, you *do* think it's a good idea. It's quite evident in your eyes. And Hildie…I'm pretty capable at this type of thing. Trust me on that. I've been blending in for years."

Frau Heinz tried but was unable to contain her mirth.

"I was planning on leaving next week, anyway. So now I'll leave a day or two after we get back. This will give me a goal to work towards."

"Are you sure?"

"Does he have to go to the rally with this brigade commander?" Neil asked.

"No. Most of the boys are going with their fathers. They'll assemble as a brigade in Nürnberg."

"Good. Like I said, I'll be his uncle…from Austria, who's been abroad in Canada for many years."

"Austria?"

He winked at her. "I don't think you need to know any more than that."

Frau Heinz sat still for quite some time, her eyes off in the distance. Finally she placed her calloused hand over his. "Thank you."

He turned his hand over, squeezing hers. "It'll be fun."

"Tell me that after you get back."

Neil went into the bedroom, straightening his things. He found the saltwater-stained photo of Fern, Gregor Faust's granddaughter, propping it up by his comb so he would see her picture each morning.

Hang in there, Fern. I'm coming. And I *will* get you out.

* * *

On Saturday, Peter and Neil made a morning trip to see the brigade commander, a shifty punk in Neil's estimation. Together, they informed the young commander that Neil—Dieter Dremel, actually, Peter's uncle—would escort Peter and they would join the brigade at the parade grounds on Monday. Peter, beaming, sat in the passenger seat of the old Adler as they made the short trip back to the farm to pack the truck.

Then, on Sunday morning, Frau Heinz saddled the two men with enough food to feed an entire platoon of real soldiers for a week. In order to fashion a tent, Neil and Peter took tarps, ropes and implements from the barn. Gabi pitched in, placing a stack of blankets behind their seats that would later be made into their bedrolls. Frau Heinz gave Neil some final instructions, surprising him with a bear hug before she moved around the old converted flatbed Adler truck to embrace her son.

Gabi appeared from the other side of the vehicle. She put out her hand to shake Neil's and, as her mother was hugging Peter on the other side of the truck, she pulled Neil into an embrace, kissed him on the lips, and used her left hand to squeeze his rear end. Neil was wide-eyed as he pulled backward. She winked at him and disappeared into the house, sashaying her hips over the entire distance.

That was earlier, but Neil couldn't quite stop thinking about the kiss—and about Gabi.

And now that they were finally in Nürnberg, the quiet Heinz farmhouse seemed like a memory of nirvana to Neil. To say the area around the Imperial Grounds was a veritable zoo would have been an incredibly disparaging remark to zoological facilities the world over. All his life Neil had despised large crowds, especially when they became mob-like. Some of the people camped around the rim of the grounds had been there for weeks in anticipation of the big event. Poor sanitation ruled the day. Neil would have thought, after years of putting on the same event, that the moronic Nazi hierarchy would have had enough sense to know that a hundred thousand people in a confined area have the ability to create a sizeable amount of garbage and bodily waste.

But the hierarchy wasn't concerned with conditions. They wanted to whip these adolescents into a frenzy, and capture film of it for the world.

Fortunately, many of the assemblage were farmers, and makeshift sanitation and sewage areas had been designated at a low spot in the bottoms area of a shallow valley. Anyone caught urinating outside of the designated area risked a serious beating, as Neil witnessed within an hour of being there. Peter was clearly nervous over the crowd's pulsating tension, and Neil reassured him that, if they were to mind their own business and make no waves, they would be fine. Thankfully there was no sign or mention of the Nazi-sponsored orgy. As with many things, it turned out to be a rumor.

A passing horse-mounted guard of some sort stopped and gave Neil the third degree for not wearing any National Socialist insignia. Without ever speaking a word, Neil nodded apologetically after each of the guard's insults. Once the mounted ass moved on, Neil and Peter locked the truck and went on a quest for swastika-laden paraphernalia. They made their way across two teeming fields to the towering façade of the stadium where, on the outer edge, each district was represented with a check-in booth below the massive rear pillars.

Neil stood back and watched as young Peter registered, retrieving complimentary National Socialist armbands and hand flags. Neil chatted with another boy's father as he stood waiting, introducing himself as Dieter Dremel. The father and son were from Düsseldorf, in the north. An amiable fellow, the father eventually picked up on Neil's foreign accent and became quite excited when Neil told him he had lived for many years in Canada. When Peter returned, handing Neil his armband and flag, Neil told the man where they were parked and shook his hand. His newfound friendship might come in handy later.

Now donning the proper National Socialist attire, Neil and Peter set about building their base camp. The weather was comfortable but humid. Neil, thinking it might rain later, felt they should not waste time in erecting their shelter. They gathered wood from a pile of smashed apple crates, stacking the flat slats two high in an effort to raise their sleeping surface from the ground. Afterward, Neil showed Peter how to construct a sturdy shelter, pulling the guy wires tight at each of the four corners to give it strength against the rain and wind.

Once complete, the two men sat on the flatbed of the old Adler and ate their evening meal of salty pork, sourdough bread, and a jar of cooked green beans. The gentleman from Düsseldorf and his eleven-year-old son arrived just before sundown, carrying a wooden crate of American Coca-Cola, the familiar Coke logo tarnished by branded swastikas that still smelled of burnt wood.

"Where did you get those?" Peter asked, ogling the sugary liquid.

"They were handing them out up by the stadium," the other boy answered. "The man said they were compliments of Adolf Hitler, paid for from his personal bank account!"

Neil fought not to roll his eyes.

As the boys swilled cola after cola, Neil and the other gentleman stood by the truck, smoking and chatting. The clouds that Neil thought might bring rain broke just as the sun set majestically, the gloaming pink and purple on the western horizon. Neil learned that the man's name was Albert Wahler. He was a middle manager at a Düsseldorf steel factory. As dusk set in, Neil managed to move Wahler past his fascination with North American culture. Wahler glanced about conspiratorially and leaned close.

"You've heard the rumor, haven't you?"

"What rumor?" Neil asked, thinking about what Frau Heinz had told him about the mass impregnation of thousands of young women.

"The Führer will be here, *tomorrow.*" Wahler inhaled the last of his cigarette before flicking it underneath the truck. "He usually comes at the end of the rally but, this year, the rumor is that he is coming at the beginning, specifically to address the youth. *His* youth."

"That's sure to cause a commotion," Neil said flatly.

"It'll be a sight to see, that's for certain. When he came to Düsseldorf last year, women were fainting at the very sight of him."

"He's just a man," Neil said quickly, feeling his face tighten. "Takes a dump every morning just like the rest of us."

Wahler seemed apprehensive at such loose talk. "But he has done so *very* much in such little time. The economic miracle he has wrought is almost Biblical."

"I'm not ready to call it Biblical, Albert," Neil said, careful to keep his tone conversational. "His methods may work in the short term, but what about long-term? I've read about all of this sabre rattling over Czechoslovakia and the Sudetenland. And then I hear about Great Britain and France's misgivings with his positions and actions. I think he means to take us to war, and soon."

"I don't care for some of the things I've read, and some I have actually seen. However..." Wahler paused, seemingly gathering his words. "Now I have a job, a good one. My three children have bountiful food. My wife has hot water to cook and clean with and my family has shelter and clothing. No one can argue this. The times are good."

"Good for *some.*"

"Well, I have to think of my own family."

Neil nodded, understanding the man's position. "That makes sense, but why does he insist on taking more and more land?"

Again, Wahler appeared shaken by even having to ponder such things. He swallowed thickly as he moved close to speak. "The Sudetenland will be the very last. Hitler's one aim was to unite all the Germanic-speaking people. Once he completes the annexation, his goals will be accomplished."

"Hmmm," Neil mused. He pinched off his cigarette before dropping the nub in one of the growing number of empty Coke bottles. "For our sake, I hope so. If he'll stop at that, and remain peaceful, we may have a chance to flourish."

Wahler's tone was not one of pride or indignation. He appeared to have great respect for "Dieter Dremel" and his opinion. So the following question seemed genuine. "And if he persists?"

Neil shook his head, thinking for a moment. "From all I can tell, the military he has built is impressive. Very impressive. But twenty years removed from the war, I'm not so sure the world is ready for *us* to be a conquering Germany."

"And the Americans? What is their attitude on this? We hear…of course…that they support our actions, that they're our ally. But you having lived in Canada, you must have heard the truth, if it's otherwise."

Neil chewed on the inside of his lip. "As best I can tell, the Americans are sitting on the sidelines right now, but I don't think they're at all supportive of us. However, if Hitler stops at the Germanic lands, and continues to aid the world economy through Germany's own growth, I would imagine things will settle down."

"Do you think they will intervene if he doesn't stop?"

"Almost certainly." Neil eyed Albert Wahler. "If Hitler doesn't stop…if he keeps going…if he goes for France or Great Britain, then our greatest hope is for a patriotic German to kill him in the name of Germany."

Wahler's mouth fell open. He glanced around before leaning close. "I know you've been away for some time, and I like you Dieter…I really do. But, please…for your sake…and mine…and my son's…please *never* say such a thing around us again."

Wahler began to walk to his son.

"Wait," Neil called out. "Come back. I'll be careful about what I say."

"I can't risk being party to such talk," Wahler hissed.

"I'm sorry. I won't do it again."

"Please don't."

"You're scared of the Nazis, aren't you?" Neil asked.

"My God, man," Wahler said. "You must have been away most of your life. One doesn't talk of such things."

"I'm sorry if I've made you uncomfortable. I'm still learning."

"Fine, but can we please talk about something else?"

The men took the conversation to brighter areas and, after the boys had drunk four colas each, they built a fire and sat around it until nearly midnight.

Neil's side ached from all the activity, but that night, as he laid his head down on his bedroll, he had to admit that the day had been a unique adventure. He truly felt better for meeting Albert Wahler and his son and, most of all, Neil had enjoyed his father-like time with Peter.

But tomorrow, as Neil silently pondered, it would be time to get back to work. He had a feeling that this event might present a few unique opportunities.

Neil's final thoughts before sleep claimed him were of Gabi Heinz, and the kiss.

And he slept well.

Chapter Thirty-Four

FROM THE TIME THEY OPENED THEIR EYES to the first golden rays of late summer sunshine, the electricity in the air on Monday made the entire area around the Imperial Grounds buzz with rampant anticipation. The rumor of Hitler's possible appearance was now openly and incessantly talked about. It even put a kick in Neil's step—for a completely different set of reasons.

After a cold breakfast of day-old bread and canned nectarines, Peter donned his Hitler Youth uniform, looking as if he might be sick at any moment. While Neil despised the Nazi youth movement, he couldn't admit such a thing to Peter. He certainly didn't want Peter to have a bad day, so he assisted his young friend in making his uniform perfect, adjusting Peter's straps and helping him spit-shine his boots to a mirror gloss. After insisting Peter brush his teeth, scrub his face and comb his hair, Neil straightened the young man's sash before stepping back and nodding.

"You look like a future colonel."

Peter dipped his head. His cheek twitched. He seemed to be on the verge of crying.

"You okay?" Neil asked, resting his hand on Peter's shoulder.

"I'd rather stay here with you."

Neil lifted Peter's chin. He eyed the young man sternly, making his voice match. "You're a young man now, Peter. You'll learn that, as we get older, we often have to do things we don't like."

"*Shit* we don't like," Peter said.

Neil nodded. "Yes, Peter…shit. But shit or not, the best thing to do is to do it, and do it *well*. Do you understand?"

"Not really."

"You grow whenever you can, wherever you can. Then, when you're old enough, *you* will have the clout and the influence to make a difference. And once you're to that age, you do everything you can to make that difference. Does that make sense?"

"Yes, sir."

"Have you ever heard of Abraham Lincoln?"

Peter shook his head.

"He was an American president. He said, 'Whatever you are, be a *good* one.'"

Peter took a deep breath and nodded.

"When you're done, I'll be right here waiting on you." Neil squeezed Peter's shoulder.

Peter's brigade commander came by shortly after and collected him for drill and ceremony practice, informing the parents that their boys would not be back until nightfall. Peter stared apprehensively at Neil, but Neil pumped his fists in a "be tough" fashion, telling him to remember what Abe Lincoln said. As Peter fell into ranks with the others from his brigade, Neil shadowed them at a distance. They marched in a giant column to an enormous field on the far side of the Imperial Stadium. Neil found a hill a full kilometer away. What he witnessed from the vantage point, the unbelievable scale of it, left him staggered.

The field was as long as an aircraft runway. It had been roped off and guarded to prevent it from being disturbed by the campers, meaning, unlike the trampled campground, the parade field was still covered in brilliant green grass. The Hitler Youth brigades linked together with remarkable precision, dress-right-dress, in a formation at least a mile long and wide. Neil narrowed his eyes, counting five hundred youth in one section. He used his index finger to count the sections before doing the multiplication. Once finished, he was so stunned by his product that he did the calculation again.

There were at least 75,000 Hitler Youth on the parade field.

Neil did his best to get over his shock so he could listen to the voice booming over the loud speaker. After several mundane announcements, a uniformed man approached the microphone, smoothing his hair before donning military headgear. He yelled the command of attention. Every one of the thousands of scarlet flags whipped through the air, standing straight up and down. As if on cue, a strong wind blew from the east, whipping each of the flags in unison. Never in Neil's life had he seen such precise, singular iconography. The swastika was everywhere, stark and bold. The German eagle was the secondary symbol, virile and strong. The panoramic result was breathtaking.

And scary.

Neil smoked a cigarette as other fathers and guardians joined him up on the vantage point. The man on the speaker was a high-ranking military leader of some sort. Though it was tough to hear everything he was saying due to the distortion from the speakers, Neil could tell that the gist of the oratory was preparing this massive assemblage for the arrival of *der Führer*. The leader kept referring to Hitler as "our most special guest," and said he was expected sometime in the early afternoon.

Neil left the hill and walked to the far side of the oval stadium, where the military presence was located. Each of the staff vehicles was adorned with more Nazi flags, as well as insignia identifying the importance of the man who rode inside. At the head of the column was a sleek black Mercedes. On the front bumper was a flag, snapping in the breeze, marked with a different kind of insignia. Neil recognized the insignia as that of the few elite *Reichsleiters*. Other than the Führer himself, Reichsleiter was the highest Nazi rank in all of Germany and included such officials as Goebbels and Himmler. The insignia was a dual oak leaf cluster over a scarlet red background. The driver, who Neil identified as a senior SS NCO in his early thirties, leaned against the front bumper, smoking a cigarette and cajoling a teenage girl who'd tried to pass by with a basket of food.

Neil concealed his interest by pretending to view an adjacent display, a schematic demonstrating the Imperial Stadium and each day's events. He stood in front of it while he watched the driver break discipline with his libidinous actions. Using what had to be his most persuasive tone, the driver was trying his best to charm the young woman to take a walk in the woods with him so he could teach her the "true meaning of life." As the driver preoccupied himself with his coaxing, Neil ambled past the Mercedes in a casual manner, spying a handsome briefcase in the center of the back seat. The vehicle was locked. The teenage girl, appearing quite scared, managed to disentangle herself and scurry away just as Neil passed. The driver, his face flushed, turned to the driver at the next car.

"Dumb little slut doesn't know what she needs."

"So teach her," the other driver said.

"She'll be back. Betcha. She wants me."

Neil glared at the Reichsleiter driver for a moment before disappearing into the tent city on the south end of the Imperial Stadium.

* * *

The 75,000-plus Hitler Youth had been inside the gaping mouth of the stadium, waiting in complete and obedient silence for well over an hour—sheer misery for anyone, and especially for adolescent boys. Earlier, at high noon, they had marched in wide columns to their pre-assigned locations, singing cadences in unison, their voices echoing through the buildings and monuments. Like every other parent or guardian in the area, Neil had stood in a line at what was known as the Great Road, watching the boys as they performed their precision maneuvers while flooding into the colossal, horseshoe arena. He observed the numerous cameras, shooting the formations as the unit directors shouted to the operators to focus only on those *Jungvolk* with distinct Aryan features. Neil waited until he spotted Peter's brigade guidon, peering through the masses until he saw the boy. And there he was, almost squarely in the middle, marching in step and singing his cadence as he had been taught—and was required—to do.

Once Peter passed, Neil walked back to the truck and retrieved his dirty undershirt from the day before, ripping it and stuffing a third of it into his pocket. He hustled away from the truck and scoured the campsites until he found what he needed, a book held by what must have been someone's grandfather. The man was asleep, snoring away on a blanket, his skin bright pink from the early autumn sun. Beside him was a pile of beer bottles, and clutched over his midsection was the book. Neil tapped the man's bare foot, waiting until he lifted his head and shaded his eyes.

"May I use a blank page from your book?" Neil asked.

The man blinked a number of times, seemingly confused as he clawed from under his alcohol-induced slumber. Without a word, he handed Neil the book. Neil flipped it open, finding a blank page at the very back of the book and ripping it out. He tossed the book back to the befuddled man and walked away.

Next, Neil searched for a pencil. He had an ink pen in the truck, but in order to make the note genuine he needed a pencil. After considerable searching, he snatched one from the dashboard of a car parked not too far from the Heinz truck.

The Hitler Youth had now been situated in the stadium for over ninety minutes. Thankfully, they were no longer silent. Now they were replying en masse to the various charges from the latest dignitary on the microphone. Neil walked back to the southwestern end of the stadium, at the Great Road, seeing the undisciplined SS driver of the Reichsleiter's Mercedes, right where he had left him. From a great distance, he watched as the man occasionally nipped from a flask. Satisfied, Neil turned and walked southeast until he arrived at the railroad tracks, following them into a shallow valley. It was the perfect spot for a naughty rendezvous and quite some distance away.

Up the opposite hill was a row of homes, the closest ones to the Nazi parade grounds. To his left was a ravine with a creek, thick with brambles, and above the creek the railroad tracks. To his right was a long, thick stretch of overgrown forest. He did a full circle, satisfied that no one was nearby. Neil hung the large scrap of his T-shirt from a tree limb just outside of a copse of conifers before heading back to the stadium. He timed the walk; it took three minutes each way.

Neil went back to the Heinz's Adler truck and produced the smaller scrap from the T-shirt. He tied the scrap to a string and used a stick to shove the scrap into the neck of the gasoline receptacle on the old Adler. He pushed the stick all the way down before using the string to pull it back out. Most of the rag was now soaked in gasoline. Neil wrapped the rag over itself so the gas would distribute through the entire scrap of cloth.

After washing his hands twice under their jug of water, Neil wrote a note, short and sweet, on the book paper with the pencil. He labored to create a juvenile female's handwriting. The message was quite clear, and Neil couldn't suppress a grin as he folded it over on itself three times. From the bottom of his flannel shirt, Neil yanked a piece of red thread, tying the note in a dainty bow. And then he waited.

The charges and replies had ceased coming from inside the stadium. The only sound that emanated was the same voice over the loudspeaker, instructing the formations to remain still, and to wait patiently for their special guest. The voice, quite unapologetically, informed the masses that the guest would arrive when he was ready, and that their unyielding endurance and quiet patience signified manly discipline. Neil recalled his days in the Army, standing stone-still in formation. It was no picnic. And on this day, to make matters worse, the temperature was quite warm, the sun beating down as if it were July.

Neil searched the toolbox on the Adler. From the wooden split rails on the sides of the flatbed, he removed a foot-long section of flat steel bar. Using a file from the toolbox, he smoothed the edges of the steel and cut a hook into the end. Neil locked the passenger door of the Adler, sliding the bar down between the window seal. After a minute of moving it around, he found the catch, pulling upward and watching as the door unlocked. Just like back in the States.

Shortly after two o'clock, a murmur went through the campground. Neil heard the horns of a distant band. He then began to see people scurrying from the campground in the direction of the Great Road, yelling "Heil" with their right arms raised, offering the Nazi salute.

The scene was frenetic, the electricity palpable.

Adolf Hitler had arrived.

Neil gathered his items: the note, the steel bar, the gas-soaked rag. He wrapped the rag in waxy sandwich paper and moved with the crowd. Because thousands had rushed from the campground area, the eastern edge of the road was ten deep in family members trying to glimpse the man who had titled himself their Führer, meaning, among similar definitions, *person in charge*. Hitler had used the name long before his meteoric rise to power, touting his Reich as a coming thousand-year epoch—the longest reign in recorded world history.

Neil didn't give Hitler's reign ten more years. Someone, or some people, would end it. They had to.

Hurrying around the tail end of the vehicle column, Neil arrived on the western side of the Great Road. There was a crowd there, too, but it was only a few deep. He was able to push himself to the human barrier of Hitler's own bodyguard regiment, known as *Leibstandarte*. Before Neil allowed himself to scan the crowd for Hitler, he first studied the bodyguards.

Several years before, when he and his team had yearned to assassinate the emerging Austrian madman, Neil read various intelligence reports about these Leibstandarte. He learned that they had been chosen, not for their skill, but rather for their size and looks. Each man possessed a chiseled face and light-colored eyes. Most had blond or light brown hair, and all were well over six feet tall. Neil studied their moves as Hitler presumably remained in the center automobile. The Leibstandarte surrounded it, jamming the crowd backward with their billy sticks.

Neil narrowed his eyes as he focused on one in particular, herding a large number of women backward. He used his baton as a barrier, pressing backward, but with his free left hand he took advantage of the frenzy, copping cheap grabs of various female body parts. Neil shook his head. Hitler was using thugs for protection, not professionals.

He turned, scanning the nearby area. There were two giant towers, adorned with enormous Nazi flags, signifying the main entrance that led to Zeppelin Field and the grandstand from where the Führer would soon speak. There was no one guarding the base of the towers, and the height was no less than eighty feet. Any assassin worth his salt could be perched at the top, concealed by the popping scarlet flags, aiming an accurate rifle at Adolf Hitler's swollen head. It would be a suicide mission, no doubt, but it could be done.

Leaving the world a better place…

Neil refocused on his current task. Hitler was out of his car now, snapping off Nazi salutes and smiling at the pulsating crowd. As Neil knew from film reels, Hitler was like a seasoned stage actor, his gesticulations incredibly pronounced for greater effect. He was shorter than Neil might have imagined, perhaps an inch or two below an average man's height. From the other autos, important-looking Nazi officers emerged, falling into place behind their Führer. Neil couldn't believe his eyes with what followed. Out of a blackened panel truck at the tail end of the convoy, four soldiers removed two Bengal tigers, the great cats' muscles rippling against the leather restraints as they roared at the frenzied onlookers.

It was clear to Neil that everything about this "world leader" was carefully, meticulously choreographed. The late entrance. The imposing, good-looking bodyguards. The surrounding, overabundant Nazi iconography. And even the two Bengal tigers. This little Austrian, Adolf Hitler, was a megalomaniac, a true lunatic and a narcissist to boot. He'd taken a downtrodden, starving people and given them abundant food and a purpose. A situation not unlike throwing gasoline on a smoldering fire. And while he had no time to concern himself with it right now, Neil knew that Adolf Hitler was no simple extremist.

And as Hitler strode toward the Zeppelin Field, accepting flowers and blown kisses from his adoring masses, Neil turned and headed back to where the officials' cars were parked. He had a "date" with the horny chauffeur of the sleek black Mercedes.

Chapter Thirty-Five

DIDIER VON HERBORN EXAMINED HIS MUD-CAKED boots, thoroughly pissed off that he had to stand watch over the car in this thick, foul sludge, which was probably created by human excrement. When he had first been bestowed the "honour" of being a chauffeur to a Reichsleiter, Didier naively believed the job would be loaded with bountiful moments of glitz and glam. Exotic nights spent in places like Berlin and Munich, bedding skinny women with insatiable appetites for sex and liquor. Important meetings with Himmler and the Führer himself, when each man might even turn to Didier for his sage, real man's advice.

"Didier, we're collectively stumped and we value your brilliant mind...what would you do about the confounding currency situation in Danzig?"

Didier had also daydreamed that perhaps he would even be chosen by one of the senior party members to impregnate their daughter. He'd heard similar rumors and, after all, Didier possessed the traits of a perfect Aryan specimen.

His delusions couldn't have been farther from reality.

In one year on the job, almost to the day, all Didier had ever gotten from Hitler was a quick glance. And damn it, wouldn't you know, it had been during a private moment when Didier just happened to be removing a nagging booger from the tip of his perfectly shaped nose. How was he to have known Hitler was going to turn his way at that moment? Didier had only wanted to make certain that it wasn't hanging out grotesquely. So he'd scratched it out, horrified as Hitler turned to him and frowned, the way a parent might frown to his child in a church setting.

Didier now hated his job.

So, as the music and the roar from the stadium reached a fever pitch, it was a surprise to Didier to see the small child, a boy of no more than five, appear from the rows of cars to hand him a note tied in a red thread bow. As the boy sprinted away, Didier turned his attention to the note. He pulled the thread and allowed it to fall to the mud as he unfolded the paper, seeing the words scrawled by what looked like an adolescent hand.

Didier's immediate and urgent erection pressed against his tropical wool uniform trousers. The note was from the teenage girl he'd sweet-talked earlier. She'd had to hurry away but now wanted to meet him during all the commotion. She wanted to kiss him and then feel him on top of her, doing the pleasurable thing that some of her older girlfriends were now doing. She wanted her first time to be special, with a handsome, Aryan soldier such as himself.

Hervorragend!

Didier von Herborn struggled to breathe. The girl was waiting for him in the low area below the tracks, probably on a blanket with her skirt hiked up around her waist.

The roars from the stadium were now coming in rapid succession. After gathering himself, Didier scurried to the next car, screaming in the face of his junior NCO friend that the young tart had called for him, just as Didier had said she would.

"Cover for me," Didier panted. "Don't tell a soul I'm gone."

Pulling his tunic down to cover the jutting steel rod in his pants, Didier sprinted through the rows of cars in the direction of the rendezvous spot with the little *Schlampe* who was so hot-to-trot. He only hoped he could last longer than a few seconds. His last time—with a hooker in Frankfurt's red light district—had been a painfully succinct, crab-contracting disaster.

* * *

Neil stood on the edge of the lot where the Reichsleiter's car was parked. Stifling his laughter, he watched the chauffer hustle through the lot, covering his midsection, moving with great haste to get to the lower field for his sex-fueled rendezvous with the dirty-minded teenager. Neil shot a look at his watch, marking the time so he would know exactly how long he had.

The chauffer disappeared over the crest of the hill, having already been gone a full minute. Moving around the boundary of the lot, Neil made his way to one of the military transport vehicles, this one with a canvas top. The roars coming from inside the stadium were now deafening. "Heil" pulsated over and over, echoing through the thousands of vehicles in the shallow valley. Neil took the gasoline rag and wedged it under one of the ribs of the transport truck's canvas top. He folded some of the canvas over the rag, produced a box of matches, and lit the rag.

He hurried away, taking only thirty seconds to move all the way around the lot, close to the Mercedes he planned to enter.

Neil peered around the area, seeing four posted drivers, each of them staring the direction of the stadium, their mouths parted as they, too, were dumbfounded by the deafening roars emanating from what must have been the world's largest ever assemblage of adolescent boys. The music and chants quieted. An eerie silence descended over the parade grounds. Neil rotated his eyes to the truck. It was burning brightly.

From the stadium, someone introduced the savior to the German Empire, the founding father of the Thousand Year Reich, the Führer, *our Führer*...Adolf Hitler!

The next was the loudest roar yet—Neil actually felt the sound waves go through his body. His only problem was that each of the posted sentries had their backs to the flaming truck. He checked his watch. Four more minutes. The crowd quieted again. There was a long pause. Then, a voice.

Adolf.

The guards listened in awe, staring at the stadium as if they were absorbing the spoken voice of a supernatural being. Neil saw that the canvas was now fully aflame, and could be burned out in a matter of minutes. He timed a pause in Hitler's speech, ducking down and screaming the German word *"Feur!"* for fire.

The drivers heard him, because they repeated the word. Neil emerged from his spot to see them scurrying to the five-ton truck. One man sprinted in the direction of a tent, probably in search of water. The closest driver to the Reichsleiter's car hurried to the burning truck, putting Neil in motion.

Neil rushed to the Mercedes, crouching down as he checked the doors. Predictably, they were all locked. Whipping the freshly-filed steel bar from his trousers, he wedged it between the felt window seal and the glass, feeling for the lock catch. This time it only took him ten seconds. He replaced the bar and opened the door, reaching backward to unlock the back door. After diving inside, he glanced at the men trying to beat back the truck's dying flames with quilts.

The Mercedes smelled new, adorned with cream leather seats and black carpet. Neil knelt on the seat with his shoes in the air so he wouldn't leave any footprints. He snapped open the briefcase and thumbed through a stack of papers, none of which seemed to hold any value. He opened the front pocket of the briefcase, feeling his heart lurch when he noticed a thin, passport-size leather book. Following another quick look out the window, he studied the identification. It was owned by a man named Baldur von Schirach. The document was adorned at the top by the typical German eagle, and stamped in various places in red and black ink. But true to what Neil had hoped from the insignia on the fender, at the bottom of the document, in old Germanic typeface, was the word "Reichsleiter." Neil clearly remembered from his research that only fifteen or so Reichsleiters existed, each of them reporting directly to Adolf Hitler himself. And next to the title, the last name scrawled legibly, was Hitler's signature.

Neil might as well have found a gushing oil well.

He tucked the identification into his pocket, replacing the briefcase just as he had found it. After a glance at his watch, showing that he was almost out of time, Neil eased out of the car and shut the door. The fire was now out, each of the drivers standing around the smoldering struts of the once covered truck, blaming one another for the responsibility of the vicious ass-chewing they knew they would soon receive. Neil hunched low, backing away from the area until he had cleared the cars and trucks, and as he spun around he was surprised to find himself staring directly into the face of the chauffeur he had deliberately misled. The man's cheeks were florid. He stared Neil up and down before turning his eyes to the smoking truck.

"What the hell were you doing in the official parking area?" he roared, poking Neil's chest in the tender area.

Doing his best not to wince, Neil glanced at the burned truck, his mind racing. A thought came to him. He hardened his face and voice as he turned back around. "Say, are you the one that my little Nicole is after?"

"What?"

"You heard me!" Neil snapped. "I don't care who you drive for. Are you the sweet-talking sonofabitch my Nicole wrote the note to? The one who made the filthy suggestions that inflamed her?"

The SS driver narrowed his eyes, cocking his head. "*Your* Nicole?"

"Yes, dammit! She's my daughter." Neil placed his hands on his hips in a defiant pose. "We live beyond the railroad tracks over there, and my wife heard her telling her younger sister about a handsome SS man she was meeting to do all sorts of untold things with. Sick, beyond her years, sexual things!"

The indignation disappeared from the driver's face instantly. He poked his lips out and shook his head. "No, that wasn't me."

Neil did a full circle, his eyes searching. "Well, we spoiled her little rendezvous, but then she got away from us and we think she's up here looking for the man. She's like a bitch in heat for him. If I find her *or* that bastard…"

The driver was momentarily stunned before a smile creased his face. He patted Neil's back, now speaking affably as he, too, scanned the area. "Believe me, I will keep a close lookout for your Nicole."

"Make sure you do. She's up here somewhere. Send her home."

"Have no fear."

Neil began to walk away, closing his eyes in relief.

"Sir," the driver called out.

Neil froze. *Oh shit.* He slowly turned around.

The SS cocked his head. "Sir, what is your accent? It sounds strange."

"I'm Austrian by birth, but we moved to Canada after the Great War. We came back to raise our children in the Reich." Neil popped his right hand straight out, giving the Nazi salute. "Heil, Hitler!"

The soldier returned the salute and quickly scurried away. Neil headed back to the campground with his prize identification in his pocket. Before he got too far, he glanced back to see the horny driver. He was ignoring the burned truck. Instead, Neil could see him, once again covering his tunic, scrambling all around the parking area, peering behind every vehicle, no doubt looking for Canadian-raised "Nicole," the teenager who was still hot-to-trot.

And from the stadium Neil could hear Hitler, fully-oiled as he was well into his deceitful speech.

* * *

It was late in the evening when Peter and Neil finally arrived at the farm. The old Adler truck creaked to a stop before Neil watched Frau Heinz emerge from the farmhouse and bear hug her son. Peter was quite conflicted after the rally, and understandably so. He was only an adolescent and adolescents are impressionable. It would be almost impossible for him not to have been swayed by the otherworldly pageantry he'd witnessed, and by the carefully scripted speeches he'd heard. Peter's brigade commander awarded each of the attendees a Hitler Youth Knife and scabbard. Peter had worn it home, on his belt, touching it occasionally.

After Frau Heinz shooed Peter inside, instructing him to brush his teeth and go straight to bed, she came around the truck to Neil. He was smoking a cigarette, his left hand massaging his aching side. Frau Heinz stared at him; the two shared a moment of silence.

"How's your side?" she finally asked.

"Sore but getting better."

"How was the rally?"

"Unimaginable," Neil answered truthfully. "And nothing inappropriate happened. You have my word."

She leaned her head back, viewing the stars in her relief. "Did Peter do well?"

"He was the model companion. You have a fine young man for a son."

"Thank you," she said. "Thank you for looking after him."

"No…thank you," Neil countered. "For saving me, hiding me, and letting me get to know each of you. I'll always be better for it." He glanced around. "Where's Gabi?"

Frau Heinz frowned. "I made her go to sleep. Have you decided when you'll leave?"

"Thursday." By waiting until Thursday, he'd have a few more days to heal. He'd also then have a full week to locate the hidden children, and doing so should be a snap with his newly acquired identification.

Surprising Neil, Frau Heinz hugged him before he went inside. Before he fell asleep, he tucked his prestigious Nazi identification away with the other forged papers.

Considering what the day had meant to Peter and his mother, and with his new treasure, Neil considered the trip a rousing success. With such a priceless identification, setting up transport for the children should be a breeze. He could now afford to relax just a bit—there was plenty of time remaining.

Or, so he thought.

Chapter Thirty-Six

SINCE MEETING WITH ANTONIO AT THE AIRFIELD, the Wilhelm Kruger murder investigation had ground to a halt. Twice Thomas had run into Gerhard Michener, and neither time did Michener even ask the identity of the deceased. He must have still been too nervous about Thomas' threat, afraid that if he were to push the old retiree too hard, Thomas would follow through and wreck his little empire with an enormous steel ball. On each occasion, Michener nodded upon hearing Thomas' intentionally bland update, clapping Thomas on the back, offering his unending support before he disappeared in a hurry.

Aside from Michener's lack of interest, it hadn't been easy to conceal the secret of the cadaver's identity from everyone else. Fortunately, Thomas still had the coroner on his side. Two other officials, both from the polizei in various departments, had requested the identity of the deceased. Deliberately misleading the officials, Thomas and the coroner informed them that they had yet to discover it—making the cadaver a "Max Mustermann", the German equivalent of a John Doe. The coroner helped Thomas, and further muddied the case, by asking if any men fitting the dead man's description had been reported as missing. Without a missing person, there was very little pressure to solve the case. Thomas thanked the heavens that Wilhelm Kruger's defection had been decades ago.

Wanting more on the victim, Thomas reached out to the Brits through an old associate at the consulate in Munich. Typically tight-lipped, especially in dealing with the growing threat of the Nazi regime, his associate's contact finally—and unofficially—acknowledged that Kruger had indeed defected during the Great War, working as an urban farmer in London over the balance of years. Kruger also had a rap sheet, mostly consisting of petty crimes, and was known to consort with an unsavory international crowd, primarily in the Shoreditch area of London. A day after Thomas' inquiry with the consulate, his contact called Thomas back to inform him that there was, indeed, a missing persons report filed in London for "Willi" Kruger. The report was filed by his Irish-born wife, two days after Thomas discovered the body. This was the final piece of evidence he sought, confirming for Thomas that the cadaver in his possession was indeed the man in question. But it still revealed nothing to him as to the why.

Why would a man who had worked so hard to leave Germany come back?

It was then that Thomas connected all of this with Antonio at the Velden airfield, and his revelation about the magically occurring midnight fuel purchases. Thomas concluded that the fatal trip had almost certainly not been Kruger's first trip back. If not for growing animosity between England and Germany, Thomas would have sought permission to go to London and interview the wife. Even though Gerhard Michener was giving Thomas a wide berth, Thomas had no illusions about the shitstorm that would occur if he were to make such a request. No, he would have to content himself with running the investigation from Germany.

After scouring what little information that remained of pilot Wilhelm Kruger's German military background, Thomas found nothing of pertinent interest, finally deciding that the only solution to this case was to focus on locating the shooter. Sometimes the easiest solution presents the most difficult problem, like the fastest trail to the top of the mountain. Yes, it's short, but it's also straight up. Thomas knew, at this point, that only the shooter could clear up the mystery. He also knew that, as the case grew colder, the likelihood of solving it began to decrease exponentially. And Thomas began to get that dreadful, familiar feeling that this one was going to go into the stack marked "unsolved." To Thomas, such a hollow denouement was unthinkable. This case was his last chance to live—he needed to create some sort of break.

And during the nearly three weeks Thomas had been in Nürnberg, sleeping four hours a night on a cot at one of the polizei's outpost stations in the quiet town of Roth, three canvass teams of two had been moving in a grid pattern southward, going door to door inside the triangle of space Thomas theorized the black airplane would have traveled. They reported in after each and every day, and after each and every day the report was the same: *nichts*.

After tightening the scope of the search to the much smaller area where Thomas now believed the De Havilland Hornet Moth had run out of fuel, they were still coming up zeroes. There was still an area left to be searched, but Thomas was beginning to darken about the prospects of finding the airplane, or the man in question.

Thomas reexamined Willi Kruger's cold purple body with his friend the coroner, probing every square inch of the deserter, looking for something, anything, which might give him an additional clue.

There were no more clues.

One day Thomas traveled by train, far north to the industrial city of Hannover, searching out Wilhelm's old school friends, ignoring the curious stares as he questioned them about a man they had long since forgotten. That trip yielded next to nothing. People remembered Willi

Kruger as a shrewd opportunist. The word "snake" was used several times, especially by the women.

After his unfruitful trip north, Thomas traveled south, this time by car, back to the airfield at Zorneding, interviewing the mop-headed air chief who had seen the alleged aircraft fly by during the morning of the murder. His story remained the same: strange aircraft; flying south—too low for a climb over the Alps. Thomas explained his theory on the fuel, and his research that had yielded the range of the Hornet Moth. The air chief agreed that, if Thomas' assumptions were correct, the airplane had likely been flying on fumes. But the air chief knew of no other airfields to the south, and had heard nothing of a crash or an emergency landing.

All roads led to nowhere.

Thomas scrutinized every shred of information in his possession, but his results were still the same. He had nothing other than a frosty cadaver, and now his case—his final case—was just as cold.

After breaking the seal on the bottle of English gin, Thomas filled his highball glass to the top, staring at the clear liquid for a full minute. It had been thirty years since he had ingested alcohol, back when he was burning the candle at both ends, using booze as a sleep aid. It would serve the same purpose tonight: the gin would relax him, and would also serve as a sort of private wake. A wake because, if the final few square kilometers yielded no evidence, his case was dead. A wake because, if no evidence turned up, it was time to turn the investigation over to the Office of Special Investigations.

And after he turned it over, Thomas knew what was in store for him.

Once the Nazis discovered that he knew the identity of the man as a known deserter—and had kept it hidden—they would demand he be punished. By his actions, he would be summarily judged as an enemy of the state, and would most likely be executed by firing squad.

Thomas coughed a quantity of blood into his fresh handkerchief.

And if the Nazis didn't kill him, whatever was going on inside his body surely would.

Curiously, he wasn't at all frightened; Thomas had long ago made his peace with death.

He took the highball into his hand and took a small sip. The pine needle-taste of the gin assaulted his senses as the innocuous-looking liquid seared his tongue and throat. Even though it had been thirty years, the taste was as familiar as something he might drink every day. He turned the highball up, gulping the remainder of the gin before smacking the heavy glass onto the bedside table. Thomas screwed the cap back on the bottle and extinguished the flame on the kerosene lantern. He slid into the tightly made bed and stared into the darkness.

He would tell Michener tomorrow, but not until the end of the day. The canvassing crews were finishing their search near the towns of Miesbach and Hausham, almost to the political border with annexed Austria. The plots of land there were large, and it would only take them another full day to speak to the residents and farmers on their list. And if, by the end of the day, they had again found nothing, Thomas vowed to walk into Gerhard Michener's office and tell him everything.

And accept his fate.

There in the dark, Thomas cursed himself for a fool, drinking liquor like some scorned teenager. He was very disappointed in himself, not because of the drinking—but because he couldn't crack the case.

As he pulled the gray wool blanket up over his shoulders, in the back closet of the station at Roth, Thomas murmured a word of prayer, on behalf of various nieces and nephews he hadn't spoken to in over twenty years. At the end of his prayer, he petitioned for something, unlike he had done since his childhood.

"Please give me a break in this case, Lord. I beg you. I want to perform just one more time. I want to be useful. Please…"

Thomas ended his prayer.

It took ten minutes for Thomas to feel the gin's full effect, giving him the gift of six hours of deep sleep.

* * *

Central London was dreary on Tuesday morning. The temperature was cool, the wind was blowing, and a growing mist swirled around the buildings, making umbrellas useless. Preston Lord jerked the napkin from the inside of his collar and pushed the grapefruit backward. He stood and took a final swig of his coffee as the waiter rushed over, holding his jacket and his overcoat for him. Lord despised hats, instead choosing to walk in the damp and press the water from his hair upon arrival. He dropped a few shillings on the white tablecloth of his hotel restaurant and shoved the front door open before the doorman could. He was on a mission, and this was the last day he would stand idly by while Scotland Yard fed him their same lines of bullshit.

Sure, his time in London had been rather enjoyable. He'd had some fun with a few of the girls, eaten decadent food, imbibed his share of their reddish ale, and even managed to take in two shows—but a week-and-a-half was enough. It wasn't that he hadn't tried. He'd worked every single angle, from putting word on the street through snitches, to going cell-to-cell with recently apprehended criminals. He'd interviewed the employees of the Queen Mary before she sailed again, and had even managed to have Reuter's picture run in the paper with the promise of a large reward. The tips that had trickled in had all been garbage.

Lord stuffed his hands deep in his pockets as he walked past the statues in Trafalgar Square. The mist had collected on his face and hair, running freely like tears he hadn't known since he was a boy. He'd certainly *caused* many a tear, but to Lord, crying was the ultimate sign of weakness—a completely impotent, craven emotion. After a quick right just past the station at Charing Cross, Lord walked down the grade of the mews, staring at the brown water of the Thames. At the lower road, he turned again, entering the side door of the ancient Scotland Yard building. The guard at the desk nodded as Lord paid him no heed. He walked through the building as if he owned it, eventually striding into the anteroom at the chief superintendent's office, throwing his overcoat at the secretary, ignoring her objections about his bursting in, which he did. Loudly.

Gregory Highsmith sat behind his desk, stirring his tea. He glanced up at Lord and frowned before turning his attention back to a sheaf of papers.

"I need you to throw *everything* into this search, and I want it done this morning," Lord demanded, stabbing a rigid finger into the ancient walnut desk.

The tinkling of the silver spoon inside the bone china was the only sound for half a minute. Highsmith tapped the spoon on the rim, placed it into the saucer, and took a sip. He settled himself back into the creaky chair and pursed his lips. "Well, we all have needs, don't we, Mister Lord?"

"You're going to stop dicking around and put some real heat to this," Lord said. "You know exactly who is backing me, and you know your damned hierarchy in their ivory tower is complicit as well. I haven't gone back up the chain to tell them I am getting *shit*, but I will, this morning, tell them that I am getting *shit*, unless you do some actual work, and tell your tepid investigators to stop feeding me *shit*."

Highsmith sipped his tea again and knitted his brow. He touched his phone. "Please, feel free to call anyone, because I'm still not quite sure what it is you're after. In fact, my man on the street tells me you seem to be more interested in cotching around, drinking French wine and shagging pay-by-the-hour harlots than you are finding your man."

Lord felt the flush in his cheeks. So they *had* followed him. Arrogant, sneaky, East End, poor-bred Cockneys. As he was taught years before in freshman debate, when wrong, do not engage. Change tack. He straightened and said, "The break has to come today, or a mountain of shit is coming down, and so help me I will see to it that you're going to be buried squarely under it."

"You enjoy the utilization of that fecal word, don'cha?"

"Just get them in here, Highsmith. Do it now."

"Tell ya what, we'll sort it out down the way," Highsmith said, gesturing to the hallway.

Fifteen minutes later, they met in what the police called the war room. The ambient noise was dampened because the windowless room was lined with tattered cork. Newspaper clippings, pictures, sketches, and scraps of paper littered the walls. There was so much flimsy paper hanging by brass tacks that any sudden movements would cause the nearest wall to undulate from the slight change in wind. It made it feel as if the room was alive and breathing.

The top inspector had just gone through all reported criminal activity, most of which Preston Lord had already heard, some of it ad nauseam. Highsmith sat across the table, reading from the reports and generally ignoring the exchange. Highsmith's inspector opened a new folder.

"Henrietta Glancy, a known hooker in Somerstown, strangled."

Lord rolled his eyes. "No."

"Phillip Day, attorney from the city, missing several weeks now. A few people close to him think he swapped identities and has gone off to the United States, to Texas, in search of a wife."

Lord shrugged irritably. "What does that have to do with my investigation?"

"William Hawkley, pub owner who broke up a knife fight in Southwark, bled to death from an abdominal wound."

"No."

The inspector sat up, enunciating clearly as he said, "Major Clayton Paige, an American Army pilot shot and, we strongly believe, killed *elsewhere*. He was found behind a pub near Dartford."

All eyes stared at Lord.

"New ones," Lord answered testily. "And why the hell do you repeat *that* one every time?"

Highsmith and the inspector shared a look before the inspector kept going. "Michael Forsythe, father-son dispute. Son dead, also from a knife wound, out in Barking."

"No," Lord breathed.

"Here's a new one: Wilhelm Kruger, went by Willi, missing city farmer with a lengthy rap sheet, presumed dead. Wife reported him missing. The report's old but just filtered through last night. Immigrants don't get as much attention." The inspector pulled out the next folder.

"Here's another new one: Spencer Benjamin...a strongman type from—"

Lord was in the middle of lighting a cigarette. "Wait a minute," he said, shaking out the match. "Wilhelm Kruger?"

"Yes."

"German name," Lord whispered, his eyes dancing.

"So?"

"Is there anything else with it?" Lord asked.

"I'll have to go pull the file."

"Do it," Lord said, standing.

"While we wait, Mister Lord," Gregory Highsmith said with a mocking grin, "you wanna hear some more about Clayton Paige, the American pilot who was shot in the face at close range before his body was moved?"

Preston Lord did not respond.

Chapter Thirty-Seven

THOMAS LUNDREN, HIS HEAD THROBBING from the alien liquid he'd ingested the night before, chose to eat his breakfast in his truck. He had just come from the main police station, checking in to see if anything new had arrived—it hadn't—and he was finishing his last bite of Limburger cheese as he pulled into the lot behind the two-story converted office that was the Roth police barracks. From the compartment next to his leg, Thomas produced a towel, wiping his mouth. He drank water from his canteen, more than usual, probably from the effects of the alcohol. Thomas wore a concerned expression as he stepped from his truck. The day was cool and gray, like the harbinger of the news he was going to have to break as soon as the canvassing crews finished their work.

He climbed the brick stairs to the police barracks and, just as Thomas stepped inside and was scraping his boots on the mat, he was nearly accosted by the watch officer.

"Herr Lundren!"

Thomas looked him up and down, frowning. The watch officer was an excitable type, as Thomas had learned over the past weeks. "What is it, son?"

"One of your men, Hammerschmidt, he called for you. His team found a lead. A strong one."

Fighting to remain calm, Thomas put his hand on the officer's shoulder. "Settle down and tell me what was said."

The watch officer handed him a scrap of paper with five digits on it. "They're standing by with a witness right now, awaiting your call."

Thomas accepted the paper and moved behind the desk. He picked up the phone and jiggled the cradle for an operator. While he waited, he turned his head back to the watch officer. "Who is the witness?"

"He's a veterinarian."

* * *

The two police cars raced up Mare Street in the dilapidated Shoreditch neighborhood, north of central London. Both carloads of men exited, slamming doors as the residents of the largely Germanic neighborhood leaned out of their windows in anticipation of who was about to be arrested. Nellie Kruger was on her hands and knees, working a row of black earth in a section of her missing husband's peculiar city farm. Preston Lord pressed past the rest of the men, spewing his rough German as he trampled into the rows of the vegetables. Nellie stood, smearing her face with the back of her gloved hand as she tried to stave off a droplet of perspiration.

"Police, are ya? We can speak German if ya like," she said in her Irish accent. "But it sounds like ya speak it better than I do, so we might wanna jost stay in the so-called Queen's English."

Lord considered her. She was almost certainly younger than she appeared, aged by a hard life and a personal vice or two. He gave her his most disarming smile and asked if he could speak to her in private. She dropped her gloves onto the ground and led him into the same room where Neil had first met with Willi, a converted kitchen that doubled as an office. Highsmith and the others lit cigarettes and milled about the inner city farm while the American went to work.

"Miss Kruger, tell—"

"Missus."

Lord cleared his throat. "*Missus* Kruger, tell me about your Wilhelm. Where do you think he could be?"

She tilted her head. "A yank?"

"Yes."

Nellie Kruger shrugged before reaching into her apron and coming out with a lumpy, hand-rolled cigarette. Without offering him one, she lit it with a kitchen match and exhaled the rancid smoke in Preston Lord's face. "I assume Willi's dead. Couldn't keep his pecker outta any woman with half-open legs, and it wouldn't be the first time an angry husband tried to do him some harm."

"Are you aware of a specific affair he had in which you think the husband may have tried to kill him?"

"Not recently."

Lord frowned. "When did you report him missing?" This was a question he'd already been told the answer to—Scotland Yard *claimed* four days ago—and he didn't believe it for a second.

Nellie crossed the kitchen and retrieved a calendar, marked by the advertisement of a local insurance debit man. She smacked it on the table and clamped the cigarette between her lips. Lord studied her as she ran her finger over the days. She didn't appear to be grieving at all. But if her husband was a habitual cheater, then that could explain it.

She stabbed a date with her finger. "He left here over three weeks ago. I expected him back two or three days after that and reported him missing around that time at the station down the way."

Preston Lord balled one of his hands into a fist as his other hand pulled downward on his face. "More than two weeks ago?"

"That's wot I said," she answered, straightening and blowing smoke at Lord again. "It usually would depend on wot he claimed he had to do, but probably actually depended on whether or not he could find some young German tart to go to bed with him."

Lord narrowed his eyes, struggling to digest all she was telling him. "Wait a minute. One thing at a time. You said he *left* here? What do you mean, 'left here'? To go buy a bottle of liquor, or actually *left*, as in, left the area?"

She opened her hands, seemingly confused. "I told the man at the King's Cross station all'a this."

"All'a what?" he demanded.

She licked the tip of the cigarette, making it hiss. "Ya really don't know, do ya?"

"Know what?"

"That Willi flew his airplane to Germany once every coupla weeks."

Lord was thunderstruck. He blinked several times, finally licking his dry lips. "Tell me about it...*all* about it, please."

Two minutes later, after hearing the remainder of her revelations, Preston Lord burst from the back of the house. He stalked directly to Highsmith, grabbing his lapels and jamming him up against the wall of the building on the far side of the alley. As the other policemen yelled their protests, Lord put his face inches from Highsmith's, growling his accusations.

"You withheld information from me. You hid it all. He was a war defector and flies to Germany all the damned time, you lying sonofabitch." With each accusation, Lord shook the older policeman, making his head hit the ancient stone wall. "You knew it all along!" he shouted over and over.

By the time he had shaken Highsmith five times, the other policemen yanked Lord away, one of them pressing a pistol into his neck. Once Highsmith had stepped away, they shoved Lord to the filthy ground and held him down by his arms and legs. Chief Superintendent Highsmith straightened his overcoat and smoothed his hair, reassuring his men he was fine and completely undamaged by the "skinnymalink Yank".

Highsmith moved over Lord, his voice low and calm as he rested his muddy shoe on the American's chest.

"Mister Lord, I was simply following m'orders. My instructions weren't to withhold anything, but to purposefully slow you down."

"Why?" Lord asked, wriggling himself to a standing position as the other detectives maintained grips on his arms.

"Because if your man, and we believe his name is Reuter, wants to kill that madman Adolf Hitler, then Godspeed to him." He licked his hand, combing his hair into a neat part. "I was told to give him a good week's head start, but that quickly expanded once we realized what a little wanker you really are."

Lord couldn't believe what he had just heard. "Who told you the bullshit theory about Hitler?"

"Maybe that bomber pilot you *murdered* told us. Maybe it was his ghost." Highsmith gestured to the west. "You and your government over there want to sit back and watch that maniac Hitler ransack Europe, you go ahead. But that doesn't mean we will, you fockin' wanker."

The detectives released Lord. He removed his overcoat and shook the dirt off as he walked back to the door where Nellie Kruger stood. She handed him a scrap of paper with an address on it. Lord stuffed it into his pocket and walked back to Highsmith, keeping his distance.

"Whatever the SIS told you, they're wrong. Dead wrong."

"You can leave whenever you like," Highsmith said. "From here on, you're on your own."

Lord brushed past the wall of detectives, turning east.

"And do not break any more of our laws, Mister Lord," Highsmith yelled out. "Because from this point on, you no longer have Her Majesty's backing. It'd do me great pleasure to throw your arse in the clink."

There was a Tube station in Hackney. It took ten minutes for Lord to walk there, fuming the entire way.

* * *

The Janzens sat on the opposite side of the table. The wife was shivering. The husband's eyelids appeared leaden, as if being roughed up at gunpoint wasn't enough to excite him. The gash above his eye would have gotten most people's undivided attention. Now that he'd forced his way into the farmhouse, Preston Lord stared at the bound couple, thinking about that prick Highsmith and his policemen. Could they have followed him here? After all, it would have been Lord's opposite number in England's Secret Intelligence Service who would have told them to create the delay. No, Lord decided, they'd washed their hands of him. The roadblock had been lifted and, as long as he didn't burn London to the ground, he should be fine.

"You and Wilhelm Kruger were partners in a smuggling operation?" Lord asked Henry Janzen.

"Yeah." The man didn't look up at all. Simply stared at a spot on the table, as if life had ended years before.

"And he did the flying, and you performed the maintenance on the airplane?"

"Yeah."

Lord questioned him for five minutes, learning nothing of substance.

"What was your part in all of this?" Lord asked the wife. She was pushing fifty, quite attractive with her Nordic features and streaks of gray in her blonde hair.

"I had no part in it," she answered. But Lord saw the flicker. It was the same unconcealed spark one might see in a weak poker player's eyes.

"That's not what I heard," Lord said offhandedly, attempting to smoke out her information.

Her eyes widened.

She's very attractive, Lord thought to himself, studying her further. Then he remembered what Nellie Kruger had said about her husband and his affinity for women. Lord glanced at Mr. Janzen, a stick-in-the-mud if there ever was one. Lord cleared his throat, deciding to take a wild stab as he motioned his thumb at her husband.

"C'mon now, Missus Janzen. You know what's been going on...and I know what's been going on...but does Mister Janzen know what's been going on?"

Her blue eyes were perfectly round with trepidation when her husband turned to her. "What did you do?" he whispered.

She answered him in rapid-fire Danish, shaking her head as she spoke. It was a denial of some sort. Mr. Janzen twisted his lips with the sour expression of an oft-cuckolded husband who has learned that his wife has betrayed him, yet again. *Okay*, Lord thought, congratulating himself. *Score one for Preston.*

"So, the weekly flights to Germany had tailed off and your relationship with Wilhelm was strained, especially since you suspected he'd been sleeping with your wife?" Lord said to the husband.

After the husband glared at his wife for nearly half a minute, he turned his attention to Lord. "Piss on you," he said in a calm voice. "Kill us both right here and right now. Please."

The wife was the key. Lord watched her as the husband attempted to bait Lord into action, and who could blame him? The poor bastard wasn't much to look at, and just learned that his business partner had been servicing his wife. But Lord had a strong inclination that she had something to tell, and judging by the strain on her face, it wouldn't take much to get it out of her.

Sliding his pistol under his belt, Lord reached into his pocket and retrieved his jack knife. He flicked the three-inch blade open, twisting it in the light for both of them to see. He eased out of his chair and walked behind Henry, pressing the blade to his neck and yanking his head back.

"On the last night when Wilhelm left here, who was his passenger and where were they going?" Lord growled.

Henry Janzen pushed his own head further backward, giving Lord full access to his neck. Lord pressed the tip of the blade in just under the ear, nicking Henry Janzen. The man grunted but didn't move.

"Who?" Lord bellowed.

"Do it," the man yelled. "Just kill me!"

"No!" screamed his wife. "Leave him alone…please."

"Who was it?" Lord asked, holding the blade firmly to the husband's neck while he stared at the wife.

The only sounds were her sobs.

"Who?" Lord yelled, nicking the husband again.

"An American," cried the wife. "I don't know his name, but Willi bragged that the man had lots of money and wanted to go to the south of Germany, into Austria."

"What else?" Lord demanded, inflamed that he was now actually onto Reuter's scent. "What else did Willi tell you?"

"Nothing," she yelled. "Please don't hurt him."

"Why didn't he tell you more?"

Her face twisted and her head shook back and forth.

"Was it because you were too busy in bed together?"

Mrs. Janzen's face said it all.

Lord pulled the knife away, continuing to hold a clump of Henry Janzen's hair. "When did they leave, Missus Janzen? On what date?"

She dipped her head as tears fell from her face, darkening her apron. "I don't know. Two weeks ago? Three weeks?"

Preston Lord snapped the knife shut with a solid click. He used a napkin from the table to dab the small cuts before he smacked Henry's face affectionately. "Henry, I have but one question, and then I will leave you to your wife, because I know you have a lot to talk about."

Henry swiveled his eyes upward.

"Could Willi's airplane make it all the way from here to Austria?"

Henry rotated his menacing glare to his wife, and then back to Lord. He said nothing.

Lord jerked his pistol from his waist and circled the table. He grabbed the woman under the chin and pressed his Beretta to the side of her head. "Speak!"

Mrs. Janzen began to shriek.

Mr. Janzen, however, barely reacted. He waited without expression until his wife's screams subsided. When they did, he spoke barely above a whisper, saying, "The airplane couldn't make it that far. Willi would have refueled."

"Where?"

"If the man had lots of money, like my *wife* says," Mr. Janzen said, glowering at her, "Willi probably planned to rob him, and he would have done that when he refueled at the airfield in Velden."

"Rob him?" Lord made a clucking sound as he shook his head, a sideways grin emerging. "So *that* was what did him in."

"What?" Frau Janzen demanded.

"Robbing my acquaintance would have been old Wilhelm's final mistake, you can bet on that. My acquaintance would've killed him dead for trying that."

Mrs. Janzen cried out, opening her mouth as more tears erupted. "Willi isn't dead. He just hasn't come back yet."

Preston Lord took one of Henry Janzen's cigarettes and lit it. As he exhaled smoke, he said, "We all meet our match someday, Missus Janzen. And I'm almost positive Willi met his."

Henry Janzen tugged at his ropes. "Will you please untie me?"

Lord held up a finger. "Velden, you say?" He then spelled out the name for confirmation.

Henry Janzen nodded.

Lord stepped behind him and sliced the binding rope. He donned his overcoat and walked from the house. There was a late train back into London, and from there he would need to arrange transport into Germany.

To Velden.

Chapter Thirty-Eight

PETER HEINZ SWUNG THE AXE BEAUTIFULLY. The shiny head of the red and silver tool arced through the damp air, impacting the seasoned piece of elm and splitting it in two. Neil walked to the wood and picked up one of the halves, placing it on the stump and clapping twice.

"That's how you do it. Did you feel the difference?"

Peter smiled. "Yes. I didn't even swing it very hard."

"Exactly," Neil said. "It's the speed of the axe and the weight of the head that does the work. If you try to muscle it, you'll be out here until spring. Hit this one."

Peter struck the halved piece of wood, and even though he was off center, he split it top to bottom. "Not so good."

"That wasn't bad. At least you swung it properly," Neil said in what sounded almost like native Bavarian German. "It's just that your aim was a bit off. Happens to everyone. Just keep your eye on the spot you want to hit." He lifted the two pieces, one small and one large. "This small piece will be a good starter log, and the big one will burn for a few hours."

It was nearly dark. A few droplets of rain had fallen earlier, but now only the gray sky loomed low over the farm as the day's light waned in its last hour. The smell of beef stew had been wafting from the house for an hour, causing both men's stomachs to rumble, and as soon as Neil finished giving Peter his lesson, he planned to eat the largest meal since his accident.

"Can you swing it yet?" Peter asked while proffering the axe, smiling as he always did, displaying his large, gapped teeth.

Neil took a step back. "When you get older, one of the best things you'll do is to learn your limitations. I've had three weeks of healing. The pain is almost gone and I can get around, but I think I'll probably need three more weeks before I can do something as swift as swinging an axe."

Peter nodded and dropped the axe straight down, planting it in the stump. "You look like you'd be good at this."

"You're the one who's good at it."

Peter grabbed one of Neil's suspenders and tugged on it. "What can we do tomorrow?"

"You'll have school again, *then* homework."

"After that."

"I can help you with your chores."

"After that!"

Neil tousled Peter's hair. "Maybe we'll take a walk somewhere."

"A walk?" Peter cried. *"Zu langweilig."* After decrying Neil's boring idea, Peter's face ignited with an idea. "Let me drive the truck in the lower field, again."

Neil touched his finger to his mouth, hushing Peter. "I don't want your mother to know I taught you to drive it—she'd kill me."

"Okay, I promise I won't tell," Peter whispered in that excited, child-like undertone which is louder than a normal tone of voice.

Neil glanced around conspiratorially. He leaned over, placing his hands on his knees and beckoned Peter close, speaking in a hushed voice. "We'll do a full circle of the property, and I'll let you go through all the gears."

"You promise?"

"Under one condition?"

"What's that?"

"You pay close attention to everything I tell you. I'm leaving Thursday so you might as well learn to drive the right way."

Lowering his head, Peter kicked a stone. "I don't want you to leave."

"I have to."

"No, you don't."

"I do, Peter. And Thursday is the day," Neil said firmly. "We can't bargain about this."

"What's the rush?"

"It's a bit of an emergency, Peter. In fact, if I was feeling well enough, I'd have already left."

"Will I ever see you again?"

"I truly don't know. I hope so."

Peter was quiet for a moment. Finally he said, "I want to do two circles of the property."

"Two?"

"Please," Peter replied, looking up at Neil.

For a moment, Neil was stricken with thoughts of his unborn son. Then, rather than being overcome with sadness, he realized what a treasure this time with Peter had been.

Neil stuck out his hand and Peter shook it. "Two laps, it is."

"Fantastich!"

"Also, I don't think it's good to have secrets from your mother, but this is one that she'd probably understand."

"I'll pay attention."

"Let's go eat that roast."

As they crossed the yard, Peter tossed an old ball to Neil, clapping his hands for Neil to throw it back. Hildie Heinz was certainly an excellent mother, but over the past few weeks, Neil could tell Peter craved male companionship, the way all men do. Their trip to Nürnberg, while bizarre in its purpose, had been an excellent time for the two men to get to know one another. Sometimes a man simply needs another man to correct him, laugh with him, and even crack a crude joke or two, if only to remind them that they're members of the coarser sex.

When Neil reached the porch, Gabi appeared from the steep drop that led to the lower fields where she had been tending to some of the grazing cattle. Her fair cheeks were splotchy and she was out of breath. Neil stopped to wave at the pretty farm girl.

Before he realized there was terror on her face.

"What is it?" Neil asked.

"Men," she hissed. "Two carloads of them, down near the crash."

"What are they doing?" Neil asked, turning to peer through the growing darkness.

"Looking all around, pointing at everything, examining the area. I think they know," she cried.

Frau Heinz must have heard her because she opened the storm door from the house, staring at the lower fields. Neil used the only tree on the valley side of the yard as cover. He stood behind it, peering around the thick trunk as he looked downward into the flood plain. The light of the day was fading fast, making the people in the lower field appear as silhouettes. The men were three hundred feet from the crash site, standing with hands on hips, one of them pointing in the sky and all around the fields.

Neil turned, finding Peter watching for his reaction. Gabi's expression was still one of alarm, and her mother's was a hardened, scornful glare. Neil hurried to the house, pushing past Frau Heinz. He walked to the bedroom, throwing several items from his grip into a small handbag. The family congregated in the door of the bedroom. As he worked, Neil spoke without turning.

"You should be able to hide my grip and the rest of my things. If they find them, just tell them they were your husband's." He found the tin and removed two more diamonds, large ones, and placed them on his bedside table. "Hide these too." It only took him a minute to get the items he needed. After buttoning the small bag, Neil pulled on his light jacket and his bowler's cap. He spun around to view Frau Heinz standing defiantly in the doorway, Gabi and Peter behind her. Both of Frau Heinz's hands were firmly planted on the doorjamb.

"You're not leaving," she said.

"If they catch me here, Hildie, they'll kill you *and* your family."

Frau Heinz stood her ground. "Stop packing that bag."

"There's no time."

"We're going to hide you."

"No, you're not."

"The hell we're not."

Neil turned back to his bag and continued packing.

* * *

The lower Heinz field was damp with rich, brown earth. Each footstep in the dirt sent earthworms wriggling, doing their best to burrow back down into the safety of the fertile soil. Above the field in a wide panorama, the western sky was deep gray and quickly fading to black. And Hörst Baldinger, the local veterinarian who'd "seen something," was speaking far too quickly for Thomas' taste. Fast-talkers were typically someone Thomas would be wary of.

Earlier today at first light, the canvassing crew, upon questioning Hörst at a farm five kilometers away, had noted the way his eyes had widened when asked about an airplane. After several minutes of questioning, Hörst had finally acquiesced, saying an airplane had crashed and that he thought it was a part of a military exercise that he wasn't supposed to discuss. This was the same tale he was telling now.

Thomas stepped away, leaving the vet going on and on about seeing an airplane come in low and crash. He was giving so much detail that some of it was conflicting. Now, Thomas' investigative crew and a few men from the local constabulary began to look wearily at one another as Hörst prattled on.

Thomas had stopped believing Hörst twenty minutes earlier.

Oh, he believed the vet knew something, but when he began to contradict himself about the airplane, Thomas wrote off his own personal interrogation and decided to let his associates handle him. What interested Thomas the most was this location's proximity to Hausham and Miesbach. Earlier, when the call came in, Thomas had rushed to the map, viewing the veterinarian's location: Hausham. It had been almost exactly where Thomas' calculations predicted the plane's fuel would run out.

The western ridge was nearly as dark as the sky above, most of the departed sun's radiance diffused by the heavy layer of high clouds. Thomas looked in that direction, seeing the silhouettes of a farmhouse and barn perched on the crest. He squatted down, scooping the tilled earth and holding it to his nose, smelling it. Usually the land this close to the mountains wasn't as arable as the foothills near his home in Velden. But this was a choice piece of property, fed by streams from the mountain snow and containing just enough rich earth to allow crops to flourish. Thomas knew these things from his time as a boy, helping three generations of Lundrens tend to a farm that would later be wiped out in only two growing seasons by a destructive fungus. He turned his head to listen to the exchange.

"If a plane landed here, then where is it?" asked the policeman who had first found the veterinarian.

"It landed...crashed rather, somewhere near here. I saw it as it came down." Hörst Baldinger sounded as if he were drunk. Thomas had seen him nipping covertly from the flask, time and time again.

Thomas dropped the earth from his hands, clapping them together. He stepped to Hörst and silenced everyone. "So, if you saw this plane crash-land, what were you doing here in the first place?"

Hörst's eyes cut to the right. He was either trying to recollect, or trying to make something up. "I was trimming a hoof."

"What hoof?" Thomas asked.

"The hoof of a horse."

"Whose horse?"

Despite the cool air, sweat emerged on the oily head of the veterinarian. Time slowed to a crawl as Hörst licked his lips. Finally, he pointed up the ridge with a shaky hand. "The Heinz family."

Thomas turned his head slowly, drinking in the lights of the farmhouse and the shadowy outline of the barn. "The Heinz family," he repeated.

"Yes."

"Is this their field?"

"Yep."

"Fine." Thomas motioned to the cars parked on the service road. "Then let's all go and visit the Heinz family."

* * *

"Stop packing," Gabi demanded.

Ignoring her, Neil fastened the bag. When he turned, he witnessed Gabi pointing his Colt at him with a trembling hand. Her finger was not on the trigger.

"You're not leaving," she said again, this time using her jagged English. Her mother reached for her arm but Gabi shrugged her off.

Neil held Gabi's gaze for a moment, chuckling despite the tension. After a moment he reached into the side of the handbag, holding up several pistol magazines. "Remind me, Gabi, assuming we someday have time, to show you how to load that pistol."

Gabi twisted the empty pistol, studying the empty slot in the grip before allowing her mother to take it.

"I aimed it at the veterinarian," Gabi said.

"Good thing he didn't know," Neil remarked.

Frau Heinz spun the Colt around properly, holding it out to Neil by the barrel. "To run now would be foolishness."

Neil accepted the handgun, holding it to his side. He stared at Gabi, who stared back. There was an emotion in her eyes Neil hadn't yet seen.

Peter pushed past and clung to Neil's side.

Frau Heinz shoved them all out of the way and crossed the room, pulling back the dusty curtain to peer into the lower field. "They're still down there. What do you think about the barn?"

Neil cocked his head, frowning. "What about it?"

"As a place to hide?" Frau Heinz asked.

"My leaving is the best option. That's your field down there. It's only a matter of time before they come up here, and they *will* look in the barn."

"They won't know where to look."

"This is a bad idea, Hildie."

Frau Heinz snapped her thick fingers. "You don't know what I'm referring to. Go to the second stall. Underneath the hay, you'll find a cellar door. It's a hidden cellar, built by my husband many years ago. Go down there and wait." She grabbed Peter's collar. "Go with him and cover the trap door with hay. Cover it well. Run!"

Neil jammed one of the magazines into the grip of his Colt. He jerked the slide backward, watching a round as it slammed home. "If they make trouble, any at all, scream to the top of your lungs and I'll come running."

Frau Heinz shooed him on. "They won't know anything if you'll *just* move your stubborn ass!"

Neil eased away from the farmhouse, hearing Frau Heinz and Gabi discussing how to conceal his things. He squatted as he peered into the fields below. Peter appeared behind him.

"Are you scared?" Peter asked.

"Yes," Neil answered, glancing around the tree.

"Scared of those men?"

Neil looked at Peter. "No, Peter, not really. I'm scared of getting your family in trouble."

"Mama will run them off."

Neil could see the headlights of the cars. They began to move, turning onto the service road, nearly a mile away. They were gaining speed.

"They're coming," Neil whispered. "We need to hurry." He scurried across the yard with Peter by his side. "You have to get back inside before they get up here."

Once inside the barn, they sprinted to the stall. Peter exposed the cellar and Neil whipped the door open, flinging himself down into the blackness as he fell to his good side.

"Are you okay?" Peter asked.

Neil stood, brushing dirt from his pants. "I'm fine. Don't act scared, Peter. Be curious, but not scared. Understand?"

"Yes."

"Good. Now, close the door, cover me, and haul ass!"

Peter did as he was told.

Chapter Thirty-Nine

THE HEINZ FAMILY STARED AT THE GROUP OF MEN. Thomas stepped forward and removed his hat, motioning for the others to follow suit. This was the type of family that kept Germany moving. Down-to-earth, practical people who did a full day's work six, and often seven, days a week. He had no idea if they were party members, nor did he care. It wasn't Thomas' style to come in heavy-handed. He eyed each of the Heinzes.

The woman was probably about fifty, big and stout. She had a tan, lined face that appeared to be all business. The daughter was plain in her work clothes and pinned-up hair, but she still managed to be quite pretty with her large hazel eyes and delicate features. Thomas focused on the boy. Not that he felt the boy knew anything; rather, the Heinz boy wore an expression like Thomas once wore, as had countless other boys before him. Seeing the assemblage of frowning, important-looking men with guns on their hips makes most boys feel as if somehow they are being left out. Like watching a posse chase out after a bandit, and feeling like the only man in town who didn't get an invite.

The boy eyed Thomas. Thomas smiled briefly before turning his eyes to the mother.

"An airplane crash, you say?" Frau Heinz asked, holding the screen door open.

"Yes'm," Thomas answered. "Herr Baldinger, who I would imagine you know…" Thomas motioned him forward "…said there may have been a crash on your property down there in the fields."

Thomas watched as the Heinz woman looked at the veterinarian. There was no malice in her eyes, only the expression a mother might wear when she has learned her child has told an umpteenth fib. "You must be referring to the airplane we saw flying around a few weeks ago," she said, turning her eyes back to Thomas.

"Actually, it was over three weeks ago. So, you *did* see it?" Thomas asked, a note of hope entering his voice.

Frau Heinz grasped her son's shoulders and pulled him forward. "This is Peter, my son. That airplane has been all he could talk about since then. It flew low all around here and then disappeared over the mountain pass, over at Tegernsee."

Thomas turned and glared at Hörst, the veterinarian. He was staring at Frau Heinz dumbly, his lips parted. Thomas turned back. "Could your boy please describe this airplane?"

Peter looked at the expectant men. His Adam's apple bobbed as he struggled to swallow. "It was a black airplane," he said, his pre-pubescent voice croaking. "It flew low and slow all around the valley and then, like Mama said, went through the lowest pass over there." He pointed to the southwest.

"Could you see the pilot?" Thomas asked.

"No, sir."

"That pass?" Thomas asked, turning to the dark shapes of the mountains and pointing.

"It's too dark to see it, but the pass is right there," Peter said, pointing thirty degrees to the right of where Thomas aimed his hand. "Like Mama said, it looked like the plane went right through the peaks."

"That pass goes straight into Österreich," one of the policemen said.

"Österreich is Deutschland now," said another.

Thomas ignored their comments. He lowered his eyes to the ground and closed them. Why on earth would this veterinarian fool tell them the plane had crashed?

"You're certain?" Thomas asked the boy.

"Yes," Peter replied. "The plane didn't crash."

Thomas nodded. "I hate to be an inconvenience, but would you mind if we look around?"

The mother's face was neutral as she held the screen door open wide. Two other policemen went into the house. Thomas donned his hat and pulled on the brim out of respect before taking the other two policemen to the barn.

Hörst wiped sweat from his forehead and stepped up the two steps to the farmhouse, close to Frau Heinz.

"How did you know about an airplane?" she hissed.

"Your boyfriend mumbled it in his feverish pain. And I want ten thousand reichsmarks to change my story," he rasped. "To hide your transgressions and that...that English-speaking man."

Frau Heinz curled her lip and motioned Peter back into the house. With her girth she pushed Hörst from the steps and then stood nose-to-nose with him in the yard. "This is my family you're playing with, you devious bastard."

"I'm not playing."

"You're endangering their lives."

"Not if I get my money, I'm not."

"I'll get you, Hörst. Do you hear me? You just remember that when you lay your filthy head down at night. I will get you for this."

Hörst spat brownish juice at her feet and smiled, showing the wad of tobacco in the corner of his disgusting mouth. "Yeah, sure, tough old bitch...so, we got a deal?"

"You'll have your money. Just get them out of here."

Hörst spat again before taking a swig from his flask. He crossed the yard and disappeared into the barn.

Frau Heinz stared after him, her eyes welling with tears.

* * *

The cellar was damp and cool, marked by the familiar earthy smell of cellars the world over. Neil was motionless, holding the Colt in both hands as he had over the previous ten minutes. Several minutes before he had heard voices as the men had walked through the barn. Days before, in a prescient move, Neil and Peter had moved the disassembled airplane parts from the barn, concealing them under hay bales in the grazing field. That move had proven wise—but hiding in this cellar felt idiotic. If Peter hadn't fully covered the cellar door, or if these men were meticulous in their search—or if one simply stepped on the door and felt its hollowness—then Neil would have to decide whether to exit peacefully, or to come out shooting.

Neil continued to aim the Colt upward as the voices returned. Though the sounds were muffled, he heard someone say something about "*die Laternen,*" meaning "the lanterns." The cellar door had gaps between the boards, and while the top of the door was covered in hay, it displayed the sudden illumination through the gaps. Neil controlled his breathing, trying to listen, praying they wouldn't find the door.

"Just a hallucinating old drunk," he heard one voice say.

"But the family acted odd," another voice said. "Like they knew more."

"With the Nazis running roughshod, everyone acts odd nowadays," remarked a third voice.

"Careful talking like that," the second one replied.

Neil tensed as he heard boots scrape in the stall above him.

"What's that?" one voice yelled.

Neil heard someone distant yell something about being mistaken.

"How could you be mistaken about something as distinct as an airplane crash?" asked a voice just above the door. Neil could see the shadows playing through the thin strips of light.

The other voice became clearer. Neil recognized it, guttural and rough as a cob. "Because sometimes when I get drunk I see things." It was the veterinarian—the damned drunken veterinarian that had performed the surgery on him. Neil gritted his teeth as uncontrolled anger coursed through his veins.

The boots in his stall moved away. Neil moved up the ladder, turning his ear so he could hear the exchange.

"Do you realize that you've wasted a full day of our investigation with your bullshit?"

"But, I wasn't bullshitting. Sometimes when I see these things I really believe…" The voices trailed off.

Neil took deep breaths, wondering what that crooked animal doctor was up to by leading a team of investigators here.

Another voice. "The house and the barn are clean. This is a damn wild goose chase."

Footsteps, going away.

In another minute, car doors slammed, engines started, and gravel crunched as the cars drove off.

Neil waited. He didn't relax. Just waited.

Several minutes later, he shielded his eyes as the trap door opened. It was Gabi. "They're gone." Her smile was triumphant but her eyes held concern. Neil tucked the Colt into his waistband and climbed out, wincing as the pain from his fall finally hit him.

"Are you okay?" she asked.

"It was the veterinarian, wasn't it?"

She pinched her lips to one side and nodded. "Yes."

"Tell me his name again."

"Hörst Baldinger. He's always been a loose cannon. Apparently he told some policemen from Nürnberg that a plane had crashed in the lower field."

"Nürnberg?"

She nodded. "Does this have to do with your gunshot wound?"

Neil turned his head to stare outside into the darkness. He didn't answer her, although he knew the airfield where he'd shot Willi was near Nürnberg.

"Where's your mother?" he asked. "Where's Peter?"

"Peter's in the kitchen, waiting on you. Mama…"

"Go on."

"She's in her bedroom crying."

Neil tapped out a cigarette and lit it. Gabi held out her hand for one. He started to object but she must have read his look because she said, "I bought those for you so don't even think about trying to deny me one. I'm a grown woman."

Unable to find humor in the moment, Neil gave her a cigarette and lit it. They stepped into the night air and didn't speak for a bit. In the distance, he could see the cars driving away. Neil looked up at the starless sky, watching the movement of the clouds as he reflected on the situation. God, how he hated that he'd involved these nice people in his problems. And now, due to the veterinarian's actions, he'd probably endangered their lives.

"So you're not going to talk?" she asked, pulling him from his reverie.

"Just thinking," Neil whispered, dropping his cigarette and grinding it under his foot

"Well, think out loud, will you?"

"I just regret that I've involved you and your family in this mess."

"I don't," Gabi said with an impish grin. She dragged on her cigarette and said, "Boring as hell around here."

"Looking for excitement can get a person in trouble, Gabi."

"Don't lecture me," she said, a strange note to her voice. "Oh...who's the picture of?"

"What picture?"

"The little girl on Peter's dresser. I hid it with your other things."

"Just someone I want to remember."

"Is she dead?"

"I hope not," Neil breathed.

As he scanned the area with his eyes, her next question gave him a jolt. She asked, "Who shot you?"

"What?"

"You heard me."

"Gabi..."

"You *were* shot—there's no debating that. So who did it?"

Neil was silent.

"Who?" Gabi snapped.

"A man."

"Very good. That really narrows it down."

"I didn't know him, Gabi."

"He was a complete stranger?"

"Sort of."

"'Sort of' means 'no'."

"Damn if you're not persistent."

Gabi smiled.

Neil spoke quickly and monotone. "That was his airplane, okay? I hired him to fly me to Austria. He landed in a place called Velden and tried to rob me, but not before he shot me. But he didn't rob me. I took his airplane and crashed it in your field. That's the truth." He opened his arms. "Satisfied?"

"You left something out. I'm not going to ask you if you shot him." She pulled in a long drag from the cigarette. "I'm not going to ask you because I know the answer already." She wagged her finger back and forth and said, "Because, even out here in the dark, I can see the answer in those dual-colored eyes of yours."

"I need to talk to your mother."

Just as he started to walk inside, Gabi grabbed his wrist and turned him to her. She flicked her cigarette away in a streaking tangerine arc. Then she stood on her tiptoes, put her hands around Neil's neck and kissed him. Neil nearly fell over as she pressed her sweet tongue into his mouth. He was suddenly quite aware of her breasts and her midsection as she pressed against him, and even though he didn't want to, he gently removed her hands and pulled himself backward.

"Why'd you do that?" she asked.

Neil touched the back of his hand to his lips. He held the hand to his nose, inhaling her scent. Then Neil turned and walked to the house.

He went directly to Frau Heinz's room and there, between the sobs of a woman who, for many years, had done a yeoman's job of being both father and mother, he listened as she relayed the story about Hörst, obviously shaken to her very core.

"Ten thousand reichsmarks?" Neil asked.

She dabbed her eyes with a handkerchief. "I don't have that kind of money. I'll have to mortgage everything."

Neil gave her a hug, probably something she wasn't used to receiving. The crying began again as Frau Heinz spent twenty minutes sobbing into Neil's shoulder. Over the course of her release, she mentioned her sweet babies, and how she just wanted to keep them safe.

And while Neil did a good job of comforting this woman who had been so good to him, his mind raced at light speed as he thought about that wicked sonofabitch Hörst Baldinger.

Neil's anger hadn't abated at all. Like a fire doused with gasoline, it grew.

And grew.

Chapter Forty

IT WAS JUST AFTER THREE IN THE MORNING. The crisp air invigorated Neil as he rode with the window down on the old Adler truck. He had taken special care to slowly roll the vehicle away from the Heinz's barn and to the top of the service road. With his foot on the clutch and the vehicle in third gear, he allowed the Adler to roll several hundred meters from the barn before he popped the clutch and started the engine. He hadn't wanted to wake Peter or Gabi. But Frau Heinz knew all about his leaving. In fact, she had given him the keys and the look they had shared said everything.

Neil puttered northbound, connecting with the road to Hausham, a cigarette dangling from his lips as the cool September evening whipped his now shaggy black hair. He could smell the tang of the nearby crops in the sweet night air. After several kilometers, just as Frau Heinz told him he would, he saw the church with the bell tower, the structure lit by a solitary electric spotlight. Hanging over the front of the bell tower, probably covering a cross, was a Nazi flag, blazing red in the spotlight. Neil pulled into the parking lot and retrieved the bundle from the truck. He walked around the church and connected with the east-west street located a block north. It was more of a rutted trail than a proper thoroughfare.

He began to walk east. At such an early hour, a person might question whether or not the town was inhabited. Other than the spotlight at the church, there were no lights anywhere. And while there were no stars out, the sky held a faint glow, making it a deep shade of grey. His eyes were now adjusted to the dark and, up ahead on the eastern limits of the town, he clearly saw the two-story ramshackle building, just as Frau Heinz told him he would.

Once he was close, Neil was able to make out the hand-painted sign that read *Baldinger Veterinary & Husbandry*.

Moving into the blackness between two buildings, Neil placed the bundle at his feet. He closed his eyes, hearkening back—back to the Great War, when his meditations would give him peace. Back to his time as a teenager, in the Sierras, when he learned all the secrets.

He halted his train of thought, closing his eyes.

Your actions escaping the ship were crude, clumsy. You nearly died.

Then in London, in the Tube…pathetic. You were lucky. Nothing more.

But now, after weeks of solitude and sobriety, there's no more excuse. You must do better. Think of Jakey. Think of Emilee. Think of little Fern.

And think of the good Herr Baldinger, inside, awaiting you.

Awaiting what you bring him…

After opening his eyes, Neil retrieved his bundle.

He walked around the building, making a wide arc, seeing nothing of interest. He went back to the front door, prepared to pick the lock as he pulled open the outer screen door. But with a quiet turn of the knob, the front door proved unlocked. He eased the door open to make sure there was no bell attached to it. There wasn't. Once inside, Neil heard the racket, coming from up the rickety stairs. It was deep and throaty, grating at its edges.

Snoring.

The night air had cleansed Neil's sinuses and, even over the animal stenches of Hörst's place of work, Neil could easily smell the cloying odor of a sleeping drunkard's breath. As he slept forty feet away, Hörst's ninety-proof exhalations had wafted throughout the entire two-story structure, infusing the inside air with sweet nastiness.

Staring up the stairs, Neil opened his bundle. After putting the wads of money in his pocket, he gripped the freshly sharpened kitchen blade in his hand and began to move. Using the outer edges of the stairs, he climbed without a sound.

The Pale Horse cometh.

* * *

In Hörst Baldinger's dream, the oily woman disappeared into a vapor of nothingness, replaced by an unbroken horse, set on trampling him. The funny thing about it was that Hörst knew he was dreaming but, just in case he wasn't, he hurried to get away from the crazed colt. Many years before when he was at university, back in his sober days, Hörst and nine other students had watched in horror as one of their professors was trampled to death by a spooked old nag. Horses can kill a man at any time. Perhaps that's why, whenever he was attending a horse and the owner wasn't nearby, Hörst would beat on it incessantly—just to show the beast who was the boss.

In the dream, he struggled as the steed worked him up against a hard wall of some sort, making it difficult for him to breathe. Claustrophobic, Hörst panicked, yelling out. Just as he felt the nag might crush him, instead, it nipped him on the neck. And the nip was painful, damned painful, like the metallic pinch of sharp scissors.

Something strange began to happen, as thousands of hands appeared from the blackness, smacking his face. Then voices. Odd voices.

"Wake up, you sonofabitch," came the deepest of them.

Hörst opened his eyes. His kerosene lamp was lit, burning low. The horse turned to vapor, morphing into a human shape. It was the man Hörst had patched up over three weeks ago; the man Hörst had led the investigators on a wild goose chase for earlier in the day.

But now the man was perched on top of him, straddling him tightly with his knees pressed against Hörst's ribcage. Hörst tried to push the man off. His efforts were in vain.

"I would *not* do that if I were you," the man warned. There was something odd about the situation—more odd than waking up with a strange man astride him—more odd than the fact that the man appeared to have blood smeared on his face in an odd pattern—and this oddness convinced Hörst to obey the man. The oddness was the man's hand, clamped to the side of Hörst's neck, the source of the pinching pain in his dream.

But his hand wasn't on Hörst's neck.

It was *inside* it.

"Do not move, Hörst. I'll show you why." The man adjusted his hand. In a flash, he reached to the rickety bedside table and held something cold to Hörst's neck. While he couldn't see it, his left ear detected a rushing sound, like water through a pipe. Then the man replaced his right hand and lifted the glass that had contained whiskey only a few hours earlier.

It was half-full of thick red blood. Hörst's blood.

Suddenly the veterinarian wasn't able to breathe. He felt lightheaded and nauseous as he leaned his head back into the pillow and clenched his eyes shut.

"I have no idea how to say it in German, but in English, the critical pathway of yours that I have punctured is known as the jugular."

"*Jugularvene*," Hörst moaned, his tears beginning.

"Well, that's easy," the man answered. "Probably comes from Latin. Anyway, my pinkie finger is in there now and it's making a pretty good seal. I made only a tiny hole, but boy does it gush when uncorked."

Hörst began to sob and shudder. "I will die. I will die like a stuck pig here in my bed."

"A drunken stuck pig," the man added. "But I doubt you'll die here. If I let you go right now, I'm guessing you'll die pounding on a neighbor's door. But you'll probably ruin their porch in the process. Blood isn't easy to remove, especially from wood."

Hörst arched his back, crying and wailing like a toddler in the midst of a conniption fit. The man on top of him remained in place, pinkie finger acting as a plug in Hörst's dike of life. When Hörst began to regain his senses, he slowed his crying, speaking with a trembling lip. "Why are you doing this?"

"It's simple. You weren't to say a word to anyone about me. That was our deal, and I take deals *very* seriously."

"But they don't know the whole truth. I did it as a warning, to get the money."

"I'd already paid you." Then, the man removed his finger and blood spurted out of Hörst's neck like a west Texas oil well. Hörst screamed: a primal, guttural sound. After a moment the man replaced his finger before lowering his enraged face to Hörst's. "You will never tell another soul that I was here. If anyone comes around asking again, stick to the story that you were drunk and hallucinating."

Hörst nodded gingerly, careful not to dislodge the man's finger.

"Do I have your solemn word this time?"

"Yes, of course."

"If you don't obey, Hörst, I swear on everything holy to me that I will come back and kill you. And I promise you it won't be nearly as painless as this."

"I believe you," Hörst answered quickly.

The man grasped Hörst's left hand and held his pinkie right beside his own. In a quick motion, he removed his own while jamming Hörst's inside the hole.

"Where's your bag?" the man asked. "The one with the needle and thread you used on me."

Minutes later, as Horst talked him through the three-stitch procedure, the man took a damp rag and wiped the skin. "No blood flowing out. I would imagine if you keep some pressure on it, it'll clot up."

"There's a lot of pressure on the *Jugularvene*," Hörst whimpered. "Are your stitches tight?"

The man peered closely. "They look fair enough to me. Not pretty, but not leaking, either."

Hörst was ashen gray, sucking on a cigarette as he sat wavering on the side of the bed. He held a wad of gauze tightly on the puckered seam of the three stitches. The man washed his hands in the bowl before tossing the pink rag on the German's lap.

"I'm ready to leave now. Do we have an understanding?"

"Yes, we do."

"And you know what I will do to you if you renege?"

"No, I don't. And I don't want to."

The American's smile was humorless. He pulled on his coat and left with nary a sound.

As soon as the man was gone, Hörst had a very good cry—while holding steady pressure on his wound.

Chapter Forty-One

NEIL SAT ALONE IN THE SMALL KITCHEN of the Heinz farmhouse. In front of him was a piece of paper with two paragraphs of text, written in pencil, the language German. He was proud of how well his German had returned in the past weeks but, at this moment, melancholy occupied his mind far more than senseless pride. He placed his cigarette in the ashtray and wrote one final paragraph, this one to Peter and Gabi. Wanting to go on but knowing not to, Neil wrapped his feelings up with a final sentence of thanks, placing only an N at the bottom of the page. He stacked ten thousand reichsmarks on the paper, along with another note instructing Frau Heinz to use only someone she trusted to remove the aircraft parts before spring. Or better yet, bury them.

He walked to the window. In the lowermost field, the one adjacent to the field that had hosted his abrupt arrival on the Heinz property, he could see the two women of the Heinz family working with the mule and wagon next to them. He didn't know what they were doing, but he knew that whatever it was, it needed to be done. They were some of the most efficient workers he had ever met.

Earlier in the morning, when he had returned from his session with the veterinarian, Neil had patted the back of Frau Heinz's hand as she had sat there, trembling as she took her morning coffee. He told her she never had to worry about Hörst the veterinarian again.

"And you don't think he will seek revenge? He's crazy, you know," she'd said.

Neil shook his head. "He won't *ever* bother you again."

Frau Heinz had sipped her coffee and nodded. Her face was stolid, but her eyes had glistened with the prospect that old Hörst had gotten his comeuppance.

Now, Neil walked back to the bed where he'd healed. The room was again Peter's—all of Neil's things had been put away. He thought of the many games of checkers he had shared with the boy. Thought of their conversations. Even today, Peter was at school, proudly presenting a paper on Bismarck that Neil had helped him write.

Neil felt as if he might get emotional—uncharacteristic for him. It was time to go—he had a mission to complete. He buttoned his flannel shirt to the top and slung the new canvas bag over his shoulders, so that it was held across his chest. With one final glance about the small farmhouse that had become his home, Neil stepped out the door and into the yard.

Staying to the far side of the yard, he made his way to the south. As he began to walk, he heard a voice. It was Gabi.

Neil cringed as he turned. She was approaching on the horse, probably coming to the house to retrieve something.

"What are you doing?" she demanded, staring at the bag.

Neil cut his eyes away. He said nothing.

"Where are you going?"

"I'm leaving, Gabi. I have to."

Gabi dropped off the horse and walked to him, her eyes never wavering as she wiped her hands on her trousers. "You *don't* have to. You said you'd leave tomorrow."

"Yes, I do. My being here is too risky for your family."

"No, it's *not.*"

Neil wasn't going to argue with Gabi. Leaving the Heinz family—especially her—was killing him. But time was against him, along with the men who were searching for him.

"Stay one more day," she pleaded.

"I can't."

"You can."

"Gabi, I'm leaving. I'm sorry."

Tears began to well in Gabi's eyes before she slapped him across the face. Neil took it without response. Gabi covered her mouth with her hand, sobbing as she turned and ran into the house.

Not quite understanding what had just happened, Neil resumed his walk, heading due south, walking straight toward the looming Alps, making a path through the fields and woods. He made a deliberate effort to push the Heinz family from his mind, concentrating on the task ahead.

No matter how hard he tried, he still felt sick.

Utterly sick.

* * *

By lunchtime Neil had reached the rutted road at a town called Kreuth, situated below a soaring peak. He stopped at the mercantile to purchase some food, asking the older man inside about the road through the mountains. The man informed him that the road led through Aachen Pass, and then to a lake known as Aachensee, inside the now informal northern border of Österreich. Neil decided not to ask about Innsbruck until he reached the lake. No sense in leaving a trail in the event he might be followed.

A mile outside of Kreuth, just as he began the steep portion of the ascent to the pass, Neil heard a foreign sound. He turned his head to see a dog just behind him, its claws clicking on the macadam. The dog seemed to be a mix of Shepherd and some type of hound, with auburn hair and black, floppy ears. The dog appeared quite old, with significant gray around the muzzle, but didn't seem to be mangy or underfed. Neil stopped and watched as the dog approached his hand, licking it. Exasperated, he knelt, quickly determining that *he* was actually a *she*. Neil didn't want to pet the dog because there was no sense in encouraging what was obviously someone else's pet. Three times he used his harshest voice, pointing back toward Kreuth and telling the old dog to go home. Each time, she would sit, looking at him with droopy eyes and a solidified countenance.

He tried English. She lay down, content to listen.

He switched back to German. She rested her head on her paws, cocking an eye at him.

He could yell to the heavens. But this dog had made up her mind, and she was coming with him.

Finally, opening his hands in a resigned fashion, Neil patted his knees to beckon her. He rubbed her ears and off they went, together, headed upward in the Aachen Pass. Although he would never admit it, even to himself, Neil was thrilled with his new companion. The wrenching melancholia of leaving the Heinz family had twisted his stomach on itself like a sour sponge. As he climbed, the memories of each Heinz family member crept back in, floating through his head: the father-like, manly moments with Peter; Frau Heinz's stiff, hard-to-detect approvals when Neil did something she was fond of; and of course, Gabi, with all her inner beauty, doggedness and strength.

He pressed forward, physically and mentally.

The afternoon brought clouds followed by a light, swirling rain as he neared the pass. The upper levels of the adjacent mountains were jagged, churning spires of dry snow, their peaks towering over each side of the winding road. The cold rain had quickly become almost unbearably frigid, and he began to be flecked with pellets of ice as he neared the crest of the road. Neil wore work gloves and wrapped a muffler around his face. An occasional automobile passed, but he did not thumb a ride. Whenever they sensed a car, Neil and his new friend moved to the side, hiding from view.

When the light of day began to recede, at the top of the ascent, Neil left the road, leading the dog through several inches of slush in search of a crevice to bed down. This was the worst environment to sleep in, but Neil's energy had given out in the cold and elevation. Several hundred feet off the road, in a flat area, he found something better than a crevice. Located directly under a perilous rock overhang was a cave of sorts. It had a wide mouth, but gradually narrowed into the mountain like a horizontal wedge. Neil pushed into the cave's bowels, finding stacks of dry wood, a tattered bedroll, and even a small pile of garbage. Not surprisingly, there had been others here before him. Names and phrases adorned the rock wall, painted by travelers. One had even coined the cave *Gasthaus*

Bergspitze, or Mountain Top Inn. Whatever it was, Neil was thrilled to have found it.

It took him a half-hour to get the space situated to his liking. He searched the nearby area, finding a dead tree that was mostly dry. It had grown from a crevice in the rock under another ledge and died, probably from lack of water or nutrients. He twisted the slightly damp log out and dragged it back to the cave, doing the same with several other large pieces of wood. Satisfied he had enough firewood, Neil began to gather rocks, making his aching side feel as if it might split open at any moment. The dog, seemingly impervious to the cold, followed him every step of the way, curiously watching his every move, her brown eyes drinking in his actions as if he were the most important man in the world.

Neil took the stones to the back of the cave, stacking the largest ones on the ground. Like he'd been taught as a boy in the Sierras, he built a two-foot-high windbreak, leaving himself enough space between the wall of the cave and his temporary wall to slide through. The light of the day was now gone, so Neil went to work with the available dry wood, creating a pyramid in the sheltered space.

The dog made herself at home on the bedroll as Neil worked. He stacked the small pieces of wood, along with several smaller branches from the tree, arching larger sticks over the top. He found some paper in the garbage pile, sliding it underneath. Satisfied, he removed his only box of matches, staring at them. After his swim in the Atlantic, his lighter was still out of naphtha, something he'd kicked himself over since his crash landing. He hadn't smoked a single cigarette during his walk, saving the last of the Heinz household matches for just this type of emergency.

Neil lit a match. Out it went as the chilly wind swirled in the semi-protected space. A second match. Out. He exhaled loudly, crouching over the would-be fire, trying to shield the wind. A third. A fourth. A fifth.

"Damn it," he growled. He looked at the dog. She was curled into a nearly perfect circle, her head tucked over her back legs. Her eyes looked up to him, giving him a, "Sorry, mister, but you're on your own with all this," look. Neil followed her lead, lying flat on the ground, surrounding the wood with his body. From the backside, he held the matches directly adjacent to the paper, lighting one and watching as it set the paper aflame. He waited, watching as the once enemy wind began to work for him, fueling the flame as the kindling and pine needles began to burn. Two minutes later, the wood was alight.

After allowing all of the pieces to catch, Neil stacked the larger wood in a square around the small fire, building it like a log cabin, but leaving space for air. He put the damp logs on the bottom so they could dry out and eventually provide fuel late in the night. As the larger pieces began to burn, he dragged the long limbs to the wide mouth of the cave, using two boulders as a lever and his body as the force to crack the limbs into workable pieces of wood. When finished, Neil had more than enough wood to last him the night.

The fire was now raging so hard that Neil actually had to slide the bedroll backward—with his new friend still lounging on top. He removed his quilt and his other jacket, situating them so he could use them when he was ready to sleep. The way he had constructed his sleeping area turned out to be correct. What wind did infiltrate was forced to go through the heat of the fire, making the back of the cave warm enough that eventually he had to unbutton his coat. From his experience, snow or ice at this altitude, upon melting, was generally safe to drink. After retrieving a quantity of ice pellets to make sufficient drinking water in his canteen, he mounded ice for the dog for her hydration. When she would take in no more, Neil finally allowed himself a chance to relax. He lit a cigarette from the fire and smiled as the dog inched her way into his lap, placing her front paws over his legs and resting peacefully.

Neil decided to just sit and think for a bit. It couldn't be past eight in the evening. Even though he was exhausted and sore from the walk, if he were to sleep now, he would be awake during the most frigid portion of the night. Instead, he ate two cans of beans, pouring the third and last can out on a flat rock for the dog. They shared his small loaf of sourdough and, seemingly sated, they both reclined at the back of the cave as the fire danced and crackled.

Having another cigarette, Neil thought back to the years he had shared with Jakey Herman. A childhood rivalry burgeoned into an adult male bond that only two men with such a union can understand. There had been no secrets between them. Joyous moments and sorrows: each was shared, dissected, and discussed. Jakey and his women; Neil and his constant struggle in the secret depths of the War Department. Their differences bound them even closer.

The Army had split the two men up after training, but after Neil had developed a bit of influence at the Unconventional Warfare School, per his recommendation, the adjutant had located Jakey. From that point forward, they were always in the same unit. And before the United States even entered the Great War, a small faction of their unit went to France, helping the French and Belgian armies see the battlefield through a different eye. It wasn't long before Neil and Jakey flouted their advisory duties—just like Sergeant Wingo and Major Hamilton had in Gallipoli— and waded into the fray. What Neil possessed in tenacity and instinct, Jakey more than equaled in cunning. A kind man, first to part with his basic necessities to help another, he could be equally fierce if he thought the other person was his adversary.

Neil remembered the fateful night, inside the German border, when Jakey had saved his life. Neil had been working on an improvised bomb, creating it from kerosene and fertilizer he'd lifted from a Saarlander's barn. Despite the cold, he remembered the sweat dripping from his nose as he completed the bomb's placement underneath a German armory. Jakey had been standing sentry on the path from the rear. An unseen soldier on guard must have heard them, sneaking to their position from the front. He'd slipped up on Neil, ordering him to stand at the tip of his bayonet.

Neil could remember the fierce expression the soldier had worn— that had been Neil's night to die. The soldier had questioned Neil as he prodded the underside of his jaw with the sharp point of the knife. When Neil would say no more, the German told him to turn. Of course, Neil refused and watched as the soldier pulled the bayonet back, coiling his arms, ready to run Neil through. Without a second to spare, Jakey rushed in from the soldier's side, as silent as Neil could ever have managed, tackling him. After tumbling to the ground, Neil watched Jakey slit the man's throat. And as the German soldier lay dying under him, Jakey whispered a brief sermon into his ear, eventually closing the soldier's stunned eyes and dragging his body under the armory, next to the fertilizer bomb.

"Jakey saved me that night," Neil said aloud. "He saved me then, and again when he sent me the letter." The dog lifted her head as he stroked her between the ears. Neil stared at her, sharing the moment.

"What shall we call you?" It didn't take long for Neil to inventory his German. "Schatze," he nearly yelled. The dog tilted her head.

"You like that name?" he asked. "Okay, Schatze, I believe it's time you and me get some shuteye." Neil groaned at the first movement after a long time of sitting in the same position. The fire was doing its job but, just in case, he stacked three more thick logs over the top, placing four more damp ones at a hand's reach. The damp logs continued to dry, hissing as they expelled water in the form of steam.

Neil nestled on the mat and pulled his quilt over him, layering his other clothes on top. Below his sweater, which would act as his pillow, Neil placed his Colt. It was locked and loaded.

Schatze waited patiently and, once Neil was settled on his side, his head resting on his arm, she curled in the shallow of her new master's torso. Deeply saddened by the way he'd left the Heinz family, Neil was thankful to have Schatze by his side. Man's best friend can certainly take the edge off. They were both asleep in only a few minutes. Neither moved until well after seven the following morning.

Chapter Forty-Two

THE SAME LOW-PRESSURE SYSTEM that had produced rain and ice for Neil was now swamping Velden, Germany with flooding storms. Preston Lord sat in the town's only café, sipping coffee as he waited. The heavy woman at the constable's home, who Lord assumed to be the man's wife, informed Lord that the constable didn't come home last night because he had been out "on a case." Judging by the size of the town, the only such case that would require an all-nighter would be, perhaps, chicken thieves. Or, maybe during the worst of crime waves, horse thieves? Even through his derision, Lord had to give it to the Germans; they made good coffee—this brew was the best he'd had in months. Strong and thick, and certainly better than any of the impotent java he'd had in tea-crazy London.

The trip across the Channel hadn't been as tricky as he thought it might. There was still limited travel available for foreigners into the growing police state and, after a tense call back to Washington, Lord had been afforded a diplomatic slot on a Lufthansa flight. The security officer from the American Embassy in Berlin had met him at the cavernous Tempelhof Airport terminal, giving him a small case loaded with German reichsmarks and a message from Director Mayfield.

Lord had connected to a smaller aircraft for the short trip to Nürnberg, reading the letter in his private seat, a cool pilsner beer in the other hand. The message, probably received by teleprinter, had been neatly retyped by someone at the embassy. Despite the message's sterile appearance, the voice was clearly Mayfield's. He bitched about the lack of an update; bitched about the suspicious death of an American bomber pilot in London; bitched about the complaints he had received from the "insipid Scouser" in Great Britain's parliament. But the tenor of the note, the primary message, was urgency. Mayfield wrote that other departments, probably aided by leaks from the nervous Brits, were beginning to ask questions and that the target needed to be found and taken care of in days, not weeks. There were talks of a German accord with Czechoslovakia—a peaceful resolution. Mayfield said it was all window-dressing:

"According to every shred of intel I've received, Hitler's intentions are still the same. He is going east by force, accord be damned. Then he's coming west. We will deal with that in time."

He can't go any direction if he's dead, Lord mused. *I wonder what Hitler would think if he knew that I, an American from the United States Department of War, am right here, in his beloved fatherland, and am probably his biggest asset at the moment.*

Lord chuckled at the irony.

"Destroy This Communiqué" was typed across the bottom of the letter and it didn't escape Lord's notice that Mayfield had been careful not to outright reveal the United States' current position on Hitler. He hinted at it, but maintained plausible deniability through the crafting of his words. While embassy pouch was typically a reliable method of communication, an intercept, especially in Nazi Germany, was not without question.

But Lord knew what Mayfield wanted; he could read between the lines. He wanted Adolf Hitler in power, for the time being, because he wanted a war between Germany and Russia. It was coming. And an assassination of Hitler might tilt the axis in favor of good sense. That was something the U.S. couldn't afford. At least, not for the moment. Not with the Russian bear rattling its considerable saber.

Lord reread the letter again before folding it and placing it inside his suit pocket. He always kept documents that were to be destroyed. Always. He knew, especially in Washington, that blackmail was the most valuable currency available. Most politicians would rather die than be caught, Lord thought, smiling to himself.

The elderly server refilled his coffee and asked him if he wanted anything to eat. Lord's German was that of a fifth-grader. He'd had four semesters at university but didn't get to practice very often. *"Nein, danke,"* he answered, giving her a thoroughly fake smile. The door to the café banged open, bringing with it the sound of the splattering rain. Lord turned his attention to the slovenly creature who ambled in, deciding that it had to be the local constable.

Upon seeing the dumpy, stain-ridden man with the Nazi armband, the server hustled behind the counter and tapped the man who must have been her husband, manning the griddle. He looked at their new customer, nodded quickly. The griddle man immediately cracked four eggs, throwing them on the sizzling skillet. After that, Lord watched the griddle man as he retrieved a thick slab of ham from the icebox, throwing it into the center of the eggs, disturbing the yolks. This seemed to be a custom breakfast, made only for a feared regular. Lord swiveled his head back to the man he presumed to be the constable. Sure enough, under the man's mottled barn coat, a massive revolver hung western style. The man grunted as the server poured his steaming coffee. As if impervious to the scalding liquid, he turned it up, guzzling so quickly that a portion of it ran down his neck.

The constable was sitting fifteen feet from Lord and it took about a second per foot for the smell to finally make its way over. Whiskey. Lots of it. So that was his "all night case." Lord idly wondered how often the constable gave his wife that same excuse.

Lord let the constable get two cups of coffee down his gullet before he approached. Just as Lord tapped the constable on his shoulder, the cook slid the steaming, oversize breakfast in front of the lawman. Ignoring Lord, the constable went for the salt and pepper. Lord tapped him again. Twisting his head with an irritated, red-eyed glare, the constable growled something undecipherable.

"Sprechen Sie English?" Lord asked, doing nothing to hide his accent, not that he could if he wanted to.

"Nein," came the reply. And then the constable fired off another phrase that Lord didn't understand but guessed, solely by tone, that the phrase was akin to the English phrase "piss off."

Lord reached into his pants pocket and removed a wad totaling one hundred reichsmarks. The small bills were wrapped in a rubber band, a perfect attention-getter. He tossed them onto the sticky counter and stabbed them with his left index finger.

Again he asked, "Sprechen Sie English?"

The constable held a hunk of egg-soaked ham in front of his mouth as his eyes alternated between the food, the money, and Lord. He jammed the food into his large oral cavity and spoke as he chewed. "A little."

"The money is yours, but I want a half-hour of your time in return." Lord gestured to a booth near the back of the café. The constable smacked his mug on the counter for a refill. In another minute, he shambled to the booth with his freshened coffee and plate of arterial hardeners. The woman hurried back with a refill for Lord and a fresh set of silverware for the constable, who accepted it before waving her away.

"What the hell do you want?" the constable grumped, twisting the wad of bills from Lord's grasp. He snapped the rubber band and inspected the money before arching his eyebrows and pocketing it.

"I'm looking for two men."

"So?"

"I want your help."

"You're American."

"Why do you say that?"

Another large bite. The constable allowed a gulf in the conversation as he gnawed on his food. Finally, he managed to get the large portion down his throat and said, "I spent seven months in an American prisoner camp on the Belgian border. Those who didn't learn English died. I learned." He sucked his teeth. "So, as you might guess, I *hate* Americans."

"Even Americans who want to give you money?"

"How much money?"

"Much more than what I've paid you."

After shoveling in a mouthful of egg, the constable said, "Exceptions can always be made."

Despite his grubby appearance, the constable's English seemed excellent. Lord felt he might have found his man—assuming the constable knew anything about the airfield where the German defector would have refueled. Greedy people are an operative's easiest mark, and this one made no bones about his desires. Lord repeated his need. "I'm looking for two men."

"You said that already. What's in it for me?"

"Another hundred, for now. And *no one* can know I'm here."

"Do you speak German?"

"Some, but since I'm paying you, I don't feel like making the effort."

The constable sawed another piece of ham. He sandwiched it between pieces of butter-drenched bread and stuffed his mouth so full he was forced to breathe through his nose. He sounded like a bulldog with breathing problems. After a full minute of chewing, he managed to swallow before swilling his coffee. *"Wasser!"* he yelled over his shoulder. He turned back to Lord.

"Tell me about these men."

"One is American. Dark hair. He has one blue eye, and one green. Dapper. Big guy. Dangerous."

"And the other?"

"The other I've never seen, but I know he was a German pilot back during the war and flies here from England."

The constable's head snapped up. His green eyes, rimmed in hangover red, focused as his pupils constricted. "A pilot who flies from England?"

"Yes."

The eyes continued to stare at Lord before the constable nodded once, stirring the remaining egg. He began to chuckle, his great belly bouncing up and down as the liquid inside his stomach could be heard sloshing.

"Well?" Lord demanded.

"I know everything about these two men," the constable said. He ran his bratwurst index finger through the yolk, slurping it with his mouth. "But it's gonna cost you far more than another hundred, doughboy."

The Department of War man's mouth broke into a wide grin, displaying his perfectly square teeth, which appeared as if they had been leveled with a belt sander.

Preston Lord had, *indeed*, found his man.

* * *

Many years had passed since Neil had known such hunger.

It took him and Schatze a little more than a full day to make it to Innsbruck. They arrived, worse for the wear and famished, late in the afternoon on Thursday, more than 24 hours after he'd departed the Heinz farm. Earlier today, following a late start due to the weather, it took five hours to walk down the icy mountain from the pass. The temperature rose sharply with the decrease in elevation, along with warmer weather that had pushed in. After stopping to eat the last can of beans, which he shared with Schatze, Neil eventually hitched a ride from the town of Jenbach. An elderly man with an old farm truck was happy to give them a lift in return for twenty of Neil's reichsmarks.

The back of the truck was a welcome mode of transportation for the long ride down into the Karwendelgebirge Valley. Neil napped as Schatze wedged her head through the slats of the truck's side, enjoying the wind in only the way a dog can do. The truck bed was loaded with dirty beets and potatoes, providing a comfortable, if a bit lumpy, surface to nestle into. In fact, the lumps actually massaged Neil's aching muscles as the old truck bounced its way down the river road toward Innsbruck. Once he'd awoken from his nap, Neil had been so hungry that he even tried to munch on an uncooked potato. He managed one choking bite, tossing the potato over the side of the truck as Schatze stared at him curiously.

Neil wasn't that hungry.

It was after six in the evening when they jumped down from the truck at the outskirts of Innsbruck. Neil thanked the old man, paying him as promised. Then he turned to Innsbruck, reminding himself that this was where his friend had died.

As they walked into the valley city, the lowering sun burned in the southwest between two mountains, splashing a riot of golden light over the picturesque town encircled by towering Alps. Neil and the dog followed the river, which rushed past in a peculiar color of sea green. A bridge sign pronounced the waterway's name as the Sill River.

Innsbruck itself was rustic and handsome, not unlike some of the mountain resorts Neil and Emilee had visited in the Sierras. As Neil and his new companion moved farther into the city, they found significant crowds of people on the sidewalks. The shops and restaurants grew swankier as the center of Innsbruck crept closer. Neil kept his head down, feeling quite out of place in the well-heeled resort with his shaggy hair, unshaven face and terribly soiled clothes. With Schatze loping along beside him and the now dirty canvas bag over his back, he looked less like an intruder and more like a tramp. And tramps attract cops. The very last thing Neil needed was a run-in with a polizei with nothing better to do.

"Ich bin Dieter Dremel," Neil murmured over and over, honing his name and accent in the event he was stopped and questioned. As he passed through the center of town, right where the Sill River snaked, Neil noticed two teenage boys skipping rocks for bounces and distance. He rubbed his stubbly face and took a deep breath. *Time to be an Austrian.* From the bridge he whistled for their attention and asked them where Berchtoldshofweg was. Without batting an eyelash at his words—making Neil exhale in relief—the shorter of the two boys pointed west, the direction Neil had been heading.

"Keep going to the outskirts of town and it'll be on the right," the boy yelled.

"Vielen dank!" Neil yelled back, watching as the boys forgot about him and resumed their arguing over the previous skip. Neil and Schatze picked up their pace.

As they were just departing the inner city, they passed by a cozy-looking restaurant in a row of what looked like fine establishments. Neil and Schatze kept on the other side of the road, by the river. In front of the restaurant, a long black Mercedes eased to a stop with a faint chirp from the drum brakes. The uniformed driver exited, circling the automobile to open the suicide rear door, giving avenue to a pair of exquisite legs that immediately appeared. They were attached to an equally attractive woman. She stood and straightened her dress, her head adorned with a cherry red hat and black lace veil. Behind her was a tall man with light blond hair. He shrugged off the chauffer, donning his tunic on his own and buttoning it slowly. He was in the *Schutzstaffel*—the SS. Neil tried to see his rank, knowing immediately that the man was an officer—but unable to discern the rank from the distance.

The SS officer frowned when he noticed Neil, the tramp, looking back at him. Neil lowered his head, silently cursing himself for gawking at the foreign sight. He continued his shuffle along the river path.

Smoke billowed from the SS's mouth as he flicked his cigarette in Neil's direction. He glared for a moment before shaking his head and murmuring something to his lady. After she straightened his belt, the SS officer touched the woman on her rear end, guiding her into the eatery as the setting sun reflected off of his gleaming boots. Neil glanced back to see the officer look at him again before disappearing into the restaurant.

There was something unnerving about the SS officer's chilly stare.

Once more, Neil looked back at the restaurant. There was no sign of the man.

Neil continued on.

* * *

Standartenführer Anton Aying of the Schutzstaffel paused inside the front door of the restaurant. His date, the wife of a wealthy—and much older— Munich businessman, turned and stared at him as the host had already reached their table. She shrugged impatiently.

"Go and sit, my dear," Aying told her. "You choose the wine." After he slept with her tonight, he'd make damn sure her husband found out about this tryst—as well as all the other men she'd spread her long legs for. She was far too into herself. Fifteen minutes with her and Aying was already annoyed.

Setting his irritation with the Bavarian princess aside, he stepped into the bar area of the restaurant, seeing a Hauptscharführer at the end of the long curved bar. The man's eyelids seemed a bit heavy. Aying didn't know the senior NCO personally, but did recognize his face as he recalled the man's reputation. He was known for his diligence and cruelty. In fact, Aying remembered him from several months before, when the Hauptscharführer had brutally beaten a well-known Innsbruck painter, who was also a reputed homosexual. The painter succumbed several days later to his injuries. Though the painter's sexual orientation was never proven, the message to the undesirables had been sent with an exclamation.

Yes, the Hauptscharführer would do just fine for what Aying had in mind.

Aying's rank, Standartenführer, was the SS equivalent to a full colonel. The Hauptscharführer at the bar was roughly equivalent to a first sergeant—a senior NCO position. While the Hauptscharführer was a ranking NCO, Aying was miles up the SS food chain.

"Hauptscharführer," Aying barked as he walked behind him at the bar.

The Hauptscharführer nearly fell out of his chair upon seeing Aying. Aying was prominent in Innsbruck and a near legend among the ranks of the SS. Stumbling to his feet, the Hauptscharführer snapped to attention, boot heels clicking, and barked out a sharp phrase that essentially promised to fulfill whatever request Aying might have for him.

"Are you waiting for someone?" Aying asked, eyeing the three empty glasses in front of the Hauptscharführer's spot at the bar.

"No, sir. I've the evening off, sir, and was…uh…just having a beer or two."

Aying sniffed, estimating that the Hauptscharführer had ingested several more than a few. "Well, I'm not deliberately trying to interrupt your evening off, but I wonder if you might do me a *personal* favor?"

"Anything, sir," the man replied, nearly breathless. "Anything at all."

Aying tossed several bills on the counter and gestured to the bartender, telling him that the Hauptscharführer was leaving. Aying led his fellow SS outside, pointing west. "Just minutes ago, a man walked by with a scraggly dog in tow. The man looked a bit like a vagabond, what with his soiled clothes and scruff. But he seemed well-fed and…and…"

"Sir?"

Aying couldn't quite put his finger on what he'd seen. "The man had knowing eyes, Hauptscharführer, if that makes sense. Frankly, I don't like the way the *Hurensohn* looked at me." Aying described the man in detail, along with the dog. "Go and find him, Hauptscharführer. Find him and bring him to me."

"Here, sir?"

"Out back. I'll alert my driver to watch for you. Do you have a vehicle?"

The Hauptscharführer swallowed. "I, er…"

"Say it, man. There's not much time."

"I used the Sturm motorcycle, sir. And I…I didn't request permission."

Aying gave the man a sour smile. "Then I suggest you satisfy my request, Hauptscharführer. If so, I'll forget your transgression." Aying looked for the NCO's sidearm. "Do you have a weapon?"

"My knife, sir. And there's an MP-35 concealed in the sidecar."

"Handcuffs?"

"In the sidecar, also."

"Very good, Hauptscharführer," Aying said, tapping out a cigarette. "Haul ass and find him. Beat him, if you must. But I'd like him alive."

"If he runs?"

"Then, by all means, shoot him. I trust your judgment. Go now."

The Hauptscharführer hurried across the street, to where the motorcycle was parked.

"Hauptscharführer!" Aying called out.

The man halted, staring expectantly at Aying. "Sir?"

Aying lit his cigarette, blowing smoke from his nose and mouth. *"Töte den Hund."*

It meant, "Kill the dog."

Chapter Forty-Three

FIVE MINUTES LATER, JUST AS THE BOY HAD SAID HE WOULD, Neil found Berchtoldshofweg. The road was marked by a massive stone on the corner, the name hand-painted on the rock. Thankfully, Neil reached it without any problem from the local polizei. The road was made of hard-packed gravel. It started as a slight incline through a narrow field but, upon reaching the trees, it climbed steeply. Neil looked upward at the mountainside, wondering how far the home was located up the road. Summoning his remaining energy, he turned to make his way up the road when the sound of a motor grabbed his attention.

The flat and meandering road that had led him from town had been quiet, other than a few cars heading into Innsbruck. Neil peered back towards town. Between the trees, he saw a motorcycle with a sidecar coming his way. The vehicle was painted dark gray and was ridden by a man in a gray uniform.

A gray SS uniform.

The driver wasn't approaching at high speed. He was puttering along, his head scanning as if he were looking for someone.

Wasting no time, Neil crossed the road, dropping down into the walled basin of the River Sill. The drop was six feet and left Neil on a slightly elevated sandbar at the river's edge. Schatze stood at the river wall until Neil reached up and deposited her softly with him on the sandbar. He ducked down and waited for the motorcycle to pass.

As he crouched there, he wondered if the rider might be looking for him? He recalled the visual exchange between himself and the SS officer just minutes before. Even though he'd only gotten a few glimpses of the rider, Neil was almost certain he wasn't the same dapper SS he'd seen earlier. The SS must have hundreds of men stationed in Innsbruck, perhaps even thousands. The rider might be on scheduled patrol or could simply be heading to see a lady friend. Setting positive thoughts aside, Neil also admitted that the officer he'd seen earlier could have sent this rider to find him and Schatze. And if the rider had keen eyes, he might have seen Neil and Schatze drop down into the river basin.

As the old adage went—if you can see the enemy, the enemy can see you.

Neil removed the Colt from his bag and took a series of steadying breaths. The engine was closer but the pitch hadn't changed—meaning the rider hadn't sped up or slowed down. Neil glanced upstream, back towards the city. The sandbar led nearly the entire way beside the wall. And approximately 200 meters from where Neil stood, poking through the northern river wall, was a large drainage pipe that led back under the road. The pipe appeared to be at least three feet in diameter.

"Come on, girl," Neil said, concealing his pistol at his side as he scurried to the pipe.

* * *

The SS Hauptscharführer rode barely above idle, pondering the peculiar request from Standartenführer Aying. What was it about the hobo that had set Aying's curiosity aflame? Well, it was of no matter. This was a golden opportunity for the Hauptscharführer to be awarded with the highest enlisted rank in the Innsbruck and Hall im Tyrol administrative area. The previous top enlisted man, carrying the rank of Stabsscharführer, had just been promoted back to Berlin. Any enlisted SS adorned with this highest of enlisted ranks enjoyed nearly the same benefits as an SS officer. To the Hauptscharführer, that meant more booze, more women and the freedom to beat—or kill— damn near anyone he wanted.

So, it was critical he find this tramp and bring him back to Aying. After, of course, he killed the dog.

Something up ahead had caught the Hauptscharführer's eye. Admittedly, he was a bit cloudy after all the beers, not to mention the schnapps he'd been nipping since before lunch. But, had he just seen a dog drop down over the river wall? The dog had disappeared slowly, as if being let down by invisible wires. Unsure of himself, the Hauptscharführer slowed the BMW motorcycle and eased it into the grass. He rubbed his eyes, staring at the spot where the supposed dog had been. Nothing.

Taking the MP-35, the Hauptscharführer slid a magazine into its side and chambered a round. He walked to where he thought he'd seen the dog, seeing fresh depressions in the green grass. Leading with the submachine gun, he carefully peered over the edge of the river wall, spotting two sets of footprints in the river sand.

One belonged to a dog. The other to a man. The footprints led back to the east, and terminated at a drainage pipe that ran under the road.

The Hauptscharführer glanced over his left shoulder. The vagrant and his dog were in the drainage pipe and were going to emerge on the other side.

And that's where they'd die.

He sprinted across the road, the MP-35 at the ready.

* * *

Neil heard the motorcycle stop before the engine was shut off. Damn.

Thankfully, Schatze didn't seem unnerved in the close quarters of the drainpipe. She leaned against Neil, probably calmed by his presence. While the pipe offered Neil plenty of room for movement forward and backward, it would prove extremely difficult to turn around, especially with his stitches. The bottom of the pipe was covered in at least six inches of dirt, silt and rock. This took away precious free space a man of Neil's size would need to change direction. He'd pushed Schatze in and gone in head first, meaning he was facing away from the river, to the north side of the road.

Neil knew it was only a matter of time before the SS would see their footsteps leading to the pipe. The question was: would the man follow the footsteps, or try to intercept Neil on the north side of the road?

While it was far from an educated guess, Neil gambled that since this particular SS rated a motorcycle, he was in a senior position. A high-ranking officer or NCO must possess some sort of intellect, correct? Thus, Neil took the chance that the SS would attempt to intercept him and Schatze on the *north* side of the road. A flimsy theory but, at the moment, it was the best Neil could come up with.

Testing his ability to turn and shoot backward, Neil finally settled in, satisfied he could shoot without hitting Schatze. He attuned his ears to listen for his hunter.

But all he heard was the quiet murmur of the River Sill.

Where was the SS? What was he doing?

* * *

The SS Hauptscharführer eased his way into the summer undergrowth at the north side of the road. He was sweating. To his left was a steep and winding road that led up the base of the nearest mountain. To his right was the mouth of a road that branched off in three directions, leading to a populous area known as Hötting, overlooking Innsbruck.

Just ahead were the numerous ditches that converged to dump their water in the drainage pipe. They were dry at the moment, as was the basin at the mouth of the pipe. The Hauptscharführer placed his finger on the trigger and began to creep down into the catch basin.

* * *

Schatze growled. It was quiet, more of a rumble from her throat. She was facing north, her ears perked in that direction. Neil calmed her, keeping his

Colt aimed to the north. If the SS were to appear at the pipe, Neil estimated the shot to be no more than thirty feet.

This situation didn't call for a summoning of his Shoshone training. This was a real-life reckoning, putting Neil on the precipice of killing—or being killed. Here, there was nowhere to go, nothing to do—other than survive. Though Neil hadn't seen them in action, he knew the SS were chosen for their distinct traits, and one of those traits was ferocity.

This man who was pursuing Neil was almost certainly doing so with bad intentions. Capture, torture, interrogate, death—it was the SS routine. While Neil had confidence in himself, he knew all about torture. They would eventually break him.

And that would lead to the children being found. Found by the SS.

Such an outcome was not an option. Neil would rather die.

As Schatze growled again, he gripped the Colt with both hands and focused his aim on the mouth of the pipe.

A bead of sweat dangled on Neil's right eyebrow. He ignored it, every ounce of his being trained on the flaxen disc of daylight thirty feet ahead.

* * *

The Hauptscharführer didn't like this. He was now able to see the silt just inside the mouth of the pipe, and it appeared undisturbed. So the tramp was either hiding in the pipe or had backed out the other end. The Hauptscharführer doubted the latter. The tramp would have no way of knowing which direction the Hauptscharführer had taken. And it was just like some old hobo to hide in a pipe—to take the easy way out and shy away. And who shies away?

A coward.

While the Hauptscharführer wanted to please his superior, he also enjoyed killing. And cowards were near the top of his list of undesirables. Why go to the trouble of soiling his own hands on some worthless vagrant by bringing him in? Perhaps, instead, he'd kill the filthy bastard and concoct a story that would leave himself looking like a hero? Maybe a verbal exchange with the tramp, outing him as a sicko pedophile, followed by a chase and a killing?

Heureka!

Recalling that he had a battered old Dreyse pistol in his bag—the one the Hauptscharführer had used to brutalize the artist, beating him about the head and face—the SS decided he could plant the pistol on the vagrant's dead body. He'd simply tell Aying that the vagrant had pulled it on him and—*voila!*—the killing was justified. The Hauptscharführer suppressed a menacing chuckle.

Time to die, you dirty prick.

The determined SS gripped the MP-35, twisting as he dropped down to the opening of the pipe. He landed perfectly, facing south in a ready shooting position as he pulled the trigger.

Bullets pumped from the MP-35 like angered wasps.

* * *

Whatever rifle the SS held spit fire as soon as the man's feet struck the ground at the north end of the pipe. The tri-slotted muzzle brake produced a muzzle flash that resembled a snake's mouth—twin fangs and a spitting tongue. It was a sight Neil had seen before, and among the scariest sights on earth.

Neil's right index finger had already answered the call, returning fire with the Colt. Fighting not to close his eyes, Neil had begun low and walked each shot upward, expending four rounds that had knocked the SS backward.

The noise!

Neil shuddered over the intense ear pain from the blasts in the enclosed space but remained focused on his target. The SS was splayed unnaturally backward, his exploded right leg folded underneath him, as if he had a new joint mid-shin.

His head collapsed onto his extended arms as Neil took a series of great breaths. There must have been fifteen rounds that had roared through the pipe, all of them too high. He rotated his eyes upward, seeing the long striations where the bullets from the submachine gun had sparked across the top of the pipe.

Shooting high with a submachine gun was a common misstep. Thank God.

Neil turned. Schatze had backed away and was cowering as low as she could, trembling with her tail underneath her. Neil hurriedly checked her to make sure she wasn't hit. Satisfied she was unharmed, he offered what reassurance he could before scurrying forward and viewing his aggressor as the ringing in his ears reached a fever pitch.

Indeed, the man was a senior SS of some sort. Though it had been some time since Neil had viewed Schutzstaffel rank, he assumed the man was an NCO in his mid or late thirties. He was quite dead. Neil decided to deal with the body later. For now, he made his way up to the road, seeing no cars in either direction. He hurried to the BMW, bringing the already warm engine to life on a single kick. As Schatze emerged above the catch basin, Neil popped the clutch and roared across the road, driving the motorcycle down into the undergrowth. He looked all around, satisfied that the SS machine couldn't be seen from the road.

Now, with a few more minutes on his hands, Neil sat in the catch basin and comforted the dog for a moment. Then, he undressed the bloody corpse and covered the dead man's body in saplings and leaves. Neil stuffed his own clothes down in the sidecar and donned the bloody, undersized clothes of the SS. Unable to lace the man's boots, Neil removed the laces and tied off the top of the boots around his calves. Though he might pass a casual glance, Neil knew he'd never pass any sort of visual muster. But he'd also seen no traffic emerge from Berchtoldshofweg, so he might not have to.

There was no choice. If he attracted more trouble, he'd simply have to deal with it.

Neil hoisted the now calm Schatze into the sidecar and slowly puttered through the undergrowth to the turnoff at Berchtoldshofweg.

He studied both sides of the steep road. The undergrowth was too thick and loaded with mountain rocks in the ditches to attempt to ride the side and stay hidden. He'd have to take the road and hope for the best.

Pulling the gray SS garrison cap down over his shaggy hair, Neil twisted the throttle, let out the clutch, and roared up the steep climb.

Chapter Forty-Four

SINCE NEIL'S NEW ADDRESS WAS 2 BERCHTOLDSHOFWEG, he didn't think the house would be very far from the bottom. He was wrong. Though the motorcycle didn't have an odometer, Neil estimated that the cabin was several kilometers up the impossibly steep road. Thankfully, Schatze loved the windy ride. Whatever fear she'd had over the gunfight melted away as her tongue flapped in the breeze. And despite his fear of being discovered, Neil would have been lying if he'd said he wasn't grateful not to have made the climb on foot.

The driveway dropped off the left side of the steep mountain road. Neil silenced the bike, holding in the clutch as he let it coast down the driveway, parking beside a detached garage and well out of sight of the road. Pistol in hand, Neil petted Schatze and listened. His ears were still ringing but his hearing had come back for the most part. Other than the birds in the trees, he heard nothing.

After lifting Schatze from the sidecar and petting her a few times, Neil dug into his bag and retrieved the round ring with three old-fashioned keys. They'd been given to him in New York by the Jewish forger. Silencing the keys in his hand, Neil walked across the driveway and viewed the house, silhouetted by the sundown occurring on its opposite side.

The house was charming.

Made of stacked river stone, it was built in cottage style, almost perfectly square, topped off with a shake roof. The rear of the house faced to the west. Neil peered to the side of the cottage. Although it was nestled on a level lot that reached about 50 feet beyond the cottage, the back yard appeared to fall straight off at its rear. As Schatze sniffed all around, Neil moved back to the front of the cottage. He studied the sizeable, unattached garage he'd parked next to. It was covered in the same shake shingles as the roof of the cottage. The garage was barred shut, the end of the bar marked by a large padlock.

Neil turned back to the cottage. It had several flower boxes on the front windows, bursting with petunias in full red bloom. The stoop was covered in a clean, brushy mat, and the hedges around the front of the cottage were neatly trimmed.

The house certainly didn't appear to be vacant.

Neil eased up the walk, chewing the inside of his lip. After climbing the low stoop, he knocked. Nothing. Knocked louder. Nothing. He yelled a German "hallo" several times. *Nichts.*

Making a full rotation, Neil still saw no one, so he decided to try the keys. He tried one. Didn't fit. He shook his head. Was he at the wrong address? He tried the second key—it *did* fit. He turned it. The thick wooden door opened. After calling out again, Neil stepped inside the darkened cottage and listened to the silence. Schatze waited politely on the front stoop. Standing inside, Neil removed his pistol and allowed his ears to adjust to the silence, alert for the slightest noise, his head and eyes on a swivel. All he could hear was the faint ringing in his ears.

The cottage smelled pleasant and lived-in. After a minute, Schatze groaned as she lowered herself to the ground, unwilling to stand for the duration of her new master's cautious entry.

It took Neil only a moment to clear the cabin's three darkened rooms—the large room with a kitchen, a bedroom, and a bathroom off to the side. Satisfied, he came back to the entry, clicking his tongue to beckon the dog. He found a switch and flipped it, surprised that the electricity was connected and working. The main room, just like the entire house, was small. It had a low ceiling and, against the far wall, a large rock fireplace. On the back wall of the house were two windows covered in drapes. He pulled both open, allowing the gloaming to seep in.

Neil walked back outside, further concealing the BMW behind the garage. Unless someone searched the property, they wouldn't see it even if they came to the front door. But when would the SS be missed? Was he on an actual mission or just out for the evening? Neil recalled the heavy smell of alcohol coming from the dead man's settling body.

The catch basin where the man's body was located was well off the road. Neil doubted anyone would find it in the next few hours. After dark, he'd have to go back down and retrieve the corpse. For now, he decided he was safe for the moment. He went back inside.

The back windows afforded a fine view of the grassy back yard and the mountains in the distance. The kitchen was part of the main room, only separated by a small row of cabinets with a working surface on top. He opened several cabinets in the kitchen, finding plates and utensils. He walked to the simple bedroom with the one bed. It looked inviting. He stepped into the bathroom, noticing that the massive claw-foot tub had gas heat. Without hesitation, Neil opened the water full force and lit the heat to the tub.

As the tub filled with clean, clear water, he locked the front door and went back into the kitchen, filling a bowl with water and placing it on the floor for Schatze. He found a can of beef stew and a can opener, pouring the stew into another bowl so she could replenish herself after their journey. While she ate, Neil opened another can of stew meat, devouring all of it cold, even turning the can up to drink the remaining juice. He opened another, repeating the process. As he finished his meal, he spied a container of Naphtha, next to a row of pipes. He used it to refill his lighter. It took several tries before the memento lighter produced flame and, when it did, he lit a cigarette. Feeling markedly better, he went back to the bathroom.

The bathtub was halfway full. Neil checked the water temperature and increased the heat. He removed his two sets of clothes from his bag, placing them on the bed. After rummaging around in the bathroom, he finally located a bar of gritty soap in the cabinet, which he placed beside the tub with a washcloth and a towel. When the tub was nearly full, he turned off the water, stripped his clothes and climbed in. The water was lukewarm but heating rapidly.

Sheer bliss.

Neil moaned as he finally acknowledged the pain and soreness from the pink, raised scars on his side. He had made certain to walk normally, and not favor his side, because he remembered from his Army days how an uneven gait could wind up causing more problems, especially with one's hips and back. But, in forcing himself to walk normally, he had tortured the freshly repaired wounds, making them feel as if they might burst open at any moment. And now, with the heat of the water, his skin expanded, stretching the stitches to their limit and making his wounds ache more.

Closing his eyes, he forced himself to lie back as the flame heaters went to work on the water. Schatze padded into the room, still licking her chops from the stew delicacy and the full bowl of water she had just ingested. She perked her ears upon seeing Neil nearly submerged. He opened one eye, telling her to lie down, which she did. In another minute, she was asleep and snoring. Neil slowed his mind to a crawl, knowing he needed rest before he could move into action, and he might as well start to convalesce at this very moment.

The bath water was finally scalding hot. He turned off the heat before sitting straight up in the water and scrubbing himself with the soap and washcloth. Neil dunked his head then soaped his shaggy hair and face, using the washcloth to vigorously scour every square inch of his body. When he felt like he was finally clean, he pulled the chain and allowed the water to drain completely. Again, he turned the water on full force, along with the heater, and repeated the process, two more times. He did it until the water was as clear as glass, when he was finally able to pronounce himself unsoiled. Neil was a fastidiously neat man and, since he had jumped from the Queen Mary, he'd not had one chance to properly clean himself. As soon as the final cycle was full, he rested in the hot water, turning his head to see Schatze still sleeping on the floor. She appeared to be dreaming, whimpering and making a running motion.

Poor dog, Neil thought. Probably wonders what the hell she got herself into.

He retrieved his trimmers and carefully snipped the stitches on his head, removing them between pinched fingernails. He repeated this process with the larger thread on his body, wincing as he yanked each one out, a few of them clinging to tiny chunks of flesh. Finished, Neil leaned back, rubbing the healing wounds and feeling good to have finally removed the painful sutures.

Then Neil's mind turned back to his mission. He didn't know how to go about finding Jakey's allies, but it would be his first order of business. The forger had told Neil they were awaiting his arrival. Neil assumed they would be Jewish, meaning they were most likely in hiding. Judging by the papers he'd read when he'd been with the Heinz family, a conflict with Czechoslovakia was looming. If that kicked off, life in Austria would probably take a major turn to wartime frugality—and possibly further action against the Jewish population.

Most importantly, Neil had seven days until the September 15th deadline. Seven days to arrange transport and get the children away from the Reich.

First he'd need to find a way to hide the dead SS and the motorcycle. After that, rest be damned, Neil needed to get a lay of the land and make hasty plans to exchange his diamonds. He needed to create a normal image for himself—starting with a good haircut—after which he'd begin to search for Jakey's contacts, in the event they didn't find him first. Rubbing his beard, Neil wondered if the SS officer he'd seen would recognize him once he was properly groomed and wearing suitable attire.

He thought about the SS officer and his woman heading into the restaurant, about the way the man had dubiously eyed him. He would have to study the way the locals dressed, and of course the—

Neil heard a scraping noise, as did Schatze.

The dog appeared bewildered for a moment before she stood and growled, the hairs between her shoulder blades bristling like a porcupine's. Before he could react, she bolted from the bedroom.

Shit.

The Colt was on the bed and here he was lazing in the tub, naked in more ways than one. How many hundreds of lessons had he learned from the Shoshone Indians, as well as in nearly every block of defense training during his time in the Army, that stated, "Always be ready. Never let your guard down. And *expect* the unexpected."

Clichés, but for a very good reason.

He listened as he stood, hearing nothing. As he stepped from the heated water, he was surprised to see Schatze pad back into the bedroom, tail wagging, bringing with her a girl in a long coat, her head wrapped in a kerchief. Neil stood there, dripping wet, staring at the girl, his mouth falling open dumbly. He almost spoke English, but thanks to nearly four weeks of practice, he stammered his words in German.

"Who are you?"

The girl's enormous brown eyes moved up and down, pausing once, wide-eyed, before she looked at his face in a type of hopeful curiosity. "Are you...Dieter Dremel?" she asked.

Neil grabbed the towel, wrapping it around his midsection before he croaked, "Ja."

Her face broke into a wide smile, which she quickly tempered. "I am Madeline," she whispered. "Thank God you're finally here! We've only got one more week."

Chapter Forty-Five

NEIL STEPPED FROM THE TUB while Madeline turned around. He tightened the towel around himself and walked into the bedroom. Madeline turned to him and focused on the bright pink scars at Neil's side.

"Were you hurt? Is that why you're so late?" she asked. Her eyes moved to the base of the tub, to the scattering of snipped stitches.

While flummoxed by his contact's unannounced arrival, Neil managed a polite smile, his German recovering. "It's Madeline, correct?"

"Yes."

"Madeline, would you mind if I get dressed before we speak? When I'm dressed, I'd like to learn a bit more about you before I tell you all that happened."

"Of course," she replied, eyes averted. "I have coffee in the kitchen. Shall I make a pot?"

"Please."

Madeline walked from the room with Schatze in tow. "You'll find a closet full of clothes in the wardrobe," she said from the other room. "The doctor guessed your sizes based on all he'd heard."

"All the doctor has heard?" Neil whispered, confused.

He let the towel fall away as he leaned against the bed, feeling faint. The overheated water combined with the rush of fear, as well as his weariness from the trip and all that had happened, made his world spin.

Taking great gasps of air, and recalling his personal charge before he "visited" the veterinarian a few nights ago, Neil vowed to eradicate the amateur slip-ups from here forward. He shut the door. It only took Neil a moment to decide to trust the young woman named Madeline. What other motivation might she have?

He hurriedly dressed in a surprisingly well-fitting shirt and slacks. Back in the bathroom, he eyed his beard and long hair, trying to remember what he looked like when properly groomed. With a subtle change to his hair color and new clothes, Neil felt he could avoid any association with the tramp who'd staggered through town only a few hours ago.

That tramp had killed an SS. Police would be on the lookout.

Once Neil had brushed his teeth, he grabbed his cigarettes and walked into the cabin's main room. A percolator on the gas stove filled the house with the aroma of strong coffee. Madeline knelt in front of the fireplace, putting the finishing touches on an unlit stack of logs that would soon become a fire. Neil looked her over.

Without the concealment of the long coat she had worn, Neil realized she was tiny. She wore a patterned dress and ankle-height lace-up shoes with thick wool socks spilling over the tops. The outfit might have been fashionable twenty years ago. Her raven hair was pulled tightly to the back of her head, woven and held into place by pins. She turned to him.

"The coffee is on. I hope you don't mind that I'm making a fire. It's only September but it gets quite cold in the evenings here."

"Thank you," Neil answered, returning her smile. He handed the lighter to her and watched as she lit the paper she had stuffed under the kindling.

Madeline studied his lighter for a moment. She blinked rapidly and handed it back. "What a...a...sw-sweet dog," she said, tripping on her words. She rubbed Schatze behind the ears and wiped a tear away with her other hand.

Neil frowned at Madeline for a moment before looking down at Schatze. "I'm afraid I can't take credit for her manners. She was obviously someone's pet. She took up with me on the walk from Germany and simply wouldn't turn back."

"Walk?"

"Excuse me?"

"You *walked* from Germany?"

"I did." Neil gave her the briefest of explanations, promising to tell her the details later.

"Well, you have a car, now," she said. "A very nice car."

"Out in the garage?"

"Yes."

Madeline poured coffee for them both and they sat at the small kitchen table, with Schatze lying beneath them, touching both of their feet. Neil lit a cigarette and pushed the pack to Madeline. She declined. He could see why Jakey might have been involved with her. She was older than he had first thought. Her lack of size somehow made her seem juvenile, but now, studying her face, he guessed she was around thirty years of age. If she decided to fix her hair and dress up, Neil predicted she would be a stunner.

"Tell me about Jakey," he said, exhaling his smoke away from her.

Her expressive brown eyes flickered and cut away, just as they had earlier. She tightened her lips over her teeth, obviously struggling. "Not just yet. I'm not ready."

"My lighter?" Neil asked, sliding it on the table. "Similar to Jakey's? Is that what got to you?"

"Please," she said in a strained voice. "Not now."

"I understand," he answered, looking around the cabin. "Do you live here?"

"I stay here occasionally. I usually live down in town, with a doctor and his family. They're sympathetic to the cause."

"Jewish?"

Madeline shook her head.

Neil dragged on his cigarette. "They're not Jewish?"

"Let me give you a quick lesson. I'm Jewish, by birth. But I don't practice the Jewish faith. Make sense?"

"Yes."

"But to the Nazis, I'm still just a despicable Jew. Like me, there are other Jews still here in Austria. Some do practice the Jewish faith, but now only in secret. And according to the Reich's outrageous Nürnberger laws, there are several degrees of Jews. I'm actually what they classify as a *Mischling*...a half-breed. Regardless," she finished with a weary smile, "in the end, to them, I'm *still* just a Jew."

"Sounds extremely harsh. I'm guessing there's persecution behind all this classification."

She laughed a laugh that was devoid of humor. "You could certainly make that assumption. The last year has been hell on earth. Even Austrians risk vicious persecution associating with Jews." She reset herself. "But there *are* sympathizers—good people—like the doctor and his family. Then, there are the apathetic, which is where most of the locals lie. I can't say I blame them—they have their own problems without creating more by running to the defense of others." The corners of her mouth ticked downward. "And then there are persecutors. Locally, the persecutors are chiefly Nazi."

"Today, when I first walked through town, I saw a man...an SS officer. He stared at me, maybe because he thought I was a vagrant."

"And?"

"Well, I kept on going. A bit later, when I neared the turnoff to come up here, another SS appeared on a motorcycle. He was coming from town, slowly, as if he were looking for someone."

"Oh, no," she said, hand over her mouth. "They're already on to you?"

He made a calming motion with his hands. "I'm not so sure they are, per se."

"What happened?"

Neil eyed her. "Do you really want to hear this?"

"Remember who my beau was? I think I can handle it."

Chuckling despite the situation, Neil said, "Well...the SS who was looking for someone...he's now growing cold in the catch basin down by the river."

This time both hands flew over her mouth. "You killed him?"

"It was that or die."

"Did anyone see?"

He shook his head, touching the back of her hand. "No one saw. I brought the motorcycle here."

"There's a Schutzstaffel motorcycle *here*?" she asked, incredulous.

"And a sidecar. Schatze loved riding in it."

"What about the body?"

"I need to move it tonight. And the motorcycle."

"Could we make it look like he died somewhere else?"

"I've been thinking about that," Neil said, crushing out the tiny nub of a cigarette. "I think it would be best if I somehow dispose of both the body and motorcycle so they're not found."

"And how do you do that?"

"I'm working on it."

There was a gulf in the conversation. Finally, she said, "You killed an SS soldier."

"I did."

A grin formed on her face as she poured more coffee. Neil lit another cigarette and the two sat there in silence, thinking independently.

* * *

Standartenführer Anton Aying had finished his sumptuous meal and was ready to bed his married date and be done with her. She'd aggravated him more by the minute. As she droned on about the intricacies of navigating Munich society, Aying snapped his fingers to the waiter.

"Yes, sir?" the waiter asked.

"Bring the bill and get my driver in here."

The driver arrived in less than a minute. Aying told him to bend down so he could whisper to him. "Have you been approached by the SS Hauptscharführer I sent looking for the hobo?"

The driver shook his head.

"Have you seen the Hauptscharführer?"

"I saw him leave on the motorcycle, but I haven't seen him since."

"How long has it been?"

The driver produced his pocket watch. "Nearly three hours, sir."

Aying rubbed his chin, recalling how drunk the man had been. "Get his name for me. I'll speak to his commander tomorrow."

"I will, sir. There are some soldiers in the bar next door who probably know his name. If you'll recall, he's the one who brutalized that homo artist until—"

"I remember. Just make it fast because we're leaving soon."

"Yes, sir," the driver replied, disappearing.

Aying massaged his nose, thinking about the Hauptscharführer. He was probably passed out in a ditch. "Dumb drunk bastard."

"Excuse me?" his date asked.

"Are you ready?" he snapped.

"To go dancing?"

"No dancing tonight, *Liebling*." Aying tapped his watch. "We've got to get right down to business and then I'll have my driver take you home."

"Up to the chalet? But I thought I was staying down here in town with you tonight."

"Change of plans." He lit a cigarette and shrugged. "You can go home now, if you like."

The woman pouted. "You said I could stay with you."

"Something's come up." He took her hand, moving it to his leg, sliding it upward. "Well? Do you want to go home, or do you at least want to stop by my place for a drink?"

She eyed him sullenly. "You better have champagne."

"Diamant Bleu cuvée, my dear."

She stared at him blankly.

"Trust me, darling, you might know about the inbreeds in Munich's ruling class, but I know champagnes. And Diamant Bleu is among the best."

"You're not being very nice tonight," she remarked. "I sense a trace of hatefulness."

"See if you say that twenty minutes from now." Aying led her from the restaurant. Despite his reassurance to her, he vowed to seek tonight's pleasure only for himself.

He also reminded himself to furtively reveal this fling to the woman's husband. What did Aying care, anyway? It's not as if her industrialist husband could do anything about it. He'd be left to take his anger out on her, and her alone.

Content that he would soon lose himself in 7 seconds of bliss, Aying settled into the back seat of the Mercedes and guided his date's head to his lap.

Chapter Forty-Six

NEIL HAD DOWNED A FULL POT OF COFFEE TO KEEP himself awake. Despite the sleep he desperately craved, the body of the SS and his motorcycle had to disappear. The motorcycle had come first, simply because Neil didn't want to dispose of the corpse until after most people were asleep. After finding a well-stocked toolbox in the detached garage, it had taken Neil several hours to break the BMW into smaller, more manageable parts. As a nighttime chill had descended on Innsbruck, Neil loaded the trunk of his new car with pieces from the BMW. He and Madeline made two trips down the base of the mountain, dumping the petroleum-free metal components into a deep portion of the Sill, well downstream. An exhausted and breathless Neil buried several pieces downhill from the garage, including the engine block and the fuel tank. Satisfied with the shallow grave, Neil covered the area with pine straw, sweeping a light over the surface. He was confident it wouldn't be found.

Just as they'd done with the motorcycle parts, Neil drove Madeline down the hill to retrieve the body. It was now past midnight. The setup of the car he'd been provided was rather foreign to Neil, but it was certainly high quality. According to Madeline, it was German, made by Horch.

While they hadn't been too nervous disposing of the BMW parts in such a remote area of the river, they were far more concerned about this Schutzstaffel's cadaver. Neil wasn't willing to sink the man in the river. With the coming fall snows, Neil felt the river would probably run swift at times. He couldn't risk the man's body washing up in a week or two. Because of that, Neil decided to employ a method he'd read about years before.

After questioning Madeline about the area farms, he decided that the large dairy farm north of the town of Götzens was their best bet. They drove to the bottom of the hill, switching off the headlamps as they pulled into the underbrush on the left side of the road. Neil had insisted on going alone but Madeline, displaying her feistiness, wasn't to be argued with. When he opened the door and smelled the earthy catch basin, Neil's blood ran cold as he recalled how close he'd come to death earlier in the evening.

"You okay?" she asked.

"I will be. Come on."

They picked their way down to the catch basin, finding the corpse where Neil had left it. Getting the man out wasn't easy. Had Neil been fully healthy, he could have carried him out alone. But his side wasn't quite up to it, yet. So the twosome dragged the dead, partially-clothed SS all the way back to the trunk of the Horch. No sooner had they reached the car than they heard voices.

Neil froze, pointing to the road. Madeline nodded. It sounded like a man and a woman, walking from town.

"They're drunk," Madeline whispered.

Neil peered down the last little bit of Berchtoldshofweg, seeing the two silhouettes on the main road as they passed over the drainpipe and approached the turn-off.

"They can't see us," Madeline whispered. No sooner had she said it than the couple turned right, coming up Berchtoldshofweg. They were fifty meters away.

"Shit," Neil hissed. He glanced down at the corpse. Neil knelt, shoving the dead SS under the rear of the car. When he stood back up, Madeline grasped him and situated herself on the trunk of the Horch.

"Pretend to kiss me," she whispered.

Neil obeyed, leaning over Madeline and kissing the side of her face. She panted heavily as she pulled him down to her.

"Hey...looks like everyone's having a good time tonight!" the drunken man yelled as he passed by. He whistled and cat-called as he and his woman staggered up Berchtoldshofweg. Neil and Madeline maintained their ruse until the couple was well up the street.

"Do you know them?" Neil whispered, still leaning over her.

"I know who the man is. He's the son of the man who owns the house at the top of the road."

"Would he have recognized you?"

She shook her head. "He doesn't know me."

Awkwardness crept in after the pretend kiss. It was made worse by loading an underwear-wearing, bloody corpse into the trunk of the Horch. Afterward, it took them twenty minutes to drive to Götzens. Neil's biggest concern centered around possible roadblocks. If the SS were looking for their own man, Neil was certain they'd not hesitate to search the car.

At Madeline's direction, Neil used quiet back roads, finally arriving at the large dairy farm, bordered on all sides by a long, barbed-wire fence. He pulled the Horch into a forest road across from the fence, extinguishing the lights.

"Which way does the summer wind typically blow?"

"*Föhn* wind," she said. "It's well known and blows from the south."

"You're sure?"

"Yes, why?"

"Most farmers put their decomposition pit downwind of summer winds. The pits smells the worst in the summer, so the farmers would rather not smell the rotting flesh when they're out having a picnic with the family." Neil twisted in his seat and pointed. "It's probably going to be somewhere near the north end of the property." He eyed her. "I guess it's silly to ask you to wait here."

"Good guess."

They exited the Horch and began to walk, crossing inside the barbed wire fence and following the curving property line around to the north. Many of the cattle, illuminated by moonlight, were sleeping. But some were night grazing, evidenced by their clattering cowbells. A few of the cows began ambling toward Neil and Madeline.

After at least twenty minutes of walking, they noticed a rancid smell.

"Oh," Madeline moaned, covering her nose and mouth. "Is that it?" she asked, her voice muffled by her hand.

Neil winced, too. There was no other smell on earth like that of rotting flesh. He dreaded what lay ahead for him. "Yeah...that's gotta be it."

It took twenty minutes to get back to the car. They drove to the nearest spot outside the fence and parked in the adjacent woods. Then they dragged the corpse across at least 300 meters of road and cow pasture. Despite the cool, both people were soaking wet when they arrived with the body at the fetid pit.

Madeline held a fold of her dress over her nose and mouth. "So they just dump dead cows in here?"

"They have to put them somewhere. Cows are like people—they die."

Despite its unpleasantness, decomposition pits are common at large farms. This particular pit was well made, and it appeared the farmer took the time to cover the carcasses with lime and a layer of dirt. As long as Neil left no evidence of tonight's burial, he felt it was highly unlikely the farmer would come digging around his own decomposition pit out of curiosity.

"Ugh!" Madeline cried. "What's that on the ground?"

"Nightcrawlers." They were everywhere.

"Nightcrawlers. Why?"

He looked at her. "Why do you think?"

Madeline rushed away, vomiting in the nearby grass.

Retching occasionally, Neil found a covered bin containing powdered lime. Next to the bin was a shovel. He found his spot at the edge of the pit, digging a shallow grave in the mercifully soft soil. After Madeline had recovered as best she could, they shoved the corpse into the grave. Neil tossed lime over the body and quickly covered it with soil.

"Pray for rain," he said.

"Why?"

"It might cover our tracks."

No longer bashful around his new friend, Neil stripped off everything other than his undershirt and shorts for the ride home. Madeline followed suit, thankfully wearing a frilly, non-revealing undergarment of some sort.

With the windows open to blow out the stench, the two people drove in silence for much of the ride. As they began to ascend Berchtoldshofweg, they looked at each other and burst out laughing.

"Welcome to Austria, Dieter Dremel!" Madeline said.

"I must say, it's been an interesting arrival," Neil replied.

* * *

Neil allowed Madeline to bathe first. He sat at the kitchen table, smoking cigarettes and steadily drinking water to rehydrate himself. Schatze had followed Madeline into the bathroom. They finally emerged, with Madeline in a man's pajamas and an oversize robe. Neil went next, hurrying but cleaning himself thoroughly. When he came back out in a new set of flannel pajamas and a robe, he found Madeline dozing with her head on the table. Schatze was at her feet. Neil began to quietly switch off the lights.

Madeline awoke. "I've been instructed to take you to the doctor right away."

"Now?"

"First thing tomorrow."

"Then why don't you sleep in the bedroom?" Neil whispered. "I can sleep out here on the couch. We'll go when we wake up."

"I like the couch," Madeline replied, standing and stretching. "And Doctor Kraabe will be able to help you with your injuries."

"I'm fine, now."

"No, you're not," she said, switching on the lamp beside the couch. "You were making all sorts of weird noises when we were lugging that scumbag around that pasture."

"I'm fine."

"Still, I want him to look at you."

He nodded resignedly. "So...without discussing Jakey, tell me what's been going on here." Again she winced upon hearing Jakey's name. Neil understood—quite well—the pain she was coping with. Even the simple sound of the name of a lost loved one stung, like a feather-light touch to an open wound. Neil didn't want to get into Emilee's murder, either, so he decided to honor this woman's wishes and keep the conversation away from sorrow.

Madeline flopped down on the couch and loosened her robe. Schatze collapsed at her feet, sighing loudly. "The Germans have essentially taken over here," Madeline said. "The Austrians, in the government and mostly the civilians, have been complicit. They call it *Anschluss*...a friendly 'link-up.' The cooperation has allowed the Nazis to arm the Austrian military, as well as many volunteers and reserves. Most of the locals were panting for Hitler to take over, thinking he would bring his *miracle* here."

Neil watched her. Her passion for her subject danced like fire in her easy-to-read chocolate eyes. He saw the flame burn white hot when she spoke of the Austrian government and their self-serving capitulation to Hitler and the Nazis. She told a story about the ballot for registered Austrian voters concerning the Anschluss. The check box for "yes" was five times the size of the check box for "no."

"And who would dare vote no?" she asked. "Those who disagreed simply abstained from voting. The ballots weren't secret, and a no-vote would land you on the Nazi rolls as a dissenter. And that, my new friend, earns you a trip to one of the *camps*."

"Okay...I get all that." He wanted to move the conversation to more pressing items. "One thing that has me up at night is arranging transport for the children. I need to know exactly how far from town they're hidden. Do you know? The reason their location is important is because it seems that getting them out by cargo train makes the most sense."

She stared at him, her eyes slowly widening.

"You do know what I'm referring to?" Neil asked.

"The children?"

"Yes."

"You're asking where they are?" Madeline asked, her voice changing in octave.

"Yes. Before I knew about any of this, I received a note from...you know...but the second page was gone. There was no location of the children mentioned on the first page."

"I know all about the note." Madeline pressed both hands on her forehead, shutting her eyes and making a moaning sound. "I thought you would arrive knowing the location."

"I have absolutely no idea. I don't know anything about this area at all."

"No one told you? None of your contacts along the way?"

"No...they said you and your contacts here would have all the details."

"This nightmare just gets worse and worse," she groaned.

"What are you talking about?"

"We *don't* know where the children are."

"Are you certain no one knows?"

"Believe me when I say we've looked everywhere. And scoured. And combed. Knowing Jakey..." she seemed to trip on the word. "Knowing *his* diligence, there's no guessing where he might have hidden them."

"So, no one here knows? None of the people in your organization?"

"No!" Madeline cried. "When Jakey arrived in Innsbruck with the children, they knew they were in for a considerable wait until we arranged for the ship to Palestine."

"Well, why the hell didn't Jakey tell anyone where they were?"

"At first we knew. He'd hidden them in an old warehouse by the rail depot. But that was unsafe so he moved them. And on the night he moved them...he was..." She dipped her head as the tears resumed.

"Don't get upset, Madeline. I'll help you find them, okay? That's why I'm here." Something occurred to him. "Wait...how would he have known to send the letter?"

"It was on my pillow that night when I came home. I didn't even know he was dead at the time."

"So he had a premonition?"

Madeline appeared on the verge of a breakdown. "The meeting he was scheduled to have that night was extremely dangerous. He knew that, hence the letter. I wouldn't have sent it had he come home."

"Did Jakey live with the doctor, too?"

"We both did, in a room in the basement. We only lived there for a short while."

"May I see it when we go see the doctor?"

"Jakey told me you're the best in the world and you want to search a basement room as a *start?* I know every centimeter of that room." She lurched from the couch and began pacing the floor. Schatze stood, worry in her eyes at the sudden change in the atmosphere.

"Jakey said you were a professional," Madeline said in a shrill voice, throwing up her hands. "He spoke of you constantly, as if you were some sort of god. Whenever there was trouble, without fail, he would always say, 'Neil would know what to do.' 'Neil would know what to do.' 'Neil would know what to do'." She stopped, her eyes joined with Neil's. "So, don't you know?"

Neil stood. He walked to Madeline and hugged her. It was almost like being in a room with himself. He understood her pain, her anguish. "It's okay, Madeline. I'll figure it out. It's okay."

Madeline buried her face into his flannel pajama shirt, wailing. Neil comforted her, patting her on her back, gently rocking her. For ten full minutes, Madeline sobbed, her body shuddering in grief. Neil wondered if she had even had the opportunity to grieve since Jakey's death. Perhaps not. She obviously had no family here and said she sometimes stayed in this cabin, probably so she could simply have a good cry.

He held her that way until her tears ceased. She seemed embarrassed as he led her to the sofa. Without hesitating, she stretched out, pulling the quilt from the top of the sofa and covering herself.

"I need to sleep," she whispered, turning over.

After extinguishing the lamp, Neil placed two more logs on the smoldering fire and let Schatze out to do her business. Then he collapsed on the bed.

Though plenty of things puzzled him, one question stood out above the rest: What happened to the second page of Jakey's note. If Madeline was the first person to receive it, who'd taken the second page before she found the envelope on her pillow?

After a moment, Schatze leapt up on the bed and settled right in beside him. Neil tabled his worries in the interest of rest.

The cabin's three inhabitants slept very hard that night.

Chapter Forty-Seven

PAIN. It wasn't the familiar discomfort from the wound on Neil's side—although, as soon as he moved, that ached, too. No, this pain was on Neil's exposed arm: a gouging, scratching hurt. He opened his eyes, watching as the blackness faded to blurry gray, and then transformed into the full spectrum of colors as the warmth of the cozy, much-needed sleep slid away like a blanket. Finally, he recognized Schatze, staring at him, her hot breath warming his face with each blast from her lungs. Neil pulled his arm away from her and lifted his sleeve, seeing the red marks from where she'd scratched him. He sat up, the many details of yesterday coming back to him. Schatze whined and hopped down, walking to the door. He nodded, stumbling across the bedroom and checking his watch. It was past lunch. He whistled. When had he last slept this late—without booze?

Neil rubbed his eyes, realizing he'd just been dreaming about being back in the Heinz house. While the entire family had been in his dream, Gabi had been the star. At the end of the dream, he and Gabi were sitting at the kitchen table, sharing a piece of chocolate cake and talking. Simply talking.

The dream had been fantastic.

After splashing frigid water on his face from the faucet, Neil staggered into the main room. Madeline was sitting at the kitchen table, a glass of water in front of her. She looked up from an open book and smiled brightly. "You slept—"

"Past noon. I know. I'm embarrassed."

"Well...you did walk all the way from Bavaria yesterday. Then, last night, you disposed of a dead body in a cow pit."

"Ugh, don't remind me," Neil grunted. Just the mention of it brought back the smell.

Madeline opened the back door, laughing as Schatze sprinted outside and squatted within seconds. "Poor dog. She's probably craving some normalcy."

"I know the feeling," Neil mumbled, rubbing his damp face. "You and the doc did a good job with the clothes. Did you happen to buy me a razor?"

"And shaving soap," Madeline replied. "Go get cleaned up, shave, and make yourself look presentable. We're going to Doctor Kraabe's in a bit, but not before I make you breakfast."

"Breakfast this late?"

"Breakfast is good anytime."

"True." Neil stepped to the kitchen table, lighting a cigarette before rubbing his eyes and forehead. "Is there more coffee?"

"On the stove."

"Mind if I have some before getting cleaned up? My head's filled with cobwebs."

"Not at all."

"I really want to hurry," Neil said. "I feel as if we're losing precious minutes. Sleeping like that makes me feel guilty."

"The shipments of children have been going on for some time now. Their food and water is carefully rationed, along with medicine. They will have enough, and probably a bit more than they need, through the deadline."

"Still...the fact that we don't know where they are..."

"You'll feel better once you meet Doctor Kraabe."

Neil shuffled into the kitchen and poured a cup, taking a long drag of his cigarette before following it with a sip of the hot liquid. A bountiful breakfast, a good night of sleep, a cup of coffee and a cigarette. Some days were certainly better than others. He looked at the eggs and cheese and the thinly sliced German bacon known as speck. "Did you buy all this food just for me?"

"Like I said, I've tried to keep the cottage ready. You have shaving tackle, local-style clothes, an automobile, this nice house...everything has been thought out for you. From this moment forward, we can focus on finding the children," she said, cracking an egg. Neil noticed her demeanor was much brighter than the night before.

He drew on the cigarette, glancing around, drinking in the cottage and backyard in the full sunlight. If Emilee were with him, he could blink once and think he was on holiday in a rented cabin. But she wasn't. And this was no holiday. He was in Nazi-occupied Austria, and Emilee was dead. Her murderer was dead, too.

And, as Neil reminded himself, he was the chief suspect. Along with that, hundreds of children might die if he didn't rescue them—soon.

Well, my bright mood just blackened considerably.

He opened the door for Schatze, noticing the puddles on the stone patio. "Did it rain?"

"You didn't hear it? Around six this morning it rained buckets."

Neil relaxed upon hearing about the rain. Hopefully it washed away any evidence of yesterday's killing and last night's corpse disposal.

"Do you know the Fausts?" he asked, getting back to business.

Madeline finished cracking eggs and began beating them. "Who?"

"The Fausts. Gregor and Petra Faust."

"No. Why?"

"They escorted me across the Atlantic. They're a part of your movement...organization. Whatever you call it."

She pinched her lips together and went back to work. "I'll let the doctor explain all that."

"I have a lot to learn, it seems."

"Go on now," she commanded. "Now that you have your coffee, go clean up. We'll eat quickly and go. The weather is beautiful today, especially after the rain. Cool and clear. Wear one of the wool suits we got you. Maybe the brown one."

Neil paused at the bedroom door, staring at Madeline. She had her back to him. The entire convoluted situation seemed surreal. Jakey's death. The Lex Curran killing and subsequent setup. The dead German pilot. The Heinz family. The dead SS. And now here he was, in the center of the Alps, playing house with a hiding Jewish woman and preparing to search for hundreds of innocent children who were at risk of starvation and persecution. In his clandestine life, Neil had participated in many far-fetched, unconventional activities. But this mission, and the situations he had already encountered, certainly topped them all.

"Go!" Madeline playfully yelled, pointing a dripping whisk at him. He nodded, hurriedly topping off his coffee before he made his way to the bedroom.

* * *

Thirty minutes later, a clean-shaven Neil sat at the kitchen table in a brown wool suit. The suit fit well enough through the upper body but was at least an inch too short at the legs. He'd tugged downward on the pants and decided they would make do. Sated, he pushed his plate away and unbuttoned the snug-fitting vest, feeling a certain kinship to the plump porker he'd just eaten. Neil's legs and calves were tender and sore, reminding him of his advancing age and the weakened physical condition caused by his injuries. Neil made a silent vow to get back in shape as soon as this was all over. He snugged his hands behind his head and stared at his temporary roommate.

"Tell me about Doctor Kraabe."

Madeline leaned forward. "You needn't concern yourself with his character. He's a fine man with impeccable morals and he'll inform you of a number of things you might find helpful."

"I'm looking forward to meeting him."

"When we ride over there, I'll have to hide in the car."

"Why?"

"No one knows where I am."

"You didn't hide last night."

"It was dark."

"What if we get stopped?" Neil asked.

"We won't."

"We could," Neil countered. "What if the SS are looking for their man?"

"It'll be fine," she replied.

"Just in case...if we get questioned, what do we do?"

"The senior soldiers and SS might know me but I doubt the rank and file have a clue about who I am. If we do get stopped, you have all the legal paperwork, with the proper stamps and seals, right?"

"Yes."

"Fine. Just stick with your cover about having lived abroad for many years, but now you're back for good. They won't hassle a wealthy Austrian with a nice car unless you're doing something very wrong."

"And if they ask about you?"

"Tell them I'm a hooker," she answered, twisting her mouth into a smile. "And that's why I'm hiding in the floorboard."

"Okay." He leaned forward in the chair. "What's the situation like in town, now that the German military is here?"

"Well, first you have the people who live here year-round, the residents. They welcomed the Nazis, for the most part. Innsbruck is a tourist town, so plenty of people don't live here—the vacationers—and they're a mixed bag of political beliefs and what not."

Neil stood and re-buttoned the vest. "Go on."

"Then you have the outright complicit—they're the locals who've gotten into bed with the Germans—and there are plenty, believe me. They cannot be trusted. And then, of course, you have the Nazis themselves. Nearly all are fanatical, and the politicians or military Nazis can take everything you own with a wave of their evil wand." She stood. "It's best to keep your head down and not to draw attention to yourself."

"Are there many who are sympathetic to the Jews?"

"Doctor Kraabe is, and there are others, but most are too scared to show it. I can't say I blame them," she said flatly.

"Ready?" he asked.

Outside, Neil walked behind the garage and looked at the partial grave of the BMW motorcycle. As he thought, the rain made the ground appear even. He walked back up to the garage, viewing the Horch in the daylight.

Lengthy and painted gray with glossy black trim, it had a look of elegance and exclusivity. Neil frowned at the mud on the tires and sides, reminding himself to wash the car later. Inside the car, a faint whiff of last night's activity overpowered the smell of new leather. He rolled down the windows and waited on Madeline.

At the bottom of the steep road, where they'd loaded the corpse of the SS, Madeline crouched into the floorboard, tucking her knees up to her body and placing her chin on top of them.

"If we get stopped, that'll be hard to explain."

"I'm a hooker, remember? You're embarrassed."

"Which way do I go?"

"Left, back into town. Cross the river at the first bridge and stay on Holzhammerstrasse. You'll see a small park on the left, and several blocks after you'll see the Kraabe mansion. You won't miss it—huge and white with black shutters."

Neil drove slowly, watching as the people moved about the town like any American city. There was no visible military or SS presence and, thankfully, no roadblocks. Madeline peered up through the side window.

"You're doing fine. It's only a block away."

Neil drove on.

* * *

Standartenführer Anton Aying leaned back at his desk, propping his polished boots on the shiny oak. He asked the telephone operator to put him through to the Waffen-SS detachment barracks situated just a few kilometers away. The detachment was basically a half-sized *Kompanie*, with the other half serving in Salzburg. The local group was commanded by a fresh-faced, ambitious Obersturmführer named Beck. According to what Aying had heard, Beck's family were influential industrialists, hailing from Stuttgart. Therefore, since his arrival several weeks ago, Aying had deliberately ignored him—something he did with any underling who attempted to ride a high horse. But today, Aying needed Beck's assistance. The entire matter was more curiosity than anything, Aying realized, worrying about some beaten-down tramp.

"But I just didn't like the way the prick stared at me," he whispered as the phone buzzed.

When the phone was eventually answered, Aying announced who he was, then instructed the clerk to find Beck. The breathless young man could be heard running from the phone, yelling to the others that Standartenführer Aying was on the phone.

Aying couldn't help but smile.

"Sir! This is Obersturmführer Beck, sir! I'm at your undying service, sir!"

"I hate an ass-kisser, Beck," Aying lied, studied his nails. "Last night, I sent one of your men, a Hauptscharführer, on a small job. Frankly, I was not pleased when he didn't return to me as I instructed."

The young SS leader sucked in a sharp breath. "You're referring to Hauptscharführer Ludwig, aren't you?"

"Was he the one who killed the painter?"

"I wasn't here yet, sir. But, yes, from the many tales I've heard, he was."

"Then, may I ask you this? While he was a bit in-the-bag, why in the hell would that dumb shit not do as I told and report back to me?"

Beck paused. When he spoke, his tone was different, worried. "Sir, Ludwig hasn't been seen since late yesterday afternoon. We did learn that he went into town and drank at a restaurant. The last report we have was Ludwig riding a *Kompanie* motorcycle, driving along the river to the west."

"And he *hasn't* returned?" Aying asked sharply, lowering his feet to the floor.

"No, sir. According to the others here, such behavior from him is highly uncharacteristic. We've begun looking for him."

Aying glanced at his watch. It had been more than sixteen hours since he'd sent Ludwig on his mission to find the tramp. Even if Ludwig, in his drunkenness, had passed out somewhere, he should have surfaced by now. Meaning, in Aying's mind, something foul had probably occurred.

"And you don't think he would have deserted?" Aying asked.

"Absolutely not, sir. While I didn't know him all that well, I trust those here who say he had a hard-on for his role as a Schutzstaffel."

"Watch your language, Beck. You sound like a savage," Aying admonished, ever the hypocrite. He used similar language every waking hour.

"Understood, sir. It won't happen again."

"What is your unit protocol for a situation such as this?"

"Normally, sir, we don't alert outside authorities for a full twenty-four hours. But, well...since you're involved..."

"But you're now searching?"

"With our own men, sir."

"Just be silent a moment. I'd like to think."

Aying leaned his head back. Could the vagrant have killed the Hauptscharführer, a man armed with a submachine gun and a motorcycle? Highly unlikely. Given the rocky, unforgiving terrain, Aying would give far better odds on finding the Hauptscharführer dead in a ditch, the victim of a drunken crash. He'd read dozens of reports of SS dying on motorcycles. But the vagrant shouldn't be ruled out, either. Anything is possible. Aying lifted the handset.

"Beck, I don't like alerting anyone other than Schutzstaffel to our internal business. And that goes especially for problems. Makes us seem weak. Understand?"

"Of course, sir."

"So, stop whatever search you're performing and send your entire detachment west. They're to search for Ludwig, the motorcycle, and a tramp of approximately forty to fifty years of age. He had a large, scraggly dog with him that was brown and grey. The tramp was probably two meters tall. His hair was dark and he had a heavy beard. He was wearing old, soiled clothing. Do you have all that?"

"I'm making notes. Got it, sir. You sent Ludwig after this tramp, you say?"

"Not pertinent. If you find the tramp, arrest him and bring him to me. And make sure you shoot his dog on sight. Probably has rabies."

"And when we find the Hauptscharführer?"

"I have a feeling he's dead. But if he's alive, of course, bring him to me."

"Dead, sir?"

"He was drunk. He either wrecked or…"

"Sir?"

"He either wrecked or that vagrant *killed* him."

There was another long pause. "Sir, may I ask what gives you that feeling?"

"No, you may not. Update me before eighteen-hundred hours." Aying hung up the phone. Again, he propped his boots on the desk and removed a cigarette from his case. He briefly viewed the fine engraving on his new lighter before igniting the cigarette and puffing thoughtfully.

Isn't it strange when life sends you little mysteries? Aying reclined in the swivel chair and blew smoke rings into the still office air.

Chapter Forty-Eight

DOCTOR KRAABE'S HOME WAS INDEED A MANSION. Neil exited the car and drank in the fine points of the manor. The house was stately, but built like a bomb shelter. Made of deep gray granite, it had been designed in the Gothic Revival style that was so popular in the 19th Century. If it didn't have so many bright flowers and bushes, it might even seem spooky. Doctor Kraabe must have employed groundskeepers to keep the massive home and surrounding yard, which covered at least four normal lots, in its pristine condition.

Neil leaned back into the car. "Are you coming?"

"I'll go in the back. Just go up to the front door."

After removing his hat, Neil held it to his stomach in a polite gesture and pressed the buzzer. A short, older woman with high cheekbones and wide eyes answered the door. She wore a uniform and spoke accented German.

"*Guten Tag, gnädige Frau.* I'm here to see the doctor. My name is Dieter Dremel."

The lady nodded politely. She ushered Neil into the foyer and instructed him to wait a moment. Neil gazed at the oil painting above him, knowing nothing of its painter, but considering its beauty. It wasn't but a few seconds before a tall, slightly hunched man appeared from what looked like the living room. He wore a shabby two-piece gray suit with a loosened tie, and the expression on his face showed surprise.

"Dieter Dremel?" he asked, cocking an eye at Neil.

"That's me," Neil answered.

As the two men measured one another, Madeline appeared. "It *is* him, doctor! He arrived last night."

Kraabe took Neil's hand and pumped it violently up and down. *"Freut mich!"* he exclaimed over and over.

"Shall we sit?" Madeline asked.

They sat in the doctor's home office, evidenced by the clay models of body parts and the numerous medical books, some in English, which surrounded them. The maid brought them hot tea and water. Neil stood and whispered something to the maid. She nodded and disappeared. Neil sat and exchanged niceties with the doctor until the maid returned with an open pack of Austrian cigarettes and an ashtray. Neil lit one and, although it was stale, he exhaled in relief as he nestled into his chair, wincing slightly as his side hitched.

Madeline pointed to Neil's side. "He's been badly injured, doctor." She pursed her lips like a busybody older sister. "That's why he was so late arriving."

"I'm fine," Neil said.

"Injured? Show me," Kraabe commanded in a tone reserved for doctors used to getting their way.

Neil shook his head. "Doctor, I'm here to help, and honestly, I'm anxious to get on with things."

Doctor Kraabe snapped his bony fingers, his face hardening in an instant. "Show me right now. How the hell can you help us if you're hurt?"

Neil paused before sticking his cigarette between his teeth and pulling the three layers of clothing up over the pinkish, healing scars. Doctor Kraabe turned the lamp to Neil's side and perched his glasses on his nose, pulling his head back to an optimum viewing distance. With a surprisingly rough motion, he fingered the front and back wounds, humming lowly.

"Gunshot," he finally murmured.

"Yes," Neil answered, suppressing a grunt as the doctor roughly tugged at the exit wound.

"I wasn't asking." Kraabe made Neil turn and then instructed him to raise both arms above his head and stretch side to side, bending his torso.

Neil was limited in his motions.

The doctor sat back in his chair and removed his glasses, putting the stem into the corner of his mouth. "Extinguish that cigarette."

"Pardon?"

"Put it out," Kraabe commanded.

Neil crushed the cigarette out.

"Did a doctor patch you up?"

"Veterinarian," Neil said in English, unsure of the word. "How do I say that in German?"

"*Ein Tierarzt*," Kraabe replied. "That's why he used such heavy-gauge filament. Do you feel well?"

"Sore, but yes, I feel very well. I walked over the northern range of the Alps to the first valley."

"No fever? No vomiting?"

"No."

"Congestion. Blood in mucus or urine or any blood whatsoever?"

"None."

"Well, you may feel a sight better than when it first happened, but the bones and cartilage aren't yet fully healed," Doctor Kraabe stated. "And even though the manufacturers don't want people to know it, those little death sticks you keep placing in your mouth slow the healing process."

"Cigarettes?"

"Yes. Don't smoke another one."

Neil turned to Madeline and frowned. She was resting her chin on the back of her hands, smirking at him. Neil let out a long, resigned breath. "Okay, doc, no more cigarettes."

"I'm quite serious," Kraabe said.

"So am I," Neil replied. He gestured to Madeline. "I need to ask him about the past. Understand? Do you want to stay in the room?"

Madeline's smirk dissolved. "I'll step out for a few minutes." She grabbed the cigarettes and walked away. Neil thought he heard her going up or down a set of stairs. He turned.

"What can you tell me about my friend Jakey? What exactly happened to him?"

Kraabe poured tea for both of them, spooning in some sugar for himself before sliding the tray to Neil. The doctor sat back in an ancient leather chair, settling until he found what must have been his favorite position, and then he pondered the question for a moment as he stared over Neil's shoulder. "Jacob was as meticulous as the finest surgeon, at times. Rough as a corn cob at others." Kraabe glanced at Neil, smiling sympathetically. "He had, once again, nearly completed what was thought to be an impossible task, but somehow they found him out."

"Who did?"

"The Nazis, but I don't know specifically who. Jacob hardly ever divulged particulars. He knew the heat was on, but wanted to complete his business regardless. He'd just moved the children to their final hiding location when he was killed."

"What exactly happened?"

"He died in an explosion. After the fact, the authorities claimed he was a twisted Jewish martyr, killing good Germans by blowing himself up." The doctor shook his head. "It was, of course, a lie. Madeline saw the explosion, but she won't talk about it."

"Did anyone die with him?"

"Yes. Two women, prostitutes, and a German Army colonel, Krausse. Krausse was working with us, helping Jacob with the particulars—for money, of course. And the prostitutes were Krausse's, but I don't need to tell you that." Kraabe sipped his tea. "And that's really all I know."

"Do you have any remote idea where the children are?"

Kraabe's smile was humorless. "If I did, you wouldn't be here."

"Madeline was surprised that I didn't know."

"She's grieving," Kraabe replied. "I've tried not to weight her down with more worry."

Neil pulled the tattered envelope from inside the jacket of his coat. He slid the single sheet of paper out, pinching it between his fingers.

"This was from Jakey. There was a second page, but it wasn't sent. I was hoping that you, or someone here, held it back to ensure that I would come."

Kraabe slowly shook his head back and forth, eyes closed. "There was never a second page."

"How do you know that?"

"I broke the seal before she ever saw it," Kraabe answered.

"And there was no second page? Are you sure?"

Kraabe leaned forward, placing his cup in a saucer. "Jacob planned it this way. Right now we're likely doing exactly as he hoped."

"Why didn't he tell you where the children are?"

"I'm not exactly sure. First, he was killed before he could tell me. And, second, I'm not sure Jacob would have trusted me, or anyone, with that information."

"So by keeping it a secret, he protected their lives."

"Presumably," the doctor said. "Assuming you can find them."

"But why would he have risked all those children on the hope that I would come? If I'd have decided not to come, wouldn't they die?"

The doctor frowned. "I don't know what might happen. My best guess is they'll run out of food and reveal themselves. There still might be hope at that point, but not much."

"What will the Nazis do if they find them?"

"That's hard to say. But it won't be good," Kraabe said, his face saying more than his words.

Neil stared at the note, finally folding it and replacing it in his pocket. "Tell me about Jakey's contacts here."

Kraabe held his tea and cocked his head. "The German military are a funny group. Stoic. And unlike what most people outside of this area think, they're quite different from my Austrian brethren." He took a sip, still staring off into the distance. "They don't do business with just anyone. They have to know you first. Believe it or not, despite what's going on right now, Germans can be generous, brilliant and funny. But the outer veneer they carry is sometimes that of a sheet of ice—*especially* since the Nazis took over."

Neil gulped his tea and habitually reached for the cigarettes, catching himself and putting his hands on his woolen pants. He pushed the powerful craving from his mind and leaned forward. "But where do I start, and who do I start with?"

"I couldn't tell you. Jacob had everything under control before the explosion. Now, the local commanders have all changed."

"Do you know them?" Neil asked.

"Yes, I do. The German officers do not trust their own medical corps, so they bully their way into my office when they're sick or injured, usually from a drunken accident or a venereal disease. The senior man, the one who replaced Krausse, arrived three weeks ago. His name is Cleebron," Krausse said, waving his hand as if shooing a gnat. "He's nothing—a paper tiger. You'll need to meet his executive officer, Falkenberg. He's the one actually running the show. In any other time and circumstance, I would like to study the man a bit. I do not make him as a true Nazi, but rather a skilled actor."

"Why do you say that?"

"Well, let's just say that my friend Sigmund Freud, the famed neurologist and psychotherapist, would love to spend a day or two with Oberst Falkenberg."

Neil had no idea what Kraabe was trying to say. "Please stop speaking in riddles. What is Falkenberg like?"

"Falkenberg loves himself, Dieter. He loves his money. His power. And his own looks. That is what gives him satisfaction, and only the things that can feed those three ideals mean a damn to him. Understand?"

"Then he's ripe for a bribe."

Doctor Kraabe placed the cup into the saucer and slid it onto the silver service. "I must say I love the American passion for simplicity."

Neil knew a thinly veiled insult when he heard one, but he took it in stride. He leaned back in his own chair and twirled his hand for Kraabe to go on.

"You're right, Dieter, he is the perfect *mark*, as you might say. But it's those around him who may create problems for you. Especially a man named Anton Aying. He has the polizei, the Burgermeister and the business leaders *all* in his pocket."

"Who is Aying?" Neil asked.

"He's the top local Schutzstaffel...the SS. Are you surprised that he holds the mantle of power?"

Neil dipped his head for a moment before telling Kraabe what had happened yesterday.

Frowning, Kraabe asked, "Are you certain there were no witnesses?"

"One can never be certain, but I don't believe there were."

"And the SS who saw you in town?"

"Was an officer. It wasn't the same man I killed."

"Could the officer describe you?"

"My clothes were filthy. My dog was next to me. I had a beard. I was exhausted. I looked like a vagrant."

"And you think the officer sent the SS on the motorcycle?"

"Yes."

"You're *sure* he wasn't the same man?"

"Positive."

"Then you must change your appearance to the point that the first man cannot identify you. As far as the missing SS, I wouldn't worry too much unless the body is found. And I'll know if it is. Otherwise, they'll consider him a deserter." Kraabe seemed satisfied. "Down here on the south end of the Reich, desertion has become a common theme. Lots of Germans making their way to the Mediterranean."

"I'll cut my hair and color it. With decent clothes and erect posture, I should look nothing like the laggard who loped through town after a night in the Alps."

"I hope that'll be enough."

Neil leaned forward. "Tell me more about the SS commander, Aying."

"Standartenführer Anton Aying. Very polished, very dangerous. I've heard he's insatiable in regard to women. He, like Falkenberg, enjoys the finer things in life. And it's rumored he even has Adolf Hitler's ear, and has visited him on numerous occasions at his retreat above Berchtesgaden."

"Interesting."

"There's one very important thing to note," Kraabe said, lifting his crooked finger. "Aying and Falkenberg despise one another. We're talking genuine hate. Supposedly, it goes back many years to wherever they served in Germany—an incident occurred."

Madeline reappeared. "Have you two finished talking about what happened?"

"We have," Kraabe answered.

Neil stood. "May I please see the room?"

"Our room?" Madeline asked.

Neil nodded. "I'd like to spend some time in there, alone, if you don't mind."

Madeline swallowed but nodded. Her hand began to nervously massage her neck.

Kraabe led Neil through the large home, the wooden floors creaking under their weight. In the kitchen, the doctor led him into a large pantry. He moved several cans, depressing an unseen trigger embedded in the wall. The entire wall swiveled backward to reveal a narrow stairwell, leading downward. A solitary light bulb was already lit, marking the passage.

"Down the stairs is a wine cellar. The back rack of wine lifts up a notch, then pull it to you. The room is behind it."

Neil grinned ruefully, thinking about Cleveland Mixton's underground hideaway in Arizona. Jakey had thought it out, helping Cleveland engineer it, fastidiously carving every corner into the hard rock of the Sonoran desert. This seemed very similar.

341

"Jakey built all of this, didn't he?"

Kraabe's wan smile provided the confirmation.

Neil walked down into the chilly cellar. Just as the doctor promised, the sturdy wooden wine rack lifted up and, when pulled, revealed the room. It was just large enough to be comfortable, running about fifteen feet on all sides. Neil pulled the chain on a bedside lamp, illuminating the wood-paneled room in amber.

The bed was a single, covered neatly in a quilt. While it probably pained her, Neil assumed Madeline still slept down here on the nights when she wasn't at the cottage. Beside the bed, on one side, was a magazine. On the side closest to Neil was a hardcover book, written in Hebrew. Neil touched it, dragging his fingers over it. On the far wall was a bookshelf. He looked at the titles, stopping at the large picture book of Paris. He remembered when Jakey purchased it, on their way home from the last trip they'd ever taken together, the one just before Neil and Emilee had been married.

Neil tugged the book out and recalled the heady conversations between him and his friend over the course of their Parisian journey. They'd talked on the train across the United States. Conversed on the voyage over the Atlantic. Told stories as they ambled the streets of every arrondissement in Paris. The one-month holiday had been nothing more than a thirty-day chat and neither man grew weary of it. True best friends. Neil dipped his head, feeling the grief coming on.

There's no time for that crap right now, Barkie. Get your ass in gear and find those kids. It's all up to you now. They're waiting...

It was as if Jakey stood in the room with Neil. The clear voice. The note of humor even in the face of calamity. The encouragement. Bolstered by his friend's spirit, Neil began by studying every item in the room.

He emerged an hour later, no wiser about the location of the children.

"Go back home," Kraabe instructed. "We'll start fresh in the morning."

"I don't want to lounge around while those children are stuck somewhere," Neil countered.

"You must rest your mind. You've been through a great deal," the doctor replied. "Reflect on your friend. Remember him. Perhaps if Madeline is up to it, the two of you can talk about him. Doing so may trigger an idea that will lead us to the children."

Dejected, Neil and Madeline departed for the cottage soon after.

* * *

Hours later, as the vestiges of the day's direct sunshine radiated onto the backyard of the cottage, Neil sat alone at the yard's edge. In front of him, after a precipitous drop-off, was a broad vista of blue Austrian sky, supported by the lush green valley and the shimmering aqua of the River Sill. Next to Neil was a stone fire pit he'd erected after changing into work clothes, built with rounded stones from the edge of the yard. He'd built the fire two hours before, allowing it to blaze in order to burn off any moss and algae from the rocks. Now the fire and coals were low, providing smooth, even heat to the pork tenderloin that was stretched across the oiled grate, slow-cooking a foot over the low flame.

Neil had found several books in the cottage, and was reading one about the 1866 Austro-Prussian War. He'd never studied Austria, and had no idea of how many lands the Austro-Hungarian Empire had once controlled. Regardless, his mind wasn't fully engaged in the reading.

Putting his finger on his page and closing the book, he sipped from his glass of water and drank in the view, his thoughts drifting to the children who were ostensibly hidden nearby. There was still time to find them—or so everyone had said. Despite all the assurances, Neil still felt the suffocating fear that something could have gone wrong. What if they had miscalculated their food and water? What if sickness had set in? Neil could think of dozens of potential problems associated with hiding human beings in the same location.

To find them, he needed to learn more about Jakey's time here. To do that, he'd have to blend in. That's what he was working on.

Around the base of the lawn chair were the trimmings of his shaggy black hair. Madeline had cut it for him and was in the house looking for a pair of small scissors to trim around his ears. Once that was done, she would paint light brown hair dye over his ears and bangs, attempting to lighten his dark hair. He ran his hand through his greatly shortened hair, feeling better already, though a cigarette would brighten his mood threefold.

Neil leaned his head back in the sun's radiance. The temperature at this altitude was chilly, and would probably approach freezing after sunset. But for now the low and unabated western sun was powerful, warming his face and his clothing as he sat facing its setting path. And below the sun, the view was magnificent. The cottage sat at least a thousand feet over the valley. On both sides, in the distance, were majestic Alpine peaks, their tips shimmering with quicksilver from the blown snowcap. The yard was quiet, so quiet that occasionally an early autumn leaf would fall in the surrounding trees and Neil could hear it touching branches on its journey to the earth. He closed his eyes and allowed his hearing to become more acute, the way he'd been taught long ago. Distant birds could be heard, singing their beautiful melodies. The fence gate at the driveway gently creaked, pressed inward by the occasional cool breeze. Neil took another sip of water and enjoyed the trance. He welcomed it.

His search of Jakey's quarters had been fruitless. Tomorrow he would make an appearance in public, speaking to the men Kraabe had told him about, men who Jakey consorted with, men who might have another clue about the children's whereabouts.

Men who might very well want to kill Neil.

The other burgeoning mission, this one Neil's own, was to find Jakey Herman's killer, to get a confession, and then avenge Jakey. Violently. Whoever he was, the bastard was going to get a triple dose, for Jakey, for Emilee, and for Neil's unborn son.

Neil planned to savor his revenge.

His eyes were still closed as he allowed his head to loll backward. He could almost fall asleep.

Madeline should be back by now.

Neil needed to get this haircut finished so he could tend to the cooking meat. *Where is she?*

"Neil?"

About time. He opened his eyes. The sun's glare made Madeline a shadow as she stood in front of him. He put his forearm in a position to shade his eyes and blinked rapidly.

"We need to hurry. The meat's just about done," he said, allowing the empty glass to fall to the grass as he sat up and brushed loose hair from his shoulders. "Burned pork isn't very good."

"Neil, it's *me.*"

He stood so quickly that a jag of lightning pain, the type from weeks before, shot through his side. In front of him, lit by the sun, stray hairs flitted about in the afternoon breeze. But once he moved to his left, the sun was no longer directly in his eyes. Neil could now see clearly.

He couldn't believe who he was seeing. Standing before him was none other than Gabi Heinz.

Part Three:
THE ALIYAH

Chapter Forty-Nine

THOUGH THIS TRIP HAD CONTAINED A NUMBER OF bombshells, Neil hadn't yet received a jolt such as this one. The jolt, of course, had been provided by Gabi Heinz. She stood before him, a hopeful expression on her face as she clutched her hands in front of her.

"Gabi," he said, breathless, futilely attempting to get his thoughts in order. "Gabi, what the *hell* are you doing here?"

She moistened her lips and took a half step in his direction. "I'm here for you."

"But how did you know where to find me?"

"After your surgery, while you slept, I went through your things. Rude, I know, but it's the truth. I found the waterlogged papers with this address, and I found the note from your friend. I knew this was where you were coming. I knew it all along."

Neil looked at her the way he might look at a child who had misbehaved, but had shown incredible intelligence in doing so. "Gabi…Gabi…what will your mother think? She's probably sick with worry."

"She urged me to come."

Neil cocked his head. "Say that again."

"Mama loved you." Gabi took a step closer. "Her heart's been broken for so many years that she wanted me to have something she's been missing." Gabi appeared on the verge of tears, touching the back of her finger under her nose before continuing. "And after you left, we sat up very late, and I told her my feelings for you and told her I knew where you were going."

"And?" Neil asked, feeling as if his racing heart might explode at any moment.

"And she told me to come to you, and to tell you how I feel."

It was the way she said the last part: passionately—lustily. Neil's lips parted as he drank in her beauty. He could feel his own excitement coursing through his body as he stood there, dumbfounded by her simple beauty of flushed cheeks and large, desiring eyes.

The back door slammed. Neil's trance shattered like thin glass. He turned his head. It only took a few seconds for Madeline to cross the yard, her face cloudy as she arrived with scissors in each hand.

"Who is this?" Madeline asked, her tone containing a trace of hostility.

Gabi looked Madeline up and down. Neil did the same, correctly guessing what Gabi was thinking. Madeline wore an apron around her dress, her sleeves rolled up, prepared to finish his haircut. The scene appeared quite familial.

To Neil, the pregnant silence lasted a full year. Maybe two.

Finally, Gabi turned back to Neil, her head shaking side to side. "You slick bastard," she whispered, speaking English.

Neil smiled, and even though he wasn't one percent in the wrong, it was a guilty smile. The same guilty smile that every other man on earth would have offered, as if implanted in the male DNA as the default expression to give in any similar situation.

He made a tamping-down motion with his hands. "Gabi, it's not what it looks like."

"It's exactly what it looks like." Gabi turned, huffing across the yard and through the gate, grabbing a tattered suitcase she must have rested there. Neil ran after her.

She stalked up the short driveway and had just turned onto the mountain road when he caught up to her. He grabbed her elbow, causing her to windmill backward with her arm, striking him on the side of his face. She swung again, spinning all the way around when she missed. Neil then grasped her from behind, wrapping his arms around her as she sobbed. He made a shushing sound into her ear and turned her to face him.

"Gabi, listen to me, damn it."

She pulled away, her face pink and glistening of tears. "Was it just too long to go without a woman in your bed?" she shouted, her words firing at a machine-gun pace. "What, did you just stop off at the local brothel on the way into town and pick her up?"

"I'm not going to explain until you calm down."

Gabi shoved him backward and wiped her free-flowing tears. "I can't believe you. I came all this way for you."

"It's not what you think."

"Isn't it?"

Neil stood there, saying nothing.

Gabi pinched her lips together and stared off through the whispering pines. Finally she nodded and turned to him. "Okay, I'm calm. So, explain."

And Neil did.

* * *

A half-hour later, the three of them sat at the kitchen table, the two girls watching as Neil sawed into the overdone pork tenderloin. With each slice, he grunted upon seeing the gray center of the meat. Madeline couldn't have cared less about the tenderloin. She occasionally stole glances at Gabi, the doe-eyed German girl. She had to be in her early twenties, and had an innocent yearning about her, which made Madeline despise her even more. Earlier, when they had returned to the backyard, Neil had sent the German girl to the bathroom to wash up. Madeline had stood by the burnt tenderloin with her hands on her hips, watching across the yard as Neil gave the girl another hug. She knew women well enough to know why—*exactly* why—the German girl had come here. She wanted to claim him as her own. And, as Madeline grudgingly admitted, who could blame her? He was handsome, mysterious, and from a faraway land.

Just like Jakey had been.

Those attributes noted, Madeline had absolutely zero designs about starting something with Neil—Dieter. She simply viewed him as a ray of hope, and it made her jealous that this German girl, who probably had never endured a fingernail of the hardships that Madeline had, also viewed him the same way. Add to that the fact that the German was beautiful, and blonde, and played the dumbfounded, innocent victim so well—it made Madeline want to knock her teeth backward and pull her hair until she screamed.

The violent thought made Madeline grin, just before she received a compliment from the German girl.

"Thank you for the food. The vegetables are delicious."

Madeline's malicious smirk dissolved, fading to a semi-frown as she was unsure of the genuineness of the accolade. She offered a cheap replica of a thankful nod before turning her gaze to the male in the room.

He appeared uncomfortable, rubbing his hands together as he blurted out a trite question to Madeline. "Have you ever been over the northern range to where Gabi is from?"

Bullshit, stock small talk annoyed Madeline to no end, and she didn't hide it from her expression or tone when she said no.

"And had you been here to Innsbruck before?" he asked Gabi.

She shook her head as she chewed green beans.

Neil gnawed on a piece of the leather-like meat, gesturing to Gabi. "Innsbruck is picturesque, but I'm not so sure I don't like where you're from better. While still mountainous, it's not quite the same as here, especially since Innsbruck is in such a steep valley." He managed to get the meat down before he placed his knife and fork on his plate. "I've always enjoyed seeing how land looks just before a big mountain range. Once, I drove from Chicago back to California, and Denver was exactly—"

"What is *your* problem?" Gabi suddenly asked Madeline, cutting Neil off.

Madeline threw her fork onto her plate and eyed Gabi, taken aback at her sudden forcefulness. She recovered quickly. "Don't you dare take a tone like that with me, *Mädchen*. Why don't you ask Neil what my problem is?"

Gabi's mouth was puckered tightly as she turned to Neil, arching her eyebrows. Neil glanced over at Madeline, resignedly placing his napkin on the table. "Madeline is half-Jewish, Gabi. Like I touched on earlier, she's endured countless persecution and her family has been taken away. The Nazis did all this."

Madeline listened to Neil's words, feeling oddly relieved and exonerated as he spoke them. She used her fingers to push back stray wisps of hair, combing them into the mass of hair that was held tightly at the back of her head. She didn't say a word; she simply watched Gabi's reaction.

Gabi blinked several times before turning to Madeline. "You mailed the letter."

"What letter?"

"The one to Neil, when he was in San Francisco, from his best friend who died."

Madeline's eyes instantly filled with tears. "He was my fiancé."

Gabi considered this for a moment. She nodded, sipped her water and looked down into her lap, pausing for an uncomfortable amount of time. "I'm terribly sorry for how I just acted. And more so for how you've been treated."

Madeline pushed her food to the center of the table. She stood and walked to the cupboard, retrieving an old pack of cigarettes she kept for when she was in the mood. She came back to the table, lighting one and sliding the pack to Neil. He opened his eyes widely.

"You'll live," Madeline remarked.

Neil nodded thoughtfully, but declined. He slid the pack to Gabi. She lit one.

Madeline stole glances at Gabi. It must have taken tremendous courage to leave her home like she did, crossing the mountains and going into another land. Even still, she wasn't completely sold on the German girl's value system. It wouldn't be fair to judge her solely as a German, because many Germans had proven to be good people. It was the minority Nazis who had caused such strife. *I might as well just ask.*

"How do you feel about Jews?"

Gabi shrugged, taking a moment before answering. "If you strip away the National Socialist views which have been forced on me and every other person in my country, I feel about Jews like I do any other person. But as far as how I feel about the discrimination that is taking place, I find it disgusting. I don't expect you to believe me, but it's the truth and that's all I have," Gabi said, maintaining eye contact. "There's a sweet old man in Hausham, the nearby town. He owned a confectionary and had to close it for the trouble the Nazis made for him. I always liked him. It wasn't fair and it made me sad because he didn't deserve any of it. I heard he was severely beaten and no one has seen him since."

Madeline was about to speak when Gabi continued. "But if you want an apology from me, you *won't* get one. My family is not Nazi. In fact, we despise the party. We keep to ourselves and work our land as we always have. I cannot apologize for what I haven't taken part in, but I am sorry...deeply sorry that such an unjust persecution is happening to anyone, including you."

The words flowed from the young lady with conviction and maturity that belied her age. Madeline listened to each syllable, drinking each one in until she felt like there was a leaden weight on her shoulders that was heavier than she could carry. She crushed out her cigarette and stood, trying to muster a smile as more tears welled in her eyes. Not knowing what to do, but needing privacy, she crossed the room and rushed into the bedroom, flopping onto the made bed and howling into one of the pillows.

The pain was there, always there, centimeters underneath the surface. Pain for Jakey. Pain for her family. The pain of knowing that a life she had once had was gone, and would *never* return. The people were gone. Their property was no longer theirs. All the good memories ruined. She sobbed, her body shuddering as her brain flashed wretched images like a picture show gone bad. Seconds later, she heard the door click shut and felt the mattress depress.

It was Gabi. The German girl gently patted Madeline's upper back, comforting her. She leaned down, making a shushing sound like a mother might comfort her sick child. It surprised Madeline that the soothing actually helped. In fact, it felt wonderful. After several minutes, Madeline was cried out. Having been through so many tragedies, she was well in touch with her emotions on the sad side of the ledger. Once the tears ceased, her sarcastic edge would typically disappear and, if only for a while, her old self would emerge. Before the tragedies, before the persecution, Madeline had been happy. She removed her damp hand from underneath her face and clasped Gabi's hand, squeezing it.

It was a gesture of gratitude.

* * *

Neil ate a full meal while they were in the bedroom. Sure, the pork was overcooked, but it still tasted better than food from a can or that tepid chicken broth he'd subsisted on for two weeks. Burnt or not, the meat was coated with the flavorful caramelized coating that only a grill can provide. He ate with gusto.

To hell with it.

As he cleaned up, the silence in the bedroom was slowly replaced by murmurs of voices. Once the kitchen was clean, Neil sipped some Austrian iced tea—it was surprisingly very sweet—and fought his craving of a cigarette. Dr. Kraabe was correct; it was a bad habit. Neil planned to heed the doctor's advice, as irritating as the cravings might be. After another twenty minutes, he lit the wood he had stacked earlier and sat on the hearth, massaging Schatze behind her ears until she fell asleep. As the seasoned alder took flame, cracking and popping, he took an inventory of what he had learned thus far.

There were two questions in Neil's mind, and a third that was pointless in answering until he answered the first two. First, where had Jakey hidden the children and their caretakers? Neil was no closer to learning this than he had been when he first left San Francisco, and the fact that he was physically closer—and still didn't have a clue—made him feel that much farther from the answer. The second question was who had killed Jakey, and why. Third, and secondary to the first, was how to move the children once he found them. Since Neil had made a career in shipping, he felt he could probably lean on experience to figure that one out when the time came.

Find the children and get them anything they need; find Jakey's killer; avenge Jakey; move the children. Preferably in that order. Thus far, however, as J. Harrison Musselwhite would say in his Arkansan drawl, Neil "hadn't peed a drop."

If he could just get a little time to focus, Neil was confident he could make progress. If he could concentrate without distraction, keeping the details of his missions to himself, he knew he'd have a clear advantage. He was like a hare, fast and agile. The pursuing fox might be faster in the stretch, but the fox had no idea when the hare might turn. If the hare timed it just right, the fox would be left rolling in the dirt and still hungry, while the hare would be alive to run again. The hare didn't use anyone else to accomplish this, and only *he* knew when that vital turn was coming.

Neil eyed the bedroom. There were two important women in there who depended on him. And while he needed to keep them safe, he also worried that their presence might hinder his abilities.

The bedroom door suddenly creaked open and Gabi and Madeline exited. "I'm going to drive her to the doctor's house," Gabi said.

"Drive her? What if someone sees you? And you don't know where you're going."

"No one will see me. Madeline will show me the way. I know how to drive. I'm a big girl. Please just stay here and keep doing whatever it is you're doing," she said in a tone that indicated she didn't want an argument.

Madeline's body was covered in her coat, draped over her shoulders. She had undone her hair, and it flowed halfway down her back and shoulders, concealing much of her face. When she turned to Neil, he could see the pain in her eyes.

"I'm sorry for the way I acted," Madeline said, hardly audible.

"You need not apologize," Neil said. "Gabi…"

"I'll be just fine." The two women exited.

It was nearly an hour before Gabi returned. She sat at the table and drank iced tea as she relayed the entire story of her conversation from earlier. Madeline had told her everything, about her family, about her feelings of depression, and about Jakey Herman. A quick study, Gabi had a near thorough understanding of everything that was going on, telling Neil that Madeline would be better off if she could continue to talk about her pain as she had done tonight.

"She's been bottling up her grief. She told me that tonight was the first time she had truly let it all out," Gabi said, shaking her head.

"Is she okay?"

"It took a lot out of her but, yes, I think she'll wake up tomorrow and feel much better for it."

"Did she talk about how Jakey died?"

"No. But I will speak with her about that soon." Gabi's voice had an edge of finality.

Neil rubbed his tired eyes. It was rare for him to feel helpless, or at least it had been before Emilee's murder, but now the feeling was becoming much more familiar to him. He uncovered his eyes and gazed at the beauty sitting next to him.

Gabi held her empty glass on the table, using her hand to move it in slow circles. There was a question forming on her face. Neil waited patiently.

"The only thing I cannot figure out is…" she paused, knitting her eyebrows as she focused on Neil, "why exactly are you here?"

Gabi had spoken for the better part of twenty minutes, without a break, and Neil had listened, rapt. Now, her abrupt query jolted him back to reality. He fumbled irritably for words, realizing that he didn't have an adequate answer.

"Well, because my friend asked me to come here, as his dying wish."

She squeezed her eyelids shut and shook her head. It was an expression of impatience, almost as if he hadn't been quite bright enough to understand the deeper meaning of her words. "I know about that, but what I don't know…what Madeline didn't know to tell me…and what I think *you* don't know to tell me…is *why* your friend Jacob chose *you*. Why ask Neil Reuter, a man who had to come all the way from San Francisco? Among all the Jews and their friends, there must be a host of supremely capable people. So, why did Jacob choose *you* to find these children?"

Neil was surprised at Gabi's sudden edge. "Well, I speak German and I've been behind the lines before—back when there was a war going on. Jakey knew that, because he'd been with me. And I'm pretty damned good at this type of thing. I'm using my own money, a considerable sum. And I'm not Jewish. There's three reasons."

"And they couldn't have found all that anywhere else? Madeline told me the money was a non-issue."

"So what's your point?"

"My point is exactly what I already asked. It's a question of why they chose you. It...doesn't...make...sense."

Angered, Neil rapped on the table. "What is all this? All of the sudden it's interrogate-Neil-Reuter-night?" Schatze lifted her head at the sudden change in tone.

"Dieter Dremel," Gabi replied softly.

"Okay, interrogate-Dieter-Dremel-night."

She looked at him. "Why did he choose you, Neil? I'm not trying to bring you down, but the question bothers me, and you should stop mourning Jakey, at least temporarily, so that you can dispassionately come to the root of the question, too." She brightened. "If you figure out *why*, then perhaps you can decipher this puzzle you're trying to solve."

Neil moved to the fireplace, the flame warming his face. He paid heed to her question, running it over and over through his mind. She was right. After all of the elaborate preparation, which could even include framing him for Lex Curran's death, what was so damned important about getting *him* to Austria to find these children? Sure, he was qualified for the mission. And because he wasn't Jewish, and could assimilate, he was able to do these things in broad daylight. But there had to be others who could have done it as well, perhaps even better.

And not taken nearly two months to arrive.

He turned to Gabi.

"I agree that Jakey's motivation is peculiar. I'll think about it. For now, I just don't know." He moved over her. "Now, Gabi, why are *you* here?"

She grasped his hand. "Because I love you, Neil."

That got him.

Neil was silent. Oddly warm inside, but silent.

"I mean it," Gabi said.

"I've learned that you don't mince words," Neil whispered. He gathered himself, clearing his throat. "Before you allow your emotions for me to set, I need to tell you something."

"Tell me what?"

He shut his eyes. He took deep breaths.

At the start of his adult life, his plum assignment as the general's attaché quickly led to special military schooling. That led to his place on the battlefield, then to undercover military work, first as an intelligence combatant and then a sapper. Eventually it turned into a shadowy existence straight out of the plot of a Saturday matinee. In those nickel flicks, the hero, someone like Spencer Tracy, a cigarette dangling from his full lips, would always say exactly what Neil was about to say, but the hero would say it with such aplomb.

Neil's voice cracked when he said it.

"I'm a professional killer."

The short sentence Neil had never before uttered was now out, lingering, floating around the couple like a phantasm.

Gabi, to her credit, took the news well. She tilted her head, eyeing him quizzically.

"Before my wife's death, Gabi, my job was to kill men who were enemies of the United States. It didn't start that way, but that's what it evolved to. It doesn't sadden me. I vetted each target beforehand and, even though I roundly despise the bastards I worked for, I still support many of their beliefs. The earth is a cleaner, safer place minus the men I've put into its soil."

"I like it when you speak the truth."

"That's it? No questions?"

"What else is there to say?"

She gave his hand a final squeeze before she stood and crossed the room, entering the bedroom and closing the door behind her. Neil heard the water running in the tub. Thirty minutes went by, dragging on longer than the sum total of his entire journey. He watched the fire lose its flame, smoldering in a lump of orange coals. Before, when the girls had been in the bedroom, he had been in the mission, inventorying his thoughts like the professional he was, preparing for his next set of tasks. But now, over that unending half-hour while she was in the bedroom and bath, all Neil could think of was this young German woman who had left her family for him, and the fact that she claimed to love him. Just when he thought he might have to go outside for some air, the bedroom door opened halfway.

He sat still, not breathing. The door was ajar; the room behind it dark. Everything remained silent and still for a full minute. Schatze lay curled in a ball, sleeping. Neil looked at the bedroom door again. He stood, slowly crossing the main room, standing just outside the bedroom. Inside, the quilt and sheet rustled.

"I drew another bath for you."

Neil's throat was nearly swollen shut and, after a strained swallow, he entered the diminutive bathroom and pushed the door shut behind him. He brushed his teeth before entering the tub, dunking himself before using soap to clean his hair, his ears and every square inch of his body. Neil realized his night clothes were in the bedroom so, after toweling dry, he cracked the door and asked Gabi to hand them to him.

"You don't need your clothes," she said. "Come to bed."

Neil's breathing was coming in large gasps which he did his best to silence. He slid under the covers and pulled the quilt to his neck. Gabi immediately rolled to him and he could tell by the touch of her skin that she, too, wore nothing. The smell of the same soap he had just used danced on her skin. She pressed her lips to his, a small peck growing into a passionate kiss. Gabi's leg probed both of his, silky smooth and sliding up and down, petting him with her foot. Her hand moved from his neck, down the muscles of his chest, over his stomach and below his navel. She locked her leg over his body, moving astride him, allowing the quilt to roll backward.

There was scant light in the room, but enough that Neil could see her staring down at him. She placed her hands on his chest and moved slowly, sliding forward and backward. The sensation was almost unbearable. She made soft sounds before taking Neil's hands and moving them to her thighs. Despite the absence of light, Neil could see her smile.

They rolled over, never losing contact with one another. Neil kissed her. She dragged her mouth to his neck, licking him up and down before again locking her mouth on his as she increased her movements under him. As the physicality of their intimate actions increased, Neil could feel his ribs throbbing, and the pain somehow added to his excitement. When he neared his zenith, Gabi moaned softly and increased her grip on him, pulling him closer as they both released in a hail of gasps before collapsing onto the damp sheets.

Gabi kissed him lightly on his chest before he rolled off of her. She nestled into the crook of his arm and whispered one last phrase for the evening.

"No matter what you've done, I still love you. *Ich liebe dich.*"

Chapter Fifty

EARLIER THAT FRIDAY, Thomas Lundren had been in the Austrian town of Wörgl. It was the type of place he might have wanted to live in his youth. There were abounding outdoor activities and, because of that, everyone seemed so cheerful. The shopkeepers and locals, easy to mark due to their deeply bronzed skin, greeted Thomas everywhere he went. Without prompting, they offered advice on activities he might enjoy on the slopes or the surrounding lakes. The local economy was tourism, and the residents obviously knew it. In a matter of weeks, Wörgl would be teeming with skiers and tourists, using it as their home base for skiing on the nearby ski runs, the most famous being Kitzbühel.

But sporting was not Thomas' reason for being here.

Once again, a map was spread out before him, this one of the three states of western Austria. Thomas was currently facing due north, at a café with an elevated outdoor patio. He had sent his detail forward to investigate several suppositions that needed to be looked into, even though he felt they would probably bear no fruit.

Sometimes Thomas simply needed to be alone with his thoughts.

The accommodating waiter had given Thomas five glasses of water. Four held the map down in the cool afternoon breeze. One was cupped in his hand as he leaned over the map, staring at the pass that the airplane was to have flown through. The first town south of the pass, on mostly level ground, was Wörgl, and that's why Thomas had chosen to come here. While he doubted Kruger's killer had immediately descended into Wörgl, Thomas felt it important to stop and view the physical surroundings as well as the map.

Thomas still believed Kruger and the other man had flown directly from England, where, years before, Kruger was said to have defected to. They likely stopped in Velden with the intention of refueling. Antonio, the airfield worker, said they didn't take any fuel and Thomas believed him. While they were there, something went wrong and Kruger was shot, right at the spot he was found. Due to the spattering of blood, the man had not been shot in the airplane and then dumped.

There were traces of one other blood type, a short distance away. Thomas assigned that blood to the "pilot," the one he'd seen struggling with the airplane. Since Wilhelm Kruger had been a pilot in the Great War, it was quite reasonable to assume he had been the one flying on that night, before his death. So then, after the killing, the shooter would have been forced to fly to get away—especially if he was too injured to run. *Yes, that makes sense*, Thomas thought. The man was either a novice pilot or very unfamiliar with that aircraft. All of these hypotheses Thomas could live with.

But what he kept coming back to was the story from the veterinarian. Why would he make such a thing up? And, if the vet had been so drunk he'd hallucinated a plane crash—something Thomas struggled to believe—why would he immediately change his tune when he heard the contrasting tale from the Heinz boy?

The veterinarian was vermin, without a doubt. Thomas wouldn't trust the man to scrawl his own name, much less take care of one of his animals. But there seemed to be some truth to his story, especially the way he had first relayed it down in that lower field. And then, after they had searched the Heinz home and barn, the man had abruptly changed his story and seemed eager to leave. But why? In all Thomas' years of investigation, never before had he seen a witness so quickly flip, and then be so sure about it.

Leaning back and stretching in the sun, Thomas felt the sea change in his leanings.

It had taken his crossing the political border into Austria to feel more strongly that the airplane had actually come to a rest somewhere north of the Alps, in *Germany*. There was certainly a chance the airplane had had enough fuel to make it to Austria. There was a chance the pilot had stopped and refueled somewhere else. There were always chances.

But that didn't coincide with Thomas' research on the range of the Hornet Moth on a single tank of fuel. The fuel would have run out north of the pass, very close to where the veterinarian said the plane crashed.

Many years ago, when all else failed, Thomas learned to trust his gut instinct. And right now it was telling him that he had gone too far south. Somehow the crooked veterinarian, and maybe even the Heinz boy at the farm, held the key to what really happened.

Thomas stayed at the café another hour, eating a light pastry before retiring to the hotel for the night. The other officers arrived at sundown, empty-handed as Thomas thought they might be. His men went out for a night on the town. But Thomas stayed in his chamber, reading, although he couldn't have recounted a word of what he read. His mind was still in Hausham, occupied with the unsavory veterinarian and his strange story.

After five hours of fitful sleep, Thomas sat straight up at three in the morning on Saturday. Following a brief coughing spell, he wore his nightshirt to the end of the hallway in the small inn, enjoying a hot bath and a shave at the same time. After cleaning his teeth, Thomas accepted a hot mug of tea from the elderly man in the office. He left a sealed note for his chief man, instructing him and the officers to split up and question the citizenry in the valley toward Zell am See, and in the other direction towards Innsbruck.

Thomas wrote that he was going back to Hausham, and that he had additional questions for Hörst Baldinger, the veterinarian.

The old truck puttered north, up the steep incline toward the pass at Kufstein. Inside was Thomas Lundren, his face bright, as his instinct told him that a break in the case was very near.

* * *

At seven in the morning, the parking lot of the main police station in Nürnberg buzzed with activity. While the black Mercedes patrol cars came and went, Preston Lord watched as a gaggle of officers yelled at one another, dividing into what looked like two sides with clearly differing opinions. They all wore the same police uniforms and, after two full minutes of arguing and a few vulgar gestures, both sides went their separate ways. Who knew what the argument was about? Who cared? Lord sat in the constable's old DKW rattletrap, not deliberately hiding, but sitting low in the seat to avoid any unwanted questioning. Before Constable Sauer had gone inside, he placed an official-looking paper on the dashboard, covered in stamps and signatures, adorned several times by the far overused National Socialist swastika.

And while Lord had seen the swastika in newsreels and photos, he was staggered by the frequency of the Nazi symbol across the Germanic land, especially in a large city like Nürnberg. On light poles, hanging from buildings, in car windows, on children's arm bands, hanging in front of schools and businesses: the icon was everywhere he turned. Sitting in the liquor-pervaded cabin of Sauer's car, Lord looked around, counting one…two…three…four…five Nazi symbols. All of them clearly visible, and this was only in an isolated parking lot, sandwiched between two taller buildings.

Twenty minutes had passed since the constable went inside. Since their meeting at the café, Sauer had told Lord all about the discovery of the body at the airstrip. The body was discovered at Velden, the very same airstrip that the Danish partner of Wilhelm Kruger said he would use to stop and refuel. After working through a loose timeline, Lord was almost certain that the body was found the morning after Kruger left England. It was too fantastic to have been a coincidence and the reasoning was simple: Reuter had needed to come to Germany, covertly. He'd found his man, hitched a ride with him, and killed him once he was inside the Reich.

Unless, by chance, the body was actually Neil Reuter's.

"No," Lord spoke to the empty car, a rueful grin on his face. "I'm lucky, but not that lucky."

But why would Reuter have left Wilhelm Kruger's carcass lying out in the open like that? And who'd flown Kruger's airplane? Reuter didn't know how to fly—at least Lord didn't think so. None of it made sense. He shook his head and dug underneath the seat, finding Sauer's flask and swigging from it. *Kentucky bourbon of piss-poor quality,* Lord thought, taking a second swig. The truth was: Lord had no way of knowing how that shooting had gone down. If Reuter was the killer—and that was highly likely—any number of things could have happened to necessitate a hasty getaway.

Lord recalled the cuckolded Danish husband, Henry Janzen, mentioning that Kruger may have tried to rob Neil. That had to have been it. The pilot landed in Velden to refuel, then tried to rob his passenger, having no idea who he really was.

Bang-Bang!

A dead body on the runway.

Dumb move, Willi Kruger.

The other troubling aspect was the airplane. The constable had told Lord that the old policeman had shot at it as it sped down the runway and flew away. On the drive to Nürnberg, Lord scoured Reuter's file for any information regarding flight training. There was none. Perhaps he had learned on his own—entirely possible. But, if that were the case, why use Kruger to get into Germany? Why not fly himself? It didn't make sense at all.

Another swig.

Just as Lord had nestled deep into the worn seat, he saw the lumbering, pear-shaped constable crossing the parking lot, triumph all over his face. *The man better never take up poker,* Lord mused, already hating him. Sauer jerked the door open, plopping onto the seat with a whoosh as his hand automatically reached underneath for the flask. Lord watched his face darken a fraction as he had to move his hand to the right of where it was supposed to be. He removed the flask and shot his evil eye at the American as he took a swig.

"Well?"

Sauer lowered the flask and let out a rancid, yet satisfied breath. "It's a very quiet operation that no one is supposed to know about. But the desk man knows me. We went out back for a cigar." Sauer's face took on an uncharacteristic apprehensive look. "It ended up costing me a twenty to get him to talk."

Lord knew full well Sauer probably only paid five reichsmarks. "Fine," he grumbled, throwing a wad of the strange-looking fives on the seat. "*What* did he tell you?"

"The man I told you about, Lundren, once a high-ranking policeman, was named special investigator just for this case. He supposedly has a solid reputation, but he's had difficulties finding anything meaningful about the murder. That said, something happened recently. He's not here because he got called to the south part of Bavaria. Something urgent."

"They say why?"

Sauer took another nip and shrugged. "Said there was a witness."

"Have they identified the body?"

"Nope."

Lord held his hand out for the flask. The constable reluctantly handed it over. After a long pull, Lord said, "I find it hard to believe they weren't able to figure out Kruger's identity." He gnawed on a fingernail. "Hell, maybe the dead man is Reuter."

"Didn't you say your American had different-colored eyes?"

"Green and blue."

"Well, the dead body down at the morgue has bad teeth and brown eyes. They don't have his name yet, but his description is in the report. He's also got an uncircumcised prick."

Lord eyed Sauer for a moment. He dug into Reuter's file, pulling out the medical information. There it was, circumcised. He shook his head, constantly surprised by the directions his job sometimes took him. Lord poked the page. "The cadaver's not Reuter. I knew it wouldn't be. Reuter killed that guy, I'd bet anything."

Sauer twisted his girth to face Lord. "We should find Lundren. He may just lead you to your man. And I wouldn't mind settling a score with that old bastard."

"Did you say the south of Bavaria?"

"Yeah."

"What's there?"

"Resorts and baths mainly, at the base of the mountains."

Lord spit out a piece of a fingernail. "The videos I've seen in the news about Adolf Hitler, where he hosts world leaders. It's in the mountains, isn't it?"

"Yeah, near Berchtesgaden."

"And where is that?" Lord knew all this, but he was bringing his patsy along, letting him think he was the intelligent one.

"In the *south* of Bavaria."

"Can you find out where this special investigator was called to?"

"Thomas Lundren."

"Yeah, Lundren."

"Maybe." Sauer paused, cutting his eyes. "I'll need more money."

Preston Lord reached inside his overcoat and peeled off 100 reichsmarks in twenties, dropping them on the wine-colored seat. As Sauer was exiting the car again, Lord pulled him back in by the tail of his threadbare barn coat.

"Whatever you do, don't raise suspicion about why you want to know this."

Sauer grinned, his face sinking back into his multiple chins as he bared his stained teeth. "It's not a problem. I made it clear that I hate the old fart. My buddy thinks this is all personal."

After Sauer had left, Lord pinched his bottom lip as his mind raced. He knew his theories were racing off in a reckless direction, but they made sense. While there was a chance he might be off target, he would bet a quarter of his trust fund that Neil Reuter was planning to kill Adolf Hitler at his retreat in southern Bavaria. The same retreat that was always on the news, as the fanatical German hosted whomever the world leader of the week might be.

And Neil Reuter would kill him there, in his home, because Reuter had just that kind of style—and so did Preston Lord.

Which enabled him to think like Neil.

Or, so he thought.

* * *

Thomas parked between the Hausham Catholic Church and the ramshackle, two-story building with a hand-painted sign displaying Baldinger Veterinary & Husbandry. It was nearly noon, a sunny *Altweibersommer* day—the German equivalent to Indian summer. The warm breeze carried the pleasant smells of hay and hops. He stretched, allowing the sun's radiation to reenergize him. While he was quite comfortable with waking early, especially at his advanced age, a fitful, coughing night of sleep had taken its toll on him. Perhaps after speaking with the veterinarian, he could find a fortified lunch somewhere in town. It seemed ages since he'd had a good meal, and on this warm day he was craving overcooked vegetables and a pork dish, with good bread, just like his Greta had once prepared every Sunday.

Shaking the doleful recollections from his mind, he stepped to the wooden slat sidewalk, tipping his hat to a group of young women as they passed. When they disappeared around the corner, he faced the building, noticing that the front door of Baldinger's practice was wide open. A thin screen door was all that kept the flies out, though they were bouncing off the thin gauge screen as if it were a trampoline. Thomas stepped inside, immediately smelling the musty animal scent along with something he couldn't readily place. Behind the main counter was a large nazi flag, hanging from the rafters. To the right, a man leaned against a pallet of stacked feed bags, smoking a hand-rolled cigarette. Thomas nodded to him.

"Don't know where the hell he is," the man grumped. "Called his name three times."

Thomas marked the man as a farmer, judging by his tattered, earth-stained clothes. Thomas poked his head out the screen door, looking at the small sign hanging from twine. It indicated that Hörst Baldinger should be in. A number of flies swarmed away from the screen door and, when Thomas opened it, they whizzed inside. The same thing had happened moments before when he had first come in.

"Is he usually open on Saturday?"

"Yes, and this waiting is getting to me," the farmer said. "Damned Hörst was supposed to be out at our place by eleven. My Freda's got hoof rot and needs to get the elixir in her." He tugged his wide brim hat on his head, setting his jaw. "I'll bet that bastard's probably drunk somewhere. Do me a favor, you see him, tell him Von Berg was here and he better get his butt out to Kampe while the sun's high."

"I will," Thomas answered. "Good luck with your Freda." Thomas watched as the man pushed the screen door open, cursing under his breath as his muddy boots clunked down the wooden sidewalk.

More flies darted in.

Thomas massaged his freshly-shaven face. He walked behind the main room, opening a swing door to what must have been the operating room. In the center of the room was a stained table—over to the side was a large steel sink. In the sink Thomas found an empty bottle of liquor and a large, clean scalpel. He peered out of the grimy back window, seeing nothing of interest. With nowhere else to look, Thomas walked back to the center of the building before eyeing the stairs.

As he climbed, the smell that had been intermixed with the musty, animal scent grew stronger with every step. Acrid. Coppery. Metallic. He knew that odor. In his years as a police officer, he'd smelled it many times before.

Not good.

The upstairs was a simple layout. A hallway with two doors, both of them open, the left one beaming rays of daylight. Thomas called out several times as he eased his way toward the openings. As he passed, he felt something in the corner of his eye in the room on the left but, being a patient lawman, he stuck his head in the darkened room on the right. There was a string above his head, which he pulled. The room was used for storage, darkened because of the boxes stacked over the windows. Everything from medicines to liquor was stored there, with no apparent rhyme or reason as to its order.

Thomas clicked the light off, taking a long, slow breath. For some reason, he was uncharacteristically unnerved about what he might see in the other room. When he'd passed, from the corner of his left eye, he had thought he'd seen flesh, along with carmine. And for a policeman, when combined with the overpowering smell, such hues typically weren't a good sign.

Thomas took three steps across the hall, swiveling his head to the right. As he took in the gruesome sight, he knew he'd been correct about the odor:

Blood.

Sickeningly sweet. Earthy. Pungent.

It was a smell unlike any other on earth, the odor of an abattoir. The carmine he'd glimpsed was full on red in the wet spots, blackish at its edges and deep garnet where it had dried on the sheets. The noontime light shone through the open second-floor window, allowing Thomas to view the disgusting scene in great detail. Hörst Baldinger's hands were handcuffed to the metal rails of the cheap single bed, his feet bound by ropes to the base legs. He was spread-eagle, wearing no clothes. Covering his body, primarily on his torso, were cuts. All in all, there were probably more than fifty of them. Some were small, less than a centimeter. Others were as wide as a man's hand, including the deadly incision that had nearly severed his neck.

And the flies…

The elderly policeman placed his hat over his mouth in a futile effort to help him focus. Who had done this? Thomas' first guess was the man who'd killed Kruger. Perhaps Baldinger had known more than he'd let on. Perhaps that man had come back and made certain that the veterinarian lived to tell no more tales. But how would the man in the airplane have known what Baldinger had seen, and told?

Thomas narrowed his eyes as he stared at the vet's slashed neck. Just above the gash, two black stitches stood out. Thomas stepped beside the bed, avoiding the sticky blood on the floor, lightly touching the sutures. Flies buzzed away from the feast at the movements of his hand, immediately diving back in for more. The small scar was over Baldinger's jugular vein, and didn't appear to have been sewn together professionally. It was puckered out, like when someone who didn't know how to sew attempted to mend a hole in their trousers. But it had clotted and begun to heal, and Thomas was nearly certain it hadn't been on the veterinarian's neck when he had made his proclamations to the investigators about the black airplane.

More flies swarmed as Thomas touched the pale, bloodless arm. Burn marks. He could see where the hair was singed, scorched backward from the rounded tip of what might have been a cigar. Thomas inspected the other arm. There were marks there as well, and on the man's legs. Thomas also noticed dark black scorching around the tip of the man's penis.

He'd been tortured. Severely.

But why, if the veterinarian had only seen the airplane, would the man from the airfield need to torture and kill him? Maybe he wanted to know what the vet had told the policemen. Plausible, but something about it didn't quite fit.

Thomas stepped back from the body, staring out the window into the town of Hausham, regretfully giving up his dreams of a fortified lunch. Then a thought struck him. *The Heinz family!* Perhaps Baldinger mentioned them to his tormentor, and that's where he'd gone next.

Though he'd like to call this in, the closest polizei who could truly help Thomas were far away, and there was no time to wait. He ran down the stairs, pulling the heavy door shut and flipping the sign by the door to signify that the veterinarian was away, which certainly was the truth.

Through his coughing fit, Thomas recalled exactly where the Heinz family lived. They were smack dab in the valley south of Hausham, nearly at the base of the Alps that he had just crossed over.

Chapter Fifty-One

WHILE THOMAS LUNDREN RUSHED TO HER FAMILY HOME, Gabi Heinz was over the south range, in the city of Salzburg. She'd done much of the day's driving as Neil worked on a plan in his mind. Many times during the slow drive to the city built over some of the world's finest salt mines, an uncomfortable hush had permeated the Horch. Whenever she spoke, Neil had asked for silence. Complete silence. Gabi had sulked as Neil stared at the passing mountains, developing the strategy, working on contingencies, and then cementing each one in its own category, so that no matter what happened, he wouldn't have to waste a precious second to think, but only react. This went on for nearly the entire drive.

They took a room at the Österreichischer Hof, a grand hotel on the banks of the River Salzach. On the building's top floor, their chamber was designed in Viennese grandeur. The room was dominated by a high, curved ceiling, adorned with a baby blue calligraphic frieze like something out of a children's book. Gabi lay asleep on the bed, the coverlet pulled over her.

They hadn't gotten much sleep the night before.

Neil sipped coffee from the china service, staring out the window at the late afternoon Saturday traffic on Elisabethkai. He produced the saltwater-stained business card from the Hasidic forger back in New York. With his mouth full of eggs, the New York forger had told Neil to call the man on the card, and he would instruct Neil how to reach the forger's cousin. Neil rang the number on the generic card, speaking German to the woman who answered. The ensuing conversation was quick—Neil expressed his desires; the woman took his number and hung up. After ten minutes, a man called back. His tone was cautious. Neil told the man he needed assistance with documents. He was greeted with silence.

"I'm a customer of your cousin from New York," Neil offered. "*Mein name ist Dieter Dremel.*"

"Dieter Dremel?"

"Yes."

"Herr Dremel, during your life in North America, where did you spend Christmas Eve in 1932?"

"Excuse me?"

Silence.

"Hang on." Neil viewed the ceiling, his mind hearkening back. "Christmas Eve of thirty-two was when my wife and I visited San Diego."

"When you were a child, you saw your cousin break his ankle jumping off a seawall. His name, please."

"Jonathan."

"Very good, Herr Dremel. Where are you right now?"

"Somewhere safe," Neil replied. "Where can I meet your document man?"

"I will call you back. Or he will. Give me your number, please."

Neil waited a half-hour, hearing only the soft murmur of Gabi's breathing. He allowed the Colt to dangle by his knee as he gazed out the window, awaiting the call. The mountains directly in front of him made up the geographical area known as Ober Salzburg. Rectangular shapes intermittently dotted the evergreen-covered mountainsides. Neil scanned each mountain, wondering if Hitler's compound was visible from where he sat.

Several years before, Neil had read a book that was almost certainly an allusion to Adolf Hitler's early days in office, although Hitler was never named by the book's author. It was written shortly after Hitler's power grab, about a hunter who finds himself with the perfect vantage point to kill a European dictator at his mountain hideaway. The author, who the Department of War vetted afterward, had a background in covert services.

Standing, Neil leaned against the window, eyeing one structure in particular, high on a mountaintop. After a moment he dipped his head.

"Hitler's not why you're here. That ship sailed years ago," he whispered.

Damn, he could use a cigarette right now. Badly. He walked to his bag and removed the pouch. From inside he produced the picture of Fern, and Jakey's tattered letter. Neil brushed his finger across the picture of the tiny, dark-haired girl. "Where are you, honey?" he whispered, trying not to imagine how unsettling months of hiding probably was for a child.

He then studied Jakey's note, each and every word. He turned it backward, upside down, looking for anything. There was something about the wording…

The phone rang.

"Yes?"

"Call for you, sir."

"Put it through." *Please be the forger.* "Hello?"

"Wilkommen mein Freund!" a jovial voice said.

"Thank you. Are you the cousin of my friend in New York?"

"Yes, of course. I won't say his name, but the last time I saw him he was nearly exploding from his clothes. The man enjoys his food."

"He hasn't changed. Where might I meet you? I have an important item for you to examine, and I need help quickly. I haven't much time."

The man hummed for a moment. "I have a thought. Do you know the festival on the east end of town? It's enormous...impossible to miss."

"We saw the signs."

"Meet me there this evening at seven. Go to the largest beer tent and stand at the southernmost portion of the tent. I will be there, wearing more swastikas than anyone."

"Interesting."

"A man like me doesn't survive in our current state without being very flexible regarding outward appearance."

The meeting was set.

Gabi was still sleeping when Neil hung up the phone and walked to the desk. He viewed the four remaining diamonds, the largest ones. On the table, in a briefcase, was the sum total of what the other diamonds had yielded earlier today. When he and Gabi had first arrived in Salzburg, just before lunch, Neil walked into the center of the city, finding the most exclusive jeweler in town. After relentlessly assuring the cautious young attendant that he was in no way a criminal or a Nazi, the fellow had taken him to the back, leading him up a set of partially hidden stairs. In an office overlooking the Kurpark, an aged jeweler had spread the remainder of the diamonds on a sheet of purple felt, bending a desk lamp over them as he examined them with an eyeglass.

"Where did you get these?" he asked without looking up.

A flash of panic seized Neil as he thought they might be fakes, but that was impossible. He'd already sold some in London and also Germany. "Does it matter?"

The man shrugged and placed them, one at a time after examination, into a pile.

"Are you the owner?" Neil asked.

"Not anymore," the man answered, studying the diamonds. He was obviously Jewish, wearing a yarmulke.

"Who is the owner?"

"The father of the young man who helped you. He purchased the store from me many years ago, when we saw what was coming. It's a bit of a false front but I refuse to leave my home."

"Do the authorities know you're here?"

"Only if you tell them."

"I will not," Neil replied.

After what seemed an hour, the old man had summoned the younger clerk by jingling a bell. He whispered something to the clerk, who nodded. The clerk was gone for twenty minutes. During that time, Neil tried to get the old man to tell him what the diamonds were worth.

"The bank is only open until noon. Let's first see if he can make the withdrawal in time." The jeweler spoke German, but his accent sounded unlike anything Neil had yet heard.

The sound of the bolt turning was finally heard from down the stairs. Breathless, the young man appeared with the type of cheap briefcase a bank gladly gives to their best clients. Neil opened it, thumbing the neat stacks of bills. "How much?"

"Nine hundred thousand reichsmarks," answered the old man, stacking his hands on top of one another. "About a third of their market value in the free world, but you won't find a better deal in Hitler's empire."

Neil had sucked back a burst of anger at the low price. He rubbed his face as he spoke. "Why so low?"

The man removed his yarmulke and massaged his scalp. "The stones will have to be exported to be sold. Fine items such as diamonds have lost tremendous value under Hitler. He is building a war machine, in case you haven't noticed. Values shift like sands with public consciousness, and currently, items such as freedom and liberties and rights hold much greater worth than mere hardened rocks."

That thought had stuck with Neil the remainder of the day. After the transaction was complete, he departed the store and used his time efficiently, visiting a camera shop, and then an equipment co-op on the edge of town, specializing in construction and excavating materials. After a final shopping trip to a general store, he'd come back to the grand hotel to find Gabi sleeping. It was then that Neil ordered the coffee and phoned the forger, making his plans while overlooking the greenish water of the River Salzach.

When the forger called, Gabi had awoken from her nap. Now that she was awake, Neil lurched into action. His face was tight and pinched, his actions hurried as he hustled around the expansive suite, transferring his purchased items into several flour bags.

"What are you doing?" Gabi asked, sitting up in bed.

"If you didn't hear, the meeting with the forger is set. Once he gets me what I need, every second will be dedicated to finding those children. If you want to go home from here, I won't blame you."

He was in the middle of pouring the last bit of powder into the third bag of flour when she touched his shoulder. He sealed the bag and turned to her.

"Do you not remember the things I said to you at my house?" she asked. "About the life I would like to lead, if it's only for a day?"

Neil closed his eyes for a moment. "Gabi, that kind of talk sounds great coming out of a person's mouth, believe me. I know because I've said it. But you're going to learn some things in the next ten years of your life that are going to give you—"

"Stop it," she snapped, cutting him off. "Don't you dare tell me that I'm too young to know how I feel. I'm aware of my emotions and can damn well make decisions for my life. Do you understand me?"

"Gabi."

She jabbed his chest with her index finger. "Do—you—understand—me?"

"Of course I do, Gabi. I'm not trying to be patronizing when I suggest you might want to go home. When I was out running my errands, I saw the soldiers and their automatic weapons, and it finally hit me how close this little tinderbox is to igniting." He touched her cheek. "I'm brusque only because I want what's best for you, for your future."

"And yours?"

"I'm no one's future, Gabi."

Gabi moved close to him, grasping his hands.

"What is it?" he asked.

Gabi kissed him. "You're my future, Neil."

"You're kind, Gabi, but this is real life. What I'm planning is reckless and deadly."

"Tell me the plan. I want to *actively* participate."

"No."

"Yes, dammit."

As she had done with him several times before, when she spoke zealously, her eyes rimmed with tears and her lip trembled.

Why not?

"As you say, Gabi."

"No. I want *you* to say it."

"Gabi, I will welcome your help."

"And not just some tawdry job like sitting by a phone. A real, active part. I want to do something meaningful. Even if it kills me."

"You will have a real, active role in the plan."

She nodded, wearing a decidedly triumphant expression.

There was an hour left before their meeting—plenty of time. Neil carefully relayed his plan and everything he knew to Gabi. She asked profound questions, bringing up several points, from angles he would have never considered.

Thirty minutes later, they departed. They were headed to meet the forger at the festival on the east end of town, in the largest beer tent, southernmost section.

* * *

Earlier that afternoon, still shaken by the veterinarian's brutal slaying, Thomas Lundren had eased to a halt under the large shade tree outside of the Heinz farmhouse. Most of the leaves were still green, with only a few beginning to display hints of their grand autumnal transformation. Chickens scurried to him, expecting to be fed. He shooed them back and removed his hat, rapping on the screen door. He noticed that the upper portion of the screen was ripped. It had not been ripped when he had been here only a few days prior. Thomas waited, hearing nothing inside. He knocked again, louder this time.

Nothing.

Ambling to the eastern edge of the upper yard, the old policeman stared out over the fields where the now dead veterinarian had said the airplane had crashed. The warmish day baked the normally damp earth in the Indian summer sunlight. There was no one to be seen, only a flock of blackbirds eating the remnants of thresh from one of the tilled sections. Thomas walked to the barn, calling out several times. He patted a whinnying horse on its muzzle, stopping at the middle stall, his heart sinking into his stomach.

In the back of the stall was a trap door. It was wide open, the hay bunched around the top. They hadn't seen it on their previous visit. He grabbed a lantern, hanging from a sixteen-penny nail, using a match from his pocket to light it. Thomas knelt over the cellar space, holding the light down inside. Crates of jarred foods were stored in there and nothing else. There was sufficient space to easily hide a man.

After extinguishing the lantern, he walked back to the house. With the screen open, he peered through the wavy glass, seeing no one. He walked around the entire house, scanning the windows and surrounding areas, but the only life nearby were the chickens clamoring at his feet. At the back porch, Thomas walked up the three steps and cupped his hands over the glass as he looked into the back room of the darkened house, seeing someone.

The lady who lived there, Frau Heinz, was flat on the floor. There was blood all around her.

Chapter Fifty-Two

THIS WAS THE EXACT SAME ROUTE NEIL HAD TAKEN when he walked into Austria. Preston Lord sat shotgun in the rattletrap DKW while the constable drove. They hadn't spoken once since leaving the Heinz farm. When they had finished there, as they had walked back to the car, Lord had seen the trepidation in Sauer's eyes. He'd been fine with the murder of the sleazy veterinarian, but he'd blanched as Lord had worked on the tough old Heinz woman. Lord could see where killing a woman might be a shock for even the most hardened man. But it was of no matter. Like that fat old kraut woman, the constable had now served his purpose—if he was hurting, he wouldn't be for long.

They were nearing the crest of the road, less than a kilometer from where Neil and Schatze had weathered the icy evening a week before. Lord shifted several times in his seat, feigning discomfort. He kept peering through the rocky formations for just the right place and, when he saw it, he asked Sauer to pull off the road.

"Why?" It was the first thing Sauer had mumbled since they had left.

"Gotta take a piss."

Sauer eased off the side of the road. The right side had a short wooden guardrail, and beyond it, a steep alpine drop of at least a thousand feet. Lord twisted in the seat, snatching the keys from the ignition.

"The hell you doing?" the constable yelled.

"Just so we trust each other," Lord answered, jiggling the keys before dropping them in his pocket. "I don't want you leaving me up here." He lurched from the car, crossed the road and walked through a small passage between two tall rock formations. Behind the rocks, he found a number of crevices and loose stones. It was the perfect spot. True to his word, he relieved himself while peering through a crevice, only able to see the back of the dusty black DKW.

Lord retrieved his Beretta from his jacket pocket and tucked it in his waistband behind him. Just as he began to walk back to the car, he stuck his hands in each side coat pocket, his right wrapping around the textured bone of his razor-sharp flip knife, the one he used on the veterinarian and the Heinz woman. His left hand gripped the cold steel of one of his contingency items, courtesy of the asylum-like weapons laboratory back in Maryland.

When he stepped through the two rock formations, he saw that the DKW was empty. Lord spun, looking all around. Perhaps the constable was relieving himself as well, but there was no sign of him. Lord sensed danger. Suddenly the frigid, rarefied air made an earthquake of a shiver go through him. He whipped out his pistol, moving behind the auto in case the constable was hidden, scanning the rock formations on the far side of the road where he'd just been.

"Drop the gun," came the constable's ragged voice from behind him. Lord stiffened, realizing what the sneaky bastard had done. He had eased over the edge, behind the guardrail. Without even turning around, Lord could picture the constable, standing on a precipice, aiming his long Mauser revolver at him. This was a bad situation.

"Drop it now or I'll shoot you dead, you skinny bastard," the constable warned, his voice rising. "I just watched you kill two people in cold blood, so don't think for a second that I'll even hesitate."

Lord sucked crisp air in through his nose and dropped his pistol onto the gravel. He turned, seeing Sauer coming over the rail, just as he had pictured.

"The knife, too."

Lord obeyed, wincing as his prized Boker rattled on the battered macadam.

"Move over there. Move!" The constable motioned Lord to the other side of the road. He gathered up Lord's Beretta and the knife, dropping them in the pockets of his barn coat.

"How much money you got in that case of yours?"

"Are you going to arrest me, or just kill me?" Lord asked.

"If I was gonna kill you, why would I ask?"

"About fifty thousand in reichsmarks, large bills."

"Counterfeit?"

Lord let out an exasperated breath. "How stupid do you think we are? No, not counterfeit. We have many ways of obtaining your soon-to-be worthless money."

"I'd be damn careful 'bout letting your mouth outtalk your ass," the wily constable warned.

Preston Lord was a trained field psychologist, an expert in understanding motivations and inclinations. The constable wasn't book-smart by any means, but did possess raw intelligence and street smarts, not unlike a wild animal that had survived many years through cunning alone.

And the constable knew the type of man Lord was, knew who he worked for, and definitely knew Lord had no qualms about killing. Knowing these things, the constable would know if he left Lord alive, it would likely be a fatal mistake.

Despite what he'd just said about the money.

And that was why, Lord decided, that the constable was going to shoot him, right here and now. If Lord had the time and the sense of humor, he would have laughed at the irony. Both men had been secretly plotting to kill the other, their reasons completely opposite. Lord's was simply for convenience. The constable had served his purpose and was now an additional, and incredibly irritating, liability. The constable, on the other hand, wanted the windfall that awaited him in the trunk. And he wanted to live.

It was a classic standoff, and the German *thought* he had the upper hand.

"Despite what you said, you *are* going to shoot me," Lord stated.

"Walk over 'tween those rocks, back to where you pissed. Slow. Try to run, you're gonna receive seven-point-six-three millimeters square in your back."

Lord eyed his adversary, running through his own narrow list of options. The "contingency" was in his left pocket. The man in engineering had warned him that it wasn't yet ready for the field. If it didn't work, Lord knew he would soon become a part of this mountain. But what other choice did he have?

After a few realistic protestations, Lord acquiesced to the constable's demand and swiveled around to his left. When his body had rotated ninety degrees, this shielded his left hand from the constable's eye. With an artful sleight of hand, Lord retrieved the item from his pocket.

Using the item was incredibly easy. Just one thing to do.

As the constable began to move behind him, Lord heaved the item up in the air so that it arced over his head, traveling behind him. He was aiming blindly, but felt the item would hit close enough to do its work.

He heard the constable shout something as his head went up to track the olive-colored object flying through the air. It was perfectly round, not quite as big as a baseball but heavier. The constable probably didn't sense danger until he saw Lord diving to his right, behind a mossy boulder.

By that point it was too late.

The grenade which, after several more improvements, would later become known as a Beano, struck the gravel at the edge of the road, six feet in front of the constable. It exploded. Jagged shards of shrapnel and rock impacted Sauer's puffy body, ripping into his flesh and knocking him backward, skidding onto the pavement as instant death enveloped him.

Preston Lord emerged from behind the boulder, sniffing the sulfurish smell of explosives and the slaughterhouse aroma of freshly butchered meat. He touched both of his ears, slowly working his jaw, idly wondering if his eardrums were blown. The engineering technician who'd given him the impact grenade had told Lord about the testing that had been done with chimpanzees. Many had been blown to bits because of the grenade's tricky fuse. While the grenade was supposed to arm itself from a harsh throwing motion, some of the test grenades had been known to arm during simple jostling, resulting in a chimp in a million pieces. But the beauty of the new grenade, which outweighed the danger, was its trademark impact detonation. A man needn't worry about cooking off the fuse, as he would be forced to do with a standard grenade. The state-of-the-art weapon had worked perfectly. It had saved Preston Lord's life. He might even give a rare commendation to the technician nerds upon his return to D.C.

But, for now, time was of the essence. He dragged the heavy constable's leaking corpse behind the car, quickly rifling through each of his pockets. Lord retrieved his own pistol and knife, finding them both nicked and scarred, but still in working order. There was a badge and a wallet, as well as the wad of money Lord had bribed the man with. All of these items, plus matches and a cigar, Lord kept. He then struggled to heft the constable over the wooden guardrail after dragging him twenty feet up the hill. That spot would be the perfect release point to allow the corpse to build enough momentum to tumble out of sight.

Lord patted the constable on his back, told him to burn in hell, then used his foot to send him rolling. He watched in fascination as the massive, obese body slowly spun, gaining speed and taking rocks with it. Before it came to a rest in a crevice far below, blood and brain could be seen hurtling outward with each cartwheel of the falling side of beef. And, with it being so close to winter, Preston Lord felt certain no one would find the body until spring, if ever.

A car approached from the Austrian direction. It was a man and a woman, dressed to the nines. Lord had just opened the driver's door of the car, giving the couple a wave and a smile. They waved back to him, probably assuming that he had stopped to take in the view, or relieve himself. They didn't seem to notice the smattering of debris, or the smeared blood, on the worn pavement of the Aachener Pass road.

Once he'd eased into the driver's seat of the DKW, Lord took the constable's tattered cigar, bit off the tip, and lit it. His first order of business would be to purchase some black paint to cover the lettering on the doors of the constable's car. After that, before he thought about locating Neil Reuter, Lord was going to use some of the reichsmarks to splurge on the best hotel room in Innsbruck. He was going to gorge himself on every decadent food the hotel offered, and then he was going to get laid by Innsbruck's finest whore.

Tomorrow, after he slept until at least noon, his work could resume.

* * *

Thomas jiggled the doorknob at the back of the Heinz house. Locked. There was no time to try to preserve evidence. He stepped backward, firing three shots into the dingy brass knob with his revolver, kicking the door open. Holding his pistol at the ready, he cleared each room of the small farmhouse before coming back and standing over the Heinz woman. Her chest and stomach were black with blood; the injuries appeared to be hours old. Thomas removed his hat, holding it over his heart. Murders were never easy, especially when they involved a woman or a child.

After a moment of silence, his mind went to the woman's children. Children in the familial sense, but the girl was certainly no child. The boy had been nearing the age of accountability. Thomas was stricken as he pondered what might have happened to them. After seeing all he had seen in the span of a few hours, he felt he might be sick, moving away in his need of fresh air.

Thomas stopped.

The woman had made a sound.

He turned and knelt beside her, taking her hand. The resiliency of the human spirit never ceased to amaze him. This woman, surrounded by a bucket of her own blood, was still clinging to a shred of life.

"Frau Heinz, can you hear me?"

She mouthed a yes.

"Where are your children?"

The woman's lined eyes squeezed shut as she appeared to be fighting her emotions. She opened them and clenched his hand with stunning strength. "Help Peter," she rasped. "Get him before they do."

"They?"

"They'll kill him."

"Who?" He wanted to press harder, but didn't want to exacerbate her situation any more than it already was. Her mouth was parched and her dry tongue poked through her cracked lips as she murmured her answer.

"An American man."

"An American? The man from the airplane? The one I questioned you about?"

She managed to shake her head back and forth. "No," she whispered forcefully. "This was a bad man."

"What did he look like?"

"Thin. Fancy. Vicious. A German man was with him…a constable…a *Hinterwäldler*. They did this to me."

Thomas narrowed his eyes, briefly looking away. "A constable?"

She nodded. And her use of the word *Hinterwäldler* indicated that he was from the country and uncultured.

Thomas stared into the front room, his mind racing. He turned his head back to Frau Heinz, hearing her breathing change. It sounded as if there was blood in her lungs, and her breaths were now coming in quick succession.

"Frau Heinz," he said. "Please listen to me. Did you know the man from the airplane?"

She managed to nod as she mouthed yes.

"Why was he here?"

"Gabi," she whispered.

"Your daughter." He knelt closer, fearing the woman would fall unconscious any second.

Her voice was a whisper. "They're in Innsbruck."

"Innsbruck? The man from the airplane took your daughter there?"

She nodded.

"But he's *not* the man who did this to you?"

The woman's eyes opened wide and bored into his. "No," she said in her loudest voice yet. "The man with Gabi is a good man. Neil..." She wheezed for a moment. "Neil Reuter." After a thick swallow, she continued. "The two men who did this to me are after him...after my Gabi." She closed her eyes again, her voice reducing to a whisper. "Go get Peter...school. Please..."

"I will, ma'am. I'll find your Peter for you." Thomas gripped both her hands in his. "Frau Heinz, what is Reuter's plan?"

"Jewish children."

"Jewish children?"

"Yes," she whispered. "Hundreds of them. He had a letter."

Thomas nearly lost equilibrium as his world spun. Peter could presumably fill him in on everything else, if he was still alive, but there was one critical piece of information he would have no way of knowing. Thomas shook the woman's hands, his voice rising an octave. "Frau Heinz, one more thing. Did you tell the men who did this to you that the man from the airplane and your daughter are in Innsbruck?"

There was no sound, but her lips opened enough that any German could see she mouthed the word "Ja." Her grip loosened, her eyes narrowed, and she uttered the final words of her life. "Help Peter. Help Gabi."

Thomas held her hand for five more minutes, crouched beside the tough old farm woman as her life ended in a spate of ragged, wet breaths. He was frozen, not by fear, but by his own ethics as he pondered how to handle the situation. When Thomas found himself in the midst of a complex problem, and that was an understatement in this case, he preferred to be alone, with a pad of paper, so he could sketch out every angle of the puzzle and address each individually. And while he didn't have that luxury at the moment, Thomas decided that, if he could locate Peter Heinz, he would not call in the murders of the veterinarian and this woman. He would let them be found by others, and by that time, he would be over the political border, again inside the now-German territory of Austria.

In the rational part of his mind, he knew his not disclosing everything about the initial killing of Wilhelm Kruger might have been what caused this woman's murder. However, his instinct told him otherwise. There was an undercurrent of something sinister at play. If Frau Heinz wasn't out of her mind, and he didn't think she had been, then the men who had done this, and who had sliced and diced Hörst Baldinger, weren't standard thugs. He had a strong feeling that Sauer, the Velden constable, was one of them. He also knew Sauer certainly wasn't the brains of the outfit. Sauer was likely recruited by the vicious, fancy American who seemed to be seeking this other American named Reuter—Neil Reuter.

A good man.

Thomas thought back to the English money and aircraft. He thought about Wilhelm Kruger, a former deserter. And then he pondered what Frau Heinz had said—that Neil Reuter was helping Jewish children. The mystery was both deep and wide. If Thomas were to involve the polizei, and eventually the Sipo, they would almost certainly plow into this case like bulls in a china shop. Life—if it were to get in their way—would have no value to them.

Especially the lives of Jewish children.

"Help Peter. Help Gabi," he whispered. Those were the woman's dying words.

Thomas understood his own emotions well enough to know that this wasn't his subconscious acting things out in a way that was beneficial only to him. He truly believed in what he was doing.

As he left the farmhouse, Thomas repeated Frau Heinz's dying words, again and again.

"Help Peter."

"Help Gabi."

"Neil Reuter...a good man."

Chapter Fifty-Three

THE OLD OPEL BLITZ TRUCK BOUNCED on the rutted road that led north to Hausham. It was late in the afternoon; Saturday school should be out by now. Since Hitler had seized control, in addition to the calisthenics he had forced upon the nation's youth, school had been extended by a full day every other week. His belief was that the Germans, and all in his Aryan empire, should be smarter than the remainder of the world. He was a fanatic about the youth, constantly harping that in his thousand-year Reich the true investment should be bestowed on the children, for it was they who would carry the legacy. While Thomas didn't disagree with the fundamentals of investing in the young, anyone with half a mind could see the multiple prongs of Hitler's efforts were all pointing in the direction of sustained global war. Thomas had seen it far too many times in his life. It couldn't have been any more clear to him had Hitler possessed a pair of bloody fangs like a vampire, overcome by bloodlust.

Thomas shook his head in an effort to clear it. The thoughts dominating his mind were dark, intensified by in the harrowing events of the last several hours. As he rounded a bend, he narrowed his eyes at a small figure in the distance. With the shifter in neutral he eased the truck into the high grass at the side of the rutted Hausham road where he shut off the ignition and stepped out. There were only two residences on this entire road, and one of them he hadn't yet reached, so the figure had to be young Peter Heinz.

Thomas closed his eyes, murmuring a prayer for strength. Oh, how he dreaded this. He opened his eyes, taking deep breaths and steadying himself. One could do this a thousand times and, if he had any kind of heart, it would never grow any easier.

The Heinz boy stopped a hundred meters away.

"Peter Heinz?" Thomas yelled, coughing afterward.

The boy didn't move.

"I'm one of the policemen that came to your house." Thomas rasped, holding his handkerchief to his mouth before saying, "I need to speak with you, son."

Peter moved cautiously, taking half steps until he was across the road from Thomas.

"Son, I'm…I'm afraid I have some very bad news for you."

"Gabi," Peter said.

Thomas shook his head. "No, son. I don't know anything about her. But...well...I'm afraid your mother has...she's...she's passed away."

The adolescent young man blinked only once. He opened his mouth, pausing for a moment before finally speaking. "Passed away?"

"I'm buffering too much," Thomas said. "I'm sorry to tell you this, son, but she was murdered. I just discovered her." Thomas moved across the road, grasping the young man and pulling him into a bear hug. To his surprise, the boy accepted the hug but didn't cry, probably in shock. After a moment Thomas pulled back and held the boy's shoulders.

"I don't know who did it, yet. But I promise you, I'll find out. They will be made to pay for what they've done."

Twin streams of tears trickled down the boy's face. Otherwise, he was still and quiet.

Thomas examined Peter. The sadness was surely there, festering, and would probably come out in droves later. But this young man seemed destined to be a warrior. In his short life, it appeared he had already learned to compartmentalize his emotions. It looked to Thomas as if the news the boy had just received, instead of sending him to his knees, had been like a great combustible log thrown onto his internal fire.

"Son, I know what you just heard is horrible beyond words. But I need you to do something for me, something very important."

Peter pointed toward the house. "I want to see my mother."

"No, son. No," Thomas answered with resolve, guiding Peter to a sitting position on the hard, jutted road. Thomas took a knee beside him, keeping his hand on the boy's shoulder. "But if you really want to help me, perhaps you can help me understand why someone would have wanted to hurt her."

"Okay," Peter whispered, still staring in the direction of the house.

Thomas spent ten minutes questioning the young man, learning all about Neil Reuter and his alias of Dieter Dremel. Thomas learned about the airplane crash, Reuter's injury, and the emergency surgery performed by the now dead veterinarian. Satisfied Peter Heinz had told him the unmitigated truth, Thomas removed a folded envelope from his trouser pocket, pressing it into the young man's hand. "I want you to go back into Hausham, Peter, and find the *local* constable. Give that note to him. He'll probably take you to Miesbach, or perhaps even Rosenheim, and that's fine. Tell him, and any other police, every single thing you know. Tell him to protect you from danger. Can you do that?"

Peter stood, continuing to stare in the direction of his home.

Thomas placed his hand on Peter's arm. "I'm going after whoever did this." He turned Peter back in the direction of town. "Go on, now. You are being very brave, but you don't have to. It's okay to grieve and be upset."

Peter hesitated for a moment. Then he dipped his head and headed back toward Hausham. Thomas watched him walk, his books slung over his shoulder, held by their strap.

Thomas dipped his head, trying to gather himself.

After Peter had rounded the bend, the old lawman pulled himself back up into the Opel. He backed up, doing a three-point turn on the rutted road before heading south, thinking about the chain of events that would soon occur.

The Hausham constable would read the note and would learn about the Heinz woman and the veterinarian. And once the higher authorities learned about it, they would swarm both crime scenes, looking for any scrap of a clue about where Thomas had gone. Perhaps Peter's testimony would lead them to Innsbruck, perhaps not. But that was okay with Thomas. If he were yanked off the case, he would simply accept his fate. On the other hand, if they had no way of knowing where it was he had gone, well, that was fine with him too.

The warmth of the day was quickly replaced by a chill as the sun disappeared behind the mountains in the distance. Thomas rolled up his window and hummed a soothing hymn to himself as he neared the northern range of the mountains he was set to cross. He would need fuel soon, and that's when he would find a place to sleep. He would go to Innsbruck in the morning, when he was rested and his mind was clear.

It wasn't clear at the moment. Thomas was so very sad for young Peter Heinz.

* * *

Peter waited until he could no longer hear the old man's truck. He stopped, standing on the crown of the road as he stared at the minimalist buildings of Hausham, two kilometers away. He dug into his pocket, retrieving the envelope, seeing the smudges and fingerprints from the policeman's dirty hands. Peter carefully refolded the envelope, replacing it in his pocket. He took several deep breaths before his body began to shudder. Dropping to his knees in the center of the road, Peter Heinz's cries became angered wails as he beat the ground with the side of his fist.

He was an orphan now. His tears were for his mama—she had deserved better. She'd worked so hard, through sickness and occasional injury, always putting herself last in order to provide for him and Gabi. Mama had held his head many nights as he lay sweating with a fever or after a bad dream. And while her hands were rough and calloused, there was something ever so gentle about them as she smoothed his hair backward, comforting him as she rocked gently, back and forth.

Peter would never experience her again.

He cried for nearly an hour. Cold darkness set in.

Under the light of a rising moon, Peter stood, wiping his nose with his sleeve. The tears had run out. He stared at the lights of Hausham. He touched the envelope in his pocket. He turned around, glowering in the direction of the farm.

Peter pulled the letter out. He ripped it open. He read the letter in the light of the moon.

After pocketing the letter again, he slung his books into the brambles, well off the rutted road.

Peter Heinz sprinted to the farm.

Chapter Fifty-Four

THE FESTIVAL WAS KNOWN AS THE SALZBURGFEST and, as the forger had said, it was impossible to miss. Neil dressed as plainly as he possibly could, wearing oversize glasses he had purchased earlier in the day. They were off the shelf, providing little magnification, but with Neil's already good vision, they quickly gave him a headache.

Gabi and Neil arrived at a quarter before seven. It was nearly dark, the wide expanse of the festival lit by lights strung diagonally over the dusty walking areas. If they had been in the United States, Neil might have thought he was at the state fair back in Sacramento. Just like back home, carnival barkers yelled from their tent, proclaiming their game, ride or activity as the best at the entire fest. Beer tents were the rule of the night, dominating every thoroughfare with their broad dimensions and the live music played on each tent's stage. And, of course, Nazi flags hung everywhere.

Neil spotted two soldiers, both members of the SS. They were standing at the corner of two of the temporary thoroughfares, chatting, their arms resting on their slung machine guns. Having no idea if the authorities were searching for him, he decided to use a risky maneuver to find out.

"Are you ready to get your feet wet?" he asked Gabi.

Once Neil had explained the "feet wet" idiom, Gabi nodded once. "Do you even need to ask such a question?"

"Then here's what I want you to do."

Neil moved between two darkened tents as Gabi strode to the two SS soldiers. She'd purposefully dressed in her blandest clothes but couldn't conceal her beauty. The two soldiers straightened upon seeing her, both of them gushing when she stopped to chat. They'd been standing by a table, which she sat on, crossing her legs. Neil watched the conversation progress. Then they both shook their heads, shrugging off what she was telling them.

One of them grabbed her elbow.

Neil could hear his heart in his ears. *No, c'mon you two, don't be assholes.*

Gabi smiled good-naturedly. She tried to disentangle herself as a few items fell from the table.

The other soldier touched her back, his hand sliding down to her rear end. They were trying to move her off the street, laughing as they jousted with her, as if forced sexual encounters were just as normal a part of the festival as candied apples. Then she said something sharply and it got their attention. Both soldiers smiled. One lifted his sleeve and tapped his wristwatch. Gabi pointed to the other side of the festival, making a big show of tapping his watch before she rubbed his arm.

She walked away from them, her fake smile dissolving as she stalked by Neil, turning left by the nearest beer tent. Neil waited a moment and followed. He caught her sitting at a table by a cotton candy confectioner. The owner of the tent began to protest their using his empty table until Neil threw three reichsmarks at him.

Gabi rested her face on her hand, speaking through heaving breaths. "I did it. When I first approached them, I told them there was an American man here. They couldn't have cared less. It didn't even register."

"What did those bastards try to do to you?"

"Are you surprised? It's been this way for nearly five years now."

"How did you get away?"

"Told them my sister is young and curious about being with a real man. Told them I'd go get her and be right back."

"And they bought it?"

"One doesn't have to be bright to be in the *Schutzstaffel*."

"Then we haven't much time," Neil said, proud of her cunning. "Let's hurry."

"Wait," Gabi said, removing a balled piece of paper from the front pocket of her dress. She unwrinkled the paper, handing it to Neil. "There was a stack of these papers on the table."

The paper contained a description of a man, approximately 40 to 50 years of age. He was sizeable, at least two meters, and had dark hair and a beard. He was thought to be a vagrant and was seen with a large and scraggly dog. Below, the text read that the man was to be considered dangerous and should be arrested on sight and brought to the Schutzstaffel, Innsbruck directorate. If the man resisted, he was to be shot and killed.

Gabi read the description and shook her head. "They won't know you're the man from Innsbruck. You certainly don't look like a vagrant and there are plenty of men in that age range, who are that tall, who have dark hair."

She was right. But it demonstrated another layer of danger in this mission—and another potential obstacle to finding those children. Neil wanted to get far away.

They had to make a circuitous route to avoid the two horny SS soldiers, taking a wide arc around the festival to where the forger had instructed them to meet him. There was, of course, a beer tent at the southernmost point, and standing at the back of the tent was a smallish man in an old-fashioned three-piece suit. He wore a wide-brimmed fedora and had a bushy gray goatee that belied his youngish face. Neil approached him.

"Guten abend."

"And good evening to you," the small man answered in quiet English, bowing before both of them. He didn't remove his hat, as would have been custom. The forger was holding a large glass of beer, which he finished in several gulps, leaving a lacing of foam hanging from his moustache.

"I have no use for many of the Austrians but, I must say, like their cousins to the north, they do make excellent beer." He flashed a charming smile at Gabi and turned to Neil.

Neil wanted to leave. "We just had a little run-in with two SS goons and I'd like to get out of here before they come looking. Is there somewhere quiet we might go?"

The smile faded from the forger. He stepped closer, placing the empty mug on the end of a picnic bench. "I need to see your papers."

Neil glanced around before reaching into his clothes, removing the salt-stained Dieter Dremel forgeries. The forger leaned down, squinting as he gazed at them. Seemingly satisfied, he pointed to the darkness. "My lair is only a few minutes away."

They walked away from the festival, the forger taking Gabi's arm. She was at least three inches taller than him. "Isn't it too late for an *Erntedankfest?*" she asked.

"Long before I was the product of a joyful evening between my parents, the people of Salzburg decided to celebrate harvest—first, with the traditional *Erntedankfest*, then, several weeks later, the St. Rupert's Day Festival. Over the years, the two festivals combined, making one very long party. Though I'm not officially welcome, I cannot help but enjoy the atmosphere."

They awaited a line of traffic at an intersection, headed back into the city. "Who was St. Rupert?" Neil asked, not really caring, but having nothing else to speak about.

They began crossing as the forger answered him. "He was the founder of the city, essentially the patron saint of salt."

Gabi and the forger talked as they walked arm in arm, in step with one another. Neil slowed as they entered a darkened street. He glanced around, looking back at the city, thinking about the letter from Jakey. *There was something…*

Something…

Like a speeding automobile, a notion flitted through his mind, never slowing for Neil to get a look at it. He stopped and closed his eyes, concentrating.

"What's wrong?" It was Gabi. She had walked back to him, standing with her head cocked. The forger stood thirty feet away.

"St. Rupert."

"What about St. Rupert?"

Neil's eyes moved above the buildings, rotating between the blackish mountain peaks surrounding the salt city. He shook his head and looked at her. "I don't know. I just keep thinking about Jakey and the letter, and I don't know why, but something about the mention of that saint triggered something in my brain."

"Do you need a minute?"

"No, let's go on." Neil followed them, his mind still somewhat preoccupied. The forger, after glancing both ways in the alleyway, entered the back door of what smelled like a restaurant. There was a darkened hallway, and a tough-looking cook peered from the lighted kitchen. When he saw the forger, he nodded and went back to his work on the grill. The forger opened a hidden door, gesturing upward.

Neil and Gabi climbed a narrow set of creaky stairs, emerging into a partially finished attic. The forger excused a non-existent mess, busying himself with tidying the already fastidiously neat space. There were no windows, the room lit by three solitary bulbs, each hanging by wires from the timber ceilings. There was a cot, a reading chair and, in the corner, a makeshift toilet with exposed pipes from the top and the bottom. In the corner of the attic was a slanted table like an engineer might use. It had an adjustable light and a large magnifying glass on a swivel.

"What did you do before?" Neil asked.

"I owned an art restoration company. For years, many of the finest museums in Austria brought their pieces to me. Vases, paintings, sculptures. I could repair them so that even the artist would have thought it was his or her own work."

"And the Nazis took your business from you?" Gabi asked.

The forger dipped his head. "I didn't wait on them. I closed my shop and disappeared." He brightened. "But my wife and my babies made it out. They're awaiting me, and you, in a sense."

"How many children do you have?" Gabi asked.

"Nine."

Neil and Gabi looked at one another. Such an answer provided a moment of needed levity. "How old are you?" Neil asked.

"Twenty-nine."

Gabi grinned as Neil shook his head, stupefied. "Wow," was all Neil managed.

"Potent," Gabi added, drawing an amused look from Neil.

"Why did you stay in Austria?" Neil asked.

"Because my work here isn't done. And that's why you're here. Now, may I see what it is you've brought me?"

As Neil removed the documents again, the forger grunted, peeling off the fake goatee to reveal a young, albeit red and irritated, face. He removed the passé fedora, displaying a tight, dense head of dark brown hair. The forger leaned over and studied the stained Dieter Dremel documents. "All of this is quite standard. Reproducing each one should be simple. I could have them for you in an hour."

Neil nodded as if this was satisfactory. "There's more."

"From my cousin?"

"No. Something I acquired from the Nazi leadership."

There was a collective pause. "If you're trying to pique my curiosity," the forger said, "you've managed."

Neil reached under his shirt and removed the stolen Nazi credentials from the pouch, placing them before the forger unopened. The man's thin fingers moved to the emblazoned booklet before he looked at Neil.

Neil winked.

The forger opened the identification, and then he was motionless for a half a minute. He turned his head to Neil but didn't speak for a moment, apparently having trouble swallowing. Finally he asked, "Is this genuine?"

"You tell me."

The forger snatched it off the small table and hurried to the worktable. He switched on the white light and adjusted the magnifying glass. Just then, there was a knock downstairs. The forger rushed down, returning up the creaking stairs with a silver service of steaming coffee.

"Pour us some, would you?" he asked Neil, hurrying back to his worktable and peering at the document from every conceivable angle.

Neil poured three cups of coffee, handing Gabi hers. He placed a cup next to the forger.

The forger straightened. "About the identification…" He pressed his lips together, seeming as if he might burst at any moment. His hand rested on the booklet. "Do you realize what this is?"

"Yes. I have the official identification of a Reichsleiter. Specifically, the Reichsleiter of the Hitler Youth."

The forger closed his eyes, displaying a tight smile like a professor filled with pride over the precocity of his star pupil. "Precisely, my Herr Dieter. The identification of one of the most powerful men in all the Reich. In fact, only twelve or thirteen such men are known to exist." The forger's eyes took on a reproachful look. "Does he know you stole it?"

"I'm sure he knows it's missing. It was taken at a most opportune time, and I left no traces. Would he possibly get in trouble if his contemporaries, or even Hitler, thought he lost it?"

The forger's face answered that question.

"Then, no, even if he does think it is missing or stolen, I would hazard he will not report it."

"He might even contact a forger to make a copy," the forger said with a chuckle. "So what shall I do with this prized document?"

"Alter it."

"But Herr Dremel, another Reichsleiter, or Hitler himself, would know you aren't genuine."

Neil placed his china coffee cup back on the service, moving close to the forger, touching his shoulder. "That's fine, but I won't be using it to get close to a Reichsleiter. I only need it to get what I want in Innsbruck."

"So Dieter Dremel is a Reichsleiter?"

Neil turned to Gabi, nodding. "Yes, he is. He's Reichsleiter of External Clandestine Services or, in other words, a man few would know exists."

"How much time do you have?"

"Precious hours."

The forger sat down at the drafting table, removing what looked like a surgeon's scalpel from a leather pouch. "Then I need to get to work. Would it trouble you if I ask for privacy? I'd hate to mar this treasure and I work best alone."

Neil and Gabi had spaghetti downstairs while the forger plied his art.

* * *

Much later that Saturday evening, in a cozy, fire-lit Innsbruck bar on the south side of the river, Colonel Leo Falkenberg cradled his Märzen lager in his hand, swaying softly to the sound of the music coming from the piano in the adjacent room. His hand rested just under the skirt of his date, a young Italian girl he had met earlier in the day. It was almost time to leave, and he was quite drunk. Tomorrow was to be a busy day, what with the military inspection he was due to perform. He would need to bed this one quickly before sending her on her way. He was confident she'd pursue him at a later date.

And tonight, he needed the rest.

Just as he was about to stammer a lurid suggestion in his limited Italian, a striking young lady entered from the main room of the saloon. She wore an exquisite outfit and her pretentious, haughty carriage mimicked that of a cinema star. Falkenberg snatched his hand from underneath the Italian's ruffles and widened his eyes as the striking lady stopped in front of him.

"Colonel Falkenberg?"

"At your service," he whispered, rapt.

She removed a folded note from the gap between her luscious cleavage. "This is for you." One of her hazel eyes winked at him before she turned and departed.

Falkenberg stood, walking to the window to watch as the lady disappeared up the street. He'd never seen her before and, despite his drunkenness, was surprised at the ferocity of his erection. As he turned back to his date, he saw only her back as she exited the bar in a huff, leaving with him the tail end of her torrent of Italian curses. She turned at the door, making a gesture that could only be described as vulgar.

Turning away, Falkenberg drained his beer. It was probably for the best. He'd had so many women since arriving in Austria that he had, upon a guiltless and introspective examination, neglected his military duties. Falkenberg smoothed his hair down, telling himself, from here forward, to slow down and focus on his duty.

But Leo Falkenberg's duty had nothing to do with the Reich or the Wehrmacht. His duty was to himself, and himself only.

As the room slowly whirled in a haze of alcohol, he remembered the note, barely hanging in his left hand. He sat down, steadying himself as he unfolded it, reading it three times with all the concentration he could muster. Upon finishing, he carefully refolded the note and placed it in his golden cigarette case, afterward sitting perfectly still for a full minute. Falkenberg's hand was over his mouth as he pondered the note's contents.

Then, Oberst Leo Falkenberg dropped twenty reichsmarks on the table, donning his officer's *Schirmmutze* hat as he exited the bar and staggered toward his new home. He would take a headache powder and sleep late tomorrow morning, inspection be damned. Falkenberg needed a complete night of rest.

Because tomorrow promised to be a landmark day.

And it had nothing to do with inspection and everything to do with the note he'd just received.

Chapter Fifty-Five

NEIL WORE ANOTHER OF HIS NEW SUITS, this one a toned-down gray. There was a chilly mist falling so he mated a charcoal waistcoat with his suit, topping off the outfit with a near-black fedora. Though he couldn't have cared less about fashion, it was rather important he look the part. Gabi and Madeline were sitting on the sofa in the cottage, staring at him as he adjusted his hat in the mirror. Schatze slumbered between the women.

"There's a pistol for each of you," Neil said, pointing to the cushions underneath them. "If anyone at all comes through either of these doors—"

"We are to shoot them without hesitation," the two women said simultaneously, cutting him off. Their collective tone was devoid of humor.

Neil nodded. "Look, I know you both want to help, but in this case, there's absolutely nothing you can do. A man like this Falkenberg fellow is already going to be skittish. Let me speak to him first, then, *together*, we can decide what to do."

Madeline crossed her arms. "Why are you going ahead with this ruse when you don't even know where the children are? It makes no sense."

"You're right, Madeline, it doesn't *seem* to make sense." *What the hell has made sense in the last two years?* "But once we find the children—and we *will*—we'll have precious little time to extract them. Doing this now will save us later. And besides," Neil said, remembering the déjà vu-like feeling he'd had last night when he heard of St. Rupert, "something about the hiding place is right in front of us. I can feel it."

"I can't," Madeline said flatly.

Neil stepped to the door, opening it as a damp blast of wind blew into the room. "I'll be back. This afternoon I want to study every single item we have of Jakey's. There has to be a clue we've missed."

He left.

Neil's mind was preoccupied with Jakey and where he might have hidden such a large number of children along with their caretakers. And if Jakey had purposefully held back the second page to the letter, as Doctor Kraabe suggested, then Jakey would also have left Neil a clue. Frustrated with himself, Neil hammered the steering wheel with his palm, his gut telling him that there was a sign right under his nose.

Innsbruck began to slide by. "Focus," Neil whispered, clearing his mind for this meeting. The children's location would have to wait. And, fortunately, there was time—albeit not much. Besides, setting the table with Falkenberg would add enormous pressure to find the children.

Neil worked best under pressure.

He parked the Horch behind the Innstrasse restaurant where he was due to meet Oberst Falkenberg, afterward striding purposefully through the dingy adjacent alley. Bits of splashed mud pocked his highly-shined brogues. Families milled about under the covered pathways in front of the restaurants and closed shops. Many had been to morning mass and were now in town for a Sunday meal. Madeline told Neil that, before the Anschluss with Germany, the restaurants were only open for Sunday lunch, but now were forced to stay open on Sunday evenings, and to serve alcohol *all* day. And in copious amounts. Soldiers, no matter their nationality, love their booze, Neil mused. Put them in charge and it's going to flow freely. After several deep breaths, he removed his hat, swaggering into the restaurant.

Upon his entry, two Heer soldiers near the door stood, eyeing him up and down. Neil ignored them, heading to the only other patron in uniform. The man was dining alone. Before him was a bowl of creamy soup with what looked like large potato balls in the liquid.

The man barely looked up, gesturing with his spoon to the opposite chair. Neil handed his fedora and coat to the older lady who shuffled over. He asked for hot tea and nothing else and then he sat, staring at Leo Falkenberg.

The colonel was blowing on a spoonful of soup. After ingesting it, he turned his icy blue eyes to Neil. "Who is she?"

"She?"

"You know who I'm referring to…the girl who brought me the note."

Neil crossed his arms and leaned back in the chair. "No one can know I'm here, Leo. No one."

Oberst Leo Falkenberg shrugged, cutting a potato ball with his spoon and eating half in one bite. "Hot," he hissed, sucking air. After managing to swallow the massive *Kartofeln*, he dabbed his mouth with his napkin and said, "I don't even know who the hell you are. The local records say you've been gone for years, which is confirmed by your curious accent. But you do pay your taxes—a good thing because, otherwise, I would be forced to jail you."

Neil watched him as he spoke. He wasn't classically handsome, but there was something regal about him. His face was slightly off kilter, but deeply-tanned with tight skin and prominent cheekbones. He was probably nearing fifty, doing everything he could to appear forty—Neil spotted a millimeter of gray roots at the base of his slicked-down, smooth brown hairstyle. As Falkenberg eyed him, Neil accepted his tea and chose to remain silent.

"In your note, you said you needed something from me, and would offer a great reward in return," Falkenberg said, pushing the soup back and yanking the napkin from his collar. He leaned back, mimicking Neil's posture.

"True on both accounts."

"Would the girl be a part of the bounty?"

"No, Leo. You have no shortage of women here in Innsbruck."

"We shall discuss compensation in due time. Let us first discuss your request."

Neil tilted his chin upward, pulling air in through his nostrils. *And so it begins...*

"I need a short cargo train, ready to go at a moment's notice, at a secluded rail yard. I need paperwork for a clear, unobstructed passage to Yugoslavia. I need to know the exact—and I mean *exact*—routing of the train to Yugoslavia. I need twenty able-bodied men, and enough accompanying covered trucks to carry them. I need five kilos of Baratol or a similar, and equally effective, explosive, along with detonators, wire, and the sort." Neil lowered his chin. "I need an absolute green light to do whatever the hell I want, whenever the hell I want. And I need all of this—by this exact time tomorrow."

Falkenberg's tilted face was stolid. He moved his tongue over his front teeth. Then he emitted a chuckle. It became a giggle before it transformed into full-blown laughter. He laughed aloud, his white teeth sparkling as he pressed his oiled hair back with both hands, looking to his soldiers, a maestro, using his hands to encourage their laughter.

Neil glanced at the soldiers. There was no way they could have heard. They were simply laughing with their boss. He turned back to Falkenberg, who was still laughing. Neil smiled.

Keep it up, asshole. You're in for a big surprise.

When Falkenberg's laughter finally subsided, he pulled his soup back in front of him and cut another potato, grinning as he chewed.

Neil leaned forward, making his tone harsh as he leveled his finger at the soldiers. "Send them outside."

"Are you daft, man? You do *not* give orders to me."

"Do it, Leo," Neil said. "Do it now, or you *will* be sorry."

Falkenberg eyed Neil, the way a professional poker player might when he has more chips and a fine hand but his challenger has pushed his entire stack of chips to the center of the table—when the challenger's smugness triggers an unsettling feeling. After what felt like a full minute, Falkenberg snapped his finger to the NCO, a *Feldwebel*. The NCO rushed over, popping his heels together in the presence of his superior.

"Pat him down."

Neil stood, lifting his arms. "Weapons only, Leo. He cannot see the document I am here to show you."

The NCO listened to this and turned to Falkenberg. Falkenberg nodded with closed eyes, followed by the NCO patting Neil down, taking time under his arms and at his ankles. The NCO straightened.

"Nichts, mein Herr."

"Then take your man and go outside. Remain by the door and keep your ears open." The NCO dipped his head and obeyed, pushing his subordinate out in front of him. The proprietors were in the back room, probably reviewing their last will and testament, leaving Neil and Colonel Falkenberg all alone. Neil poked the tablecloth with his index finger.

"So, about my request, it would be highly advisable for you to demonstrate your compliance."

Falkenberg lifted the polished silver candleholder, exposing his teeth and studying their reflection. After spiriting away a fleck of pepper with the fingernail of his pinkie, he shook his head, as if he were already bored with this. "Let's just say, Dremel, I could possibly accommodate your request, just for argument's sake."

Neil removed the National Socialist Party identification booklet from his jacket pocket, laying it flat on the table, the swastika visible between his fingers. "Go on, please."

"What sort of monetary enticement would you be able to provide?" Falkenberg asked, his eyes darting downward at the booklet.

"Leo," Neil said with familiarity, "at this stage in the Reich's development, world perception is nearly as important as the strengthening of our own empire, wouldn't you agree?"

Falkenberg canted an eyebrow. "I wouldn't have an opinion on such things. I am a soldier."

"Well, it is, trust me. Right now all of the talk is about the Sudetenland and Czechoslovakia, and Poland."

"So?"

"In a matter of months Yugoslavia will be the next topic, and we need to give the world a reason to condemn its regime, and to celebrate our stabilizing presence when we engulf their country and her critical ports."

Falkenberg shrugged. "This is drivel. Why should I care for such things?"

"Intelligence, Leo, reports that you had some of the highest raw reasoning scores in officer training. Surely you can see the path upward more clearly than your contemporaries, or should I seek someone else?"

Falkenberg seemed indifferent for a moment before anger flashed over his face. His voice rose as he spoke. "You speak like you have some sort of authority over me, you piss ant. And now, sir, you're on the verge of being arrested."

"Oberst?" the NCO said, poking his head inside. Falkenberg shooed him away.

With a single finger, Neil slid the altered Reichsleiter credentials across the table. Falkenberg went for them but Neil flattened his palm over them, making him wait. "Leo, my existence is one of the Reich's greatest secrets. I've spent many years of my life in North America, priming them for what is to come, setting the proper political and economic landmines to those associated with resisting the Reich. I've fixed elections. I've eliminated enemies. I've crashed corporations. I've done it all, *all* in the name of our Führer's vision, and if you don't get in lock step with me, right now, and keep my existence as secret as it currently is, you, *mein neuer Freund*, will be shot before the evening falls. That's a promise."

Falkenberg seemed to measure Neil's every word. When Neil removed his hand, Falkenberg lifted the credentials and opened them. No matter how hard he might have tried, he was unable to contain the widening of his eyes as he processed the identification with the monolithic phrase Reichsleiter. He was no doubt thinking of the other, more famous Reichsleiters: Bormann, Goebbels, Himmler.

Neil's heart was on the verge of stopping. His mouth was dry. His palms were wet. But he remained impassive and unmoving, watching Falkenberg.

The German colonel placed the credentials back on the table only to snatch them back up and hold them very close to his face. He seemed to study each letter. Neil held his breath, hoping beyond hope that the Salzburg forger had done the trick with his meager set of tools. After a gulf of time Falkenberg narrowed his eyes, closing the booklet and carefully replacing it on the table.

Neil waited, finally allowing himself to breathe. He kept his palms flat on the table, fearful the German colonel might see his tremors.

Finally, Falkenberg dipped his head, a gesture of respect. "*Mein Reichsleiter*, thank you for choosing me."

Neil snatched the ID from the table and replaced it in his pocket. "I'm Dieter Dremel, wealthy local. Got it?"

"But of course."

"You may hear other things about me. This is by design. The denizens of the Thousand Year Reich cannot know its own people are staging such an event." Neil chewed a corner of his lip, as if he were proud of the layers of deception he had worked so hard to create. "Do you understand this, Leo?"

An enthusiastic nod. "Yes, of course."

"If anyone asks about what you are doing, I will assume you have enough intelligence to think up a credible excuse."

"I certainly can, *mein Reichsleiter*."

"Call me Dieter."

"Of course, Dieter."

"You will be handsomely compensated. The benefit of my office is a budget that is staggering, even to those in our Führer's personal directorate." Neil tossed a wad of ten thousand reichsmarks, skittering over the table and onto Falkenberg's lap. "Another ninety thousand when the train, the trucks and the men are standing by. The remainder will be given to you after the train is in Yugoslavia."

Falkenberg had questions, Neil could tell. But now he was afraid, afraid to push.

Or was he setting a trap?

The German swallowed thickly. It seemed genuine. He gulped water before whispering, "And did you say there will be *more* money, a remainder?"

"Another hundred thousand. Two hundred grand for a day's work, all within your authority." Neil smoothed the lapels of his damp suit. "I hope you have what it takes, Leo."

"Of course I do, mein…excuse me, Dieter," Falkenberg said, clearing his throat. "And in this operation, what is the train to be used to transport?"

"If you ever breathe a word of this…"

"Never," Falkenberg said with respectful force.

"Children, Leo. Jewish children. They're orphans, being taken to Palestine. They will be detained and imprisoned in Yugoslavia in order to set off a world condemnation of the Slavs."

"Savagery."

"They won't be harmed."

"Well, who will ever know?"

"I have the press of many nations primed. There will be eyewitnesses, photographs and even newsreels." Neil forced a smile as he opened his hands. "Most people can find it in their heart to empathize with a child."

"But won't the Reich look bad for causing the children to flee in the first place?"

"Good question. But, no. We've prepared propaganda packages that deflect any anti-Semitism to the Russians and the Brits. Jews aren't only fleeing the Reich."

Falkenberg's hand massaged his neck at the collar. "Well, I'm in no position to question your methods. Your request is possible, but could be difficult for even me to fulfill."

"I have faith *in* you. And money *for* you."

Falkenberg's eyes looked away. "I'm certain I can come through."

Neil leaned closer. "There was a man working for me, the man who smuggled the children here. He was a Jew...and he was murdered *without* my directive."

Falkenberg's eyes widened. "A Jew, you say? Working *for* you?"

"Leo...we have many, many Jews in our employ. The Führer has his beliefs, but *I'm* in the business of getting things done. This man was highly skilled and was killed in connection with the very request I'm making of you."

"He was killed in the explosion, wasn't he?" Falkenberg whispered, staring off in the distance.

Narrowing his eyes, Neil said, "You know about it?"

"It's the reason I'm here. My previous colleague died in an explosion with a Jew and two whores." Falkenberg nodded and clucked his tongue. "This explains everything. My predecessor was rumored to be taking money from Jews who were trying to escape."

Neil's hands strained on the edge of the table, his veins blue and bulging. "Who did it, Leo? Who killed my man?"

Falkenberg's eyes moved over Neil's shoulder, their pupils constricting as the skin tightened on his face in a grimace. Another blast of chilly, damp air made the candles flicker as Leo slyly pointed. "Probably him."

Neil turned. A man stood in the far entrance by the bar. He cut a dashing figure, wearing the striking uniform of an SS Standartenführer. Like Falkenberg, the SS man was equivalent to a colonel. He removed his polished hat, the *Tötenkopf*—the SS death's head—glaring with its vacuous eyes. Two junior SS men flanked the Standartenführer, standing appropriately, just behind him. The man surveyed the empty restaurant, handing his overcoat and hat to one of his men as he settled his gaze on Neil and Falkenberg.

Neil remembered him, quite well.

He was the man he'd seen upon first arriving in Innsbruck. The man who'd almost certainly sent the other SS after Neil, the SS who was currently decomposing with dead cows south of town.

The Standartenführer strode directly toward their table, glowering at Neil the entire way.

* * *

Thomas Lundren turned west, seeing the sign that announced Innsbruck as only eight kilometers away. He coughed into a white handkerchief, eyeing the fresh red blood spattering the cloth. Thomas lifted his eyes back to the slick road, his heart pounding in his chest. It didn't beat fast due to his worsening condition; it raced due to his nearly uncontained excitement.

A lawman's instinct is sometimes his greatest ally. And a conscientious lawman learns to separate instinct from hope.

This was not hope. Something was happening in Innsbruck. Something bigger than Thomas. And every fiber of his sick being was telling him—screaming—that time was of the essence.

He pressed his foot on the accelerator, pushing the old Opel as fast as it would go.

Chapter Fifty-Six

THE SS STANDARTENFÜHRER WOVE HIS WAY through the tables. He'd be upon them in fifteen seconds. Neil whipped his head back to Falkenberg. "Who is that man?"

"His name is Aying and he's very powerful and influential here in Innsbruck, and in the SS." Falkenberg's voice lowered. "And he's about as dangerous a prick as you'll ever meet."

"He can't know who I am," Neil hissed.

Aying halted at their table, clicking his heels and staring down at Neil as if he could see into his soul. After a moment, he turned his gaze to Falkenberg, speaking loudly. "Leo Falkenberg, did you clear the restaurant of the fine Innsbruckers with only your annoying presence, or did you break my rules and do it by force?"

Falkenberg glared up at him. Neil felt the palpable tension as a chilly quarter-minute passed.

Aying squeezed Neil's shoulder, too hard for social grace. "And you, sir. Have we met?"

Neil glanced up and shook his head.

"Standartenführer Anton Aying," the SS man said, offering his hand.

Neil took it, giving it a quick, firm shake.

"Stand up, man."

Neil stood, eye-to-eye with the tall SS man.

"What's your name?"

"Dieter Dremel."

Recognition flooded Aying's face. "Ahh, Herr Dremel, the owner of the home up on Berchtoldshofsweg."

Though his heart skipped about three beats, Neil made certain to look politely unimpressed. "You know where I live?"

"But of course, Herr Dremel. The charming cottage up on the hill. Several of my officers requested its use for their own, and when we checked we learned that you've been abroad for many years." Aying canted his chin downward. "Allegedly."

Neil ignored the insinuation. He turned to Falkenberg, giving a quick nod before moving to leave. Aying caught Neil by his arm.

"While I've not been successful in meeting with you at your home, I feel convicted that we've met before."

"I don't believe so, Standartenführer, but I'm happy to make your acquaintance," Neil said, allowing his tone to belie the compliment.

"You seem to have acquired a great deal of the Canadian accent, although yours sounds more in line with American." Aying rounded his lips. "I don't hear the dragging 'oh' sounds in your speech."

"As you know, ninety percent of Canada lives on the border with the United States." Neil smiled with his mouth only. "Hopefully my native Austrian accent will come back to me in short order."

Aying held fast. "And here you are, fresh in from Canada...*allegedly*...already lunching with the *good* Oberst Falkenberg?"

Neil was uncomfortable, not unlike an unprepared witness being grilled in a vicious cross-examination by a skilled attorney. "We didn't dine together. I met Oberst Falkenberg earlier and was simply catching up on what our German friends are doing here, and asking how I can help."

Aying averted his eyes to Neil's lapel, grasping it and giving it a little shake. "Are you a member of the party? Where's your insignia?"

"I'm not an official member, yet," Neil answered. "But, as I said, I just recently returned. I will register at once."

"Hmmm," Aying mused. "That would have been my first order of business."

Oberst Falkenberg stood and moved around the table, stepping into Aying's space. Neil homed in on the electric stare-down which took place; it was obvious to him the two men loathed one another, just like Doctor Kraabe had indicated.

"Do you need something here, Aying?" Falkenberg snapped.

"Don't you dare question my actions," Aying retorted.

Falkenberg took a step closer, edging Aying backward. "Let go of Herr Dremel's arm. He is a personal friend of mine."

Aying laughed, at both of them, as he released his grip on Neil. "Leo, Leo, Leo..." he said, his voice trailing away in a childlike admonishment. "You should stick to your trite little job and stop pissing in ponds that are too vast for your lacking *Schwanz.*"

Neil watched as the two alpha males jousted, throwing veiled threats back and forth in a testosterone-fueled debate. As their strife turned mildly humorous, Aying removed a pack of cigarettes from his jacket, American Lucky Strikes, shaking one out and holding it pinched between his lips. His hand came up out of his pocket in a flash, pressing three times on a lighter.

Etched into the side of the golden lighter was an image of the Eiffel Tower.

Neil stared it at it, catatonic.

It was Jakey's lighter.

Unless it was a copy, it was the mate, the fraternal twin to the Thorens Automatic Lighter in Neil's own pocket. Jakey purchased the one with the Eiffel Tower at the same time Neil bought his, the exact same type of lighter but, instead of featuring the Eiffel Tower, Neil's was engraved with Paris's famous Arc de Triomphe.

Neil felt his throat closing but he struggled not to display any outward emotion. He managed to swallow, glancing around the room to hide his expression. He had to know. He had to find out. *Think, Neil. Think!*

The two officers were still quarreling, something about a local political directorate and who had authority over it. Neil could feel the sweat growing on his forehead and under his collar. His hands were trembling and his mouth felt like the Gobi desert. Aying turned to him, narrowing his eyes.

"Are you ill?"

Neil managed to lick his lips. He needed to see the lighter again.

"Dieter Dremel, what on earth is the matter with you?" Aying demanded.

"Cigarette," Neil croaked.

"What?"

"May I have a cigarette?"

The SS shook one out, exhaling loudly, seemingly irritated at having to offer any gesture that might be taken for kindness. Almost immediately, Neil felt bolstered, as if a great jolt of adrenaline had energized him. He made a show of patting his pockets before holding out his hand. "May I use your lighter? Mine seems to have disappeared." Neil focused on Aying's hand as it came up out of his trouser pocket with the gold lighter.

Anton Aying resumed the argument as he absently handed the lighter to Neil. Neil turned as if it were windy, cupping his hand over the cigarette as he brought the lighter up. He twisted it around. On the opposite side of the lighter was an engraving of two letters in a fancy French script: "J" for Jacob and "H" for Herman. Neil remembered the warm Parisian day as they had sat on a park bench, discussing the new en-vogue author Hemingway while their lighters were noisily engraved at the small stand on the walking path next to the Seine, in the shadow of the Eiffel Tower.

"What is so interesting?" Aying asked. As Neil had been focused on the lighter, and the realization that he was standing in the presence of Jakey's killer, he had been too consumed to realize that Falkenberg had taken his seat, leaving Aying to stare at him.

Neil kept his eyes downward, handing the lighter back. "I was just enjoying the taste of the Lucky Strike. They're hard to come by here."

Aying frowned, stuffing Jakey's lighter back in his pants pocket. "Hard to come by, only if you don't know what you're doing," he said, leading Neil away and hitching his thumb at the colonel. "I've been through the population rolls a half a dozen times, Dremel. You are one of the wealthiest men in Innsbruck and, when I finally meet you, you're consorting with a man like Falkenberg. In my mind, it means you either have poor judgment or there's something amiss with your situation."

Neil couldn't hide it. Not his desire to help Madeline and Doctor Kraabe, nor his love for Gabi, nor even his yearning to find the hidden Jewish children could have provided him enough self-restraint to resist lashing out at his lifelong friend's killer. He took a step closer but turned his head at the last moment.

"No, Neil! Not yet. Deny yourself just this once. Remember, timing is everything, old boy. Aying's time will come."

It was Jakey's voice. Standing there in his favorite linen pullover shirt, purchased for two cigarettes in Morocco. Jakey's tension transformed to good humor as his thin lips twisted in amusement over the unusual situation. *You'll have your moment in good time, but if you have it now, then my death will be in vain.* He motioned with his finger back and forth, from his heart to Neil's. *I've given you all you need. Complete the mission, then have your fun with this prick.* Jakey winked.

Neil turned back to Aying, glaring at him through slit eyes. He could feel himself trembling, the Lucky Strike dangling from his own lips, the smoke drifting up between them like a lace divider.

"Are you utterly mad?" Aying asked with a curled lip.

"I feel like I might be sick." Neil clutched his stomach, gagging.

Standartenführer Aying leapt backward. "Get outside, man!"

Neil exited in a rush, causing the two SS men to snap to their feet as he passed. He staggered into the mist of the street, everything spinning. He could feel his breaths coming in ragged gasps, fully overcome as the reality of his discovery began to sink in. Across Innstrasse and a strip of wet grass, just in front of the concrete wall containing the River Sill, was a damp park bench. He needed to sit and think, to process the situation and to reclaim a sane progression of his thoughts.

Still grasping the Lucky Strike, though not wanting to resume the unhealthy habit, he flicked it as he stumbled through a row of diagonally parked cars, watching as it twirled to a stop next to a set of large, dirty tires. His eyes moved up from the tires, taking in the entire vehicle, a converted truck. The tag was German, marked by the initials MB for Miesbach. It had a flat, plywood bed with split rails and a missing gate. It was manufactured by Adler.

Neil knew the truck quite well.

It was the Heinz's farm truck.

Frozen, Neil's only action was a rapid series of blinks, his mind already on overload from the run-in with SS Standartenführer Aying.

Had Hildie Heinz driven here? Maybe she'd come to reclaim Gabi? Maybe she had important news about the manhunt.

Doing his best to set aside what he'd just learned, Neil circled the truck, studying the obvious clues. The dirt and mud on the tires were fresh. The bottom of the truck was still dripping. There were fresh streaks on the windshield from the worn wipers. Neil estimated it had very recently been parked, meaning Frau Heinz, and perhaps Peter, were probably close by.

Rotating his head, he looked up and down the mostly empty street. Two blocks northbound, on the curving road that led to Hall im Tyrol, he saw a thin figure walking the other way.

Peter Heinz. Damn it, Hildie!

Neil had warned her that this mission was treacherous, and here she was driving into the center of town and letting her boy wander about while wolves like Anton Aying prowled the streets. Neil growled in frustration as he looked back at the restaurant, making certain no one was watching. He hurried down the sidewalk until he caught up to Peter, not wanting to yell out. He grasped the teenager's shoulder, whispering his name as he spun him around.

Peter's face was emotionless until he drank in Neil's image with widening eyes. Then Peter's face took on a look of horror, followed by relief. The boy exploded into tears, nearly collapsing as he fell against Neil, locking his arms around his waist. Neil frowned, pulling the boy to him as the sobs wracked him with tremors, his mouth buried into Neil's chest as he moaned. Neil patted Peter's back, confused as to why this homecoming would cause such emotion.

Something was wrong. Badly wrong.

Neil moved Peter backward, quieting him until he could ask the question, "Peter, where's your mother? Where's Hildie?"

Peter's eyes widened again. It was the expression of someone who thought the other should have known the answer to the question. His wet mouth hung open in horror, and finally Peter yelled out, "She's dead. They killed her. They killed my mother!"

* * *

Thomas knew he didn't have much time in Innsbruck. Because today, or tomorrow at the latest, the numerous investigators would swarm in after piecing together the murders of Hildie Heinz and the veterinarian, Baldinger. Thomas would be thrown off the case and probably tossed in jail. He scanned the mostly-deserted streets of the rainy city, reckoning that he probably had twelve to eighteen hours before he was arrested—at best. Until then, Thomas planned to keep looking.

Having just arrived in town, he was following Herzog Ottostrasse to the southwest, creeping along in his truck, wondering if he should begin with the hotels and pensions. The bright colors of the row buildings were muted by the low gray clouds and wet weather, tugging down his previously excited mood like leaden weights. Innsbruck was larger than he thought it might be, leaving him slightly overwhelmed. Thomas viewed the numerous buildings across the bluish-green water of the quick-moving River Sill, distressed at the amount of area he would have to search.

Something caught his eye. Across the river sat a young man on a bench, staring directly at Thomas.

The river and split rail fences were the only boundaries between Thomas and the young man, a separation of perhaps a hundred feet. While many parts of his body had begun to deteriorate, Thomas had always been blessed with good distance vision, and even in the light mist, his eagle eyes did not fail him on this day. Because the young man sitting on that river bench was the Heinz boy—Peter Heinz. Thomas skidded the old Opel Blitz to a stop on the empty street, taking in the surprising sight.

Peter was not alone. Sitting next to him was a tall, handsome, dark-haired man.

Thomas narrowed his eyes, peering through the mist at the man.

He was patting Peter between the shoulder blades in a consoling manner. Peter turned and said something to the man, gesturing to Thomas. The man twisted his head to look at Thomas, and that's when Thomas realized he was now staring eye-to-eye with the man from the airplane.

Again.

The man Hildie Heinz told him about. The mysterious man who'd kept Thomas awake at night for weeks.

The man who killed Wilhelm Kruger.

A good man.

* * *

"There's the policeman," Peter mumbled, aiming his finger across the Sill.

An instant jolt of fear shot through Neil, but when he processed what Peter had said, he automatically assumed he was speaking of the regular Innsbruck Polizei. Perhaps Peter had already encountered them since arriving. Then he followed Peter's pointing finger across the river and joined eyes with a man he hadn't seen in a month.

For the third time in ten minutes, Neil's heart redlined.

Because stopped across the river in an old pickup was the man from the airstrip in Velden. Neil never forgot a face, especially a face that belonged to a man who'd fired a rifle at him. His mind lurched back to that fateful morning. The old man had arrived just after Neil had shot Willi the German, and Neil clearly remembered his brief encounter with the old man, seconds before his first—and last—stint as the pilot of an airplane.

And Peter just said the man was a policeman.

A policeman?

The man exited the truck, seemingly transfixed as he stared across the river. Neil's eyes were riveted on him until Peter broke the reverie, his voice distant, defeated.

"I bet he's here because I didn't do as he told me to."

"What did he tell you to do?" Neil breathed, his eyes remaining on the old man.

"He told me to tell the police about my mother." Peter rubbed his eyes. "But I didn't. I drove the truck here, instead."

Neil considered the possibilities of escape. He looked to his left. The nearest bridge accessible to the policeman was nearly a kilometer away. However, if he was able to get turned around, there was another bridge only a hundred meters behind him. But his truck was on a one-way street, and another car was approaching from behind.

"Come on," Neil said, pulling Peter from the bench. They hurried back across Innstrasse, staying to the left of the restaurant. Neil heard the grinding of gears. He looked over his shoulder to see the old man motioning to the driver behind him as he struggled to turn the old truck around.

There wasn't much time.

They splashed through the back-alley puddles to the Horch. Neil yelled for Peter to get in and get down. He grimaced as the engine refused to crank. The smell of petrol filled the cabin.

"Why are we running away?"

"That man is trouble," Neil grunted as he removed his foot from the accelerator, turning bleary eyes to Peter. He made a conscious decision to no longer mince words with the boy. "Peter, get your butt down in the floor and be quiet until I get us out of here."

The excitement seemed to have taken immediate effect on Peter. His color had returned, appearing as a rosy flush on his cheeks. He nodded, twisting himself into an impossibly small ball in the floorboard of the Horch, not unlike Madeline had done days before.

Neil growled his frustration, keeping his foot off the gas as he turned the skinny key—*start you old nag!*—of the Horch. After what seemed minutes, the engine sputtered twice, wheezing under the starter's power, finally catching and sending puffs of white smoke pluming down the alley. Neil backed from the parking space before roaring out of the alleyway and onto Höttinger. He pushed the engine hard as the Horch accelerated up the hill, doubling back onto Riedgasse, heading north, away from the cottage in the event his pursuer suspected where he was headed. Once he was five blocks north, Neil slowed to a normal speed and began to breathe again, scanning for the policeman's truck.

He needed to get Peter to the cabin but feared the location might be compromised. After a moment's thought, Neil made the decision to risk it. What choice did he have? He'd have to debrief the boy—not in a harsh manner, but he had to know what Peter told the old man. And was the old man truly a cop? Or was he just telling Peter that to gain his trust? After all, he *had* been at the airport the night Neil killed Willi the pilot. Maybe the old man was in cahoots with Willi, and was here for revenge. That would be better for Neil. Far better. A pissed-off crook would be considerably easier to deal with than a policeman—especially in a police state.

Whipping right onto Innstrasse, Neil removed his fedora and sat low in the seat. As he rolled down the street, he spotted the Opel Blitz. It was parked and Neil could see the old man hurrying into the back alley where Neil and Peter had disappeared. They drove past the alley, Neil noting the German plates on the Blitz. He had to slow in heavy traffic two blocks later. The traffic was caused by the line for valet service under the shallow portico at the posh Tyroler Inn.

Relaxing somewhat, especially with the old man on foot and chasing his tail, Neil fell in line behind a limousine, waiting for a coming auto to pass so he could go around the mini traffic jam.

"Everything okay?" Peter asked.

"Just fine, Peter," Neil answered in as soothing a voice as he could manage. "Just a few more minutes. While we wait, tell me what you know."

"I only know about my mother," he said, his voice hitching. "And that veterinarian."

Neil turned. "What about him?"

"The old man, the policeman, wrote down that the veterinarian, Doctor Baldinger, had also been murdered."

Motionless for a moment as he digested this news, Neil finally and numbly nodded his understanding. He felt the desperate need to examine the situation but knew he first needed to get away. He watched his mirrors and the adjacent streets, looking for the old man. Although he hadn't yet returned to his truck, Neil was on edge over how long the traffic was taking to clear away.

Hurry up, damn it!

The crowd under the portico was heavy as people, their stomachs stuffed with Sunday lunch, struggled to stay dry while they awaited their ride.

The people…

With nothing else to do but wait, Neil's eyes suddenly zoomed in on one person...

The earth ceased its rotation, screeching to an abrupt halt.

There was no sound. No movement. Everything stopped, all except for the motion of one human being. He was the only operational organism in the universe, and he stood fifty feet in front of Neil Reuter.

The man reached into his overcoat with both hands, removing a cigarette from one pocket and a box of matches from another. Cupped his hands. Lit the cigarette. Smoothed his hair. Stared downward at the rear end of the frozen lady in front of him. The corner of his mouth turned up. Picked a bit of tobacco off of his tongue. Glanced around.

Leering.

A demon in tailored clothing.

Preston Lord.

Preston Lord, United States Department of War.

Preston Lord, Operational Director of Covert Services.

Preston Lord, scourge of the earth.

The earth resumed its rotation. Sounds occurred again. The coming auto passed. Neil coughed, wracked with a spasm from the sudden shock. When it passed he blinked the blur from his eyes, studying the man under the awning.

Yes...it's him—it's Preston Lord, here in Innsbruck.

With the road momentarily clear, Neil floored the Horch, passing the assembled line of cars with his head turned to the left so Lord couldn't see him.

Peter had obviously seen the change in Neil's demeanor. "What's wrong? Did you see the policeman again?"

Realizing he was speeding, Neil eased off the gas pedal. He twisted both hands on the steering wheel as he made his way toward the cottage, nearly overcome by the substantial events of the last ten minutes. The meeting with Falkenberg. Learning that Anton Aying was Jakey's killer. Finding Peter. Hearing about Frau Heinz's death. Seeing the man from the airstrip. Learning that veterinarian had been murdered. And then, like a toxic cherry on top, discovering that Preston Lord had tracked him here.

Laboring to call on his past, Neil did as he'd been taught, deliberately pushing aside the multitude of problems and focusing on only one thing: escape. He motored smoothly, checking mirrors, vigilant for anything out of the ordinary.

"Are you sure you're okay?" Peter asked.

Though he was doing a fine job of focusing on driving, Peter's query brought all the problems flooding back. As Neil turned the Horch onto the ascending road to the cabin, he decided to let Peter in on the truth.

"Everyone knows I'm here, Peter. Everyone." Neil glanced down at his young friend, shaking his head. "Holy shit, Peter," Neil said in English before switching back to German. "In all my years, with all I've done, I've never had the noose clamp down like this before. Ever."

"Yes," Peter echoed in English. "Holy shit."

Neil somehow managed to return Peter's wan smile.

"Remember when you taught me to chop the wood?" Peter asked after a moment.

Neil drove on in silence.

"Do you *remember* when you taught me to chop the wood?"

"I remember."

"You told me not to swing too hard and to let the axe do all the work."

Neil turned back to Peter.

"Maybe you shouldn't swing too hard. Maybe you already have the tools." Peter's eyes were bright and wide. "Let your tools do all the work."

"Remind me of that later, okay, Peter?"

They pulled into the driveway and stopped at the top of the hill. Neil sat motionless for a moment, still gripping the steering wheel. He closed his eyes, again running down the laundry list of what he was going to have to deal with.

My God, he thought. Aying, the SS man I'd already been warned about, is Jakey's killer. Peter is here. Hildie is dead, murdered. A man purporting to be a policeman—who knows I killed Willi Kruger—is here looking for me. And...Neil hammered the steering wheel...Preston Lord is here, too. And that can mean only one thing.

He's here to kill me, and who knows who he may have brought with him?

Neil opened his eyes, resuming his plan of one thing at a time. He glanced back down the road. It was clear. They hadn't been followed so, for now, the escape was a success. Now, on to the next task—reuniting Gabi with Peter, and telling her the news. A dollop of dread blunted Neil's soul.

Pressing the clutch, Neil allowed the Horch to coast down the hill. He stopped in front of the cottage, switching off the engine.

"Peter, I think you better let me tell your sister about your mother."

Peter Heinz, still in the floorboard, nodded before he dipped his head into his folded arms.

* * *

Madeline and Gabi, with nothing else to do, had absently been muddling their way through a hand of gin rummy when they heard the car outside. The two women, along with Schatze, rushed to the front door, opening it and waiting. After a moment, the driver's door opened and Neil exited, his hat in his hand.

He was ashen.

"Everything okay here?" Neil called out.

"Yes, of course," Madeline answered.

Neil walked around the car, opening the passenger door. Peter exited, running around the car and up the stone walkway, nearly tackling his sister as they collided in an embrace. As she hugged her brother, Gabi stared at Neil in bewilderment. Neil moved inside, watching the reunion with a pained face. He motioned Madeline to go to the bedroom and, because she probably sensed something was amiss, she quickly complied. After a moment, Neil pulled the Heinzes apart and spoke several dreadful sentences.

Gabi's face was a mask of horror. Then she fainted.

Chapter Fifty-Seven

HAVING LOST PETER HEINZ AND THE MAN known as Neil Reuter, Thomas Lundren drove around Innsbruck again, eventually spotting the Heinz family's Adler truck parked on the main thoroughfare by the river. He parked his own truck in a back alley before walking around to view the converted Adler, sticking out like a sore thumb among the fine automobiles lining the rainy streets of the resort city.

The questions were overflowing from his mind, cascading like water over a dam on the verge of bursting. Why had the Heinz boy come here? Had the man from the airstrip, Reuter, been at the farm all along and driven the boy here just now? Could the boy have been lying to Thomas before? Was Frau Heinz out of her mind when giving her deathbed confessional?

Thomas again recalled what she had said: The man with Gabi is a good man. A very good man.

As Thomas had stared out over the river, Reuter had seemed to be consoling the boy. Then the American had looked up and seen Thomas, and he'd been startled.

Thomas recalled what Frau Heinz had said about the men who had tortured her, gripping him with her calloused hands: *An American man...a bad man. A German man was with him...a constable. They did this to me.*

They had also, presumably, killed the veterinarian. "A good American...with Peter Heinz. Another American, a bad man, and with him a German constable," Thomas whispered. He stepped from the old Adler to the park bench where Peter had been sitting with Reuter.

The two men are after him, and after my Gabi.

The two men, the bad American and the constable, *are after him...*"him" being the good American named Reuter.

Thomas watched the rushing water of the River Sill, the mist having no effect on its strong flow. He scooped a pebble from the ground, tossing it into the water as his mind went all the way back to that late summer morning behind his house when he found Wilhelm Kruger lying dead on the airstrip. Reuter had registered utter shock upon seeing Thomas. And Kruger was a deserter—and by all accounts, gutter-slime—from the Luftwaffe, back then named the *Luftstreitkräfte*. How did he fit into this puzzle? And who was the constable who helped the "bad American" kill Hildie Heinz? Was it Constable Sauer, or was it someone else? Sauer had his hand in the illicit fuel sales all along—it had to be him.

Thomas' eyes flickered. A thought passed through his brain before he was able to grasp it. He had just missed something. Something important.

He dipped his head, knowing he should involve, at a minimum, the local police. There was something brewing in Innsbruck, between two Americans, the Heinz children and a German policeman. Thus far, to Thomas' knowledge, three people had already died as a result of this situation: Wilhelm Kruger, Hörst Baldinger and Hildie Heinz.

Thomas removed the locket from his pocket. He opened it, wiping the first droplets of mist from the image of his Greta's face. "What do I do, Greta?" Thomas breathed. "Should I give the case up to save those children?"

Help Peter. Help Gabi.

That's what Hildie Heinz had told him with her final breath. She had begged *him* to do it.

Once, many years before, Thomas had busted up a counterfeiting ring. The ring, he later found, had tentacles that went well into the senior ranks of the polizei. And while no violence had occurred, he had managed to pull the curtain off the ring by being fastidiously secretive about the entire affair. He had not even told his most trusted deputy. Why? Because Thomas knew that greed was among the most intoxicating of human motivators and, in a case like that, he only trusted himself.

He stared at the picture of his wife, listening for her words. He could envision her, in their kitchen, handing him a cup of hot cocoa and pressing her lips together the way she would do when deep in thought.

"You've come this far, Thomas. If you feel you cannot be effective, get help. But if you believe you can still do it, then do so, and move swiftly."

Thomas clicked the locket shut, wiping the moisture from his face as he donned his wide-brimmed fedora. He decided to leave his truck parked where it was, walking back across the bridge and into the old city. Most of the shops were closed, leaving only hotels and restaurants open for business. It was time to perform the most basic of police techniques. Thomas was going to go door-to-door, inquiring about Americans in Innsbruck.

Since Thomas was a good Lutheran, and with today being Sunday, he prayed he would catch a break.

* * *

It was a heartrending gathering. Peter and Gabi Heinz sat on the couch, their wailing now reduced to soft crying as both leaned forward, their heads cradled by their hands. Their other hands, Peter's right and Gabi's left, were joined. Both Neil and Madeline had tried to console them, but Gabi had politely pushed them away. Neil understood. Sometimes grief makes a person want to be alone with their thoughts. Schatze, however, had been welcomed into the fold. She sat between them, licking their clasped hands every few moments. Occasionally one of the Heinz siblings would pet her, appreciative of her concern.

With his Colt visible in his waistband, Neil held the curtain back, staring up the driveway and down the hill. He sipped from a heavy mug of coffee, his voice a whisper to Madeline. "We have to leave here. Ten more minutes, tops."

"The man who saw you and Peter, he's from where?"

"He's from Velden. He saw me in the airplane that I later crashed at their farm," he said, motioning to Gabi and Peter, his chuckle devoid of humor. "I'd just shot the man who flew me into Germany, in self-defense. He'd shot me a few moments before. And that's when the old man arrived, just as I was leaving."

"How do you know he's a policeman?"

"I don't know for sure, but that's what Peter told me. The old man is the one who claims he discovered their mother."

Madeline drank from her cup and looked away. "What makes you think he isn't the one who killed her?"

"Because he wrote a note for—"

"He *wasn't* the one who killed Mama," Peter said, cutting Neil off. Madeline and Neil exchanged glances. They had no idea they were speaking loud enough to be heard.

Peter stood. "He came to the farm once before, looking for you…when you hid in the barn cellar."

"He was one of the ones that evening down in the field," Neil said nodding, putting the pieces together. "The one who the veterinarian led up to the farm before he tried to bribe your mother."

Gabi nodded, wiping her tears. "He seemed like a nice old man who was just doing his job."

Something struck Neil. He raised his hand to summon silence. His mind went to the glimpse he'd had of Preston Lord, standing in front of the grand Tyroler Inn. Neil, nor his team, knew much about Lord. On the occasions when forced to meet with him, Neil always felt there was an icy disconnect deep inside him. The kind of numb, psychopathic detachment that makes a person seem less than human.

If Lord had picked up the trail in London, then followed Neil to Germany under a diplomatic cover, he would have probably learned of the investigation into the murder of a pilot in Velden. A pilot who lived in England. He would have learned that Willi Kruger's Hornet Moth had originated near London. Lord would have calculated the airplane's range and determined that it would have run out of fuel somewhere in southern

Bavaria. He would have located the investigator on the Kruger case, presumably the old man Neil and Peter had just seen, and he would have heard about a veterinarian in a town called Hausham who had claimed to know something, which he most certainly did.

Lord, if Neil was surmising correctly, wouldn't have done things by-the-book, like his German counterparts, and a weak man like the veterinarian would have spilled everything he knew after only a few seconds of painful torture. So, Neil thought, seeing it clearly now, Lord would have found out about the Heinz farm, rushed there, tortured Hildie Heinz for information and, like he probably did the veterinarian, killed her to cover his tracks. Then Preston Lord, in his typical arrogant fashion, breezed into Innsbruck, thinking his tail was clear as he promptly checked into the finest hotel in town.

Sonofabitch!

Peter pushed something into Neil's hand. It was the note from Thomas Lundren to the Hausham constable. Neil read it quietly, his lips parting a fraction as he took in the high points: According to Hildie, the American man who had assaulted her had been working with a German policeman—a constable. So was the policeman they'd just seen, Lundren, the one Lord was working with? Or was there another cop involved and, if so, where was he? Besides, if Lundren authored the note, why would he rat on himself?

Neil focused on Peter. "Peter, you are certain the old man...Lundren...was trying to help?"

Peter used the back of his arm to wipe his eyes. "I know I'm not grown yet, but this is one time you should *all* listen to me. He told me about Mama..." A shiver went through him. "He stood there and hugged me after he told me." Peter squeezed his eyes shut and lowered his head.

Neil nodded, staring again at the note. He walked to the far side of the room.

"What is it?" Madeline asked.

"One second," he whispered as his mind's fog began to burn away.

It wouldn't be hard for Lord to learn about Neil—or Dieter Dremel. Neil had been in two restaurants, the butcher shop, and had spoken to a number of people since his arrival. His accent, while much better than before, still stood out. People commented on it often. His multi-colored eyes didn't help either. Someone would identify him, probably connecting him with the Horch, and maybe even the mountain cabin.

Neil thought about Standartenführer Anton Aying, Jakey's killer. He knew about this residence and he knew all about the wealthy Dieter Dremel.

Lord was a pro and was almost certainly here under diplomatic immunity. And Lord would surely find Anton Aying—the two twisted individuals would be attracted by a magnetic pull.

"We've got a few hours at the most," Neil said, grabbing everyone's attention with his hard-edged tone.

"How do you know that?" Madeline asked, seemingly bewildered with Neil's swings of temperament.

"I just do." He turned to Gabi. "I'm sorry about your mother—so sorry—but you need to get your things. We need to get out of here, and fast."

"But we can't just—"

"Now!"

He rushed into the bedroom. As the others hurried around the house, grabbing the bare essentials, Neil stopped what he was doing. He jerked open the bedside table, removing the documents he had hidden behind the drawer. Nestled with the passports and credentials was the letter from Jakey. Neil put the identifications in his jacket before opening the letter, staring at it.

"Talk to me, Jakey," he said, staring at the letter again...

July 2, '38

Barkie-Boy:

Do you still get mad when I call you that? Probably the last time you'll hear it, especially if you're reading this letter. But, as you and I know so well, the sun also rises again.

I need a giant favor. And after what you've been through, you're just the man. I need you to go to the city I've been working in and move a few hundred children to safety. They're well hidden but they will run out of food and supplies 75 days from the date I write this.

If this important envelope made it to you in S-F, it means my job isn't done. It means I bought the farm. The whys and wherefores of the mission will be explained to you. Will you do it? I need you Pale Horse. We need you. These are innocent people: women and children. And after all you've been through, I thought you might like the distraction.

You must liberate them to the transport ship by September 15th. Not before and not after. It's too dangerous to have them out in the open. All you need to do is find secure transport from→

The lack of the second page had at first been frustrating. But, as Kraabe had informed him, there had never been a second page. Jakey probably knew there was a chance the envelope might be intercepted. And if it was, he wouldn't want to give away the children's location. So what exactly was Jakey trying to convey? Neil read the note again, word by word—*c'mon Jakey!*—scrutinizing it for clues.

"We're ready," Madeline said, breathless as she leaned into the doorway.

"Stand guard by the door and wait. I need quiet."

"I thought we had to hurry?" she snapped.

"I'm sorry. Just take this and stand guard by the door," he said, handing her his Colt.

She took the pistol and slammed the bedroom door shut.

Neil studied the note, reading each sentence forward and backward. While he found no hidden phrases when read backward, he noticed an inefficiency about the letter. Every single sentence in the letter had a purpose, except the one at the end of the first paragraph:

But, as you and I know so well, the sun also rises again.

Neil gnawed on a fingernail, unable to make any sense of it. He kept reading.

If this important envelope made it to you in S-F, it means my job isn't done.

And what was it about that line that didn't seem right?

This was a *letter*.

It was only *held* by the envelope. Why would the damned envelope be important?

Neil picked up the tattered envelope, flipping it over as he stared at the cracked remnants of the wax seal. The glued-down folds of the envelope displayed the slightly askew cuts made by a pair of scissors. The envelope was handmade. Neil remembered during his time as a boy when many envelopes had been made by hand, but not anymore. Whoever had made it had done a fine job, because only a close inspection would have revealed it as having been handmade. But this one was—Neil was certain of it.

He opened the envelope, holding it to the scant light of the bedroom. Of course it was empty. He hurried across the room, yanking the curtain backward as he lifted the envelope into the gray light of the window.

There was writing inside!

Neil sprinted from the bedroom, not hearing the loud inquisitions from the two women. After yanking the top drawer from the cabinet, ignoring the loud crash and scattering of silverware, he found the pair of scissors he was looking for and carefully cut the envelope open. Gabi, Madeline, and Peter gathered around the narrow bar of the kitchen counter as Neil flattened the cross-shaped paper on the countertop. In the center of the paper, written faintly in lead pencil, was a sequence of numbers.

Madeline traced her finger under the numerals. "Groupings of numbers. What do they mean?"

Neil studied them for a moment, finally straightening, staring at Madeline. "It means Jakey is still talking to us." He put his arm around Madeline, giving her a quick hug before he carefully refolded the envelope and placed it in his jacket.

At Neil's urging, they all loaded into the Horch, leaving the cottage for the final time.

Chapter Fifty-Eight

NEIL HAD HALFWAY EXPECTED ROADBLOCKS on the downhill drive to Doctor Kraabe's valley home. Perhaps even formations of Panzer tanks, their 75-millimeter barrels ready to blow the Horch all the way back to the Zwickau factory where it had been manufactured. But there was no resistance, other than a gentle rain. Regardless, he took a circuitous route and, upon arriving at the mansion, he jockeyed the Horch around the two Kraabe cars to the very back of the home so it wouldn't be visible from the street.

The four passengers, with Schatze leading the way, burst into the Kraabe household. Madeline explained to the doctor all that had happened, hurriedly introducing Peter and Gabi and telling him about the murder of their mother. Doctor Kraabe took them into the sitting room, calming everyone and, with his trademark compassion, asking the Heinz siblings to relay their accounts of what had happened.

Neil, meanwhile, dashed through the kitchen, past the hidden doors, and down into Jakey's former room. He pulled the wine rack door shut behind him, welcoming the chilly solitude of the subterranean room. Once he'd unfolded the envelope's remains, Neil studied the sequence again, afterward allowing his eyes to take in every book in the room. The numbers appeared to be a simple book code. Neil and Jakey had used such a code to communicate on a number of occasions. Unless another person had the book—and it had to be of the *exact* same printing and edition— the numbers of the code were completely useless.

There were probably a hundred books in the small space, their collective mass dampening all sounds like a foot-thick layer of insulation. If he had the time, which he didn't, Neil would spot-check every single book, trying the code until he found the one that worked.

Assuming the correct book was even here.

After perusing the titles, Neil slid two books off the shelf next to the bed. One was a picture book titled *Paris*. Neil remembered exactly when Jakey had purchased it, on the Olympic as they sailed from New York to England. That was the summer he and Jakey had spent their holiday in Paris, carousing, drinking, enjoying the other's company and letting off much-needed steam from their war experience.

The other book, *A Farewell to Arms* by Ernest Hemingway, was one Neil had purchased that summer in Paris. After he was finished with it, Jakey had read it and obviously kept it. Neil remembered the dusty American bookstore on the Rue du Rivoli. He and Jakey had purchased a number of books there, reading in the adjacent brasserie, lazing around with a glass of—

Wait! An alarm sounded in Neil's head.

Paris. Hemingway.

Neil lifted the note, his eyes moving to the sentence that didn't belong.

But, as you and I know so well, the sun also rises again.

The Sun Also Rises! It was a book by Ernest Hemingway, perhaps the one they had discussed the most that summer. Hemingway, like Jakey and Neil, was a war veteran, and many of his remembrances synced perfectly with theirs, like a keystone.

The clue had been as plain as day the entire time but, in a forest-for-the-trees blindness, Neil had never even noticed it. He began to study the title of every haphazardly stacked book, frantically searching for the code novel. He knocked over shelves, looked under the bed, checked every crack and crevice. There were no other Hemingway books.

Neil rushed back upstairs, finding everyone seated in the sunroom. Peter was resting against Gabi as she stroked his hair. Schatze had her paws in Madeline's lap. Doctor Kraabe was leaning against a bookcase, lecturing the group about something.

"Yes?" Kraabe asked, frowning at Neil's boisterous entry.

Neil jabbed a finger at Madeline. "I need one of Jakey's books. *The Sun Also Rises* by Ernest Hemingway. That's the key to the code."

She stood, a look of concern coming over her face. "They're all down there. Didn't you see it?"

"Damn it!" Neil yelled. "I looked at every single book three times. It's *not* there. Where else could it be?"

Doctor Kraabe ambled to his library, coming back with a handsome, black-bound copy of the novel. Neil took it. It was in German. He nearly rejected it, but then realized that the code would have worked just as well in a German book. All it did was reference a page number, and then a letter. You simply counted the letters from the top left until you found the correct one. He asked everyone to stay put, rushing into the study where he began to work the code.

The first letter was represented by the number 12-32. Neil flipped to page 12, carefully counting to the thirty-second letter. F. He scribbled it down. The next letter would probably need to be a vowel, or an L, or an R. The following letter in the code directed him to 50-90. Neil went to page fifty, taking his time as he counted to the ninetieth letter. It was a Q. He cursed. Perhaps he had counted too fast. He repeated the process.

Q again.

Neil flung the book across the room, spewing curse words. Doctor Kraabe appeared, Madeline in tow.

"That's not the damned book! It would be Jakey's own. I know how he thought," Neil said, his frustration boiling over. "He wouldn't have used your book."

Doctor Kraabe donned his spectacles, opening his hand for the envelope. With an exasperated breath, Neil handed it to him. "Perhaps you're not doing it properly," the doctor mused.

Neil closed his eyes, doing his best not to lash out. He explained the way the code worked, silently reminding himself that there was no harm in the doctor trying. "Try it backward. Maybe he flipped the page and letters on me. We used to do that kind of thing sometimes."

Neil glanced at Madeline. "While he's doing that..." He grabbed Madeline's hand and rushed her downstairs into the hidden room. Books lay everywhere on the floor. He gestured around. "Madeline, think carefully. Where might Jakey have hidden the book?"

Her chocolate eyes flickered before widening. "The note, and the code, was for *you*."

"So?"

"So, he would have hidden the book somewhere where *you* would know to find it."

Agreeing with her logic, Neil sat on the bed. He removed the note from his pocket, looking for any other clues in the text. He found none. The stairs creaked and Doctor Kraabe appeared in the doorway, hunching over due to the low height. Gabi and Peter appeared behind him, followed by Schatze who padded into the room and hopped right on the bed. Kraabe handed Neil the cross-shaped envelope, shaking his head.

"Thanks for trying," Neil mumbled. Everyone was silent as Neil began to rummage through the books. He lifted *A Farewell to Arms*. Perhaps Jakey had only been trying to tip him off as to the author. Taking his time, Neil tried the code, regular and inverse, shaking his head each time. The only sound from the assemblage was a dejected group exhalation each time the code didn't work.

Closing his eyes, Neil tried to think like his best friend. What would have had meaning to Neil? What clue might Jakey have left Neil that would be triggered by some sort of meaning?

And why would he have chosen a Hemingway book?

Neil rattled off the facts: Hemingway was a veteran. He had a succinct writing style. He often wrote about Europe. Neil and Jakey had first discovered his writing when they were in Paris.

Paris.

Neil kicked the books aside until he again found the large picture book. Predictably, on the cover was a gold embossed image of the Eiffel

Tower, similar to the one on Jakey's lighter. He opened the book, riffling through the pages, finding nothing. Neil rubbed his face, unsure of what to do. Gabi pushed into the crowded room, kneeling on the bed so that her arms reached over Neil's shoulders. She turned the book back so that they could view the page inside the front cover. In the spot where people often write their name, or a note if the book is a gift, were the words "Sweet Dreams" in black ink. The words were stark and appeared to have been penned recently. The handwriting was Jakey's.

Neil whipped his head to Madeline. "Which side of the bed did Jakey sleep on?"

"Right where you are."

Neil jerked Jakey's pillow from the bed, shaking it. He threw it across the room and pulled the thin mattress off the bed frame. No book. Again he looked under the bed. Nothing but dust bunnies. Undeterred, Neil stared at each person until a thought came to him. Once, during a block of instruction on covert measures in Lancashire, England, the instructor taught the select students how to hide objects in a mattress. Neil pulled the mattress to him, carefully running his fingers through the seams until he found a small opening. The thread had been cut and removed, and only a meticulous inspection would have yielded the discovery. He pressed his fingers into the slit, his fingers passing the stuffing until they impacted something hard. He pinched his fingers together, grasping its thickness, removing a battered book, holding it up for everyone to see.

On the green spine, printed in silver, was *The Sun Also Rises*, by Ernest Hemingway.

Madeline put her hand over her mouth, suppressing a sound that was both a laugh and a cry.

Jakey's hour had come.

Neil asked to be alone. Grudgingly, the assembled group moved away, climbing the stairs as he pushed the door shut behind them. Schatze curled up beside him, keeping her eyes on her master. The solitary bulb swayed gently, moved by the breeze from the door. Neil steadied it, writing on a tablet with a thick pencil. He placed the splayed envelope to his right, studying the code for a moment as he ran his hand underneath.

"What do you have to tell me, Jakey?"

12-32 50-90 13-1 101-27 28-5 37-10 67-8 91-41 28-78 34-3 51-17 70-10 70-10

Jacob "Jakey" Herman's best friend went to work, flipping to page twelve, using the pencil to mark the letters as he counted. The first letter was an S. Again, Neil ran the possibilities in his head as he turned to the fiftieth page. The next letter would need to be a vowel or an H, L, N, P,

Q, T, or W. A few other scant possibilities existed, but in such a short message, he doubted it.

The word was *coast*, the 90th letter an "O."

Neil's heart leapt. This had to be the correct book. Even after finding the book hidden in the mattress, having endured such a roadblock-laden voyage, Neil had begun to feel uncharacteristically discouraged at every turn. Now, however, he knew he was at the precipice of a major turning point. Jakey's puzzle was about to be revealed. Concrete plans could be made. People set in motion. Actions taken.

Children saved.

Neil took his time, penciling each letter before going back and double-checking his work. Two letters became four, four became seven, and before five minutes passed, the simple thirteen-letter code was cracked.

SOUTHMINEHALL

He lifted the pad of paper, cocking his eye.

Southminehall?

Neil bellowed for everyone to come back, which they did. Quickly. A herd of buffalo would have created less of a racket.

Doctor Kraabe pressed his way to the front, donning the spectacles hanging from the chain around his neck. He held the pad away, staring at it, trying to make sense of it. After a protracted period of thought, he removed his glasses and looked at Neil, shaking his head in bewilderment.

Neil squeezed his eyes shut.

The Heinzes looked at it. Peter spewed a few ideas that were gently rejected. Gabi stared at Neil, a calming smile on her face. "Relax," she told him without saying a word. Neil touched her hand and nodded.

Madeline took the pad. She was shorter than everyone, even Peter, allowing them all to peer over her shoulder as she rotated the pad, looking for any other way the message might be read. Just as she appeared ready to give up, she squawked like a bird, following it with laughter.

"What?" Neil demanded.

"So simple," she laughed, and cried.

"Apparently not to me," Neil remarked.

"This is typical Jakey Herman…sweet and simple. Where's the pencil?"

Neil placed it in her hand and they all watched as she drew vertical lines between South and Mine and Hall.

South Mine Hall.

"I'd seen those three words," Neil said, trying not to sound as irritated as he felt. "But they didn't make sense to me."

Madeline turned to the doctor, her eyes boring into his. "Think, doctor. Think about each word." After a moment, recognition flooded his face. He smiled triumphantly and smacked his forehead.

"What?" asked Neil. "What the *hell* does it mean?"

Madeline was momentarily overcome by the final message from Jakey. Gabi rubbed Madeline's shoulders as she gathered herself, finally regaining her composure.

"Jakey wants us to go to the south mine in Hall. Hall is the name of a town. It's ten kilometers to the east. Like the hundreds of other stripped-out mines around here, that mine was abandoned years ago. It's where my papa first worked as a teen."

"Would that be a suitable place to hide the children?"

Madeline wiped her tears, nodding. "It is, as far as remoteness and privacy is concerned. The Salzburg train passes near the mine, but otherwise, it's very difficult to reach."

After several minutes of celebration, Neil silenced everyone. The moment was steeped in significance, especially considering the heartbreak endured by Madeline and the Heinz children. "I'm sorry for what each of you has endured. The losses in this room are overwhelming."

He allowed that to sink in before he eyed each person, poking a rigid finger into the palm of his hand for emphasis. "We're very close, but this is where it gets tricky. If we foul just one thing up, all of our efforts, all of Jakey's efforts, and those who've died, will have been in vain." Neil paused. "Those children are counting on us."

Madeline motioned up the stairs. "It's already dark out. And with all the rain, I don't think I'd attempt to find it tonight."

"There's still time," Doctor Kraabe added. "One more night won't harm them. I trust Jacob's calculations. He would not have made an error."

After vigorously rubbing his face, Neil nodded. "Could you please have your lady put on some coffee? We've much work to do. And I need to ring Oberst Falkenberg."

* * *

Doctor Kraabe drove his Mercedes painfully slow. Peter again sat in the front floorboard, seemingly brighter on this pleasant September morning. Neil, however, felt none too comfortable, contorted into an odd position on the rear floor of the luxury automobile, his mind awash in all that needed to be done. He felt like they had been driving for an hour.

Neil closed his eyes, picturing Gabi having a discussion with Emilee. How would they greet one another? What would they talk about? Neil believed Emilee would like Gabi, once she got over the fact he was involved with her. She would at first think Gabi was too young—that would, without a doubt, be her first comment. Neil smiled to himself, thinking of the hell Emilee would give him. But after some time, Neil could imagine Emilee hugging him, resting her chin on his shoulder, telling him she only wanted him to be happy. If Neil had died first, he would have wanted the same for her.

Last night, at Madeline's urging, Neil and Gabi slept in Madeline and Jakey's bed. They didn't make love. They stayed up until well after midnight, the cellar room pitch black as they lay there, facing one another, baring their souls. Neil talked about Emilee, and Lex Curran, and some of the things he regretted from his past life as an assassin. While he had once easily justified his secret life, meting out justice in the name of his country's best interest, now he wasn't so sure. After seeing the way the Nazi government was treating the Jews and other humans they considered undesirable, Neil realized how dangerous a violent régime could be. What gave them the right to eliminate a human being that had done nothing wrong? And how was Neil much different? Who was he to judge who was an enemy of his country? Had he killed some unsavory men? Sure. Was he right in doing so? Two months before, in the buzz between his drunkest moments, he would have said yes.

"And now?" Gabi had asked him.

"I wasn't right. While I thought I knew for sure the bad those men had done, I rarely saw it with my own eyes."

His mind had turned to Preston Lord, the architect of the team. Lord had determined who was eliminated, Neil's team simply followed through.

Neil recalled a request in the waning days of 1935, before Cleveland Mixton's cancer and before Neil's grief. Some of the killings had begun to seem a bit gray. Lord's next target turned out to be an overstuffed lawyer from Maryland—his sins against the state were allegedly buried so deeply that only a man with Lord's considerable power might find them. Neil had been suspicious, and his discreet query uncovered proceedings between the lawyer, his client, and Preston Lord's family fortune.

It was then Neil realized he and his team had been nothing more than a cat's paw for Lord. His team fancied themselves like a bishop, or perhaps a rook, striking from great distance on the chess board, true power players.

Now, upon detached reflection, they seemed to have been nothing more than Lord's pawns.

Nonessential.

Disposable.

It surprised Neil that Lord hadn't ordered him killed before now. And what was Lord doing here that was critical enough to merit a personal visit?

Neil reflected on his own reason for being here. While, at first, Neil was a bit taken aback by the simplicity of what he had been brought here to do, he'd finally come around to examining the underlying reasoning. It *was* upright. It *was* the right thing to do. These were children, innocent children. They should have every right to live. And every chance.

"Do you still believe you made the right decision in coming here?" Gabi had asked.

"Absolutely." Neil had propped up on his elbow. "Do you remember the picture of the little girl you asked me about?"

"Yes."

"Her name is Fern." Neil recalled the story of how he'd come to have Fern's picture. "When I think about that frail little girl, I think about the son I never knew."

Neil and Gabi held each other for a while before, out of the blue, Gabi began to cry, the pain of her mother's death finding her in the blackness.

Preston Lord had struck again. Thankfully she cried herself to sleep.

The Mercedes slowed to a stop, bringing Neil back to the present and the mission at hand.

"This is as far as I can drive," Doctor Kraabe said.

"Am I clear to get up?" Neil whispered.

Peter leaned over the seat. "I'll say. We're in the middle of a dark forest."

Neil opened the rear door, veritably tumbling out of the car. He stood and stretched, rubbing the scars on his side before taking the map from the front seat. Glancing around, he saw that they were in a shallow depression, and parallel to the rocky road was a trickling brook. Once he located their position on the map, he put his finger where the mine opening should be, on the other side of what the map represented as heavy relief. He pointed to the dashes of blue sky over the ridge, capped by tall pine trees, telling them that the mine's mouth should be right over the hill.

"How did the workers get there every day?" Peter asked.

Neil waited for the doctor to answer. When he didn't, Neil spoke as he retrieved the implements and lanterns from the boot of the Mercedes. "Peter, from what Madeline told me, the mine workers here were only one step up from captive slaves. They were probably taken in by train and forced to work incredibly long hours with no option to leave. I'd hazard that they even had armed guards at the mouth of the cave."

"That's no way to treat people."

Neil and Doctor Kraabe shared a look. Neil tousled the teenager's hair. "Well, that's why we're here today. That's why we need your best, Peter."

The three men set out up the steep, pine needle-covered incline. Doctor Kraabe had brought a large bag full of medical supplies in case they were needed. As they walked, Peter peppered both men with numerous questions, many of them reflective of a mind that was advanced beyond Peter's age. Doctor Kraabe, seeming to enjoy the academic queries, fed Peter from a seemingly endless supply of hard candies he kept in his pocket. Neil answered what questions he could, more concerned with checking behind them. No one was following.

The ridge was more than a small hill. It was the spine leading to one of the high mountains surrounding the valley. The mountain was three times higher than the ridge, but when hiked from the valley floor, with an older man, a teenager, and a recently injured man in middle age—all carrying implements and supplies—the climb was arduous.

After a water break on the ridge, the trio descended a rock path, following an overgrown trail through brambles to a wide gravel opening. And there, in the side of a sheer limestone face, were two entrances. The wide entrance was covered with heavy, dried tree trunks, held by massive metal posts. It would take either a crane or ten men to remove each log. To the left of the wide entrance was a short, medieval door-sized entrance, covered only with heavy timbers. Various hand painted signs warned the good *Volk* of Tyrol to keep away. According to the person who had painted the signs, there was a danger of asphyxiation, danger of cave-ins, danger of floods. Someone, using different paint, had added that the resident dragon, named Wilhelm, was quite friendly, though.

Neil pulled in great breaths through his nose. Wood smoke. The gentle breeze was coming from the south, from the spine they'd just traversed. The mine seemed to wind under the spine. If the children were indeed here, they could vent a fire through one of the many vertical air vents. Neil looked for the origin of the smoke but couldn't see it.

He moved close to the large entrance and noted fresh gouges on the timbers of the smaller opening. Someone had moved them recently.

Neil gave Peter the task of getting the two lanterns lit while he and Kraabe removed the timbers from the small doorway. It was nearly high noon by the time they were ready to enter. Neil went first, followed by Peter, then the doctor. The smaller door led to a similarly shaped tunnel. The smell of earth and something else, an acrid odor, was immediately noticeable. As they moved inside, the temperature plummeted. Every hundred feet or so were arched passages, on the right, connecting with the main tunnel. The smaller tunnel was supported with iron and wood, while the large tunnel was cut straight from the limestone.

Neil made his two helpers wait at each access passage while he checked for signs of life. First passage. Nothing. Second passage. Nothing. Eighth. Nothing. Twelfth. Nothing. But the smell of smoke was stronger.

By the time they'd reached the seventeenth access passage, they had to creep due to the ice. It was there that Neil again passed through, expecting the same damp blackness he'd been encountering at each passage.

But this time there were crates filling the void. Hundreds of them.

Neil turned, his voice straining as he told the doctor and Peter to stay put. Nothing appeared outwardly dangerous, but he didn't want Peter or the doctor to die because of a booby trap.

Confused, Neil walked to a long, narrow box, situated at the highest point of the rows and rows of boxes and crates. The box was made of pine, a swastika burned into the top. On the side it was marked: *Deutsche Waffen und Munitions Fabrik, Berlin/Potsdam*. He moved his lantern around the crate, seeing nothing that would indicate a booby trap. Following a deep breath, he opened the box, finding twenty shiny-new Parabellum Pistols, held dress-right-dress by an inner rack. He closed it and reset the hasp. Shutting his eyes, Neil lifted the crate. Nothing.

Did the same in the next row, rifles, nothing.

Grenades, *nichts*.

An impossibly heavy crate holding only four MG-34's. No booby trap.

He could hear Peter and Kraabe scraping around, probably getting impatient.

Neil walked behind the rows of crates, moving his lantern to the depths of the tunnel. There was no sign of any children or their caretakers. And the smoke smell was powerful.

Suddenly, Neil realized there was no ice here. A few hundred feet back, in the smaller tunnel, there had been. Figuring Kraabe and Peter had turned back, Neil began to walk deeper in the tunnel. It wasn't far until he saw the lumps.

Halting, the lantern swaying, it only took a moment for Neil to realize the lumps were human beings. A brief jag of dread went through him as he thought they might be dead. But after just a short moment, Neil saw one of the lumps move. The lump was a little boy of perhaps four. He lifted his head, the irises of his eyes illuminated by the lantern. Then, as if he knew he'd disobeyed, he buried his head in his arms and burrowed between those around him.

Neil lifted the lantern. The children, and their caretakers, went on as far as he could see.

Speaking German, Neil's voice cracked as he said, "Don't be afraid. I'm your friend. I'm Jacob Herman's friend. I'm here with others. We've come to rescue you."

Numerous heads popped up and Neil couldn't help but laugh with joy.

Chapter Fifty-Nine

IN INNSBRUCK, GABI AND MADELINE KILLED TIME in the study of the Kraabe mansion. While they'd chatted idly after the men had left, they'd finally run out of topics to discuss. Regardless of their current cooperation, there was still the faintest sheen of frost between them. The thick volumes of medical textbooks, the countless anatomical models, and the heavy Oriental rug beneath them seemed to absorb nearly every sound. Every sound other than the metronomic rhythm from the study's massive antique Swiss clock.

Tick. Tick. Tick.

Schatze lay between the women, quite contented, occasionally grunting when she switched positions and resumed her slumber. Gabi tried to read. Madeline sat, eyes closed, not sleeping.

Tick. Tick.

Madeline opened her eyes, looked at Gabi. Gabi was staring at her. "What?" Madeline asked.

Gabi closed the book, an impish expression dancing over her face. "Well, I was thinking about something." She slid closer. "Neil talked about the German policeman coming after him. The older man."

"Yes, so?"

"Think about who else is here in Innsbruck…the American."

"The one who…"

Gabi knotted her lips together and nodded. "The one who probably killed my mother. Neil said he's dangerous and unpredictable."

"Okay? Where are you going with all this?" Madeline asked, sitting up.

"Lord is the American's name, and we know he's staying at the posh hotel—"

"The Tyroler Inn."

"Right. And then there's the SS man, Aying. He's the ranking Schutzstaffel in town. Probably wouldn't be too hard to find him."

Madeline's gaze rotated downward. "Aying I know about, all too well."

"Exactly. Don't you see our connection?"

"Lord took your mother. Aying took my man."

"Correct." Gabi slid the book onto the table. "Madeline, if we had to, we could make certain Neil was free of these two men…these obstacles. And, in the process, perhaps we could exact our own revenge."

Madeline eyes were slits. "And, pray tell, how do we do that?"

Tick. Tick.

Gabi removed lipstick from her purse, applying a light coating and pressing her lips together. She then tugged downward on the sides of her matronly dress before lifting her breasts, simulating a low-cut, busty outfit. "On the farm, do you know how my mother would ensnare a pesky hare?"

"How?"

"She'd appeal to his greedy nature and set a trap."

"Neil would never let us," Madeline answered, shaking her head.

"Well, who says Neil's in charge?"

Tick. Tick.

Madeline's brown eyes widened. "I thought you loved Neil."

"I do."

"But you'd defy him?"

"Absolutely. If I thought it was for the best."

"And you think this is for the best?"

There was a period of silence as Gabi's eyes glistened. "I'm grieving my mother, Madeline. She's on my mind nearly every second. And, to be brutally frank, I doubt this situation here is going to end well."

Madeline didn't respond other than a nod.

"So," Gabi said, forcing a mirthful expression, "Let's just get ready in the event we need to cause a diversion...and I'm not asking *anyone's* permission. Those days are now behind me forever." She stood and offered her hand. "So, why don't you and I put our minds *together*?"

Tick. Tick.

"Do you have a plan?" Madeline asked, as Gabi's hand floated in front of her.

"It's coming to me."

Madeline accepted Gabi's hand. "Where do we start?"

Gabi led Madeline through the house as they gathered items from various rooms. In the doctor's closet they found a sewing box and also a small stool. Together the women carried everything back to the study.

Madeline went first, trying on a dress Gabi had purchased in Salzburg, modeling it on the stool. As the two women opened up about their past, Gabi went to work, pinning hems and cutting sleeves. Every now and then she would stand back, envisioning the way the dress would look through the eyes of the men they hoped to seduce.

Tick. Tick.

* * *

One of the caretakers was Irish. She spoke for the group as the hundreds of children gathered around Neil, hugging him, tugging at his clothes and laughing.

"First, is everyone here okay?" Neil asked, breathless in his excitement.

The caretaker, her face black with soot, nodded and grimaced at the same time. "As good as can be. We've recently had some stomach sickness going around but we still have food and clean water and medicine."

"Is everyone still here?" Neil asked, his hands touching the head of the boy who was currently clamped on his leg.

"Yes. We do a count three times a day."

Neil knelt, greeting the children in German, telling them everything would be okay. They surrounded him, their tiny bodies pressing against him in their exuberance. There was the obvious odor of human beings about them, but to Neil it was the sweetest smell in the world.

"How did you manage?" he asked the caretaker, accepting a hug from a child.

"It wasn't easy. This tunnel goes much deeper and branches off. We created a sanitary area as best we could. We have a makeshift kitchen. We bury trash and waste near one of the air vents. We've even taught lessons to combat the boredom."

"And you still have food?"

"We've a few hundred cans remaining. We also have flour and other ingredients. But we would have run out soon—maybe another four or five days. We were instructed how many calories to feed per day."

"It's so cold in here," Neil said.

"Blankets, heavy clothes and hot water. That's all we've had."

Another of the children, a young boy, put his arms around Neil's neck. To him, the children's collective innocence was among the most pure characteristics known to man. And their touch was medicine to Neil's soul.

The Irish caretaker began to cry. "It's been so long. I can't tell you how many times we almost voted to come out and give up. What happened? Why did it take seventy-two days?"

Neil stood, giving her a reassuring hug as he apologized. He didn't think revealing what had happened to Jakey was a good idea. "I have a few people with me, one of whom is a doctor. Keep everyone here, okay? I'll be back in just a few minutes. And please keep everyone quiet. We're not out of the woods, yet."

After disentangling himself, Neil hurried past the weaponry, reminding himself to ask if Jakey had put it there. It had to be Jakey. When Neil reached the ice, he began to speak Peter's and Doctor Kraabe's names. No response. He stepped into the smaller passage and called out again, even risking yelling.

Nothing. Maybe the limestone absorbed his yells.

Neil walked back into the main tunnel, hurrying up the incline, noticing the gear grooves in the narrow gauge track.

"Doctor Kraabe! Peter!"

He was getting close to the mouth of the tunnel.

Have they walked back out?

The tunnel leveled out.

"Kraabe!"

"Peter!"

A rat scurried across the path.

Neil removed his Colt as unease began to set in. He could now see the broken light between the giant timbers of the opening. He turned at the next pass-through, walking to the much brighter side tunnel.

As Neil made a left turn in the smaller passage, he saw a long revolver aimed between his eyes.

The revolver was steady. The revolver was sure. And the man holding it was ready.

The Colt hung impotently in Neil's right hand beside him.

Between Neil and the man with the revolver was Doctor Kraabe, his hands clasped on his head as he knelt. The doctor's eyes were down. Ashamed.

Peter sat against the wall of the small passage, his knees pulled up to him. An unworried look inhabited his face.

"Drop that pistol to your right," the armed man said in German.

With the help of the sunlight beaming in from the mouth of the passage, Neil recognized the man, so he complied.

"Now get your hands up."

This was the third time Neil had joined eyes with this individual. He was the old man, the cop, from the airfield in Velden.

"Let's go," the old man commanded with a wag of the revolver. "Outside, to the light."

He instructed Peter to go first and Kraabe second. Then, after swearing to Mother Mary in a voice that defined validity, the old man guaranteed Neil a bullet in the back if he did anything untoward. Remembering the bullet that hit the airplane instrument on that fateful morning of his first solo flight, Neil believed him.

The old man followed the threesome out of the tunnel.

And he coughed the entire way.

* * *

Peter and the old man did all the talking on the short walk from the tunnel. The old man, between fits of coughing, murmured several times to Peter that after he took care of this "situation," he would see that he was cared for properly. Neil and Doctor Kraabe trudged out obediently. Outside, the day had grown quite warm, made to feel even warmer after the frigidity of the tunnel. The old man instructed Neil and Kraabe to move to his left and kneel while keeping their hands on their heads. He sent Peter to a canvas bag, lying on the path fifty meters away, to retrieve two pair of handcuffs.

Peter hesitated.

"Go ahead, son. Then I want to get to the bottom of all of this."

Peter did as he was told. The old man aimed the ridiculously long pistol at Neil, standing fifteen feet away as he said, "Cuff both of them, son, and lock the cuffs tightly. Do the younger man first." The old man coughed into his sleeve, watching Peter as he cuffed Neil. Then Peter moved on to Kraabe.

There was a wry smile on the old man's face. "I've been a policeman for eighty percent of my life, Peter. Please go back to the younger gentleman and cuff his left hand properly."

Peter closed his eyes, his chest falling with a great exhalation. He walked back to Neil, squeezing the handcuff tightly. The old man moved behind both men, shaking the cuffs as their hands were on the back of their heads. He moved around and looked at Neil. *"Sprechen sie Deutsche?"*

Neil nodded, his eyes cast at the pine and leaf mottled forest floor.

"Und Sie?"

"Bestimmt," Doctor Kraabe answered with a frown, as if this were an insulting opening query.

The old man instructed them both to sit. He continued to aim the pistol at Neil. "Stay still."

"They're helping find the children," Peter objected.

"Let's talk about it, Peter," the old man said, beckoning him to his side. "Who is this man?" he asked, gesturing to Doctor Kraabe.

"Doctor Kraabe," Peter answered.

"What kind of doctor?"

"Medical," Kraabe said.

"And what about him?" the old man asked, gesturing to Neil.

"I know him much better," Peter replied.

"From Germany, correct?"

"Yes, sir."

"I remember him from Germany, too," the old man said to Neil. "From the airstrip, in Velden."

Neil nodded.

"Why?" the old man asked.

Kraabe shrugged and nodded at Neil. Neil turned back to the old man and said, "That man you found—his name was Willi—was nothing more than my hired ride from England. I paid him in good faith. We landed there to refuel and he tried to rob me. When I resisted, he shot me first, then I shot him. You witnessed the aftermath."

The old man narrowed his eyes, turning his head as if he were trying to hear more clearly. "And?"

"And nothing. That was all there was to it. I hired Willi to fly me into Germany and he turned on me. Knowing the conditions there, I didn't think it wise to hang around for the inquisition that would follow."

"Was that man, Willi, involved in what you're doing now?"

"Do you know what am I doing now? Do you know why we're at this mine?" Neil asked.

After coughing again, a bit less severe since he appeared to have caught his breath, the old man turned to Peter. "Peter, I need to trust you for a moment."

Peter nodded. The old man tilted his head in the manner of a person who wants greater assurance.

"You can absolutely trust me," Peter said earnestly.

"Good. Take a short walk up the hill and I'll call out to you when I want you to come back."

"What are you going to do?"

"I'm not going to hurt them, son. You have my word. I just want to have a conversation that I don't want you to hear."

Peter turned to Neil, plaintively, and said, "But I'm involved in all of this."

"Go ahead, Peter," Neil said. "Give us five minutes."

Peter whirled and stalked away, angrily kicking sticks and stones.

"My name is Thomas Lundren," the old man said to Neil. "I'm German. I was a career police officer, retired when you and I first *met*. After what I saw at the airstrip, the current commissioner allowed me to come back and work this case."

"How do we know that you aren't the one who killed Hildie Heinz?" Neil asked.

Straightening, Thomas said, "While I'm an imperfect person and a sinner in the eyes of the Lord, I have never, *ever* killed an innocent person in my life and certainly never a woman. So, no, I did not kill that young man's mother. She died while I held her hand."

"Did you speak to her?" Doctor Kraabe asked.

"I did. In fact, I was surprised at what she told me."

Again, Neil chose silence. "And?" Kraabe asked testily.

"She said she'd been knifed by another American man, thin and vicious and dressed slickly. He was accompanied by a cob-rough German constable whose identity I can most likely guess."

Neil lifted his blue and green eyes. They danced to the left and the right before he spoke. "That confirms my suspicions. I *know* the man who killed her, the American."

"I thought you might."

"He's here to kill me."

"I figured that as well, Herr *Reuter*."

Kraabe's head snapped up.

"Hildie give you that, too?" Neil asked.

"Yes, she did."

Neil and Doctor Kraabe shared an agreeable look. Neil turned back to the retired police officer, opening up in a way he rarely did. "Thomas, not that you would care, but this task we're performing is...well, it's a humanitarian effort."

"Frau Heinz said it involves Jewish children."

Neil smiled as he looked at Kraabe. "They're in there. I found them."

"Are they well?" Kraabe breathed, his eyes wide.

"They're fine. A little sickness. Nothing serious."

Doctor Kraabe appeared momentarily stunned. Then he tilted his head back, laughing quietly, his eyes weeping tears of joy. Neil watched the doctor's reaction, feeling emotional himself. Then he looked up at the old man.

"I've done a lot of bad in this life, Thomas. Truly. But right now, we're all on the precipice of something wonderful."

"Tell me about these children."

Neil gave Thomas the short version. "So, now, if you'll trust me, it's up to me and my friends to get them away from the Reich."

Thomas stood above both men. His thick gray stubble shifted as something resembling a smile appeared underneath. He un-cocked the long pistol, holstering it. Then he reached into his pocket, dangling a set of keys in front of Neil and Kraabe, the scant rays of midday sun glinting off of their metal.

"Frau Heinz, in her final breaths, said some nice things about you, Herr Reuter."

"She was a fine woman."

Thomas considered both men, again focusing on Neil. "So, after all of this, after all that's gone on...why did your friend choose *you*? You were so far away."

"All I know is he *did*," Neil answered. "I can't make sense of it otherwise."

"It's his *aliyah*," Doctor Kraabe added.

Thomas frowned. "His what?"

"His aliyah."

Neil turned to the doctor.

"Aliyah means 'ascension' in Hebrew. The oldest meaning signified ascension through death," Doctor Kraabe said, again staring up through the whispering pines. "And, more recently, to the Jewish people, it means the pilgrimage back to their holy land."

"And me?" Neil asked.

"For you, Neil, I think it means your redemption."

After a bout of coughing, Thomas knelt behind Doctor Kraabe, unlocking his hands. He did the same for Neil, beckoning them both to stand. After formally introducing himself, and shaking their hands, he motioned his hand to the trail and the tunnel. "Now, shall we collect that brave young man and make the trek inside to see these precious children? And as we walk, perhaps the three of you could explain how you plan to extract these darlings from the resident Nazi sovereignty?"

Neil nodded, a hint of good cheer coming across his face. "We'll tell you everything."

"Good," Thomas answered. "I've been toiling over this mystery for over a month. And it would have killed me if I had died before figuring it out."

"About that," Kraabe said. "Let's talk about that cough of yours."

"Later," Thomas answered firmly.

When Peter rejoined them, the four men headed into the tunnel. After collecting Neil's pistol and Kraabe's supplies, they spent several hours with the women and children. Doctor Kraabe treated several minor injuries and ordered Prontosil, an antibiotic Jakey had left with the caretakers, be given to eleven children suffering with chronic cough.

Though the children and their caretakers had to remain in place for the time being, the four rescuers reassured them that they'd be leaving here very soon.

Chapter Sixty

IT WAS EARLY EVENING AND MORE STORMS HAD MOVED IN. Water splashed as Thomas stamped his feet in a shallow puddle, standing just off of Innstrasse, staring at the portico of the elegant Tyroler Inn. He walked around to the back of the hotel, looking at all the exits and, in the process, finding the parking area. As he moved around the far side of the building, he noticed something familiar. Parked at the rear edge of the lot, sandwiched between two larger autos, was a Dampf-Kraft-Wagen, known as a DKW. The DKWs, in their numerous styles, were common cars. But this one drew Thomas' keen eyes, aided by the rain that made the auto's dingy black paint glisten as if it were new and still wet. On the door of the DKW, in an arc, was the shadow of the word *Polizist*, German for constable.

Thomas walked to the door, running his hand over the black paint that had been used to paint over the word. Such a sight was not uncommon; old, used police cars were often sold near the end of their useful life. But Thomas felt he knew this particular constable's car. He moved to the rear, staring at the Austrian license plate. The flat-head screws were twisted tightly into the bumper. Thomas touched the surface around one of the screws, pulling his wet finger back with the residue of paint and metal filings. The plate had been installed recently and Thomas would bet his farm and livestock it was stolen.

He checked the far side of the building. There was a fire escape above, and only one rear door on the first floor. He walked around to the main entrance. As soon as he stepped through the first set of doors, an overly solicitous doorman took Thomas' coat and hat. As soon as the coat was off, the doorman turned up his nose upon seeing Thomas' plain worker's clothes, asking him if he might be in the wrong place. Thomas ignored him, pushing through the rotating main door into the swank lobby.

Brahms played softly, coupled with the din of a large crowd of guests forced to stay inside on such a dreary evening. In the center of the lobby, sitting at a round, gilded table, four beautiful people appeared to be laughing at a joke or a funny story, doing their best not to spill their fancy cocktails. The men wore extravagant suits and polished shoes with shiny buckles. The women were decked out in dresses of the finest, flashiest design, matched with all the requisite accouterments. Thomas passed the group, taking note of the large number of military officers and SS. He headed to the concierge desk. The uniformed man working behind the massive walnut counter was smoking a cigarette, reading something, concealing it below the shelf. Upon sensing Thomas' presence, the concierge snapped to attention with a beaming smile. The smile quickly faded as he eyed Thomas.

"Good evening," Thomas said.

The concierge arched his brows.

Thomas placed his hands on the counter. "I need your help."

"You're not a guest." It wasn't a question.

Thomas flipped his aged badge onto the counter top. "I'd suggest you do whatever it is you need to do to improve your attitude. I'm pressed for time."

Shaking his head in irritation, the concierge moved from behind the desk. He stopped before Thomas, clasping his hands in front of him in a practiced manner. "I'm Fritz. How might I assist you?"

"Fritz, I need to see your guest list."

The concierge pursed his lips and closed his eyes. "Police or not, I cannot allow that without a judge's order and I have precedence to back me up. We have many influential guests here in our hideaway city who...well, as you can imagine...they don't want their identities known for obvious reasons. And many are ranking party officials, I might add."

Thomas tucked the badge into his pocket, curling his finger to the concierge. "Come close, Fritz."

The concierge rolled his eyes and leaned closer, turning his ear.

"You get that damned list right now or I'm hoofing it over there to the Hofgarten and speaking to my SS friends, who have great interest in what I'm doing by the way, and I'm telling them Fritz the concierge from the Tyroler Inn is highly uncooperative." Before the man could protest, Thomas lifted a crooked finger. "I'll also report you as a sexual deviant of the juvenile persuasion, a thief, an enemy of the National Socialist Party, and a sworn opponent of the Anschluss." Thomas offered a thin smile. "And I'll tell them that when I told you the SS was interested in what I'm here doing, that you said 'to hell with the SS and everyone serving in it.'"

The concierge straightened, horrified.

Thomas winked. "Does that top your court order, Fritz?"

"Yes," the concierge whispered.

"Now, you can avoid all that by just getting me the list."

The suddenly sweaty Fritz rushed to the front desk, back in moments with a leather-bound book. "Use it as long as you need it," he said, nearly throwing the book at Thomas.

"Thank you, Fritz." Thomas carried it to a chair in the corner of the lobby and slowly perused the names: *Hammerschmidt from Herborn. Jaworski from Waldgirmes. Humphries from Dublin. Glinke from Wettenberg. Von Berg from Giessen. Barreto from Venice. Düking from Frankfurt.*

The next one made Thomas cock his eye: *Diplomat guest.*
Nothing else beside the title. There was no name and no address.
"Fritz!" Thomas called out.

Fritz sprinted across the lobby.

Thomas stabbed the black ink. "The diplomat?"

"Yes."

"Who is he?"

"I honestly don't know his name," Fritz said with a shaky voice.
"They have privileges of privacy and that is the unvarnished truth on the
heads of my children."

Thomas turned his eyes up to the concierge. "Relax, Fritz."

Fritz exhaled and wiped sweat from his forehead.

"Do you know the diplomat by face?"

"Yes, yes, of course. An excellent tipper and he's used
my...*services*...several times."

"Where's he from?"

The concierge hesitated, licking his lips. Thomas glared at him,
widening one eye. *C'mon Fritz, those camps are waiting.*

"I'm almost certain he's American." Fritz removed his wire-rimmed
glasses and nervously polished the lenses with a handkerchief. "Would this
have anything to do with Standartenführer Aying?"

Thomas remembered what Neil had told him about Aying. "It
might."

"Because they're probably still in the bar, together. The diplomat had
me retrieve the SS commander a short time ago." Fritz cleared his throat.
"I assume, since you're here on the SS's behalf, that you've made
Standartenführer Aying's acquaintance?"

"Why don't you let me ask the questions, Fritz?"

"Uh, certainly, sir."

"The bar, you say?"

"Yes, sir."

Thomas stood, retrieving several reichsmarks from his pocket,
handing them to Fritz along with the hotel register. He crossed the lobby,
following the smell of beer, smoke and perfume. Ragtime music began to
clash with Brahms, becoming overbearing by the time he reached the rear
of the building. A set of double French doors opened to a darkened room,
marked by purple lighting. Thomas walked inside, amazed at the noise.
Only in a resort town on a rainy Monday evening could you find a packed
bar at dinnertime.

He walked around the establishment, careful to watch where he
stepped. The bar contained multiple step-downs, barely outlined by floor
lighting that one would miss if his eyes weren't accustomed to the semi-
darkness.

Thomas didn't know the music, but it certainly was loud, coming courtesy of the live, two-piece ensemble at the back of the Berlin-style bar. A drenched man was bent over the keys of the piano, the sweat pouring off of him the way the rain had cascaded off of Thomas minutes before. He was banging on the keys with stiff fingers, somehow managing to create a cousin to actual music in his manic frenzy. Another man, this one with longish, sweaty black hair and an enormous nose, leaned over his band mate, his eyes closed, thumbing a large bass in rhythm, creating the frenetic cacophony of modern song.

Thomas made his way back to the front of the saloon, pushing up to the mahogany bar, holding a ten pinched between his fingers until the busy bartender yelled to him, taking his order. Thomas ordered a mineral water and beckoned the bright-eyed bartender in close.

"Do you get many Americans in here?"

The bartender slid the change over as he shouted his reply. "Not as many as we used to."

"Have you served any recently?" Thomas shouted.

The bartender nodded immediately. He stood on a stepstool, narrowing his eyes as he scanned the throng. Thomas watched the man's eyes, knowing he was looking for someone in particular. After ten seconds of looking, the man zeroed in, pointing to the right side of the bar. He leaned down, keeping his hand helpfully pointing at the table. "Right over there. Been in the hotel a day or two. Fancy American. He's sitting with *the* man."

"Who's that?"

"Standartenführer Aying."

Thomas tried to see them, barely catching a glimpse of their sunken round booth. "Who is Aying?"

The bartender grinned crookedly. "You're obviously not from here."

Thomas shook his head. "No."

The bartender leaned all the way over the bar so that his mouth was almost touching Thomas' ear. "He's only the most powerful man in all of Tyrol. And you don't want to be on his bad side, if you get my drift." The bartender leaned back, winking.

Thomas nodded his thanks, sliding his change back as a considerable tip. He grasped his water, never taking a sip, and crossed the bar in the direction of Aying and the American. When he was ten steps away, a large SS soldier stood, blocking Thomas' way. The lightning-like SS runes stood out boldly on the man's uniform, like a deathly stop sign to those who were unwelcome.

"I want to speak with Standartenführer Aying and the American."

"No visitors," the SS man replied.

Thomas leaned around him, making eye contact with the SS Standartenführer who had gray eyes to match his uniform. Thomas made a talking motion with his hand. The Standartenführer was smoking a cigarette; he narrowed his eyes and curled his finger at the burly bodyguard. The guard poked Thomas in his slight chest, telling him to stay put. After listening to his boss for a moment, the giant returned and leaned down to Thomas.

"What do you want?"

"The American man they're both looking for," Thomas said, gesturing to Aying and the man he presumed to be Preston Lord. "I'm looking for him, too. And I have some information they might be interested in."

The man listened to Thomas, holding a solitary finger up for Thomas to wait. As he leaned over and relayed the information, Thomas saw both men's reaction as if their seat suddenly became electrified. Aying pushed his bodyguard out of the way and curled his hand at Thomas, sliding over so he could sit.

From the depths of depression just days before, Thomas' excitement level now soared to the heavens. Both men stared at him expectantly, waiting for him to spill his guts—something he might eventually have to do. Literally.

And now the real game begins, Thomas thought, allowing his aged smile to reappear.

* * *

It was nearly seven in the evening. The heavy rain made the coming night settle over Innsbruck chillingly early. The warm sunshine of earlier was a distant memory. Neil sat at Doctor Kraabe's desk, in his study. He wrote several lines, immediately scratching over them like a madman before crumpling the paper and tossing it into the garbage can. His left hand resumed its place, pressing back through his hair as he scribbled again. Madeline and Gabi sat with Doctor Kraabe in the next room, whispering in an effort not to disturb Neil. Once, frustrated with Neil's manic solitude, Madeline had stood to intervene. Finger over her mouth, Gabi shook her head back and forth.

Don't do that, Madeline, Gabi's eyes said. *He'll explode like a stick of dynamite.*

Madeline exhaled so loudly it became a moan. She sat back down, jerking a magazine from the coffee table and thumbing through it with feigned interest.

Peter was the only one not waiting on Neil. Sitting in the kitchen, alone, Peter listened to a German radio show. It was about a detective, a

National Socialist—of course—closing in on a band of wicked Polish criminals bent on destroying the Reich.

The back door clicked open and shut. Everyone but Neil rushed into the kitchen. Gabi turned off the radio, drawing a quick protest from Peter before he caught her electric gaze.

Thomas stepped into the kitchen, his shoes and lower trousers soaked. "Where's Herr Reuter?" he asked.

Neil appeared, holding the tablet of paper with the scrawled pages. "Did you find them?"

"I did...thick as thieves, drinking in the bar." Thomas coughed, digging his fingers into his upper chest as if it might help. When he'd recovered he rasped, "Your American, Lord, has enlisted Aying's help."

"Paying him handsomely, no doubt," Neil muttered, staring at the wall as he shook his head. "Did they believe you?"

"I changed the story after hearing something that was said. Somehow, some way, Preston Lord is under the impression you're here to assassinate Adolf Hitler."

Everyone in the room turned their eyes to Neil. Neil, a knowing look on his face, nodded. "Yes, well, that's been suggested a time or two."

"Apparently Hitler is not within five hundred kilometers of here right now, and won't be anytime soon. Because of that, I got the impression that Lord's not in a huge hurry."

"Well, he's staying at the nicest hotel in town," Neil remarked. "Knowing him, he's having a working holiday." Neil glanced at the tablet in his hand. "How did you change the story?"

"Hitler's retreat, in Obersalzburg..."

"Yes?"

"I told them you were awaiting his return, and that's where you would strike." Thomas' eyes crinkled in merriment as he surveyed the room. "And I told them that I have reason to believe you're hiding out somewhere near Salzburg."

"Did they believe you?"

Thomas shrugged. "I don't see why not, but they didn't rush out of the bar, if that's what you mean." He moved closer to Neil. "So the answer is yes...I do think they both believed me, and I think before I arrived, neither man had much to go on. In fact, Standartenführer Aying has guaranteed me an agonizing death if he finds out I'm lying."

Neil and Doctor Kraabe exchanged a look. Peter scratched his head, probably struggling to return to reality after the fiction he'd just enjoyed. The two women deflated and stepped back into the sitting room. Neil motioned to the kitchen table where the four men sat. Schatze joined them, curling up at Neil's feet.

"There's a potential problem," Thomas added.

"What's that?" Neil asked.

"There are soldiers everywhere in that hotel. What if just one of them hears that Falkenberg is rallying a group of men? What if word leaks to Aying?"

Neil massaged his eyes. "We'll just have to chance it. I know of no other way."

"That's dangerous," Gabi interjected. She looked at Madeline and the two women nodded at each other.

"I agree," Neil said, missing the unspoken communication between the women. "But Falkenberg is being paid to keep this quiet. He wants the balance of his money."

"It's still a concern," Thomas replied.

"Did you tell them your name?" Neil asked.

"I most certainly did. It was necessary to do so, and to show them my special orders. Otherwise, they wouldn't have believed me."

"Very risky," Doctor Kraabe muttered.

Peter averted his eyes. "Just think about my mother and what happened to her."

"You're absolutely right, Peter," Thomas said, patting him on the back.

"Were they suspicious?" Neil asked.

"Well, since I'd had that run-in with you at the airstrip, I first told them about Willi Kruger." Thomas cleared his throat, fighting off a coughing spasm. In a hoarse voice, he said, "I told them I spoke to him *before* he expired, and he told me you were going to kill Hitler at the party rally, with the airplane."

"As in a suicide?"

"They didn't ask, but they most certainly believed that. In fact, your American, when I told them this, shook his head and said, 'I knew it,' in English."

Neil's eyes widened at Thomas' craftiness. "Very good."

"And I told them that, since you were shot, I knew you would have to lie in wait somewhere."

"Did they ask why the pilot and I had a confrontation?"

"They did, and I simply explained it as the type of thing that happens between two unsavory people."

Doctor Kraabe patted Thomas on the back. "You did very well, sir." Thomas coughed again, into a brown-mottled handkerchief, making Kraabe stare at him with great concern.

Neil placed his palms flat on the mahogany table. "Was Aying angry with you, for supposedly keeping all of this to yourself?"

"I think he was more concerned with taking over. Stopping a Hitler assassination attempt, will net him a seat beside the Führer...at least in his mind it will."

"What about Lord?" Neil asked.

Thomas accepted a glass of water from Kraabe. "He only had one point, and he made it repeatedly."

"And what was that?" Neil asked.

Thomas pointed fingers at Neil, simulating a gun. "That you have to die."

Peter furrowed his brow. "Why wouldn't Aying call in the rest of the SS to find Neil, if all this were true?"

Neil patted his young friend on the back. "Two reasons, Peter. I have zero doubt that my former employer has no desire for this story to get out. If the Nazis knew an American, in the employ of the government, was here to kill Hitler, we could become mortal enemies overnight. Lord wants the Germans focused on the Russians and peoples east of here. They might even change my identity if they were to kill me."

"So, even though the U.S. doesn't like Hitler, they want him to win?" Peter asked, screwing up his face.

"Sort of," Neil said. "*Some* in our government would like Hitler to run east for a while, to weaken the Russians."

Peter nodded his understanding. "And the second reason Aying wouldn't call in the SS?"

Neil looked at the other adults. They all answered in unison. "Money."

"Lord has almost certainly promised Aying a fortune for his cooperation," Neil added. "He'll pay it, too, assuming they can find and kill me."

The assembled group grew quiet. Neil broke the silence.

"Since Aying and Lord are busy getting loaded in the hotel bar, I think we should get the children out tonight. Too much could change in the span of another day. And this rain will provide good cover. There'll be less of a chance of someone wandering by and seeing the commotion."

Kraabe nodded at the group. "Then call Falkenberg. Let's tell him it's time to earn his money."

* * *

"*Ja?*"

"Oberst Falkenberg?"

"Nein. He is busy."

"Get him."

"Who is this?"

"It's the person he's been waiting for."

A bump as the earpiece was placed on a table. Mumbling in the background. Footsteps coming quickly. *"Falkenberg."*

"Do you have everything ready?"

"Do you have my money?"

"Yes."

"Then everything is ready."

"We need to go tonight, as in, right now."

Silence.

"Did you hear me?"

"I'm here."

"Did you hear me?"

"Ja."

"Can you make it happen?"

"I believe so."

"Not good enough."

"Yes."

"Good. Where do I meet you and your men?"

Silence.

"I haven't much time."

"My fee doubles if we go now."

"I don't have that much." A lie.

"Yes, you do." A double-bluff.

"If I can scrape together almost that much, say ninety percent of double, can we meet in one hour?" *Say yes, you asshole.*

"Why wait an hour? If you can scrape it together, we can meet in ten minutes."

"Where?"

"North side of the Hauptbahnhof, next to the church. It's secluded. There's a spur where you'll see the train and the trucks."

"One hour, and tell your men not a word escapes to anyone."

"You bring my money and we can lay siege to the city if you like."

"One hour."

Neil placed the earpiece in the cradle and turned to the expectant crowd. "The show starts...right now."

Chapter Sixty-One

UNFORTUNATELY, THE HEAVY RAIN MOVED SWIFTLY EAST, leaving in its wake chilly temperatures and a scattered sky of purple clouds racing over the swollen moon. The men were busy loading items into Thomas' Opel Blitz truck. After loading two water cans, and wincing at the pulling in his side, Neil turned to the three men. "When we get to the train, Peter will ride up front with me. Doctor Kraabe, do you want to go with us?"

"I didn't spend my last two years working on this for nothing. Of course, I'll go."

Neil nodded. "Good. Then I want you in one of the cars with the children, hopefully near the center of the train. I'm not sure how the boxcars will be set up, but in the event we have any stops, you keep your eye on what's happening. I don't know the soldiers we're working with, or Falkenberg for that matter. We'll need to be on our guard every step of the way."

Neil turned to Thomas. "Herr Lundren, since you're our policeman, I want you on the back of the train for security. We'll put Madeline back there with you, and Gabi can come to the front with me."

Thomas chewed on his lower lip for a moment. "I'm not so sure that's where I can best serve you."

Neil was loading the last of the items and, upon hearing this, he stopped and frowned. "What's that mean?"

Thomas motioned to Doctor Kraabe. "The doctor here says I've most likely got cancer of the lung...or lungs. I'm running on borrowed time."

Peter's mouth turned downward. He looked Thomas up and down and, without hesitation, put his arm around the old man. Thomas affirmed the embrace, his eyes glistening.

"How can you be so sure?" Neil asked.

Doctor Kraabe nodded but said nothing.

Neil stepped closer to Thomas. "That doesn't mean you won't get well again. You should still come with us."

Thomas shook his head. It was the type of quick, firm headshake that means only one thing. "No, I'll stay behind. I already gave the SS my name, and when they find out they've been deceived, I'm as good as dead anyway."

"Not if you escape to Yugoslavia," Neil countered.

"I'm too old and too sick to escape. It doesn't appeal to me at this stage in my life."

"So what'll you do?"

"I'll do what does *appeal* to me." The old man's silver stubble twitched as his face crinkled into a smile. "Perhaps I can be a bit of an obstruction for Aying and your Mister Lord."

Neil stared into the old man's eyes. While he would have liked to have had time to dissuade him of his plan, he knew from experience that each person is responsible for their own actions. This was Thomas Lundren's call. "So be it," Neil said, extending his hand. Once the two men shook, Neil glanced around.

"Where are the girls?"

"I think they're downstairs," Peter answered.

"We leave in five minutes." Neil thudded through the house and down the stairs. When he reached the secret passageway, the scent of perfume assaulted his nose. He pushed the door open, his eyes widening at the two creatures before him. Gabi was decked out in bright red, Madeline in black. The girls wore heels, tall ones, displaying shiny legs. Their hair was burnished and coiffed, framing porcelain doll faces accented by just enough makeup that they didn't look overdone. Central to both outfits were jutting breasts, standing out like beacons, accentuated and revealing enough to attract the eyes of any man with a heartbeat. Madeline turned away from Neil, studying her own face in the small wall mirror while Gabi zipped up Madeline's form-fitting dress from behind.

"What the hell is all this?" Neil bellowed.

Gabi turned to Neil. "Madeline, could you leave us for a moment?"

Once they were alone, Gabi walked to Neil and placed her arms around his waist. "We're going to occupy your pursuers while you move the children."

Neil didn't breathe, didn't speak, just stood there. "Are you completely insane?" he finally blurted in his native English.

Gabi turned back to the small table, donning a gold bangle. She leaned down, taking a final look in the mirror before turning back to Neil. "Remember when I told you I didn't want to be window dressing?"

Neil remained silent.

"Remember when I said I would rather live and die than lead a boring existence?"

"Yes, I remember."

"Well, I wasn't kidding."

"I can *see* that you weren't kidding. And this is how you do it?"

"Go and retrieve those precious children and get them across the border. Tell me where to meet you and I *will* be there." She eyed him in the mirror. "*After* I've done my part of this job."

Neil's tone started low and grew in volume. "They'll kill you, Gabi. They'll kill you stone dead. Preston Lord is a murderer, of the worst sort, and he'll smile at you while he disembowels you."

She turned, placing her arms over his shoulders, nearly eye-to-eye in her high heels. "Well then, I guess I'll have to be careful, won't I?"

Neil closed his eyes, willing himself to be patient. "Gabi, you're in over your head. They'll figure you out...Madeline, too."

"We'll just have to take that chance."

"Are you even listening to me?"

"I've considered your every word."

Neil lowered his eyes to the floor. "I can't stop you, can I?"

"No, you cannot. This is what I want to do. I'm no different than you, am I? Stubborn as hell and propelled by what I believe is right."

His eyes came up to hers as he noted her evident excitement over what was to come and, at that moment, he understood her better than he ever had before. His chest hitched once as he chuckled sadly, feeling oddly defeated, though he didn't know why.

"I love you, Neil. No matter what happens to me, or you, or both of us, I want you to know I've fallen in love with you. I cannot imagine ever being with another man after you."

Neil looked away, overcome with an image of Emilee, the last, and only, woman he'd ever told he loved. As he was about to respond, Gabi shook her head, touching a finger to his lips.

Then she kissed him, fully, holding his head in her hands. Finished, she pulled back from Neil, a confident smile on her face. "I won't forget anything you've said about Lord and Aying. Madeline and I are big girls. So, from this point on, just worry about your end of things. We'll be fine."

Neil went into his pocket and handed her a wad of money. "Listen closely. Meet us tomorrow, in Jesenice, in Yugoslavia. I've never been there, so I don't know any landmark to give you." He looked to the low ceiling, thinking. "The main train station. Be there, acting like a passenger, at three in the afternoon. In case one of us is delayed, do the same thing the following day. And the one after that, if need be." He stepped away and came back with a map.

"Here we are," he said, touching the map. "And here's Jesenice. In case you drive the truck, I want you to memorize the route, and a secondary route in case that one is blocked."

She took it. "I will."

"If they get tipped off to who you are—"

"Then Madeline and I will make our way there in hiding. I *can* do this, Neil."

"How will you cross the border?" he asked.

"I'll manage."

"But you won't be able to just—"

"I will manage," she interrupted.

Neil shook his head. "Promise me you'll be careful."

Gabi nodded. "I promise." She touched his face. "*You* be careful, Neil. And look after Peter."

"Peter will be fine." Neil wore a blithe smile, like a boy about to go out to play after having been cooped up by rain for three days straight. "Our part is going to be fun."

"See...we both feel that way."

"You got it? Jesenice...main train station...three in the afternoon."

"See you in Jesenice." She kissed him again.

* * *

Moments before, after she had left the underground chamber, Madeline pulled the door shut behind her and lingered in the wine cellar. There was a bit of light there, spilling in from the stairway that led up to the kitchen. As the muffled voices of Neil and Gabi floated through the cool cellar, she knelt, careful not to get dust on the tight black dress. From the bottom shelf, after quietly removing six bottles of Bordeaux, she lifted a small plank, retrieving a single item from a hidden compartment. Madeline stuffed the item into her clutch, making her way upstairs and waiting, cigarette in hand.

The item might come in handy later.

* * *

Thomas drove his truck with Doctor Kraabe in the cabin beside him. Despite Neil's objections, Peter rode with him in the bed of the old Opel, carrying Neil's second pistol while Neil held his Colt at his side. Schatze was with them, hanging her head out of the rails of the truck as it bumped over the trolley tracks on Maximilian Strasse.

The rain had apparently been pushed out by a cold front because the temperature was dropping rapidly. They drove into the Pradl neighborhood before doubling back to the Hauptbahnhof from the east. Thomas killed the lights on the truck as a passenger train departed. As soon as it passed, he crossed the tracks, following the access road to the south, just above the main yard. Neil saw the train, only six cars in total, including the engine. It was sitting to their left, nearly concealed by trees and scrub brush. Beside it were several trucks and a staff car. Neil could see the cherry glow of cigarettes, the mark of soldiers the world over, causing his worst craving since he'd quit.

"Over there," Neil said to Thomas through the back glass. Thomas stopped near the assembled group and shut off the engine. Two presumed soldiers, dressed in plain dark shirts and dungarees, took positions on the sides of the truck, both men carrying shiny black MP-35 sub-machine guns around their neck.

"Wer ist Dremel?" one of them asked.

Neil called out his presence, climbing down from the back. The soldier started to frisk him when Neil pulled back and snapped at the man in sharp German. "I'm armed and, in case Falkenberg didn't tell you, I'm in charge here."

"Disarm him and let him through," came the sound of Falkenberg's high-German accent from the darkened staff car.

When Neil didn't move, Falkenberg said, "No one is trying to double-cross you. I just want to complete our deal before we proceed."

Unsure why he trusted Falkenberg, Neil placed his Colt in the soldier's hand and headed to the staff car. Falkenberg exited the black Mercedes, eyeing Neil in the darkness. He wore dark wool slacks and a black Greek fisherman's sweater.

"Come this way," Falkenberg said, taking Neil to the side. "Is that the full amount?" Falkenberg asked, gesturing to the bag.

"It's all there, Leo. If you're going to count it, could you please get on with it? We're pressed for time."

The German colonel took the bag back to his car, opening the rear door and using his light to briefly survey the contents. After placing the bag in the trunk and murmuring something to his driver, he returned to Neil.

"What's your plan?"

Neil informed Falkenberg of the location of the mine, estimating that their cargo of children and weapons would nearly fill the boxcars.

"Weapons?"

"They'll come in handy," Neil said. "We can stack the crates behind the doors of the boxcars. Then we'll hide the children behind them."

"Where did you get them?"

"My associate purchased them before Aying killed him."

"Very well." Falkenberg had one of the soldiers retrieve the train's engineer and, without going into detail about the items they'd be loading, Neil told the location of the mine, as well as the spur the train could transfer to for loading.

"We'll need a few mine cars," the engineer volunteered.

"I agree," Neil answered. "But I didn't know where to find such a thing."

The man lit a cigar, puffing for a moment before he said, "No problem. There's a supply house right where we'll transfer off the main line to go up the spur to the mine."

Neil thanked him before Falkenberg sent him back to the train. Neil turned back to the colonel. "Do you have my Baratol?"

"I have a substitute." Neil cocked his head but Falkenberg halted him with two vertical palms. "It's better, trust me. German engineering, you know…"

"And these soldiers, we'll need them to work and, if necessary, provide defense. This train *has* to make it to Yugoslavia. There can be no failures."

Falkenberg handed Neil a bound folder. "In there you have all necessary paperwork containing every stamp and seal imaginable. In the event we're stopped—and you can count on it at the border, if not before—this will ensure safe passage."

Neil nodded, extending his hand to Falkenberg, who took it. "Let's get a move on. We've got a great deal of loading to do, and I want to get to that border before the sun comes up tomorrow."

Falkenberg summoned his men for a sterilized briefing. Everyone boarded the train, all except Thomas who, after a quick conference with Neil, set out for a destination several kilometers past the mine.

Chapter Sixty-Two

IT WAS FULLY DARK IN INNSBRUCK. The gilded gas lamps above the wooden sidewalk bathed the center of the rustic resort town in amber light. Soft Italian music wafted through the air, coming from the patio of a restaurant near the Tyroler Inn. The town oozed affluence, marked by finely-attired couples promenading hand in hand in the cool night air. Most had left their children at home in the care of a nanny from Italy or Egypt or Rumania. But the children weren't on the parents' minds this evening. This, like every night in stylish Innsbruck, was a time to be seen in one's finest, looking one's best. And none looked better than the dashing couple strutting around the corner onto Innstrasse. Their names were Madeline Seelbach and Gabi Heinz.

But, on this night, the girls had decided to be someone else. Madeline instructed Gabi not to give her name to anyone, to be perfectly coy. However, in the event she was questioned, she was still to use her Christian name, which was Gabrielle. Her last name would be Hoffman, another common German name that started with the letter H.

Madeline, while half Jewish, had a perfectly Germanic family name. Even still, having been secretive for some time, she was quite used to the usage of pseudonyms. Tonight, Madeline employed her favorite name, which she wished her mother had named her: Katarina. In the event she had to produce a family name, she would go with the decidedly German, and quite Christian, name Kreuz, meaning "cross."

While dressed to the nines, they had chosen to steer clear of formalwear, which might limit the bars they would feel comfortable in. Madeline's black dress, courtesy of Gabi's shopping trip in Salzburg, had been too large on her petite frame. But Gabi, being quite handy with a needle and thread, expertly re-seamed the outfit, perfectly accentuating the getup to Madeline's curves. She wore no jewelry other than a faux pearl necklace and a matching clasp in her hair. In her left hand was the black clutch, its slight bulge barely noticeable.

Gabi, on the other hand, wore a tight-fitting red dress with black trim, adorned with a cloche hat. Her hair was fashionably curled, so that her long locks tucked up closely to her neck and ears, showcasing the faux diamond earrings she had purchased in Salzburg. Her dress was cut above the knee and tapered to mimic the mermaid look, displaying her long legs, made even more alluring by the high, stiletto-style heels. In her gloved hand, Gabi held a black clutch, which, unlike Madeline's, contained nothing illicit.

They stopped outside of the Tyroler Inn, already drawing looks from every man within a city block.

"Are you sure you want to do this?" Gabi asked, suddenly feeling a spate of panic.

"Yes," Madeline breathed. She snapped her fingers at a passing man. "Cigarettes, please." The man almost ripped his jacket as he shoved his hand inside, producing two cigarettes and a light for both women.

"Might I accompany you both in—"

"Sorry, but no," Madeline said with a dismissive wave. The man took a final eyeful of both women before he hurried down the street like a whipped pup.

The two women giggled, the levity of the brush-off being just the tonic they needed.

When the moment had passed, Madeline's painted red lips straightened. "It's time."

"Shall we go?"

"Lead on."

The doorman beamed at the two women, opening the door adjacent to the revolving door and sweeping his gloved hand with a great flourish. The women stepped into the lobby, heading toward the rear of the hotel, as they had been instructed. The music was overpowering in the arched back hallway. People spilled out of the darkened bar. Women stood against the walls, while their suitors leaned close to their ears, trying to convince them to leave and do something their mothers had long ago warned them against. Soldiers stood in groups outside the door, laughing and gesturing wildly with their hands. Drunk, as usual.

Gabi spun just before entering the bar, whispering, "Gabrielle Hoffman. Gabrielle Hoffman. Gabrielle Hoffman." She closed her eyes, swallowing several times.

Madeline gripped her hand. "Will you calm down? This is nothing. We'll find them, sit with them a while and make sure they get very drunk. And, if need be, we'll go back to their rooms. It doesn't mean we have to go through with anything. Remember, the job is keeping them occupied."

"Revolting," Gabi answered, curling her lip.

Madeline nodded. "Well, I agree, but I'm also ten years older than you. Just wait, this won't be the last time you have to act fake to occupy a man who vexes you. And sometimes, that man is your own."

The two women crushed out their cigarettes in an urn before striding to the bar and sauntering inside.

* * *

The children and their caretakers were evacuated first. Just as he had earlier, Neil tried to spot Fern but was unable to make her out from the others. He didn't think it would be a good idea to single her out—not yet. The children's excitement was understandably uncontainable. And while a bathing system had been devised by the women, the children were still quite filthy, especially their clothing. It made them all look similar. But other than their incredibly pale skin, the children looked remarkably healthy. As they were loaded onto the train cars and given strict instruction about remaining quiet, the Irish caretaker explained to Neil the many methods they'd employed to combat sickness. Their most important item were Redoxon tablets—synthetic vitamin C. This prevented the children and caretakers from getting scurvy.

"What did Jacob tell you when he left?" Neil asked.

"He said he couldn't risk coming back until it was time to leave. He didn't want to tip anyone to our position. And he warned us that it could take weeks or even months to arrange the transport."

Neil shook his head. "I find it amazing that, after all this time, you stuck with it."

The caretaker's smile was wan. "When the alternative is imprisonment, or death, one finds the fortitude. This isn't my first time, either. I've brought three groups of children out—this will be my fourth. There are always delays so I try not to worry."

"But you've made it each time?"

"Never lost one child."

"I can't imagine what you all went through in that tunnel," Neil remarked.

"It's always hardest on the young ones."

"How many in this group are what you consider *young*?"

"We have twenty-six children under the age of three."

Neil whistled. "Any infants?"

"No, thankfully."

"Do you know one child named Fern?"

"Of course. She's with us."

Neil fought to remain passive. "Is she okay?"

The woman shrugged. "About like the others, why?"

"I met her grandparents. We can talk about it later." He pointed to the train. "Please meet with the other caretakers. I don't know what to expect tonight, but if we get stopped, you need to make sure everyone hiding behind those crates is absolutely silent. One sneeze, cough or sniffle could put all of us in a prison camp or…"

She assured him she understood.

Once the children were dispersed through the boxcars, the weapons had to be loaded. Because the mine cars weren't motorized, they had to be pushed out. A system was developed, using six of the soldiers to push and pull each loaded car to the midway point of the mine, where the track leveled out and the ice abated. At that point, two of the soldiers would transfer the items to the second mine car, pushing it the rest of the way to the waiting train. Each circuit, including the transfer, took ten minutes. Men switched after every transfer, getting a slight break on the upper half of the circuit. Good Germans they were, the system was quick and efficient.

Peter stayed with Neil at the train. Neil put him in charge of the loading, telling him to make certain each car was only loaded enough to block the view of the children.

When the doorways were full, Neil instructed the soldiers to stop loading.

"What about the remaining weapons?" an older soldier asked.

Neil shrugged. "Once we cross that border, you can come back and pilfer to your heart's delight for all I care."

Oberst Falkenberg called out to Neil. With a cigarette holder clamped between his sparkling teeth, the German spread a map on the hood of his unmarked staff car. He asked Neil to hold his hand lamp while he traced the route of the train with his finger.

"There are guard stations here and here, run by the military, which probably won't take any interest in you," Falkenberg said. The train's engineer, who was fully briefed, sauntered up behind them. "The last stop, here," indicated Falkenberg, at a point on the map at the border, "is the border checkpoint."

"And the paperwork you gave me will provide me safe passage?"

Falkenberg paused. "It should..."

Neil turned the hand lamp to Falkenberg. "I told you I needed a green light...safe, *unobstructed* passage all the way to Yugoslavia."

"And that's what I've given you. But that checkpoint, which may be benign, is out of my control. Its authority falls under the SS. If they are there and manning it, how am I to prevent a search?"

"And what do you suggest I do if they stop us?"

Falkenberg removed the cigarette holder, blowing his smoke away from Neil. "I would stop, show the papers, and then proceed. The papers are in perfect order."

"They'll search the train."

"Why?"

"They just will. Operations like this never run without a hitch," Neil said, speaking from years of experience.

"The weapons you're carrying are being moved by the military for a future operation of great importance," Falkenberg said, smiling thinly. "Threaten anyone who stops you with upsetting said operation. Tell them that Himmler will personally cut off their balls. And use that false Reichsleiter identification of yours."

Neil frowned. "False?"

"Come now, Dieter," Falkenberg said with a wink. "It fooled me at first, but not anymore. I did some checking. It's of no matter, anyway. I've been properly remunerated."

Neil didn't respond. He turned to the train's engineer.

"Can you help talk us through the border?"

"I've made enough legal crossings that, yes, I feel confident we'll be okay."

"Did they search your train each time?"

"Rarely."

"Well, if they do, just know that things could get very interesting."

The engineer pushed his cap back. "Everything's interesting these days."

"How many SS are typically there?"

"A couple, if any. Sometimes it's just civilian guards under the SS's employ."

Neil hitched his thumb to the locomotive. "How fast is she?"

The engineer turned his head and took in the length of the full train. "Pretty weighty load, even though short. We're lucky because much of our route is downhill, so I think she can make a hundred if we can keep our head'a steam."

"A hundred kilometers per hour, meaning about sixty miles an hour?"

The engineer's smile widened. "You want a hundred miles an hour, you're gonna have to go ask Hitler himself."

"And what's the distance to the border?"

"There's no straight shot, due to the mountains and hills. But this is a trip I've made many times, so I know it well…365 kilometers from where we stand."

"So about four hours?" Neil asked.

"Really depends how quickly we can get up to speed. My old iron horse might do better than the hundred I promised so, if we don't have to stop, let's call it three and a half."

Neil nodded, checking his watch. The schedule was looking good. Too good. He turned back to the colonel.

"Oberst Falkenberg, as soon as we're loaded, we're moving. Get half of your men aboard those trucks and I'll take the other half on the train. We'll rally…" Neil turned the light to the map, running his finger northwest from the border, "…here, at Winkl."

"Rally for what?" Falkenberg asked.

"Do you remember why I'm paying you for your soldiers? There's a possibility of a firefight. And they damn sure *will* fight, if need be."

Neil turned and walked into the tunnel. He needed to find Doctor Kraabe.

* * *

A hazy veil of smoke hung stagnant inside the bar. The music was so loud a person could barely hear herself think. Gabi and Madeline brushed off the attendant at the front. Though she was shaking with nerves, Gabi poked out her lips and blinked her eyes slowly, doing her best sultry Marlene Dietrich impression. As they walked to the bar, Madeline perused the room, noticing with satisfaction that nearly every set of male eyes was looking their way. They perched on the bar's high swivel chairs, turning to face the crowd. Madeline curled her finger at the bartender, ordering champagne for Gabi, a vodka and tonic for herself.

Playing for the crowd, Madeline instructed Gabi to lean into her ear, tell her something, and then laugh. Gabi said, "We look like brainless tarts." Madeline giggled, genuinely, leaning her head back as she got into the spirit of things. The high chair had caused her dress to ride up to mid-thigh. Gabi placed her right hand on Madeline's leg, still laughing, rubbing upward to the hem of the dress. Madeline rubbed the back of Gabi's neck and glanced back into the crowd, predictably seeing a gaggle of German officers leering at them, their tongues exposed, leaving them panting like a pack of overheated dogs.

The drinks arrived and Madeline toasted the evening loudly, guzzling her drink before smacking the tumbler on the bar and ordering another. When she turned back around, standing before her was a tall man in a German officer's white tunic. At Jakey's insistence, Madeline had studied the German insignia after the Anschluss, correctly identifying this man as a major in the regular Heer—the German Army.

Madeline arched her eyebrows at the man. She gauged his age to be about her own. He had a long, narrow face and deep-set brown eyes. His hair was neatly parted and freshly barbered, and his scent was that of sandalwood soap. She could tell he was the type of man who found himself far more charming and attractive than did anyone else.

The man took both of their hands, bowed, and kissed each. "Good evening, my sweethearts," he said, using the tone of local gentry who had come to nobly claim the tax that was owed to him. "My name is Karl Lollar. I'm from Stuttgart and I am most honored to meet you both."

The women looked at one another and laughed.

Karl tried to smile, but it was obvious he was being laughed at, not with. He blinked several times. "Might I inquire as to what's so funny?"

Madeline continued to stare into Gabi's hazel eyes. Gabi nodded. Madeline turned to the man. "Karl," she said, using her lacquered nail to press his shoulder backward, "I'm afraid our date might not like you trying to pick us up."

Karl swiveled his head back and forth, taking on a stilted expression that belied his efforts to remain good-natured. "Well, unless your date is Rudolf Hess, then I'm not too concerned. In fact, I'm quite adept at boxing, and grappling."

"Oh, really, Karl Lollar from Stuttgart?" Gabi asked, setting off another round of sniggering.

Karl's mouth tightened. He tugged at his collar. "Why don't you tell me who he is, so I can have a proper talk with him? Perhaps outside."

"Would you?" Madeline asked. "Because we cannot seem to find him."

Karl's good nature evaporated. "His name," he commanded.

"You really want to know?" Madeline asked.

"Indeed."

"Anton Aying," Gabi answered, ending the suspense. "Standartenführer Anton Aying, of the Schutzstaffel."

It appeared, within a second of hearing the name, that Karl Lollar of Stuttgart needed to sit on the toilet. His face became splotchy, his breathing ragged. He stammered through something akin to, "I see…I now understand."

"So, not Rudolf Hess," Madeline said, thoroughly enjoying the experience of having a German Army officer teetering on soiling his uniform in her presence, "but would you like to box and grapple with Anton? If so, we'll tell him that Karl Lollar, of Stuttgart—a major in the Heer—would like to step outside with him."

Karl shook his head to the stops as fresh springs of sweat appeared on his neck. He dug into his pocket, producing twenty reichsmarks, placing them on the counter, careful not to touch either woman. "Please *don't* tell him that, and do accept my apologies. Perhaps this will pay for your next few rounds." He smiled politely, nervously, before turning to leave. He stopped. "Shall I retrieve the honorable Standartenführer for you?"

Madeline eyed him, smoke from her cigarette wrapping around her head like a white ribbon. "Karl?"

"Yes?"

"Just leave."

Major Karl Lollar, of Stuttgart, scurried back to his table, shaking his head to the rest of the men sitting with him, mouthing "*nein*" over and over again. They were all majors or captains and, after witnessing their comrade's hasty retreat, each man turned to gawk. Eventually someone at the table managed to get the story from Karl. Upon hearing the name Anton Aying, each man spun around to concentrate on their libation.

Gabi sipped her champagne and leaned close to Madeline. "This is almost fun."

Madeline's smile dissolved. "Almost."

The girls sat in silence until they finished their drinks, occasionally catching each other's eye. A melancholy seemed to descend over Madeline.

"Smile," Gabi said.

"I know, I know. Sorry."

"What were you thinking about?" Gabi asked, crushing out a cigarette.

"Take a guess."

"He'd be proud of you."

It took a moment, but suddenly Madeline brightened at Gabi's suggestion. "Yeah, he would. He'd let me have it for being a fool, but he *would* be proud of me."

"I agree."

"Are you ready to do this?"

Gabi nodded. "I am."

"Are you sure you're up to it?"

"We're going to find out, aren't we?"

"I want Aying," Madeline said. "No matter what, I want Aying." She turned, motioning to the bartender who almost knocked over his partner to get to her.

"Do you know Standartenführer Aying?"

"Of course," the bartender yelled in return.

"Please tell me he's still here."

He pointed across the bar to the back corner. "Over there."

Madeline slumped in relief. "Still with the American?"

"The last I saw he was. They're pretty juiced up, if you know what I mean."

Madeline pushed Karl Lollar's money to the bartender, winking at him. "We have no more use for this money."

As they pushed their way through the crowded bar, Gabi leaned into Madeline's ear. "I hope, after tonight, I never see another uniform again."

"Me, too," Madeline answered flatly. "Me, too."

They reached the rear table, spotting the SS Standartenführer and the ferret-faced American facing outward in the round booth. From the table next to the booth, a junior SS man stood, blocking their way with two meaty hands.

"We're here to see the Standartenführer," Madeline said, leaning around the bodyguard like an inflamed fan of a movie star.

"Yes, and his friend," Gabi added, mimicking Madeline's eagerness.

Chapter Sixty-Three

IT WAS NEARLY MIDNIGHT. The caretakers and children had been instructed and reassured—then the weapon crates were moved to hide their presence in each boxcar. Neil directed the engineer and Peter to climb up on the engine and to await his arrival before they were to leave. Neil then walked to the rear of the train, a traditional caboose, stationing Doctor Kraabe there with four of Falkenberg's soldiers. Neil armed Kraabe from the cache of weapons, giving him a Mauser MG-34 machine gun after making sure the action worked and the firing pin was installed. Speaking more to the soldiers than Kraabe, he told them to be watchful, in the event they were covertly pursued.

"You can probably go through a thousand rounds a minute with that Swiss cheese maker but, if you do, you'll burn up the barrel," Neil said, not caring if the soldiers already knew this. "I don't think it will, but if something untoward *does* happen, use those rounds judiciously. A few bursts from that Mauser will go a long way."

Kraabe hung onto every word, a liberated smile on his face. It was like he was experiencing a second childhood.

We'll see how his face looks if lead really starts flying, Neil thought ruefully.

He found Falkenberg, asking him if his soldiers knew the train was to be defended at all costs, even against their fellow Germans.

"That's why they're wearing civilian clothes, Herr Dremel. These are elite soldiers. You could tell them to shoot their own brother and they would ask you, 'Head or heart?'" He and Neil positioned the soldiers up and down the length of the train, inside the door of the boxcars, surrounded by crates of weapons. Neil viewed each of the doors, satisfied that no one would see the dozens of children hidden behind the crates.

Falkenberg would follow the same general route in his staff car, and would keep in contact by syncing the staff car's transmitter with the radio on the train.

Ten more minutes passed before the Opel Blitz reappeared, a small amount of steam escaping from the hood. "Never knew I could drive that fast," Thomas pronounced. He followed Neil into the steam engine's control compartment, tormented by a coughing fit from the small climb. Neil glanced at Peter and the engineer, both wearing concerned looks over Thomas' paroxysm.

Holding a scarlet-blotted handkerchief to his mouth, Thomas pointed to a location on the map with his finger. "It's here, at the water tower. It'll be on your right side as you travel," he rasped. "You should be able to see it from quite a distance, but you'll have to be a crack shot."

Neil nodded, marking the spot with a grease pencil. "How high?"

"About three meters. Should be a level shot for you if you're up here."

After studying the map another moment, Neil straightened, extending his right hand. "I can't thank you enough, Thomas. You could've ended everything if you had not been open-minded."

Thomas accepted Neil's hand. "Not everything in this world is black and white. Besides, I haven't been too pleased with my own government since I was a younger man than you."

"Well, regardless, you've been invaluable." Neil turned to Peter. "Peter, say goodbye to Officer Lundren."

Obviously sensing the gravitas of the moment, Peter hugged Thomas, telling him he was the last person to ever speak to his mother. Thomas accepted the boy's hug, clapping him solidly on the back.

After a moment the old lawman pulled back and nodded with finality to the group, saying, "Good luck, because I think you're going to need it tonight."

"You're clear on what you're going to do?" Neil asked as Thomas backed down the five-rung metal ladder.

"I'm very clear." He stood on the ground, looking up at Neil as he stifled a cough. "Let's just hope I'm not too late."

As Thomas drove away, Neil could see him bent double, coughing and retching.

Having stepped back into the cab of the locomotive, Neil instructed the engineer to get the train moving. It was now nearly one in the morning. Less than four hours to freedom.

As the locomotive began to move the train, accelerating faster than normal due to the downhill grade, Neil watched Peter as he studied the engineer's actions. Schatze was on her hind legs, her front paws resting on a ledge, enjoying the growing wind from the speed of the train, blissfully unaware of what might lie ahead.

Neil left the group, moving to the rear of the locomotive. He stood on the elevated platform, letting the chill night air blow his hair backward as he removed a brand new pack of cigarettes from inside his sweater, along with his lighter. He held a cigarette between his lips as he unsuccessfully tried the lighter several times, his mind overrun in melancholia as his thoughts raced between Jakey, and then Emilee, and then their unborn child, and then Gabi, and then Madeline, and then

Thomas Lundren. As the track leveled out, Neil tossed the unlit cigarette away and went to work—he hoped it would help him clear his mind.

Below him, in a crate, was an MG-34, identical to the one he had placed in the caboose with Doctor Kraabe and the German soldiers. Neil removed it, tossing the crate and padding over the side and placing the spare barrel and accompanying asbestos glove in a notch at the edge of the platform. He ripped six individual rounds from the belt, placing them in his pocket, then set about locking and loading the machine gun with the belt of ammo from the steel box. Neil called to Peter, instructing him how to feed him the belt in the event of a firefight. A quick study, Peter understood the concept.

"See this right here," Neil said, pointing to a rectangular indention on the side of the gun. "Hot brass comes flying out from here, so make sure you stand away from it. I've seen red-hot shells actually stick to a careless soldier's cheek before, cauterizing itself to the skin."

"Ouch," Peter said, wincing.

Neil removed another cigarette from the pack, bending over behind the windbreak of the engine compartment, cupping his hands and getting one lit this time.

Peter frowned. "I thought you stopped smoking to heal."

Neil exhaled through his teeth, the white smoke disappearing in the rushing wind. He tapped Peter in the chest with his fist. "Sometimes, Peter, it's okay to break a few rules."

Peter's eyes stayed locked on Neil's for some time. Then, without expression, Peter disentangled the pack of cigarettes from Neil's hand, taking one and sticking it in his mouth. He tugged the cigarette from Neil's mouth, pressing the tip to his own and puffing until it was lit. With Neil still motionless, Peter pushed the cigarette back into Neil's lips and replied with two words.

"I agree."

Neil arched his eyebrows but offered no objection.

How could he?

It was the same feeling Neil had experienced when Peter had outmaneuvered him at checkers.

The two men smoked in silence.

After their brief smoke together, Neil spent the next hour traversing the cars, checking on the children, the soldiers and Doctor Kraabe.

* * *

Things progressed rapidly at the corner table in the Tyroler Inn Bar. The two men, Preston Lord and Anton Aying, were piss drunk. Slurred words. Fumbling fingers. To Madeline's frustration, Aying took an immediate liking to Gabi and Preston Lord to herself. After a short break, the two-piece band was playing an encore. It was nearly 1 a.m. Madeline dragged on a cigarette, rolling her eyes as Lord's fingers groped around at her midsection while he occasionally tried to kiss her face and neck.

Aying, despite his inebriation, was a bit more suave in how he went about things. He'd turned in the booth, facing Gabi. In both of his hands he held one of hers, kissing it and murmuring ridiculously flattering phrases to her. Neither man seemed the least bit suspicious about why the girls had come to them.

Ego, Madeline thought. Pure ego. How many countries have toppled due to one man's swollen self-admiration?

And it wasn't until the band stopped playing that Aying motioned for the waiter, whispering something in his ear. Minutes after that, the concierge, a different one from earlier, appeared. Aying stood, pressing a wad of bills into his hand as the concierge nodded and rushed away.

"What was all that?" Madeline asked, leaning over the table and slurring her own words in an attempt to sound genuinely drunk.

"I'm getting a suite."

"Why?" she asked, beginning to panic.

She had to be with Aying. She absolutely had to.

"Preston's already got a nice one, don't you *Liebling?*" Madeline asked.

"I do. It has a big bed, too," Lord said, rotating his eyes to Gabi.

"Just hold off on that room, okay?" Madeline asked Aying. She motioned with her head to Gabi. "We need to powder our noses. Be right back." She held Gabi's gloved hand, pushing through the diminishing crowd and into the hotel lobby restroom.

Gabi untwisted a mint from the counter and said, "Haven't we held them long enough?"

"No," Madeline hissed through clenched teeth. "Not nearly long enough, and we have to get them in *one* room together."

"Why?"

"We just do. That way we can stay in contact with each other."

"How do we keep them together?"

Madeline applied lipstick, pressing her lips together. "Never you mind, just cooperate with me when we get out there. Once we all get to the room, play them along a bit, maybe another half-hour, then tell them you have to run back to the bar for something you forgot." Madeline aimed a finger at Gabi. "But go alone. Do *not* let either man accompany you."

Gabi's eyes narrowed. "I'm confused, Madeline. What are you planning?"

Madeline gripped both of her hands, squeezing tightly, smiling reassuringly. "Just do it, okay?"

Gabi nodded, a concerned look on her face.

They reappeared at the booth to find Aying and Preston Lord standing. Just then, an attendant appeared, handing both men their overcoats and hats. Madeline put her arm around Gabi's waist, pulling her close.

"I hope neither of you are tired."

Lord's eyes went wide as his mouth fell slack. He placed a palm on the table for support. Aying, however, expressed mild distaste as he turned away. The concierge reappeared, placing a heavy gold room key into Aying's hand and murmuring something to him.

"Are we ready?" Lord asked.

"To the lift," Aying commanded.

At the elevator's door, Aying instructed his junior SS man to go home and be back at eight in the morning. The attendant closed the two gates before moving the brass throw-lever up, setting the elevator in motion. They stopped at the top floor, Preston Lord's floor. When the gates were opened, Madeline tugged on Aying's hand, simultaneously grabbing Gabi around her waist.

"The two of you should come with us," she breathed. "It'll be twice as much fun."

Gabi took the cue, moving her hand up and down Aying's chest and whispering to him, "I agree. Let's all be *good friends*, tonight."

The attendant, a short, middle-aged man with a dark Caesar's crown, breathed deeply at the sight. He looked down in embarrassment, but noticeably twisted his head to make certain he heard everything.

Aying nobly lifted his chin, cinching his arm around Gabi's waist, pulling her back into the lift. "I'm a proper man and a traditionalist. Perhaps, Herr Lord, this type of thing goes on in the United States." He irritably motioned Lord and Madeline on. "But here, *we* do things a bit differently."

As the attendant locked the gates, Madeline and Gabi joined eyes. Gabi's eyes showed remorse. Madeline's sparkly eyes displayed understanding.

She waved goodbye.

For the final time.

* * *

Madeline entered Lord's quarters, a Roman-inspired corner suite with commanding views of the mountains to the north and east. Each peak was highlighted by moon glow, casting purplish light down on the majestic formations. Lord removed his jacket and pulled out his tucked-in shirt, unbuttoning it, tossing his cufflinks to the floor. From the bar he took a bottle of unopened Scotch, breaking the seal and guzzling from it. Lips glistening, a carnivorous expression on his murine face, he crossed the floor, grasping Madeline roughly and rubbing himself against her.

Madeline pushed away from him, her mind racing through a pit of dread as she moved by the window. The evening had been a disaster. The exact opposite of what she had intended to happen had happened, and even when she tried to save it with her best, and most ribald effort, it had failed miserably. And now, here she was, stuck with this creepy American who played no role in her own personal scheme.

He crossed the room again, still swigging liquor, and this time tried to yank her dress down over her breasts. She pressed him backward, irritation on her face.

He tried again.

She shoved him.

Preston Lord slapped her without hesitation. *Pop!*

The violent action was exactly what Madeline needed. She leaned back against the paned window, staring at him, her face registering appropriate shock. The salty taste of drawn blood mingled with the saliva in her mouth. Lord's wet lips glinted as he leered at her, looking like a vampire in the darkened room. Madeline thought back to Neil's descriptions of this man, just after he had come back with Peter. Neil relayed several accounts about Preston Lord, the American he was so surprised to have just seen. Neil detailed a rumor, one he believed, about a coed Lord had allegedly raped, afterward using his influence to deflect the investigation elsewhere. Neil also relayed the tales of several of the team's killings and how, after reflection, he felt Lord had ordered the individuals killed for his own personal gain.

As her face throbbed, Lord continued to ogle her, gritting his teeth in a maniacal smile.

A monster.

Just like Aying.

Different. But same.

Madeline forced a smile. "So, you want it rough, do you?" she asked, lashing out and scraping his skinny chest in a cat's swipe, drawing blood.

He touched the claw marks, chuckling.

Madeline undid her tight black dress, pushing it to the floor, leaving her heels on.

Lord's breathing became audible as he rubbed himself through his suit pants. He took another long pull on the scotch and removed his undershirt, displaying a skinny body with sinewy muscle. He moved to her, grabbing her arm and digging his own fingernails in as he pulled her to the bedroom. Madeline sucked in a sharp breath as something occurred to her. She looked back at her dress. Her clutch lay next to it.

He tossed her on the bed, slapping her legs out of the way before fully undressing.

The next four minutes were the most repulsive of her life.

When finished, Lord lay next to her, smoking a massive cigar. He stared up at the ceiling, his hand roaming her body, displaying not a hint of tenderness. It was the touch of ownership—he knew no bounds.

"Why are you in Innsbruck?" Madeline asked, the pillow nestled under her head as she stared at him, pondering what she should do.

"I go anywhere I want," Lord replied.

"But why here?"

He twisted his head to look at her. "What's it to you?" His German, while adequate, held no effort at all to add the proper accent.

She took his hand, pushing it backward. "Why are you here? Americans are running the other way, not *coming* here."

He puffed the cigar, blowing the smoke in her direction. "I'm here to kill a man." The way he said it—it was not unlike a person ordering a bowl of soup and a sandwich.

"Why?"

"He's trying to wreck my plans."

"How's that?"

Irritation spread over him as he flicked the cigar in her direction, sending ash on her torso. "Don't worry your pretty little head about it. You wouldn't understand."

"Try me."

Lord smiled indulgently, though there was no good humor involved. "Your fellow Austrian, Hitler...even though he's a fanatical, self-absorbed, world-class lunatic, is *temporarily* needed."

"Needed by whom?"

"The United States...hell, most of the world." Lord puffed the cigar. "For the time being."

"Why?"

"Because of the Russians, you little minx. Their communism makes fascism look as pleasurable as Munchkin Country from that book *The Wonderful Wizard of Oz.*"

Madeline took two deep breaths, bolstering herself before she asked, "And what of the things Hitler and the Nazis are doing to the Jews? The expulsions. The looting and burning of businesses. The killings."

Lord eyed her before turning his eyes back to the ceiling, placing the great cigar into his mouth and puffing thoughtfully. "Once...I guess it was seven or eight years ago...I screwed a Jewish gal up under the pier at Coney Island. Turns out, the nasty little whore gave me the crabs." He snorted. "I didn't notice the crabs at first. They itched a bit, but not bad enough that I knew anything was wrong." He turned, staring at Madeline. "But those little crabs started to multiply, and the itching turned to burning and then outright agony." He grinned. "Those crabs were kinda like the Jews. A few aren't too bad, but Hitler's smart. You let those bastards start multiplying and then you're in for some real trouble. They'll take over everything." He jabbed the cigar into his mouth and said, "I've got no beef that he wants to rid the world of them."

Allowing his words to burn into her mind, she remained quiet for a moment. Finally, she nodded to herself. *That settles it.* Madeline leaned over him, hand roaming. She made her voice sultry as she asked, "Can you do it again this soon?"

"Are you kidding?" he asked, putting his cigar on the nightstand.

"In just a moment," she said, standing.

"Where are you going?"

"I hope that bar of yours has some vodka. I hate scotch."

The moonlight illuminated Madeline's petite body as she crossed the room, wearing only her heels.

Chapter Sixty-Four

ANTON AYING FUMBLED WITH GABI'S DRESS as he kissed her neck and shoulder. He'd tried very hard to romance her upon entering his suite. First, he talked to her, staring into her eyes, sounding every bit the bad actor who was trying to win a part. His flowery language bored Gabi almost to tears. Aying had popped champagne, making a great production of a feeble toast about this being one of the finest nights of his life. Gabi watched him the entire time and, although she wondered where his wife and children were, she was unable to merge her current image of this insipid man with the cold-blooded killer Neil alleged him to be.

He unzipped the back of her dress, gently easing it downward as he turned her to face him. Gabi simulated a sigh, her mind elsewhere. How could she confirm that this man was as dangerous as she'd been led to believe?

"Anton?" she whispered.

He was trying to work the form-fitting dress over her hips. Pulling back, he briefly glanced at her bare breasts before looking into her eyes. "Yes, darling?"

"Anton, you don't seem to embody the descriptions I've heard of men chosen for the SS."

Aying pulled her to him. "Why, dear, because I'm a gentleman?" He brushed her cheek with a kiss before looking at her again. "Don't believe the rumors you hear about us. We are chosen for *good* reasons, not bad. And, even then, the runes have to be earned, and it's not easy. It takes great character, and much more."

"I can only imagine," she said pleasantly before intentionally troubling her voice. "But what of the actions being taken against the Jews? How do you explain that?"

Anton Aying pursed his lips, as if he'd been asked the question a thousand times before. "My dear, if I see a toddler about to wander into the street, I help it to safety. When I see a man abusing a woman, I correct him, with great prejudice." His face and voice became firm. "But a Jew, according to our Führer, isn't even human. If you were to study some of the horrid things they've done to our people, and to our great land, you'd see that. And the world court of public opinion, especially in the media, is controlled by them. A person has to dig deep for the truth because they've prevented you, and most unknowing people in the general public of all lands, from seeing what they're truly capable of."

"So you justify it by telling yourself they're less than human?"

Aying released Gabi, stepping backward. A polite smile came over his face. "My dear, you are a creation of majestic beauty and I desperately want to make love to you tonight. In fact, I hope for a future together. When I take you to the state gala in Munich, the Führer himself will be awestruck by your Aryan beauty. So, please, stop pontificating over such weighty subjects. It's harming the mood."

"Well, what if you had wound up with my friend tonight? Would you have been as pleased?"

His significant irritation began to show as their tender moment slipped away. He pulled close to her again, trying to get it back. "Katarina was grand, darling…a beautiful girl. And I'm certain our American friend is having a wonderful time right now, as should *we*."

Gabi used her hand to ease him backward. "But you think I'm prettier."

"You have substantially more qualities that attract me," he crooned. "Isn't that a diplomatic way to put it?"

She canted her head. "You won't offend me when you tell me this." She swallowed, softening her face with a smile. "But purely for her sake, so I can tell her later, had she and I wound up with the opposite man tonight, would you have enjoyed making love with Madeline?"

Aying closed his eyes, a hand moving to his forehead. "My dear…"

"Just answer, please."

"Well, of course I would. She was attractive and funny, and while a bit salacious for my—"

Gabi's words dropped like an executioner's blade. "She's Jewish."

To his credit, Standartenführer Anton Aying didn't overreact. He stopped rubbing his forehead but maintained a soft grip on Gabi with his other hand. A pinched smile appeared on his mouth before he spoke. "You're just trying to have a little fun with me, aren't you?"

Since the time Gabi was eight years old, she'd been controlled, often overpowered, by a directness that most people in society weren't comfortable with. Even in Germany, where candor and straightforwardness were prized, Gabi's occasional blunt manner had often bordered on rude or shocking. And her directness was magnified when she was cross.

Like right now.

"Do you remember Jacob Herman?" Gabi asked, challenging Aying, studying his eyes. "Jacob 'Jakey' Herman?"

Aying released her. He retrieved his cigarettes from his jacket, hanging from the wingback chair. As he lit one, with Jakey's lighter, he stared at her over the flame. Silence settled in the room as he puffed, his chest visibly moving with each breath. Gabi refused to move, standing with her dress around her waist, her own breasts rising and falling with her increased breathing. The moment was electric.

Finally, he said, "I remember him."

"You killed him."

"Yes, I did."

"He was Katarina's lover. Her real name is Madeline."

The Schutzstaffel officer blinked once. "I must say I'm a bit hurt right now. You truly are one of the most beautiful women I've ever laid eyes on. Tonight was going to be very special." His chest hitched once as he laughed quietly. "And you have balls, I'll give you that—a fine, albeit misguided, Aryan woman."

"Go to hell."

He dragged deeply on the cigarette, the tobacco popping and crackling in the quiet hotel room. Then he spoke with smoke escaping his mouth, a deadly dragon. "Did you know that the woman you speak of, that slut with the American, Jacob Herman's jewess, killed one of my men...gutted him in cold blood? And through your little revelation here, assuming it's true, you just *killed* her. And possibly yourself."

Gabi took a step forward. "I really don't think she cares if she dies tonight, nor do I."

"Oh?"

"She and I can die tonight and the world will never miss us, like two pebbles thrown into a large lake. But it's you, Standartenführer Aying, who is the loser *tonight*."

"Careful, young lady," he said, crushing out his cigarette. His eyes returned to her breasts as he moistened his lips. "I'm willing to allow you to rethink things, and you can start by completely disrobing."

She knew she should stop herself. She knew it.

But she couldn't.

"All we did tonight was distract you in the oldest way known to man, and you and that rat-faced little American were too *stupid* to realize it." Gabi spit the word "stupid." Then she beamed, emboldened by the look of horror that was growing on Aying's face. "And while you drooled all over me, Anton, it all went down right out there in Innsbruck, right under your big nose. You had no idea because you're not nearly as smart as you think."

He closed the distance in a fraction of a second, firing a backhanded right into her cheek, sending her sprawling. Gabi came to her elbows on the Oriental rug, the room spinning. She could hear Aying's rapid footsteps. His voice on the phone, snippets of phrases. *Get back to the Tyroler. Hurry. Call the alert platoon.* Speaking, yelling. *The Tyroler Inn. Come now!*

Gabi rolled to her backside, sitting up.

Anton Aying dropped the phone. He lurched and struck her again. Blackness.

Blackness.

Then light. Wisps at first, like open seams in a heavy drape. Gabi immediately felt the throbbing pain on the side of her face and head. As her eyes cleared, she realized Aying was cradling her head on his leg. His other leg was scissored over her arms and stomach—essentially holding her in a body lock. She felt radiant warmth, turning her head to see that, in her murkiness, he'd moved her in front of the fireplace. With no warning at all, he clamped his hand over her mouth. She waited, unsure of what he was doing. There were a few metallic sounds followed by the worst pain she'd ever experienced. Gabi wailed into his hand, trying to writhe but held fast by his legs. Suddenly most of the pain ceased.

And Gabi's nostrils were assaulted by the smell of scorched skin.

He loosened his legs, allowing her to sit up. She watched as he replaced his fiery orange sabre, known as a *Degen*, into the smoldering hardwoods of the fire. Gabi's eyes moved downward. He had pressed the tip of the Degen between her breasts, onto the shallow skin of her breastplate, leaving an indentation of blackened skin the size of a thumbnail.

Aying's hands were powerful, holding her hair and her neck. He allowed the hand from her neck to move downward, perversely kneading her breasts as he said, "I don't believe in the effectiveness of advance warnings. You now *know* the pain you're in for, and the next time, little lady, I'm going to burn off both of these pretty nipples."

Gabi hated herself for the tears. "Just kill me, you nauseating bastard," she wailed.

Aying smiled proudly. "That's my brave girl, and that's why I was attracted to you over the jewess. You're turning me on right now, my dear."

Gabi spat in his face.

Without another word, Aying retrieved the reheated Degen, holding the flat side of its tip into her left nipple and clamping his hand over her mouth.

As tough as she was, Gabi talked.

* * *

Doctor Kraabe and Neil were together in the caboose. Neil's boot was up on the rail, the inky shadows of the looming Venediger range of the Alps sliding by as the train labored up a steep grade. Kraabe leaned against the railing, staring at Neil. They had spoken for ten minutes about what to do in the event of a firefight. The conversation had resolved itself, and now both men seemed content to listen to the steel on steel and the chugging of the steam engine. The chill wind swirled around both men, invigorating them as the tension of the night had slowly abated with the metronomic train journey.

Gabi and Madeline were on Neil's mind. Jealousy was, perhaps, a quarter of Neil's worry when it came to Gabi. He hoped she wouldn't allow things to progress too far. He chuckled quietly as he thought about her strength. Had she been a male soldier, they would have no doubt nicknamed her "Cowboy," the obvious sobriquet bestowed on nearly every soldier who pressed harder than necessary to make a name for himself.

As his imagination began to head in an undesirable direction, Kraabe broke the silence.

"Why did you resume your smoking?"

Neil exhaled, dipping his chin, a resigned smile on his face. "I guess I wasn't too concerned with healing tonight, you know?"

The doctor grunted his disapproval. Another bout of silence set in.

Finally, the doctor turned to Neil. "I suppose you would like to know why."

Neil pitched his cigarette, the orange tip forming an arc before it tumbled in a hail of sparks on the crossties. "Like to know why about what?"

"Why it was you," Doctor Kraabe said flatly.

Neil thought back to when Gabi, on the night they were first intimate, threw the same question in his face. *Why you, Neil? Of all the people in the world, why would they call on an alcoholic from San Francisco?* Well, she hadn't quite said it that way, but that's the way Neil heard it. That had been only a week before—now it seemed like a year. And while the question had niggled at his brain during this entire journey, she'd been the only one who pressed him on it. He chose, and wanted, to believe that Jakey called him in because of his prowess, and their friendship. Gabi hadn't seemed quite so convinced.

"Yeah," Neil answered, removing his boot from the rail. "I would like to know why me. Do you know…for sure?"

"No, but I can make an educated guess."

Neil stared.

"I believe your friend chose you for two reasons. First, he trusted you more than any person on earth. He knew you had the skill and the means."

"But he knew the sort of shape I was in," Neil countered.

"And that, my friend, was the second reason. He did it to give you purpose. Jacob didn't know for certain that he was going to die. But, he had a feeling he might. And if he did die, Jacob wished his friend to come back to life…and finish what had been started." The doctor gripped Neil's shoulder, giving it a strong squeeze.

"In my estimation," Kraabe concluded, "Jacob's wish came true."

Neil stared up in the sky as the train ticked steadily southward.

* * *

Madeline glided across the room, away from the bed. Still in heels, still nude, she retrieved the item from her clutch. Then, she deflected attention from the item with a silken scarf that had been draped over a chair back. She wrapped it around her neck, twirling through the room as she worked her way back to Lord. Her eye caught a glimpse of him as she did so. His leer was back, a primal stare, dominating what was otherwise an intelligent, almost bookish face. Something must have happened to him as a child, Madeline mused, without any sort of empathy. Perhaps he'd been unloved, or possibly abused. Or maybe he was merely nasty, and it was all by his own choice. And the reason she felt no compassion for the man is because she believed it was the latter. To her, it seemed as if he was in control, supremely, of his own actions.

Like right now, as he grabbed for her, his fingers were not tilted back so she would only feel the pads of his fingertips. No, they were tensed, providing pain as his fingernails raked over her pelvis.

"Whose scarf is this?" she asked, swirling it down to the bed sheets.

"It was a woman's, a high-priced whore." Preston Lord pulled her, digging his hands into her waist as he positioned her on top of him. Once again, his fingernails bit into her skin as they began to move together. The first time had been for his surface sexual pleasure. This one, Madeline knew from experience with a number of twisted men, would be for his base desires. The warped ones.

His hands worked upward, yanking and twisting her breasts so hard she cried out. He pushed up and down, muttering the word "harder" in English.

Madeline's left hand slipped into the tangle of sheets behind her…

* * *

Standartenführer Anton Aying grabbed Gabi around the neck, nearly crushing her larynx. They stood at the door of his room, his gray eyes alight with maniacal energy.

"Make one unnecessary sound and I will kill you where you stand," he growled, his nose touching hers. He flung the door open and pulled her along as she fumbled to get her dress back up over her burned chest. Without waiting for the elevator attendant, Aying tugged at her, pulling her into the stairwell and ascending. They exited at the top floor, seeing a row of twelve doors on each side of the hallway.

Aying cursed before picking up the phone by the elevator, jiggling it and waiting with loud, audible breaths. Through the fabric Gabi touched her hand to her chest, feeling the raw, burnt spots where the Degen had scorched her skin.

"This is Standartenführer Aying. What room is Preston Lord in? What?" he yelled. "He's a diplomat, and if you don't tell me, you die!" He listened for a moment then dropped the phone on the floor.

"Let's go."

They began to walk toward the end of the hallway.

* * *

"Harder, bitch," Lord grunted. He pinched her side with enough force to leave a bruise. She could feel his legs tense; he was preparing to change positions.

It was time.

"Preston?" Madeline stopped moving. His face contorted in a mask of anger.

"What the hell are you stopping for?"

"I need you to listen to me for a moment."

He grunted in frustration. "What the hell is this? We're supposed to be screwing, not talking."

"I want you to know something."

He became silent.

Madeline smiled at him.

"What the hell is wrong with you?" he yelled.

"Preston, I'm Jewish."

His lips parted as his eyes flicked back and forth to each of hers, no doubt unconcerned with the fact that she was Jewish, but quite concerned with why she would be telling him this—in this way. Madeline knew that a man with his intelligence quotient, despite all his misgivings, would surely realize there would be more to this admission than merely proud Judaism.

He began to try to move her off of him, but she clamped his narrow frame with her thighs, her hands remaining behind her back.

Madeline said, "You told me Jews were less than human but, before I told you I'm Jewish, you certainly seemed to be enjoying yourself."

Her shoulders and arms jerked slightly as she completed a movement behind her back.

Lord cocked an eyebrow.

One second.

Two seconds.

Both hands came around her body. Her right hand dropped a ring on his chest—it had a slightly crooked pin sticking from its end. In her other hand was a brand new German M-39 fragmentation grenade.

"Compliments of Neil Reuter *and* Jakey Herman," Madeline said in accented English. Her hands covered the grenade, pressing it into his stomach as she tilted her head backward, laughing loudly, luxuriously.

Preston Lord's eyes bulged as he shrieked like a young girl.

* * *

The shockwave knocked Gabi to the floor and threw Aying spinning against a recessed doorjamb. They had been two doors away when the door splintered and blew outward, the explosion sounding like the end of days in the confines of the narrow hallway. Gabi brought herself to all fours, staring open-mouthed at the shattered door. The room number remained, upside down on a barely clinging nail. Her mind raced backward, thinking of the things Madeline had said earlier.

Before she could finish her thought process, guests began to emerge from their rooms, hurrying past and to the stairs as a quickly recovering Aying directed them, no doubt wanting privacy so he could see what had actually occurred.

After the last man and woman passed them—the woman in hysterical tears and the man wiggling his index fingers in both of his ears—Aying held a crooked finger to Gabi's face, commanding her to stay still, despite the fact she could barely hear. She defied Aying by coming back to a standing position and worked her mouth open and shut, trying to get her own hearing back.

He kicked the broken door before stepping into the darkened space. Gabi could see, while even though the lights had blown out, enough light spilled in through the shattered windows from Innstrasse to illuminate the smoky scene. Aying touched a handkerchief to his mouth as he turned and came back, his face stolid. Before he reached her, however, his eyes widened as he stared at something beyond her, in the direction of the stairs.

Gabi read his gaze, turning her head. Standing there, in the hallway with a long revolver aimed squarely at the Standartenführer, was Thomas Lundren.

He held the pistol on Aying while he dug into his pants pocket with his left hand, throwing his keys at her. "Gabi, can you hear me?"

She nodded, rubbing her ears with both of her hands. "Speak loudly," she yelled.

Thomas coughed, a deep, throaty cough, the pistol never wavering. "I take it Madeline was in there?"

Gabi nodded, wanting to cry but not able to muster the emotion.

He nodded soberly, his eyes still locked on Aying. "My truck is out back. Take it and drive it as fast as it will go. You remember where?"

Gabi's face twitched as she thought about her confession downstairs, minutes earlier. She hitched her thumb to Aying. "He knows, Thomas."

Thomas' eyes flicked to Gabi before going back to Aying. He nodded knowingly. "Just go, Gabi. I've got him now."

After walking a short distance she stopped. She turned back to Anton Aying, his eyes blazing fury. Gabi matched the electric look in a long glare before she turned to Thomas, brushing his stubbly cheek with the back of her hand. She lingered a moment before nodding her thanks and running barefoot down the hallway. The elevator arrived with two hotel officials and the attendant. Their faces registered appropriate shock when they saw Thomas holding a gun on Standartenführer Anton Aying. Gabi hurried into the elevator, telling the three men that Thomas was a policeman and to take her down immediately.

She gave them a rushed, purposefully confused version of the events that had occurred, repeatedly telling the shift manager that the old man was with the polizei, and that he had the situation now under control. In the lobby, the manager ordered her to stay put. Despite their yells of protest, Gabi rushed from the hotel, finding Thomas' Opel Blitz just past the rear awning.

It wasn't much different than her mother's old Adler. Gabi ground the gears before wheeling the Opel into a U-turn, speeding through the deserted Innsbruck streets as sirens wailed in the distance.

Chapter Sixty-Five

STANDARTENFÜHRER AYING TOOK A STEP FORWARD. Thomas cocked the old pistol, the well-oiled cylinder dutifully clicking into place, aligned with the strike-plate and barrel. The sirens terminated downstairs, outside the hotel. At the end of the hall, a picture that had been hanging precariously fell to the floor. Thomas didn't flinch.

"Old man, are you completely senile?" Aying snapped. "Do you realize what that girl is up to?"

Thomas dipped his chin, a quick nod. "Yes, I do."

"And do you realize her friend, a *jewess*, just killed our American ally, and herself? Can you not see what type of sub-humans we're dealing with here?"

Thomas shouted his reply in the event Aying's hearing was damaged. "Perhaps she felt her cause was greater than her own life. Perhaps you killed her lover, a man who was no threat to any peace-loving person. Perhaps the American had already killed two German citizens, and she did us all a favor."

Aying bore his teeth, his face taut as he roared, "I am the authority here, not you!" He quivered visibly, pounding his chest in a Napoleonic manner. "I make those decisions, no one else. Do you hear me, you tainted relic? Do you?"

Thomas listened to the little diatribe without emotion, but just as Aying finished yelling, he saw his eyes briefly divert. Expecting to see men from the fire brigade, Thomas glanced backward. He was surprised to see a large man in an SS overcoat. The man was lifting a machine-pistol and, from many years of experience, Thomas could literally feel the man's intention to kill. Thomas whipped around, yanking off a round from the old revolver, watching the white-hot finger of flame reach from the barrel of the long pistol. The SS man squeezed off a few rounds but it was too late. Thomas' bullet had struck him in his upper chest, sending him wheeling over like he'd been punched by Max Schmeling.

As he turned back, Thomas saw nothing but a blur of gray as Aying had already launched himself. The two men went down in a heap. Struggling to get his pistol up, Thomas quickly realized he was no match for the younger, stronger man. Aying controlled Thomas' shooting hand and struck Thomas with his other hand until he lost consciousness.

When he came to, Thomas' thoughts were muddled. The only sure reality was that his coughing was severe and he was still prone on the floor. He looked up to see the ornate hall lighting, still not working from the blast, illuminated by moving light from hand-lamps. Covering his mouth until his hacking stopped, Thomas twisted his head to see Aying. Men stood all around him, listening as the Standartenführer railed on and on about hurrying to the Yugoslavian border, to the Jesenice rail crossing.

Thomas glanced at his watch and forced his hazy mind to do the calculations. The train couldn't be but about two hours from the border, if the engineer had been correct. Gabi's timing was going to be close. If she were to average 130 kilometers per hour, she should reach the border just as the train would. But given the top speed of an Army transport truck, there was no way Aying could catch up to the train at this point with the type of distance he would be forced to—

"And you tell that prick from the Luftwaffe we'll be there in fifteen minutes," Aying proclaimed, halting Thomas' train of thought. "I want as many men crammed on that bird as we can get, and we're to land in the first clearing near that border crossing."

Thomas deflated. Neil and those aboard the train, as well as Gabi in the truck, were forced to take a circuitous route due to the rugged mountains. Thomas wasn't sure of the exact distance, but assuming an airplane flew at three hundred kilometers per hour, Aying would almost certainly beat everyone to the border.

"And what of him, sir?" an SS man asked, pointing a finger down at Thomas as if he were road kill.

Aying snapped his fingers at the junior man, taking his machine gun. He stared down at Thomas, piercing him with his gray eyes.

"Old man, I only wish I had more time to make you suffer."

Thomas stared straight up toward the heavens, a genuine smile creasing his face. *Here I come, Greta!*

Aying fired two shots into Thomas' chest and one into his head. Thomas' mission, and his suffering, was complete.

* * *

Two hours later, Gabi had the truck in high gear, holding the accelerator to the floor. The speedometer needle had disappeared, meaning she was doing better than the 100 kilometers per hour the gauge registered. It wasn't long before she crested the long grade and, once headed downhill, the old truck revved until it sounded as if it might explode. She was navigating by road signs, having memorized each stop on the way to Jesenice—*thank you, Neil, for making me study that map.* Towns shot by her in the black of the night. Schwaz. Wörgl. Zell am See. She watched the fuel indicator in the old truck—nothing more than a floating ball. It was hovering low. Gabi kept her foot down. Once things leveled out, near the town of Villach, the train tracks rejoined the main road, to her left. Gabi decreased speed a bit, fearful she might have passed the train. If she had, she would have to find an unpatrolled section of the border and cross on foot.

Wouldn't she?

Earlier, she'd seemed so confident about crossing. Now, having endured such extreme pain and sorrow, she'd lost a great measure of her confidence.

As she sped out of Villach, a light on a roadhouse flashed like a strobe. Gabi closed the distance and, just when she was nearing the roadhouse, the light stopped flashing. The old truck rumbled as she pushed it even harder. She whizzed past the roadhouse, seeing the hard triangle of white light. It was aimed to illuminate a train. The light hadn't been a strobe after all.

A train had been passing, blocking the light with each passing car.

She squinted her eyes, trying to see ahead of her. At her speed, she was looking so far forward that she didn't realize she was already beside the train, alerted by the rumble of the caboose thirty meters to her left. Gabi wheeled the stubborn window down and began to pull and push the headlamp switch.

Standing on the rear deck of the caboose, barely illuminated, was a group of men. They were aiming rifles at her. One of them gestured to the others and she watched as each man ceased his aim. Then one man disappeared into the caboose.

She matched the speed of the train for another kilometer before sparks erupted under the train.

It was stopping.

She slowed, pulling the truck to the side of the road as the train finally squealed to a halt. Gabi exited the truck, her knees on the verge of buckling. When she saw Neil climbing down the black steel of the train's ladder, a torrent of emotion swept through her. Though he frowned as he approached, he embraced her tightly, holding her for a long moment before he pulled back.

"Are you okay?"

Gabi was unable to hold back her tears.

"Gabi, where's Madeline?"

She squeezed her eyes shut.

"Gabi, what happened?"

"She's gone, Neil."

Neil dipped his head with a murmur of exhalation.

"I talked, Neil. He tortured me and I told him everything. He knows…" Gabi buried her head in Neil's chest and sobbed, his sweater muffling the sounds.

After a moment Neil lifted her head. "Who killed Madeline?"

Gabi wiped her eyes. "I think she killed herself. There was an explosion, upstairs in his hotel room. It killed them both."

Neil looked away. After a moment, as if accepting this, he nodded and said, "So she planned it." His hand moved to Gabi's upper chest, probing carefully as the center burn was visible in the moonlight. "And that...that sonofabitch, Lord...he tortured you." It wasn't a question.

Gabi's brow lowered as she turned her head side to side. "No, Neil. Madeline was with Preston Lord. *Aying* burned me." She pulled the side of her wrinkled dress down, wincing as she showed him both of the fresh burns. "It's Aying who knows everything...I'm so sorry."

"Where's Aying now?"

"When I left, the policeman, Herr Lundren, was holding him off."

Neil's heterochromatic eyes danced, moving all around her. While they had been talking, Falkenberg had walked up, listening at a distance, his car idling in front of the train. During the gulf in the conversation he said, "No single policeman is going to hold back Aying and his SS."

Gabi turned to him. "There were more SS arriving just as I left."

Falkenberg threw his leather gloves to the dewy grass in disgust. "Damn that man." He nodded knowingly. "He'll be there. He'll be at the border."

"Airplane?" Neil asked.

"That's my guess," Falkenberg replied. "How long ago did you leave, *mein Liebling?*"

"About two hours."

Falkenberg nodded. "Okay. Assume he took fifteen minutes to dispatch your policeman friend. Then, another fifteen to get an aircraft ready. He'd be bringing the alert platoon, which is lucky for you because they're, in my opinion, a bunch of self-important greenhorns. But even still, they have the finest—"

"Did you say 'lucky for *me*'?" Neil asked with a great deal of heat. "You mean *us*?"

Falkenberg cupped his hand over a cigarette, illuminating his face as he lit it. After a few puffs, he said, "We've gotten you here. The border is only ten minutes ahead. If Aying isn't already there, the cursory guards at the crossing won't be able to stop you. They've no doubt been notified, but there are no switches there, so just have your engineer blow through at full speed while you light up with fully automatic fire to keep the border guards' heads down."

"And if Aying *is* there?"

Falkenberg turned his head to Gabi, politely smiling. "Begging your pardon, my dear, but greenhorns or not, if Aying is already there with the ready platoon, I'd hazard that you're roundly *gefickt*. He'll blow the track."

"Leave the truck here and go get on the caboose," Neil said to Gabi. "Have Kraabe put something on your burn. Peter's in there, too." When she didn't move he said, "Gabi, please go. We must hurry."

As she walked away, Neil moved toe-to-toe with Falkenberg. "I realize you probably don't want to be found associating with me, but you and your men are in plainclothes. I've got hundreds of innocent children, plus a woman, a teenager, an old doctor, and a train engineer under my care. I refuse to allow them to perish because *you* didn't hold up your end of the bargain." Falkenberg opened his mouth to speak but Neil continued. "I'm offering ten thousand reichsmarks, cash, for each of your men who will come with me."

There was a half-minute of silence.

"What do you say, Falkenberg?"

"I'd like to see the money."

"It's on the train."

"I'd still like to see the money," Falkenberg persisted.

Neil wet his lips. "Look, I realize that you and I probably wouldn't be close friends in normal circumstances. But, believe it or not, Falkenberg, I like you. You don't bullshit around. You may not care for me, and that's fine. For once, however, do me a favor and *just* trust me. I've got the money and don't mind paying it. There's no more time."

The German's eyes crinkled at their edges. He turned to his driver, snapping his fingers. "Assemble all the men right here, right now." He turned back to Neil.

"You're aware, my friend, that my personal fee just doubled?"

Neil's mouth twisted into a sour smirk. "I'd expect nothing less."

* * *

Standartenführer Anton Aying was crouched just behind the two cockpit seats of the Junkers Ju-86. The moon was low and to their right, bathing the cockpit in indigo light as the co-pilot navigated by map, occasionally calling out heading adjustments to the pilot. Behind Aying, fifteen SS were split on two benches. Each man was well equipped with a spanking new Beretta 1938 sub-machine gun, ammunition, and two grenades. Some of the SS, their faces sweaty and their eyes wide, appeared ready to fight that instant. Others slept.

Aying turned and eyed his men, recalling from his fighting experience in the Great War how soldiers prepare for deadly situations in a multitude of ways. If there was to be a deadly situation on this night, finding that blasted train—immediately—was imperative.

The pilot cut power as he began their descent. The sudden lack of engine roar allowed Aying to hear what the pilots were saying.

"Did you just say 'the airfield at Villach'?" Aying demanded, pulling on the co-pilot's harness.

"Yes, sir," the man, a Hauptmann, equivalent to a captain, yelled back. "It's about ten kilometers from the border."

Aying shook his head emphatically. "Bullshit! You will land this aircraft in a field or on a road close to the railway's border crossing. I literally want to be right there when that train comes through."

The pilot, a major, turned in his seat, screwing up his face at Aying. "Sir, while we're airborne *I am in charge* of this aircraft. Now, you can do whatever the hell you want to me when we get back, but I'll take a reprimand over death any day. Because there's a *good* chance we'll die if we try to land in some unknown place, especially at night. Electric lines, towers, ditches, livestock...there are all sorts of potential landmines and we're still well over half-full with fuel."

Aying nodded as if he understood. The two pilots turned and resumed their flying.

After thinking it through for only a few seconds, Aying calmly pulled out his Luger, cocked it, and fired it into the pilot's head just behind his right ear. He turned to the dumbfounded co-pilot and wagged the smoking pistol at him. "Listen to me, Hauptmann, I've got over four hundred hours at the stick. Do you want to land the plane, or do you want me to do it?"

The co-pilot gaped at his dead pilot, being held off the controls by Aying's left hand. He glanced at the pistol, then at Standartenführer Anton Aying. "I'll do it," he yelled enthusiastically. After moving his index finger over the map, the man nodded to himself before adding a measure of power and banking slightly to the right.

Aying turned to the ready platoon, all of whom were now wide-eyed. "You see what happens to men who disobey orders in a time of war?" he yelled. "Listen up because here are *your* orders. We're going to halt a train and then we're going to..."

Chapter Sixty-Six

NEIL INSTRUCTED THE ENGINEER TO STOP THE TRAIN two kilometers from the border. Up ahead, white lights marked the border crossing. From this distance there seemed to be no evidence of increased activity. Neil hopped off the engine and walked to Falkenberg's staff car. Falkenberg lit his lighter, aiding Neil's vision as he checked his watch.

"I've instructed the engineer to move forward at full speed eighteen minutes from now." Neil was leaning on the car and twisted his head back to the border. "We probably could have just plowed straight through, but there is no way of knowing that there isn't something blocking the tracks. I can't risk a derailment with all those children aboard."

"There appears to be no activity," Falkenberg said, peering through his binoculars. "But, I can't tell if they've blocked the tracks."

"We'll find out. Take your four men over there, where you can lay a field of fire if needed," Neil indicated, pointing to a cluster of railcars to the east of the border crossing. "Don't shoot unless someone opens fire on us. Make sure you're shooting only in the arc between your position and the crossing. I'll instruct your other soldiers of your position so we don't cut each other apart."

"Let's assume for a moment Aying isn't here. What about the border guards?"

Neil hoisted the two canvas bags slung over his back. "Just go take up the position by those railcars. I'll handle the guards...I've got some mouse traps to set."

"So all I need to do is take my four boys to the boxcars and prepare to shoot?"

"If anyone shows aggression toward the train."

Falkenberg crushed out the cigarette in the car's ashtray. He considered Neil a moment before he said, "Good luck, friend." He extended his hand, which Neil took.

As Falkenberg's car eased away with its lights darkened, Neil jogged back to the train, absently realizing his side finally felt almost back to normal. Perhaps the loading of the train broke up the last of the major scar tissue. There was no pain at all.

"How about that," he muttered to himself as he stopped before the assembled group of Heer soldiers.

"Where do you want us, sir?" an old, craggy-faced noncom asked.

"I'm going to make my way down to the crossing. After I do, I want you to tactically follow, but halt about five hundred meters before the crossing. From there, you'll fan out in intervals ten to fifteen meters wide to the *west* side of the tracks. Essentially, you'll make an arc," Neil said, scratching a diagram on the ground next to the train. He showed them where Falkenberg and his four would be, on the eastern flank, warning the soldiers not to confuse them with an enemy. "Go ahead and assume that there will be resistance, but do *not* shoot first. If you do see gunshots, be mindful of Falkenberg and his men to the east. With that in mind, your job is to cut our aggressors to shreds."

A young soldier, probably no more than eighteen, looked around at his comrades, his voice high with tension. "So we're going to just kill our fellow Germans? Our fellow soldiers?"

Neil nearly answered but waited. Instead, the craggy-faced noncom—he looked forty going on sixty—answered the soldier in a raspy smoker's voice. "Didn't you hear what Falkenberg said earlier, boy? He offered this man's bounty money and you didn't turn back then."

"Well..." the young soldier stammered. "The fighting part didn't seem real then. But now he's talking about us fighting our own soldiers."

"The SS aren't soldiers," the noncom shot back. "And the longer you serve, you'll learn that the only place they belong is in a prison, nasty pack of hoods they are."

After waiting for the NCO to finish, Neil spoke to the young soldier. "If you don't want to be a part of this, hand over your ammo and head back the other way. You don't have to participate, but," he glanced at his watch, twisting to see it in the moonlight, "we've got about thirteen minutes before the train starts moving and we have to be in place well beforehand."

Without much deliberation the soldier stepped back into ranks. Neil asked who was senior and, again, the craggy-faced NCO spoke up.

"Fine," Neil answered with a courteous nod. "Give me a few minutes' head start. Move tactically as you proceed...I'd use the ditches to prevent showing your silhouettes. Fan out when you get to five hundred meters and stay locked, loaded and on full alert at all times. The SS could *already* be here for all we know."

As the men set about preparing their weapons and grenades, Neil began moving forward, using the darkness to the right of the road. As he moved, loaded with his equipment and cooled by the chill night air, he felt as if he'd gone back twenty-five years in time. His feet touched the earth with only a whisper. With every step, even in the darkness, his vision seemed to grow more acute, discerning minute differences in color and brightness. Inside of five seconds he evaluated all facets of the border crossing, scanned the entire starlit sky for aircraft, and calculated the countless permutations of his plan. Neil could have easily been back in California, a teen in the bosom of the Shoshone, playing hide-and-seek with his summer friends, his body nothing more than a floating shadow.

The Pale Horse ran again.

He heard the thud of hand drums in the distance. He felt the touch of the elder's hand, gently guiding him, teaching him. *Don't just let your instinct come to you; listen for it; summon it; grasp it.*

Neil could hear his spirit's iron guidance, as loud as if someone were yelling the instructions in his ear. *Jink left. Duck right. Go to ground and crawl.*

When he was only a hundred meters out, he checked his time. There were eight minutes until the train was due to move. Things were looking good. Neil scanned the area, seeing no one else. Perhaps he would get a break on this night. Maybe Aying was well behind, or couldn't get his airplane, or simply went home and went to sleep.

Doubtful...

He stopped, focusing on the lighted border crossing.

For a moment there was nothing. Then two men appeared from behind the small building. They were talking. Neil couldn't hear what they were saying, but their conversation seemed relaxed. Just two bored men pulling all-night guard, simply trying to stay awake, the tales getting deeper as the night wore on.

Neil closed his eyes for a moment, recalling the highest canon of his training at the hand of the Shoshone.

Peace.

It wasn't always a possibility, but he was taught to seek it whenever possible.

Neil turned his eyes back to his left, to the railcars, focusing on them. After a moment he saw the faint movement of a hand moving side to side. Falkenberg. He looked to the rear, up the tracks, unable to see the remainder of soldiers but trusting that they were in position.

His eyes turned back to the crossing...

When one of the guards was lighting a cigarette and the other was leaning against a wall on the verge of dozing, Neil dashed through the shadows and leapt onto their platform, aiming two of the cache's inky Walther pistols, one at each man. The guard leaning against the wall saw Neil first, straightening as one hand went to his sidearm while his eyes went to the phone on the brick wall.

"Don't move, gentlemen," Neil said in soothing German. He cocked both pistols with his thumbs, western style. The guard who was smoking developed a case of slack-jaw, sending his cigarette tumbling to the ground. The other one still held his hand on his holstered pistol, his eyes alternating between Neil and the phone.

"I know what you're thinking," Neil said to the one with his hand on his pistol. "And it won't work. Just getting that holster open will take at least a second, by which time you will be down on the tracks, on your back, replete with several unnecessary entry and exit wounds." He turned to the other man. "And you, you'll see me shoot him, and you'll try to duck for cover. And even if you make it, there are fifteen soldiers covering us right now. They'll burn you to the ground if you try to run."

The one guard removed his hand from his holster. The other put his hands up without being asked to do so, mimicked by his friend.

"Very good, gentlemen. It's time for you to leave your post." Neil stepped closer. "Stand face-to-face, a half-meter apart. Go ahead. Good. Now, clasp your raised hands as if you're going to play a game of mercy. Very good, boys. They must put the sharp ones out here on the border. Now, don't move yet, or my friends might start shooting." Neil removed two sets of cuffs from the four he had stashed in his bag. He cuffed the guards' hands together, disarming them afterward.

"Okay, boys, the mother of all firefights might just take place here, so I want you to start walking down these tracks, toward Yugoslavia. Keep walking until you're well away from here."

"What if a train comes?" one asked.

"Then I'd suggest you get the hell off the tracks. *Move out.*"

The two men, face-to-face, made their way off the concrete platform and down onto the tracks. Neil could hear them arguing and the gravel crunching as they walked to the south. He leaned inside the shack, finding the lights, blipping them three times before leaving them off altogether. He yanked the phone from the wall, hiding it under a desk in the shack, and then he went to work.

Neil placed the cans of Amatol on each side of the tracks, down in the adjacent gravel ditches. There were five cans altogether, so he placed two on the eastern side and three on the road side, linking them all together by detonation wire and attached to the pre-drilled blasting cap in the top of each can. He took special care to thread the det-wire under the tracks in case the train went by without his needing to fire it. Using the fast-reel spool, Neil backed across the road, finding a suitable spot in the high weeds as he twisted the two leads onto the friction detonator. He checked his watch.

Four minutes.

* * *

"Sir, there's the train tracks and the border crossing," the co-pilot said, pointing.

Aying could see it, two kilometers away to the north, the only lighted building in the area. Suddenly the light at the crossing flashed three times before the crossing went dark.

"Reuter!" Aying bellowed, punching the back of the pilot's seat.

"Who, sir?"

"Kill your engines."

"But, sir…"

Aying jammed the pistol into the co-pilot's neck. "You've got more than enough altitude and your load is light. Now, kill the engines and land dead-stick on that adjacent road or I'll do it."

The Junkers slowed as the engines wheezed and went eerily quiet. Aying turned to the soldiers and said, "When you exit this aircraft, shoot *anything* that moves."

* * *

Neil surveyed the area from his position in the high grass, able to occasionally see the German soldiers under the NCO's command still fanning into the last of their positions. Unable to go back any farther due to the detonation cord's length, Neil motioned the closest soldier forward. The soldier who arrived was the young complainer from before. Neil, frustrated at the young man's earlier hesitation, did his best to be enthusiastic at the soldier's presence.

"Ever fired one of these before?" Neil asked.

"No, sir," the post-teen answered, staring wide-eyed at the detonator.

"You grab this handle and spin it as fast and hard as you can. Can you do that?"

The boy nodded.

"Good. And don't do it, under any circumstance, until you hear me yell…" Neil searched for a word, his eyes scanning the area. "What's a good code word I can yell to you that we won't hear out here otherwise?"

"*Todeskuss*," the soldier answered immediately.

Neil translated it directly in his mind as "kiss of death." "Perfect," he answered. "Even if we move, you stay down and stay here, got it?"

"Yes, sir."

Neil clapped the boy's back before he stood to run to the soldiers behind him, hoping this was all a pointless exercise. As he was reaching a prone soldier fumbling with his rifle, a whooshing sound could suddenly be heard. Neil turned to see a tri-motor airplane, its black German cross visible in the moonlight, gliding in to land on the very road where he had just stood. It was landing to the north, and passed the guard station with only feet to spare. Puffs of smoke erupted as the tires barked their brief protest upon a rather rough touchdown.

Aying.

Neil stifled a curse, realizing that, had he blown the Amatol at the aircraft's passing, all that would be left of the airplane would be a massive fireball and a few shards of scrap metal. But because it had come in dead-stick, he hadn't heard it till it was too late.

Rotating his head side to side, Neil viewed the young men cinching their rifles to their shoulders, each here only because of his blood money. He felt nauseous and, in an effort to fight the sickness, he began to move. Snippets of wartime memories flashed through his mind as he ran. Neil remembered the horrid images of bodies flying, cartwheeling through the air, missing hands or feet. He saw men rushing across a field, brave snarls on their face, replaced in an instant by expressions of despondency as bullets pierced their bodies. The old saying was "war is hell," and whoever coined that phrase had almost certainly served in a trench.

And now the war was back.

As the aircraft rolled farther up the road, Neil found the grizzled senior NCO and slid down next to him, using the high grass as cover. "The men on that airplane are here to kill us. I hope you know that."

The NCO turned to him, his voice low and hard. "I got no problem shootin' my fellow Germans, if that's what you mean, as long as they're SS."

"You and your men pick them off as they file out of the airplane. Wait for my shot." Neil nestled the new Gewehr rifle into the crook of his shoulder, grumbling as the aircraft continued its roll.

"They're going to be out of our range," the NCO said, watching helplessly.

The aircraft was still moving even though the engines were off—probably a tactical decision if they'd seen the soldiers awaiting their arrival. Knowing the SS couldn't yet hear him, he yelled to the NCO's group of soldiers to close the distance. Everyone got to their feet and trundled forward.

"Wait for my first shot!" Neil shouted as he rushed through the damp knee-high grass. When he was two hundred meters away—which might as well been have two hundred miles with an un-zeroed rifle—the men began boiling from the two rear doors of the Junkers aircraft like ants doused in vinegar.

"Damn it!" Neil grunted. Either Aying knew Falkenberg's men were already out here, or the SS made a habit of disembarking all aircraft with strategic haste. Neil grudgingly scored one for the Schutzstaffel. They were almost certainly highly trained and would be a game opponent.

After six SS had made it out, Neil knelt and began to pepper the aircraft with semi-automatic fire. Shots began to ring out across the way, marked by orange dots as Falkenberg had moved his own group north and pinned down the six who had already emerged. Another two SS came out of the aircraft and one paid his life for it, crumpling onto the black strip of asphalt. The SS man screamed, holding his hands to his face before quickly going silent.

"Who's got that rocket launcher?" Neil yelled to the old NCO. Orders could be heard being barked to Neil's left. He saw a man bouncing forward with a long tube, taking up a belly position twenty-five meters ahead. Neil kept laying fire toward the rear door, doing his best to keep the remaining occupants inside the would-be death trap.

He reloaded as quickly as possible, eyeing the soldier with the rocket launcher. *Fire the damned thing.*

His wish was granted, marked by white light and a whoosh. Neil watched as the rocket shot forward, guided as if on a wire. It struck the tail of the Junkers, blowing it off in an explosion of sparks and ripping metal. The aircraft spun, doing a half-turn. Since the rocket struck the back of the aircraft, there was no effect on the fuel. Neil watched as the remaining occupants rolled out of the now wide-open back of the airplane, scattering immediately.

Instead of killing the remaining SS, the poor shot with the rocket launcher had provided them with an easy escape from the confines of the airplane.

Neil rushed forward, followed by the NCO and his men. Moving under the cover provided by Falkenberg's group, they managed to pin down most of the SS. One tried to make his way forward to a large dirt mound using a low-crawl, but a bullet from a shooter to Neil's left knocked his helmet off. A second bullet from Neil's rifle ended the man's life.

The other SS were getting organized, working themselves into a full circle perimeter, shooting outward in their own arc of responsibility. Their efforts began to pay dividends. After a bullet whizzed by Neil's head, he heard screams to his left, seeing one of his Heer men stand, frantically holding his spurting neck before a second shot silenced him forever.

"We need to pull back and somehow get them into the kill zone by the tracks," Neil said to the senior NCO. "Tell your men to start pulling back toward the border. I'll stay here and lay down cover fire." Two rounds impacted in front of Neil, throwing dirt and debris into his face so hard it opened cuts. He wiped his face and said, "Once you're in position, open up a firestorm and I'll pull back."

The old NCO slid backward, shouting clipped commands. Neil reloaded, waiting. When the men began to pull back, he began firing carefully aimed shots at each of the SS men in the perimeter. By now, they were more than a hundred meters away, but Neil's vantage point was partially hidden and slightly above them—an ideal location. He thought he hit one man, seeing him begin to roll violently. After that, Neil noticed a figure in the center of the perimeter, crawling person to person. Neil focused on the man...

It was Anton Aying.

Cinching the rifle into his shoulder, Neil took deep breaths. He paused, aimed carefully, squeezed off a round. A flash of dirt flew to the front and right of Aying. Neil's rifle was un-zeroed, meaning it was Kentucky windage time. Neil lifted the rifle a degree, moving it slightly to the left. Just then, the senior NCO and his men must have gotten into position as a high volume of cover fire from Neil's right began to cause the SS men to adjust their position. Neil remained focused on the man he thought to be Aying. He was moving on all fours, but Neil tracked him, aiming high and left. He squeezed off a round, watching as the man crumpled, holding his arm and screaming.

Gotcha, you bastard.

Score one for Jakey.

The SS soldiers must have been aware that the remainder of the men had pulled back, because once they saw the next round emerge from Neil's location, two stood and began to charge. Neil fired at once, making one man dive for cover. The other was coming hard, his boots pounding only twenty meters away as Neil rotated to him. Just as the SS raised his machine gun to shoot, a bullet from the right sent him careening. It wasn't a kill shot, but it did the trick. Neil squeezed off a finishing round, hitting the SS man in the side of the head. Knowing he had but seconds to pull back, Neil stood and sprinted in a curving direction around the cover fire, watching frenzied tracer rounds streak by in both directions.

Once Neil reached the grizzled old NCO, he pointed out fire now coming from *behind* the remaining SS men. It had to be from Falkenberg. He and his group had continued flanking to the north and now approached downward, pushing the SS soldiers from behind.

A light appeared behind all of them.

The train.

"Cover me!" Neil yelled as he crouched and moved laterally to the soldier with the friction device. Neil crashed into the dewy weeds next to him, wiping sweat from his face and saying, "Don't blow it until I tell you to. We need to make sure as many of them as possible move into that kill-zone, because we only get one shot at this." Neil hurriedly reloaded. "When you twist that device, get your head down because the gravel in those ditches is gonna fly like hot shrapnel."

The young soldier never answered him.

As the firefight raged, Neil turned to the silent young man. His rifle was still aimed north. From his position, he'd probably fired the shot that had saved Neil from the rushing SS soldier. He tilted the young man's helmet back, seeing where a round had struck him through the eye.

"Damn it," Neil breathed.

He grasped the soldier's shoulders, rolling him flat. The young man's face was still flushed from the heat of battle although his life had left him. A regular Army soldier, probably conscripted, he was hardly different than Peter Heinz. And he'd had the balls to speak up earlier, not understanding the complex set of morals at play on this night. Upon hasty reflection, Neil wasn't sure he understood, either. And somewhere, this dead soldier probably had a mother and father, and maybe a girlfriend. They each had a picture of him, and since there was no war, yet, they each probably thought he was safe in his bunk on this evening. But he wasn't in his bunk and he wasn't safe at all. No, he was on the Yugoslavian border, killed while trying to earn 10,000 reichsmarks that he probably would have sent home.

Neil punched the earth.

War is hell.

Knowing more would die if he didn't keep his wits about him, he forced himself to refocus. The SS appeared to be progressing on each side of the track, in and around the three-meter wide ditches. They were advancing into the ideal spot, or so they thought. From their new vantage point, they could fire on their objective, the train, and find a respite from the semi-automatic fire coming from their enemy in all directions.

They couldn't have been more mistaken.

Neil grasped the friction detonator, subconsciously twisting the contact nuts to make sure the wires were tight. The train was five hundred meters away, accelerating slower than Neil would have liked. He watched as the last of the SS soldiers found their way into the ditches. Gunfire emanated from various positions in the ditch as the SS used the old trench warfare technique of repositioning after each few shots. Neil's allies, the Heer soldiers, grew frustrated and were expending too many rounds for Neil's taste, but the train was too close to make an effort at correction.

As the train's powerful lamp began to add light to the tracks and the ditches, Neil was able to make out two SS soldiers carrying rocket launchers like the one the Heer soldier had used earlier. The two SS took up positions just under the cover of the ditch.

The train was two hundred meters away.

Neil could hear someone in the ditch shouting orders to the men with rocket launchers. He was demanding that they be patient.

"Good advice," Neil breathed.

He waited. He waited.

It had been twenty years since he'd done something like this. Yes, he had killed, but the killings had all been surgical. Precise. But tonight he was at war, as he had been twenty years before. Twenty years full of pain, friendships, sorrow, marriage, love and death.

Twenty years.

This type of killing was much different. Each minute could be the exact opposite of the one before. Most plans go out the window once the lead starts flying. Heart rates go up. Sweat pours from one's body. No one thinks about their bank account, or whether or not they watered their garden before they left for the day. Each second becomes a victory, and dealing out death merely adds more time to the clock.

He looked left. The train was very close.

He looked right. The kill zone was fully populated.

War is hell, indeed.

Neil twisted the friction detonator.

The explosion—just as they had always been back during the war—was far bigger than Neil thought it would be. Five balls of blue and orange flame exploded from the ditch, sending gravel, bodies, rail debris, and earth hurtling outward at hundreds of miles per hour. Neil ducked down, his body registering pain as the rocks tore into him. He lifted his head, fearful that the explosion might have damaged the track. Biting his hand in anticipation, Neil yelled a victory cry as the steam train thundered past. The tracks bent under the train's weight, the rail bed having been eroded by the explosion. But the train's path was true, clearing the smoke in a vortex of its speed and mass. Neil shouted to the figures on the caboose's rear platform. He stood, holding his rifle above his head, shaking it as he saw Doctor Kraabe, Peter and, of course, Gabi.

Despite his elation, Neil quickly realized he'd dispensed with battlefield protocol—the type of thing that had gotten many a man killed. He dropped prone and reached into the dead soldier's collar, snatching his *Erkennungsmarke* from his neck—Germany's version of dog tags. With the tags in his pocket, Neil skittered away. There seemed to be no movement from the ditches. Neil crept forward. The senior NCO was on his feet, crouched as he passed thirty meters to Neil's left. When Neil reached the ditch, the NCO was kicking at a hunk of meat that was once someone's torso. "They've all had it," he pronounced with finality.

"Assuming they were all in the ditches," Neil said, moving himself into the cover of the ditch.

The NCO tapped out a cigarette. "Was that Baratol?"

"Something similar," Neil replied absently, his eyes narrowed as he searched the stretches of land surrounding the tracks. The NCO's soldiers were standing from their positions, chattering the way soldiers do after a battle, clumped in groups and lighting cigarettes.

But something seemed wrong to Neil. The SS who had been shouting instructions to the two rocket launchers had not sounded like Aying. And, in Neil's mind, had Aying been in the ditch, it would have been him who would have been giving orders.

As the NCO lit his cigarette with a match, a brief flurry of shooting could be heard near the parked railcars. Neil sprinted in that direction, hearing a series of confused yells. Shouting his presence as he neared, Neil watched as four soldiers converged and crouched around another.

Falkenberg.

Neil pushed into the group, noting that Falkenberg's breathing was coming in wet gasps. Blood gushed through a soldier's pressed hand as he tried to contain the bleeding. Neil knelt down and asked what happened.

"Aying," Falkenberg's driver said without hesitation. "Cowardly bastard never moved forward with his men. He must've been hiding in the weeds, and after the explosion and the train getting through, we stood to advance and he shot our colonel right in the back."

Neil gripped Falkenberg's hand and whispered thanks, doing so in English.

"See that my family receives the money," Falkenberg rasped.

"Jawohl," Neil agreed. He asked the soldiers to keep their rifles trained in case Aying was still around. But Neil remained in his kneeling position next to Falkenberg, the two men gripping hands until Falkenberg's hand went slack and his breathing ceased. Neil placed the German colonel's hand over his chest and pulled downward to close his eyes. After dipping his head for a moment, his own eyes closed, Neil turned to Falkenberg's driver.

"You're *sure* it was Standartenführer Aying? You're certain?"

"Absolutely. By the time it happened, we turned and fired but he was sprinting that way," the soldier said, pointing north. "His silhouette was unmistakable."

"Did he appear to be injured?"

"If he was, he was still able to run. What a coward."

* * *

Fifteen minutes later, as Neil summed up with the old senior NCO, another younger NCO approached. His face was haggard and from his mouth hung a blood-stained cigarette. Neil soon saw why—his hand was covered in blood.

The older NCO ripped open a bandage, handing it to him. "What happened to your hand?"

"Shrapnel from the explosion."

"What's the count?"

The younger NCO shook his head. "It's hard to tell because of the damage, but we think we've got the remains of about fifteen SS bodies, and we know we lost four ourselves, including the colonel."

"Nineteen dead," the senior NCO whispered, looking at Neil in a way that was not at all accusatory. It was a look one professional soldier gives to another when discussing the horrors of their unfortunate fraternity.

"Go muster the men by the railcars," the older NCO said. "Assemble the dead as best you can."

"Our money?" the younger NCO asked unapologetically.

"Taking care of it right now," Neil said.

The younger NCO walked away.

Neil hefted a bag from beside his feet, handing it to the wizened NCO. He explained how it should be split up and insisted that the dead soldiers' first of kin, Falkenberg included, should receive their money as quickly as possible.

"What should I tell them?" the senior NCO asked.

"Tell them the truth."

Neil lit his own cigarette and asked the first of two final questions. "What's your name?"

"Feldwebel Ernst Gauss."

The second question. "Are you a Nazi, Ernst?"

The NCO straightened. "I am *not*. I'm just a career soldier working to feed my family."

"I'd go to war with you, any day, Ernst." They shook hands. "For now, I'd suggest you haul ass."

"What do you recommend I tell our command? Should I *also* tell them the truth?"

Neil tossed his barely smoked cigarette, blowing his final drag into the cool morning air. "Aying will be on the warpath, you can bet on that. I'd play dumb and just say you were doing as you were told by Falkenberg."

The two men nodded their agreement one final time. The NCO headed north with his men, back into the Reich.

Neil walked south, into freedom.

Chapter Sixty-Seven

THE CITY OF JESENICE, YUGOSLAVIA BUZZED on Tuesday morning, the citizenry blissfully unaware of the battle that had taken place a short distance to the north mere hours before. Neil walked the entire ten-kilometer distance from the border, enjoying the peace of being in the free country. No one bothered him, and few seemed to take note of his scruffy appearance. As he walked, he thought about his journey—his aliyah, as Doctor Kraabe had termed it. Today was the fifty-sixth day since Meghan Herman had walked back into his life. Since that day he'd stopped drinking; he traveled a third of the way around the world; been gravely wounded by a German defector's pistol; piloted an airplane; crashed an airplane; was operated on by a man who specialized in farm animals; fallen in love; come within feet of Adolf Hitler; and helped a group of persecuted children escape from Nazi-occupied Austria.

It had been a busy, and wonderful, two months.

Neil stopped at a crosswalk, doing a full revolution as he tried to locate the city's center. The city was dominated by smokestacks from the steel industry. Surrounded by mountains, and not too dissimilar from the topography of Innsbruck, Jesenice had a decidedly different feel to it. All business, certainly—but with the anticipation of a coming war, the people still walked with the bounce of freedom in their step. It seemed an eternity since Neil had felt such true optimism in the air. He finally found a local who spoke English. The man pointed Neil past a large fountain to the central train station, situated near the Jesenice city seat.

As Neil approached the station, a burgundy car skidded to a stop in front of him, making Neil's hand shoot to his back, gripping the Walther resting underneath his thick sweater. Neil backed away as a man emerged from the other side, smiling broadly.

It was Gregor Faust, his contact from the Queen Mary.

Faust wore desert khakis. In his hand was his omnipresent cigar. He leaned his meaty arms on top of the car as he stood on the running board. "The others were beginning to worry that you didn't make it, Mister Reuter, but I knew you would."

Neil removed his hand from his pistol. He simply stood there staring, too exhausted to muster a reaction.

"Are you okay?" Faust asked, his merriment evaporating.

Neil nodded.

"Hop in. We'll be there in minutes."

"Is everyone okay?"

"Of course they are, thanks to you."

The vehicle was driven by a young man Neil had never seen before. After rolling down his own window, Neil didn't hear a word Faust said, his massive girth twisted as he jawed at Neil, his mouth going a mile a minute. Neil took deep breaths, in through his nose, out through his mouth, trying to remain calm. He wanted to see Gabi, and check on her wounds. Peter crossed his mind, as did Faust's granddaughter Fern. Then Emilee, then his unborn son. Neil closed his eyes, lowering his chin to his chest as he suppressed a shudder.

So many heavy thoughts…

The car skidded to a stop just outside of town. They were below the train station, parked in front of a new-looking depot situated off of a single spur. There were several other cars and trucks parked in front. Faust came around the car, holding the door open for Neil. After exiting and steadying himself, Neil dug into his pocket.

"We need to get inside," Faust said, glancing around.

"Before we do." Neil pressed the young German soldier's dog tags into Faust's hand. "Use your influence, please. See that this young man's family is taken care of."

"I'm Jewish. I have no influence in Germany."

"Please," Neil said. "You're a smart man. I know you'll think of something. Promise me."

"I promise," Faust said after a pause, clearly nonplussed. "Are you ready to see the fruits of your labor?"

"Ready." Neil followed Faust and the tall driver inside. He knew this would be a powerful moment.

They entered the frigid building, walking through two sets of rooms before coming to a large warehouse. The door they entered put them on a platform ten feet above the room. The far wall was dominated by roll-up doors over loading docks. The warehouse was chock full of people, most of them children.

Neil studied the faces.

From his vantage point he first saw Petra Faust, the tall and regal wife of Gregor. She was smiling, something he never witnessed during their time together on the ship. Standing next to Petra was the Russian woman who'd boarded Neil's plane in Chicago. She waved.

They weren't the only ones there.

Doctor Kraabe clapped before giving Neil two thumbs up. Peter Heinz stood on his seat and cheered—and had to put down his bottle of Coca-Cola to do so. Neil had to remind himself to breathe as he turned to the next person, the small, goateed forger from Salzburg. He'd removed his yarmulke and waved it about as he yelled. Neil shook his head, stunned and overwhelmed.

But it was the children who melted Neil's heart. They'd been cleaned up and were cheering and clapping in frenetic joy. Most of them were holding food, many of them with their precious little mouths full as they yelled. Such innocence—*how could anyone harm a child?*

The adults joined in the cheers, hooting and hollering. There were thirty others Neil didn't recognize, but they celebrated his arrival like he was some long lost hero.

And making her way from the crowd, climbing the grid metal stairs, was Gabi, with Schatze by her side. Other than the bandage on her chest, Gabi looked healthy and radiant as she bear-hugged him until the cheering died down. Schatze licked Neil's hand.

"I didn't think you'd made it," Gabi whispered to him.

"I always do, Gabi," he whispered back, his voice cracking. "I always do."

Gabi held him for a full minute. Neil didn't move. He accepted her hug, eyes closed, enjoying the sublimity of the moment.

Twenty minutes later, after introductions and congratulations were complete, after Neil's facial wounds had been cleaned, the adults sat at a long row of picnic tables pushed together. The children ate in groups on blankets. Peter sat in their midst, laughing with them. They ate a breakfast of bread, cheese, salted fish and fresh fruits. Somewhere, somehow, they had managed to obtain fresh orange juice, and Neil swilled a full liter on his own. After eating, Gabi gripped his hand underneath the table, frowning at him as he smoked a cigarette.

Gregor Faust, who upon closer examination was dressed like a desert bushman from the Kalahari, stood at the head of the table and tapped a spoon against his orange juice. The room fell silent. He made eye contact with everyone before finally looking to Neil.

"Mister Reuter, please accept my bountiful thanks for essentially giving up everything you owned to come and assist us. You gave up your business, your home, your life. And it means more to me, personally, than I could ever muster words to explain."

Afraid to speak, Neil nodded.

"We *all* thank you from the bottom of our collective hearts."

Neil nodded his thanks as applause broke out again.

Faust continued, "I also want you to know that the full sum of money you spent on this journey will be reimbursed to you."

Neil spoke. "That's not necessary."

"But it is. You see, this was never about money."

"I agree," Neil said. He breathed deeply before he replied. "And to me, this was never political. It began with my friend, Jakey, and soon transformed into a mission of mercy for these children." Neil reached into his breast pocket and produced the picture of Fern. "She kept me going."

Gregor Faust's eyes sparkled when Neil turned the picture around. After a few steadying breaths, Faust said, "Would you like to meet her?"

Neil's expression provided the answer.

Faust crossed the room, retrieving a thin young girl who'd been laughing with her friends. She came with him, displaying timidity when she approached Neil. Faust encouraged her to shake Neil's hand, which she did.

Neil Reuter was overcome.

Overcome with so many emotions. After a moment, Fern hugged him.

Neil Reuter's life was complete.

* * *

Gabi awoke to light rain pattering the sill of the open window in their hotel room. Something about awakening to rain struck her with melancholy for her mother. Each night since learning of her mother's death, Gabi had dreamed about her. But the dreams hadn't been nightmares—they'd been beautiful, with her mother seeming radiant and happy. Seeing her that way, if only in a dream, helped Gabi cope.

Despite getting decent sleep, she was still exhausted and quite sore, especially around the tender burns on her chest. Ignoring the pain, Gabi swirled in the sheets, stretching as an involuntary grin occupied her face while she reminisced about the spirited love she and Neil had made the evening before. As tired as he must have been, he loved her again and again, saying and doing the most beautiful things. Though the memory was quite warm, in the dull light and cool damp of the rainy morning, the encounter seemed only another dream. She glanced around the room, wondering where Neil was. The clock read ten o'clock; he had probably gotten dressed and gone downstairs for coffee.

Gabi lurched when she saw the briefcase.

It was the briefcase full of money from Gregor Faust and his organization. Millions. And yesterday, Neil had placed it in the hotel safe. But now it was here, and perched on top was an envelope of the hotel's stationary.

Gabi stood, sensing something was wrong.

Her name, in Neil's distinctly masculine handwriting, was written on the front envelope. And next to the envelope was a freshly cut flower.

* * *

Fern's Diary

I am on a big ship on a beautiful blue sea. This morning, the sun came up right in front of the ship and I stood there watching it with a huge smile on my face. As the sun rose, I ate a fruit called a tangerine. It was so good and tasty, just like all the other food I've eaten since we left the cave.

A few of the children are still weak but no one is very sick now. We have medicine and food and nice soft beds even though we have to share. My best friend Julia and I don't care. We wake up smiling because we know we're away from the cave.

I've been a little sad because I found out that the man named Jacob died in an accident after he hid us. But his friends came and rescued us and now we are on our way to Zion. The headmistress warned us that Zion is not perfect and our families might not ever come for us. I'm trying not to think of that too much.

But she said in Zion we will be around others who love us. I believe her. And I also take back what I said so many times about there being no love in that cave. There was lots of love in that cave. And I think love is what rescued us.

Chapter Sixty-Eight

1976 - Manhasset, NY, USA
THE GATHERING TOOK PLACE EVERY YEAR, on the Saturday closest to September 19th. The year was 1976, the United States' Bicentennial. The family had just finished a feast of a German dinner, prepared in a manner taught by Hildie Heinz many years before. Gabrielle Lightsey, still eye-catching despite her age, walked from the dining room to the kitchen. Her husband Frank was loading a cigar case.

"Are you sure you won't stay?" she asked.

It was the same scene every year and Frank played his part perfectly. He glanced up at her and smiled. "Please, don't worry about me. I'm going to try to get in on the Saturday card game at the club and I need to get there early."

Gabrielle touched his arm, rubbing it, a kind look on her face. "You're welcome to stay. In fact, I wish you would."

He pinched his lips together, a look of gratitude. It only took a moment before he shook his head, giving her a peck on the forehead. "I'll be late. Don't wait up." She watched out the window as he wended down the curved drive, past the brick columns, negotiating his sedan into the early evening Long Island traffic.

Back in the dining room, Peter passed photos and mementos around the table, removing them one at a time from a painted curio box. Many of the pictures were courtesy of the German government. In 1954, while Germany was still in the midst of reconstruction, Gabrielle and Peter had traveled back for a meeting arranged by their New York congressman. The Federal Republic of Germany, while not anxious for their account to become public, had been incredibly accommodating, recording their entire story in the private German archives. After Peter and Gabrielle declined a quiet offer of a settlement for their mother's land, the government happily provided pictures of every person they requested.

For everyone else's benefit, Peter and Gabrielle recalled snippets of what they remembered about the people in the photos. Gabrielle talked about Madeline's fierce spirit. Peter recalled Thomas Lundren's kindness and his dogged determination to get to the root of the case. They told stories about Neil, about their mother, and even about the crooked Nazi veterinarian Hörst Baldinger.

"In case you don't remember, this is Doctor Kraabe," Gabrielle said, pointing to the picture of the doctor in his earlier days. "He lived until

1952, though I didn't know he had passed away until we went back. He was extremely kind to all people."

Neil Jr., now thirty-seven years old and still a bachelor, had remained quiet up until this point. He considered the picture of the distinguished doctor for a moment before he lifted a close-up photo of the angular, unsmiling man with dark hair.

"This was my father," he said, showing the picture to his latest girlfriend.

"His eyes look different," she remarked, pointing at the light and dark shade of each one in the sepia photo.

"They were different in color," Gabrielle said, nervously fingering the locket around her neck. "His father was German, his mother Shoshone. He joked that his eyes split the difference."

A silence came over the room as the younger Neil continued to study the photo. His girlfriend lifted another photo. "Why is there a picture of a dog in here?"

Peter and Gabrielle laughed together. "Schatze," Peter said. "She was already quite old when Neil found her, and then she lived on until 1948. The vet estimated she was at least seventeen when she died—a miracle for a large dog."

Neil Jr. opened both falsified passports, smiling at the American names his mother and Peter had used to flee. "Who made these?" he asked.

"A talented Austrian forger," Peter answered. "A Jewish forger."

Gabrielle and Peter told the story which, even condensed, took several hours to tell. Everyone present, other than Neil's girlfriend, had heard it before. But no one cared. They were captivated. Every time the tale was told, new details emerged. And as fantastic as it was, no one doubted a word.

Finished, Peter reached into the curio box and carefully handed a yellowed envelope to his sister.

Gabrielle, a wan smile on her face, accepted it, smoothing it with both hands.

"Read the letter," Peter said to her.

She shook her head, her eyes glistening.

Peter and Neil Jr. looked at one another. Peter's wife gripped his arm but he shooed her away. "Look, Gabi, someday one of us is going to die, and if you kick the bucket first, I'll just read it then. So why not read it now? It's been nearly forty years. You've told us everything. I've told all I remember. Now, all that's left is the letter."

"It was a letter meant for only me," she whispered, her moist hazel eyes staring into some faraway place.

"Mom," Neil Jr. said, touching her hand. "If you don't want to do it, we'll all understand. But I've never heard my father's voice. All I know are the limited things you've told me. Hearing his words might tell me a little something about myself."

She dipped her head, pressing the locket to her lips. Her eyes were squeezed tightly shut. She took sharp breaths through her nose, exhaling through her mouth. Then, doing something she'd never before done, Gabrielle removed the paper and carefully unfolded the brittle letter. Inside were the pressed remains of what was once a pink flower, which she gently placed on the table. She sniffled several times, looking at all eyes to make sure everyone was listening. As she read the letter, she unintentionally allowed a hint of her accent to come forward.

My sweet Gabi,

Forgive me for not telling you this face-to-face. I can do a number of things, but breaking bad news to you is not one of them. I'm leaving, Gabi, and I will not be back. Don't hold out hope for my return. Hope can be a good thing, as well as a bad thing. This time there is no hope, for me at least. If you think long and hard about all I've said, you'll know where I'm going. It's a place from which I will never return, but that's fine. This is the way it should end. My Shoshone ancestors sometimes practiced something called self-immolation—death by fire. While it sounds gruesome, I now have an understanding of their motivation. It's an end on their terms, on my terms.

As much as I would like to, there is no way I could have made a life with you. My country will not be at all happy with what I've done, but more important than that, I'm damaged goods. I simply cannot forward on with the weight of all I've done, and the pain of Emilee's death. But something happened to me I never thought possible: I fell in love, Gabi. I fell in love with you. You showed me more in a matter of weeks than any person ever before. You're a special lady, Gabi, and I hope you will someday find a man deserving of your special, powerful brand of love.

Even though I lost my wife and unborn son, and even though I am now losing you, my life feels complete. I wish I could have left a child on this earth, but that just wasn't in the cards. Perhaps my memory will live on with you.

Take this money and get away, Gabi. Tell no one about it. You told me you wanted to live a bold life before you died, and that you were fully capable of anything. Well, now's your chance. Use that brain of yours and get the hell away from the Nazis. They're bad news and something horrible is staring your country right in the face. That's a promise. So, please, if you ever listened to me, listen now. Forget about the farm; forget about your things. Take Peter and run like hell.

I love you, Gabi. I love you so very much. I wish there were a stronger way to demonstrate this to you. I'd scream it to the world if it would do any good. Life is terribly unfair at times and I've questioned why I met you when I did. Why did fate bring me the perfect woman when I couldn't have her? I know, had things been different, we could have spent our lives together in happiness. But for the brief time we had together, you mended the hole in my heart. And your gift to me, the ability to love again, is the greatest gift I have ever received.

Go on now. Go boldly.

Much Love,

Neil

P.S. I am so very proud of you. You certainly "lived" while I knew you.

Gabrielle placed the letter flat on the table, two streams of tears steadily running down her face. Neil's girlfriend stood, walking behind and hugging Gabrielle. "Mrs. Lightsey, you should feel good that you did as he wished." She pointed to Neil Jr. "And look at the gift he left you, and me."

Gabrielle patted the young woman's hand, feeling as if, for just a moment, Madeline Seelbach had entered the room. She looked to her son, her voice hitching as she smiled through her tears. "You're too old to be single, Neil. Will you please marry this girl and give me some grandchildren?" It was just the levity the room of people needed.

Neil Jr. stood and walked to his mother, putting his arm around her. He gave her shoulders a squeeze. "Tell us the last part, mom. Tell us the part that always leaves you feeling a little better."

She wiped the tears from her face, blinking rapidly. Once she had gathered herself, she again made brief eye contact with every person individually. "The children, every one of them, made it safely to Palestine." She smiled. "As far as I know, they're all in Israel today."

"And the other part," Peter said. "What we learned."

"Well, when we went back to Germany, we did ask about whatever became of Anton Aying."

"Did they tell you?" Neil's girlfriend asked, moving back to her chair. "Not officially."

"C'mon Gabi…tell them what they told us, *unofficially*," Peter said.

The wisp of a smile creased Gabrielle's face as she began to tell the tale…

* * *

Several Days After the Children Reached Jesenice

Standartenführer Anton Aying sat at his desk, reading the fourth draft of the report from his attaché. Aying was due in Berlin on Monday, and knew he'd better make damn well sure his powder was dry before he arrived at the swastika-adorned Prinz-Albrecht-Strasse to deliver his report. With a red pen, he made copious notes in the margin, threatening to jail his attaché if he didn't get it right on the next draft. Disgusted, Aying tossed the paper onto his desk and lit a cigarette with Jacob Herman's gold lighter.

Aying spun his chair around to stare at the Nordkette Mountains to the north of Innsbruck. The snow on the caps was growing and, before long, would stretch all the way down into the valley. Aying rubbed his bandaged arm, wondering if he would be in Innsbruck to see the snow, or if he'd find himself in the bowels of the Spandau Prison in Berlin.

"Sir," the voice crackled on his intercom.

"What?" Aying snapped, irritated at the interruption of his first tranquil moment of the day.

"Sir, I have a Sturmbannführer Fahlpferd here to see you?"

"Fahlpferd?" Aying said with a frown at the unusual name. "I don't know him, nor does he have an appointment."

"Yes, sir."

Aying breathed deeply and resumed his fatalistic ruminations about next week. He propped his boots on the painted windowsill, visualizing the exchanges that would take place, shaping them to paint himself in a flattering light.

"Sir," the intercom buzzed again.

"Damn it!" Aying bellowed. "What is it? I'm very busy."

"Sir, he says he has information..." there was a pause and Aying could hear someone speaking to his assistant. "Sir, he says he has a solution, excuse me, a *resolution* for you regarding some events last week near Yugoslavia. He said one of the troops of his storm unit apprehended a man you're looking for."

Aying spun around, his eyes wide. He stared at the intercom for ten seconds, finally lifting the phone. "Send him in."

The door opened and shut. In strode a man in an SS major's uniform, an eye-patch over one eye. His gloved hand held a cigarette to his face, puffing as he walked. He stopped squarely in front of Aying's desk and lowered the cigarette. With his free hand he reached into his pants pocket, producing and tossing a gold lighter, almost identical to Aying's own, onto the black leather blotter. The lighter was adorned with an engraving of the Arc de Triomphe, done in the same style as the engraved Eiffel Tower on Jacob Herman's lighter.

Aying stared at the lighter, knowing exactly who this man was and why he was here. When he raised his eyes, he saw a Walther pistol pointing directly at him from the man's waist level. He watched as the man dropped his cigarette on the floor, removed the SS officer's hat and the eye patch, tossing them aside, revealing one blue eye, one green. The man, of course, was none other than Neil Reuter, though Aying still could only think of him as Dieter Dremel.

"So you couldn't leave well enough alone?" Aying asked, his cutting tone belying the thudding in his chest.

"One of my missions has been accomplished, Aying," Neil said in unaccented American English. "And now I intend to complete the second one."

"And that would be what?" Aying countered in what sounded like a Welsh-tinted accent.

"Your lighter, the fraternal twin to mine…it belonged to my best friend, Jakey Herman."

"Ah, yes, Mister Herman." Aying could feel his temper coming up. "Well, he's gone now, Dremel, or Fahlpferd, or whatever you'd like me to call you." Aying grinned. "And your Jewish friend squealed like a panicky little pig when I killed him." Aying watched with satisfaction as Dremel flinched. "So what is this so-called second portion of your mission, Herr Dremel?"

"As you no doubt know, my name's Neil Reuter, of San Francisco, California. I'm an agent with the United States Department of War, and I've come back to avenge the death of my friend."

Aying calmly placed his palms on the desk. "How did you get here? There are many safeguards beyond simply wearing that uniform…if I have a traitor working here who helped you, perhaps that can be your first bargaining chip."

"I lived a portion of my life with the Shoshone…American Indians— wonderful, peaceful people. They taught me how to mimic the traits of my quarry. Trust me, Aying, getting to you was the easiest thing I've done in some time."

"Well, Mister Reuter of San Francisco, agent of the United States Department of War, he of unclean *savage* blood…you may have had an easy time getting to me, but there is a serious flaw in your plan."

"Oh? And what is that?"

"You may have gotten to me, but you've made a grave miscalculation of your escape. It's impossible. This is not the United States, where criminals roam the land without fear of retribution." Aying smiled thinly. "If you harm me, you *will* die. That I can promise."

Neil stared back at Aying, holding the Walther as steadily as if it were on a mount.

"Well?" Aying asked.

Neil said nothing.

The German flicked his eyes down to the Walther—the American's finger was on the trigger. Suppressing a spate of panic, Aying swallowed thickly. "You obviously have information, Herr Reuter, that I can use. And I can aid you through the power of this office. We can help one another. You help *me* out of the mess you created, and I will provide you *safe* passage from the Reich. We can pin everything on that cretin Falkenberg. Now, let's stop with unprofitable talk of vengeance, let's put the gun away, and let's work out an exchange like the civilized, cultured men we are."

"Thought I was a savage?"

Aying shrugged. "My temper. You'll pardon me. Now, put the gun away. Let's trade information and I will make way for your escape."

Neil continued to hold the pistol on Aying.

"What is your problem? Are you deaf? Put the gun away and I will help you escape, free of any charges of wrongdoing. It's your only choice."

Neil Reuter, of San Francisco, began to laugh. Low at first, rising to throaty, and ending quite malevolent.

"What's so funny?" Aying demanded, gripping the armrests of his chair as he felt sweat under his tight collar.

The American's laughter grew as tears welled in his eyes, finally running down his face.

"What is it?" Aying yelled.

The laughter ceased as if chopped off by a falling blade, transforming into an eerily calm voice as the American said, "And who said I cared *anything* about escaping?"

The blood left Aying's face, leaving him grey, matching his eyes and uniform.

* * *

1976 - Manhasset, NY, USA

"So," Gabrielle summed up, "They told us that story. Then they told us, officially, Aying was listed as having been killed…shot…in a so-called training accident." Gabrielle rubbed the locket. "His date of death was only a few days after we last saw Neil. Five other men were killed that day, too, in this *purported* training accident."

"He got Anton Aying," Neil Jr. said proudly, rapping his knuckles on the table. "My dad got that evil sonofabitch."

Gabrielle inserted the brittle flower and refolded the delicate letter, kissing it once. She murmured, "Yes, I believe he did."

When everyone had left the room, Gabrielle replaced everything in the curio box. She touched her hand to the top of the box, staring into the distance, remembering Neil's touch, his voice, his spirit. She walked into the study, removing a painting of her mother's farm that revealed a wall safe. Once the safe was opened, she deposited the curio box inside.

Before she closed the safe, Gabrielle touched her locket. After a moment, she opened it, staring at the engraving of the letter "N." Gabrielle went back into the curio box and retrieved the letter again. Sitting on the comfortable reading chair in the study, she reread the letter, taking her time, allowing her mind to drink in every word. Then she closed her eyes, picturing Neil as he'd lain in Peter's bed, healing from his injuries. She thought of his dashing figure when dressed in his suit. She remembered how he had looked the night they first made love. How his rare smile had always ignited her soul.

Gabrielle held the letter to her heart and closed her eyes as she shuddered in her tears.

THE END

Acknowledgments

So many people had their hands in the creation of this book. I wrote the first draft seven years ago and have worked on it time and time again. It's always been one of my favorite stories and bloomed from a true story I read about an underground network used to smuggle Jewish children from the growing Nazi threat. While so many stories ended tragically, I couldn't write one like that. I had to create a bit of victory around this difficult subject. And please don't feel bad for Neil. Believe me, he got the victory he wanted.

First and foremost, I'd like to thank my former agent, Bob Thixton. He championed this book and gave me advice to make it better. Bob, again, I apologize for my impatience.

Thanks to Mitch Compton, pilot extraordinaire, for his advice on how a non-pilot might fly a taildragger. We had fun creating that sequence.

Don McKale, a globally renowned Hitler and Third Reich expert, helped me understand day-to-day life inside the Third Reich. Don, I appreciate your friendship and all you've done to help me.

Kelly Durham, esteemed author (buy his books, you won't be disappointed!) gave me great advice on a number of historical items. Thanks, Kelly, once again. You've helped me a great deal and I'm proud of all you've accomplished.

Liz Latanishen, mommy-to-be and editor-in-chief, I appreciate your keen eye and perspective. You always improve my stories with your fine work.

Dina Dryden, the polisher, thanks again for a great job on this book. I appreciate your friendship and your help.

To so many others who assisted me with this book: Ralph Rowland, Mickey Dorsey, Bob Sides, Ann Brown, A.J. Norris, Frank O'Brien, John Taylor, David Barabas—thank you so very much. Each of your insights helped make this story better than it was before.

This book's contest winners consisted of the following fantastic readers: Kayla Kurucz, Bruce Leland, Dennis Tyler and Bill Nathanson. I hope each of you enjoyed the read. Readers, keep your eyes peeled for an email from me. You never know when you might be asked to pre-read.

Finally, a big thanks to all readers who've purchased and read this book. This story is quite special to me because it deals with a number of real world issues despite its fiction. I hope you enjoyed it. God bless.

C.

About the Author

Chuck Driskell credits the time he spent as a U.S. Army
paratrooper as what initially fueled his love of writing.
During the week, he works in marketing. Seven mornings a
week, usually very early, he writes, exercising his fantasies
and spinning his yarns.

Chuck lives in South Carolina with his tolerant wife
and two loving children. *Final Mission: Zion*
is Chuck's eleventh novel.

Made in the USA
Columbia, SC
03 November 2018